Library of America, a nonprofit organization,
champions our nation's cultural heritage
by publishing America's greatest writing in
authoritative new editions and providing resources
for readers to explore this rich, living legacy.

DONALD BARTHELME

Donald Barthelme

COLLECTED STORIES

Come Back, Dr. Caligari
Unspeakable Practices, Unnatural Acts
City Life
Sadness
Amateurs
Great Days
FROM *Sixty Stories*
Overnight to Many Distant Cities
FROM *Forty Stories*
Uncollected Stories

Charles McGrath, *editor*

THE LIBRARY OF AMERICA

DONALD BARTHELME: COLLECTED STORIES
Volume compilation, notes, and chronology copyright © 2021 by
Literary Classics of the United States, Inc., New York, N.Y.
All rights reserved.

No part of this book may be reproduced in any manner whatsoever without
the permission of the publisher, except in the case of brief
quotations embodied in critical articles and reviews.

Published in the United States by Library of America.
Visit our website at www.loa.org.

Come Back, Dr. Caligari © 1964 by Donald Barthelme. *Unspeakable Practices, Unnatural Acts* © 1968 by Donald Barthelme. *City Life* © 1970 by Donald Barthelme. *Sadness* © 1972 by Donald Barthelme. *Amateurs* © 1974 by Donald Barthelme. *Great Days* © 1979 by Donald Barthelme. *Overnight to Many Distant Cities* © 1983 by Donald Barthelme. Reprinted by arrangement with Counterpoint Press and the Estate of Donald Barthelme.

Sixty Stories © 1981 by Donald Barthelme. *Forty Stories* © 1987 by Donald Barthelme. Reprinted by arrangement with the Estate of Donald Barthelme.

"Edwards, Amelia," "A Man," "Basil from Her Garden," and "Tickets" © 1972, 1985, 1989 by Donald Barthelme. Reprinted by arrangement with Counterpoint Press.

This paper exceeds the requirements of
ANSI/NISO Z39.48–1992 (Permanence of Paper).

Distributed to the trade in the United States
by Penguin Random House Inc.
and in Canada by Penguin Random House Canada Ltd.

Library of Congress Control Number: 2020947381
ISBN 978-1-59853-684-3

First Printing
The Library of America—343

Manufactured in the United States of America

Contents

Introduction by Charles McGrath xvii

COME BACK, DR. CALIGARI
Florence Green is 81 3
The Piano Player 14
Hiding Man 17
Will You Tell Me? 27
For I'm the Boy Whose Only Joy Is Loving You 36
The Big Broadcast of 1938 43
The Viennese Opera Ball 55
Me and Miss Mandible 63
Marie, Marie, Hold On Tight 75
Up, Aloft in the Air 81
Margins 93
The Joker's Greatest Triumph 98
To London and Rome 106
A Shower of Gold 114

UNSPEAKABLE PRACTICES, UNNATURAL ACTS
The Indian Uprising 125
The Balloon 132
This Newspaper Here 137
Robert Kennedy Saved from Drowning 142
Report 151
The Dolt 156
The Police Band 162

Edward and Pia 165
A Few Moments of Sleeping and Waking 172
Can We Talk 179
Game 182
Alice 187
A Picture History of the War 194
The President 204
See the Moon? 208

CITY LIFE

Views of My Father Weeping 221
Paraguay 233
The Falling Dog 240
At the Tolstoy Museum 246
The Policemen's Ball 257
The Glass Mountain 260
The Explanation 265
Kierkegaard Unfair to Schlegel 275
The Phantom of the Opera's Friend 284
Sentence 289
Bone Bubbles 295
On Angels 302
Brain Damage 305
City Life 318

SADNESS

Critique de la Vie Quotidienne 335
Träumerei 343

The Genius 347

Perpetua 354

A City of Churches 361

The Party 366

Engineer-Private Paul Klee Misplaces an Aircraft Between Milbertshofen and Cambrai, March 1916 370

A Film 375

The Sandman 383

Departures 390

Subpoena 399

The Catechist 402

The Flight of Pigeons from the Palace 408

The Rise of Capitalism 419

The Temptation of St. Anthony 424

Daumier 431

AMATEURS

Our Work and Why We Do It 449

The Wound 454

110 West Sixty-First Street 458

Some of Us Had Been Threatening Our Friend Colby 463

The School 467

The Great Hug 471

I Bought a Little City 474

The Agreement 480

The Sergeant 484

What to Do Next 491

The Captured Woman 496

And Then   506

Porcupines at the University   512

The Educational Experience   517

The Discovery   520

Rebecca   524

The Reference   529

The New Member   534

You Are as Brave as Vincent van Gogh   540

At the End of the Mechanical Age   544

GREAT DAYS

The Crisis   553

The Apology   558

The New Music   563

Cortés and Montezuma   576

The King of Jazz   584

The Question Party   588

Belief   594

Tales of the Swedish Army   598

The Abduction from the Seraglio   601

The Death of Edward Lear   605

Concerning the Bodyguard   609

The Zombies   613

Morning   617

On the Steps of the Conservatory   622

The Leap   629

Great Days   636

(FROM) SIXTY STORIES

Eugénie Grandet   649

Nothing: A Preliminary Account   658

A Manual for Sons   662

Aria   684

The Emerald   687

How I Write My Songs   715

The Farewell   720

The Emperor   725

Thailand   728

Heroes   732

Bishop   738

Grandmother's House   743

OVERNIGHT TO MANY DISTANT CITIES

They called for more structure . . .   753

Visitors   755

Financially, the paper . . .   763

Affection   765

I put a name in an envelope . . .   771

Lightning   772

That guy in the back room . . .   780

Captain Blood   782

A woman seated on a plain wooden chair . . .   787

Conversations with Goethe   790

Well we all had our Willie & Wade records . . .   793

Henrietta and Alexandra   795

Speaking of the human body . . . 800
The Sea of Hesitation 801
When he came . . . 810
Terminus 812
The first thing the baby did wrong . . . 816
The Mothball Fleet 818
Now that I am older . . . 822
Wrack 824
On our street . . . 831
The Palace at Four A.M. 835
I am, at the moment . . . 842
Overnight to Many Distant Cities 844

(FROM) FORTY STORIES

Chablis 851
On the Deck 854
Opening 857
Sindbad 860
Rif 866
Jaws 871
Bluebeard 875
Construction 881
Letters to the Editore 887
January 892

UNCOLLECTED STORIES

Basil from Her Garden 903
Edwards, Amelia 912

A Man 917
Tickets 922

Chronology 929
Note on the Texts 937
Notes 945

Introduction

BY CHARLES MCGRATH

DONALD BARTHELME was, by his own design, a hard writer to categorize. Even at the height of his fame, in the late '70s and early '80s, there were readers who just didn't get him, or suspected his work was a hoax or a joke they weren't in on. At *The New Yorker*, where he was a regular contributor for decades, clerks in the library were expected to type up on index cards brief summaries of every article, fact or fiction, that appeared in the magazine. Barthelme's cards sometimes contained just one word: "gibberish."

By most standards, many of his stories aren't stories at all. They don't have plots, or even realistic, believable characters, and they touch on human emotion only indirectly. Barthelme loved arcane vocabulary, and called such pieces "slumgullions"—stews, that is. In the manner of visual artists like Duchamp and Rauschenberg, they incorporated all sorts of found materials: snippets from ad copy, old travel guides, textbooks, and instruction manuals, even other writers. The range of references and allusions in his stories is vast and encyclopedic: cheesy movies, nineteenth-century philosophers, opera, country-and-western, military history, art, architecture, softcore pornography. For a while he even took to illustrating his work with engravings and pictures clipped from old books and magazines. He once wrote, only half-joking, that "the most essential tool for genius today" was rubber cement.

Many of the stories feel like riffs, jazzy improvisations on the way people speak: musician-talk, military lingo, art-jargon, academic highbrow. He was like his character Hokie Mokie, in the story "The King of Jazz," of whom it is said, he "can just knock a fella out, just the way he pronounces a word. What intonation on that boy! God almighty!" Still other stories are retellings, or reimaginings, of older stories: Captain Blood, Bluebeard, the Hunchback of Notre Dame. Barthelme's version of Balzac's *Eugénie Grandet* includes a reference-book summary of the novel; a woodcut of Eugénie herself, holding a ball for some reason; and the word "butter" repeated ninety-seven times.

Barthelme was also fascinated by the trite and clichéd, and sometimes incorporated snatches of writing that were deliberately clumsy and hackneyed, or else close to incomprehensible, like this one, from "Paraguay," a story that also includes lengthy cribbings from obscure books:

> Relational methods govern the layout of cities. Curiously, in some of the most successful projects the design has been swung upon small collections of rare animals spaced (on the lost-horse principle) on a lack of grid. Carefully calculated mixes: mambas, the black wrasse, the giselle. Electrolytic jelly exhibiting a capture ratio far in excess of standard is used to fix the animals in place.

One of his favorite devices was the list, an occasion for tossing in all sorts of rag-picked stuff just for its own sake: "two ashtrays, ceramic, one dark brown and one dark brown with an orange blur at the lip; a tin frying pan; two-litre bottles of red wine; three-quarter-litre bottles of Black & White, aquavit, cognac, vodka, gin, Fad #6 sherry; a hollow-core door in birch veneer on black wrought-iron legs; a blanket, red-orange, with faint blue stripes; a red pillow and a blue pillow; a woven straw wastebasket; two glass jars for flowers; corkscrews and can openers; two plates and two cups, ceramic, dark brown; a yellow-and-purple poster; a Yugoslavian carved flute, wood, dark brown; and other items." Many stories of this assembled sort have an almost painterly quality; they remind you of Warhol sometimes, in their fascination with found objects and cultural detritus, and of Kurt Schwitters, in their collage-like layering of seemingly random elements.

But toward the end of his career Barthelme wrote stories so minimal and pared-down they were almost abstract, just alternating lines of overheard conversation preceded by a dash. Almost from the beginning, there were also stories that were monologues, stories that took the form of a catechism or a Q&A, stories that were out-and-out parodies, stories within stories, stories in the form of numbered lists, stories disguised as essays or interviews, and one story that consists of a single unfinished sentence seven pages long. Barthelme even wrote a few stories that seemed old-school, with real people and actual beginnings, middles, and ends. Late in his life he wrote a prize-winning children's book, and though his gifts were not really novelistic, he nevertheless wrote four novels—extended, book-length narratives that paid a certain homage to the old conventions of the novel while also undermining them from within. If there's a constant in his career, it's restlessness and a dread of seeming predictable.

Barthelme hated labels, but grudgingly accepted that "postmodernist" might not be too far off the mark, and biologically, at least, he really was one. His father, Donald, Sr., was an architect who ardently championed the work of Walter Gropius, Mies van der Rohe, Frank Lloyd Wright, and Le Corbusier. Modernism in the Barthelme household was practically a religion. The family lived in a modern house, designed by Don, Sr., so radical in its time and place, a Houston suburb in the '50s, that people used to park outside and gawk. The furniture was modern, and so were the paintings and the books. The father was impatient and imperious, and he and his namesake, his eldest child, were frequently at odds. But Barthelme nevertheless inherited from his father an unassailable conviction that there had been a revolution in art, and that there was no going back to the old ways.

The contemporaries Barthelme allied himself with were of a similar bent, anxious to dispense with the tired and old-fashioned: Walter Abish, Robert Coover, William Gass, William Gaddis, Jerome Klinkowitz, John Hawkes, John Barth, Joseph McElroy, Susan Sontag, and Thomas Pynchon. In 1983 he famously invited them all to a meal at a SoHo restaurant. (Pynchon, it goes without saying, was a no-show.) The occasion came to be known as the Post-Modernists' Dinner, and probably entailed a lot of wine and a certain amount of unspoken invidiousness, since some of his contemporaries resented Barthelme's success at *The New Yorker* and privately accused him of selling out. Barthelme differed from his fellow postmoderns in at least two respects. He had little use for the notion of "metafiction," so much in vogue back then: the idea that writing should call attention to its own made-upness. And he lacked the high seriousness of so many postmods, their habit of making grand pronouncements. Barthelme accepted that the age in which he found himself was not a golden one.

He never pretended to greatness, and he made fun of those who did. His fallback, his signature, is always humor. For all his avant-gardism, and occasional difficulty, he is a very funny writer, even a jokey one at times. He's more entertaining to read, and requires less heavylifting, than many of the postmoderns, and he enjoyed more popular success than just about any of them.

For much of the 1970s, in fact, if slush-pile submissions to *The New Yorker* were any indication, Barthleme was the most widely imitated writer in America. I was a young editor then and every week would come across a dozen or so wannabe Barthelmes. In 1973 one enterprising forger even managed to sell a passable Barthelme imitation—not to *The New Yorker* but to one of the little quarterlies. "Quite a worthy effort, as pastiches go," Barthelme said of it, "and particularly successful in reproducing my weaknesses." (For a while one of Barthelme's brothers, Frederick, was among the imitators, and it wasn't until he found a very different voice of his own that he, too, went on to become a regular *New Yorker* contributor.) But Barthelme's heyday was short-lived. In a few years his imitators had been replaced by writers trying to copy Raymond Carver (Frederick Barthelme went through a phase of that, too) and the slush pile now overflowed with stories set in trailer parks.

The Barthelme example proved to be not just harder to copy than it looked but also so original it didn't lead anywhere. You can see glints and traces of Barthelme in writers like Donald Antrim, Mary Robison, George Saunders, Nicholson Baker, and Dave Eggers, but Barthelme never inspired a whole school of fiction writing the way Carver did. Where Carver is rooted in the deepest tradition of American realism, Barthelme seems to come out of nowhere. Before becoming a full-time writer, he worked as a museum director and editor of an arts magazine, and his roots, such as they were, were as much in the visual arts as in literature. He's a one-off, and that turns out to be his greatest claim on posterity: he's like no one else. He also embodies, more inventively and more entertainingly than any of his contemporaries, that moment in American fiction when so many writers were seized by a need to kill off their ancestors, throw out the old forms, and make everything new. One of his best stories, "A Manual for Sons," later part of a novel, is a sort of guidebook to that moment: it's about how to cope with dead fathers who won't stay dead.

That Barthelme had such a long and fruitful relationship with *The New Yorker*—publishing 129 stories there over twenty-six years, not to mention dozens of "Notes and Comment" pieces, and even filling in as a temporary film reviewer in the '70s— now seems remarkable, for he was in many ways the least likely *New Yorker* contributor ever. He was consciously arty, for one thing, with a formidable, bristling intellect, at a time when the magazine maintained a tone of studied casualness and unpretentiousness. He cultivated a long, mustache-less beard, which made him look like an Amish farmer or else Captain Ahab. Nor was his work especially well liked by many on the staff. The writer and editor William Maxwell said he just didn't get what Barthelme was up to, but whatever it was, it wasn't fiction, and the magazine's then managing editor used to stalk testily around the office and quiz people: Did they really understand this Barth-helm, or however he said his name?

But he had two important allies: Roger Angell, the editor who discovered him, and William Shawn, the magazine's editor-in-chief, who readily embraced Barthelme, as he did so many experimental writers. In the beginning, what Shawn and Angell saw in Barthelme was probably another humorist, in the tradition, say, of S. J. Perelman, whose work Barthelme began to admire when he was still in high school, and who got him to start reading *The New Yorker* in the first place. His first published piece in the magazine, in the issue of March 2, 1963, was not one of his slumgullions but what *The New Yorker* called a "casual," a piece of light humor—in this case, a parody of an Antonioni screenplay. As Barthelme's work began to evolve in new and more daring directions Shawn and Angell stuck with it—they even relaxed, just for him, some of the magazine's usual fussiness about punctuation—and the relationship proved mutually beneficial, as it did with so many longtime *New Yorker* contributors. In this case, Barthelme got an audience, something like a steady income (though it was never enough, and he was frequently in debt to the magazine), and the freedom to experiment. The magazine got a controversial but also widely admired writer who helped dispel the cloud of the so-called *New Yorker* story: the magazine's reputation—outdated then but still lingering—for publishing stories that were mostly plotless evocations of suburban ennui.

Barthleme's plotlessness was of a different, more disconcerting sort. It left readers without any of the bearings supplied by traditional fiction. Sometimes you didn't have a clue as to where you were. Here, for example, is the beginning of "The Indian Uprising," a famous early story that is in part a response to the Vietnam War, though you could be forgiven for not guessing that right away:

> We defended the city as best we could. The arrows of the Comanches came in clouds. The war clubs of the Comanches clattered on the soft, yellow pavements. There were earthworks along the Boulevard Mark Clark and the hedges had been laced with sparkling wire. People were trying to understand. I spoke to Sylvia. "Do you think this is a good life?" The table held apples, books, long-playing records. She looked up. "No."

But even the most collage-like of his stories were not mere abstractions, devoid of feeling or meaning. Barthelme distrusted the means of traditional fiction but not its end—to help make sense of things, a job rendered even more difficult, he thought, by the cluttered and cheapened culture in which he found himself. To a surprising extent, some of his work is even autobiographical. Barthelme drank too much and often felt guilty about it, and drinking, or regret about drinking, is a not uncommon theme in his work. He was also lonely and lovelorn; he married three times, and had a great many affairs. Romantic disappointment and sexual longing are even more frequent themes in the stories, and sometimes the drinking and the disappointment are combined: "Our evenings lacked promise. The world in the evenings seems fraught with the absence of promise, if you are a married man. There is nothing to do but go home and drink your nine drinks and forget about it."

One of Barthelme's better collections was called *Sadness*, and sadness is the default mood in most of his work. Not full-blown despair of the sort you find in Beckett, a writer Barthelme greatly admired, but melancholy, regret, disappointment, a sense of belatedness and unrequited longing, a feeling that life seldom turns out the way you'd hoped. But Barthelme's sadness is tempered by his omnipresent humor, and by a sense that, on second thought, maybe things aren't so bad after all. His story "The Leap of Faith" is probably inspired by that moment in Beckett's *The Unnameable* when the narrator says, "I can't go on. I'll go on." Barthelme's version, though unmistakably in Beckett's manner, is less urgent and angst-ridden. Two characters are talking about whether or not to make a leap of faith—to find something, anything, worth believing in. "I can't make it," one of them says, but then they agree to keep trying, to try again another day. It ends this way:

—Another day when the singing sunlight turns you every which way but loose.
—When you accidentally notice the sublime.
—Somersaults and duels.
—Another day when you see a woman with really red hair. I mean really red hair.
—A wedding day.
—A plain day.
—So we'll try again? Okay?
—Okay.
—Okay?
—Okay.

There's always another day in Barthelme, a redemptive sense of open-endedness, and a belief that small miracles are sometimes possible. Barthelme's great story "The School" is set in a nursery school where a series of escalating catastrophes takes place. First the orange trees planted by the children die. Then the pet snakes and the herb garden—after, that is, the deaths of the gerbil, the white mice, the salamander. It gets worse: the puppy, the Korean orphan, heart attacks, a suicide, a drowning among the parents. The sense of impending doom is macabre but somehow hilarious at the same time. And then the not-quite-miracle takes place. There's a knock at the door, the new gerbil walks in, and the children cheer wildly. It's not precisely what they were hoping for—they wanted the teacher and his teaching assistant to have sex right there in front of them—but for now it's enough.

There are lots of such moments in Barthelme—not happy endings, exactly, but provisional ones, a hopefulness conjured sometimes out of nothing more than the author's wish not to leave us (and himself) too far down in the dumps. For all his difficulty and occasional impenetrableness, Barthelme was at heart a generous writer who thought that his main task, especially in what he saw as a belated and diminished time, was to sneak up on the readers and startle them with a little dose of pleasure and surprise.

He wasn't just good at endings. Unlike many writers, he also had a knack for titles: "Some of Us Had Been Threatening Our Friend Colby," "Kierkegaard Unfair to Schlegel," "Our Work and Why We Do it," "The Falling Dog," "Nothing: A Preliminary Account." He gave his collections irresistible names like *Come Back, Dr. Caligari* and *Unspeakable Practices, Unnatural Acts*, and he fussed over them. He designed the jackets and cover art himself, chose his own typefaces, tweaked and retweaked the contents and their order. If so many of his stories are collage-like, the same is true, on an even larger scale, for the collections themselves. The final one, *Overnight to Many Distant Cities*, even has mysterious interchapters, italicized fragments that function much the same way as those little newspaper snippets and ticket stubs in the collages of Braque and Picasso. They add a kind of texture, a connection to the world outside the picture frame or, in this case, the frame of the book. Barthelme puts it this way on the first page, right after the table of contents: "They called for more structure, then, so we brought in some big hairy four-by-fours from the back shed and nailed them into place with railroad spikes."

He thought of the collections not as compendiums—periodic sweepings-up of whatever work he had on hand—but as carefully arranged wholes where everything from the title to the cover art to the flap copy to the unsmiling, Ahab-like author photo at the back contributed to a unified effect. (For that reason, this edition departs from the usual Library of America custom of presenting a writer's work chronologically,

INTRODUCTION

and instead reprints each of his nine collections exactly as it first appeared, with some uncollected stories added at the end. A disadvantage to this arrangement is that the first book, *Come Back, Dr. Caligari*, is uneven and even a little offputting at times. Readers brand new to Barthelme might want to start with the second, *Unspeakable Practices, Unnatural Acts*, one of his strongest and most entertaining collections, and then go back after they've got their feet wet.) The individual volumes really are different in tone and feeling from one another—some more serious, some more playful—and, read in order, they don't just show an arc of development, they offer a clue to Barthelme's own thinking about what he was doing. He never wasted much, and in later books even repurposed old material, but he also made things harder for himself by rejecting anything that seemed easy or formulaic. The later work is gloomier, more death-haunted than the earlier, but never without that glimmer of hopefulness. The last line of that final individual collection, *Overnight to Many Distant Cities*, is a kind of cosmic weather prediction, promising but open-ended: "Tomorrow, fair and warmer, warmer and fair, most fair . . ."

COME BACK, DR. CALIGARI

To my mother and father

Florence Green Is 81

DINNER WITH Florence Green. The old babe is on a kick tonight: *I want to go to some other country,* she announces. Everyone wonders what this can mean. But Florence says nothing more: no explanation, no elaboration, after a satisfied look around the table bang! she is asleep again. The girl at Florence's right is new here and does not understand. I give her an ingratiating look (a look that says, "There is nothing to worry about, I will explain everything later in the privacy of my quarters Kathleen"). Lentils vegetate in the depths of the fourth principal river of the world, the Ob, in Siberia, 3200 miles. We are talking about Quemoy and Matsu. "It's a matter of leading from strength. What is the strongest possible move on our part? To deny them the islands even though the islands are worthless in themselves." Baskerville, a sophomore at the Famous Writers School in Westport, Connecticut, which he attends with the object of becoming a famous writer, is making his excited notes. The new girl's boobies are like my secretary's knees, very prominent and irritating. Florence began the evening by saying, grandly, "The upstairs bathroom leaks you know." What does Herman Kahn think about Quemoy and Matsu? I can't remember, I can't remember . . .

Oh Baskerville! you silly son of a bitch, how can you become a famous writer without first having worried about your life, is it the *right kind* of life, does it have the right people in it, is it *going well*? Instead you are beglamoured by J. D. Ratcliff. The smallest city in the United States with a population over 100,000 is Santa Ana, California, where 100,350 citizens nestle together in the Balboa blue Pacific evenings worrying about their lives. I am a young man but very brilliant, very ingratiating, I adopt this ingratiating tone because I can't help myself (for fear of boring you). I edit with my left hand a small magazine, very scholarly, very brilliant, called *The Journal of Tension Reduction* (social-psychological studies, learned disputation, letters-to-the-editor, anxiety in rats). Isn't that distasteful? Certainly it is distasteful but if Florence Green takes her money to another country who will pay the printer? answer me that. From an article in *The Journal of Tension Reduction*: "*One source of concern in the classic encounter between patient and psychoanalyst is the patient's fear of boring the doctor.*" The doctor no doubt is also worrying about his life, unfolding with ten minutes between hours to smoke a cigarette in and wash his hands in. Reader, you who have already been told more than you want to know about the river Ob, 3200 miles long, in Siberia, we have roles to play, thou and I: you are the doctor (washing your hands between hours), and I, I am, I think, the nervous dreary patient. I am free associating, brilliantly, brilliantly, to put you into the problem. Or for fear of boring you: which? *The Journal of Tension Reduction* is concerned with everything from global tensions (drums along the Ob) to interpersonal relations (Baskerville and the new girl). There is, we feel, too much tension in the world, I myself am a perfect example, my stomach is like a clenched fist. Notice the ingratiating tone here? the only way I can relax it, I refer to the stomach, is by introducing quarts of Fleischmann's Gin. Fleischmann's I have found is a magnificent source of tension reduction, I favor the establishment of comfort stations providing free Fleischmann's on every street corner of the city of Santa Ana, California, and all other cities. Be serious, can't you?

The new girl is a thin thin sketchy girl with a big chest looming over the gazpacho and black holes around her eyes that are very promising. Surely when she opens her mouth toads will pop out. I am tempted to remove my shirt and show her my trim midsection sporting chiseled abdominals, my superior shoulders and brilliantly developed pectoral-latissimus tie-in. Jackson called himself a South Carolinian, and his biographer, Amos Kendall, recorded his birthplace as Lancaster County, S.C.; but Parton has published documentary evidence to show that Jackson was born in Union County, N.C., less than a quarter mile from the South Carolina line. Jackson is my great hero even though he had, if contemporary reports are to be believed, lousy lats. I am also a weightlifter and poet and admirer of Jackson and the father of one abortion and four miscarriages; who among you has such a record and no wife? Baskerville's difficulty not only at the Famous Writers School in Westport, Connecticut, but in every part of the world, is that he is slow.

"That's a slow boy, that one," his first teacher said. "That boy is what you call *real slow*," his second teacher said. "That's a *slow son of a bitch*," his third teacher said. And they were right, right, entirely correct, still I learned about Andrew Jackson and abortions, many of you walking the streets of Santa Ana, California, and all other cities know nothing about either. "*In such cases the patient sees the doctor as a highly sophisticated consumer of outré material, a connoisseur of exotic behavior. Therefore he tends to propose himself as more colorful, more eccentric (or more ill) than he really is; or he is witty, or he fantasticates.*" You see? Isn't that sensible? In the magazine we run many useful and sensible pieces of this kind, portages through the whirlpool-country of the mind. In the magazine I cannot openly advocate the use of Fleischmann's Gin in tension reduction but I did run an article titled "Alcohol Reconsidered" written by a talented soak of my acquaintance which drew many approving if carefully worded letters from secret drinkers in psychology departments all over this vast, dry and misunderstood country . . .

"That's a *slow son of a bitch*," his third teacher remarked of him, at a meeting called to discuss the formation of a special program for Inferior Students, in which Baskerville's name had so to speak rushed to the fore. The young Baskerville, shrinking along the beach brushing sand from his dreary Texas eyes, his sad fingers gripping $20 worth of pamphlets secured by post from Joe Weider, "Trainer of Terror Fighters" (are they, Baskerville wondered, like fire fighters? do they fight terror? or do they, rather, inspire it? the latter his, Baskerville's, impossible goal), was even then incubating plans for his novel *The Children's Army* which he is attending the Famous Writers School to learn how to write. "You will do famously, Baskerville," said the Registrar, the exciting results of Baskerville's Talent Test lying unexamined before him. "Run along now to the Cashier's Office." "I am writing doctor an immense novel to be called *The Children's Army*!" (Why do I think the colored doctor's name, he with his brown hand on the red radishes, is Pamela Hansford Johnson? Why do I think?) Florence Green is a small fat girl eighty-one years old, old with blue legs and very rich. Rock pools deep in the earth, I salute the shrewdness of whoever filled you with Texaco! Texaco breaks my heart, Texaco is particularly poignant. Florence Green who was not always a small fat girl once made a voyage with her husband Mr. Green on the *Graf Zeppelin*. In the grand salon, she remembers, there was a grand piano, the great pianist Mandrake the Magician was also on board but could not be persuaded to play. The Zeppelins could not use helium; the government of this country refused to sell helium to the owners of the Zeppelins. The title of my second book will be I believe *Hydrogen After Lakehurst*. For the first half of the evening we heard about the problem of the upstairs bathroom: "I had a man come out and look at it, and he said it would be two hundred and twenty-five dollars for a new one. I said I didn't want a new one, I just wanted this one fixed." Shall I offer to obtain a new one for Florence, carved out of solid helium? would that be ingratiating? Does she worry about her life? "He said mine was old-fashioned and they didn't make parts for that kind any more." Now she sleeps untidily at the head of the table, except for her single, mysterious statement, delivered with the soup (*I want to go to some other country!*), she has said nothing about her life whatsoever . . . The diameter of the world at the Poles is 7899.99 miles whereas the diameter of the world at the Equator is 7926.68 miles, mark it and strike it. I am sure the colored man across from me is a doctor, he has a doctor's doctorly air of being needed and necessary. He leans into the conversation as if to say: Just make *me* Secretary of State and then you will see some action. "I'll tell you one thing, there are a hell of a lot of Chinese over there." Surely the very kidneys of wisdom, Florence Green has only one kidney, I have a kidney stone, Baskerville was stoned by the massed faculty of the Famous Writers School upon presentation of his first lesson: he was accused of formalism. It is well known that Florence adores doctors, why didn't I announce myself, in the beginning, from the very first, as a doctor? Then I could say that the money was for a very important research project (use of radioactive tracers in reptiles) with very important ramifications in stomach cancer (the small intestine is very like a reptile). Then I would get the money with much less difficulty, cancer frightens Florence, the money would rain down like fallout in New Mexico. I am a young man but very brilliant, very ingratiating, I edit with my left hand a small magazine called . . . did I explain that? And you *accepted* my explanation? Her name is not really Kathleen, it is Joan Graham, when we were introduced she said, "Oh are you a native of Dallas Mr. Baskerville?" No Joan baby I am a native of Bengazi sent here by the UN to screw your beautiful ass right down into the ground, that is not what I said but what I should have said, it would have been brilliant. When she asked him what he did Baskerville identified himself as an American weightlifter and poet (that is to say: *a man stronger and more eloquent than other men*). "It moves," Mandrake said, pointing to the piano, and although no one else could detect the slightest movement, the force of his personality was so magical that he was not contradicted (the instrument sat in the salon, Florence says, as solidly as Gibraltar in the sea).

The man who has been settling the hash of the mainland Chinese searches the back of his neck, where there is what appears to be a sebaceous cyst (I can clear that up for you; my instrument will be a paper on the theory of games). What if Mandrake *had* played, though, what if he had seated himself before the instrument, raised his hands, and . . . what? The Principal Seas, do you want to hear about the Principal Seas? Florence has been prodded awake; people are beginning to ask questions. If not this country, then what country? Italy? "No," Florence says smiling through her emeralds, "not Italy. I've *been* to Italy. Although Mr. Green was very fond of Italy." "*To bore the doctor is to become, for this patient, a case similar to other cases; the patient strives mightily to establish his uniqueness. This is also, of course, a tactic for evading the psychoanalytic issue.*" The first thing the All-American Boy said to Florence Green at the very brink of their acquaintanceship was "It is closing time in the gardens of the West Cyril Connolly." This remark pleased her, it was a pleasing remark, on the strength of this remark Baskerville was invited again, on the second occasion he made a second remark, which was "Before the flowers of friendship faded friendship faded Gertrude Stein." Joan is like one of those marvelous *Vogue* girls, a tease in a half-slip on Mykonos, bare from the belly up on the rocks. "It moves," Mandrake said, and the piano raised itself a few inches, magically, and swayed from side to side in a careful Baldwin dance. "It moves," the other passengers agreed, under the spell of posthypnotic suggestion. "It moves," Joan says, pointing at the gazpacho, which sways from side to side with a secret Heinz trembling movement. I give the soup a serious warning, couched in the strongest possible terms, and Joan grins gratefully not at me but at Pamela Hansford Johnson. The Virgin Islands maybe? "We were there in 1925, Mr. Green had indigestion, I sat up all night with his stomach and the flies, the flies were something you wouldn't believe." They are asking I think the wrong questions, the question is not where but why? "I was reading the other day that the average age of Chiang's enlisted men is thirty-seven. You can't do much with an outfit like that." This is true, I myself am thirty-seven and if Chiang must rely on men of my sort then he might as well kiss the mainland goodbye. Oh, there is nothing better than intelligent conversation except thrashing about in bed with a naked girl and Egmont Light Italic.

Despite his slowness already remarked upon which perhaps inhibited his ingestion of the splendid curriculum that had been prepared for him, Baskerville never failed to be "promoted," but on the contrary was always "promoted," the reason for this being perhaps that his seat was needed for another child (Baskerville then being classified, in spite of his marked growth and gorgeous potential, as a child). There were some it was true who never thought he would extend himself to six feet, still he learned about Andrew Jackson, helium-hydrogen, and abortions, where are my mother and father now? answer me that. On a circular afternoon in June 1945—it was raining, Florence says, hard enough to fill the Brazen Sea—she was sitting untidily on a chaise in the north bedroom (on the wall of the north bedroom there are twenty identically framed photographs of Florence from eighteen to eighty-one, she was a beauty at eighteen) reading a copy of *Life*. It was the issue containing the first pictures from Buchenwald, she could not look away, she read the text, or a little of the text, then she vomited. When she recovered she read the article again, but without understanding it. What did *exterminated* mean? It meant nothing, an eyewitness account mentioned a little girl with one leg thrown alive on top of a truckload of corpses to be burned. Florence was sick. She went immediately to the Greenbrier, a resort in West Virginia. Later she permitted me to tell her about the Principal Seas, the South China, the Yellow, the Andaman, the Sea of Okhotsk. "I spotted you for a weightlifter," Joan says. "But not for a poet," Baskerville replies. "What have you written?" she asks. "Mostly I make remarks," I say. "Remarks are not literature," she says. "Then there's my novel," I say, "it will be twelve years old Tuesday." "Published?" she asks. "Not finished," I say, "however it's very violent and necessary. It has to do with this Army see, made up of children, young children but I mean really well armed with M–1's, carbines, .30 and .50 caliber machine guns, 105 mortars, recoilless rifles, the whole works. The central figure is the General, who is fifteen. One day the Army appears in the city, in a park, and takes up positions. Then it begins killing the people. Do you understand?" "I don't think I'd like it," Joan says. "I don't like it either," Baskerville says, "but it doesn't make any difference that I don't like it. Mr. Henry James writes fiction as though it were a painful duty Oscar Wilde."

Does Florence worry about her life? "He said mine was old-fashioned and they didn't make parts for that kind any more." Last year Florence tried to join the Peace Corps and when she was refused, telephoned the President to complain. "I have always admired the work of the Andrews Sisters," Joan says. I feel feverish; will you take my temperature doctor? Baskerville that simple preliterate soaks up all the Taylor's New York State malmsey in reach meanwhile wondering about his Grand Design. France? Japan? "Not Japan dear, we had a lovely time there but I wouldn't want to go back now. France is where my little niece is, they have twenty-two acres near Versailles, he's a count and a biochemist, isn't that wonderful?" The others nod, they know what is wonderful. The Principal Seas are wonderful, the Important Lakes of the World are wonderful, the Metric System is wonderful, let us measure something together Florence Green baby. I will trade you a walleyed hectometer for a single golden micron. The table is hushed, like a crowd admiring 300 million dollars. Did I say that Florence has 300 million dollars? Florence Green is eighty-one with blue legs and has 300 million dollars and in 1932 was in love, airily, with a radio announcer named Norman Brokenshire, with his voice. "*Mean*while Edna Cather's husband who takes me to church, he's got a very good job with the Port, I think he does very well, he's her second husband, the first was Pete Duff who got into all that trouble, where was I? Oh yes when Paul called up and said he wouldn't come because of his hernia—you heard about his hernia—John said *he'd* come over and look at it. Mind you I've been using the *down*stairs bathroom all this time." In fact the whole history of Florence's radio listenership is of interest. In fact I have decided to write a paper called "The Whole History of Florence Green's Radio Listenership." Or perhaps, in the seventeenth-century style, "The Whole and True History of Florence Green's Radio Listenership." Or perhaps . . . But I am boring you, I sense it, let me say only that she can still elicit, from her ancient larynx, the special thrilling sound used to introduce Cap-tain Midnight . . . The table is hushed, then, we are all involved in a furious pause, a grand parenthesis (here I will insert a description of Florence's canes. Florence's canes line a special room, the room in which her cane collection is kept. There are hundreds of them: smooth black Fred Astaire canes and rough chewed alpenstocks, blackthorns and quarterstaffs, cudgels and swagger sticks, bamboo and ironwood, maple and slippery elm, canes from Tangier, Maine, Zurich, Panama City, Quebec, Togoland, the Dakotas and Borneo, resting in notched compartments that resemble arms racks in an armory. Everywhere Florence goes, she purchases one or more canes. Some she has made herself, stripping the bark from the green unseasoned wood, drying them carefully, applying layer on layer of a special varnish, then polishing them, endlessly, in the evenings, after dark and dinner) as vast as the Sea of Okhotsk, 590,000 square miles. I was sitting, I remember, in a German restaurant on Lexington, blowing bubbles in my seidel, at the next table there were six Germans, young Germans, they were laughing and talking. At Florence Green's here-and-now table there is a poet named Onward Christian or something whose spectacles have wide silver sidepieces rather than the dull brown horn sidepieces of true poets and weightlifters, and whose poems invariably begin: "Through all my clangorous hours . . ." I am worried about his remarks, are his remarks better than my remarks? We are elected after all on the strength of our glamorous remarks, what is he saying to her? to Joan? what sort of eyewash is he pouring in her ear? I am tempted to walk briskly over and ask to see his honorable discharge from the Famous Writers School. What could be more glamorous or necessary than *The Children's Army*, "An army of youth bearing the standard of truth" as we used to sing in my fourth-grade classroom at Our Lady of the Sorrows under the unforgiving eye of Sister Scholastica who knew how many angels could dance on the head of a pin . . .

Florence I have decided is evading the life-issue. She is proposing herself as more unhappy than she really is. She has in mind making herself more interesting. She is afraid of boring us. She is trying to establish her uniqueness. She does not really want to go away. Does Onward Christian know about the Important Lakes of the World? Terminate services of employees when necessary. I terminate you, brightness that seems to know me. She proceeded by car from Tempelhof to a hotel in the American zone, registered, dined, sat in a chair in the lobby for a time observing the American lieutenant colonels and their healthy German girls, and then walked out into the street. The first German man she saw was a policeman directing traffic. He wore a uniform. Florence walked out into the traffic island and tugged at his sleeve. He bent politely toward the nice old American lady. She lifted her cane, the cane of 1927 from Yellowstone, and cracked his head with it. He fell in a heap in the middle of the street. Then Florence Green rushed awkwardly into the plaza with her cane, beating the people there, men and women, indiscriminately, until she was subdued. The Forms of Address, shall I sing to you of the Forms of Address? What Florence did was what Florence did, not more or less, she was returned to this country under restraint on a military plane. "Why do you have the children kill everybody?" "Because everybody has already been killed. Everybody is absolutely dead. You and I and Onward Christian." "You're not very sanguine." "That's true." For an earl's younger son's wife, letters commence: *Madam* . . . "We put in the downstairs bathroom when Ead came to visit us. Ead was Mr. Green's sister and she couldn't climb stairs." What about Casablanca? Santa Cruz? Funchal? Málaga? Valletta? Iráklion? Samos? Haifa? Kotor Bay? Dubrovnik? "I want to go to some *other* place," Florence says. "Somewhere where *everything is different*." For the Talent Test a necessary but not a sufficient condition for matriculation at the Famous Writers School Baskerville delivered himself of

"Impressions of Akron" which began: "Akron! Akron was full of people walking the streets of Akron carrying little transistor radios which were turned on."

Florence has a Club. The Club meets on Tuesday evenings, at her huge horizontal old multibathroom home on Indiana Boulevard. The Club is a group of men who gather, on these occasions, to recite and hear poems in praise of Florence Green. Before you can be admitted you must compose a poem. The poems begin, usually, somewhat in this vein: "Florence Green is eighty-one/ Nevertheless she's lots of fun . . ." Onward Christian's poem began "Through all my clangorous hours . . ." Florence carries the poems about with her in her purse, stapled together in an immense, filthy wad. Surely Florence Green is a vastly rich vastly egocentric old-woman nut! Six modifiers modify her into something one can think of as a nut. "But you have not grasped the living reality, the essence!" Husserl exclaims. Nor will I, ever. His examiner (was it J. D. Ratcliff?) said severely: "Baskerville, you blank round, discursiveness is not literature." "The aim of literature," Baskerville replied grandly, "is the creation of a strange object covered with fur which breaks your heart." Joan says: "I have two children." "Why did you do that?" I ask. "I don't know," she says. I am struck by the modesty of her answer. Pamela Hansford Johnson has been listening and his face jumps in what may be described as a wince. "That's a terrible thing to say," he says. And he is right, right, entirely correct, what she has said is the First Terrible Thing. We value each other for our remarks, on the strength of this remark and the one about the Andrews Sisters, love becomes possible. *I* carry in my wallet an eight-paragraph General Order, issued by the adjutant of my young immaculate Army to the troops: "(1) You are in this Army because you wanted to be. So you have to do what the General says. Anybody who doesn't do what the General says will be kicked out of the Army. (2) The purpose of the Army is to do what the General says. (3) The General says that nobody will shoot his weapon unless the General says to. It is important that when the Army opens fire on something everybody does it together. This is very important and anybody who doesn't do it will have his weapon taken away and will be kicked out of the Army. (4) Don't be afraid of the noise when everybody fires. It won't hurt you. (5) Everybody has enough rounds to do what the General wants to do. People who lose their rounds won't get any more. (6) Talking to people who are not in the Army is strictly forbidden. Other people don't understand the Army. (7) This is a serious Army and anybody that laughs will have his weapon taken away and will be kicked out of the Army. (8) What the General wants to do now is, find and destroy the enemy."

I want to go somewhere where everything is different. A simple, perfect idea. The old babe demands nothing less than total otherness. Dinner is over. We place our napkins on our lips. Quemoy and Matsu remain ours, temporarily perhaps; the upstairs bathroom drips away unrepaired; I feel the money drifting, drifting away from me. I am a young man but very brilliant, very ingratiating, I edit . . . but I explained all that. In the dim foyer I slip my hands through the neck of Joan's yellow dress. It is dangerous but it is a way of finding out everything all at once. Then Onward Christian arrives to resume his yellow overcoat. No one has taken Florence seriously, how can anyone with three hundred million dollars be taken seriously? But I know that when I telephone tomorrow, there will be no answer. Iráklion? Samos? Haifa? Kotor Bay? She will be in none of these places but in another place, a place where *everything is different*. Outside it is raining. In my rain-blue Volkswagen I proceed down the rain-black street thinking, for some simple reason, of the Verdi *Requiem*. I begin to drive my tiny car in idiot circles in the street, I begin to sing the first great *Kyrie*.

The Piano Player

Outside his window five-year-old Priscilla Hess, square and squat as a mailbox (red sweater, blue lumpy corduroy pants), looked around poignantly for someone to wipe her overflowing nose. There was a butterfly locked inside that mailbox, surely; would it ever escape? Or was the quality of mailboxness stuck to her forever, like her parents, like her name? The sky was sunny and blue. A filet of green Silly Putty disappeared into fat Priscilla Hess and he turned to greet his wife who was crawling through the door on her hands and knees.

"Yes?" he said. "What now?"

"I'm ugly," she said, sitting back on her haunches. "Our children are ugly."

"Nonsense," Brian said sharply. "They're wonderful children. Wonderful and beautiful. Other people's children are ugly, not our children. Now get up and go back out to the smokeroom. You're supposed to be curing a ham."

"The ham died," she said. "I couldn't cure it. I tried everything. You don't love me any more. The penicillin was stale. I'm ugly and so are the children. It said to tell you goodbye."

"*It?*"

"The ham," she said. "Is one of our children named Ambrose? Somebody named Ambrose has been sending us telegrams. How many do we have now? Four? Five? Do you think they're heterosexual?" She made a *moue* and ran a hand through her artichoke hair. "The house is rusting away. Why did you want a steel house? Why did I think I wanted to live in Connecticut? I don't know."

"Get up," he said softly, "get up, dearly beloved. Stand up and sing. Sing *Parsifal*."

"I want a Triumph," she said from the floor. "A TR–4. Everyone in Stamford, every single person, has one but me. If you gave me a TR–4 I'd put our ugly children in it and drive away. To Wellfleet. I'd take all the ugliness out of your life."

"A green one?"

"A *red* one," she said menacingly. "Red with red leather seats."

"Aren't you supposed to be chipping paint?" he asked. "I bought us an electronic data processing system. An IBM."

"I want to go to Wellfleet," she said. "I want to talk to Edmund Wilson and take him for a ride in my red TR–4. The children can dig clams. We have a lot to talk about, Bunny and me."

"Why don't you remove those shoulder pads?" Brian said kindly. "It's too bad about the ham."

"*I loved that ham*," she said viciously. "When you galloped into the University of Texas on your roan Volvo, I thought you were going to *be somebody*. I gave you my hand. You put rings on it. Rings that my mother gave me. I thought you were going to be distinguished, like Bunny."

He showed her his broad, shouldered back. "Everything is in flitters," he said. "Play the piano, won't you?"

"You always were afraid of my piano," she said. "My four or five children are afraid of the piano. *You taught them to be afraid of it.* The giraffe is on fire, but I don't suppose you care."

"What can we eat," he asked, "with the ham gone?"

"There's some Silly Putty in the deepfreeze," she said tonelessly.

"Rain is falling," he observed. "Rain or something."

"When you graduated from the Wharton School of Business," she said, "I thought *at last!* I thought *now we can move to Stamford and have interesting neighbors*. But they're not interesting. The giraffe is interesting but he sleeps so much of the time. The mailbox is *rather* interesting. The man didn't open it at 3:31 P.M. today. He was five minutes late. The government lied again."

With a gesture of impatience, Brian turned on the light. The great burst of electricity illuminated her upturned tiny face. Eyes like snow peas, he thought. Tamar dancing. My name in the dictionary, in the back. The Law of Bilateral Good Fortune. Piano bread perhaps. A nibble of pain running through the Western World. Coriolanus.

"Oh God," she said, from the floor. "Look at my knees."

Brian looked. Her knees were blushing.

"It's senseless, senseless, senseless," she said. "I've been caulking the medicine chest. What for? I don't know. You've got to give me more money. Ben is bleeding. Bessie wants to be an S.S. man. She's reading *The Rise and Fall*. She's identified with Himmler. Is that her name? Bessie?"

"Yes. Bessie."

"What's the other one's name? The blond one?"

"Billy. Named after your father. Your Dad."

"You've got to get me an air hammer. To clean the children's teeth. What's the name of that disease? They'll all have it, every single one, if you don't get me an air hammer."

"And a compressor," Brian said. "And a Pinetop Smith record. I remember."

She lay on her back. The shoulder pads clattered against the terrazzo. Her number, 17, was written large on her chest. Her eyes were screwed tight shut. "Altman's is having a sale," she said. "Maybe I should go in."

"Listen," he said. "Get up. Go into the grape arbor. I'll trundle the piano out there. You've been chipping too much paint."

"You wouldn't touch that piano," she said. "Not in a million years."

"You really think I'm afraid of it?"

"Not in a million years," she said, "you phony."

"All right," Brian said quietly. "All *right*." He strode over to the piano. He took a good grip on its black varnishedness. He began to trundle it across the room, and, after a slight hesitation, it struck him dead.

Hiding Man

ENTER EXPECTING to find the place empty (I. A. L. Burligame walks through any open door). But it is not, there is a man sitting halfway down the right side, heavy, Negro, well dressed, dark glasses. Decide after moment's thought that if he is hostile, will flee through door marked EXIT (no bulb behind EXIT sign, no certainty that it leads anywhere). The film is in progress, title *Attack of the Puppet People.* Previously observed films at same theater, *Cool and the Crazy, She Gods of Shark Reef, Night of the Blood Beast, Diary of a High School Bride.* All superior examples of genre, tending toward suggested offscreen rapes, obscene tortures: man with huge pliers advancing on disheveled beauty, cut to girl's face, to pliers, to man's face, to girl, scream, blackout.

"It's better when the place is full," observes Negro, lifting voice slightly to carry over Pinocchio noises from puppet people. Voice pleasant, eyes behind glasses sinister? Choice of responses: anger, agreement, indifference, pique, shame, scholarly dispute. Keep eye on EXIT, what about boy in lobby, what was kite for? "Of course it's never *been* full." Apparently there is going to be a conversation. "Not all these years. As a matter of fact, you're the first one to come in, ever."

"People don't always tell the truth."

Let him chew that. Boy in lobby wore T-shirt, printed thereon, OUR LADY OF THE SORROWS. Where glimpsed before? Possible agent of the conspiracy, in the pay of the Organization, duties: lying, spying, tapping wires, setting fires, civil disorders. Seat myself on opposite side of theater from Negro and observe film. Screen torn from top to bottom, a large rent, faces and parts of gestures fall off into the void. Hard-pressed U. S. Army, Honest John, Hound Dog, Wowser notwithstanding, psychological warfare and nerve gas notwithstanding, falls back at onrush of puppet people. Young lieutenant defends Army nurse (uniform in rags, tasty thigh, lovely breast) from obvious sexual intent of splinter men.

"Don't you know the place is closed?" calls friend in friendly tone. "Didn't you see the sign?"

"The picture is on. And you're here."

Signs after all mean everyone, if there are to be exceptions let them be listed: soldiers, sailors, airmen, children with kites, dogs under suitable restraint, distressed gentlefolk, people who promise not to peek. Well-dressed Negroes behind dark glasses in closed theaters, the attempt to scrape acquaintance, the helpful friend with the friendly word, note of menace as in *Dragstrip Riot*, as in *Terror from the Year 5000*. Child's play, amateur night, with whom do they think they have to deal?

"The silly thing just keeps running," alleges friend. "That's what's so fascinating. Continuous performances since 1944. Just keeps rolling along." Tilts head back, laughs theatrically. "It wasn't even any good then, for chrissake."

"Why do you keep coming back?"

"I don't think that's an interesting question."

Friend looks bland, studies film. Fires have started in many areas, the music is demure. I entrust myself to these places advisedly, there are risks but so also are there risks in crossing streets, opening doors, looking strangers in the eye. Man cannot live without placing himself naked before circumstance, as in warfare, under the sea, jet planes, women. Flight is always available, concealment is always possible.

"What I *meant* was," continues friend, animated now, smiling and gesturing, "other theaters. When they're full, you get lost in the crowd. Here, if anybody came in, they'd spot you in a minute. But *most* people, they believe the sign."

I. A. L. Burligame walks through any open door, private homes, public gatherings, stores with detectives wearing hats, meetings of Sons and Daughters of I Will Arise, but should I boast? Keep moving, counterpunching, examination of motives reveals appeal of dark places has nothing to do with circumstance. But because I feel warmer. The intimation was, *most* people do what they are told, NO LOITERING, NO PARKING BETWEEN 8 AM AND 5 PM, KEEP OFF THE GRASS, CLOSED FOR REPAIRS KEEP OUT. Negro moves two seats closer, lowers voice confidentially.

"Of course it's no concern of mine . . ." Face appears gentle, interested, as with old screw in *Girl on Death Row*, aerialist-cum-strangler in *Circus of Horrors*. "Of course I couldn't care less. But frankly, I feel a certain want of seriousness."

"I am absolutely serious."

On the other hand, perhaps antagonist is purely, simply what he pretends to be: well-dressed Negro with dark glasses in closed theater. But where then is the wienie? What happens to the twist? All of life is rooted in contradiction, movement in direction of self, two spaces, diagonally, argues hidden threat, there must be room for irony.

"Then what are you doing *here*?" Friend sits back in sliding seat with air of having clinched argument. "Surely you don't imagine *this* is a suitable place?"

"It looked good, from the outside. And there's no one here but you."

"Ah, but I *am* here. What do you know about me? Nothing, absolutely nothing. I could be anybody."

"So could I be anybody. And I notice that you too keep an eye on the door."

"Thus, we are problematic for each other." Said smoothly, with consciousness of power. "Name's Bane, by the way." Lights pipe, with flourishes and affectations. "Not my real one, of course."

"Of course." Pipe signal to confederates posted in balcony, behind arras, under EXIT signs? Or is all this dumb show merely incidental, concealing vain heart, empty brain? On screen famous scientist has proposed measures to contain puppet people, involving mutant termites thrown against their flank. The country is in a panic, Wall Street has fallen, the President looks grave. And what of young informer in lobby, what is his relevance, who corrupted wearer of T-shirt, holder of kite?

"I'm a dealer in notions," friend volunteers. "Dancing dolls, learn handwriting analysis by mail, secrets of eternal life, coins and stamps, amaze your friends, pagan rites, abandoned, thrilling, fully illustrated worldwide selection of rare daggers, gurkhas, stilettos, bowies, hunting, throwing."

"And what are you doing here?"

"Like you," he avers. "Watching the picture. Just dropped in."

We resume viewing. Role of Bane obscure, possible motives in igniting conversation: (1) Agent of the conspiracy, (2) Fellow sufferer in the underground, (3) Engaged in counterespionage, (4) Talent scout for Police Informers School, (5) Market research for makers of *Attack of the Puppet People*, (6) Plain nosy bastard unconnected with any of the foregoing. Decide hypotheses (1), (2), and (6) most tenable, if (6), however, simple snubs should have done the job, as administered in remark "People don't always tell the truth," in remark "I notice you too keep an eye on the door." Also discourse has hidden pattern, too curious, too knowledgeable in sociology of concealment. Cover story thin, who confines himself to rare daggers, gurkhas, bowies, hunting, throwing in this day and age when large-scale fraud is possible to even the most inept operator, as in government wheat, television, uranium, systems development, public relations? Also disguise is commonplace, why a *Negro*, why a Negro in *dark glasses*, why sitting in the dark? Now he pretends fascination with events on screen, he says it has been playing since 1944, whereas I know to my certain knowledge that last week it was *She Gods of Shark Reef,* before that *Night of the Blood Beast, Diary of a High School Bride, Cool and the Crazy.* Coming: *Reform School Girl* on double bill with *Invasion of the Saucer Men.* Why lie? or is he attempting to suggest the mutability of time? Odor of sweetness from somewhere, flowers growing in cracks of floor, underneath the seats? Possible verbena, possible gladiolus, iris, phlox. Can't identify at this distance, what does he want? Now he looks sincere, making face involves removing glasses (his eyes burn in the dark), wrinkling forehead, drawing down corners of mouth, he does it very well.

"Tell me exactly what it is you hide from," he drops, the *Enola Gay* on final leg of notorious mission.

Bomb fails to fire, Burligame reacts not. Face the image of careless gaiety, in his own atrocious phrase, couldn't care less. Bane now addresses task *con amore*, it is clear that he is a professional, but sent by whom? In these times everything is very difficult, the lines of demarcation are not clear.

"Look," pleads he, moving two spaces nearer, whispering, "I know you're hiding, you know you're hiding, I will make a confession, I too am hiding. We have discovered each other, we are mutually embarrassed, we watch the exits, we listen for the sound of rough voices, the sound of betrayal. Why not confide in me, why not make common cause, every day is a little longer, sometimes I think my hearing is gone, sometimes my eyes close without instruction. Two can watch better than one, I will even tell you my real name."

Possible emotions in the face of blatant sincerity: repugnance, withdrawal, joy, flight, camaraderie, denounce him to the authorities (there are still authorities). And yet, is this not circumstance before which the naked Burligame might dangle, is this not real life, risk and danger, as in *Voodoo Woman*, as in *Creature from the Black Lagoon*?

Bane continues. "My real name (how can I say it?) is Adrian Hipkiss, it is this among other things I flee. Can you imagine being named Adrian Hipkiss, the snickers, the jokes, the contumely, it was insupportable. There were other items, in 1944 I mailed a letter in which I didn't say what I meant, I moved the next day, it was New Year's Eve and all the moving men were drunk, they broke a leg on the piano. For fear it would return to accuse me. My life since has been one mask after another, Watford, Watkins, Watley, Watlow, Watson, Watt, now identity is gone, blown away, who am I, who knows?"

Bane-Hipkiss begins to sob, cooling system switches on, city life a texture of mysterious noises, starting and stopping, starting and stopping, we win control of the physical environment only at the expense of the auditory, what if one were sensitive, what if one flinched in the dark? Mutant termites devouring puppet people at a great rate, decorations for the scientists, tasty nurse for young lieutenant, they will end it with a joke if possible, meaning: it was not real after all. Cheating exists on every level, the attempt to deny what the eye reveals, what the mind knows to be true. Bane-Hipkiss strains credulity, a pig in a poke, if not (6) or (1) am I prepared to deal with (2)? Shall there be solidarity? But weeping is beyond toleration, unnatural, it should be reserved for great occasions, the telegram in the depths of the night, rail disasters, earthquakes, war.

"I hide from the priests" (my voice curiously tentative, fluting), "when I was the tallest boy in the eighth grade at Our Lady of the Sorrows they wanted me to go out for basketball, I would not, Father Blau the athletic priest said I avoided wholesome sport to seek out occasions of sin, in addition to the sin of pride, in addition to various other sins carefully enumerated before an interested group of my contemporaries."

Bane-Hipkiss brightens, ceases sobbing, meanwhile film begins again, puppet people move once more against U. S. Army, they are invincible, Honest John is a joke, Hound Dog malfunctions, Wowser detonates on launching pad, flower smell stronger and sweeter, are they really growing underneath our feet, is time in truth passing?

"Father Blau took his revenge in the confessional, he insisted on knowing everything. And there was much to know. Because I no longer believed as I was supposed to believe. Or believed too much, indiscriminately. To one who has always been overly susceptible to slogans they should never have said: *You can change the world*. I suggested to my confessor that certain aspects of the ritual compared unfavorably with the resurrection scene in *Bride of Frankenstein*. He was shocked."

Bane-Hipkiss pales, he himself is shocked.

"But because he had, as it were, a vested interest in me, he sought to make clear the error of my ways. I did not invite this interest, it embarrassed me, I had other things on my mind. Was it my fault that in all that undernourished parish only I had secreted sufficient hormones, had chewed thoroughly enough the soup and chips that were our daily fare, to push head and hand in close proximity to the basket?"

"You could have faked a sprained ankle," Bane-Hipkiss says reasonably.

"That was unfortunately only the beginning. One day in the midst of a good Act of Contrition, Father Blau officiating with pious malice, I leaped from the box and sprinted down the aisle, never to return. Running past people doing the Stations of the Cross, past the tiny Negro lady, somebody's maid, our only black parishioner, who always sat in the very last row with a handkerchief over her head. Leaving Father Blau, unregenerate, with the sorry residue of our weekly encounter: impure thoughts, anger, dirty words, disobedience."

Bane-Hipkiss travels two seats nearer (why two at a time?), there is an edge to his voice. "Impure thoughts?"

"My impure thoughts were of a particularly detailed and

graphic kind, involving at that time principally Nedda Ann Bush who lived two doors down the street from us and was handsomely developed. Under whose windows I crouched on many long nights awaiting revelations of beauty, the light being just right between the bureau and the window. Being rewarded on several occasions, namely 3 May 1942 with a glimpse of famous bust, 18 October 1943, a particularly chill evening, transfer of pants from person to clothes hamper, coupled with three minutes' subsequent exposure in state of nature. Before she thought to turn out the light."

"Extraordinary!" Bane-Hipkiss exhales noisily. It is clear that confession is doing him good in some obscure way. "But surely this priest extended some sort of spiritual consolation, counsel . . ."

"He once offered me part of a Baby Ruth."

"This was a mark of favor?"

"He wanted me to grow. It was in his own interest. His eye was on the All-City title."

"But it was an act of kindness."

"That was before I told him I wasn't going out. In the dark box with sliding panels, faces behind screen as in *Bighouse Baby*, as in *Mysterious House of Usher*, he gave me only steadfast refusal to understand these preoccupations, wholly natural and good interest in female parts however illicitly pursued, as under window. Coupled with skilled questioning intended to bring forth every final detail, including self-abuse and compulsive overconsumption of Baby Ruths, Mars Bars, Butterfingers, significance of which in terms of sexual self-aggrandizement was first pointed out to me by this good and holy man."

Bane-Hipkiss looks disturbed, why not? it is a disturbing story, there are things in this world that disgust, life is not all Vistavision and Thunderbirds, even Mars Bars have hidden significance, dangerous to plumb. The eradication of risk is the work of women's organizations and foundations, few of us, alas, can be great sinners.

"Became therefore a convinced anticlerical. No longer loved God, cringed at words 'My son,' fled blackrobes wherever they appeared, pronounced anathemas where appropriate, blasphemed, wrote dirty limericks involving rhymes for 'nunnery,' was in fine totally alienated. Then it became clear that this game was not so one-sided as had at first appeared, that there was a pursuit."

"Ah . . ."

"This was revealed to me by a renegade Brother of the Holy Sepulcher, a not overbright man but good in secret recesses of heart, who had been employed for eight years as cook in bishop's palace. He alleged that on wall of bishop's study was map, placed there were pins representing those in the diocese whose souls were at issue."

"Good God!" expletes Bane-Hipkiss, is there a faint flavor here of . . .

"It is kept rigorously up-to-date by the coadjutor, a rather political man. As are, in my experience, most church functionaries just under episcopal rank. Paradoxically, the bishop himself is a saint."

Bane-Hipkiss looks incredulous. "You still believe in saints?"

"I believe in saints,
"Holy water,
"Poor boxes,
"Ashes on Ash Wednesday,
"Lilies on Easter Sunday,
"Crèches, censers, choirs,
"Albs, Bibles, miters, martyrs,
"Little red lights,
"Ladies of the Altar Society,
"Knights of Columbus,
"Cassocks and cruets,
"Dispensations and indulgences,
"The efficacy of prayer,
"Right Reverends and Very Reverends,
"Tabernacles, monstrances,
"Bells ringing, people singing,
"Wine and bread,
"Sisters, Brothers, Fathers,
"The right of sanctuary,
"The primacy of the papacy,
"Bulls and concordats,
"The Index, the Last Judgment,
"Heaven and Hell,

"I believe it all. It's impossible not to believe. That's what makes things so difficult."

"But then . . ."

"It was basketball I didn't believe in."

But there is more, it was the first ritual which discovered to me the possibility of other rituals, other celebrations, for instance *Blood of Dracula*, *Amazing Colossal Man*, *It Conquered the World*. Can Bane-Hipkiss absorb this nice theological point, that one believes what one can, follows that vision which most brilliantly exalts and vilifies the world? Alone in the dark one surrenders to *Amazing Colossal Man* all hope, all desire, meanwhile the bishop sends out his patrols, the canny old priests, the nuns on simple errands in stately pairs, I remember the year everyone wore black, what dodging into doorways, what obscene haste in crossing streets!

Bane-Hipkiss blushes, looks awkward, shuffles feet, opens mouth to speak.

"I have a confession."

"Confess," I urge, "feel free."

"I was sent here."

Under their noses or in Tibet, they have agents even in the lamaseries.

"That reminds me of something," I state, but Bane-Hipkiss rises, raises hand to head, commands: "Look!" As Burligame shrinks he *strips away his skin*. Clever Bane-Hipkiss, now he has me, I sit gape-mouthed, he stands grinning with skin draped like dead dishrag over paw, he is white! I pretend imperturbability. "That reminds me, regarding the point I was making earlier, the film we are viewing is an interesting example . . ."

But he interrupts.

"Your position, while heretical, has its points," he states, "but on the other hand we cannot allow the integrity of our operation to be placed in question, willy-nilly, by people with funny ideas. Father Blau was wrong, we get some lemons just like any other group. On the other hand if every one of our people takes it into his head to flee us, who will be saved? You might start a trend. It was necessary to use this" (holds up falseface guiltily) "to get close to you, it was for the health of your soul."

Barefaced Bane-Hipkiss rattles on, has Burligame at last

been taken, must he give himself up? There is still the sign marked EXIT, into the john, up on the stool, out through the window. "I am empowered to use force," he imparts, frowning.

"Regarding the point I was making earlier," I state, "or beginning to make, the film we are watching is itself a ritual, many people view such films and refuse to understand what they are saying, consider the . . ."

"At present I have more pressing business," he says, "will you come quietly?"

"No," I affirm, "pay attention to the picture, it is trying to tell you something, revelation is not so frequent in these times that one can afford to diddle it away."

"I must warn you," he replies, "that to a man filled with zeal nothing is proscribed. Zeal," he states proudly, "is my middle name."

"I will not stir."

"You must."

Now Bane-Hipkiss moves lightly on little priest's feet, sidewise through rows of seats, a cunning smile on face now revealed as hierarchical, hands clasped innocently in front of him to demonstrate purity of intent. Strange high howling noises, as in *Night of the Blood Beast*, fearful reddish cast to sky, as in *It Conquered the World*, where do they come from? The sweetness from beneath the seats is overpowering, I attempted to warn him but he would not hear, slip the case from jacket pocket, join needle to deadly body of instrument, crouch in readiness. Bane-Hipkiss advances, eyes clamped shut in mystical ecstasy, I grasp him by the throat, plunge needle into neck, his eyes bulge, his face collapses, he subsides quivering into a lump among the seats, in a moment he will begin barking like a dog.

Most people haven't the wit to be afraid, most view television, smoke cigars, fondle wives, have children, vote, plant gladiolus, iris, phlox, never confront *Screaming Skull*, *Teenage Werewolf*, *Beast with a Thousand Eyes*, no conception of what lies beneath the surface, no faith in any manifestation not certified by hierarchy. Who is safe in home with *Teenage Werewolf* abroad, with streets under sway of *Beast with a Thousand Eyes*? People think these things are jokes, but they are wrong, it is dangerous to ignore a vision, consider Bane-Hipkiss, he has begun to bark.

Will You Tell Me?

Hubert gave Charles and Irene a nice baby for Christmas. The baby was a boy and its name was Paul. Charles and Irene who had not had a baby for many years were delighted. They stood around the crib and looked at Paul; they could not get enough of him. He was a handsome child with dark hair, dark eyes. Where did you get him Hubert? Charles and Irene asked. From the bank, Hubert said. It was a puzzling answer, Charles and Irene puzzled over it. Everyone drank mulled wine. Paul regarded them from the crib. Hubert was pleased to have been able to please Charles and Irene. They drank more wine.

Eric was born.

Hubert and Irene had a clandestine affair. It was important they felt that Charles not know. To this end they bought a bed which they installed in another house, a house some distance from the house in which Charles, Irene and Paul lived. The new bed was small but comfortable enough. Paul regarded Hubert and Irene thoughtfully. The affair lasted for twelve years and was considered very successful.

Hilda.

Charles watched Hilda growing from his window. To begin with, she was just a baby, then a four-year-old, then twelve years passed and she was Paul's age, sixteen. What a pretty young girl! Charles thought to himself. Paul agreed with Charles; he had already bitten the tips of Hilda's pretty breasts with his teeth. Hilda thought she was too old for most boys Paul's age, but not for Paul.

Hubert's son Eric wanted Hilda but could not have her.

In the cellar Paul continued making his bombs, by cellar-light. The bombs were made from tall Schlitz cans and a plastic substance which Paul refused to identify. The bombs were sold to other boys Paul's age to throw at their fathers. The bombs were to frighten them rather than to harm them. Hilda sold the bombs for Paul, hiding them under her black sweater when she went out on the street.

Hilda cut down a black pear tree in the back yard. Why?

Do you know that Hubert and Irene are having an affair? Hilda asked Paul. He nodded.

Then he said: But I don't care.

In Montreal they walked in the green snow, leaving marks like maple leaves. Paul and Hilda thought: What is wonderful? It seemed to Paul and Hilda that this was the question. The people of Montreal were kind to them, and they thought about the question in an *ambiance* of kindness.

Charles of course had been aware of the affair between Hubert and Irene from the beginning. But Hubert gave us Paul, he thought to himself. He wondered why Hilda had cut down the black pear tree.

Eric sat by himself.

Paul put his hands on Hilda's shoulders. She closed her eyes. They held each other with their hands and thought about the question. France!

Irene bought Easter presents for everyone. How do I know which part of the beach Rosemarie will be lying upon? she asked herself. In Hilda's back yard the skeleton of the black pear tree whitened.

Dialogue between Paul and Ann:

—You say anything that crawls into your head Paul, Ann objected.

—Go peddle your hyacinths, Hyacinth Girl.

It is a portrait, Hubert said, composed of all the vices of our generation in the fullness of their development.

Eric's bomb exploded with a great splash near Hubert. Hubert was frightened. What has been decided? he asked Eric. Eric could not answer.

Irene and Charles talked about Paul. I wonder how he is getting along in France? Charles wondered. I wonder if France likes him. Irene wondered again about Rosemarie. Charles wondered if the bomb that Eric had thrown at Hubert had been manufactured by his foster son, Paul. He wondered too about the strange word "foster," about which he had not wondered previously. From the bank? he wondered. What could Hubert have meant by that? What could Hubert have meant by "from the bank"? he asked Irene. I can't imagine, Irene said. The fire sparkled. It was evening.

In Silkeborg, Denmark, Paul regarded Hilda thoughtfully. You love Inge, she said. He touched her hand.

Rosemarie returned.

Paul grew older. Oh that poor fucker Eric he said.

2

The quality of the love between Hubert and Irene:

This is a pretty good bed Hubert, Irene said. Except that it's not really quite wide enough.

You know that Paul is manufacturing bombs in your cellar don't you? Hubert asked.

Inge brushed her long gold hair in her red sweater.

Who was that man, Rosemarie asked, who wrote all those books about dogs?

Hilda sat in a café waiting for Paul to return from Denmark. In the café she met Howard. Go away Howard, Hilda said to Howard, I am waiting for Paul. Oh come on Hilda, Howard said in a dejected voice, let me sit down for just a minute. Just a minute. I won't bother you. I just want to sit here at your table and be near you. I was in the war you know. Hilda said: Oh all right. But don't touch me.

Charles wrote a poem about Rosemarie's dog, Edward. It was a sestina.

Daddy, why are you writing this poem about Edward? Rosemarie asked excitedly. Because you've been away Rosemarie, Charles said.

At Yale Eric walked around.

Irene said: Hubert I love you. Hubert said that he was glad. They lay upon the bed in the house, thinking about the same things, about Montreal's green snow and the blackness of the Black Sea.

The reason I cut down the black pear tree Howard, which I've never told anyone, was that it was just as old as I was at that time, sixteen, and it was beautiful, and *I* was beautiful I think, and we both were *there* the tree and me, and I couldn't stand it, Hilda said. You are still beautiful, now, at nineteen, Howard said. But don't touch me, Hilda said.

Hubert was short in a rising market. He lost ten thousand. Can you pay the rent on this house for a while? he asked Irene. Of course darling, Irene said. How much is it? Ninety-three dollars a month, Hubert said, every month. That's not much really, Irene said. Hubert reached out his hand to caress Irene but decided not to.

Inge smiled in the candlelight from the victory candle.

Edward was tired of posing for Charles's poem. He stretched, growled, and bit himself.

In the cellar Paul mixed the plastic for another batch of bombs. A branch from the black pear tree lay on his worktable. Seeds fell into his toolbox. From the bank? he wondered. What was meant by "from the bank"? He remembered the kindness of Montreal. Hilda's black sweater lay across a chair. God is subtle, but he is not malicious, Einstein said. Paul held his tools in his hands. They included an awl. Now I shall have to find more Schlitz cans, he thought. Quickly.

Irene wondered if Hubert really loved her, or if he was merely saying so to be pleasant. She wondered how she could find out. Hubert was handsome. But so was Charles handsome for that matter. And I, I am still quite beautiful, she reminded herself. Not in the same way as young girls like Hilda and Rosemarie, but in a different way. I have a mature beauty. Oh!

From the bank? Inge wondered.

Eric came home for the holidays.

Anna Teresa Tymieniecka wrote a book to which I. M. Bochénski contributed a foreword.

Rosemarie made a list of all the people who had not written her a letter that morning:

> George Lewis
> Peter Elkin
> Joan Elkin
> Howard Toff
> Edgar Rich
> Marcy Powers
> Sue Brownly
> *and many others*

Paul said to the man at the hardware store: I need a new awl. What size awl do you have in mind? the man asked. One about this size, Paul said, showing the man with his hands. Oh Hilda!

What is his little name? Charles and Irene asked Hubert. His name, Hubert said, is Paul. A small one, isn't he? Charles remarked. But well made, Hubert noted.

Can I buy you a drink? Howard asked Hilda. Have you had any *grappa* yet? It's one of the favorite drinks of this country. Your time is up Howard, Hilda said ruthlessly. Get out of this café. Now wait a minute, Howard said. This is a free country isn't it? No, Hilda said. No buddy, a free country is precisely what this is not insofar as your sitting at this table is concerned. Besides, I've decided to go to Denmark on the next plane.

The mailman (Rosemarie's mailman) persisted in his irritating habit of doing the other side of the street before he did her side of the street. Rosemarie ate a bowl of Three-Minute Oats.

Eric cut his nails with one of those 25¢ nail cutters.

The bomb Henry Jackson threw at his father failed to detonate. Why did you throw this Schlitz can at me Henry? Henry's father asked, and why is it ticking like a bomb?

Hilda appeared in Paul's cellar. Paul, she asked, can I borrow an axe? or a saw?

Hubert touched Irene's breast. You have beautiful breasts, he said to Irene. I like them. Do you think they're too mature? Irene asked anxiously.

Mature?

3

Ann the Hyacinth Girl wanted Paul but could not have him. He was sleeping with Inge in Denmark.

From his window Charles watched Hilda. She sat playing under the black pear tree. She bit deeply into a black pear. It tasted bad and Hilda looked at the tree inquiringly. Charles started to cry. He had been reading Bergson. He was surprised by his own weeping, and in a state of surprise, decided to get something to eat. Irene was not home. There was nothing in the refrigerator. What was he going to do for lunch? Go to the drugstore?

Rosemarie looked at Paul. But of course he's far too young for me, she thought.

Edward and Eric met on the street.

Inge wrote the following letter to Ann to explain why Ann could not have Paul:

Dear Ann—

I deeply appreciate the sentiments expressed by you in our recent ship-to-shore telephone conversation. Is the Black Sea pleasant? I hope so and hope too that you are having a nice voyage. The Matson Line is one of my favorite lines. However I must tell you that Paul is at present deeply embedded in a love affair with me, Inge Grote, a very nice girl here in Copenhagen, and therefore cannot respond to your proposals, charming and well stated as they were. You have a very nice prose style on the telephone. Also, I might point out that if Paul loves any girl other than me in the near future it will surely be Hilda, that girl of girls. Hilda! what a remarkable girl! Of course there is also the possibility that he will love some girl he has not met yet—this is remote, I think. But thank you for the additional hyacinths anyway, and we promise to think of you from time to time.

Your friend,
Inge

Charles lay in bed with his wife, Irene. He touched a breast, one of Irene's. You have beautiful breasts Irene, Charles said. Thank you, Irene said, Charles.

Howard's wire to Eric was never delivered.

Hubert thought seriously about his Christmas present to Charles and Irene. What can I get for these dear friends that will absolutely shatter them with happiness? he asked himself. I wonder if they'd like a gamelan? a rag rug?

Oh Hilda, Paul said cheerfully, it has been so long since I've been near to you! Why don't the three of us go out for supper?

Hubert had a dinner engagement with the best younger poet now writing in English in Wisconsin.

Charles! Irene exclaimed. You're hungry! And you've been crying! Your gray vest is stained with tears! Let me make you a ham and cheese sandwich. Luckily I have just come from the grocery store, where I bought some ham, cheese, bread, lettuce, mustard and paper napkins. Charles asked: Have you seen or heard from Hubert lately by the way? He regarded his gray tear-stained vest. Not in a long time, Irene said, Hubert's been acting sort of distant lately for some strange reason. Oh

Charles, can I have an extra ninety-three dollars a month for the household budget? I need some floor polish and would also like to subscribe to the *National Geographic*.

Every month?

Ann looked over the ship's rail at the Black Sea. She threw hyacinths into it, not just one but a dozen or more. They floated upon the black surface of the water.

"But I can't stand the pain. Oh, why doesn't God help me?"

"Can you give me a urine sample?" asked the nurse.

Paul placed his new awl in the toolbox. Was that a shotgun Eric had been looking at in the hardware store?

Irene, Hubert said, I love you. I've always hesitated to mention it though because I was inhibited by the fact that you are married to my close friend, Charles. Now I feel close to you here in this newsreel theater, for almost the first time. I feel intimate. I feel like there might be some love in you for me, too. Then, Irene said, your giving me Paul for a Christmas present was symbolic?

Inge smiled.

Rosemarie smiled.

Ann smiled.

Goodbye, Inge, Paul said. Your wonderful blondness has been wonderful and I shall always remember you that way. Goodbye! Goodbye!

The newsreel articulated the fall of Ethiopia.

Howard cashed a check at American Express. What shall I do with this money? he wondered. Nothing financial has meaning any more now that Hilda has gone to Denmark. He returned to the café in the hope that Hilda had not really meant it.

Charles put some more wine on to mull.

Henry Jackson's father thought candidly: Henry is awfully young to be an anarchist isn't he?

Put those empty Schlitz cans over there in the corner by the furnace Harry, Paul said. And thank you for lending me your pickup truck in this cold weather. I think you had better get some snow tires pretty soon though, as I hear that snow is predicted for the entire region shortly. Deep snow.

Howard to Hilda: If you don't understand me, that's okay, but I am afraid you do understand me. In that case, I think I will have dreams.

Where are you going Eric with that shotgun? Hubert asked.

It is virtually impossible to read one of Joel S. Goldsmith's books on the oneness of life without becoming a better person Eric, Rosemarie said.

Eric, take that shotgun out of your mouth! Irene shouted. Eric!

4

Oh Hubert, why did you give me that damn baby? Paul I mean? Didn't you know he was going to grow?

The French countryside (the countryside of France) was covered with golden grass. I'm looking for a bar, they said, called the Cow on the Roof or something like that.

Inge stretched her right and left arms luxuriously. You have brought me so much marvelous happiness Paul that although I know you will go away soon to consort once more with Hilda, that all-time all-timer girl, it still pleases me to be here in this good Dansk bed with you. Do you want to talk about phenomenological reduction now? or do you want a muffin?

Edward counted his Pard.

From the bank? Rosemarie asked herself.

I have decided Charles to go to the Virgin Islands with Hubert. Do you mind? Since Hubert's position in the market has improved radically I feel he is entitled to a little relaxation in the golden sun. Okay?

The Black Sea patrol boat captain said: *Hy*acinths?

The new black pear tree reached sturdily for the sky on the grave, the very place, of the old black pear tree.

He wondered whether to wrap it as a gift, or simply take it over to Charles and Irene's in the box. He couldn't decide. He decided to have a drink. While Hubert was drinking his vodka martini it started to cry. I wonder if I'm making these drinks too strong?

The snow of Montreal banked itself against the red Rambler. Paul and Hilda embraced. What is wonderful? they thought. They thought the answer might be in their eyes, or in their mingled breath, but they couldn't be sure. It might be illusory.

I wonder how I might become slightly more pleasing to the eye? Rosemarie asked. Perhaps I should tattoo myself attractively?

—Hilda I do think it's possible now for us to be together, to *stay* together even, even to live together if that is your wish. I feel that we have come to the end of a very trying time, a time in which we were tried see? and that from this day forward everything will be fine. We will have a house and so on, et cetera et cetera, and even children of our own perhaps. I'll get a job.

—That sounds wonderful, Aaron.

Eric?

For I'm the Boy Whose Only Joy Is Loving You

ON THE trip back from the aerodrome Huber who was driving said: Still I don't see why we were required. You weren't required Bloomsbury said explicitly, you were invited. Invited then Huber said, I don't see what we were invited *for*. As friends of the family Bloomsbury said. You are both friends of the family. A tissue of truths he thought, delicate as the negotiations leading to the surrender. It was not enough Bloomsbury felt, to say that his friends Huber and Whittle were as men not what he wished them to be. For it was very possible he was aware, that he was not what they wished him to be. Nevertheless there were times when he felt like crying aloud, that it was not right!

She was I thought quite calm Bloomsbury said. You also Huber said turning his head almost completely around. Of course she has been trained to weep in private Bloomsbury said looking out of the window. Training he thought, that's the great thing. Behind them aircraft rose and fell at intervals, he wondered if they should have waited for "the take-off," if it would have been more respectful, or on the other hand less respectful, to have done so. Still I thought there'd certainly be weeping Whittle said from the front seat. I have observed that in situations involving birth, bereavement or parting forever there is usually some quantity of weeping. But he provided a crowd Huber said, precluding privacy. And thus weeping Whittle agreed. Yes Bloomsbury said.

Ah Pelly where do you be goin'? T' grandmather's, bein' it please yer lardship. An' what a fine young soft young warm young thing ya have there Pelly on yer bicycle seat. Ooo yer lardship ye've an evil head on yer, I'll bet yer sez that t'all us guls. Naw Pelly an' the truth of the matter is, there's nivver a gul come down my street wi' such a fine one as yers. Yer a bold one yer worship if ye doon cock a minnow. Lemme just feel of her a trifle Pelly, there's a good gul. Ooo Mishtar Bloomsbury I likes a bit o' fun as good as the next 'un but me husbing's watchin' from the porch wi' 'is field telescope. Pother Pelly it won't be leavin' any marks, we'll just slither behind this tree. Ring me bicycle bell yer lardship he'll think yer after sellin' the Eskimo Pies. That I will Pelly I'll give 'er a ring like she nivver had before. Ooo yer grace be keerful of me abdominal belt what's holdin' up me pedal pushers. Never fear Pelly I dealt wi' worse than that in my time I have.

Of course it's inaccurate to say that we are friends of the family Huber said. There no longer being any family. The family exists still I believe Whittle said, as a legal entity. Were you married? it would affect the legal question, whether or not the family *qua* family endures beyond the physical separation of the partners, which we have just witnessed. Bloomsbury understood that Whittle did not wish to be thought prying and understood also, or recalled rather, that Whittle's wife or former wife had flown away in an aircraft very similar to if not identical with the one in which Martha his own wife had elected to fly away. But as he considered the question a tiresome one, holding little interest in view of the physical separation already alluded to, which now claimed his attention to the exclusion of all other claims, he decided not to answer. Instead he said: She looked I thought quite pretty. Lovely Whittle acknowledged and Huber said: Stunning in fact.

Ah Martha coom now to bed there's a darlin' gul. Hump off blatherer I've no yet read me Mallarmé for this evenin'. Ooo Martha dear canna we noo let the dear lad rest this night? when th' telly's already shut doon an' th' man o' the hoose 'as a 'ard on? Don't be comin' round wit yer lewd proposals on a Tuesday night when ye know better. But Martha dear where is yer love for me that we talked about in 19 and 38? in the cemetary by the sea? Pish Mishtar Hard On ye'd better be lookin' after the Disposall what's got itself plogged up. Ding the Disposall! Martha me gul it's yer sweet hide I'm after havin'. Get yer hands from out of me Playtex viper, I'm dreadful bored wit' yer silly old tool. But Marthy dear what of th' poetry we read i' the' book, aboot th' curlew's cry an' th' white giant's thigh, in 19 and 38? that we consecrated our union wit'? That was then an' this is now, ye can be runnin' after that bicycle gul wi' th' tight pants if yer wants a bit o' the auld shiver n' shake. Ah Marthy it's no bicycle gul that's brakin' me heart but yer sweet self. Keep yer paws off me derriere dear yer makin' me lose me page i' th' book.

Rich girls always look pretty Whittle said factually and Huber said: I've heard that. Did she take the money with her? Whittle asked. Oh yes Bloomsbury said modestly (for had he not after all relinquished, at the same time he had relinquished Martha, a not inconsiderable fortune, amounting to thousands, if not more?). You could hardly have done otherwise I suppose Huber said. His eyes which fortunately remained on the road during this passage were "steely-bright." And yet... Whittle began. Something for your trouble Huber suggested, a tidy bit, to put in the Postal Savings. It would have gone against the grain no doubt Whittle said. But there was trouble was there not? for which little or no compensation has been offered? Outrage Bloomsbury noted stiffened Whittle's neck which had always been inordinately long and thin, and stiff. The money he thought, there had been in truth a great deal. More than one person could easily dispose of. But just right as fate would have it for two.

A BEER WINE LIQUOR ICE sign appeared by the roadside. Huber stopped the car which was a Pontiac Chieftain and entering the store purchased, for $27.00, a bottle of 98-year-old brandy sealed on the top with a wax seal. The bottle was old and dirty but the brandy when Huber returned with it was tasty in the extreme. For the celebration Huber said generously offering the bottle first to Bloomsbury who had in their view recently suffered pain and thus deserved every courtesy, insofar as possible. Bloomsbury did not overlook this great-hearted attitude on the part of his friend. Although he has many faults Bloomsbury reflected, he has many virtues also. But the faults engaged his attention and sipping the old brandy he began to review them seriously, and those of Whittle also. One fault of Huber's which Bloomsbury considered and reconsidered was that of *not keeping his eye on the ball*. In the matter of the road for instance Bloomsbury said to himself, any Texaco Gasoline sign is enough to distract him from his clear duty, that of operating the vehicle. And there were other faults both mortal and venial which Bloomsbury thought about just as seriously as this. Eventually his thinking was interrupted by these words of Whittle's: Good old money!

It would have been wrong Bloomsbury said austerely, to have kept it. Cows flew by the windows in both directions. That during the years of our cohabitation it had been *our* money to cultivate and be proud of does not alter the fact that originally it was her money rather than my money he finished. You could have bought a boat Whittle said, or a horse or a house. Presents for your friends who have sustained you in the accomplishment of this difficult and if I may say so rather unpleasant task Huber added pushing the accelerator pedal to the floor so that the vehicle "leaped ahead." While these things were being said Bloomsbury occupied himself by thinking of one of his favorite expressions, which was: *Everything will be revealed at the proper time.* He remembered too the several occasions on which Huber and Whittle had dined at his house. They had admired he recalled not only the tuck but also the wife of the house whose aspect both frontside and backside was scrutinized and commented upon by them. To the point that the whole enterprise (friendship) had become, for him, quite insupportable, and defeating. Huber had in one instance even reached out his hand to touch it, when it was near, and bent over, and sticking out, and Bloomsbury as host had been forced, by the logic of the situation, to rap his wrist with a soup spoon. Golden days Bloomsbury thought, in the sunshine of our happy youth.

It's idiotic Huber said, that we know nothing more of the circumstances surrounding the extinguishment of your union than you have chosen to tell us. What do you want to know? Bloomsbury asked, aware however that they would want *everything*. It would be interesting I think as well as instructive Whittle said casually, to know for instance at what point the situation of living together became untenable, whether she wept when you told her, whether you wept when she told you, whether you were the instigator or she was the instigator, whether there were physical fights involving bodily blows or merely objects thrown on your part and on her part, if there were mental cruelties, cruelties of what order and on whose part, whether she had a lover or did not have a lover, whether you did or did not, whether you kept the television or she kept the television, the disposition of the balance of the furnishings including tableware, linens, light bulbs, beds and baskets, who got the baby if there was a baby, what food remains in the pantry at this time, what happened to the medicine bottles including Mercurochrome, rubbing alcohol, aspirin, celery tonic, milk of magnesia, No-Doze and Nembutal, was it a fun divorce or not a fun divorce, whether she paid the lawyers or you paid the lawyers, what the judge said if there was a judge, whether you asked her for a "date" after the granting of the decree or did not so ask, whether she was touched or not touched by this gesture if there was such a gesture, whether the date if there was such a date was a fun thing or not a fun thing—in short we'd like to get the feel of the event he said. We'd be pepped to know, Huber said. I remember how it was when my old wife Eleanor flew away Whittle said, but only dimly because of the years. Bloomsbury however was thinking.

Have ye heard the news Pelly, that Martha me wife has left me in a yareplane? on th' bloody Champagne Flight? O yer wonderfulness, wot a cheeky lot to be pullin' the plog on a lovely man like yerself. Well that's how the cock curls Pelly, there's naught left of 'er but a bottle of Drene Shampoo in th' boodwar. She was a bitch that she was to commit this act of lese majesty against th' sovereign person of yer mightiness. She locked 'erself i' th' john Pelly toward th' last an' wouldn't come out not even for Flag Day. Incredible Mishtar Bloomsbury to think that such as that coexist wi' us good guls side by side in the twentieth century. An' no more lovey-kindness than a stick, an' no more gratitude than a glass o' milk of magnesia. What bought her clothes at the Salvation Army by th' look of her, on the Revolving Credit Plan. I fingerprinted her fingerpaintings she said and wallowed in sex what is more. Coo, Mishtar Bloomsbury me husbing Jack brings th' telly right into th' bed wi' 'im, it's bumpin' me back all night long. I' th' bed? I' th' bed. It's been a weary long time Pelly since love 'as touched my hart. Ooo your elegance, there's not a young gul in the Western Hemisphere as could withstand the grandeur of such a swell person as you. It's marriage Pelly what has ruined me for love. It's a hard notion me Bloomie boy but tragically true nonetheless. I don't want pity Pelly there's little enough rapport between adults wi'out clouding th' issue wi' sentiment. I couldn't agree more yer gorgeousness damme if I haven't told Jack a thousand times, that rapport is the only thing.

Although customarily of a lively and even ribald disposition the friends of the family nevertheless maintained during these thoughts of Bloomsbury's attitudes of the most rigorous and complete solemnity, as were of course appropriate. However Whittle at length said: I remember from my own experience that the pain of parting was shall I say exquisite? Exquisite Huber said, what a stupid word. How would you know? Whittle asked, you've never been married. I may not know about marriage Huber said stoutly, but I know about words. Exquisite he pronounced giggling. You have no delicacy Whittle said, that is clear. Delicacy Huber said, you get better and better. He began weaving the car left and right on the highway, in delight. The brandy Whittle said, has been too much for you. Crud Huber said assuming a reliable look. You've suffered an insult to the brain Whittle said, better let me drive. You drive! Huber exclaimed, your ugly old wife Eleanor left you *precisely because* you were a mechanical idiot, she confided in me on the day of the hearing. A mechanical idiot! Whittle said in surprise, I wonder what she meant by that? Huber and Whittle then struggled for the wheel for a brief space but in a friendly way. The Pontiac Chieftain behaved very poorly during this struggle, zigging and zagging, but Bloomsbury who was preoccupied did not notice. It was interesting he thought that after so many years one could still be surprised by a flyaway wife. Surprise he thought, that's the great thing, it keeps the old tissues tense.

Well Whittle said how does it feel? It? Bloomsbury said, what is *it*?

The physical separation mentioned earlier Whittle said. We want to know how it feels. The question is not what is the feeling but what is the meaning? Bloomsbury said reasonably. Christ Huber said, I'll tell you about *my* affair. What about it? Bloomsbury asked. It was a Red Cross girl Huber said, named Buck Rogers. Of what did it consist? Whittle asked. It consisted Huber said, of going to the top of the Chrysler Building and looking out over the city. Not much meat there Whittle said disparagingly, how did it end? Badly Huber said. Did she jump? Whittle asked. I jumped Huber said. You were always a jumper Whittle said. Yes Huber said angrily, I had taken precautions. Did your chute open? Whittle asked. With a sound like timber falling Huber said, but she never knew. The end of the affair Whittle said sadly. But what a wonderful view of the city Huber commented. So now, Whittle said to Bloomsbury, *give us the feeling*.

We can discuss Bloomsbury said, the meaning but not the feeling. If there is emotion it is only just that you share it with your friends Whittle said. Who are no doubt all you have left in the world said Huber. Whittle had placed upon Huber's brow, which was large and red, handkerchiefs dampened in brandy, with a view toward calming him. But Huber would not be calmed. Possibly there are relatives Whittle pointed out, of one kind or another. Hardly likely Huber said, considering his circumstances, now that there is no more money I would hazard that there are no more relatives either. Emotion! Whittle exclaimed, when was the last time we had any? The war I expect Huber replied, all those chaps going West. I'll give you a hundred dollars Whittle said, for the feeling. No Bloomsbury said, I have decided not. We are fine enough to be a crowd at the airport so that your wife will not weep but not fine enough to be taken into your confidence I suppose Huber said "bitterly." Not a matter of fine enough Bloomsbury said reflecting meanwhile upon the proposition that the friends of the family were *all he had left*, which was he felt quite a disagreeable notion. But probably true. Good what manner of man is this! Whittle exclaimed and Huber said: Prick!

Once in a movie house Bloomsbury recalled Tuesday Weld had suddenly turned on the screen, looked him full in the face, and said: You are a good man. You are good, good, good. He had immediately gotten up and walked out of the theater, gratification singing in his heart. But that situation dear to him as it was helped him not a bit in this situation. And that memory memorable as it was did not prevent the friends of the family from stopping the car under a tree, and beating Bloomsbury in the face first with the brandy bottle, then with the tire iron, until at length the hidden feeling emerged, in the form of salt from his eyes and black blood from his ears, and from his mouth, all sorts of words.

The Big Broadcast of 1938

Having acquired in exchange for an old house that had been theirs, his and hers, a radio or more properly radio *station*, Bloomsbury could now play "The Star-Spangled Banner," which he had always admired immoderately, on account of its finality, as often as he liked. It meant, to him, that everything was finished. Therefore he played it daily, 60 times between 6 and 10 A.M., 120 times between 12 noon and 7 P.M., and the whole night long except when, as was sometimes the case, he was talking.

Bloomsbury's radio talks were of two kinds, called the first kind and the second kind. The first consisted of singling out, for special notice, from among all the others, some particular word in the English language, and repeating it in a monotonous voice for as much as fifteen minutes, or a quarter-hour. The word thus singled out might be any word, the word *nevertheless* for example. "Nevertheless," Bloomsbury said into the microphone, "nevertheless, nevertheless, nevertheless, nevertheless, nevertheless, nevertheless, nevertheless." After this exposure to the glare of public inspection the word would frequently disclose new properties, unsuspected qualities, although that was far from Bloomsbury's intention. His intention, insofar as he may be said to have had one, was simply to put something "on the air."

The second kind of radio talk which Bloomsbury provided was the *commercial announcement.*

The Bloomsbury announcements were perhaps not too similar to other announcements broadcast during this period by other broadcasters. They were dissimilar chiefly in that they were addressed not to the mass of men but of course to her, she with whom he had lived in the house that was gone (traded for the radio). Frequently he would begin somewhat in this vein:

"Well, old girl" (he began), "here we are, me speaking into the tube, you lying on your back most likely, giving an ear, I don't doubt. Swell of you to tune me in. I remember the time you went walking without your shoes, what an evening! You were wearing, I recall, your dove-gray silk, with a flower hat, and you picked your way down the boulevard as daintily as a real lady. There were chestnuts on the ground, I believe; you complained that they felt like rocks under your feet. I got down on my hands and knees and crawled in front of you, sweeping the chestnuts into the gutter with my hand. What an evening! You said I looked absurd, and a gentleman who was passing in the other direction, I remember he wore yellow spats with yellow shoes, smiled. The lady accompanying him reached out to pat me on my head, but he grasped her arm and prevented her, and the knees of my trousers tore on a broken place in the pavement.

"Afterwards you treated me to a raspberry ice, calling for a saucer, which you placed, daintily, at your feet. I still recall the coolness, after the hot work on the boulevard, and the way the raspberry stained my muzzle. I put my face in your hand, and your little glove came away pink and sticky, sticky and pink. We were comfortable there, in the ice cream parlor, we were pretty as a picture! Man and wife!

"When we got home, that evening, the street lights were just coming on, the insects were just coming out. And you said that next time, if there were a next time, you would wear your shoes. Even if it killed you, you said. And I said I would always be there to sweep away the chestnuts, whatever happened, even if nothing happened. And you said most likely that was right. I always *had* been there, you said. Swell of you to notice that. I thought at the time that there was probably no one more swell than you in the whole world, anywhere. And I wanted to tell you, but did not.

"And then, when it was dark, we had our evening quarrel. A very ordinary one, I believe. The subject, which had been announced by you at breakfast and posted on the notice board, was *Smallness in the Human Male*. You argued that it was willfulness on my part, whereas I argued that it was lack of proper nourishment during my young years. I lost, as was right of course, and you said I couldn't have any supper. I had, you said, already gorged myself on raspberry ice. I had, you said, ruined a good glove with my ardor, and a decent pair of trousers too. And I said, but it was for the love of you! and you said, hush! or there'll be no breakfast either. And I said, but love makes the world go! and you said, or lunch tomorrow either. And I said, but we were everything to each other once! and you said, or supper tomorrow night.

"But perhaps, I said, a little toffee? Ruin your teeth then for all I care, you said, and put some pieces of toffee in my bed. And thus we went happily to sleep. Man and wife! Was there ever anything, old skin, like the old days?"

Immediately following this commercial announcement, or an announcement much like this, Bloomsbury would play "The Star-Spangled Banner" 80 or 100 times, for the finality of it.

When he interrogated himself about the matter, about how it felt to operate a radio of his own, Bloomsbury told himself the absolute truth, that it felt fine. He broadcast during this period not only some of his favorite words, such as the words *assimilate*, *alleviate*, *authenticate*, *ameliorate*, and quantities of his favorite music (he was particularly fond of that part, toward the end, that went: da-da, da da da da da da da-a), but also a series of commercial announcements of great power and poignancy, and persuasiveness. Nevertheless he felt, although he managed to conceal it from himself for a space, somewhat futile. For there had been no response from her (she who figured, as both subject and object, in the commercial announcements, and had once, before it had been traded for the radio, lived in the house).

A commercial announcement of the period of this feeling was:

"On that remarkable day, that day unlike any other, that day, if you will pardon me, of days, on that old day from the old days when we were, as they say, young, we walked if you will forgive the extravagance *hand in hand* into a theater where there was a film playing. Do you remember? We sat in the upper balcony and smoke from below, where there were people smoking, rose and we, if you will excuse the digression, smelled of it. It smelled, and I or we thought it remarkable at the time, like the twentieth century. Which was after all our century, none other.

"We were there you and I because we hadn't rooms and there were no parks and we hadn't automobiles and there were no beaches, for making love or anything else. *Ergo*, if you will condone the anachronism, we were forced into the balcony, to the topmost row, from which we had a tilty view of the silver screen. Or would have had had we not you and I been engaged in pawing and pushing, pushing and pawing. On my part at least, if not on yours.

"The first thing I knew I was inside your shirt with my hand and I found there something very lovely and, as they say, desirable. It belonged to you. I did not know, then, what to do with it, therefore I simply (simply!) held it in my hand, it was, as the saying goes, soft and warm. If you can believe it. Meanwhile down below in the pit events were taking place, whether these were such as the people in the pit had paid for, I did not and do not know. Nor did or do, wherever you are, you. After a time I was in fact distracted, I still held it in my hand but I was looking elsewhere.

"You then said into my ear, get on with it, can't you?

"I then said into your ear, I'm watching the picture.

"At this speech of mine you were moved to withdraw it from my hand, I understood, it was a punishment. Having withdrawn it you began, for lack of anything better, to watch the picture also. We watched the picture together, and although this was a kind of intimacy, the other kind had been lost. Nevertheless it had been there once, I consoled myself with that. But I felt, I felt, I felt (I think) that you were, as they say, angry. And to that row of the balcony we, you and I, never returned."

After this announcement was broadcast Bloomsbury himself felt called upon to weep a little, and did, but not "on the air."

He was in fact weeping quietly in the control room, where were kept the microphone, the console, the turntables and the hotplate, with "The Star-Spangled Banner" playing bravely and a piece of buttered toast in his hand, when he saw in the glass that connected the control room with the other room, which had been a reception room or foyer, a girl or woman of indeterminate age dressed in a long bright red linen duster.

The girl or woman removed her duster, underneath she was wearing black toreador pants, an orange sweater, and harlequin glasses. Bloomsbury immediately stepped out into the reception room or foyer in order to view her more closely, he regarded her, she regarded him, after a time there was a conversation.

"You're looking at me!" she said.

"Oh, yes," he said. "Right. I certainly am."

"Why?"

"It's something I do," he said. "It's my you might say *métier*."

"*Milieu*," she said.

"*Métier*," Bloomsbury said. "If you don't mind."

"I don't often get looked at as a matter of fact."

"Because you're not very good-looking," Bloomsbury said.

"Oh I say."

"Glasses are discouraging," he said.

"Even harlequin glasses?"

"Especially harlequin glasses."

"Oh," she said.

"But you have a grand behind," he said.

"Also a lively sense of humor," she said.

"Lively," he said. "Whatever possessed you to use that word?"

"I thought you might like it," she said.

"No," he said. "Definitely not."

"Do you think you ought to stand around and look at girls?" she asked.

"Oh, yes," Bloomsbury said. "I think it's indicated."

"*Indicated*," she cried. "What do you mean, *indicated*?"

"Tell me about your early life," Bloomsbury said.

"To begin with I was president of the Conrad Veidt fan club," she began. "That was in, oh, I don't remember the year. His magnetism and personality got me. His voice and gestures fascinated me. I hated him, feared him, loved him. When he died it seemed to me a vital part of my imagination died too."

"I didn't mean necessarily in such detail," he said.

"My world of dreams was bare!"

"Fan club prexies are invariably homely," Bloomsbury said.

"*Plain*," she suggested. "I prefer the word plain. Do you want to see a picture of Conrad Veidt?"

"I would be greatly interested," Bloomsbury said (although this was not the truth).

The girl or woman then retrieved from her purse, where it had apparently remained for some time, perhaps even years, a page from a magazine. It bore a photograph of Conrad Veidt who looked at one and the same instant handsome and sinister. There was moreover printing on the photograph which said:

If CONRAD VEIDT offered you a cigarette, it would be a DE REZKE—of course!

"Very affecting," Bloomsbury said.

"I never actually met Mr. Veidt," the girl (or woman) said. "It wasn't that sort of club. I mean we weren't in actual communication with the star. There was a Joan Crawford fan club, and *those* people now, *they* were in actual communication. When they wanted a remembrance . . ."

"A remembrance?"

"Such as Kleenex that had been used by the star, for instance, with lipstick on it, or fingernail clippings, or a stocking, or a hair from the star's horse's tail or mane . . ."

"Tail or mane?"

"The star naturally, *noblesse oblige*, forwarded that object to them."

"I see," Bloomsbury said.

"Do you look at a lot of girls?"

"Not a *lot*," he said, "but quite a number."

"Is it fun?"

"Not *fun*," he said, "but better than nothing."

"Do you have affairs?"

"Not *affairs*," he said, "but sometimes a little flutter."

"Well," she said, "I have feelings too."

"I think it's very possible," he said. "A great big girl like you."

This remark however seemed to offend her, she turned on her heel and left the room. Bloomsbury himself felt moved by this meeting, which was in fact the first contact he had enjoyed with a human being, of any description, since the beginning of the period of his proprietorship of the radio, and even before. He immediately returned to the control room and introduced a new commercial announcement.

"I remember" (he enunciated), "the quarrel about the ice cubes, that was a beauty! That was one worth . . . remembering. You had posted on the notice board the subject *Refrigeration*, and I worried about it all day long, and wondered. Clever minx! I recalled at length that I had complained, once, because the ice cubes were not *frozen*. But were in fact unfrozen! watery! useless! I had said that there *weren't enough ice cubes*, whereas you had said there were *more than enough*.

"You said that I was a fool, an idiot, an imbecile, a stupid!, that the machine in your kitchen which you had procured and caused to be placed there was without doubt and on immaculate authority the most accomplished machine of its kind known to those who knew about machines of its kind, that among its attributes was the attribute of conceiving containing and at the moment of need whelping a fine number of ice cubes so that no matter how grave the demand, how vast the occasion, how indifferent or even hostile the climate, how inept or even treacherous the operator, how brief or even nonexistent the lapse between genesis and parturition, between the wish and the fact, ice cubes in multiples of sufficient would present themselves. Well, I said, perhaps.

"Oh! how you boggled at that word *perhaps*. How you sweated, old girl, and cursed. Your chest heaved, if I may say so, and your eyes (your eyes!) flashed. You said we would, by damn, *count* the by damn ice cubes. As we, subsequently, did.

"How I enjoyed, although I concealed it from you, the counting! You were, as they say, magisterial. There were I observed twelve rows of three, or three of twelve, in each of four trays. But this way of counting was not your way of counting. You chose, and I admired your choice, the explicitness and *im*plicitness of it, to run water over the trays so that the cubes, loosened, fell into the salad bowl, having previously turned the trays, and thus the cubes, bottoms up, so that the latter would fall, when water was run upon the former, in the proper direction. That these matters were so commendably arranged I took to be, and even now take to be, a demonstration of your fundamental decency, and good sense.

"But you reckoned wrong, when it came to that. You were never a reckoner. You reckoned that there were in the bowl one hundred forty-four cubes, taking each cube, individually, from the bowl and placing it, individually, in the sink, bearing in mind meanwhile the total that could be obtained by simple multiplication of the spaces in the trays. Thus having it, in this as in other matters, both ways! However you failed on this as on other occasions to consider the imponderables, in this instance the fact that I, unobserved by you, had put three of the cubes into my drink! Which I then drank! And that one had missed the bowl entirely and fallen into the sink! And melted once and for all! These events precluded sadly enough the number of cubes in the bowl adding up to a number corresponding to the number of spaces in the trays, proving also that *there is no justice*!

"What a defeat for you! What a victory for me! It was my first victory, I fear I went quite out of my head. I dragged you to the floor, among the ice cubes, which you had flung there in pique and chagrin, and forced you, with results that I considered then, and consider now, to have been 'first rate.' I thought I detected in you . . ."

But he could not continue this announcement, from a surfeit of emotion.

The girl or woman, who had become a sort of camp follower of the radio, made a practice during this period of sleeping in the former reception room underneath the piano, which being a grand provided ample shelter. When she wished to traffic with Bloomsbury she would tap on the glass separating them with one finger, at other times she would, with her hands, make motions.

A typical conversation of the period when the girl (or woman) was sleeping in the foyer was this:

"Tell me about your early life," she said.

"I was, in a sense, an All-American boy," Bloomsbury replied.

"In what sense?"

"In the sense that I married," he said.

"Was it love?"

"It was love but it was only temporary."

"It didn't go on forever?"

"For less than a decade. As a matter of fact."

"But while it did go on . . ."

"It filled me with a somber and paradoxical joy."

"Coo!" she said. "It doesn't sound very American to me."

"*Coo*," he said. "What kind of an expression is that?"

"I heard it in a movie," she said. "A Conrad Veidt movie."

"Well," he said, "it's distracting."

This conversation was felt by Bloomsbury to be not very satisfactory, however he bided his time, having if the truth were known no alternative. The word *matriculate* had engaged his attention, he pronounced it into the microphone for what seemed to him a period longer than normal, that is to say, in excess of a quarter-hour. He wondered whether or not to regard this as significant.

It was a fact that Bloomsbury, who had thought himself dispassionate (thus the words, the music, the slow turning over in his brain of events in the lives of him and her), was beginning to feel, at this time, disturbed. This was attributable perhaps to the effect, on him, of his radio talks, and also perhaps to the presence of the "fan," or listener, in the reception room. Or possibly it was something else entirely. In any case this disturbance was reflected, beyond a doubt, in the announcements made by him in the days that, inevitably, followed.

One of these was:

"The details of our housekeeping, yours and mine. The scuff under the bed, the fug in the corners. I would, if I could, sigh to remember them. You planted prickly pear in the parlor floor, and when guests came . . . Oh, you were a one! You veiled yourself from me, there were parts I could have and parts I couldn't have. And the rules would change, I remember, in the middle of the game, I could never be sure which parts were allowed and which not. Some days I couldn't have anything at all. Is it remarkable, then, that there has never been another? Except for a few? Who don't count?

"There has, I don't doubt, never been anything like it. The bed, your mother's bed, brought to our union with your mother in it, she lay like a sword between us. I had the gall to ask what you were thinking. It was one of those wonderful days of impenetrable silence. Well, I said, and the child? Up the child, you said, 'twasn't what I wanted anyway. What then did you want? I asked, and the child cried, its worst forebodings confirmed. Pish, you said, nothing you could supply. Maybe, I said. Not bloody likely, you said. And where is it (the child) now? Gone, I don't doubt, away.

"Are you with me, old bush?

"Are you tuned in?

"A man came, in a hat. In the hat was a little feather, and in addition to the hat and the feather there was a satchel. Jack, this is my husband, you said. And took him into the bedroom, and turned the key in the lock. What are you doing in there? I said, the door being locked, you and he together on the inside, me alone on the outside. Go away and mind your own silly business, you said, from behind the door. Yes, Jack said (from behind the door), go away and don't be bothering people with things on their minds. Insensitive brute! you said, and Jack said, filthy cad! Some people, you said, and Jack said, the cheek of the thing. I watched at the door until nightfall, but could hear no more words, only sounds of a curious nature, such as grunts and moans, and sighs. Upon hearing these (through the door which was, as I say, locked), I immediately rushed to the attic to obtain our copy of *Ideal Marriage*, by Th. H. Van De Velde, M.D., to determine whether this situation was treated of therein. But it was not. I therefore abandoned the book and returned to my station outside the door, which remained (and indeed why not?) shut.

"At length the door opened, your mother emerged, looking as they say 'put out.' But she had always taken your part as opposed to my part, therefore she said only that I was a common sneak. But, I said, what of those who even now sit in the bed? laughing and joking? Don't try to teach thy grandmother to chew coal, she said. I then became, if you can believe it, melancholy. Could not we two skins, you and me, climb and cling for all the days that were left? Which were not, after all, so very many days? Without the interpolation of such as Jack? And, no doubt, others yet to come?"

After completing this announcement and placing "The Star-Spangled Banner" on the turntable, and a cup of soup on the hotplate, Bloomsbury observed that the girl in the reception room was making motions with her hands, the burden of which was, that she wanted to speak to him.

"Next to Mr. Veidt my favorite star was Carmen Lambrosa," she said. "What is more, I am said to resemble her in some aspects."

"Which?" Bloomsbury asked with interest. "Which aspects?"

"It was said of Carmen Lambrosa that had she just lived a little longer, and not died from alcohol, she would have been the top box office money-maker in the British Cameroons. Where such as she and me are appreciated."

"The top box office money-maker for what year?"

"The year is not important," she said. "What is important is the appreciation."

"I would say you favored her," Bloomsbury observed, "had I some knowledge of her peculiarities."

"Do I impress you?"

"In what way?"

"As a possible partner? Sexually I mean?"

"I haven't considered it," he said, "heretofore."

"They say I'm sexy," she noted.

"I don't doubt it," he said. "I mean it's plausible."

"I am yours," she said, "if you want me."

"Yes," he said, "there's the difficulty, making up my mind."

"You have only," she said, "to make the slightest gesture of acquiescence, such as a nod, a word, a cough, a cry, a kick, a crook, a giggle, a grin."

"Probably I would not enjoy it," he said, "now."

"Shall I take off my clothes?" she asked, making motions as if to do so.

With a single stride, such as he had often seen practiced in the films, Bloomsbury was "at her side."

"Martha," he said, "old skin, why can't you let the old days die? That were then days of anger, passion, and dignity, but are now, in the light of present standards, practices, and attitudes, days that are done?"

Upon these words from him, she began to weep. "You looked interested at first," she said (through her tears).

"It was kind of you to try it," he said. "Thoughtful. As a matter of fact, you were most appealing. Tempting, even. I was fooled for whole moments at a time. You look well in bull-fighter pants."

"Thank you," she said. "You said I had a grand behind. You said that at least."

"And so you do."

"You can't forget," she asked, "about Dudley?"

"Dudley?"

"Dudley who was my possible lover," she said.

"Before or after Jack?"

"Dudley who in fact broke up our *ménage*," she said, looking at him expectantly.

"Well," he said, "I suppose."

"Tell me about the joy again."

"There was some joy," Bloomsbury said. "I can't deny it."

"Was it really like you said? Somber and paradoxical?"

"It was all of that," he said gallantly, "then."

"Then!" she said.

There was a moment of silence during which they listened, thoughtfully, to "The Star-Spangled Banner" playing softly in the other room behind them.

"Then we are, as they say, through?" she asked. "There is no hope for us?"

"None," he said. "That I know of."

"You've found somebody you like better?"

"It's not that," he said. "That has nothing to do with it."

"Balls," she said. "I know you and your letchy ways."

"Goodbye," Bloomsbury said, and returned to the control room, locking the door behind him.

He then resumed broadcasting, with perhaps a tremor but no slackening in his resolve not to flog, as the expression runs, a dead horse. However the electric company, which had not been paid from the first to the last, refused at length to supply further current for the radio, in consequence of which the broadcasts, both words and music, ceased. That was the end of this period of Bloomsbury's, as they say, life.

The Viennese Opera Ball

I DO not like to see an elegant pair of forceps! Blundell stated. Let the instrument look what it is, a formidable weapon! *Arte, non vi* (art, not strength) may be usefully engraved upon one blade; and *Care perineo* (take care of the perineum) on the other. His companion replied: The test of a doctor's prognostic acumen is to determine the time to give up medicinal and dietetic measures and empty the uterus, and overhesitancy to do this is condemnable, even though honorable ... I do not mean that we should perform therapeutic abortion with a light spirit. On the contrary, I am slow to adopt it and always have proper consultation. If on the other hand a bear kills a man, someone said, the Croches immediately organize a hunt, capture a bear, kill it, eat its heart, and throw out the rest of the meat; they save the skin, which with the head of the beast serves as a shroud for the dead man. Among the Voguls the nearest relative was required to seek revenge. The Goldi have the same custom in regard to the tiger; they kill him and bury him with this little speech: *Now we are even, you have killed one of ours, we have killed one of yours. Now let us live in peace. Don't disturb us again, or we will kill you.* Carola Mitt, brown-haired, brown-eyed and just nineteen, was born in Berlin (real name: Mittenstein), left Germany five years ago. In her senior year at the Convent of the Sacred Heart in Greenwich, Conn., Carola went to the Viennese Opera Ball at the Waldorf-Astoria, was spotted by a *Glamour* editor.

I mean, the doctor resumed, we should study each patient thoroughly and empty the uterus before she has retinitis; before jaundice has shown that there is marked liver damage; before she has polyneuritis; before she has toxic myocarditis; before her brain is degenerated, *et al.*—and it can be done. Meyer Davis played for the Viennese Opera Ball. Copperplate printers, said a man, deliver Society Printing in neat, stylish boxes. They are compelled to slipsheet the work with tissue paper, an expense the letterpress printer may avoid, if careful. Boxes, covered with enameled paper for cards and all kinds of Society

Printing, are on sale to carry the correct sizes. No matter how excellent your work and quality may be, women who know the correct practice will not be satisfied unless the packages are as neat as those sent out by the copperplate printers. The devil is not as wicked as people believe, and neither is an Albanian. (Carola Mitt soon dropped her plans to be a painter, made $60 an hour under the lights, appeared on the covers of *Vogue*, *Harper's Bazaar*, *Mademoiselle* and *Glamour*, shared a Greenwich Village apartment with another girl, yearned to get married and live in California. But that was later.)

The *Glamour* editor said: Take Dolores Wettach. Dolores Wettach is lush, Lorenesque, and doubly foreign (her father is Swiss, her mother Swedish); she moved at the age of five from Switzerland to Flushing, N.Y., where her father set up a mink ranch. Now about twenty-four ("You learn not to be too accurate"), Dolores was elected Miss Vermont in the 1956 Miss Universe contest, graduated in 1957 from the University of Vermont with a B.S. in nursing. Now makes $60 an hour. While Dolores Wettach was working as a nurse at Manhattan's Doctors Hospital, a sharp-eyed photographer saw beyond her heavy Oxfords, asked her to pose. Dying remarks: Oliver Goldsmith, 1728–74, British poet, playwright and novelist, was asked: Is your mind at ease? He replied: No, it is not, and died. Hegel: Only one man ever understood me. And he didn't understand me. Hart Crane, 1899–1932, poet, as he jumped into the sea: Goodbye, everybody! Tons of people came to the Viennese Opera Ball. At noon, the first doctor said, on January 31, 1943, while walking, the patient was seized with sudden severe abdominal pain and profuse vaginal bleeding. She was admitted to the hospital at 1 P.M. in a state of exsanguination. She presented a tender, rigid abdomen and uterus. Blood pressure 110/60. Pulse rate 110—thready. Fetal heart not heard. Patient was given intravenous blood at once. The membranes were ruptured artificially and a Spanish windlass was applied. Labor progressed rapidly. At 6 P.M., a 5-pound stillborn infant was delivered by low forceps. Hemorrhage persisted following delivery in spite of hypodermic Pituitrin, intravenous ergotrate, and firm uterine packing. Blood transfusion had been maintained continuously. At 9 P.M. a laparotomy was done, and a Couvelaire uterus with tubes and ovaries was removed by

THE VIENNESE OPERA BALL 57

supracervical hysterectomy. The close adherence of the tubes and ovaries to the fundus necessitated their removal. Patient stood surgery well. A total of 2000 C.C. of whole blood and 1500 C.C. of whole plasma had been administered. Convalescence was satisfactory, and the patient was dismissed on the fourteenth postoperative day. Waiters with drinks circulated among the ball-goers.

Carola Mitt met Isabella Albonico at the Viennese Opera Ball. Isabella Albonico, Italian by temperament as well as by birth (twenty-four years ago, in Florence), began modeling in Europe when she was fifteen, arrived in New York four years ago. Brown-haired and brown-eyed, she has had covers on *Vogue*, *Harper's Bazaar* and *Life*, makes $60 an hour, and has won, she says, "a reputation for being allergic to being pummeled around under the lights. Nobody touches me." I entirely endorse these opinions, said a man standing nearby, and would only add that the wife can do much to avert that fatal marital *ennui* by independent interests which she persuades him to share. For instance, an interesting book, or journey, or lecture or concert, experienced, enjoyed and described by her, with sympathy and humor, may often be a talisman to divert his mind from work and worry, and all the irritations arising therefrom. But, of course, he, on his side, must be able to appreciate her appreciation and her conversation. The stimuli to the penile nerves may differ in degrees of intensity and shades of quality; and there are corresponding diversities in the sensations of pleasure they bestow. It is of much importance in determining these sensations whether the stimuli are localized mainly in the frenulum preputti or the posterior rim of the glans. *Art* rather than *sheer force* should prevail. (There is an authentic case on record in which the attendant braced himself and pulled so hard that, when the forceps slipped off, he fell out of an open window onto the street below and sustained a skull fracture, while the patient remained undelivered.) The Jumbo Tree, 254 feet high, is named from the odd-shaped growths at the base resembling the heads of an elephant, a monkey and a bison. Isabella told Carola that she "would like most of all to be a movie star," had just returned from Hollywood, where she played a small part ("but opposite Cary Grant") in *That Touch of Mink* and a larger one in an all-Italian film, *Smog*. Besides

English and Italian, Isabella speaks French and Spanish, hates big groups. What kind of big groups? Carola asked. *This* kind, Isabella said, waving her hand to indicate the Viennese Opera Ball.

Smog is an interesting name Carola said. In the empty expanses of Islamabad, the new capital that Pakistan plans to erect in the cool foothills of the Himalayas, the first buildings scheduled to go up are a cluster of airy structures designed by famed U.S. architect Edward Stone. Set in a cloistered water garden, the biggest of Stone's buildings will house Pakistan's first nuclear reactor—one of the largest sales made by New York's American Machine & Foundry Co. Fifteen years ago, AMF was a company with only a handful of products (cigarette, baking and stitching machines) and annual sales of about $12,000,000. Today, with 42 plants and 19 research facilities scattered across 17 countries, AMF turns out products ranging from remote-controlled toy airplanes to ICBM launching systems. Thanks to AMF's determined pursuit of diversification and growth products, its 1960 sales were $361 million, its earnings $24 million. And in the glum opening months of 1961, the company's sales and earnings hit new first-quarter highs. AMF's expansion is the work of slow-spoken, low-pressured Chairman Morehead Patterson, 64, who took over the company in 1943 from his father, Rufus L. Patterson, inventor of the first automated tobacco machine. After World War II, Morehead Patterson decided that the company had to grow or die. Searching for new products, he turned up a crude prototype of an automatic bowling-pin setter. To get the necessary cash to develop the intricate gadget, Patterson swapped off AMF stock to acquire eight small companies with fast-selling products. The Pinspotter, perfected and put on the market in 1951, helped to turn bowling into the most popular U.S. competitive sport. Despite keen competition from the Brunswick Corp., AMF has remained the world's largest maker of automatic pin setters. With 68,000 machines already on lease in the U.S. (for an average annual gross of $68 million), AMF last week got a $3,000,000 contract to equip a new chain of bowling centers in the East. Is there another Pinspotter in AMF's future? Chairman Patterson cautiously admits to the hope that perhaps the firm's intensive research into purifying

THE VIENNESE OPERA BALL 59

brackish and fouled water might produce another product breakthrough. "Companies, like people," says Patterson, "get arteriosclerosis. My job is to see that AMF doesn't." Morehead Patterson did not attend the Viennese Opera Ball.

Carola Mitt said: Among other things, I means the ego; it is also the symbol, in *astronomy*, for the inclination of an orbit to the ecliptic; in *chemistry*, for iodine; in *physics*, for the density of current, the intensity of magnetization, or the moment of inertia; in *logic*, for a particular affirmative proposition. Lester Lannin also played for the Viennese Opera Ball. Nonsense! said a huge man wearing the Double Eagle of St. Puce, what about sailing, salesmen, salt, sanitation, Santa Claus, saws, scales, schools, screws, sealing wax, secretaries, sects, selling, the Seven Wonders, sewerage, sewing machines, sheep, sheet metal, shells, shipbuilding, shipwrecks, shoemaking, shopping, shower baths, sieges, signboards, silverware, sinning, skating, skeletons, skeleton *keys*, sketching, skiing, skulls, skyscrapers, sleep, smoking, smugglers, Socialism, soft drinks, soothsaying, sorcery, space travel, spectacles, spelling, sports, squirrels, steamboats, steel, stereopticans, the Stock Exchange, stomachs, stores, storms, stoves, streetcars, strikes, submarines, subways, suicide, sundials, sunstroke, superstition, surgery, surveying, sweat and syphilis! It is one of McCormack's proudest boasts, Carola heard over her lovely white shoulder, that he has never once missed having dinner with his wife in their forty-one years of married life. She remembered Knocko at the Evacuation Day parade, and Baudelaire's famous remark. Mortality is the final evaluator of methods. An important goal is an intact sphincter. The greater the prematurity, the more generous should be the episiotomy. Yes said Leon Jaroff, Detroit Bureau Chief for *Time*, at the Thomas Elementary School on warm spring afternoons I could look from my classroom into the open doors of the Packard plant. Ideal foster parents are mature people who are not necessarily well off, but who have a good marriage and who love and understand children. The ninth day of the ninth month is the festival of the chrysanthemum (Kiku No Sekku), when *sake* made from the chrysanthemum is drunk. Kiku Jido, a court youth, having inadvertently touched with his foot the pillow of the emperor, was banished to a distant isle, where, it is said, he was nourished by the dew of the chrysanthemums which abounded there. Becoming a hermit, he lived for a thousand years. Husbands have been known to look at their wives with new eyes, Laura La Plante thought to herself. Within the plane of each individual work—experienced apart from a series—he presents one with a similar set of one-at-a-time experiences each contained within its own compartment, and read in a certain order, up or down or across. Far off at Barlow Ranger Station, as the dawn was breaking, Bart slept dreamlessly at last. *Peridermium coloradense* on spruce (*Picea*) has long been considered conspecific with *Melampsorella caryophyllacearum* Schroet., which alternates between fir (*Abies*) and *Caryophyllaceæ*. Evidence that these rusts are identical consists largely of inoculation results of Weit and Hubert (1,2), but these have never been fully confirmed. Take Dorothea McGowan the *Glamour* editor said. Dorothea McGowan is the exception in the new crop: she speaks only English and was born in Brooklyn. Her premodeling life took her as far from home as Staten Island, where she finished her freshman year at Notre Dame College before taking a summer job modeling $2.98 house dresses. A few months later, her first photographic try at a cover made *Vogue*; this year she set some kind of a record by appearing on four *Vogue* covers in a row (nobody but her mother or agent could have told that it was the same girl). Twenty-year-old Dorothea ("My middle initial is E, and Dorothy sounded so ordinary") makes $60 an hour, has her own apartment in New York, studies French at Manhattan's French Institute twice a week ("so that when my dream of living in Paris comes true, I'll be ready for it"). Dorothea has been sent, all expenses paid, to be photographed in front of the great architectural monuments of Europe, among Middle East bazaars and under Caribbean palms. She is absolutely infatuated with the idea of being paid to travel. I never saw so many autumn flowers as grow in the woods and sheep-walks of Maryland. But I confess, I scarcely knew a single name. Let no one visit America without first having studied botany.

Carola was thrilled by all the interesting conversations at the Viennese Opera Ball. The Foundation is undertaking a comprehensive analytical study of the economic and social positions of the artist and of his institutions in the United States. In part this will serve as a basis for future policy decisions and

THE VIENNESE OPERA BALL

program activities. The contemplated study will also be important outside the Foundation. The climate of the arts today, discussion in the field reveals, is complex and various. Pack my box with Title Shaded Litho. Pack my box with Boston Breton Extra Condensed. Pack my box with Clearface Heavy. (C) Brasol, 261–285; Buck, 212–221; Carr, *D*, 281–301; Collins, 76–82; Curle, 176–224; A. G. Dostoevsky, *D Portrayed by His Wife*, 268–269; F. Dostoevsky, *Letters and Reminiscences*, 241–242, 247, 251–252; F. Dostoevsky, *New D Letters*, 79–102; Freud, *passim*; Gibian, "D's Use of Russian Folklore," *passim*; Hesse—see; Hromadka, 45–50; Ivanov, 142–166 and *passim*; King, 22–29; Lavrin, *D and His Creation*, 114–142; Lavrin, *D: A Study*, 119–146; Lavrin, "D and Tolstoy," 189–195; Lloyd, 275–290; McCune, *passim*; Mackiewicz, 183–191; Matlaw, 221–225; Maugham, 203–208; Maurina, 147–153, 198–203, 205–210, 218–221; Meier-Graefe, 288–377; Muchnic, *Intro . . .* , 165–172; Mueller, 193–200; Murry, 203–259; Passage, 162–174; Roe, 20–25, 41–51, 68–91, 100–110; Roubiczek, 237–244, 252–260, 266–271; Sachs, 241–246; Scott, 204–209; Simmons, 263–279 and *passim*; Slonim, *Epic . . .* , 289–293 and *passim*; Soloviev, 195–202; Strakosch, *passim*; Troyat, 395–416; Tymms, 99–103; Warner, 80–101; Colin Wilson, 178–201; Yarmolinsky, *D, His Life and Art*, 355–361 and *passim*; Zander, 15–30, 63–95, 119–137. Carola said: What a wonderful ball! The width of the black band varies according to relationship. For a widow's card a band of about one-third inch (No. 5) during the first year of widowhood, diminishing about one-sixteenth inch each six months thereafter. On a widower's card one-quarter inch (No. 3) is the widest, diminishing gradually from time to time. For other relatives, the band may vary from the thickness of No. 3 to that of the "Italian." No. 5 band is now considered excessive, but among the Latin races is held to be moderate, and if preferred, is entirely correct. To administer the agreement and facilitate the attainment of its ends, a Committee on Trade Policy and Payments will be set up with all member countries represented. The judicial form contemplated in the agreement is that of a free trade zone to be transformed gradually into a customs union. As Emile Myerson has said, *"L'homme fait de la métaphysique comme il respire, sans le vouloir et surtout sans s'en douter la plupart du temps."* No woman is worth more than 24 cattle, Pamela Odede B.A.'s father said. With this album Abbey Lincoln's stature as one of the great jazz singers of our time is confirmed, Laura La Plante said. Widely used for motors, power tools, lighting, TV, etc. Generator output: 3500 watts, 115/230 volt, 60 cy., AC, continuous duty. Max. 230 V capacitor motor, loaded on starting—1/2 hp; unloaded on starting—2 hp. Control box mounts starting switch, duplex 115 V receptacle for standard or 3-conductor grounding plugs, tandem 230 V grounding receptacles, and wing nut battery terminals. More than six hundred different kinds of forceps have been invented. Let's not talk about the lion, she said. Wilson looked over at her without smiling and now she smiled at him. This process uses a Lincoln submerged arc welding head to run both inside and outside beads automatically. The rate of progress during the first stage will determine the program to be followed in the second stage. The *Glamour* editor whose name was Tutti Beale "moved in." What's your name girl? she said coolly. Carola Mitt, Carola Mitt said. The Viennese Opera Ball continued.

Me and Miss Mandible

13 September

MISS MANDIBLE wants to make love to me but she hesitates because I am officially a child; I am, according to the records, according to the gradebook on her desk, according to the card index in the principal's office, eleven years old. There is a misconception here, one that I haven't quite managed to get cleared up yet. I am in fact thirty-five, I've been in the Army, I am six feet one, I have hair in the appropriate places, my voice is a baritone, I know very well what to do with Miss Mandible if she ever makes up her mind.

In the meantime we are studying common fractions. I could, of course, answer all the questions, or at least most of them (there are things I don't remember). But I prefer to sit in this too-small seat with the desktop cramping my thighs and examine the life around me. There are thirty-two in the class, which is launched every morning with the pledge of allegiance to the flag. My own allegiance, at the moment, is divided between Miss Mandible and Sue Ann Brownly, who sits across the aisle from me all day long and is, like Miss Mandible, a fool for love. Of the two I prefer, today, Sue Ann; although between eleven and eleven and a half (she refuses to reveal her exact age) she is clearly a woman, with a woman's disguised aggression and a woman's peculiar contradictions. Strangely neither she nor any of the other children seem to see any incongruity in my presence here.

15 September

Happily our geography text, which contains maps of all the principal land-masses of the world, is large enough to conceal my clandestine journal-keeping, accomplished in an ordinary black composition book. Every day I must wait until Geography to put down such thoughts as I may have had during the morning about my situation and my fellows. I have tried writing at other times and it does not work. Either the teacher is walking up and down the aisles (during this period, luckily, she sticks close to the map rack in the front of the room) or Bobby Vanderbilt, who sits behind me, is punching me in the kidneys and wanting to know what I am doing. Vanderbilt, I have found out from certain desultory conversations on the playground, is hung up on sports cars, a veteran consumer of *Road & Track*. This explains the continual roaring sounds which seem to emanate from his desk; he is reproducing a record album called *Sounds of Sebring*.

19 September

Only I, at times (only at times), understand that somehow a mistake has been made, that I am in a place where I don't belong. It may be that Miss Mandible also knows this, at some level, but for reasons not fully understood by me she is going along with the game. When I was first assigned to this room I wanted to protest, the error seemed obvious, the stupidest principal could have seen it; but I have come to believe it was deliberate, that I have been betrayed again.

Now it seems to make little difference. This life-role is as interesting as my former life-role, which was that of a claims adjuster for the Great Northern Insurance Company, a position which compelled me to spend my time amid the debris of our civilization: rumpled fenders, roofless sheds, gutted warehouses, smashed arms and legs. After ten years of this one has a tendency to see the world as a vast junkyard, looking at a man and seeing only his (potentially) mangled parts, entering a house only to trace the path of the inevitable fire. Therefore when I was installed here, although I knew an error had been made, I countenanced it, I was shrewd; I was aware that there might well be some kind of advantage to be gained from what seemed a disaster. The role of The Adjuster teaches one much.

22 September

I am being solicited for the volleyball team. I decline, refusing to take unfair profit from my height.

23 September

Every morning the roll is called: Bestvina, Bokenfohr, Broan, Brownly, Cone, Coyle, Crecelius, Darin, Durbin, Geiger, Guiswite, Heckler, Jacobs, Kleinschmidt, Lay, Logan, Masei,

Mitgang, Pfeilsticker. It is like the litany chanted in the dim miserable dawns of Texas by the cadre sergeant of our basic training company.

In the Army, too, I was ever so slightly awry. It took me a fantastically long time to realize what the others grasped almost at once: that much of what we were doing was absolutely pointless, to no purpose. I kept wondering why. Then something happened that proposed a new question. One day we were commanded to whitewash, from the ground to the topmost leaves, all of the trees in our training area. The corporal who relayed the order was nervous and apologetic. Later an off-duty captain sauntered by and watched us, white-splashed and totally weary, strung out among the freakish shapes we had created. He walked away swearing. I understood the principle (orders are orders), but I wondered: Who decides?

29 September

Sue Ann is a wonder. Yesterday she viciously kicked my ankle for not paying attention when she was attempting to pass me a note during History. It is swollen still. But Miss Mandible was watching me, there was nothing I could do. Oddly enough Sue Ann reminds me of the wife I had in my former role, while Miss Mandible seems to be a child. She watches me constantly, trying to keep sexual significance out of her look; I am afraid the other children have noticed. I have already heard, on that ghostly frequency that is the medium of classroom communication, the words "*Teacher's pet!*"

2 October

Sometimes I speculate on the exact nature of the conspiracy which brought me here. At times I believe it was instigated by my wife of former days, whose name was . . . I am only pretending to forget. I know her name very well, as well as I know the name of my former motor oil (Quaker State) or my old Army serial number (US 54109268). Her name was Brenda, and the conversation I recall best, the one which makes me suspicious now, took place on the day we parted. "You have the soul of a whore," I said on that occasion, stating nothing less than literal, unvarnished fact. "You," she replied, "are a pimp, a poop, and a child. I am leaving you forever and I trust that without me you will perish of your own inadequacies. Which are considerable."

I squirm in my seat at the memory of this conversation, and Sue Ann watches me with malign compassion. She has noticed the discrepancy between the size of my desk and my own size, but apparently sees it only as a token of my glamour, my dark man-of-the-world-ness.

7 October

Once I tiptoed up to Miss Mandible's desk (when there was no one else in the room) and examined its surface. Miss Mandible is a clean-desk teacher, I discovered. There was nothing except her gradebook (the one in which I exist as a sixth-grader) and a text, which was open at a page headed *Making the Processes Meaningful*. I read: "Many pupils enjoy working fractions when they understand what they are doing. They have confidence in their ability to take the right steps and to obtain correct answers. However, to give the subject full social significance, it is necessary that many realistic situations requiring the processes be found. Many interesting and lifelike problems involving the use of fractions should be solved . . ."

8 October

I am not irritated by the feeling of having been through all this before. Things are done differently now. The children, moreover, are in some ways different from those who accompanied me on my first voyage through the elementary schools: "*They have confidence in their ability to take the right steps and to obtain correct answers.*" This is surely true. When Bobby Vanderbilt, who sits behind me and has the great tactical advantage of being able to maneuver in my disproportionate shadow, wishes to bust a classmate in the mouth he first asks Miss Mandible to lower the blind, saying that the sun hurts his eyes. When she does so, *bip!* My generation would never have been able to con authority so easily.

13 October

It may be that on my first trip through the schools I was too much under the impression that what the authorities (who decides?) had ordained for me was right and proper, that I confused authority with life itself. My path was not particularly of my own choosing. My career stretched out in front of me like a paper chase, and my role was to pick up the clues. When I got out of school, the first time, I felt that this estimate was substantially correct, and eagerly entered the hunt. I found clues abundant: diplomas, membership cards, campaign buttons, a marriage license, insurance forms, discharge papers, tax returns, Certificates of Merit. They seemed to prove, at the very least, that I was *in the running*. But that was before my tragic mistake on the Mrs. Anton Bichek claim.

I misread a clue. Do not misunderstand me: it was a tragedy only from the point of view of the authorities. I conceived that it was my duty to obtain satisfaction for the injured, for this elderly lady (not even one of our policyholders, but a claimant against Big Ben Transfer & Storage, Inc.) from the company. The settlement was $165,000; the claim, I still believe, was just. But without my encouragement Mrs. Bichek would never have had the self-love to prize her injury so highly. The company paid, but its faith in me, in my efficacy in the role, was broken. Henry Goodykind, the district manager, expressed this thought in a few not altogether unsympathetic words, and told me at the same time that I was to have a new role. The next thing I knew I was here, at Horace Greeley Elementary, under the lubricious eye of Miss Mandible.

17 October

Today we are to have a fire drill. I know this because I am a Fire Marshal, not only for our room but for the entire right wing of the second floor. This distinction, which was awarded shortly after my arrival, is interpreted by some as another mark of my somewhat dubious relations with our teacher. My armband, which is red and decorated with white felt letters reading FIRE, sits on the little shelf under my desk, next to the brown paper bag containing the lunch I carefully make for myself each morning. One of the advantages of packing my own lunch (I have no one to pack it for me) is that I am able to fill it with things I enjoy. The peanut butter sandwiches that my mother made in my former existence, many years ago, have been banished in favor of ham and cheese. I have found that my diet has mysteriously adjusted to my new situation; I no longer drink, for instance, and when I smoke, it is in the boys' john, like everybody else. When school is out I hardly smoke at all. It is only in the matter of sex that I feel my own true age; this is apparently something that, once learned, can never be forgotten. I live in fear that Miss Mandible will one day keep me after school, and when we are alone, create a compromising situation. To avoid this I have become a model pupil: another reason for the pronounced dislike I have encountered in certain quarters. But I cannot deny that I am singed by those long glances from the vicinity of the chalkboard; Miss Mandible is in many ways, notably about the bust, a very tasty piece.

24 October

There are isolated challenges to my largeness, to my dimly realized position in the class as Gulliver. Most of my classmates are polite about this matter, as they would be if I had only one eye, or wasted, metal-wrapped legs. I am viewed as a mutation of some sort but essentially a peer. However Harry Broan, whose father has made himself rich manufacturing the Broan Bathroom Vent (with which Harry is frequently reproached; he is always being asked how things are in Ventsville), today inquired if I wanted to fight. An interested group of his followers had gathered to observe this suicidal undertaking. I replied that I didn't feel quite up to it, for which he was obviously grateful. We are now friends forever. He has given me to understand privately that he can get me all the bathroom vents I will ever need, at a ridiculously modest figure.

25 October

"Many interesting and lifelike problems involving the use of fractions should be solved . . ." The theorists fail to realize that everything that is either interesting or lifelike in the classroom proceeds from what they would probably call interpersonal relations: Sue Ann Brownly kicking me in the ankle. How lifelike, how womanlike, is her tender solicitude after the deed! Her pride in my newly acquired limp is transparent; everyone knows that she has set her mark upon me, that it is a victory in her unequal struggle with Miss Mandible for my great, overgrown heart. Even Miss Mandible knows, and counters in perhaps the

only way she can, with sarcasm. "Are you wounded, Joseph?" Conflagrations smolder behind her eyelids, yearning for the Fire Marshal clouds her eyes. I mumble that I have bumped my leg.

30 October
I return again and again to the problem of my future.

4 November
The underground circulating library has brought me a copy of *Movie–TV Secrets*, the multicolor cover blazoned with the headline "Debbie's Date Insults Liz!" It is a gift from Frankie Randolph, a rather plain girl who until today has had not one word for me, passed on via Bobby Vanderbilt. I nod and smile over my shoulder in acknowledgment; Frankie hides her head under her desk. I have seen these magazines being passed around among the girls (sometimes one of the boys will condescend to inspect a particularly lurid cover). Miss Mandible confiscates them whenever she finds one. I leaf through *Movie–TV Secrets* and get an eyeful. "The exclusive picture on these pages isn't what it seems. We know how it looks and we know what the gossipers will do. So in the interests of a nice guy, we're publishing the facts first. Here's what really happened!" The picture shows a rising young movie idol in bed, pajama-ed and bleary-eyed, while an equally blowzy young woman looks startled beside him. I am happy to know that the picture is not really what it seems; it seems to be nothing less than divorce evidence.

What do these hipless eleven-year-olds think when they come across, in the same magazine, the full-page ad for Maurice de Paree, which features "Hip Helpers" or what appear to be padded rumps? ("A real undercover agent that adds appeal to those hips and derriere, both!") If they cannot decipher the language the illustrations leave nothing to the imagination. "Drive him frantic . . ." the copy continues. Perhaps this explains Bobby Vanderbilt's preoccupation with Lancias and Maseratis; it is a defense against being driven frantic.

Sue Ann has observed Frankie Randolph's overture, and catching my eye, she pulls from her satchel no less than seventeen of these magazines, thrusting them at me as if to prove that anything any of her rivals has to offer, she can top. I shuffle through them quickly, noting the broad editorial perspective:

> "Debbie's Kids Are Crying"
> "Eddie Asks Debbie: Will You . . .?"
> "The Nightmares Liz Has About Eddie!"
> "The Things Debbie Can Tell About Eddie"
> "The Private Life of Eddie and Liz"
> "Debbie Gets Her Man Back?"
> "A New Life for Liz"
> "Love Is a Tricky Affair"
> "Eddie's Taylor-Made Love Nest"
> "How Liz Made a Man of Eddie"
> "Are They Planning to Live Together?"
> "Isn't It Time to Stop Kicking Debbie Around?"
> "Debbie's Dilemma"
> "Eddie Becomes a Father Again"
> "Is Debbie Planning to Re-wed?"
> "Can Liz Fulfill Herself?"
> "Why Debbie Is Sick of Hollywood"

Who are these people, Debbie, Eddie, Liz, and how did they get themselves in such a terrible predicament? Sue Ann knows, I am sure; it is obvious that she has been studying their history as a guide to what she may expect when she is suddenly freed from this drab, flat classroom.

I am angry and I shove the magazines back at her with not even a whisper of thanks.

5 November

The sixth grade at Horace Greeley Elementary is a furnace of love, love, love. Today it is raining, but inside the air is heavy and tense with passion. Sue Ann is absent; I suspect that yesterday's exchange has driven her to her bed. Guilt hangs about me. She is not responsible, I know, for what she reads, for the models proposed to her by a venal publishing industry; I should not have been so harsh. Perhaps it is only the flu.

Nowhere have I encountered an atmosphere as charged with aborted sexuality as this. Miss Mandible is helpless; nothing goes right today. Amos Darin has been found drawing a dirty picture in the cloakroom. Sad and inaccurate, it was offered not as a sign of something else but as an act of love in itself. It has excited even those who have not seen it, even those who saw but understood only that it was dirty. The room buzzes with imperfectly comprehended titillation. Amos stands by the door, waiting to be taken to the principal's office. He wavers between fear and enjoyment of his temporary celebrity. From time to time Miss Mandible looks at me reproachfully, as if blaming me for the uproar. But I did not create this atmosphere, I am caught in it like all the others.

8 November
Everything is promised my classmates and I, most of all the future. We accept the outrageous assurances without blinking.

9 November
I have finally found the nerve to petition for a larger desk. At recess I can hardly walk; my legs do not wish to uncoil themselves. Miss Mandible says she will take it up with the custodian. She is worried about the excellence of my themes. Have I, she asks, been receiving help? For an instant I am on the brink of telling her my story. Something, however, warns me not to attempt it. Here I am safe, I have a place; I do not wish to entrust myself once more to the whimsy of authority. I resolve to make my themes less excellent in the future.

11 November
A ruined marriage, a ruined adjusting career, a grim interlude in the Army when I was almost not a person. This is the sum of my existence to date, a dismal total. Small wonder that re-education seemed my only hope. It is clear even to me that I need reworking in some fundamental way. How efficient is the society that provides thus for the salvage of its clinkers!

Plucked from my unexamined life among other pleasant, desperate, money-making young Americans, thrown backward in space and time, I am beginning to understand how I went wrong, how we all go wrong. (Although this was far from the intention of those who sent me here; they require only that I *get right*.)

14 November
The distinction between children and adults, while probably useful for some purposes, is at bottom a specious one, I feel. There are only individual egos, crazy for love.

15 November
The custodian has informed Miss Mandible that our desks are all the correct size for sixth-graders, as specified by the Board of Estimate and furnished the schools by the Nu-Art Educational Supply Corporation of Englewood, California. He has pointed out that if the desk size is correct, then the pupil size must be incorrect. Miss Mandible, who has already arrived at this conclusion, refuses to press the matter further. I think I know why. An appeal to the administration might result in my removal from the class, in a transfer to some sort of setup for "exceptional children." This would be a disaster of the first magnitude. To sit in a room with child geniuses (or, more likely, children who are "retarded") would shrivel me in a week. Let my experience here be that of the common run, I say; let me be, please God, typical.

20 November
We read signs as promises. Miss Mandible understands by my great height, by my resonant vowels, that I will one day carry her off to bed. Sue Ann interprets these same signs to mean that I am unique among her male acquaintances, therefore most desirable, therefore her special property as is everything that is Most Desirable. If neither of these propositions work out then life has broken faith with them.

I myself, in my former existence, read the company motto ("Here to Help in Time of Need") as a description of the duty of the adjuster, drastically mislocating the company's deepest concerns. I believed that because I had obtained a wife who was made up of wife-signs (beauty, charm, softness, perfume, cookery) I had found love. Brenda, reading the same signs that have now misled Miss Mandible and Sue Ann Brownly, felt she had been promised that she would never be bored again. All of us, Miss Mandible, Sue Ann, myself, Brenda, Mr. Goodykind, still believe that the American flag betokens a kind of general righteousness.

But I say, looking about me in this incubator of future citizens, that signs are signs, and that some of them are lies. This is the great discovery of my time here.

23 November

It may be that my experience as a child will save me after all. If only I can remain quietly in this classroom, making my notes while Napoleon plods through Russia in the droning voice of Harry Broan, reading aloud from our History text. All of the mysteries that perplexed me as an adult have their origins here, and one by one I am numbering them, exposing their roots.

2 December

Miss Mandible will refuse to permit me to remain ungrown. Her hands rest on my shoulders too warmly, and for too long.

7 December

It is the pledges that this place makes to me, pledges that cannot be redeemed, that confuse me later and make me feel I am not *getting anywhere*. Everything is presented as the result of some knowable process; if I wish to arrive at four I get there by way of two and two. If I wish to burn Moscow the route I must travel has already been marked out by another visitor. If, like Bobby Vanderbilt, I yearn for the wheel of the Lancia 2.4-liter coupé, I have only to go through the appropriate process, that is, get the money. And if it is money itself that I desire, I have only to make it. All of these goals are equally beautiful in the sight of the Board of Estimate; the proof is all around us, in the no-nonsense ugliness of this steel and glass building, in the straightline matter-of-factness with which Miss Mandible handles some of our less reputable wars. Who points out that arrangements sometimes slip, that errors are made, that signs are misread? "*They have confidence in their ability to take the right steps and to obtain correct answers.*" I take the right steps, obtain correct answers, and my wife leaves me for another man.

8 December

My enlightenment is proceeding wonderfully.

9 December

Disaster once again. Tomorrow I am to be sent to a doctor, for observation. Sue Ann Brownly caught Miss Mandible and me in the cloakroom, during recess, and immediately threw a fit. For a moment I thought she was actually going to choke. She ran out of the room weeping, straight for the principal's office, certain now which of us was Debbie, which Eddie, which Liz. I am sorry to be the cause of her disillusionment, but I know that she will recover. Miss Mandible is ruined but fulfilled. Although she will be charged with contributing to the delinquency of a minor, she seems at peace; *her* promise has been kept. She knows now that everything she has been told about life, about America, is true.

I have tried to convince the school authorities that I am a minor only in a very special sense, that I am in fact mostly to blame—but it does no good. They are as dense as ever. My contemporaries are astounded that I present myself as anything other than an innocent victim. Like the Old Guard marching through the Russian drifts, the class marches to the conclusion that truth is punishment.

Bobby Vanderbilt has given me his copy of *Sounds of Sebring*, in farewell.

Marie, Marie, Hold On Tight

HENRY MACKIE, Edward Asher and Howard Ettle braved a rainstorm to demonstrate against the human condition on Wednesday, April 26 (and Marie, you should have used waterproof paint; the signs were a mess after half an hour). They began at St. John the Precursor on 69th Street at 1:30 P.M. picketing with signs bearing the slogans MAN DIES!/ THE BODY IS DISGUST!/ COGITO ERGO NOTHING!/ ABANDON LOVE! and handing out announcements of Henry Mackie's lecture at the Playmor Lanes the next evening. There was much interest among bystanders in the vicinity of the church. A man who said his name was William Rochester came up to give encouragement: "*That's the way!*" he said. At about 1:50 a fat, richly dressed beadle emerged from the church to dispute our right to picket. He had dewlaps which shook unpleasantly and, I am sorry to say, did not look like a good man.

"All right," he said, "now *move* on, you have to *move along, you can't* picket us!" He said that the church had never been picketed, that it could not be picketed without its permission, that it owned the sidewalk, and that he was going to call the police. Henry Mackie, Edward Asher and Howard Ettle had already obtained police permission for the demonstration through a fortunate bit of foresight; and we confirmed this by showing him our slip that we had obtained at Police Headquarters. The beadle was intensely irritated at this and stormed back inside the church to report to someone higher up. Henry Mackie said, "Well, get ready for the lightning bolt," and Edward Asher and Howard Ettle laughed.

Interest in the demonstration among walkers on 69th Street increased and a number of people accepted our leaflet and began to ask the pickets questions such as "What do you mean?" and "Were you young men raised in the church?" The pickets replied to these questions quietly but firmly and in as much detail as casual passersby could be expected to be interested in. Some of the walkers made taunting remarks— "Cogito ergo your ass" is one I remember—but the demeanor of the pickets was exemplary at all times, even later when things began, as Henry Mackie put it, "to get a little rough." (Marie, you would have been proud of us.) People who care about the rights of pickets should realize that these rights are threatened mostly not by the police, who generally do not molest you if you go through the appropriate bureaucratic procedures such as getting a permit, but by individuals who come up to you and try to pull your sign out of your hands or, in one case, spit at you. The man who did the latter was, surprisingly, very well dressed. What could be happening within an individual like that? He didn't even ask questions as to the nature or purpose of the demonstration, just spat and walked away. He didn't say a word. We wondered about him.

At about 2 P.M. a very high-up official in a black clerical suit emerged from the church and asked us if we had ever heard of Kierkegaard. It was raining on him just as it was on the pickets but he didn't seem to mind. "This demonstration displays a Kierkegaardian spirit which I understand," he said, and then requested that we transfer our operations to some other place. Henry Mackie had a very interesting discussion of about ten minutes' duration with this official during which photographs were taken by the New York *Post*, *Newsweek* and CBS Television whom Henry Mackie had alerted prior to the demonstration. The photographers made the churchman a little nervous but you have to hand it to him, he maintained his phony attitude of polite interest almost to the last. He said several rather bromidic things like "The human condition is the *given*, it's what we do with it that counts" and "The body is simply the temple wherein the soul dwells" which Henry Mackie countered with his famous question "*Why does it have to be that way?*" which has dumbfounded so many orthodox religionists and thinkers and with which he first won us (the other pickets) to his banner in the first place.

"*Why?*" the churchman exclaimed. It was clear that he was radically taken aback. "Because it *is* that way. You have to deal with what is. With reality."

"But why does it *have to* be that way?" Henry Mackie repeated, which is the technique of the question, which used in this way is unanswerable. A blush of anger and frustration crossed the churchman's features (it probably didn't register on your TV screen, Marie, but I was there, I saw it—it was beautiful).

"The human condition is a fundamental datum," the cleric stated. "It is immutable, fixed and changeless. To say otherwise . . ."

"Precisely," Henry Mackie said, "why it must be challenged."

"But," the cleric said, "it is God's will."

"Yes," Henry Mackie said significantly.

The churchman then retired into his church, muttering and shaking his head. The rain had damaged our signs somewhat but the slogans were still legible and we had extra signs cached in Edward Asher's car anyway. A number of innocents crossed the picket line to worship including several who looked as if they might be from the FBI. The pickets had realized in laying their plans the danger that they might be taken for Communists. This eventuality was provided for by the mimeographed leaflets which carefully explained that the pickets were not Communists and cited Edward Asher's and Howard Ettle's Army service including Asher's Commendation Ribbon. "We, as you, are law-abiding American citizens who support the Constitution and pay taxes," the leaflet says. "We are simply opposed to the ruthless way in which the human condition has been imposed on organisms which have done nothing to deserve it and are unable to escape it. *Why does it have to be that way?*" The leaflet goes on to discuss, in simple language, the various unfortunate aspects of the human condition including death, unseemly and degrading bodily functions, limitations on human understanding, and the chimera of love. The leaflet concludes with the section headed "What Is To Be Done?" which Henry Mackie says is a famous revolutionary catchword and which outlines, in clear, simple language, Henry Mackie's program for the reification of the human condition from the ground up.

A Negro lady came up, took one of the leaflets, read it carefully and then said: "They look like Communists to *me*!" Edward Asher commented that no matter how clearly things were explained to the people, the people always wanted to believe you were a Communist. He said that when he demonstrated once in Miami against vivisection of helpless animals he was accused of being a Nazi Communist which was, he explained, a contradiction in terms. He said ladies were usually the worst.

By then the large crowd that had gathered when the television men came had drifted away. The pickets therefore shifted the site of the demonstration to Rockefeller Plaza in Rockefeller Center via Edward Asher's car. Here were many people loafing, digesting lunch etc. and we used the spare signs which had new messages including

> WHY ARE YOU STANDING
> WHERE YOU ARE STANDING?
>
> THE SOUL IS NOT!
>
> NO MORE
> ART
> CULTURE
> LOVE
>
> REMEMBER YOU ARE DUST!

The rain had stopped and the flowers smelled marvelously fine. The pickets took up positions near a restaurant (I wish you'd been there, Marie, because it reminded me of something, something you said that night we went to Bloomingdale's and bought your new cerise-colored bathing suit: "The color a new baby has," you said, and the flowers were like that, some of them). People with cameras hanging around their necks took pictures of us as if they had never seen a demonstration before. The pickets remarked among themselves that it was funny to think of the tourists with pictures of us demonstrating in their scrapbooks in California, Iowa, Michigan, people we didn't know and who didn't know us or care anything about the demonstration or, for that matter, the human condition itself, in which they were so steeped that they couldn't stand off and look at it and know it for what it was. "It's a paradigmatic situation," Henry Mackie said, "exemplifying the distance between the potential knowers holding a commonsense view of the world and what is to be known, which escapes them as they pursue their mundane existences."

At this time (2:45 P.M.) the demonstrators were approached by a group of youths between the ages I would say of sixteen and twenty-one. They were dressed in hood jackets, T-shirts, tight pants etc. and were very obviously delinquents from bad environments and broken homes where they had received no love. They ringed the pickets in a threatening manner. There were about seven of them. The leader (and Marie, he wasn't the oldest; he was younger than some of them, tall, with a peculiar face, blank and intelligent at the same time) walked around looking at our signs with exaggerated curiosity. "What are you guys," he said finally, "some kind of creeps or something?"

Henry Mackie replied quietly that the pickets were American citizens pursuing their right to demonstrate peaceably under the Constitution.

The leader looked at Henry Mackie. "You're flits, you guys, huh?" he said. He then snatched a handful of leaflets out of Edward Asher's hands, and when Edward Asher attempted to recover them, danced away out of reach while two others stood in Asher's way. "What do you flits think you're doin'?" he said. "What *is* this shit?"

"You haven't got any right . . ." Henry Mackie started to say, but the leader of the youths moved very close to him then.

"What do you mean, you don't believe in God?" he said. The other ones moved in closer too.

"That is not the question," Henry Mackie said. "Belief or nonbelief is not at issue. The situation remains the same whether you believe or not. The human condition is . . ."

"Listen," the leader said, "I thought all you guys went to church every day. Now you tell me that flits don't believe in God. You putting me on?"

Henry Mackie repeated that belief was not involved, and said that it was, rather, a question of man helpless in the grip of a definition of himself that he had not drawn, that could not be altered by human action, and that was in fundamental conflict with every human notion of what should obtain. The pickets were simply subjecting this state of affairs to a radical questioning, he said.

"You're putting me on," the youth said, and attempted to kick Henry Mackie in the groin, but Mackie turned away in time. However the other youths then jumped the pickets, right in the middle of Rockefeller Center. Henry Mackie was thrown to the pavement and kicked repeatedly in the head, Edward Asher's coat was ripped off his back and he sustained many blows in the kidneys and elsewhere, and Howard Ettle was given a broken rib by a youth called "Cutter" who shoved him against a wall and smashed him viciously even though bystanders tried to interfere (a few of them). All this happened in a very short space of time. The pickets' signs were broken and smashed and their leaflets scattered everywhere. A policeman summoned by bystanders tried to catch the youths but they got away through the lobby of the Associated Press building and he returned empty-handed. Medical aid was summoned for the pickets. Photos were taken.

"Senseless violence," Edward Asher said later. "They didn't understand that . . ."

"On the contrary," Henry Mackie said, "they understand everything better than anybody."

The next evening, at 8 P.M. Henry Mackie delivered his lecture in the upstairs meeting room at the Playmor Lanes, as had been announced in the leaflet. The crowd was very small but attentive and interested. Henry Mackie had his head bandaged in a white bandage. He delivered his lecture titled "What Is To Be Done?" with good diction and enunciation and in a strong voice. He was very eloquent. And eloquence, Henry Mackie says, is really all any of us can hope for.

Up, Aloft in the Air

BUCK SAW now that the situation between Nancy and himself was considerably more serious than he had imagined. She exhibited unmistakable signs of a leaning in his direction. The leaning was acute, sometimes he thought she would fall, sometimes he thought she would not fall, sometimes he didn't care, and in every way tried to prove himself the man that he was. It meant dressing in unusual clothes and the breaking of old habits. But how could he shatter her dreams after all they had endured together? after all they had jointly seen and done since first identifying Cleveland as Cleveland? "Nancy," he said, "I'm too old. I'm not nice. There is my son to consider, Peter." Her hand touched the area between her breasts where hung a decoration, dating he estimated from the World War I period—that famous period!

The turbojet, their "ship," landed on its wheels. Buck wondered about the wheels. Why didn't they shear off when the aircraft landed so hard with a sound like thunder? Many had wondered before him. Wondering was part of the history of lighter-than-air-ness, you fool. It was Nancy herself, standing behind him in the exit line, who had suggested that they dance on the landing strip. "To establish rapport with the terrain," she said with her distant coolness, made more intense by the hot glare of the Edward pie vendors and customs trees. They danced the comb, the meringue, the *dolce far niente*. It was glorious there on the strip, amid air rich with the incredible vitality of jet fuel and the sensate music of exhaust. Twilight was lowered onto the landing pattern, a twilight such as has never graced Cleveland before, or since. Then broken, heartless laughter and the hurried trip to the hotel.

"I understand," Nancy said. And looking at her dispassionately, Buck conjectured that she *did* understand, unscrupulous as that may sound. *Probably*, he considered, *I convinced her against my will.* The man from Southern Rhodesia cornered him in the dangerous hotel elevator. "Do you think you have the right to hold opinions which differ from those of President

Kennedy?" he asked. "The President of your land?" But the party made up for all that, or most of it, in a curious way. The baby on the floor, Saul, seemed enjoyable, perhaps more than his wont. *Or my wont*, Buck thought, *who knows?* A Ray Charles record spun in the gigantic salad bowl. Buck danced the frisson with the painter's wife Perpetua (although Nancy was alone, back at the hotel). "I am named," Perpetua said, "after the famous typeface designed by the famous English designer, Eric Gill, in an earlier part of our century." "Yes," Buck said calmly, "I know that face." She told him softly the history of her affair with her husband, Saul Senior. Sensuously, they covered the ground. And then two ruly police gentlemen entered the room, with the guests blanching, and lettuce and romaine and radishes too flying for the exits, which were choked with grass.

Bravery was everywhere, but not here tonight, for the gods were whistling up their mandarin sleeves in the yellow realms where such matters are decided, for good or ill. Pathetic in his servile graciousness, Saul explained what he could while the guests played telephone games in crimson anterooms. The policemen, the flower of the Cleveland Force, accepted a drink and danced ancient police dances of custody and enforcement. Magically the music crept back under the perforated Guam doors; it was a scene to make your heart cry. "That Perpetua," Saul complained, "why is she treating me like this? Why are the lamps turned low and why have the notes I sent her been returned unopened, covered with red Postage Due stamps?" But Buck had, in all seriousness, hurried away.

The aircraft were calling him, their indelible flight plans whispered his name. He laid his cheek against the riveted flank of a bold 707. "*In case of orange and blue flames,*" he wrote on a wing, "*disengage yourself from the aircraft by chopping a hole in its bottom if necessary. Do not be swayed by the carpet; it is camel and very thin. I suggest that you be alarmed, because the situation is very alarming. You are up in the air perhaps 35,000 feet, with orange and blue flames on the outside and a ragged hole in the floorboards. What will you do?*" And now, Nancy. He held out his arms. She came to him.

"Yes."

"Aren't we?"

"Yes."
"It doesn't matter."
"Not to you. But to me . . ."
"I'm wasting our time."
"The others?"
"I felt ashamed."
"It's being here, in Cleveland."

They returned together in a hired automobile. Three parking lots were filled with overflow crowds in an ugly mood. I am tired, so very tired. The man from Southern Rhodesia addressed the bellmen, who listened to his hateful words and thought of other things. "But, then," Buck said, but then Nancy laid a finger on his lips.

"You appear to me so superior, so elevated above all other men," she said, "I contemplate you with such a strange mixture of humility, admiration, revenge, love and pride that very little superstition would be necessary to make me worship you as a superior being."

"Yes," Buck said, for a foreign sculptor, a Bavarian doubtless, was singing "You Can Take Your Love and Shove It Up Your Heart," covered though he was with stone dust and grog. The crowd roared at the accompanists plying the exotic instruments of Cleveland, the dolor, the mangle, the bim. Strum swiftly, fingers! The butlers did not hesitate for a minute. "History will absolve me," Buck reflected, and he took the hand offered him with its enormous sapphires glowing like a garage. Then Perpetua danced up to him, her great amazing brown eyelashes beckoning. "Where is Nancy?" she asked, and before he could reply, continued her account of the great love of her existence, her relationship with her husband, Saul. "He's funny and fine," she said, "and good and evil. In fact there is so much of him to tell you about, I can hardly get it all out before curfew. Do you mind?"

The din of dancing in Cleveland was now such that many people who did not know the plan were affronted. "This is an affront to Cleveland, this damn din!" one man said; and grog flowed ever more fiercely. The Secretary of State for Erotic Affairs flew in from Washington, the nation's capital, to see for himself at first hand, and the man from Southern Rhodesia had no recourse. He lurked into the Cleveland Air Terminal. "Can

I have a ticket for Miami?" he asked the dancing ticket clerk at the Delta Airlines counter hopelessly. "Nothing to Miami this year," the clerk countered. "How can I talk to him in this madness?" Nancy asked herself. "How can the white bird of hope bless our clouded past and future with all this noise? How? How? How? How? How?"

But Saul waved in time, from the porch of Parking Lot Two. He was wearing his belt dangerously low on his hips. "There is copulation everywhere," he shouted, fanning his neck, "because of the dancing! Yes, it's true!" And so it was, incredibly enough. Affection was running riot under the reprehensible scarlet sky. We were all afraid. "Incredible, incredible," Buck said to himself. "Even by those of whom you would not have expected it!" Perpetua glimmered at his ear. "Even by those," she insinuated, "of whom you would have expected . . . nothing." For a moment . . .

"Nancy," Buck exclaimed, "you are just about the nicest damn girl in Cleveland!"

"What about your wife in Texas?" Nancy asked.

"She is very nice too," Buck said, "as a matter of fact the more I think of it, the more I believe that nice girls like you and Hérodiade are what make life worth living. I wish there were more of them in America so that every man could have at least five."

"Five?"

"Yes, five."

"We will never agree on this figure," Nancy said.

2

The rubbery smell of Akron, sister city of Lahore, Pakistan, lay like the flameout of all our hopes over the plateau that evening.

When his aircraft was forced down at the Akron Airpark by the lapse of the port engines, which of course he had been expecting, Buck said: "But this, this . . . is Akron!" And it was Akron, sultry, molecular, crowded with inhabitants who held tiny transistor radios next to their tiny ears. A wave of ingratitude overcame him. "Bum, bum," he said. He plumbed its heart. The citizens of Akron, after their hours at the plant, wrapped themselves in ill-designed love triangles which never contained less than four persons of varying degrees of birth, high and low and mediocre. Beautiful Ohio! with your transistorized citizens and contempt for geometry, we loved you in the evening by the fireside waiting for our wife to nap so we could slip out and see our two girls, Manfred and Bella!

The first telephone call he received in his rum raisin hotel room, Charles, was from the Akron Welcome Service.

"Welcome! new human being! to Akron! Hello?"

"Hello."

"Are you in love with any of the inhabitants of Akron yet?"

"I just came from the airport."

"If not, or even if so, we want to invite you to the big get-acquainted party of the College Graduates' Club tonight at 8:30 P.M."

"Do I have to be a college graduate?"

"No but you have to wear a coat and tie. Of course they are available at the door. What color pants are you wearing?"

Buck walked the resilient streets of Akron. His head was aflame with conflicting ideas. Suddenly he was arrested by a shrill cry. From the top of the Zimmer Building, one of the noblest buildings in Akron, a group of Akron lovers consummated a four-handed suicide leap. *The air!* Buck thought as he watched the tiny figures falling, *this is certainly an air-minded country, America! But I must make myself useful.* He entered a bunshop and purchased a sweet green bun, and dallied with the sweet green girl there, calling her "poppet" and "funicular." Then out into the street again to lean against the warm green façade of the Zimmer Building and watch the workmen scrubbing the crimson sidewalk.

"Can you point me the way to the Akron slums, workman?"

"My name is not 'workman.' My name is 'Pat.'"

"Well 'Pat' which way?"

"I would be most happy to orient you, slumwise, were it not for the fact that slumlife in Akron has been dealt away with by municipal progressiveness. The municipality has caused to be erected, where slumlife once flourished, immense quadratic inventions which now house former slumwife and former slumspouse alike. These incredibly beautiful structures are over that way."

"Thanks, 'Pat.'"

At the housing development, which was gauche and grand, Buck came upon a man urinating in the elevator, next to a man breaking windows in the broom closet. "What are you fellows doing there!" Buck cried aloud. "We are expressing our rage at this fine new building!" the men exclaimed. "Oh that this day had never formulated! We are going to call it Ruesday, that's how we feel about it, by gar!" Buck stood in a wash of incomprehension and doubt. "You mean there is rage in Akron, the home of quadratic love?" "There is quadratic rage also," the men said, "Akron *is* rage from a certain point of view." Angel food covered the floor in neat squares. And what could be wrong with that? Everything?

"What is that point of view there, to which you refer?" Buck asked dumbly. "*The point of view of the poor people of Akron,*" those honest yeomen chanted, "or, as the city fathers prefer it, the underdeveloped people of Akron." And in their eyes, there was a strange light. "Do you know what the name of this housing development is?" "What?" Buck asked. "Sherwood Forest," the men said, "isn't that disgusting?"

The men invited Buck to sup with their girls, Heidi, Eleanor, George, Purple, Ann-Marie, and Los. In the tree, starlings fretted and died, but below everything was glass. Harold poured the wine of the region, a light Cheer, into the forgotten napery. And the great horse of evening trod over the immense scene once and for all. We examined our consciences. Many a tiny sin was rooted out that night, to make room for a greater one. It was "hello" and "yes" and "yes, yes" through the sacerdotal hours, from one to eight. Heidi held a pencil between her teeth. "Do you like pencil games?" she asked. Something lurked behind the veil of her eyes. "Not . . . especially," Buck said, "I . . ."

But a parade headed by a battalion of warm and lovely girls from the Akron Welcome Service elected this tense moment to come dancing by, with bands blazing and hideous floats in praise of rubber goods expanding in every direction. The rubber batons of the girls bent in the afterglow of events. "It is impossible to discuss serious ideas during a parade," the Akron Communists said to Buck, and they slipped away to continue expressing their rage in another part of the Forest.

"Goodbye!" Buck said. "Goodbye! I won't forget . . ."

The Welcome Service girls looked very *bravura* in their brief white-and-gold Welcome Service uniforms which displayed a fine amount of "leg." *Look at all that "leg" glittering there!* Buck said to himself, and followed the parade all the way to Toledo.

3

"Ingarden dear," Buck said to the pretty wife of the mayor of Toledo, who was reading a copy of *Infrequent Love* magazine, "where are the poets of Toledo? Where do they hang out?" He showered her with gifts. She rose and moved mysteriously into the bedroom, to see if Henry were sleeping. "There is only one," she said, "the old poet of the city Constantine Cavity." A frost of emotion clouded her fuzz-colored lenses. "He operates a juju drugstore in the oldest section of the city and never goes anywhere except to make one of his rare and beautiful appearances." "Constantine Cavity!" Buck exclaimed, "even in Texas where I come from we have heard of this fine poet. You must take me to see him at once." Abandoning Henry to his fate (and it was a bitter one!) Buck and Ingarden rushed off hysterically to the drugstore of Constantine Cavity, Buck inventing as they rolled something graceful to say to this old poet, the forerunner so to speak of poetry in America.

Was there fondness in our eyes? We could not tell. Cadenzas of documents stained the Western Alliance, already, perhaps, prejudiced beyond the power of prayer to redeem it. "Do you think there is too much hair on my neck? here?" Ingarden asked Buck. But before he could answer she said: "Oh shut up!" She knew that Mrs. Lutch, whose interest in the pastor was only feigned, would find the American way if anyone could.

At Constantine Cavity's drugstore a meeting of the Toledo Medical Society was being held, in consequence of which Buck did not get to utter his opening words which were to have been: "Cavity, we are here!" A pity, but call the roll! See, or rather hear, who is present, and who is not! Present were

                Dr. Caligari
                Dr. Frank

Dr. Pepper
Dr. Scholl
Dr. Frankenthaler
Dr. Mabuse
Dr. Grabow
Dr. Melmoth
Dr. Weil
Dr. Modesto
Dr. Fu Manchu
Dr. Wellington
Dr. Watson
Dr. Brown
Dr. Rococo
Dr. Dolittle
Dr. Alvarez
Dr. Spoke
Dr. Hutch
Dr. Spain
Dr. Malone
Dr. Kline
Dr. Casey
Dr. No
Dr. Regatta
Dr. Il y a
Dr. Baderman
Dr. Aveni

and other doctors. The air was stuffy here, comrades, for the doctors were considering (yes!) a resolution of censure against the beloved old poet. An end to this badinage and wit! Let us be grave. It was claimed that Cavity had dispensed . . . but who can quarrel with Love Root, rightly used? It has saved many a lip. The prosecution was in the able hands of Dr. Kline, who invented the heart, and Dr. Spain, after whom Spain is named some believe. Their godlike figures towered over the tiny poet.

    Kline advances.
    Cavity rises to his height, which is not great.
    Ingarden holds her breath.
    Spain fades, back, back . . .
    A handout from Spain to Kline.

Buck is down.
A luau?
The poet opens . . .
No! No! Get back!

". . . and if that way is long, and leads around by the reactor, and down in the valley, and up the garden path, leave her, I say, to heaven. For science has its reasons that reason knows not of," Cavity finished. And it was done.

"Hell!" said one doctor, and the others shuffled morosely around the drugstore inspecting the strange wares that were being vended there. It was clear that no resolution of censure could possibly . . . But of course not! What were we thinking of?

Cavity himself seemed pleased at the outcome of the proceedings. He recited to Buck and Ingarden his long love poems entitled "In the Blue of Evening," "Long Ago and Far Away," "Who?" and "Homage to W. C. Williams." The feet of the visitors danced against the sawdust floor of the juju drugstore to the compelling rhythms of the poet's poems. A rime of happiness whitened on the surface of their two faces. "Even in Texas," Buck whispered, "where things are very exciting, there is nothing like the old face of Constantine Cavity. Are you true?"

"Oh I wish things were other."

"You do?"

"There are such a lot of fine people in the world I wish I was one of them!"

"You are, you are!"

"Not essentially. Not inwardly."

"You're very authentic I think."

"That's all right in Cleveland, where authenticity is the thing, but here . . ."

"Kiss me please."

"Again?"

4

The parachutes of the other passengers snapped and crackled in the darkness all around him. There had been a malfunction in the afterburner and the pilot decided to "ditch." The whole thing was very unfortunate. "What is your life-style,

Cincinnati?" Buck asked the recumbent jewel glittering below him like an old bucket of industrial diamonds. "Have you the boldness of Cleveland? the anguish of Akron? the torpor of Toledo? What is your posture, Cincinnati?" Frostily the silent city approached his feet.

Upon making contact with Cincinnati Buck and such of the other passengers of the ill-fated flight 309 as had survived the "drop" proceeded to a hotel.

"Is that a flask of grog you have there?"

"Yes it is grog as it happens."

"That's wonderful."

Warmed by the grog which set his blood racing, Buck went to his room and threw himself on his bed. "Oh!" he said suddenly, "I must be in the wrong room!" The girl in the bed stirred sleepily. "Is that you Harvey?" she asked. "Where have you been all this time?" "No, it's Buck," Buck said to the girl, who looked very pretty in her blue flannel nightshirt drawn up about her kneecaps on which there were red lines. "I must be in the wrong room I'm afraid," he repeated. "Buck, get out of this room immediately!" the girl said coldly. "My name is Stephanie and if my friend Harvey finds you here there'll be an unpleasant scene."

"What are you doing tomorrow?" Buck asked.

Having made a "date" with Stephanie for the morning at 10 A.M., Buck slipped off to an innocent sleep in his own bed.

Morning in Cincinnati! The glorious cold Cincinnati sunlight fell indiscriminately around the city, here and there, warming almost no one. Stephanie de Moulpied was wearing an ice-blue wool suit in which she looked very cold and beautiful and starved. "Tell me about your Cincinnati life," Buck said, "the quality of it, that's what I'm interested in." "My life here is very aristocratic," Stephanie said, "polo, canned peaches, *liaisons dangéreuses*, and so on, because I am a member of an old Cincinnati family. However it's not much 'fun' which is why I made this 10 A.M. date with you, exciting stranger from the sky!" "I'm really from Texas," Buck said, "but I've been having a little trouble with airplanes on this trip. I don't really trust them too much. I'm not sure they're trustworthy." "Who is trustworthy after all?" Stephanie said with a cold sigh, looking blue. "Are you blue Stephanie?" Buck asked. "Am I blue?" Stephanie wondered. In the silence that followed, she counted her friends and relationships.

"Is there any noteworthy artistic activity in this town?"

"Like what do you mean?"

Buck then kissed Stephanie in a taxicab as a way of dissipating the blueness that was such a feature of her face. "Are all the girls in Cincinnati like you?" "All the *first-class* girls are like me," Stephanie said, "but there are some other girls whom I won't mention."

A faint sound of . . . A wave of . . . Dense clouds of . . . Heavily the immense weight of . . . Thin strands of . . .

Dr. Hesperidian had fallen into the little pool in vanPelt Ryan's garden (of course!) and everyone was pulling him out. Strangers met and fell in love over the problem of getting a grip on Dr. Hesperidian. A steel band played arias from *Wozzeck*. He lay just below the surface, a rime of algae whitening his cheekbones. He seemed to be . . . "Not *that* way," Buck said reaching for the belt buckle. "*This* way." The crowd fell back among the pines.

"You seem to be a nice young man, young man," vanPelt Ryan said, "although we have many of these of our own now since the General Electric plant came to town. Are you in computerization?"

Buck remembered the endearing red lines on Stephanie de Moulpied's knees.

"I'd rather not answer that question," he said honestly, "but if there's some other question you'd like me to answer . . ."

vanPelt turned away sadly. The steel band played "Red Boy Blues," "That's All," "Gigantic Blues," "Muggles," "Coolin'," and "Edward." Although each player was maimed in a different way . . . but the affair becomes, one fears, too personal. The band got a nice sound. Hookers of grog thickened on the table placed there for that purpose. "I grow less, rather than more, intimately involved with human beings as I move through world life," Buck thought, "is that my fault? Is it a fault?" The musicians rendered the extremely romantic ballads "I Didn't Know What Time It Was," "Scratch Me," and "Misty." The grim forever adumbrated in recent issues of *Mind* pressed down, down . . . Where *is* Stephanie de Moulpied? No one could tell him, and in truth, he did not want to know. It is not he who asks this question, it is Mrs. Lutch. She glides down her glide path, sinuously, she is falling, she bursts into flame, her last words: "Tell them . . . when they crash . . . turn off . . . the ignition."

Margins

EDWARD WAS explaining to Carl about margins. "The *width* of the margin shows culture, aestheticism and a sense of values or the lack of them," he said. "A very wide left margin shows an impractical person of culture and refinement with a deep appreciation for the best in art and music. Whereas," Edward said, quoting his handwriting analysis book, "whereas, narrow left margins show the opposite. No left margin at all shows a practical nature, a wholesome economy and a general lack of good taste in the arts. A very wide *right* margin shows a person afraid to face reality, oversensitive to the future and generally a poor mixer."

"I don't believe in it," Carl said.

"Now," Edward continued, "with reference to your sign there, you have an *all-around wide margin* which shows a person of extremely delicate sensibilities with love of color and form, one who holds aloof from the multitude and lives in his own dream world of beauty and good taste."

"Are you sure you got that right?"

"I'm communicating with you," Edward said, "across a vast gulf of ignorance and darkness."

"*I* brought the darkness, is that the idea?" Carl asked.

"You brought the darkness, you black mother," Edward said. "Funky, man."

"Edward," Carl said, "for God's sake."

"Why did you write all that jazz on your sign, Carl? Why? It's not true, is it? Is it?"

"It's kind of true," Carl said. He looked down at his brown sandwich boards, which said: *I Was Put In Jail in Selby County Alabama For Five Years For Stealing A Dollar and A Half Which I Did Not Do. While I Was In Jail My Brother Was Killed & My Mother Ran Away When I Was Little. In Jail I Began Preaching & I Preach to People Wherever I Can Bearing the Witness of Eschatological Love. I Have Filled Out Papers for Jobs But Nobody Will Give Me a Job Because I Have Been In Jail*

& The Whole Scene Is Very Dreary, Pepsi Cola. I Need Your Offerings to Get Food. Patent Applied For & Deliver Us From Evil. "It's true," Carl said, "with a kind of *merde*-y inner truth which shines forth as the objective correlative of what actually did happen, back home."

"Now, look at the way you made that 'm' and that 'n' there," Edward said. "The tops are pointed rather than rounded. That indicates aggressiveness and energy. The fact that they're also pointed rather than rounded at the bottom indicates a sarcastic, stubborn and irritable nature. See what I mean?"

"If you say so," Carl said.

"Your capitals are very small," Edward said, "indicating humility."

"My mother would be pleased," Carl said, "if she knew."

"On the other hand, the excessive size of the loops in your 'y' and your 'g' display exaggeration and egoism."

"That's always been one of my problems," Carl answered.

"What's your whole name?" Edward asked, leaning against a building. They were on Fourteenth Street, near Broadway.

"Carl Maria von Weber," Carl said.

"Are you a drug addict?"

"Edward," Carl said, "you *are* a swinger."

"Are you a Muslim?"

Carl felt his long hair. "Have you read *The Mystery of Being*, by Gabriel Marcel? I really liked that one. I thought that one was fine."

"No, c'mon Carl, answer the question," Edward insisted. "There's got to be frankness and honesty between the races. Are you one?"

"I think an accommodation can be reached and the government is doing all it can at the moment," Carl said. "I think there's something to be said on all sides of the question. This is not such a good place to hustle, you know that? I haven't got but two offerings all morning."

"People like people who look neat," Edward said. "You look kind of crummy, if you don't mind my saying so."

"You really think it's too long?" Carl asked, feeling his hair again.

"Do you think I'm a pretty color?" Edward asked. "Are you envious?"

"No," Carl said. "Not envious."

"See? Exaggeration and egoism. Just like I said."

"You're kind of boring, Edward. To tell the truth."

Edward thought about this for a moment. Then he said: "But I'm white."

"It's the color of choice," Carl said. "I'm tired of talking about color, though. Let's talk about values or something."

"Carl, I'm a fool," Edward said suddenly.

"Yes," Carl said.

"But I'm a *white* fool," Edward said. "That's what's so lovely about me."

"You *are* lovely, Edward," Carl said. "It's true. You have a nice look. Your aspect is good."

"Oh, hell," Edward said despondently. "You're very well-spoken," he said. "I noticed that."

"The reason for that is," Carl said, "I read. Did you read *The Cannibal* by John Hawkes? I thought that was a hell of a book."

"Get a haircut, Carl," Edward said. "Get a new suit. Maybe one of those new Italian suits with the tight coats. You could be upwardly mobile, you know, if you just put your back into it."

"Why are you worried, Edward? Why does my situation distress you? Why don't you just walk away and talk to somebody else?"

"You bother me," Edward confessed. "I keep trying to penetrate your inner reality, to find out what it is. Isn't that curious?"

"John Hawkes also wrote *The Beetle Leg* and a couple of other books whose titles escape me at the moment," Carl said. "I think he's one of the best of our younger American writers."

"Carl," Edward said, "*what is* your inner reality? Blurt it out, baby."

"It's mine," Carl said quietly. He gazed down at his shoes, which resembled a pair of large dead brownish birds.

"Are you sure you didn't steal that dollar and a half mentioned on your sign?"

"Edward, I *told* you I didn't steal that dollar and a half." Carl stamped up and down in his sandwich boards. "It sure is *cold* here on Fourteenth Street."

"That's your imagination, Carl," Edward said. "This street isn't any colder than Fifth, or Lex. Your feeling that it's colder here probably just arises from your marginal status as a despised person in our society."

"Probably," Carl said. There was a look on his face. "You know I went to the government, and asked them to give me a job in the Marine Band, and they wouldn't do it?"

"Do you blow good, man? Where's your axe?"

"They wouldn't *give* me that cotton-pickin' job," Carl said. "What do you think of that?"

"This eschatological love," Edward said, "what kind of love is that?"

"That is later love," Carl said. "That's what I call it, anyhow. That's love on the other side of the Jordan. The term refers to a set of conditions which . . . It's kind of a story we black people tell to ourselves to make ourselves happy."

"Oh me," Edward said. "Ignorance and darkness."

"Edward," Carl said, "you don't *like* me."

"I do too like you, Carl," Edward said. "Where do you steal your books, mostly?"

"Mostly in drugstores," Carl said. "I find them good because mostly they're long and narrow and the clerks tend to stay near the prescription counters at the back of the store, whereas the books are usually in those little revolving racks near the front of the store. It's normally pretty easy to slip a couple in your overcoat pocket, if you're wearing an overcoat."

"But . . ."

"Yes," Carl said, "I know what you're thinking. If I'll steal books I'll steal other things. But stealing books is metaphysically different from stealing like money. Villon has something pretty good to say on the subject I believe."

"Is that in 'If I Were King'?"

"Besides," Carl added, "haven't *you* ever stolen anything? At some point in your life?"

"My life," Edward said. "Why do you remind me of it?"

"Edward, you're not satisfied with your life! I thought white lives were *nice*!" Carl said, surprised. "I love that word 'nice.' It makes me so happy."

"Listen Carl," Edward said, "why don't you just concentrate on improving your handwriting."

"My character, you mean."

"No," Edward said, "don't bother improving your character. Just improve your handwriting. Make larger capitals. Make smaller loops in your 'y' and your 'g.' Watch your word-spacing so as not to display disorientation. Watch your margins."

"It's an idea. But isn't that kind of a superficial approach to the problem?"

"Be careful about the spaces between the lines," Edward went on. "Spacing of lines shows clearness of thought. Pay attention to your finals. There are twenty-two different kinds of finals and each one tells a lot about a person. I'll lend you the book. Good handwriting is the key to advancement, or if not *the* key, at least *a* key. You could be the first man of your race to be Vice-President."

"That's something to shoot for, all right."

"Would you like me to go get the book?"

"I don't think so," Carl said, "no thanks. It's not that I don't have any faith in your solution. What I *would* like is to take a leak. Would you mind holding my sandwich boards for a minute?"

"Not at all," Edward said, and in a moment had slipped Carl's sandwich boards over his own slight shoulders. "Boy, they're kind of heavy, aren't they?"

"They cut you a bit," Carl said with a malicious smile. "I'll just go into this men's store here."

When Carl returned the two men slapped each other sharply in the face with the back of the hand, that beautiful part of the hand where the knuckles grow.

The Joker's Greatest Triumph

FREDRIC WENT over to his friend Bruce Wayne's house about every Tuesday night. Bruce would be typically sitting in his study drinking a glass of something. Fredric would come in and sit down and look around the study in which there were many trophies of past exploits.

"Well Fredric what have you been doing? Anything?"

"No Bruce things have been just sort of rocking along."

"Well this is Tuesday night and usually there's some action on Tuesday night."

"I know Bruce or otherwise I wouldn't pick Tuesday night to come over."

"You want me to turn on the radio Fredric? Usually there's something interesting on the radio or maybe you'd like a little music from my hi-fi?"

Bruce Wayne's radio was a special short-wave model with many extra features. When Bruce turned it on there was a squealing noise and then they were listening to Tokyo or somewhere. Above the radio on the wall hung a trophy from an exploit: a long African spear with a spearhead made of tin.

"Tell me Bruce what is it you're drinking there?" Fredric asked.

"I'm sorry Fredric it's tomato juice. Can I get you a glass?"

"Does it have anything in it or is it just plain tomato juice?"

"It's tomato juice with a little vodka."

"Yes I wouldn't mind a glass," Fredric said. "Not too heavy on the vodka please."

While Bruce went out to the kitchen to make the drink Fredric got up and went over to examine the African spear more closely. It was he saw tipped with a rusty darkish substance, probably some rare exotic poison he thought.

"What is this stuff on the end of this African spear?" he asked when Bruce came back into the room.

"I must have left the other bottle of vodka in the Batmobile," Bruce said. "Oh that's curare, deadliest of the South

American poisons," he affirmed. "It attacks the motor nerves. Be careful there and don't scratch yourself."

"That's okay I'll just drink this tomato juice straight," Fredric said settling himself in his chair and looking out of the window. "Oh-oh there's the bat symbol spotlighted against the sky. This must mean a call from Commissioner Gordon at headquarters."

Bruce looked out of the window. A long beam of yellowish light culminating in a perfect bat symbol lanced the evening sky.

"I told you Tuesday night was usually a good night," Bruce Wayne said. He put his vodka-and-tomato-juice down on the piano. "Hold on a minute while I change will you?"

"Sure, take your time," Frederic said. "By the way is Robin still at Andover?"

"Yes," Bruce said. "He'll be home for Thanksgiving, I think. He's having a little trouble with his French."

"Well I didn't mean to interrupt you," Fredric said. "Go ahead and change. I'll just look at this magazine."

After Bruce had changed they both went out to the garage where the Batmobile and the Batplane waited.

Batman was humming a tune which Fredric recognized as being the "Warsaw Concerto." "Which one shall we take?" he said. "It's always hard to decide on a vague and indeterminate kind of assignment like this."

"Let's flip," Fredric suggested.

"Do you have a quarter?" Batman asked.

"No but I have a dime. That should be okay," Fredric said. They flipped, heads for the Batmobile, tails for the Batplane. The coin came up heads.

"Well," Batman said as they climbed into the comfortable Batmobile, "at least you can have some vodka now. It's under the seat."

"I hate to drink it straight," Fredric said.

"Press that button there on the dashboard," Batman said. Fredric pressed the button and a panel on the dashboard slid back to reveal a little bar, with ice, glasses, water, soda, quinine, lemons, limes etc.

"Thanks," Fredric said. "Can I mix you one?"

"Not while I'm working," Batman said. "Is there enough quinine water? I forgot to get some when I went to the liquor store last night."

"Plenty," Fredric said. He enjoyed his vodka tonic as Batman wheeled the great Batmobile expertly through the dark streets of Gotham City.

In Commissioner Gordon's office at Police Headquarters the Commissioner said: "Glad you finally got here Batman. Who is this with you?"

"This is my friend Fredric Brown," Batman said. "Fredric, Commissioner Gordon." The two men shook hands and Batman said: "Now Commissioner, what is this all about?"

"This!" Commissioner Gordon said. He placed a small ship model on the desk before him. "The package came by messenger, addressed to you, Batman! I'm afraid your old enemy, The Joker, is on the loose again!"

Batman hummed a peculiar melody which Fredric recognized as the "Cornish Rhapsody" which is on the other side of the "Warsaw Concerto." "Hmmmmm!" Batman said. "This sounds to me like another one of The Joker's challenges to a duel of wits!"

"Flying Dutchman!" Fredric exclaimed, reading the name painted on the bow of the model ship. "The name of a famous old ghost vessel? What can it mean!"

"A cleverly disguised clue!" Batman said. "The 'Flying Dutchman' meant here is probably the Dutch jewel merchant Hendrik van Voort who is flying to Gotham City tonight with a delivery of precious gems!"

"Good thinking Batman!" Commissioner Gordon said. "I probably never would have figured it out in a thousand years!"

"Well we'll have to hurry to get out to the airport!" Batman said. "What's the best way to get there from here Commissioner?"

"Well if I were you I'd go out 34th Street until you hit the War Memorial, then take a right on Memorial Drive until it connects with Gotham Parkway! After you're on the Parkway it's clear sailing!" he indicated.

"Wait a minute!" Batman said. "Wouldn't it be quicker to get on the Dugan Expressway where it comes in there at 11th

Street and then take the North Loop out to the Richardson Freeway? Don't you think that would save time?"

"Well I come to work that way!" the Commissioner said. "But they're putting in another two lanes on the North Loop, so that you have to detour down Strand, then cut over to 99th to get back on the Expressway! Takes you about two miles out of your way!" he said.

"Okay!" Batman said, "we'll go out 34th! Thanks Commissioner and don't worry about anything! Come on Fredric!"

"Oh by the way," Commissioner Gordon said. "How's Robin doing at Exeter?"

"It's not Exeter it's Andover," Batman said. "He's doing very well. Having a little trouble with his French."

"I had a little trouble with it myself," the Commissioner said jovially. "*Où est mon livre?*"

"*Où est ton livre?*" Batman said.

"*Où est son livre?*" the Commissioner said pointing at Fredric.

"*Tout cela s'est passé en dix-neuf cent vingt-quatre,*" Fredric said.

"Well we'd better creep Commissioner," Batman said. "The Joker as you know is a pretty slippery customer. Come on Fredric."

"Glad to have met you Commissioner," Fredric said.

"Me too," the Commissioner said, shaking Fredric's hand. "This is a fine-appearing young man Batman. Where did you find him?"

"He's just a friend," Batman said smiling under his mask. "We get together usually on Tuesday nights and have a few."

"What do you do Fredric? I mean how do you make your living?"

"I sell *Grit*, a newspaper which has most of its circulation concentrated in rural areas," Fredric said. "However I sell it right here in Gotham City. Many of today's leaders sold *Grit* during their boyhoods."

"Okay," said Commissioner Gordon, ushering them out of his office. "Good luck. *Téléphonez-moi un de ces jours.*"

"Righto," Batman said, and they hurried down the street to the Batmobile, which was parked in a truck zone.

"Can we stop for a minute on the way?" Fredric asked. "I'm out of cigarettes."

"There are some Viceroys in the glove compartment," Batman said pushing a button. A panel on the dashboard slid back to reveal a fresh carton of Viceroys.

"I usually prefer Kents," Fredric said, "but Viceroys are tasty too."

"They're all about the same I find," Batman said. "Most of the alleged differences in cigarettes are just advertising as far as I'm concerned."

"I wouldn't be surprised if you were right about that," Fredric said. The Batmobile sped down the dark streets of Gotham City toward Gotham Airport.

"Turn on the radio," Batman suggested. "Maybe we can catch the news or something."

Fredric turned on the radio but there was nothing unusual on it.

At Gotham Airport the jewel merchant Hendrik van Voort was just dismounting from his KLM jet when the Batmobile wheeled onto the landing strip, waved through the gates by respectful airport police in gray uniforms.

"Well everything seems to be okay," Batman said. "There's the armored car waiting to take Mr. van Voort to his destination."

"That's a new kind of armored car isn't it?" Fredric asked.

Without a word Batman leaped through the open door of the armored car and grappled with the shadowy figure inside.

HA HA HA HA HA HA HA HA HA HA HA HA HA HA HA HA HA HA!

"That's The Joker's laugh!" Fredric reflected. "The man inside the armored car must be the grinning clown of crime himself!"

"Batman! I thought that clue I sent you would leave you *completely at sea*!"

"No, Joker! I'm afraid this leaves your plans *up in the air*!"

"But not for long Batman! I'm going to bring you *down to earth*!"

With a swift movement, The Joker crashed the armored car into the side of the Terminal Building!

CRASH!

"Great Scott!" Fredric said to himself. "Batman is stunned! He's helpless!"

"You foiled my plans Batman," The Joker said, "but before the police get here, I'm going to lift that mask of yours and find out who you *really are*! HA HA HA HA HA HA HA HA HA HA HA HA HA HA HA HA HA HA HA HA HA HA!"

Fredric watched, horror-stricken. "Great Scott! The Joker has unmasked Batman! Now he knows that Batman is really *Bruce Wayne*!"

At this moment Robin, who was supposed to be at Andover, many miles away, landed the Batplane on the airstrip and came racing toward the wrecked armored car! But The Joker, alerted, grasped a cable lowered by a hovering helicopter and was quickly lifted skyward! Robin paused at the armored car and put the mask back on Batman's face!

"Hello Robin!" Fredric called. "I thought you were at Andover!"

"I was but I got a sudden feeling Batman needed me so I flew here in the Batplane," Robin said. "How've you been?"

"Fine," Fredric said. "But we left the Batplane in the garage, back at the Bat-Cave. I don't understand."

"We have two of everything," Robin explained. "Although it's not generally known."

With Fredric's aid Robin carried the stunned Batman to the waiting Batmobile. "You drive the Batmobile back to the Bat-Cave and I'll follow in the Batplane," Robin said. "All right?"

"Check," Fredric said. "Don't you think we ought to give him a little brandy or something?"

"That's a good idea," Robin said. "Press that button there on the dashboard. That's the brandy button."

Fredric pressed the button and a panel slid back, revealing a bottle of B & B and the appropriate number of glasses.

"This is pretty tasty," Fredric said, tasting the B & B. "How much is it a fifth?"

"Around eight dollars," Robin said. "There, that seems to be restoring him to his senses."

"Great Scott," Batman said, "what happened?"

"The Joker crashed the armored car and you were stunned," Fredric explained.

"Hi Robin what are you doing here? I thought you were up at school," Batman said.

"I was," Robin said. "Are you okay now? Can you drive home okay?"

"I think so," Batman said. "What happened to The Joker?"

"He got away," Fredric said, "but not before lifting your mask while you lay stunned in the wreckage of the wrecked armored car."

"Yes Batman," Robin said seriously, "I think he learned your real identity."

"Great Scott!" Batman said. "If he reveals it to the whole world it will mean the end of my career as a crime-fighter! Well, it's a problem."

They drove seriously back to the Bat-Cave, thinking about the problem. Later, in Bruce Wayne's study, Bruce Wayne, Fredric, and Robin, who was now dressed in the conservative Andover clothes of Dick Grayson, Bruce Wayne's ward, mulled the whole thing over between them.

"What makes The Joker tick I wonder?" Fredric said. "I mean what are his real motivations?"

"Consider him at any level of conduct," Bruce said slowly, "in the home, on the street, in interpersonal relations, in jail—always there is an extraordinary contradiction. He is dirty and compulsively neat, aloof and desperately gregarious, enthusiastic and sullen, generous and stingy, a snappy dresser and a scarecrow, a gentleman and a boor, given to extremes of happiness and despair, singularly well able to apply himself and capable of frittering away a lifetime in trivial pursuits, decorous and unseemly, kind and cruel, tolerant yet open to the most outrageous varieties of bigotry, a great friend and an implacable enemy, a lover and an abominator of women, sweet-spoken and foul-mouthed, a rake and a puritan, swelling with hubris and haunted by inferiority, outcast and social climber, felon and philanthropist, barbarian and patron of the arts, enamored of novelty and solidly conservative, philosopher and fool, Republican and Democrat, large of soul and unbearably petty, distant and brimming with friendly impulses, an inveterate liar and astonishingly strict with petty cash, adventurous and timid, imaginative and stolid, malignly destructive and a planter of trees on Arbor Day—I tell you frankly, the man is a mess."

"That's extremely well said Bruce," Fredric stated. "I think you've given really a very thoughtful analysis."

"I was paraphrasing what Mark Schorer said about Sinclair Lewis," Bruce replied.

"Well it's very brilliant just the same," Fredric noted. "I guess I'd better go home now."

"We could all use a little sleep," Bruce Wayne said. "By the way Fredric how are the *Grit* sales coming along? Are you getting many subscriptions?"

"Yes quite a few Bruce," Fredric said. "I've been doing particularly well in the wealthier sections of Gotham City although the strength of *Grit* is usually found in rural areas. By the way Dick if you want to borrow my language records to help you with your French you can come by Saturday."

"Thanks Fredric I'll do that," Dick said.

"Okay Bruce," Fredric said, "I'll see you next Tuesday night probably unless something comes up."

To London and Rome

THERE WAS A
BRIEF PAUSE

THERE WAS A
LONG PAUSE

THERE WAS A
TREMENDOUS
PAUSE DURING
WHICH I
BOUGHT HER
A NECCHI
SEWING-
MACHINE

THERE WAS A
PAUSE BROKEN
ONLY BY THE
HUMMING OF
THE NECCHI

THERE WAS AN
INTERVAL

THERE WAS A
LONG INTERVAL

THERE WAS AN
INTERMISSION

Do you know what I want more than anything else? Alison asked.

What? I said.

A sewing-machine Alison said, with buttonhole-making attachments.

There are so many things I could do with it for instance fixing up last year's fall dresses and lots of other things.

Wonderful! Alison said sitting at the controls of the Necchi and making buttonholes in a copy of the New York *Times* Sunday Magazine. Her eyes glistened. I had also bought a two-year subscription to *Necchi News* because I could not be sure that her interest would not be held for that long at least.

Then I bought her a purple Rolls which we decided to park on the street because our apartment building had no garage. Alison said she absolutely loved the Rolls! and gave me an enthusiastic kiss. I paid for the car with a check drawn on the First City Bank.

Peter Alison said, what do you want to do now?

Oh I don't know I said.

Well we can't simply sit around the apartment Alison said so we went to the races at Aqueduct where I bought a race horse that was running well out in front of the others. What a handsome race horse! Alison said delightedly. I paid for the horse with a check on the Capital National Bank.

The trailer was attached by means of a trailer hitch, which I bought when it

BETWEEN RACES SO WE WENT AROUND TO THE STABLES AND BOUGHT A HORSE TRAILER

became clear that the trailer could not be hitched up without one, to the back of our new Rolls. The horse's name was Dan and I bought a horse blanket, which he was already wearing but which did not come with him, to keep him warm.

He *is* beautiful Alison said.

A front-runner too I said.

THERE WAS AN INTERVAL OF SEVERAL DAYS. THEN ALISON AND I DROVE THE CAR WITH THE TRAILER UP THE RAMP INTO THE PLANE AND WE FLEW BACK TO MILWAUKEE

After stopping for lunch at Howard Johnson's where we fed Dan some fried clams which he seemed to like very much Alison said: Do you know what we've completely forgotten? I knew that there was something but although I thought hard I could not imagine what it was.

There's no place to keep him in our apartment building! Alison said triumphantly, pointing at Dan. She was of course absolutely right and I hastily bought a large three-story house in Milwaukee's best suburb. To make the house more comfortable I bought a concert grand piano.

ON THE DOORSTEP OF THE NEW HOUSE THE PIANO MOVERS PAUSED FOR A GLASS OF COLD WATER

Here are some little matters which you must attend to Alison said, handing me a box of bills. I went through them carefully, noting the amounts and thinking about money.

What in the name of God is this! I cried, holding up a bill for $1600 from the hardware store.

Garden hose Alison said calmly.

THERE WAS AN UNCOMFORTABLE SILENCE

It was clear that I would have to remove some money from the State Bank & Trust and place it in the Municipal National and I did so. The pilot of the airplane which I had bought to fly us to Aqueduct, with his friend the pilot of the larger plane I had bought to fly us back, appeared at the door and asked to be paid. The pilots' names were George and Sam. I paid them and also bought from Sam his flight jacket, which was khaki-colored and pleasant-looking. They smiled and saluted as they left.

Well I said looking around the new house, we'd better call a piano teacher because I understand that without use pianos tend to fall out of tune.

Not only pianos Alison said giving me an exciting look.

A SILENCE FREIGHTED WITH SEXUAL SIGNIFICANCE ENSUED. THEN WE WENT TO BED FIRST HOWEVER ORDERING A PIANO TEACHER AND A PIANO TUNER FOR THE EARLY MORNING

The next day Mr. Washington from the Central National called to report an overdraft of several hundred thousand dollars for which I apologized. Who was that on the telephone? Alison asked. Mr. Washington from the bank I replied. Oh Alison said, what do you want for breakfast? What have you got? I asked. Nothing Alison said, we'll have to go out for breakfast.

So we went down to the drugstore where Alison had eggs sunny side up and I had buckwheat cakes with sausage. When we got back to the house I noticed that there were no trees surrounding it, which depressed me.

Have you noticed I asked, that there are no trees?

A SILENCE
A PROLONGED SILENCE

Yes Alison said, I've noticed.

In fact Alison said, the treelessness of this house almost makes me yearn for our old apartment building.

A TERRIBLE SILENCE

There at least one could look at the large plants in the lobby.

ABSOLUTE SILENCE FOR ONE MINUTE
SHORT SILENCE

As soon as we go inside I said, I will call the tree service and buy some trees.

Maples I said.

Oh Peter what a fine idea Alison said brightly. But who are these people in our living-room?

SILENTLY WE REGARDED THE

Realizing that the men were the piano teacher and the piano tuner we had requested, I said: Well did you try the piano?

> TWO MEN WHO SAT ON THE SOFA

Yep the first man said, couldn't make heads or tails out of it.

And you? I asked, turning to the other man.

Beats me he said with a mystified look.

What seems to be the difficulty? I asked.

> THERE WAS A SHAMEFACED SILENCE

Frankly the piano teacher said, this isn't my real line of work. *Really* he said, I'm a jockey.

How about you? I said to his companion.

Oh I'm a bona fide piano tuner all right the tuner said. It's just that I'm not very good at it. Never was and never will be.

> WE CONSIDERED THE PROBLEM IN SILENCE

I have a proposition to make I announced. What is your name? I asked, nodding in the direction of the jockey.

Slim he said, and my friend here is Buster.

Well Slim I said, we need a jockey for our race horse, Dan, who will fall out of trim without workouts. And Buster, you can plant the maple trees which I have just ordered for the house.

> THERE WAS A JOYFUL SILENCE AS BUSTER AND SLIM TRIED TO DIGEST THE GOOD NEWS

I settled on a salary of $12,000 a year for Slim and a slightly smaller one for Buster. This accomplished I drove the Rolls over to Courtlandt Street to show it to my mistress, Amelia.

When I knocked at the door of Amelia's apartment she refused to open it. Instead she began practicing scales on her flute. I knocked again and called out: Amelia!

> THE SOUND OF THE FLUTE FILLED THE SILENT HALLWAY

I knocked again but Amelia continued to play. So I sat down on the steps and began to read the newspaper which was lying on the floor, knocking at intervals and at the same time wondering about the psychology of Amelia.

SILENTLY I
WONDERED
WHAT TO DO

AN
INTERMINABLE
SILENCE,
THEN AMELIA
HOLDING THE
FLUTE OPENED
THE DOOR

WHEN I GAVE
THE SALESMAN
A CHECK ON
THE MEDICAL
NATIONAL
HE PAUSED,
FROWNED, AND
SAID: "THIS IS A
NEW BANK ISN'T
IT?"

Montgomery Ward I noticed in the newspaper was at 40½. Was Amelia being adamant I considered, because of Alison?

Amelia I said at length (through the door), I want to give you a nice present of around $5500. Would you like that?

Do you mean it? she said.

Certainly I said.

Can you afford it? she asked doubtfully.

I have a new Rolls I told her, and took her outside where she admired the car at great length. Then I gave her a check for $5500 on the Commercial National for which she thanked me. Back in the apartment she gracefully removed her clothes and put the check in a book in the bookcase. She looked very pretty without her clothes, as pretty as ever, and we had a pleasant time for an hour or more. When I left the apartment Amelia said Peter, I think you're a very pleasant person which made me feel very good and on the way home I bought a new gray Dacron suit.

Where have you been? Alison said, I've been waiting lunch for hours. I bought a new suit I said, how do you like it? Very nice Alison said, but hurry I've got to go shopping after lunch. Shopping! I said, I'll go with you!

So we ate a hasty lunch of vichyssoise and ice cream and had Buster drive us in the Rolls to the Federated Department Store where we bought a great many things for the new house and a new horse blanket for Dan.

Do you think we ought to buy uniforms for Buster and Slim? Alison asked and I replied that I thought not, they didn't seem the sort who would enjoy wearing uniforms.

A FROSTY SILENCE	I think they ought to wear uniforms Alison said firmly.
	No I said, I think not.
DEAD SILENCE	Uniforms with something on the pocket Alison said. A crest or something.
	No.
THERE WAS AN INTERVAL DURING WHICH I SENT A CHECK FOR $500,000 TO THE MUSEUM OF MODERN ART	Instead of uniforms I bought Slim a Kaywoodie pipe and some pipe tobacco, and bought Buster a larger sterling silver cowboy belt buckle and a belt to go with it.

Buster was very pleased with his sterling silver belt buckle and said that he thought Slim would be pleased too when he saw the Kaywoodie pipe which had been bought for him. You were right after all Alison whispered to me in the back seat of the Rolls.

Alison decided that she would make a pie for supper, a chocolate pie perhaps, and that we would have Buster and Slim and George and Sam the pilots too if they were in town and not flying. She began looking in her recipe book while I read the *Necchi News* in my favorite armchair.

Then Slim came in from the garage with a worried look. Dan he said is not well.

A STUNNED PAUSE

Everyone was thrown into a panic by the thought of Dan's illness and I bought some Kaopectate which Slim however did not believe would be appropriate. The Kaopectate was $0.98 and I paid for it with a check on the Principal National. The delivery boy from the drugstore, whose name was Andrew, suggested that Dan needed a doctor. This seemed sensible so I tipped Andrew with a check on the Manufacturers' Trust and asked him to fetch the very best doctor he could find on such short notice.

WE LOOKED AT ONE ANOTHER IN WORDLESS FEAR	Dan was lying on his side in the garage, groaning now and then. His face was a rich gray color and it was clear that if he did not have immediate attention, the worst might be expected.
	Peter for God's sake do something for this poor horse! Alison cried.
PAUSING ONLY TO WHIP A FRESH CHECKBOOK FROM THE DESK DRAWER, I BOUGHT A LARGE HOSPITAL NEARBY FOR $1.5 MILLION	We sent Dan over in his trailer with strict instructions that he be given the best of everything. Slim and Buster accompanied him and when Andrew arrived with the doctor I hurried them off to the hospital too. Concern for Dan was uppermost in my mind at that moment.
	The telephone rang and Alison answered. Then she said: It's some girl, for you.
RETURNING TO THE LIVING-ROOM, ALISON HESITATED	As I had thought it might be, it was Amelia. I told her about Dan's illness. She was very concerned and asked if I thought it would be appropriate if she went to the hospital.
A MOMENT OF INDECISION FOLLOWED BY A PAINFUL SILENCE	You don't think it would be appropriate Amelia said.
	No Amelia I said truthfully, I don't.
	Then Amelia said that this indication of her tiny status in all our lives left her with nothing to say.
THE CONVERSATION LAPSED	To cheer her up I said I would visit her again in the near future. This pleased her and the exchange ended on a note of warmth. I knew however that Alison would ask questions and I returned to the livingroom with some anxiety.
AN HIATUS FILLED WITH DOUBT AND SUSPICION	But now the pilots George and Sam rushed in with good news indeed. They had gotten word of Dan's illness over the radio they said, and filled with concern had flown straight to the hospital, where they learned that Dan's stomach had been pumped and all was well. Dan was resting

easily George and Sam said, and could come home in about a week.

Oh Peter! Alison exclaimed in a pleased way, our ordeal is over. She kissed me with abandon and George and Sam shook hands with each other and with Andrew and Buster and Slim, who had just come in from the hospital. To celebrate we decided that we would all fly to London and Rome on a Viscount jet which I bought for an undisclosed sum and which Sam declared he knew how to fly very well.

A Shower of Gold

BECAUSE HE needed the money Peterson answered an ad that said *"We'll pay you* to be on TV if your opinions are strong enough or your personal experiences have a flavor of the unusual." He called the number and was told to come to Room 1551 in the Graybar Building on Lexington. This he did and after spending twenty minutes with a Miss Arbor who asked him if he had ever been in analysis was okayed for a program called *Who Am I?* "What do you have strong opinions about?" Miss Arbor asked. "Art," Peterson said, "life, money." "For instance?" "I believe," Peterson said, "that the learning ability of mice can be lowered or increased by regulating the amount of serotonin in the brain. I believe that schizophrenics have a high incidence of unusual fingerprints, including lines that make almost complete circles. I believe that the dreamer watches his dream in sleep, by moving his eyes." *"That's very interesting!"* Miss Arbor cried. "It's all in the *World Almanac*," Peterson replied.

"I see you're a sculptor," Miss Arbor said, "that's wonderful." "What is the nature of the program?" Peterson asked. "I've never seen it." "Let me answer your question with another question," Miss Arbor said. "Mr. Peterson, are you absurd?" Her enormous lips were smeared with a glowing white cream. "I beg your pardon?" "I mean," Miss Arbor said earnestly, "do you encounter your own existence as gratuitous? Do you feel *de trop?* Is there nausea?" "I have an enlarged liver," Peterson offered. "That's *excellent!*" Miss Arbor exclaimed. "That's a *very* good beginning! *Who Am I?* tries, Mr. Peterson, to discover what people *really are.* People today, we feel, are hidden away inside themselves, alienated, desperate, living in anguish, despair and bad faith. Why have we been thrown here, and abandoned? That's the question we try to answer, Mr. Peterson. Man stands alone in a featureless, anonymous landscape, in fear and trembling and sickness unto death. God is dead. Nothingness everywhere. Dread. Estrangement. Finitude. *Who*

A SHOWER OF GOLD

Am I? approaches these problems in a root radical way." "On television?" "We're interested in basics, Mr. Peterson. We don't play around." "I see," Peterson said, wondering about the amount of the fee. "What I want to know now, Mr. Peterson, is this: are you *interested* in absurdity?" "Miss Arbor," he said, "to tell you the truth, I don't know. I'm not sure I believe in it." "Oh, Mr. Peterson!" Miss Arbor said, shocked. "Don't *say* that! You'll be . . ." "Punished?" Peterson suggested. "*You* may not be interested in absurdity," she said firmly, "but absurdity is interested in *you*." "I have a lot of problems, if that helps," Peterson said. "Existence is problematic for you," Miss Arbor said, relieved. "The fee is two hundred dollars."

"I'm going to be on television," Peterson said to his dealer. "A terrible shame," Jean-Claude responded. "Is it unavoidable?" "It's unavoidable," Peterson said, "if I want to eat." "How much?" Jean-Claude asked and Peterson said: "Two hundred." He looked around the gallery to see if any of his works were on display. "A ridiculous compensation considering the infamy. Are you using your own name?" "You haven't by any chance . . ." "No one is buying," Jean-Claude said. "Undoubtedly it is the weather. People are thinking in terms of—what do you call those things?—Chris-Crafts. To boat with. You would not consider again what I spoke to you about before?" "No," Peterson said, "I wouldn't consider it." "Two little ones would move much, much faster than a single huge big one," Jean-Claude said, looking away. "To saw it across the middle would be a very simple matter." "It's supposed to be a work of art," Peterson said, as calmly as possible. "You don't go around sawing works of art across the middle, remember?" "That place where it saws," Jean-Claude said, "is not very difficult. I can put my two hands around it." He made a circle with his two hands to demonstrate. "Invariably when I look at that piece I see two pieces. Are you absolutely sure you didn't conceive it wrongly in the first instance?" "Absolutely," Peterson said. Not a single piece of his was on view, and his liver expanded in rage and hatred. "You have a very romantic impulse," Jean-Claude said. "I admire, dimly, the posture. You read too much in the history of art. It estranges you from those possibilities for authentic selfhood that inhere in the present century." "I know," Peterson said, "could you let me have twenty until the first?"

Peterson sat in his loft on lower Broadway drinking Rheingold and thinking about the President. He had always felt close to the President but felt now that he had, in agreeing to appear on the television program, done something slightly disgraceful, of which the President would not approve. But I needed the money, he told himself, the telephone is turned off and the kitten is crying for milk. And I'm running out of beer. The President feels that the arts should be encouraged, Peterson reflected, surely he doesn't want me to go without beer? He wondered if what he was feeling was simple guilt at having sold himself to television or something more elegant: nausea? His liver groaned within him and he considered a situation in which his new relationship with the President was announced. He was working in the loft. The piece in hand was to be called *Season's Greetings* and combined three auto radiators, one from a Chevrolet Tudor, one from a Ford pickup, one from a 1932 Essex, with part of a former telephone switchboard and other items. The arrangement seemed right and he began welding. After a time the mass was freestanding. A couple of hours had passed. He put down the torch, lifted off the mask. He walked over to the refrigerator and found a sandwich left by a friendly junk dealer. It was a sandwich made hastily and without inspiration: a thin slice of ham between two pieces of bread. He ate it gratefully nevertheless. He stood looking at the work, moving from time to time so as to view it from a new angle. Then the door to the loft burst open and the President ran in, trailing a sixteen-pound sledge. His first blow cracked the principal weld in *Season's Greetings*, the two halves parting like lovers, clinging for a moment and then rushing off in opposite directions. Twelve Secret Service men held Peterson in a paralyzing combination of secret grips. He's looking good, Peterson thought, very good, healthy, mature, fit, trustworthy. I like his suit. The President's second and third blows smashed the Essex radiator and the Chevrolet radiator. Then he attacked the welding torch, the plaster sketches on the workbench, the Rodin cast and the Giacometti stickman Peterson had bought in Paris. "*But Mr. President!*" Peterson shouted. "*I thought we were friends!*" A Secret Service man bit him in the back of the neck. Then the President lifted the sledge high in the air, turned toward Peterson, and said: "Your liver is diseased? That's a good sign. You're making progress. You're thinking."

"I happen to think that guy in the White House is doing a pretty darn good job." Peterson's barber, a man named Kitchen who was also a lay analyst and the author of four books titled *The Decision To Be*, was the only person in the world to whom he had confided his former sense of community with the President. "As far as his relationship with you personally goes," the barber continued, "it's essentially a kind of I-Thou relationship, if you know what I mean. You got to handle it with full awareness of the implications. In the end one experiences only oneself, Nietzsche said. When you're angry with the President, what you experience is self-as-angry-with-the-President. When things are okay between you and him, what you experience is self-as-swinging-with-the-President. Well and good. *But*," Kitchen said, lathering up, "you want the relationship to be such that what you experience is the-President-as-swinging-with-you. You want *his* reality, get it? So that you can break out of the hell of solipsism. How about a little more off the sides?" "Everybody knows the language but me," Peterson said irritably. "Look," Kitchen said, "when you talk about me to somebody else, you say 'my barber,' don't you? Sure you do. In the same way, I look at you as being 'my customer,' get it? But you don't regard yourself as being 'my' customer and I don't regard myself as 'your' barber. Oh, it's hell all right." The razor moved like a switchblade across the back of Peterson's neck. "Like Pascal said: 'The natural misfortune of our mortal and feeble condition is so wretched that when we consider it closely, nothing can console us.' The razor rocketed around an ear. "Listen," Peterson said, "what do you think of this television program called *Who Am I*? Ever seen it?" "Frankly," the barber said, "it smells of the library. But they do a job on those people, I'll tell you that." "What do you mean?" Peterson said excitedly. "What kind of a job?" The cloth was whisked away and shaken with a sharp popping sound. "It's too horrible even to talk about," Kitchen said. "But it's what they deserve, those crumbs." "Which crumbs?" Peterson asked.

That night a tall foreign-looking man with a switchblade big as a butcherknife open in his hand walked into the loft without knocking and said "Good evening, Mr. Peterson, I am the cat-piano player, is there anything you'd particularly like to hear?" "Cat-piano?" Peterson said, gasping, shrinking from the knife. "What are you talking about? What do you want?" A biography of Nolde slid from his lap to the floor. "The cat-piano," said the visitor, "is an instrument of the devil, a diabolical instrument. You needn't sweat quite so much," he added, sounding aggrieved. Peterson tried to be brave. "I don't understand," he said. "Let me explain," the tall foreign-looking man said graciously. "The keyboard consists of eight cats—the octave— encased in the body of the instrument in such a way that only their heads and forepaws protrude. The player presses upon the appropriate paws, and the appropriate cats respond—with a kind of shriek. There is also provision made for pulling their tails. A tail-puller, or perhaps I should say tail *player*" (he smiled a disingenuous smile) "is stationed at the rear of the instrument, where the tails are. At the correct moment the tail-puller pulls the correct tail. The tail-note is of course quite different from the paw-note and produces sounds in the upper registers. Have you ever seen such an instrument, Mr. Peterson?" "No, and I don't believe it exists," Peterson said heroically. "There is an excellent early seventeenth-century engraving by Franz van der Wyngaert, Mr. Peterson, in which a cat-piano appears. Played, as it happens, by a man with a wooden leg. You will observe my own leg." The cat-piano player hoisted his trousers and a leglike contraption of wood, metal and plastic appeared. "And now, would you like to make a request? 'The Martyrdom of St. Sebastian'? The 'Romeo and Juliet' overture? 'Holiday for Strings'?" "But why—" Peterson began. "The kitten is crying for milk, Mr. Peterson. And whenever a kitten cries, the cat-piano plays." "But it's not my kitten," Peterson said reasonably. "It's just a kitten that wished itself on me. I've been trying to give it away. I'm not sure it's still around. I haven't seen it since the day before yesterday." The kitten appeared, looked at Peterson reproachfully, and then rubbed itself against the cat-piano player's mechanical leg. "Wait a minute!" Peterson exclaimed. "This thing is rigged! That cat hasn't been here in two days. What do you want from me? What am I supposed to do?" "Choices, Mr. Peterson, choices. You *chose* that kitten as a way of encountering that which you are not, that is to say, kitten. An effort on the part of the *pour-soi* to—" "But it chose me!" Peterson cried, "the door was open and the first thing I knew it was lying in my bed, under the Army blanket. I didn't have anything to do with it!" The cat-piano player repeated his disingenuous smile. "Yes, Mr. Peterson, I know, I know. Things are done to you, it is all a gigantic conspiracy. I've heard the story a hundred times. But the kitten is here, is it not? The kitten is weeping, is it not?" Peterson looked at the kitten, which was crying huge tigerish tears into its empty dish. "*Listen* Mr. Peterson," the cat-piano player said, "*listen!*" The blade of his immense knife jumped back into the handle with a thwack! and the hideous music began.

The day after the hideous music began the three girls from California arrived. Peterson opened his door, hesitantly, in response to an insistent ringing, and found himself being stared at by three girls in blue jeans and heavy sweaters, carrying suitcases. "I'm Sherry," the first girl said, "and this is Ann and this is Louise. We're from California and we need a place to stay." They were homely and extremely purposeful. "I'm sorry," Peterson said, "I can't—" "We sleep anywhere," Sherry said, looking past him into the vastness of his loft, "on the floor if we have to. We've done it before." Ann and Louise stood on their toes to get a good look. "What's that funny music?" Sherry asked, "it sounds pretty far-out. We really won't be any trouble at all and it'll just be a little while until we make a connection." "Yes," Peterson said, "but why me?" "You're an artist," Sherry said sternly, "we saw the A.I.R. sign downstairs." Peterson cursed the fire laws which made posting of the signs obligatory. "Listen," he said, "I can't even feed the cat. I can't even keep myself in beer. This is not the place. You won't be happy here. My work isn't authentic. I'm a minor artist." "The natural misfortune of our mortal and feeble condition is so wretched that when we consider it closely, nothing can console us," Sherry said. "That's Pascal." "I know," Peterson said, weakly. "Where is the john?" Louise asked. Ann marched into the kitchen and began to prepare, from supplies removed from her rucksack, something called *veal engagé*. "Kiss me,"

Sherry said, "I need love." Peterson flew to his friendly neighborhood bar, ordered a double brandy, and wedged himself into a telephone booth. "Miss Arbor? This is Hank Peterson. Listen, Miss Arbor, I can't do it. No, I mean really. I'm being punished horribly for even thinking about it. No, I mean it. You can't imagine what's going on around here. Please, get somebody else? I'd regard it as a great personal favor. Miss Arbor? Please?"

The other contestants were a young man in white pajamas named Arthur Pick, a karate expert, and an airline pilot in full uniform, Wallace E. Rice. "Just be natural," Miss Arbor said, "and of course be frank. We score on the basis of the validity of your answers, and of course that's measured by the polygraph." "What's this about a polygraph?" the airline pilot said. "The polygraph measures the validity of your answers," Miss Arbor said, her lips glowing whitely. "How else are we going to know if you're . . ." "Lying?" Wallace E. Rice supplied. The contestants were connected to the machine and the machine to a large illuminated tote board hanging over their heads. The master of ceremonies, Peterson noted without pleasure, resembled the President and did not look at all friendly.

The program began with Arthur Pick. Arthur Pick got up in his white pajamas and gave a karate demonstration in which he broke three half-inch pine boards with a single kick of his naked left foot. Then he told how he had disarmed a bandit, late at night at the A&P where he was an assistant manager, with a maneuver called a "rip-choong" which he demonstrated on the announcer. "How about that?" the announcer caroled. "Isn't that something? Audience?" The audience responded enthusiastically and Arthur Pick stood modestly with his hands behind his back. "Now," the announcer said, "let's play *Who Am I?* And here's your host, *Bill Lemmon*!" No, he doesn't look like the President, Peterson decided. "Arthur," Bill Lemmon said, "for twenty dollars—do you love your mother?" "Yes," Arthur Pick said. "Yes, of course." A bell rang, the tote board flashed, and the audience screamed. "He's lying!" the announcer shouted, "lying! lying! lying!" "Arthur," Bill Lemmon said, looking at his index cards, "the polygraph shows that the validity of your answer is . . . questionable. Would you like to try it again? Take another crack at it?" "You're crazy," Arthur Pick said. "Of course I love my mother." He was fishing around inside his pajamas for a handkerchief. "Is your mother watching the show tonight, Arthur?" "Yes, Bill, she is." "How long have you been studying karate?" "Two years, Bill." "And who paid for the lessons?" Arthur Pick hesitated. Then he said: "My mother, Bill." "They were pretty expensive, weren't they, Arthur?" "Yes, Bill, they were." "How expensive?" "Five dollars an hour." "Your mother doesn't make very much money, does she, Arthur?" "No, Bill, she doesn't." "Arthur, what does your mother do for a living?" "She's a garment worker, Bill. In the garment district." "And how long has she worked down there?" "All her life, I guess. Since my old man died." "And she doesn't make very much money, you said." "No. But she *wanted* to pay for the lessons. She *insisted* on it." Bill Lemmon said: "She wanted a son who could break boards with his feet?" Peterson's liver leaped and the tote board spelled out, in huge, glowing white letters, the words BAD FAITH. The airline pilot, Wallace E. Rice, was led to reveal that he had been caught, on a flight from Omaha to Miami, with a stewardess sitting on his lap and wearing his captain's cap, that the flight engineer had taken a Polaroid picture, and that he had been given involuntary retirement after nineteen years of faithful service. "It was perfectly safe," Wallace E. Rice said, "you don't understand, the automatic pilot can fly that plane better than I can." He further confessed to a lifelong and intolerable itch after stewardesses which had much to do, he said, with the way their jackets fell just on top of their hips, and his own jacket with the three gold stripes on the sleeve darkened with sweat until it was black.

I was wrong, Peterson thought, the world is absurd. The absurdity is punishing me for not believing in it. I affirm the absurdity. On the other hand, absurdity is itself absurd. Before the emcee could ask the first question, Peterson began to talk. "Yesterday," Peterson said to the television audience, "in the typewriter in front of the Olivetti showroom on Fifth Avenue, I found a recipe for Ten Ingredient Soup that included a stone from a toad's head. And while I stood there marveling a nice old lady pasted on the elbow of my best Haspel suit a little blue sticker reading THIS INDIVIDUAL IS A PART OF THE

COMMUNIST CONSPIRACY FOR GLOBAL DOMINATION OF THE ENTIRE GLOBE. Coming home I passed a sign that said in ten-foot letters COWARD SHOES and heard a man singing "Golden Earrings" in a horrible voice, and last night I dreamed there was a shoot-out at our house on Meat Street and my mother shoved me in a closet to get me out of the line of fire." The emcee waved at the floor manager to turn Peterson off, but Peterson kept talking. "In this kind of a world," Peterson said, "absurd if you will, possibilities nevertheless proliferate and escalate all around us and there are opportunities for beginning again. I am a minor artist and my dealer won't even display my work if he can help it but minor is as minor does and lightning may strike even yet. Don't be reconciled. Turn off your television sets," Peterson said, "cash in your life insurance, indulge in a mindless optimism. Visit girls at dusk. Play the guitar. How can you be alienated without first having been connected? Think back and remember how it was." A man on the floor in front of Peterson was waving a piece of cardboard on which something threatening was written but Peterson ignored him and concentrated on the camera with the little red light. The little red light jumped from camera to camera in an attempt to throw him off balance but Peterson was too smart for it and followed wherever it went. "My mother was a royal virgin," Peterson said, "and my father a shower of gold. My childhood was pastoral and energetic and rich in experiences which developed my character. As a young man I was noble in reason, infinite in faculty, in form express and admirable, and in apprehension . . ." Peterson went on and on and although he was, in a sense, lying, in a sense he was not.

UNSPEAKABLE PRACTICES, UNNATURAL ACTS

To Herman Gollob

The Indian Uprising

WE DEFENDED the city as best we could. The arrows of the Comanches came in clouds. The war clubs of the Comanches clattered on the soft, yellow pavements. There were earthworks along the Boulevard Mark Clark and the hedges had been laced with sparkling wire. People were trying to understand. I spoke to Sylvia. "Do you think this is a good life?" The table held apples, books, long-playing records. She looked up. "No."

Patrols of paras and volunteers with armbands guarded the tall, flat buildings. We interrogated the captured Comanche. Two of us forced his head back while another poured water into his nostrils. His body jerked, he choked and wept. Not believing a hurried, careless, and exaggerated report of the number of casualties in the outer districts where trees, lamps, swans had been reduced to clear fields of fire we issued entrenching tools to those who seemed trustworthy and turned the heavy-weapons companies so that we could not be surprised from that direction. And I sat there getting drunker and drunker and more in love and more in love. We talked.

"Do you know Fauré's 'Dolly'?"

"Would that be Gabriel Fauré?"

"It would."

"Then I know it," she said. "May I say that I play it at certain times, when I am sad, or happy, although it requires four hands."

"How is that managed?"

"I accelerate," she said, "ignoring the time signature."

And when they shot the scene in the bed I wondered how you felt under the eyes of the cameramen, grips, juicers, men in the mixing booth: excited? stimulated? And when they shot the scene in the shower I sanded a hollow-core door working carefully against the illustrations in texts and whispered instructions from one who had already solved the problem. I had made after all other tables, one while living with Nancy, one while living with Alice, one while living with Eunice, one while living with Marianne.

Red men in waves like people scattering in a square startled by something tragic or a sudden, loud noise accumulated against the barricades we had made of window dummies, silk, thoughtfully planned job descriptions (including scales for the orderly progress of other colors), wine in demijohns, and robes. I analyzed the composition of the barricade nearest me and found two ashtrays, ceramic, one dark brown and one dark brown with an orange blur at the lip; a tin frying pan; two-litre bottles of red wine; three-quarter-litre bottles of Black & White, aquavit, cognac, vodka, gin, Fad #6 sherry; a hollow-core door in birch veneer on black wrought-iron legs; a blanket, red-orange with faint blue stripes; a red pillow and a blue pillow; a woven straw wastebasket; two glass jars for flowers; corkscrews and can openers; two plates and two cups, ceramic, dark brown; a yellow-and-purple poster; a Yugoslavian carved flute, wood, dark brown; and other items. I decided I knew nothing.

The hospitals dusted wounds with powders the worth of which was not quite established, other supplies having been exhausted early in the first day. I decided I knew nothing. Friends put me in touch with a Miss R., a teacher, unorthodox they said, excellent they said, successful with difficult cases, steel shutters on the windows made the house safe. I had just learned via an International Distress Coupon that Jane had been beaten up by a dwarf in a bar on Tenerife but Miss R. did not allow me to speak of it. "You know nothing," she said, "you feel nothing, you are locked in a most savage and terrible ignorance, I despise you, my boy, *mon cher*, my heart. You may attend but you must not attend now, you must attend later, a day or a week or an hour, you are making me ill. . . ." I nonevaluated these remarks as Korzybski instructed. But it was difficult. Then they pulled back in a feint near the river and we rushed into that sector with a reinforced battalion hastily formed among the Zouaves and cabdrivers. This unit was crushed in the afternoon of a day that began with spoons and letters in hallways and under windows where men tasted the history of the heart, cone-shaped muscular organ that maintains *circulation of the blood*.

But it is you I want now, here in the middle of this Uprising, with the streets yellow and threatening, short, ugly lances with fur at the throat and inexplicable shell money lying in the grass. It is when I am with you that I am happiest, and it is for you that I am making this hollow-core door table with black wrought-iron legs. I held Sylvia by her bear-claw necklace. "Call off your braves," I said. "We have many years left to live." There was a sort of muck running in the gutters, yellowish, filthy stream suggesting excrement, or nervousness, a city that does not know what it has done to deserve baldness, errors, infidelity. "With luck you will survive until matins," Sylvia said. She ran off down the Rue Chester Nimitz, uttering shrill cries.

Then it was learned that they had infiltrated our ghetto and that the people of the ghetto instead of resisting had joined the smooth, well-coördinated attack with zipguns, telegrams, lockets, causing that portion of the line held by the I.R.A. to swell and collapse. We sent more heroin into the ghetto, and hyacinths, ordering another hundred thousand of the pale, delicate flowers. On the map we considered the situation with its strung-out inhabitants and merely personal emotions. Our parts were blue and their parts were green. I showed the blue-and-green map to Sylvia. "Your parts are green," I said. "You gave me heroin first a year ago," Sylvia said. She ran off down George C. Marshall Allée, uttering shrill cries. Miss R. pushed me into a large room painted white (jolting and dancing in the soft light, and I was excited! and there were people watching!) in which there were two chairs. I sat in one chair and Miss R. sat in the other. She wore a blue dress containing a red figure. There was nothing exceptional about her. I was disappointed by her plainness, by the bareness of the room, by the absence of books.

The girls of my quarter wore long blue mufflers that reached to their knees. Sometimes the girls hid Comanches in their rooms, the blue mufflers together in a room creating a great blue fog. Block opened the door. He was carrying weapons, flowers, loaves of bread. And he was friendly, kind, enthusiastic, so I related a little of the history of torture, reviewing the technical literature quoting the best modern sources, French, German, and American, and pointing out the flies which had gathered in anticipation of some new, cool color.

"What is the situation?" I asked.

"The situation is liquid," he said. "We hold the south quarter and they hold the north quarter. The rest is silence."

"And Kenneth?"

"That girl is not in love with Kenneth," Block said frankly. "She is in love with his coat. When she is not wearing it she is huddling under it. Once I caught it going down the stairs by itself. I looked inside. Sylvia."

Once I caught Kenneth's coat going down the stairs by itself but the coat was a trap and inside a Comanche who made a thrust with his short, ugly knife at my leg which buckled and tossed me over the balustrade through a window and into another situation. Not believing that your body brilliant as it was and your fat, liquid spirit distinguished and angry as it was were stable quantities to which one could return on wires more than once, twice, or another number of times I said: "See the table?"

In Skinny Wainwright Square the forces of green and blue swayed and struggled. The referees ran out on the field trailing chains. And then the blue part would be enlarged, the green diminished. Miss R. began to speak. "A former king of Spain, a Bonaparte, lived for a time in Bordentown, New Jersey. But that's no good." She paused. "The ardor aroused in men by the beauty of women can only be satisfied by God. That is *very* good (it is Valéry) but it is not what I have to teach you, goat, muck, filth, heart of my heart." I showed the table to Nancy. "See the table?" She stuck out her tongue red as a cardinal's hat. "I made such a table once," Block said frankly. "People all over America have made such tables. I doubt very much whether one can enter an American home without finding at least one such table, or traces of its having been there, such as faded places in the carpet." And afterward in the garden the men of the 7th Cavalry played Gabrieli, Albinoni, Marcello, Vivaldi, Boccherini. I saw Sylvia. She wore a yellow ribbon, under a long blue muffler. "Which side are you on," I cried, "after all?"

"The only form of discourse of which I approve," Miss R. said in her dry, tense voice, "is the litany. I believe our masters and teachers as well as plain citizens should confine themselves to what can safely be said. Thus when I hear the words *pewter, snake, tea, Fad #6 sherry, serviette, fenestration, crown, blue* coming from the mouth of some public official, or some raw youth, I am not disappointed. Vertical organization is also possible," Miss R. said, "as in

>pewter
>snake
>tea
>Fad #6 sherry
>serviette
>fenestration
>crown
>blue.

I run to liquids and colors," she said, "but you, you may run to something else, my virgin, my darling, my thistle, my poppet, my own. Young people," Miss R. said, "run to more and more unpleasant combinations as they sense the nature of our society. Some people," Miss R. said, "run to conceits or wisdom but I hold to the hard, brown, nutlike word. I might point out that there is enough aesthetic excitement here to satisfy anyone but a damned fool." I sat in solemn silence.

Fire arrows lit my way to the post office in Patton Place where members of the Abraham Lincoln Brigade offered their last, exhausted letters, postcards, calendars. I opened a letter but inside was a Comanche flint arrowhead played by Frank Wedekind in an elegant gold chain and congratulations. Your earring rattled against my spectacles when I leaned forward to touch the soft, ruined place where the hearing aid had been. "Pack it in! Pack it in!" I urged, but the men in charge of the Uprising refused to listen to reason or to understand that it was real and that our water supply had evaporated and that our credit was no longer what it had been, once.

We attached wires to the testicles of the captured Comanche. And I sat there getting drunker and drunker and more in love and more in love. When we threw the switch he spoke. His name, he said, was Gustave Aschenbach. He was born at L——, a country town in the province of Silesia. He was the son of an upper official in the judicature, and his forebears had all been officers, judges, departmental functionaries. . . . And you can never touch a girl in the same way more than once, twice, or another number of times however much you may wish to hold, wrap, or otherwise fix her hand, or look, or some other quality, or incident, known to you previously. In Sweden the little Swedish children cheered when we managed nothing more remarkable than getting off a bus burdened with packages, bread and liver-paste and beer. We went to an old church and sat in the royal box. The organist was practicing. And then into the graveyard next to the church. *Here lies Anna Pedersen, a good woman.* I threw a mushroom on the grave. The officer commanding the garbage dump reported by radio that the garbage had begun to move.

Jane! I heard via an International Distress Coupon that you were beaten up by a dwarf in a bar on Tenerife. That doesn't sound like you, Jane. Mostly you kick the dwarf in his little dwarf groin before he can get his teeth into your tasty and nice-looking leg, don't you, Jane? Your affair with Harold is reprehensible, you know that, don't you, Jane? Harold is married to Nancy. And there is Paula to think about (Harold's kid), and Billy (Harold's other kid). I think your values are peculiar, Jane! Strings of language extend in every direction to bind the world into a rushing, ribald whole.

And you can never return to felicities in the same way, the brilliant body, the distinguished spirit recapitulating moments that occur once, twice, or another number of times in rebellions, or water. The rolling consensus of the Comanche nation smashed our inner defenses on three sides. Block was firing a greasegun from the upper floor of a building designed by Emery Roth & Sons. "See the table?" "Oh, pack it in with your bloody table!" The city officials were tied to trees. Dusky warriors padded with their forest tread into the mouth of the mayor. "Who do you want to be?" I asked Kenneth and he said he wanted to be Jean-Luc Godard but later when time permitted conversations in large, lighted rooms, whispering galleries with black-and-white Spanish rugs and problematic sculpture on calm, red catafalques. The sickness of the quarrel lay thick in the bed. I touched your back, the white, raised scars.

We killed a great many in the south suddenly with helicopters and rockets but we found that those we had killed were children and more came from the north and from the east and

THE INDIAN UPRISING

from other places where there are children preparing to live. "Skin," Miss R. said softly in the white, yellow room. "This is the Clemency Committee. And would you remove your belt and shoelaces." I removed my belt and shoelaces and looked (rain shattering from a great height the prospects of silence and clear, neat rows of houses in the subdivisions) into their savage black eyes, paint, feathers, beads.

The Balloon

THE BALLOON, beginning at a point on Fourteenth Street, the exact location of which I cannot reveal, expanded northward all one night, while people were sleeping, until it reached the Park. There, I stopped it; at dawn the northernmost edges lay over the Plaza; the free-hanging motion was frivolous and gentle. But experiencing a faint irritation at stopping, even to protect the trees, and seeing no reason the balloon should not be allowed to expand upward, over the parts of the city it was already covering, into the "air space" to be found there, I asked the engineers to see to it. This expansion took place throughout the morning, soft imperceptible sighing of gas through the valves. The balloon then covered forty-five blocks north-south and an irregular area east-west, as many as six crosstown blocks on either side of the Avenue in some places. That was the situation, then.

But it is wrong to speak of "situations," implying sets of circumstances leading to some resolution, some escape of tension; there were no situations, simply the balloon hanging there—muted heavy grays and browns for the most part, contrasting with walnut and soft yellows. A deliberate lack of finish, enhanced by skillful installation, gave the surface a rough, forgotten quality; sliding weights on the inside, carefully adjusted, anchored the great, vari-shaped mass at a number of points. Now we have had a flood of original ideas in all media, works of singular beauty as well as significant milestones in the history of inflation, but at that moment there was only *this balloon*, concrete particular, hanging there.

There were reactions. Some people found the balloon "interesting." As a response this seemed inadequate to the immensity of the balloon, the suddenness of its appearance over the city; on the other hand, in the absence of hysteria or other societally-induced anxiety, it must be judged a calm, "mature" one. There was a certain amount of initial argumentation about the "meaning" of the balloon; this subsided, because we have learned not to insist on meanings, and they are rarely even looked for now, except in cases involving the simplest, safest phenomena. It was agreed that since the meaning of the balloon could never be known absolutely, extended discussion was pointless, or at least less purposeful than the activities of those who, for example, hung green and blue paper lanterns from the warm gray underside, in certain streets, or seized the occasion to write messages on the surface, announcing their availability for the performance of unnatural acts, or the availability of acquaintances.

Daring children jumped, especially at those points where the balloon hovered close to a building, so that the gap between balloon and building was a matter of a few inches, or points where the balloon actually made contact, exerting an ever-so-slight pressure against the side of a building, so that balloon and building seemed a unity. The upper surface was so structured that a "landscape" was presented, small valleys as well as slight knolls, or mounds; once atop the balloon, a stroll was possible, or even a trip, from one place to another. There was pleasure in being able to run down an incline, then up the opposing slope, both gently graded, or in making a leap from one side to the other. Bouncing was possible, because of the pneumaticity of the surface, and even falling, if that was your wish. That all these varied motions, as well as others, were within one's possibilities, in experiencing the "up" side of the balloon, was extremely exciting for children, accustomed to the city's flat, hard skin. But the purpose of the balloon was not to amuse children.

Too, the number of people, children and adults, who took advantage of the opportunities described was not so large as it might have been: a certain timidity, lack of trust in the balloon, was seen. There was, furthermore, some hostility. Because we had hidden the pumps, which fed helium to the interior, and because the surface was so vast that the authorities could not determine the point of entry—that is, the point at which the gas was injected—a degree of frustration was evidenced by those city officers into whose province such manifestations normally fell. The apparent purposelessness of the balloon was vexing (as was the fact that it was "there" at all). Had we painted, in great letters, "LABORATORY TESTS PROVE" or "18% MORE EFFECTIVE" on the sides of the balloon, this difficulty would have been circumvented. But I could not bear to do so. On the whole, these officers were remarkably tolerant, considering the dimensions of the anomaly, this tolerance being the result of, first, secret tests conducted by night that convinced them that little or nothing could be done in the way of removing or destroying the balloon, and, secondly, a public warmth that arose (not uncolored by touches of the aforementioned hostility) toward the balloon, from ordinary citizens.

As a single balloon must stand for a lifetime of thinking about balloons, so each citizen expressed, in the attitude he chose, a complex of attitudes. One man might consider that the balloon had to do with the notion *sullied*, as in the sentence *The big balloon sullied the otherwise clear and radiant Manhattan sky*. That is, the balloon was, in this man's view, an imposture, something inferior to the sky that had formerly been there, something interposed between the people and their "sky." But in fact it was January, the sky was dark and ugly; it was not a sky you could look up into, lying on your back in the street, with pleasure, unless pleasure, for you, proceeded from having been threatened, from having been misused. And the underside of the balloon was a pleasure to look up into, we had seen to that, muted grays and browns for the most part, contrasted with walnut and soft, forgotten yellows. And so, while this man was thinking *sullied*, still there was an admixture of pleasurable cognition in his thinking, struggling with the original perception.

Another man, on the other hand, might view the balloon as if it were part of a system of unanticipated rewards, as when one's employer walks in and says, "Here, Henry, take this package of money I have wrapped for you, because we have been doing so well in the business here, and I admire the way you bruise the tulips, without which bruising your department would not be a success, or at least not the success that it is." For this man the balloon might be a brilliantly heroic "muscle and pluck" experience, even if an experience poorly understood.

Another man might say, "Without the example of ———, it is doubtful that ——— would exist today in its present form," and find many to agree with him, or to argue with him. Ideas of "bloat" and "float" were introduced, as well as concepts of dream and responsibility. Others engaged in remarkably detailed fantasies having to do with a wish either to lose themselves in the balloon, or to engorge it. The private character of these wishes, of their origins, deeply buried and unknown, was such that they were not much spoken of; yet there is evidence that they were widespread. It was also argued that what was important was what you felt when you stood under the balloon; some people claimed that they felt sheltered, warmed, as never before, while enemies of the balloon felt, or reported feeling, constrained, a "heavy" feeling.

Critical opinion was divided:

"monstrous pourings"

"harp"

XXXXXXX "certain contrasts with darker portions"
"inner joy"

"large, square corners"

"conservative eclecticism that has so far governed modern balloon design"

::::::: "abnormal vigor"

"warm, soft, lazy passages"

"Has unity been sacrificed for a sprawling quality?"

"*Quelle catastrophe!*"

"munching"

People began, in a curious way, to locate themselves in relation to aspects of the balloon: "I'll be at that place where it dips down into Forty-seventh Street almost to the sidewalk, near the Alamo Chile House," or, "Why don't we go stand on top, and take the air, and maybe walk about a bit, where it forms a tight, curving line with the façade of the Gallery of Modern Art—" Marginal intersections offered entrances within a given time duration, as well as "warm, soft, lazy passages" in which . . . But it is wrong to speak of "marginal intersections," each intersection was crucial, none could be ignored (as if, walking there, you might not find someone capable of turning your attention, in a flash, from old exercises to new exercises, risks and escalations). Each intersection was crucial, meeting of balloon and building, meeting of balloon and man, meeting of balloon and balloon.

It was suggested that what was admired about the balloon was finally this: that it was not limited, or defined. Sometimes a bulge, blister, or sub-section would carry all the way east to the river on its own initiative, in the manner of an army's movements on a map, as seen in a headquarters remote from the fighting. Then that part would be, as it were, thrown back again, or would withdraw into new dispositions; the next morning, that part would have made another sortie, or disappeared altogether. This ability of the balloon to shift its shape, to change, was very pleasing, especially to people whose lives were rather rigidly patterned, persons to whom change, although desired, was not available. The balloon, for the twenty-two days of its existence, offered the possibility, in its randomness, of mislocation of the self, in contradistinction to the grid of precise, rectangular pathways under our feet. The amount of specialized training currently needed, and the consequent desirability of long-term commitments, has been occasioned by the steadily growing importance of complex machinery, in virtually all kinds of operations; as this tendency increases, more and more people will turn, in bewildered inadequacy, to solutions for which the balloon may stand as a prototype, or "rough draft."

I met you under the balloon, on the occasion of your return from Norway; you asked if it was mine; I said it was. The balloon, I said, is a spontaneous autobiographical disclosure, having to do with the unease I felt at your absence, and with sexual deprivation, but now that your visit to Bergen has been terminated, it is no longer necessary or appropriate. Removal of the balloon was easy; trailer trucks carried away the depleted fabric, which is now stored in West Virginia, awaiting some other time of unhappiness, sometime, perhaps, when we are angry with one another.

This Newspaper Here

Again today the little girl come along come along dancing doggedly with her knitting needle steel-blue knitting needle. She knows I can't get up out of this chair theoretically and sticks me, here and there, just to make me yell, nice little girl from down the block somewhere. Once I corrected her sharply saying "don't for God's sake what pleasure is there hearing me scream like this?" She was wearing a blue Death of Beethoven printed dress and white shoes which mama had whited for her that day before noon so white were they (shoes). I judged her to be eleven. The knitting needle in the long thrust and hold position she said "torment is the answer old pappy man it's torment that is the game's name that I'm learning about under laboratory conditions. Torment is the proper study of children of my age class and median income and *you* don't matter in any case you're through dirty old man can't even get out of rotten old chair." Summed me up she did in those words which I would much rather not have heard so prettily put as they were nevertheless. I hate it here in this chair in this house warm and green with Social Security. Do you know how little it is? The little girl jabbed again hitting the thin thigh that time and said "we know *exactly* how little it is and even that is money down the drain why don't you die damn you dirty old man what are you contributing?" Then I explained about this newspaper here sprinkled with rare lies and photographs incorrectly captioned accumulated along a lifetime of disappointments and some fun. I boasted saying "one knows just where nerves cluster under the skin, how to pinch them so citizens jump as in dreams when opened suddenly a door and there see two flagrantly . . ." But I realize then her dreams are drawn in ways which differ so that we cannot read them together. I threw then jam jar (black currant) catching her nicely on kneecap and she ran howling but if they come to object I have jab marks in extenuation. Nice little girl from down the block somewhere.

The reason I like to read this newspaper here the one in my hand, is because I like what it says. It is my favorite. I would be pleased really quite if you could read it. But you can't. But some can. It comes in the mail. I give it to a fellow some time back, put it in his hand and said "take a look." He took a look took a look but he couldn't see anything strawdinary along this newspaper here, couldn't see it. And he says "so what?" Of course I once was in this business myself making newspapers in the depression. We had fun then. This fellow I give it to to take a look some time back he that said "so what" is well educated reads good travels far drinks deep gin mostly talks to dolphins click click click click. A professor of ethnology at the University of California at Davis. Not in fine a dullard in any sense but he couldn't see anything strawdinary along this newspaper here. I said look there page 2 the amusing story of the plain girl fair where the plain girls come to vend their wares but he said "on *my* page 2 this newspaper here talk about the EEC." Then I took it from his hand and showed him with my finger pointing the plain girl fair story. Then he commences to read aloud from under my finger there some singsong about the EEC. So I infer that he is one who can't. So I let the matter drop.

I went to the plain girl fair out Route 22 figuring I could get one if I just put on a kind face. This newspaper here had advertising the aspidistra store not far away by car where I went then and bought one to carry along. At the plain girl fair they were standing in sudden-death décolletage and brown arms everywhere. As you passed along into the tent after paying your dollar fifty carrying your aspidistra a blinding flash of some hundred contact lenses came. And a quality of dental work to shame the VA Hospital it was so fine. One fell in love temporarily with all this hard work and money spent just to please to improve. I was sad my dolphin friend was not there to see. I took one by the hand and said "come with me I will buy you a lobster." My real face behind my kind face smiling. And the other girls on their pedestals waved and said "goodbye Marie." And they also said "have a nice lobster," and Marie waved back and said "bonne chance!" We motored to the lobster place over to Barwick, then danced by the light of the moon for a bit. And then to my hay where I tickled the naked soles of feet with a piece of it and admired her gestures of marvellous gaucherie. In my mind.

Of course I once was in this business myself making newspapers in the depression. So I know some little some about it, both the back room and the front room. If you got in the makeups' way they'd yell "dime waitin' on a nickel." But this here and now newspaper I say a thing of great formal beauty. Sometimes on dull days the compositors play which makes paragraphs like

```
(!) (!) (!) (!) (!) (!) (!) (!) (!) (!) (!) (!) (!)
* * * * * * * * * * * * * * * * * * * * *
? / ? / ? / ? / ? / ? / ? / ? / ? / ? / ? / ? / ? /
o : o : o : o : o : o : o : o : o : o : o : o : o
? / ? / ? / ? / ? / ? / ? / ? / ? / ? / ? / ? / ? /
* * * * * * * * * * * * * * * * * * * * *
(!) (!) (!) (!) (!) (!) (!) (!) (!) (!) (!) (!) (!)
```

refreshing as rocks in this newspaper here. And then you come along a page solid bright aching orange sometimes and parts printed in alien languages and invisible inks. This newspaper here fly away fly away through the mails to names from the telephone book. Have you seen my library of telephone books I keep in the kitchen with names from Greater Memphis Utica Key West Toledo Santa Barbara St. Paul Juneau Missoula Tacoma and every which where. It goes third class because I print HOTELS-MOTELS NEED TRAINED MEN AND WOMEN AMAZING FREE OFFER on the wrapper. As a disguise.

Then a learned man come to call saying "this with the newspaper is not kosher you know that." He had several degrees in Police Engineering and the like and his tiny gun dwelt in his armpit like the growths described by Defoe in *Journal of the Plague Year*. I judged him to be with some one of the governments. Not overfond of him in my house but I said in a friendly way "can I see it." He took out the tiny black gun and held it in his hand, then slapped me up against the head with it in a friendly way. He coughed and looked at the bottle of worrywine sitting on the table on the newspaper saying "and we can hear the presses in the basement with sensitive secret recording devices." And finally he said sighing "we know it's you why don't you simply take a few months off, try Florida or Banff which is said to swing at this season of the year and we'll pay everything." I told him smiling I didn't get the reference. He was almost crying it seemed to me saying "you know it excites the people stirs them up exacerbates hopes we thought laid to rest generations ago." He nodded to agree with himself laying soft hands around the windpipe of the gramophone automatically feeling for counter-bugs down its throat saying "we don't understand what it is you're after. If you don't like our war you don't have to come to it, too old anyway you used-up old poop." Then he slapped me up alongside the head couple more times with his exquisite politesse kicking my toothpick scale model of Heinrich von Kleist in blue velvet to splinters on the way out.

Can you imagine some fellow waking at dawn in Toledo looking at his red alarm clock and then thinking with wonder of a picture drawn in this newspaper here by my friend Golo. When we were in Paris Golo was a famous one because he drew with his thumbs in black black paint which was not then done yet much on brown paper and it made people stop. Now Golo has altered his name because he is wanted. Still he sends me drawings on secular subjects from here and there, when they irritate me I put them in. It is true that I dislike their war and have pointed out that the very postage stamps shimmer with dangerous ideological radiation. They hated that. I run coupons to clip offering Magnificent Butterfly Wing Portraits Send Photo, Transistorized Personal Sun Tanner, How to Develop a He-Man Voice, Darling Pet Monkey Show It Affection and Enjoy Its Company, British Shoes for Gentlemen, Live Seahorses $1 Each, Why Be Bald, Electric Roses Never Fade or Wither, Hotels-Motels Need Trained Men and Women. And I keep the money.

But what else can I do? Making this newspaper here I hold a prerequisite to eluding death which is looking for me don't you know. Girl with knitting needle simply sent to soften me up, a probing action as it were. My newspaper warm at the edges fade in fade out a tissue of hints whispers glimpses uncertainties, zoom in zoom out. I considered in an editorial the idea that the world is an error on the part of God, one of the earliest and finest heresies, they hated that. Ringle from the telephone "what do you mean the world is a roar on the part of God," which pleased me. I said "madam is your name Marie if so I will dangle your health in verymerrywine this very eve blast me if I will not." She said into the telephone "dirty old man." Who ha who ha. I sit here rock around the clock interviewing Fabian on his plateglass window incident in my mind. Sweet to know your face uncut and unabridged. Who ha who ha dirty old man.

Robert Kennedy Saved from Drowning

K. at His Desk

He is neither abrupt with nor excessively kind to associates. Or he is both abrupt and kind.

The telephone is, for him, a whip, a lash, but also a conduit for soothing words, a sink into which he can hurl gallons of syrup if it comes to that.

He reads quickly, scratching brief comments ("Yes," "No") in corners of the paper. He slouches in the leather chair, looking about him with a slightly irritated air for new visitors, new difficulties. He spends his time sending and receiving messengers.

"I spend my time sending and receiving messengers," he says. "Some of these messages are important. Others are not."

Described by Secretaries

A: "Quite frankly I think he forgets a lot of things. But the things he forgets are those which are inessential. I even think he might forget deliberately, to leave his mind free. He has the ability to get rid of unimportant details. And he does."

B: "Once when I was sick, I hadn't heard from him, and I thought he had forgotten me. You know usually your boss will send flowers or something like that. I was in the hospital, and I was mighty blue. I was in a room with another girl, and *her* boss hadn't sent her anything either. Then suddenly the door opened and there he was with the biggest bunch of yellow tulips I'd ever seen in my life. And the other girl's boss was with him, and he had tulips too. They were standing there with all those tulips, smiling."

Behind the Bar

At a crowded party, he wanders behind the bar to make himself a Scotch and water. His hand is on the bottle of Scotch, his glass is waiting. The bartender, a small man in a beige uniform with gilt buttons, politely asks K. to return to the other side, the guests' side, of the bar. "You let one behind here, they all be behind here," the bartender says.

K. Reading the Newspaper

His reactions are impossible to catalogue. Often he will find a note that amuses him endlessly, some anecdote involving, say, a fireman who has propelled his apparatus at record-breaking speed to the wrong address. These small stories are clipped, carried about in a pocket, to be produced at appropriate moments for the pleasure of friends. Other manifestations please him less. An account of an earthquake in Chile, with its thousands of dead and homeless, may depress him for weeks. He memorizes the terrible statistics, quoting them everywhere and saying, with a grave look: "We must do something." Important actions often follow, sometimes within a matter of hours. (On the other hand, these two kinds of responses may be, on a given day, inexplicably reversed.)

The more trivial aspects of the daily itemization are skipped. While reading, he maintains a rapid drumming of his fingertips on the desktop. He receives twelve newspapers, but of these, only four are regarded as serious.

Attitude Toward His Work

"Sometimes I can't seem to do anything. The work is there, piled up, it seems to me an insurmountable obstacle, really out of reach. I sit and look at it, wondering where to begin, how to take hold of it. Perhaps I pick up a piece of paper, try to read it but my mind is elsewhere, I am thinking of something else, I can't seem to get the gist of it, it seems meaningless, devoid of interest, not having to do with human affairs, drained of life. Then, in an hour, or even a moment, everything changes suddenly: I realize I only have to *do* it, hurl myself into the midst of it, proceed mechanically, the first thing and then the second thing, that it is simply a matter of moving from one step to the next, plowing through it. I become interested, I become excited, I work very fast, things fall into place, I am exhilarated, amazed that these things could ever have seemed dead to me."

Sleeping on the Stones of Unknown Towns (Rimbaud)

K. is walking, with that familiar slight dip of the shoulders, through the streets of a small city in France or Germany. The shop signs are in a language which alters when inspected closely, MÖBEL becoming MEUBLES for example, and the citizens mutter to themselves with dark virtuosity a mixture of languages. K. is very interested, looks closely at everything, at the shops, the goods displayed, the clothing of the people, the tempo of street life, the citizens themselves, wondering about them. What are their water needs?

"In the West, wisdom is mostly gained at lunch. At lunch, people tell you things."
The nervous eyes of the waiters.
The tall bald cook, white apron, white T-shirt, grinning through an opening in the wall.
"Why is that cook looking at me?"

Urban Transportation
"The transportation problems of our cities and their rapidly expanding suburbs are the most urgent and neglected transportation problems confronting the country. In these heavily populated and industrialized areas, people are dependent on a system of transportation that is at once complex and inadequate. Obsolete facilities and growing demands have created seemingly insoluble difficulties and present methods of dealing with these difficulties offer little prospect of relief."

K. Penetrated with Sadness
He hears something playing on someone else's radio, in another part of the building.
The music is wretchedly sad; now he can (barely) hear it, now it fades into the wall.
He turns on his own radio. There it is, on his own radio, the same music. The sound fills the room.

Karsh of Ottawa
"We sent a man to Karsh of Ottawa and told him that we admired his work very much. Especially, I don't know, the Churchill thing and, you know, the Hemingway thing, and all that. And we told him we wanted to set up a sitting for K. sometime in June, if that would be convenient for him, and he said yes, that was okay, June was okay, and where did we want

to have it shot, there or in New York or where. Well, that was a problem because we didn't know exactly what K.'s schedule would be for June, it was up in the air, so we tentatively said New York around the fifteenth. And he said, that was okay, he could do that. And he wanted to know how much time he could have, and we said, well, how much time do you need? And he said he didn't know, it varied from sitter to sitter. He said some people were very restless and that made it difficult to get just the right shot. He said there was one shot in each sitting that was, you know, the key shot, the right one. He said he'd have to see, when the time came."

Dress
He is neatly dressed in a manner that does not call attention to itself. The suits are soberly cut and in dark colors. He must at all times present an aspect of freshness difficult to sustain because of frequent movements from place to place under conditions which are not always the most favorable. Thus he changes clothes frequently, especially shirts. In the course of a day he changes his shirt many times. There are always extra shirts about, in boxes.
"Which of you has the shirts?"

A Friend Comments: K.'s Aloneness
"The thing you have to realize about K. is that essentially he's absolutely alone in the world. There's this terrible loneliness which prevents people from getting too close to him. Maybe it comes from something in his childhood, I don't know. But he's very hard to get to know, and a lot of people who think they know him rather well don't really know him at all. He says something or does something that surprises you, and you realize that all along you really didn't know him at all.

"He has surprising facets. I remember once we were out in a small boat. K. of course was the captain. Some rough weather came up and we began to head back in. I began worrying about picking up a landing and I said to him that I didn't think the anchor would hold, with the wind and all. He just looked at me. Then he said: 'Of course it will hold. That's what it's for.'"

K. on Crowds
"There are exhausted crowds and vivacious crowds.

"Sometimes, standing there, I can sense whether a particular crowd is one thing or the other. Sometimes the mood of the crowd is disguised, sometimes you only find out after a quarter of an hour what sort of crowd a particular crowd is.

"And you can't speak to them in the same way. The variations have to be taken into account. You have to say something to them that is meaningful to them *in that mood*."

Gallery-going
K. enters a large gallery on Fifty-seventh Street, in the Fuller Building. His entourage includes several ladies and gentlemen. Works by a geometricist are on show. K. looks at the immense, rather theoretical paintings.

"Well, at least we know he has a ruler."

The group dissolves in laughter. People repeat the remark to one another, laughing.

The artist, who has been standing behind a dealer, regards K. with hatred.

K. Puzzled by His Children
The children are crying. There are several children, one about four, a boy, then another boy, slightly older, and a little girl, very beautiful, wearing blue jeans, crying. There are various objects on the grass, an electric train, a picture book, a red ball, a plastic bucket, a plastic shovel.

K. frowns at the children whose distress issues from no source immediately available to the eye, which seems indeed uncaused, vacant, a general anguish. K. turns to the mother of these children who is standing nearby wearing hip-huggers which appear to be made of linked marshmallows studded with diamonds but then I am a notoriously poor observer.

"Play with them," he says.

This mother of ten quietly suggests that K. himself "play with them."

K. picks up the picture book and begins to read to the children. But the book has a German text. It has been left behind, perhaps, by some foreign visitor. Nevertheless K. perseveres.

"A ist der Affe, er isst mit der Pfote." ("A is the Ape, he eats with his Paw.")

The crying of the children continues.

A Dream
Orange trees.
Overhead, a steady stream of strange aircraft which resemble kitchen implements, bread boards, cookie sheets, colanders.
The shiny aluminum instruments are on their way to complete the bombing of Sidi-Madani.
A farm in the hills.

Matters (from an Administrative Assistant)
"A lot of matters that had been pending came to a head right about that time, moved to the front burner, things we absolutely had to take care of. And we couldn't find K. Nobody knew where he was. We had looked everywhere. He had just withdrawn, made himself unavailable. There was this one matter that was probably more pressing than all the rest put together. Really crucial. We were all standing around wondering what to do. We were getting pretty nervous because this thing was really. . . . Then K. walked in and disposed of it with a quick phone call. A quick phone call!"

Childhood of K. as Recalled by a Former Teacher
"He was a very alert boy, very bright, good at his studies, very thorough, very conscientious. But that's not unusual; that describes a good number of the boys who pass through here. It's not unusual, that is, to find these qualities which are after all the qualities that we look for and encourage in them. What *was* unusual about K. was his compassion, something very rare for a boy of that age—even if they have it, they're usually very careful not to display it for fear of seeming soft, girlish. I remember, though, that in K. this particular attribute was very marked. I would almost say that it was his strongest characteristic."

Speaking to No One but Waiters, He—
"The dandelion salad with bacon, I think."

"The *rijsttafel*."

"The poached duck."

"The black bean purée."

"The cod fritters."

K. Explains a Technique

"It's an expedient in terms of how not to destroy a situation which has been a long time gestating, or, again, how *to* break it up if it appears that the situation has changed, during the gestation period, into one whose implications are not quite what they were at the beginning. What I mean is that in this business things are constantly altering (usually for the worse) and usually you want to give the impression that you're not watching this particular situation particularly closely, that you're paying *no* special attention to it, until you're ready to make your move. That is, it's best to be sudden, if you can manage it. Of course you can't do that all the time. Sometimes you're just completely wiped out, cleaned out, totaled, and then the only thing to do is shrug and forget about it."

K. on His Own Role

"Sometimes it seems to me that it doesn't matter what I do, that it is enough to exist, to sit somewhere, in a garden for example, watching whatever is to be seen there, the small events. At other times, I'm aware that other people, possibly a great number of other people, could be affected by what I do or fail to do, that I have a responsibility, as we all have, to make the best possible use of whatever talents I've been given, for the common good. It is not enough to sit in that garden, however restful or pleasurable it might be. The world is full of unsolved problems, situations that demand careful, reasoned and intelligent action. In Latin America, for example."

As Entrepreneur

The original cost estimates for burying the North Sea pipeline have been exceeded by a considerable margin. Everyone wonders what he will say about this contretemps which does not fail to have its dangers for those responsible for the costly miscalculations, which are viewed in many minds as inexcusable.

He says only: "Exceptionally difficult rock conditions."

With Young People

K., walking the streets of unknown towns, finds himself among young people. Young people line these streets, narrow and curving, which are theirs, dedicated to them. They are everywhere, resting on the embankments, their guitars, small radios, long hair. They sit on the sidewalks, back to back, heads turned to stare. They stand implacably on street corners, in doorways, or lean on their elbows in windows, or squat in small groups at that place where the sidewalk meets the walls of buildings. The streets are filled with these young people who say nothing, reveal only a limited interest, refuse to declare themselves. Street after street contains them, a great number, more displayed as one turns a corner, rank upon rank stretching into the distance, drawn from the arcades, the plazas, staring.

He Discusses the French Writer, Poulet

"For Poulet, it is not enough to speak of *seizing the moment*. It is rather a question of, and I quote, 'recognizing in the instant which lives and dies, which surges out of nothingness and which ends in dream, an intensity and depth of significance which ordinarily attaches only to the whole of existence.'

"What Poulet is describing is neither an ethic nor a prescription but rather what he has discovered in the work of Marivaux. Poulet has taken up the Marivaudian canon and squeezed it with both hands to discover the essence of what may be called the Marivaudian being, what Poulet in fact calls the Marivaudian being.

"The Marivaudian being is, according to Poulet, a pastless futureless man, born anew at every instant. The instants are points which organize themselves into a line, but what is important is the instant, not the line. The Marivaudian being has in a sense no history. Nothing follows from what has gone before. He is constantly surprised. He cannot predict his own reaction to events. He is constantly being *overtaken* by events. A condition of breathlessness and dazzlement surrounds him. In consequence he exists in a certain freshness which seems, if I may say so, very desirable. This freshness Poulet, quoting Marivaux, describes very well."

K. Saved from Drowning

K. in the water. His flat black hat, his black cape, his sword are on the shore. He retains his mask. His hands beat the surface of the water which tears and rips about him. The white foam, the green depths. I throw a line, the coils leaping out over the surface of the water. He has missed it. No, it appears that he has it. His right hand (sword arm) grasps the line that I have thrown him. I am on the bank, the rope wound round my waist, braced against a rock. K. now has both hands on the line. I pull him out of the water. He stands now on the bank, gasping.

"Thank you."

Report

OUR GROUP is against the war. But the war goes on. I was sent to Cleveland to talk to the engineers. The engineers were meeting in Cleveland. I was supposed to persuade them not to do what they are going to do. I took United's 4:45 from LaGuardia arriving in Cleveland at 6:13. Cleveland is dark blue at that hour. I went directly to the motel, where the engineers were meeting. Hundreds of engineers attended the Cleveland meeting. I noticed many fractures among the engineers, bandages, traction. I noticed what appeared to be fracture of the carpal scaphoid in six examples. I noticed numerous fractures of the humeral shaft, of the os calcis, of the pelvic girdle. I noticed a high incidence of clay-shoveller's fracture. I could not account for these fractures. The engineers were making calculations, taking measurements, sketching on the blackboard, drinking beer, throwing bread, buttonholing employers, hurling glasses into the fireplace. They were friendly.

They were friendly. They were full of love and information. The chief engineer wore shades. Patella in Monk's traction, clamshell fracture by the look of it. He was standing in a slum of beer bottles and microphone cable. "Have some of this chicken à la Isambard Kingdom Brunel the Great Ingineer," he said. "And declare who you are and what we can do for you. What is your line, distinguished guest?"

"Software," I said. "In every sense. I am here representing a small group of interested parties. We are interested in your thing, which seems to be functioning. In the midst of so much dysfunction, function is interesting. Other people's things don't seem to be working. The State Department's thing doesn't seem to be working. The U.N.'s thing doesn't seem to be working. The democratic left's thing doesn't seem to be working. Buddha's thing—"

"Ask us anything about our thing, which seems to be working," the chief engineer said. "We will open our hearts and heads to you, Software Man, because we want to be understood and loved by the great lay public, and have our marvels appreciated by that public, for which we daily unsung produce tons of new marvels each more life-enhancing than the last. Ask us anything. Do you want to know about evaporated thin-film metallurgy? Monolithic and hybrid integrated-circuit processes? The algebra of inequalities? Optimization theory? Complex high-speed micro-miniature closed and open loop systems? Fixed variable mathematical cost searches? Epitaxial deposition of semi-conductor materials? Gross interfaced space gropes? We also have specialists in the cuckooflower, the doctorfish, and the dumdum bullet as these relate to aspects of today's expanding technology, and they do in the damnedest ways."

I spoke to him then about the war. I said the same things people always say when they speak against the war. I said that the war was wrong. I said that large countries should not burn down small countries. I said that the government had made a series of errors. I said that these errors once small and forgivable were now immense and unforgivable. I said that the government was attempting to conceal its original errors under layers of new errors. I said that the government was sick with error, giddy with it. I said that ten thousand of our soldiers had already been killed in pursuit of the government's errors. I said that tens of thousands of the enemy's soldiers and civilians had been killed because of various errors, ours and theirs. I said that we are responsible for errors made in our name. I said that the government should not be allowed to make additional errors.

"Yes, yes," the chief engineer said, "there is doubtless much truth in what you say, but we can't possibly *lose* the war, can we? And stopping is losing, isn't it? The war regarded as a process, stopping regarded as an abort? We don't know *how* to lose a war. That skill is not among our skills. Our array smashes their array, that is what we know. That is the process. That is what is.

"But let's not have any more of this dispiriting downbeat counterproductive talk. I have a few new marvels here I'd like to discuss with you just briefly. A few new marvels that are just about ready to be gaped at by the admiring layman. Consider for instance the area of realtime online computer-controlled wish evaporation. Wish evaporation is going to be crucial in meeting the rising expectations of the world's peoples, which are as you know rising entirely too fast."

I noticed then distributed about the room a great many transverse fractures of the ulna. "The development of the pseudo-ruminant stomach for underdeveloped peoples," he went on, "is one of our interesting things you should be interested in. With the pseudo-ruminant stomach they can chew cuds, that is to say, eat grass. Blue is the most popular color worldwide and for that reason we are working with certain strains of your native Kentucky *Poa pratensis*, or bluegrass, as the staple input for the p/r stomach cycle, which would also give a shot in the arm to our balance-of-payments thing don't you know. . . ." I noticed about me then a great number of metatarsal fractures in banjo splints. "The kangaroo initiative . . . eight hundred thousand harvested last year . . . highest percentage of edible protein of any herbivore yet studied . . ."

"Have new kangaroos been planted?"

The engineer looked at me.

"I intuit your hatred and jealousy of our thing," he said. "The ineffectual always hate our thing and speak of it as antihuman, which is not at all a meaningful way to speak of our thing. Nothing mechanical is alien to me," he said (amber spots making bursts of light in his shades), "because I am human, in a sense, and if I think it up, then 'it' is human too, whatever 'it' may be. Let me tell you, Software Man, we have been damned forbearing in the matter of this little war you declare yourself to be interested in. Function is the cry, and our thing is functioning like crazy. There are things we could do that we have not done. Steps we could take that we have not taken. These steps are, regarded in a certain light, the light of our enlightened self-interest, quite justifiable steps. We could, of course, get irritated. We could, of course, *lose patience.*

"We could, of course, release thousands upon thousands of self-powered crawling-along-the-ground lengths of titanium wire eighteen inches long with a diameter of .0005 centimetres (that is to say, invisible) which, scenting an enemy, climb up his trouser leg and wrap themselves around his neck. We have developed those. They are within our capabilities. We could, of course, release in the arena of the upper air our new improved pufferfish toxin which precipitates an identity crisis. No special technical problems there. That is almost laughably easy. We could, of course, place up to two million maggots in their rice within twenty-four hours. The maggots are ready, massed in secret staging areas in Alabama. We have hypodermic darts capable of piebalding the enemy's pigmentation. We have rots, blights, and rusts capable of attacking his alphabet. Those are dandies. We have a hut-shrinking chemical which penetrates the fibres of the bamboo, causing it, the hut, to strangle its occupants. This operates only after 10 P.M., when people are sleeping. Their mathematics are at the mercy of a suppurating surd we have invented. We have a family of fishes trained to attack their fishes. We have the deadly testicle-destroying telegram. The cable companies are coöperating. We have a green substance that, well, I'd rather not talk about. We have a secret word that, if pronounced, produces multiple fractures in all living things in an area the size of four football fields."

"That's why—"

"Yes. Some damned fool couldn't keep his mouth shut. The point is that the whole structure of enemy life is within our power to *rend*, *vitiate*, *devour*, and *crush*. But that's not the interesting thing."

"You recount these possibilities with uncommon relish."

"Yes I realize that there is too much relish here. But *you* must realize that these capabilities represent in and of themselves highly technical and complex and interesting problems and hurdles on which our boys have expended many thousands of hours of hard work and brilliance. And that the effects are often grossly exaggerated by irresponsible victims. And that the whole thing represents a fantastic series of triumphs for the multi-disciplined problem-solving team concept."

"I appreciate that."

"We *could* unleash all this technology at once. You can imagine what would happen then. But that's not the interesting thing."

"What is the interesting thing?"

"The interesting thing is that we have *a moral sense*. It is on punched cards, perhaps the most advanced and sensitive moral sense the world has ever known."

"Because it is on punched cards?"

"It considers all considerations in endless and subtle detail," he said. "It even quibbles. With this great new moral tool, how can we go wrong? I confidently predict that, although we *could* employ all this splendid new weaponry I've been telling you about, *we're not going to do it.*"

"We're not going to do it?"

I took United's 5:44 from Cleveland arriving at Newark at 7:19. New Jersey is bright pink at that hour. Living things move about the surface of New Jersey at that hour molesting each other only in traditional ways. I made my report to the group. I stressed the friendliness of the engineers. I said, It's all right. I said, We have a moral sense. I said, *We're not going to do it.* They didn't believe me.

The Dolt

EDGAR WAS preparing to take the National Writers' Examination, a five-hour fifty-minute examination, for his certificate. He was in his room, frightened. The prospect of taking the exam again put him in worlds of hurt. He had taken it twice before, with evil results. Now he was studying a book which contained not the actual questions from the examination but similar questions. "Barbara, if I don't knock it for a loop this time I don't know what we'll do." Barbara continued to address herself to the ironing board. Edgar thought about saying something to his younger child, his two-year-old daughter, Rose, who was wearing a white terrycloth belted bathrobe and looked like a tiny fighter about to climb into the ring. They were all in the room while he was studying for the examination.

"The written part is where I fall down," Edgar said morosely, to everyone in the room. "The oral part is where I do best." He looked at the back of his wife which was pointed at him. "If I don't kick it in the head this time I don't know what we're going to do," he repeated. "Barb?" But she failed to respond to this implied question. She felt it was a false hope, taking this examination which he had already failed miserably twice and which always got him very worked up, black with fear, before he took it. Now she didn't wish to witness the spectacle any more so she gave him her back.

"The oral part," Edgar continued encouragingly, "is A-okay. I can for instance give you a list of answers, I know it so well. Listen, here is an answer, can you tell me the question?" Barbara, who was very sexually attractive (that was what made Edgar tap on her for a date, many years before) but also deeply mean, said nothing. She put her mind on their silent child, Rose.

"Here is the answer," Edgar said. "The answer is Julia Ward Howe. What is the question?"

This answer was too provocative for Barbara to resist long, because she knew the question. "Who wrote the *Battle Hymn of the Republic?*" she said. "There is not a grown person in the United States who doesn't know that."

"You're right," Edgar said unhappily, for he would have preferred that the answer had been a little more recherché, one that she would not have known the question to. But she had been a hooker for a period before their marriage and he could resort to this area if her triumph grew too great. "Do you want to try another one?"

"Edgar I don't *believe* in that examination any more," she told him coldly.

"I don't believe in you Barbara," he countered.

This remark filled her with remorse and anger. She considered momentarily letting him have one upside the head but fear prevented her from doing it so she turned her back again and thought about the vaunted certificate. With a certificate he could write for all the important and great periodicals, and there would be some money in the house for a change instead of what they got from his brother and the Unemployment.

"It isn't you who has to pass this National Writers' Examination," he shot past her. Then, to mollify, he gave her another answer. "Brand, tuck, glave, claymore."

"Is that an answer?" she asked from behind her back.

"It is indeed. What's the question?"

"I don't know," she admitted, slightly pleased to be put back in a feminine position of not knowing.

"Those are four names for a sword. They're archaic."

"That's why I didn't know them, then."

"Obviously," said Edgar with some malice, for Barbara was sometimes given to saying things that were obvious, just to fill the air. "You put a word like that in now and then to freshen your line," he explained. "Even though it's an old word, it's so old it's new. But you have to be careful, the context has to let people know what the thing is. You don't want to be simply obscure." He liked explaining the tricks of the trade to Barb, who made some show of interest in them.

"Do you want me to read you what I've written for the written part?"

Barb said yes, with a look of pain, for she still felt acutely what he was trying to do.

"This is the beginning," Edgar said, preparing his yellow manuscript paper.

"What is the title?" Barbara asked. She had turned to face him.

"I haven't got a title yet," Edgar said. "Okay, this is the beginning." He began to read aloud. *"In the town of A———, in the district of Y———, there lived a certain Madame A———, wife of that Baron A——— who was in the service of the young Friedrich II of Prussia. The Baron, a man of uncommon ability, is chiefly remembered for his notorious and inexplicable blunder at the Battle of Kolin: by withdrawing the column under his command at a crucial moment in the fighting, he earned for himself the greatest part of the blame for Friedrich's defeat, which resulted in a loss, on the Prussian side, of 13,000 out of 33,000 men. Now as it happened, the château in which Madame A——— was sheltering lay not far from the battlefield; in fact, the removal of her husband's corps placed the château itself in the gravest danger; and at the moment Madame A——— learned, from a Captain Orsini, of her husband's death by his own hand, she was also told that a detachment of pandours, the brutal and much-feared Hungarian light irregular cavalry, was hammering at the château gates."*

Edgar paused to breathe.

Barb looked at him in some surprise. "The beginning turns me on," she said. "More than usual, I mean." She began to have some faint hope, and sat down on the sofabed.

"Thank you," Edgar said. "Do you want me to read you the development?"

"Go ahead."

Edgar drank some water from a glass near to hand.

"The man who brought this terrible news enjoyed a peculiar status in regard to the lady; he was her lover, and he was not. Giacomo Orsini, second son of a noble family of Siena, had as a young man a religious vocation. He had become a priest, not the grander sort of priest who makes a career in Rome and in great houses, but a modest village priest in the north of his country. Here befell him a singular misfortune. It was the pleasure of Friedrich Wilhelm I, father of the present ruler, to assemble, as is well known, the finest army in Europe. Tiny Prussia was unable to supply men in sufficient numbers to satisfy this ambition; his

recruiters ranged over the whole of Europe, and those whom they could not persuade, with promises of liberal bounties, into the king's service, they kidnapped. Now Friedrich was above all else fond of very tall men, and had created, for his personal guard, a regiment of giants, much mocked at the time, but nonetheless a brave and formidable sight. It was the bad luck of the priest Orsini to be a very tall man, and of impressive mien and bearing withal; he was abducted straight from the altar, as he was saying mass, the Host in his hands—"

"This is very exciting," Barb broke in, her eyes showing genuine pleasure and enthusiasm.

"Thank you," Edgar said, and continued his reading.

"—and served ten years in the regiment of giants. On the death of Friedrich Wilhelm, the regiment was disbanded, among other economies; but the former priest, by now habituated to military life, and even zestful for it, enlisted under the new young king, with the rank of captain."

"Is this historically accurate?" Barbara asked.

"It does not contradict what is known," Edgar assured her.

"Assigned to the staff of Baron A———, and much in the latter's house in consequence, he was thrown in with the lovely Inge, Madame A———, a woman much younger than her husband, and possessed of many excellent qualities. A deep sympathy established itself between them, with this idiosyncrasy, that it was never pressed to a conclusion, on his part, or acknowledged in any way, on hers. But both were aware that it existed, and drew secret nourishment from it, and took much delight in the nearness, one to the other. But this pleasant state of affairs also had a melancholy aspect, for Orsini, although exercising the greatest restraint in the matter, nevertheless considered that he had, in even admitting to himself that he was in love with Madame A———, damaged his patron the Baron, whom he knew to be a just and honorable man, and one who had, moreover, done him many kindnesses. In this humor Orsini saw himself as a sort of jackal skulking about the periphery of his benefactor's domestic life, which had been harmonious and whole, but was now, in whatsoever slight degree, compromised."

Rose, the child, stood in her white bathrobe looking at her father who was talking for such a long time, and in such a dramatic shaking voice.

"The Baron, on his side, was not at all insensible of the passion that was present, as it were in a condition of latency, between his young wife and the handsome Sienese. In truth, his knowledge of their intercourse, which he imagined had ripened far beyond the point it had actually reached, had flung him headlong into a horrible crime: for his withholding of the decisive troops at Kolin, for which history has judged him so harshly, was neither an error of strategy nor a display of pusillanimity, but a willful act, having as its purpose the exposure of the château, and thus the lovers, whom he had caused to be together there, to the blood-lust of the pandours. And as for his alleged suicide, that too was a cruel farce; he lived, in a hidden place."

Edgar stopped.

"It's swift-moving," Barbara complimented.

"Well, do you want me to read you the end?" Edgar asked.

"The end? Is it the end already?"

"Do you want me to read you the end?" he repeated.

"Yes."

"I've got the end but I don't have the middle," Edgar said, a little ashamed.

"You don't have the middle?"

"Do you want me to read you the end or don't you?"

"Yes, read me the end." The possibility of a semi-professional apartment, which she had entertained briefly, was falling out of her head with this news, that there was no middle.

"The last paragraph is this:

"During these events Friedrich, to console himself for the debacle at Kolin, composed in his castle at Berlin a flute sonata, of which the critic Guilda has said, that it is not less lovely than the sonatas of Georg Philip Telemann."

"That's ironic," she said knowingly.

"Yes," Edgar agreed, impatient. He was as volatile as popcorn.

"But what about the middle?"

"*I don't have the middle!*" he thundered.

"Something has to happen between them, Inge and what's his name," she went on. "Otherwise there's no story." Looking at her he thought: she is still streety although wearing her housewife gear. The child was a perfect love, however, and couldn't be told from the children of success.

Barb then began telling a story she knew that had happened to a friend of hers. This girl had had an affair with a man and had become pregnant. The man had gone off to Seville, to see if hell was a city much like it, and she had spontaneously aborted, in Chicago. Then she had flown over to parley, and they had walked in the streets and visited elderly churches and like that. And the first church they went into, there was this tiny little white coffin covered with flowers, right in the sanctuary.

"Banal," Edgar pronounced.

She tried to think of another anecdote to deliver to him.

"I've got to get that certificate!" he suddenly called out desperately.

"I don't think you can pass the National Writers' Examination with what you have on that paper," Barb said then, with great regret, because even though he was her husband she didn't want to hurt him unnecessarily. But she had to tell the truth. "Without a middle."

"I wouldn't have been great, even with the certificate," he said.

"Your views would have become known. You would have been something."

At that moment the son manqué entered the room. The son manqué was eight feet tall and wore a serape woven out of two hundred transistor radios, all turned on and tuned to different stations. Just by looking at him you could hear Portland and Nogales, Mexico.

"No grass in the house?"

Barbara got the grass which was kept in one of those little yellow and red metal canisters made for sending film back to Eastman Kodak.

Edgar tried to think of a way to badmouth this immense son leaning over him like a large blaring building. But he couldn't think of anything. Thinking of anything was beyond him. I sympathize. I myself have these problems. Endings are elusive, middles are nowhere to be found, but worst of all is to begin, to begin, to begin.

The Police Band

It was kind of the department to think up the Police Band. The original impulse, I believe, was creative and humanitarian. A better way of doing things. Unpleasant, bloody things required by the line of duty. Even if it didn't work out.

The Commissioner (the old Commissioner, not the one they have now) brought us up the river from Detroit. Where our members had been, typically, working the Sho Bar two nights a week. Sometimes the Glass Crutch. Friday and Saturday. And the rest of the time wandering the streets disguised as postal employees. Bitten by dogs and burdened with third-class mail.

What are our duties? we asked at the interview. Your duties are to wail, the Commissioner said. That only. We admired our new dark-blue uniforms as we came up the river in canoes like Indians. We plan to use you in certain situations, certain tense situations, to alleviate tensions, the Commissioner said. I can visualize great success with this new method. And would you play "Entropy." He was pale, with a bad liver.

We are subtle, the Commissioner said, never forget that. Subtlety is what has previously been lacking in our line. Some of the old ones, the Commissioner said, all they know is the club. He took a little pill from a little box and swallowed it with his Scotch.

When we got to town we looked at those Steve Canyon recruiting posters and wondered if we resembled them. Henry Wang, the bass man, looks like a Chinese Steve Canyon, right? The other cops were friendly in a suspicious way. They liked to hear us wail, however.

The Police Band is a very sensitive highly trained and ruggedly anti-Communist unit whose efficacy will be demonstrated in due time, the Commissioner said to the Mayor (the old Mayor). The Mayor took a little pill from a little box and said, We'll see. He could tell we were musicians because we were holding our instruments, right? Emptying spit valves, giving the horn that little shake. Or coming in at letter E with some sly emotion stolen from another life.

The old Commissioner's idea was essentially that if there was a disturbance on the city's streets—some ethnic group cutting up some other ethnic group on a warm August evening—the Police Band would be sent in. The handsome dark-green band bus arriving with sirens singing, red lights whirling. Hard-pressed men on the beat in their white hats raising a grateful cheer. We stream out of the vehicle holding our instruments at high port. A skirmish line fronting the angry crowd. And play "Perdido." The crowd washed with new and true emotion. Startled, they listen. Our emotion stronger than their emotion. A triumph of art over good sense.

That was the idea. The old Commissioner's *musical* ideas were not very interesting, because after all he was a cop, right? But his police ideas were interesting.

We had drills. Poured out of that mother-loving bus onto vacant lots holding our instruments at high port like John Wayne. Felt we were heroes already. Playing "Perdido," "Stumblin'," "Gin Song," "Feebles." Laving the terrain with emotion stolen from old busted-up loves, broken marriages, the needle, economic deprivation. A few old ladies leaning out of high windows. Our emotion washing rusty Rheingold cans and parts of old doors.

This city is too much! We'd be walking down the street talking about our techniques and we'd see out of our eyes a woman standing in the gutter screaming to herself about what we could not imagine. A drunk trying to strangle a dog somebody'd left leashed to a parking meter. The drunk and the dog screaming at each other. This city is too much!

We had drills and drills. It is true that the best musicians come from Detroit but there is something here that you have to get in your playing and that is simply the scream. We got that. The Commissioner, a sixty-three-year-old hippie with no doubt many graft qualities and unpleasant qualities, nevertheless understood that. When we'd play "ugly," he understood that. He understood the rising expectations of the world's peoples also. That our black members didn't feel like toting junk mail around Detroit forever until the ends of their lives. For some strange reason.

He said one of our functions would be to be sent out to play in places where people were trembling with fear inside their houses, right? To inspirit them in difficult times. This was the plan. We set up in the street. Henry Wang grabs hold of his instrument. He has a four-bar lead-in all by himself. Then the whole group. The iron shutters raised a few inches. Shorty Alanio holding his horn at his characteristic angle (sideways). The reeds dropping lacy little fill-ins behind him. We're cooking. The crowd roars.

The Police Band was an idea of a very romantic kind. The Police Band was an idea that didn't work. When they retired the old Commissioner (our Commissioner), who it turned out had a little drug problem of his own, they didn't let us even drill anymore. We have never been used. His idea was a romantic idea, they said (right?), which was not adequate to the rage currently around in the world. Rage must be met with rage, they said. (Not in so many words.) We sit around the precinct houses, under the filthy lights, talking about our techniques. But I thought it might be good if you knew that the Department still has us. We have a good group. We still have emotion to be used. We're still here.

Edward and Pia

EDWARD LOOKED at his red beard in the tableknife. Then Edward and Pia went to Sweden, to the farm. In the mailbox Pia found a check for Willie from the government of Sweden. It was for twenty-three hundred crowns and had a rained-on look. Pia put the check in the pocket of her brown coat. Pia was pregnant. In London she had been sick every day. In London Pia and Edward had seen the Marat/Sade at the Aldwych Theatre. Edward bought a bottle of white stuff for Pia in London. It was supposed to make her stop vomiting. Edward walked out to the wood barn and broke up wood for the fire. Snow in patches lay on the ground still. Pia wrapped cabbage leaves around chopped meat. She was still wearing her brown coat. Willie's check was still in the pocket. It was still Sunday.

"What are you thinking about?" Edward asked Pia and she said she was thinking about Willie's hand. Willie had hurt his hand in a machine in a factory in Markaryd. The check was for compensation.

Edward turned away from the window. Edward received a cable from his wife in Maine. "Many happy birthdays," the cable said. He was thirty-four. His father was in the hospital. His mother was in the hospital. Pia wore white plastic boots with her brown coat. When Edward inhaled sharply—a sharp intake of breath—they could hear a peculiar noise in his chest. Edward inhaled sharply. Pia heard the noise. She looked up. "When will you go to the doctor?" "I have to get something to read," Edward said. "Something in English." They walked to Markaryd. Pia wore a white plastic hat. At the train station they bought a *Life* magazine with a gold-painted girl on the cover. "Shall we eat something?" Edward asked. Pia said no. They bought a crowbar for the farm. Pia was sick on the way back. She vomited into a ditch.

Pia and Edward walked the streets of Amsterdam. They were hungry. Edward wanted to go to bed with Pia but she didn't feel like it. "There's something wrong," he said. "The wood isn't catching." "It's too wet," she said, "perhaps." "I *know* it's too wet," Edward said. He went out to the wood barn and broke up more wood. He wore a leather glove on his right hand. Pia told Edward that she had been raped once, when she was twenty-two, in the Botanical Gardens. "The man that raptured me has a shop by the Round Tower. Still." Edward walked out of the room. Pia looked after him placidly. Edward reëntered the room. "How would you like to have some Southern fried chicken?" he asked. "It's the most marvellous-tasting thing in the world. Tomorrow I'll make some. Don't say 'rapture.' In English it's 'rape.' What did you do about it?" "Nothing," Pia said. Pia wore green rings, dresses with green sleeves, a green velvet skirt.

Edward put flour in a paper bag and then the pieces of chicken, which had been dipped in milk. Then he shook the paper bag violently. He stood behind Pia and tickled her. Then he hugged her tightly. But she didn't want to go to bed. Edward decided that he would never go to bed with Pia again. The telephone rang. It was for Fru Schmidt. Edward explained that Fru Schmidt was in Rome, that she would return in three months, that he, Edward, was renting the flat from Fru Schmidt, that he would be happy to make a note of the caller's name, and that he would be delighted to call this note to the attention of Fru Schmidt when she returned, from Rome, in three months. Pia vomited. Pia lay on the bed sleeping. Pia wore a red dress, green rings on her fingers.

Then Edward and Pia went to the cinema to see an Eddie Constantine picture. The film was very funny. Eddie Constantine broke up a great deal of furniture chasing international bad guys. Edward read two books he had already read. He didn't remember that he had read them until he reached the last page of each. Then he read four paperback mysteries by Ross Macdonald. They were excellent. He felt slightly sick. Pia walked about with her hands clasped together in front of her chest, her shoulders bent. "Are you cold?" Edward asked. "What are you thinking about?" he asked her, and she said she was thinking about Amboise, where she had contrived to get locked in a chateau after visiting hours. She was *also* thinking, she said, about the green-and-gold wooden horses they had seen in Amsterdam. "I would like enormously to have one for this flat," she said. "Even though the flat is not ours." Edward asked Pia if she felt like making love now. Pia said no.

It was Sunday. Edward went to the bakery and bought bread. Then he bought milk. Then he bought cheese and the Sunday newspaper, which he couldn't read. Pia was asleep. Edward made coffee for himself and looked at the pictures in the newspaper. Pia woke up and groped her way to the bathroom. She vomited. Edward bought Pia a white dress. Pia made herself a necklace of white glass and red wood beads. Edward worried about his drinking. Would there be enough gin? Enough ice? He went out to the kitchen and looked at the bottle of Gordon's gin. Two inches of gin.

Edward and Pia went to Berlin on the train. Pia's father thrust flowers through the train window. The flowers were wrapped in green paper. Edward and Pia climbed into the Mercedes-Benz taxi. "Take us to the Opera if you will, please," Edward said to the German taxi-driver in English. "*Ich verstehe nicht*," the driver said. Edward looked at Pia's belly. It was getting larger, all right. Edward paid the driver. Pia wondered if the Germans were as loud in Germany as they were abroad. Edward and Pia listened for loudness.

Edward received a letter from London, from Bedford Square Office Equipment, Ltd. "We have now completed fitting new parts and adjusting the Olivetti portable that was unfortunately dropped by you. The sum total of parts and labour comes to £7.10.0 and I am adding £1.00.0 hire charges, which leaves a balance of £1.10.0 from your initial deposit of £10. Yours." Yours. Yours. Edward received a letter from Rome, from Fru Schmidt, the owner of the flat in Frederiksberg Allé. "Here are many Americans who have more opportunities to wear their mink capes than they like, I guess! I wish I had one, just one of rabbit or cat, it is said to be just as warm! but I left all my mink clothes behind me in Denmark! We spend most of our time in those horrible subways-metros which are like the rear entrance to Hell and what can you see of a city from there? Well you are from New York and so are used to it but I was born as a human being and not as a—" Here there was a sketch of a rat, in plan. Kurt poured a fresh cup of coffee for Edward. There were three people Pia and Edward did not know in the room, two men and a woman. Everyone watched Kurt pouring a cup of coffee for Edward. Edward explained the American position in South Vietnam. The others looked dubious. Edward and Pia discussed leaving each other.

Pia slept on the couch. She had pulled the red-and-brown blanket up over her feet. Edward looked in the window of the used-radio store. It was full of used radios. Edward and Pia drank more sherry. "What are you thinking about?" he asked her and she said she was wondering if they should separate. "You don't seem happy," she said. "You don't seem happy either," he said. Edward tore the cover off a book. The book cover showed a dog's head surrounded by flowers. The dog wore a black domino. Edward went to the well for water. He lifted the heavy wooden well cover. He was wearing a glove on his right hand. He carried two buckets of water to the kitchen. Then he went to the back of the farmhouse and built a large wooden veranda, roofed, thirty metres by nine metres. Fortunately there was a great deal of new lumber stacked in the barn. In the Frederiksberg Allé apartment in Copenhagen he stared at the brass mail slot in the door. Sometimes red-and-blue airmail envelopes came through the slot.

Edward put his hands on Pia's breasts. The nipples were the largest he had ever seen. Then he counted his money. He had two hundred and forty crowns. He would have to get some more money from somewhere. Maurice came in. "My house is three times the size of this one," Maurice said. Maurice was Dutch. Pia and Edward went to Maurice's house with Maurice. Maurice's wife Randy made coffee. Maurice's son Pieter cried in his wooden box. Maurice's cats walked around. There was an open fire in Maurice's kitchen. There were forty empty beer bottles in a corner. Randy said she was a witch. She pulled a long dark hair from her head. Randy said she could tell if the baby was to be a boy or a girl. She slipped a gold ring from her finger and, suspending the ring on the hair, dangled it over Pia's belly. "It has to be real gold," Randy said, referring to the ring. Randy was rather pretty.

Pia and Edward and Ole and Anita sat on a log in France drinking white Algerian wine. It was barely drinkable. Everyone wiped the mouth of the bottle as it was passed from hand to hand. Edward wanted to sleep with Pia. "Yes," Pia said. They left the others. Edward looked at his red beard in the shiny bottom part of the kerosene lantern. Pia thought about her first trip to the Soviet Union. Edward sat at the bar in Le Ectomorph listening to the music. Pia thought about her first trip to the Soviet Union. There had been a great deal of singing. Edward listened to the music. Don Cherry was playing trumpet. Steve Lacey was playing soprano sax. Kenny Drew was playing piano. The drummer and bassist were Scandinavians. Pia remembered a Russian boy she had known. Edward talked to a Swede. "You want to know who killed Kennedy?" the Swede said. "*You* killed Kennedy." "No," Edward said. "I did not." Edward went back to Frederiksberg Allé. Pia was sleeping. She was naked. Edward lifted the blankets and looked at Pia sleeping. Pia moved in the bed and grabbed at the blankets. Edward went into the other room and tried to find something to read. Edward had peculiar-looking hair. Parts of it were too short and parts of it were too long. Edward and Pia telephoned friends in another city. "Come stay with us," Edward and Pia said. "Please!"

Edward regarded Pia. Pia felt sick: "Why doesn't he leave me alone sometimes?" Edward told Pia about Harry. Once he had gotten Harry out of jail. "Harry was drunk. A cop told him to sit down. Harry stood up. Blam! Five stitches." "What are stitches?" Edward looked it up in the Dansk-Engelsk Ordbog. Edward had several maneuvers that were designed to have an effect on Pia. One of them was washing the dishes. At other times he was sour for several hours. In Leningrad they visited Pia's former lover, Paul. The streets in Leningrad are extremely wide. Paul called his friend Igor, who played the guitar. Paul called Igor on the telephone. Pia and Paul were happy to see each other again. Paul talked to Edward about South Vietnam. There was tea. Edward thought that he, Edward, was probably being foolish. But how could he tell? Edward washed more dishes. Igor's fingers moved quickly among the frets. Edward had drunk too much tea. Edward had drunk too much brandy. Edward was in bed with Pia. "You look beautiful," Edward said to Pia. Pia thought: I feel sick.

In Copenhagen Edward bought *The Penguin English Dictionary*. Sixteen crowns. Pia told a story about one of the princesses. "She is an archeologist, you know? Her picture comes in the newspaper standing over a great hole with her end sticking up in the air." Pia's little brother wore a black turtleneck sweater and sang "We Shall Overcome." He played the guitar. Kurt played the guitar. Kirsten played the guitar. Anita and Ole played the guitar. Deborah played the flute. Edward read *Time* and *Newsweek*. On Tuesday Edward read *Newsweek*, and on Wednesday, *Time*. Pia bought a book about babies. Then she painted her nails silver. Pia's nails were very long. Organ music played by Finn Viderø was heard on the radio. Edward suggested that Pia go back to the university. He suggested that Pia study French, Russian, English, guitar, flute, and cooking. Pia's cooking was rotten. Suddenly she wished she was with some other man and not with Edward. Edward was listening to the peculiar noise inside his chest. Pia looked at Edward. She looked at his red beard, his immense spectacles. I don't like him, she thought. That red beard, those immense spectacles. SAAB jets roared overhead. Edward turned off the radio.

Pia turned on the radio. Edward made himself a dry vermouth on the rocks with two onions. It was a way of not drinking. Edward felt sick. He had been reading *Time* and *Newsweek*. It was Thursday. Pia said to Edward that he was the only person she had ever loved for this long. "How long is it?" Edward asked. It was seven months. Edward cashed a check at American Express. The girl gave him green-and-blue Scandinavian money. Edward was pleased. Little moans of pleasure. He cashed another check at Cook's. More money. Edward sold Pia's farm for eighteen thousand crowns. Much more money. Pia was pleased. Edward sold Pia's piano for three thousand crowns. General rejoicing. Klaus opened the door. Edward showed him the money. Pia made a chocolate cake with little red-and-white flags on the top. Pia lay in bed. She felt sick. They plugged in an electric heater. The lights went out. Herr Kepper knocked on the door. "Is here an electric heater?" Edward showed him the money. Pia hid the electric heater.

Edward watched the brass slot on the door. Pia read to Edward from the newspaper. She read a story about four Swedes sent to prison for rapture. Edward asked Pia if she wanted to make love. "No," she said. Edward said something funny. Pia tried to laugh. She was holding a piece of cake with a red-and-white flag on top. Edward bought a flashlight. Pia laughed. Pia still didn't want to go to bed with Edward. It was becoming annoying. He owed the government back home a thousand dollars. Edward laughed and laughed. "I owe the government a thousand dollars," Edward said to Pia, "did you know that?" Edward laughed. Pia laughed. They had another glass of wine. Pia was pregnant. They laughed and laughed. Edward turned off the radio. The lights went out. Herr Kepper knocked on the door. "The lights went out," he said in Danish. Pia and Edward laughed. "What are you thinking about?" Edward asked Pia and she said she couldn't tell him just then because she was laughing.

A Few Moments of Sleeping and Waking

EDWARD WOKE up. Pia was already awake.
"What did you dream?"

"You were my brother," Pia said. "We were making a film. You were the hero. It was a costume film. You had a cape and a sword. You were jumping about, jumping on tables. But in the second half of the film you had lost all your weight. You were thin. The film was ruined. The parts didn't match."

"I was your brother?"

Scarlatti from the radio. It was Sunday. Pete sat at the breakfast table. Pete was a doctor on an American nuclear submarine, a psychiatrist. He had just come off patrol, fifty-eight days under the water. Pia gave Pete scrambled eggs with mushrooms, *wienerbrød*, salami with red wine in it, bacon. Pete interpreted Pia's dream.

"Edward was your brother?"

"Yes."

"And your real brother is going to Italy, you said."

"Yes."

"It may be something as simple as a desire to travel."

Edward and Pia and Pete went for a boat ride, a tour of the Copenhagen harbor. The boat held one hundred and twenty tourists. They sat, four tourists abreast, on either side of the aisle. A guide spoke into a microphone in Danish, French, German, and English, telling the tourists what was in the harbor.

"I interpreted that dream very sketchily," Pete said to Edward.

"Yes."

"I could have done a lot more with it."

"Don't."

"This is the Danish submarine fleet," the guide said into the microphone. Edward and Pia and Pete regarded the four black submarines. There had been a flick every night on Pete's submarine. Pete discussed the fifty-eight flicks he had seen. Pete sat on Edward's couch discussing "The Sound of Music."

Edward made drinks. Rose's Lime Juice fell into the Gimlet glasses. Then Edward and Pia took Pete to the airport. Pete flew away. Edward bought *The Interpretation of Dreams*.

Pia dreamed that she had journeyed to a great house, a castle, to sing. She had found herself a bed in a room overlooking elaborate gardens. Then another girl appeared, a childhood friend. The new girl demanded Pia's bed. Pia refused. The other girl insisted. Pia refused. The other girl began to sing. She sang horribly. Pia asked her to stop. Other singers appeared, demanding that Pia surrender the bed. Pia refused. People stood about the bed, shouting and singing.

Edward smoked a cigar. "Why didn't you just give her the bed?"

"My honor would be hurt," Pia said. "You know, that girl is not like that. Really she is very quiet and not asserting—asserting?—asserting herself. My mother said I should be more like her."

"The dream was saying that your mother was wrong about this girl?"

"Perhaps."

"What else?"

"I can't remember."

"Did you sing?"

"I can't remember," Pia said.

Pia's brother Søren rang the doorbell. He was carrying a pair of trousers. Pia sewed up a split in the seat. Edward made instant coffee. Pia explained *blufaerdighedskraenkelse*. "If you walk with your trousers open," she said. Søren gave Edward and Pia "The Joan Baez Songbook." "It is a very good one," he said in English. The doorbell rang. It was Pia's father. He was carrying a pair of shoes Pia had left at the farm. Edward made more coffee. Pia sat on the floor cutting a dress out of blue, red, and green cloth. Ole arrived. He was carrying his guitar. He began to play something from "The Joan Baez Songbook." Edward regarded Ole's Mowgli hair. We be of one blood, thee and I. Edward read *The Interpretation of Dreams*. "In cases where not my ego but only a strange person appears in the dream content, I may safely assume that by means of identification my ego is concealed behind that person. I am permitted to supplement my ego."

Edward sat at a sidewalk café drinking a beer. He was wearing his brown suède shoes, his black dungarees, his black-and-white checked shirt, his red beard, his immense spectacles. Edward regarded his hands. His hands seemed old. "I am thirty-three." Tiny girls walked past the sidewalk café wearing skintight black pants. Then large girls in skintight white pants.

Edward and Pia walked along Frederiksberg Allé, under the queer box-cut trees. "Here I was knocked off my bicycle when I was seven," Pia said. "By a car. In a snowstorm."

Edward regarded the famous intersection. "Were you hurt?"

"My bicycle was demolished utterly."

Edward read *The Interpretation of Dreams*. Pia bent over the sewing machine, sewing blue, red, and green cloth.

"Freud turned his friend R. into a disreputable uncle, in a dream."

"Why?"

"He wanted to be an assistant professor. He was bucking for assistant professor."

"So why was it not allowed?"

"They didn't know he was Freud. They hadn't seen the movie."

"You're joking."

"I'm trying."

Edward and Pia talked about dreams. Pia said she had been dreaming about unhappy love affairs. In these dreams, she said, she was very unhappy. Then she woke, relieved.

"How long?"

"For about two months, I think. But then I wake up and I'm happy. That it is not so."

"Why are they *unhappy* love affairs?"

"I don't know."

"Do you think it means you want new love affairs?"

"Why should I want unhappy love affairs?"

"Maybe you want to have love affairs but feel guilty about wanting to have love affairs, and so they become unhappy love affairs."

"That's subtle," Pia said. "You're insecure."

"Ho!" Edward said.

"But why then am I happy when I wake up?"

"Because you don't have to feel guilty anymore," Edward said glibly.

"Ho!" Pia said.

Edward resisted *The Interpretation of Dreams*. He read eight novels by Anthony Powell. Pia walked down the street in Edward's blue sweater. She looked at herself in a shop window. Her hair was rotten. Pia went into the bathroom and played with her hair for one hour. Then she brushed her teeth for a bit. Her hair was still rotten. Pia sat down and began to cry. She cried for a quarter hour, without making any noise. Everything was rotten.

Edward bought *Madam Cherokee's Dream Book*. Dreams in alphabetical order. If you dream of black cloth, there will be a death in the family. If you dream of scissors, a birth. Edward and Pia saw three films by Jean-Luc Godard. The landlord came and asked Edward to pay Danish income tax. "But I don't make any money in Denmark," Edward said. Everything was rotten.

Pia came home from the hairdresser with black varnish around her eyes.

"How do you like it?"

"I hate it."

Pia was chopping up an enormous cabbage, a cabbage big as a basketball. The cabbage was of an extraordinary size. It was a big cabbage.

"That's a big cabbage," Edward said.

"Big," Pia said.

They regarded the enormous cabbage God had placed in the world for supper.

"Is there vinegar?" Edward asked. "I like . . . vinegar . . . with my . . ." Edward read a magazine for men full of colored photographs of naked girls living normal lives. Edward read the *New Statesman*, with its letters to the editor. Pia appeared in her new blue, red, and green dress. She looked wonderful.

"You look wonderful."

"Tak."

"Tables are women," Edward said. "You remember you said I was jumping on tables, in your dream. Freud says that tables are figures for women. You're insecure."

"*La vache!*" Pia said.

Pia reported a new dream. "I came home to a small town where I was born. First, I ran around as a tourist with my camera. Then a boy who was selling something—from one of those little wagons?—asked me to take his picture. But I couldn't find him in the photo *apparat*. In the view glass. Always other people got in the way. Everyone in this town was divorced. Everybody I knew. Then I went to a ladies' club, a place where the women asked the men to dance. But there was only one man there. His picture was on an advertisement outside. He was the gigolo. Gigolo? Is that right? Then I called up people I knew, on the telephone. But they were all divorced. Everybody was divorced. My mother and father were divorced. Helle and Jens were divorced. Everybody. Everybody was floating about in a strange way."

Edward groaned. A palpable groan. "What else?"

"I can't remember."

"Nothing else?"

"When I was on my way to the ladies' club, the boy I had tried to take a picture of came up and took my arm. I was surprised but I said to myself something like, *It's necessary to have friends here.*"

"What else?"

"I can't remember."

"Did you sleep with him?"

"I don't remember."

"What did the ladies' club remind you of?"

"It was in a cellar."

"Did it remind you of anything?"

"It was rather like a place at the university. Where we used to dance."

"What is connected with that place in your mind?"

"Once a boy came through a window to a party."

"Why did he come through the window?"

"So he didn't pay."

"Who was he?"

"Someone."

"Did you dance with him?"

"Yes."

"Did you sleep with him?"
"Yes."
"Very often?"
"Twice."

Edward and Pia went to Malmö on the flying boat. The hydrofoil leaped into the air. The feeling was that of a plane laboring down an interminable runway.

"I dreamed of a roof," Pia said. "Where corn was kept. Where it was stored."

"What does that—" Edward began.

"Also I dreamed of rugs. I was beating a rug," she went on. "And I dreamed about horses, I was riding."

"Don't," Edward said.

Pia silently rehearsed three additional dreams. Edward regarded the green leaves of Malmö. Edward and Pia moved through the rug department of a department store. Surrounded by exciting rugs: Rya rugs, Polish rugs, rag rugs, straw rugs, area rugs, wall-to-wall rugs, rug remnants. Edward was thinking about one that cost five hundred crowns, in seven shades of red, about the size of an opened-up *Herald Tribune*, Paris edition.

"It is too good for the floor, clearly," Pia said. "It is to be hung on the wall."

Edward had four hundred dollars in his pocket. It was supposed to last him two months. The hideously smiling rug salesman pressed closer. They burst into the street. Just in time. "God knows they're beautiful, however," Edward said.

"What did you dream last night?" Edward asked. "What did you dream? What?"

"I can't remember."

Edward decided that he worried too much about the dark side of Pia. Pia regarded as a moon. Edward lay in bed trying to remember a dream. He could not remember. It was eight o'clock. Edward climbed out of bed to see if there was mail on the floor, if mail had fallen through the door. No. Pia awoke.

"I dreamed of beans."

Edward looked at her. *Madam Cherokee's Dream Book* flew into his hand.

"To dream of beans is, in all cases, very unfortunate. Eating them means sickness, preparing them means that the married state will be a very difficult one for you. To dream of *beets* is on the other hand a happy omen."

Edward and Pia argued about "Mrs. Miniver." It was not written by J. B. Priestley, Edward said.

"I remember it very well," Pia insisted. "Errol Flynn was her husband, he was standing there with his straps, his straps"—Pia made a holding-up-trousers gesture—"hanging, and she said that she loved Walter Pidgeon."

"Errol Flynn was not even in the picture. You think J. B. Priestley wrote everything, don't you? Everything in English."

"I don't."

"Errol Flynn was not even in the picture." Edward was drunk. He was shouting. "Errol Flynn was not even . . . *in* . . . the goddam *picture!*"

Pia was not quite asleep. She was standing on a street corner. Women regarded her out of the corners of their eyes. She was holding a string bag containing strawberries, beer, razor blades, turnips. An old lady rode up on a bicycle and stopped for the traffic light. The old lady straddled her bicycle, seized Pia's string bag, and threw it into the gutter. Then she pedalled away, with the changing light. People crowded around. Someone picked up the string bag. Pia shook her head. "No," she said. "She just . . . I have never seen her before." Someone asked Pia if she wanted him to call a policeman. "What for?" Pia said. Her father was standing there smiling. Pia thought, *These things have no significance really.* Pia thought, *If this is to be my dream for tonight, then I don't want it.*

Can We Talk

I WENT to the bank to get my money for the day. And they had painted it yellow. Under cover of night, I shrewdly supposed. With white plaster letters saying CREDIT DEPARTMENT. And a row of new vice-presidents. But I have resources of my own, I said. Sulphur deposits in Texas and a great humming factory off the coast of Kansas. Where we make little things.

Thinking what about artichokes for lunch? Pleased to be in this yellow bank at 11:30 in the morning. A black man cashing his check in a Vassar College sweatshirt. A blue policeman with a St. Christopher pinned to his gunbelt. Thinking I need a little leaf to rest my artichokes upon. The lady stretching my money to make sure none of hers stuck to it.

Fourteenth Street gay with Judy Bond Dresses Are On Strike. When I leaned out of your high window in my shorts, did you really think I had hurtling to destruction in mind? I was imagining a loudspeaker-and-leaflet unit that would give me your undivided attention.

When I leaned out of your high window in my shorts, did you think *why me?*

Into his bank I thought I saw my friend Kenneth go. To get his money for the day. Loitering outside in my painted shoes. Considering my prospects. A question of buying new underwear or going to the laundromat. And when I put a nickel in the soap machine it barks.

When I leaned out of your high window in my shorts, were you nervous because you had just met me? I said: Your eyes have not been surpassed.

The artichokes in their glass jar from the artichoke heart of the world, Castroville, Calif. I asked the man for a leaf. Just one, I said. We don't sell them in ones, he said. Can we negotiate, I asked. Breathing his disgust he tucked a green leaf into my yellow vest with his brown hands.

When I asked you why you didn't marry Harry you said it was because he didn't like you. Then I told you how I cheated the Thai lieutenant who was my best friend then.

Posing with my leaf against a plastic paper plate. Hoping cordially that my friend Victor's making money in his building. Then the artichokes one by one. Yes, you said, this is the part they call Turtle Bay.

Coffee wondering what my end would be. Thinking of my friend Roger killed in the crash of a Link Trainer at Randolph Field in '43. Or was it breakbone fever at Walter Reed.

Then out into the street again and uptown for my fencing lesson. Stopping on the way to give the underwear man a ten. Because he looked about to bark.

When I reached to touch your breast you said you had a cold. I believed you. I made more popcorn.

Thinking of my friend Max who looks like white bread. A brisk bout with my head in a wire cage. The Slash Waltz from "The Mark of Zorro." And in the shower a ten for Max, because his were the best two out of three. He put it in his lacy shoe. With his watch and his application to the Colorado School of Mines.

In the shower I refrained from speaking of you to anyone.

The store where I buy news buttoned up tight. Because the owners are in the mountains. Where I would surely be had I not decided to make us miserable.

I said: I seem to have lost all my manuscripts, in which my theory is proved not once but again and again and again, and now when people who don't believe a vertical monorail to Venus is possible shout at me, I have nothing to say. You peered into my gloom.

My friend Herman's house. Where I tickle the bell. It is me. Invited to put a vacuum cleaner together. The parts on the floor in alphabetical order. Herman away, making money. I hug his wife Agnes. A beautiful girl. And when one hugs her tightly, her eyes fill.

When I asked you if you had a private income, you said something intelligent but I forget what. The skin scaling off my back from the week at the beach. Where I lay without knowing you.

Discussing the real estate game, Agnes and I. Into this game I may someday go, I said. Building cheap and renting dear. With a doorman to front for me. Tons of money in it, I said.

When my falling event was postponed, were you disappointed? Did you experience a disillusionment event?

Hunted for a *Post*. To lean upon in the black hours ahead. And composed a brochure to lure folk into my new building. Titled "The Human Heart In Conflict With Itself." Promising 24-hour incineration. And other features.

Dancing on my parquet floor in my parquet shorts. To Mahler.

After you sent me home you came down in your elevator to be kissed. You knew I would be sitting on the steps.

Game

SHOTWELL KEEPS the jacks and the rubber ball in his attaché case and will not allow me to play with them. He plays with them, alone, sitting on the floor near the console hour after hour, chanting "onesies, twosies, threesies, foursies" in a precise, well-modulated voice, not so loud as to be annoying, not so soft as to allow me to forget. I point out to Shotwell that two can derive more enjoyment from playing jacks than one, but he is not interested. I have asked repeatedly to be allowed to play by myself, but he simply shakes his head. "Why?" I ask. "They're mine," he says. And when he has finished, when he has sated himself, back they go into the attaché case.

It is unfair but there is nothing I can do about it. I am aching to get my hands on them.

Shotwell and I watch the console. Shotwell and I live under the ground and watch the console. If certain events take place upon the console, we are to insert our keys in the appropriate locks and turn our keys. Shotwell has a key and I have a key. If we turn our keys simultaneously the bird flies, certain switches are activated and the bird flies. But the bird never flies. In one hundred thirty-three days the bird has not flown. Meanwhile Shotwell and I watch each other. We each wear a .45 and if Shotwell behaves strangely I am supposed to shoot him. If I behave strangely Shotwell is supposed to shoot me. We watch the console and think about shooting each other and think about the bird. Shotwell's behavior with the jacks is strange. Is it strange? I do not know. Perhaps he is merely a selfish bastard, perhaps his character is flawed, perhaps his childhood was twisted. I do not know.

Each of us wears a .45 and each of us is supposed to shoot the other if the other is behaving strangely. How strangely is strangely? I do not know. In addition to the .45 I have a .38 which Shotwell does not know about concealed in my attaché case, and Shotwell has a .25 calibre Beretta which I do not know about strapped to his right calf. Sometimes instead of watching the console I pointedly watch Shotwell's .45, but this is simply a ruse, simply a maneuver, in reality I am watching his hand when it dangles in the vicinity of his right calf. If he decides I am behaving strangely he will shoot me not with the .45 but with the Beretta. Similarly Shotwell pretends to watch my .45 but he is really watching my hand resting idly atop my attaché case, my hand resting idly atop my attaché case, my hand. My hand resting idly atop my attaché case.

In the beginning I took care to behave normally. So did Shotwell. Our behavior was painfully normal. Norms of politeness, consideration, speech, and personal habits were scrupulously observed. But then it became apparent that an error had been made, that our relief was not going to arrive. Owing to an oversight. Owing to an oversight we have been here for one hundred thirty-three days. When it became clear that an error had been made, that we were not to be relieved, the norms were relaxed. Definitions of normality were redrawn in the agreement of January 1, called by us, The Agreement. Uniform regulations were relaxed, and mealtimes are no longer rigorously scheduled. We eat when we are hungry and sleep when we are tired. Considerations of rank and precedence were temporarily put aside, a handsome concession on the part of Shotwell, who is a captain, whereas I am only a first lieutenant. One of us watches the console at all times rather than two of us watching the console at all times, except when we are both on our feet. One of us watches the console at all times and if the bird flies then that one wakes the other and we turn our keys in the locks simultaneously and the bird flies. Our system involves a delay of perhaps twelve seconds but I do not care because I am not well, and Shotwell does not care because he is not himself. After the agreement was signed Shotwell produced the jacks and the rubber ball from his attaché case, and I began to write a series of descriptions of forms occurring in nature, such as a shell, a leaf, a stone, an animal. On the walls.

Shotwell plays jacks and I write descriptions of natural forms on the walls.

Shotwell is enrolled in a USAFI course which leads to a master's degree in business administration from the University of Wisconsin (although we are not in Wisconsin, we are in Utah, Montana or Idaho). When we went down it was in either Utah, Montana or Idaho, I don't remember. We have been here for one hundred thirty-three days owing to an oversight. The pale green reinforced concrete walls sweat and the air conditioning zips on and off erratically and Shotwell reads *Introduction to Marketing* by Lassiter and Munk, making notes with a blue ballpoint pen. Shotwell is not himself but I do not know it, he presents a calm aspect and reads *Introduction to Marketing* and makes his exemplary notes with a blue ballpoint pen, meanwhile controlling the .38 in my attaché case with one-third of his attention. I am not well.

We have been here one hundred thirty-three days owing to an oversight. Although now we are not sure what is oversight, what is plan. Perhaps the plan is for us to stay here permanently, or if not permanently at least for a year, for three hundred sixty-five days. Or if not for a year for some number of days known to them and not known to us, such as two hundred days. Or perhaps they are observing our behavior in some way, sensors of some kind, perhaps our behavior determines the number of days. It may be that they are pleased with us, with our behavior, not in every detail but in sum. Perhaps the whole thing is very successful, perhaps the whole thing is an experiment and the experiment is very successful. I do not know. But I suspect that the only way they can persuade sun-loving creatures into their pale green sweating reinforced concrete rooms under the ground is to say that the system is twelve hours on, twelve hours off. And then lock us below for some number of days known to them and not known to us. We eat well although the frozen enchiladas are damp when defrosted and the frozen devil's food cake is sour and untasty. We sleep uneasily and acrimoniously. I hear Shotwell shouting in his sleep, objecting, denouncing, cursing sometimes, weeping sometimes, in his sleep. When Shotwell sleeps I try to pick the lock on his attaché case, so as to get at the jacks. Thus far I have been unsuccessful. Nor has Shotwell been successful in picking the locks on my attaché case so as to get at the .38. I have seen the marks on the shiny surface. I laughed, in the latrine, pale green walls sweating and the air conditioning whispering, in the latrine.

I write descriptions of natural forms on the walls, scratching them on the tile surface with a diamond. The diamond is a two and one-half carat solitaire I had in my attaché case when we went down. It was for Lucy. The south wall of the room containing the console is already covered. I have described a shell, a leaf, a stone, animals, a baseball bat. I am aware that the baseball bat is not a natural form. Yet I described it. "The baseball bat," I said, "is typically made of wood. It is typically one meter in length or a little longer, fat at one end, tapering to afford a comfortable grip at the other. The end with the handhold typically offers a slight rim, or lip, at the nether extremity, to prevent slippage." My description of the baseball bat ran to 4500 words, all scratched with a diamond on the south wall. Does Shotwell read what I have written? I do not know. I am aware that Shotwell regards my writing-behavior as a little strange. Yet it is no stranger than his jacks-behavior, or the day he appeared in black bathing trunks with the .25 calibre Beretta strapped to his right calf and stood over the console, trying to span with his two arms outstretched the distance between the locks. He could not do it, I had already tried, standing over the console with my two arms outstretched, the distance is too great. I was moved to comment but did not comment, comment would have provoked countercomment, comment would have led God knows where. They had in their infinite patience, in their infinite foresight, in their infinite wisdom already imagined a man standing over the console with his two arms outstretched, trying to span with his two arms outstretched the distance between the locks.

Shotwell is not himself. He has made certain overtures. The burden of his message is not clear. It has something to do with the keys, with the locks. Shotwell is a strange person. He appears to be less affected by our situation than I. He goes about his business stolidly, watching the console, studying *Introduction to Marketing*, bouncing his rubber ball on the floor in a steady, rhythmical, conscientious manner. He appears to be less affected by our situation than I am. He is stolid. He says nothing. But he has made certain overtures, certain overtures have been made. I am not sure that I understand them. They have something to do with the keys, with the locks. Shotwell has something in mind. Stolidly he shucks the shiny silver paper from the frozen enchiladas, stolidly he stuffs them into the electric oven. But he has something in mind. But there must be a quid pro quo. I insist on a quid pro quo. I have something in mind.

I am not well. I do not know our target. They do not tell us for which city the bird is targeted. I do not know. That is planning. That is not my responsibility. My responsibility is to watch the console and when certain events take place upon the console, turn my key in the lock. Shotwell bounces the rubber ball on the floor in a steady, stolid, rhythmical manner. I am aching to get my hands on the ball, on the jacks. We have been here one hundred thirty-three days owing to an oversight. I write on the walls. Shotwell chants "onesies, twosies, threesies, foursies" in a precise, well-modulated voice. Now he cups the jacks and the rubber ball in his hands and rattles them suggestively. I do not know for which city the bird is targeted. Shotwell is not himself.

Sometimes I cannot sleep. Sometimes Shotwell cannot sleep. Sometimes when Shotwell cradles me in his arms and rocks me to sleep, singing Brahms' "Guten abend, gut Nacht," or I cradle Shotwell in my arms and rock him to sleep, singing, I understand what it is Shotwell wishes me to do. At such moments we are very close. But only if he will give me the jacks. That is fair. There is something he wants me to do with my key, while he does something with his key. But only if he will give me my turn. That is fair. I am not well.

Alice

twirling around on my piano stool my head begins to swim my head begins to swim twirling around on my piano stool twirling around on my piano stool a dizzy spell eventuates twirling around on my piano stool I begin to feel dizzy twirling around on my piano stool

I want to fornicate with Alice but my wife Regine would be insulted Alice's husband Buck would be insulted my child Hans would be insulted my answering service would be insulted tingle of insult running through this calm loving healthy productive tightly-knit the hinder portion scalding-house good eating Curve B in addition to the usual baths and ablutions military police sumptuousness of the washhouse risking misstatements kept distances iris to iris queen of holes damp, hairy legs note of anger chanting and shouting konk sense of "mold" on the "muff" sense of "talk" on the "surface" konk² all sorts of chemical girl who delivered the letter give it a bone plummy bare legs saturated in every belief and ignorance rational living private client bad bosom uncertain workmen mutton-tugger obedience to the rules of the logical system Lord Muck hot tears harmonica rascal

that's chaos can you produce chaos? Alice asked certainly I can produce chaos I said I produced chaos she regarded the chaos chaos is handsome and attractive she said and more durable than regret I said and more nourishing than regret she said

I want to fornicate with Alice but it is a doomed project fornicating with Alice there are obstacles impediments preclusions estoppels I will exhaust them for you what a gas see cruel deprivements SECTION SEVEN moral ambiguities SECTION NINETEEN Alice's thighs are like SECTION TWENTY-ONE

I am an OB I obstetricate ladies from predicaments holding the bucket I carry a device connected by radio to my answering service bleeps when I am wanted can't even go to the films now for fear of bleeping during filmic highpoints can I in conscience *turn off* while fornicating with Alice?

Alice is married to Buck I am married to Regine Buck is my friend Regine is my wife regret is battologized in SECTIONS SIX THROUGH TWELVE and the actual intercourse intrudes somewhere in SECTION FORTY-THREE

I maintain an air of serenity which is spurious I manage this by limping my limp artful creation not an abject limp (Quasimodo) but a proud limp (Byron) I move slowly solemnly through the world miming a stiff leg this enables me to endure the gaze of strangers the hatred of pediatricians

we discuss discuss and discuss important considerations swarm and dither

for example in what house can I fornicate with Alice? in my house with Hans pounding on the bedroom door in her house with Buck shedding his sheepskin coat in the kitchen in some temporary rented house what joy

can Alice fornicate without her Malachi record playing? will Buck miss the Malachi record which Alice will have taken to the rented house? will Buck kneel before the rows and rows of records in his own house running a finger along the spines looking for the Malachi record? poignant poignant

can Buck the honest architect with his acres of projects his mobs of draughtsmen the alarm bell which goes off in his office whenever the government decides to renovate a few blocks of blight can Buck object if I decide to renovate Alice?

and what of the boil on my ass the right buttock can I lounge in the bed in the rented house in such a way that Alice will not see will not start away from in fear terror revulsion and what of rugs should I rug the rented house and what of cups what of leaning on an elbow in the Hertz Rent-All bed having fornicated with Alice and desiring a cup of black and what of the soap powder dish towels such a cup implies and what of a decent respect for the opinions of mankind and what of the hammer throw

I was a heavy man with the hammer once should there be a spare hammer for spare moments?

Alice's thighs are like great golden varnished wooden oars I assume I haven't seen them

chaos is tasty AND USEFUL TOO

colored clothes paper handkerchiefs super cartoons bit of fresh the Pope's mule inmission do such poor work together in various Poujadist manifestations deep-toned blacks waivers play to the gas Zentralbibliothek Zurich her bare ass with a Teddy bear blatty string kept in a state of suspended tension by a weight cut from the backs of alligators

you can do it too it's as easy as it looks

there is no game for that particular player white and violet over hedge and ditch clutching airbrush still single but wearing a ring the dry a better "feel" in use pretended to be doing it quite unconsciously fishes hammering long largish legs damp fine water dancer, strains of music, expenses of the flight Swiss emotion transparent thin alkaline and very slippery fluid danger for white rats little country telephone booths brut insults brought by mouth famous incidents

in bed regarding Alice's stomach it will be a handsome one I'm sure but will it not also resemble some others?

or would it be possible in the rented house to dispense with a bed to have only a mattress on the floor with all the values that attach to that or perhaps only a pair of blankets or perhaps only the skin of some slow-moving animal such as the slug the armadillo or perhaps only a pile of read newspapers

wise Alice tells you things you hadn't heard before in the world in Paris she recognizes the Ritz from the Babar books oh yes that's where the elephants stay

or would it be possible to use other people's houses at hours when these houses were empty would that be erotic? could love be made in doorways under hedges under the sprinting chestnut tree? can Alice forego her Malachi record so that Buck kneeling before the rows of records in his empty deserted abandoned and pace-setting house fingering the galore of spines there would *find* the Malachi record with little peeps of gree peeps of gree good for Buck!

shit

Magritte

what is good about Alice is first she likes chaos what is good about Alice is second she is a friend of Tom

SECTION NINETEEN TOM plaster thrashing gumbo of explanations grease on the Tinguely new plays sentimental songs sudden torrential rains carbon projects evidence of eroticism conflict between zones skin, ambiguous movements baked on the blue table 3 mm. a stone had broken my windshield hurricane damage impulsive behavior knees folded back lines on his tongue with a Magic Marker gape orange tips ligamenta lata old men buried upright delights of everyone's life uninteresting variations pygmy owl assumes the quadrupedal position in which the intestines sink forward measurement of kegs other sciences megapod nursemaid said very studied, hostile things she had long been saving up breakfast dream wonderful loftiness trank red clover uterine spasms guided by reason black envelopes highly esteemed archers wet leg critical menials making gestures chocolate ice pink and green marble weight of the shoes I was howling in the kitchen Tom was howling in the hall white and violet over hedge and ditch clutching oolfoo quiet street suburban in flavor quiet crowd only slightly restive as reports of the letters from Japan circulate

I am whispering to my child Hans my child Hans is whispering to me Hans whispers that I am faced with a problem in ethics the systems of the axiologicalists he whispers the systems of the deontologicalists but I am not privy to these systems I whisper try the New School he whispers the small device in my coat pocket goes bleep!

nights of ethics at the New School

is this "middle life"? can I hurry on to "old age"? I see Alice walking away from me carrying an A & P shopping bag the shopping bag is full of haunting melodies grid coordinates great expectations French ticklers magic marks

nights of ethics at the New School "good" and "bad" as terms with only an emotive meaning I like the Walrus best Alice whispered he ate more than the Carpenter though the instructor whispered then I like the Carpenter best Alice whispered but he ate as many as he could get the instructor whispered

yellow brick wall visible from rear bedroom window of the rented house

I see Alice walking away from me carrying a Primary Structure

MOVEMENT OF ALICE'S ZIPPER located at the rear of Alice's dress running from the neckhole to the bumhole yes I know the first is an attribute of the dress the second an attribute of the girl but I have located it for you in some rough way the zipper you could find it in the dark

a few crones are standing about next to them are some louts the crones and louts are talking about the movement of Alice's zipper

rap Alice on the rump standing in the rented bedroom I have a roller and a bucket of white paint requires a second coat perhaps a third who knows a fourth and fifth I sit on the floor next to the paint bucket regarding the yellow brick wall visible there a subway token on the floor I pick it up drop it into the paint bucket slow circles on the surface of the white paint

insurance?

confess that for many years I myself took no other measures, followed obediently in the footsteps of my teachers, copied the procedures I observed painted animals, frisky inventions, thwarted patrons, most great hospitals and clinics, gray gauzes transparent plastic containers Presidential dining room about 45 cm. coquetry and flirtation knit games beautiful tension beaten metal catch-penny devices impersonal panic Klinger's nude in tree tickling nose of bear with long branch or wand unbutton his boots fairly broad duct, highly elastic walls peerless piece "racing" Dr. Haacke has poppy-show pulled me down on the bed and started two ceiling-high trees astonishing and little known remark of Balzac's welter this field of honor financial difficulties what sort of figure did these men cut?

Alice's husband Buck calls me will I gather with him for a game of golf? I accept but on the shoe shelf I cannot find the correct shoes distractedness stupidity weak memory! I am boring myself what should be the punishment I am forbidden to pick my nose forevermore

Buck is rushing toward me carrying pieces of carbon paper big as bedsheets what is he hinting at? duplicity

bleep! it is the tipped uterus from Carson City calling

SECTION FORTY-THREE then I began chewing upon Alice's long and heavy breasts first one then the other the nipples brightened freshened then I turned her on her stomach and rubbed her back first slow then fast first the shoulders then the buttocks

possible attitudes found in books 1) I don't know what's happening to me 2) what does it mean? 3) seized with the deepest sadness, I know not why 4) I am lost, my head whirls, I know not where I am 5) I lose myself 6) I ask you, what have I come to? 7) I no longer know where I am, what is this country? 8) had I fallen from the skies, I could not be more giddy 9) a mixture of pleasure and confusion, that is my state 10) where am I, and when will this end? 11) what shall I do? I do not know where I am

but I do know where I am I am on West Eleventh Street shot with lust I speak to Alice on the street she is carrying a shopping bag I attempt to see what is in the shopping bag but she conceals it we turn to savor rising over the Women's House of Detention a particularly choice bit of "sisters" statistics on the longevity of life angelism straight as a loon's leg conceals her face behind *pneumatiques* hurled unopened scream the place down tuck mathematical models six hours in the confessional psychological comparisons scream the place down Mars yellow plights make micefeet of old cowboy airs cornflakes people pointing to the sea overboots nasal contact 7 cm. prune the audience dense car correctly identify chemical junk blooms of iron wonderful loftiness sentient populations

A Picture History of the War

KELLERMAN, GIGANTIC with gin, runs through the park at noon with his naked father slung under one arm. Old Kellerman covers himself with both hands and howls in the tearing wind, although sometimes he sings in the bursting sunlight. Where there is tearing wind he howls, and where there is bursting sunlight he sings. The park is empty except for a pair of young mothers in greatcoats who stand, pressed together in a rapturous embrace, near the fountain. "What are those mothers doing there," cries the general, "near the fountain?" "That is love," replies the son, "which is found everywhere, healing and beautiful." "Oh what a desire I have," cries the general, "that there might happen some great dispute among nations, some great anger, so that I might be myself again!" "Think of the wrack," replies the son. "Empty saddles, boots reversed in the stirrups, tasteful eulogies—" "I want to tell you something!" shrieks the general. "On the field where this battle was fought, I saw a very wonderful thing which the natives pointed out to me!"

On the night of the sixteenth, Wellington lingered until three in the morning in Brussels at the Duchess of Richmond's ball, sitting in the front row. "Showing himself very cheerful," according to Müffling. Then with Müffling he set out for the windmill at Brye, where they found Marshal Blücher and his staff. Kellerman, followed by the young mothers, runs out of the park and into a bar.

"Eh, hello, Mado. A Beaujolais."

"Eh, hello, Tris-Tris," the barmaid replies. She is wiping the zinc with a dirty handkerchief. "A Beaujolais?"

"Cut the sentimentality, Mado," Kellerman says. "A Beaujolais. Listen, if anybody asks for me—"

"You haven't been in."

"Thanks, Mado. You're a good sort."

Kellerman knocks back the Beaujolais, tucks his naked father under his arm, and runs out the door.

"You were rude with that woman!" the general cries. "What is the rationale?"

"It's a convention," Kellerman replies. The Belgian regiments had been tampered with. In the melee, I was almost instantly disabled in both arms, losing first my sword, and then my reins, and followed by a few men, who were presently cut down, no quarter being asked, allowed, or given, I was carried along by my horse, till, receiving a blow from a sabre, I fell senseless on my face to the ground. Kellerman runs, reading an essay by Paul Goodman in *Commentary*. His eye, caught by a line in the last paragraph ("In a viable constitution, every excess of power should structurally generate its own antidote"), has wandered back up the column of type to see what is being talked about ("I have discussed the matter with Mr. and Mrs. Beck of the Living Theatre and we agree that the following methods are tolerable").

"What's that?" calls the first mother. "On the bench there, covered with the overcoat?"

"That's my father," Kellerman replies courteously. "My dad."

"Isn't he cold?"

"Are you cold?"

"He looks cold to me!" exclaims the one in the red wrapper. "They're funny-looking, aren't they, when they get that old? They look like radishes."

"Something like radishes," Kellerman agrees. "Dirty in the vicinity of the roots, if that's what you mean."

"What does he do?" asks the one in the blue boots. "Or, rather, what did he do when he was of an age?"

Kellerman falls to his knees in front of the bench. "Bless me, Father, for I have sinned. I committed endoarchy two times, melanicity four times, encropatomy seven times, and preprocity with igneous intent, pretolemicity, and overt cranialism once each."

"Within how long a period?"

"Since Monday."

"Did you enjoy it?"

"Which?"

"Any of it."

"Some of it. Melanicity in the afternoon promotes a kind of limited joy."

"Have you left anything out?"

"A great deal." On the field where this battle was fought I saw a very wonderful thing which the natives pointed out to me. The bones of the slain lie scattered upon the field in two lots, those of the Persians in one place by themselves, those of the Egyptians in another place apart from them. If, then, you strike the Persian skulls, even with a pebble, they are so weak, that you break a hole in them; but the Egyptian skulls are so strong, that you may smite them with a stone and you will scarcely break them in.

"Oh what a desire I have," cried the general, "that my son would, like me, jump out of airplanes into aggressor terrain and find farmers with pitchforks poised to fork him as he drifts into the trees! And the farmer's dog, used for chivying sheep usually—how is it possible that I have a son who does not know the farmer's dog? And then calling out in the night to find the others, voices in the night, it's incredibly romantic. I gave him a D-ring for a teething toy and threw him up in the air, higher than any two-year-old had ever been, and put him on the mantel, and said, 'Jump, you little bastard,' and he jumped, and I caught him—this when I was only a captain and chairman of the Machine Gun Committee at Benning. He had expensive green-gold grenadiers from F.A.O. Schwarz and a garrote I made myself from the E flat on his mother's piano. Firefights at dusk on the back lawn at Leonard Wood. Superior numbers in the shower room. Give them a little more grape, Captain Gregg, under the autumnal moon."

"Now, Agnes, don't start crying! We better go see Uncle René all together right away, and he'll explain anything you need to know."

"Interesting point of view," the ladies remarked. "Does he know anything about skin?"

"Everything."

Touched by the wind, the general howls.

"He was a jumping general," Kellerman explains to the ladies, "who jumped out of airplanes with his men to fall on the aggressor rear with sudden surprise and great hurt to that rear. He jumped in Sicily with the One-Oh-Bloody-One Airborne. The German cemetery at Pomezia has twenty-seven thousand four hundred graves," Kellerman declares. "What could he have been thinking of, on the way down? Compare if you will the scene with the scene at the battle of Borodino, at the battle of Arbela, at the battle of Metaurus, at the battle of Châlons, at the battle of Pultowa, at the battle of Valmy—"

"Eh, hello, Mado. A Beaujolais."

"Eh, hello, Tris-Tris. A Beaujolais?"

"Listen, Mado, if anybody asks for me—"

"You haven't been in."

"Bless me, Father, for I have sinned. I wanted to say a certain thing to a certain man, a certain true thing that had crept into my head. I opened my head, at the place provided, and proceeded to pronounce the true thing that lay languishing there—that is, proceeded to propel that trueness, that felicitous trularity, from its place inside my head out into world life. The certain man stood waiting to receive it. His face reflected an eager acceptingness. Everything was right. I propelled, using my mind, my mouth, all my muscles. I propelled. I propelled and propelled. I felt that trularity inside my head moving slowly through the passage provided (stained like the caves of Lascaux with garlic, antihistamines, Berlioz, a history, a history) toward its début on the world stage. Past my teeth, with their little brown sweaters knitted of gin and cigar smoke, toward its leap to critical scrutiny. Past my lips, with their tendency to flake away in cold weather—

"Father, I have a few questions to ask you. Just a few questions about things that have been bothering me lately." In the melee, I was almost instantly disabled in both arms. Losing first my sword, and then my reins. And followed by a few men, who were presently cut down, no quarter being asked, allowed, or given, I was carried along by my horse, till— "Who is fit for marriage? What is the art of love? What physical or mental ailments can be hereditary? What is the best age for marriage? Should marriage be postponed until the husband alone can support a family? Should a person who is sterile marry? What is sterility? How do the male reproductive organs work? Is a human egg like a bird's? What is a false pregnancy? What is artificial insemination? What happens if the sex glands are removed? In the male? In the female? Is it possible to tell if a person is emotionally fit for marriage? Why are premarital medical examinations important? What is natural childbirth?

What is the best size for a family? Can interfaith marriages be successful? Can a couple know in advance if they can have children? Are there any physical standards to follow in choosing a mate? How soon after conception can a woman tell if she is pregnant? What is the special function of the sex hormones? What are the causes of barrenness? How reliable are the various contraceptive devices? If near relatives marry will their children be abnormal? Do the first sex experiences have a really important bearing upon marital adjustment? Can impotence be cured? Can the sex of a child be predicted? How often should intercourse be practiced? How long should it last? Should you turn out the lights? Should music be played? Is our culture sick? Is a human egg like a bird's?"

Kellerman stops at the ginstore. "We can't use any of those," the ginstoreman says. "Those whatever-it-ises you've got under your arm there."

"That's my dad," Kellerman says. "Formerly known as the Hammer of Thor. Now in reduced circumstances."

"I thought it was radishes," the ginstoreman says. "A bunch of radishes."

Kellerman kneels on the floor of the ginstore. "Bless me, Father, for I have sinned. That one was venial. But in respect to mortal sins, I would announce the following sins. Their mortalaciousness will not disappoint, is in fact so patent, so demonstrable, that the meanest confessor would, with a shy wave of the hand, accept and forgive them, in the manner of a customs inspector running his hand generously, forgivingly around the inside of a Valpak presented by a pretty girl."

"What do *you* do?" the mothers ask. "You yourself."

"I'm a bridge expert," Kellerman says kindly. "The father of a book on the subject, 'Greater Bridge,' which attempts to make complex the simple, so that we will not be bored. A Bible of bridge, if you take my meaning. Some of our boys carried it in the pockets over their hearts during the war. As they dropped through the air. Singing 'Johnny Got a Zero.'" All deliriously pretty and sexy mothers in brawny Chanel tweeds. Black-and-white hound's-tooth checks, say; black-and-white silk Paisley blouses; gleaming little pairs of white kidskin gloves. Very correct hang to the jackets. Short skirts with a clochelike slide over the hip, lots of action at the hemline—couldn't be better.

Café-ed mouths, shiny orange-brown cheeks, ribbons of green enamel eye makeup. Mrs. Subways.

"I'm cold," old Kellerman says.

"Cold," the ladies remark, pointing.

Kellerman pulls out his flask. "Winter gin," he says, "it absumeth the geniture."

"Say something professional," the ladies request.

"♠ 6   ♡ K Q J 9 4   ◊ A K 8 5   ♣ K Q 2," Kellerman says.

On the third, Hood's main army was in the neighborhood of Lost Mountain. Stewart's Corps was sent to strike the railway north of Marietta and to capture, if possible, Allatoona. Stewart, on the morning of the fifth, rejoined Hood, having destroyed two small posts on the railroad and having left French's division to capture Allatoona and destroy the Etowah Bridge. The Army of the Cumberland led the pursuit, and on the evening of the fourth it was bivouacking at the foot of Kenesaw Mountain. "And many others," Kellerman says. "Just as steamy and sordid as that one. Each sin preserved in amber in the vaults of the Library of Congress, under the management of the Registrar of Copyrights."

"With all the sticky details?"

"Rife with public hair," Kellerman says, "just to give you a whiff of the sordidness possible since the perfection of modern high-speed offset lithography."

"O sin," exclaims the general from his bench, "in which fear and guilt encrandulate (or are encrandulated by) each other to mess up the real world of objects with a film of nastiness and dirt, how well I understand you! Standing there! How well I understand your fundamental motifs! How ill I understand my fundamental motifs! Why are objects preferable to parables? How did I get so old so suddenly? In what circumstances is confusion a virtue? Why have I never heard of Yusef Lateef? 1. On flute, Lateef creates a completely distinctive sound—sensitive, haunting, but filled with a firm and passionate strength unequalled among jazz flutists. 2. On tenor saxophone, Yusef is again thoroughly and excitingly individual, combining brilliantly modern conception with a big, deep, compellingly full-throated tone. 3. The oboe, as played by Lateef, undergoes a startling transformation into a valid jazz instrument, wailing with a rich and fervently funky blues quality. 4. What is 'wailing'? What is 'funky'? Why does language subvert me, subvert my seniority, my medals, my oldness, whenever it gets a chance? What does language have against me—me that has been good to it, respecting its little peculiarities and nicilosities, for sixty years? 5. What do 'years' have against me? Why have they stuck stones in my kidneys, devaluated my tumulosity, retracted my hair? 6. Where does 'hair' go when it dies?"

Kellerman is eating one of his fifty-two-cent lunches: a 4½ oz. can of Sells Liver Pâté (thirty-one cents) and a box of Nabisco Saltines (twenty-one cents), washed down with the last third of a bottle of leftover Chablis. He lifts the curiously ugly orange wineglass, one of four (the fourth destroyed in the dishwasher) sent to Noëlie at Christmas by her Oregon aunt. He is reading an essay by Paul Goodman in *Commentary*. His eye, caught by a line in the last paragraph ("In a viable constitution, every excess of power should structurally generate its own antidote"), has wandered back up the page to see what is being talked about ("I have discussed the matter with Mr. and Mrs. Beck of the Living Theatre and we agree that the following methods are tolerable"). He nicks the little hump of pâté with the sharp edge of a Saltine. He congratulates himself on the economical elegance of the meal. Gregg meantime has attacked Fitzhugh Lee on the Louisa Courthouse road and has driven him back some distance, pursuing until nightfall. Near one of the hedges of the Hougoumont farm, without even a drummer to beat the *rappel*, we succeeded in rallying under the enemy's fire 300 men; I made a villager act as our guide, and bound him by his arm to my stirrup.

Kellerman stands before a chalkboard with a long wooden pointer in his hand. The general has been folded into a schoolchild's desk, sitting in the front row. On the board, in chalk, there is a diagrammatic sketch of a suit of armor. Kellerman points.

"A.: *Palette*."

"Palette," the old man repeats.

"Covers the shoulder joint," Kellerman says.

"The armpit?" the old man suggests.

"The shoulder joint," Kellerman says.

"Are you certain?"

"Absolutely."

The general writes in his tablet.

Kellerman points. "B.: *Breastplate*."

His father scribbles.

"Covers the—"

"Breast," old Kellerman says.

"Chest," Kellerman says.

"Mustard plaster," the old man says. "Trying to break up the clog in your little lung. Your mother and I. All through the night. Tears in her eyes. The doctor forty miles away."

"C.: *Tasset*."

"Semolina pudding you wanted. 'No,' I said. 'Later,' I said. 'Bad for the gut,' I said. You cried and cried."

"*Tasset*," Kellerman repeats. "For the upper thigh. Suspended from the waistplate by straps."

"Strap. Ah, strap!"

"D.: *Cuisse*."

"I was good with the strap. Fast, but careful. Not too much, not too little. Calculating the angles, wind velocity, air-spring density, time of day. My windup a perfect hyperbolic paraboloid."

"Covers the thigh proper," Kellerman says. "Fastened by means of—"

"Strap," the general says, with satisfaction. "Unpleasant duty. When in the course of human events it becomes necessary—"

"*You loved it!*" Kellerman says, shouting.

The Belgian regiments had been tampered with. In the melee, I was almost instantly disabled in both arms, losing first my sword, and then my reins, and followed by a few men, who were presently cut down, no quarter being asked, allowed, or given, I was carried along by my horse, till, receiving a blow from a sabre, I fell senseless on my face to the ground. Germany was unspeakably silly. Technically, I was a radar operator on the guidance system. It was a rotten job. Ten hours a day of solid boredom. I did get one trip to the wild Hebrides for the annual firing of the missile (it's called a Corporal). Confidentially, it doesn't work worth a damn. We have a saying: Its effective range is thirty-five feet—its length. If it falls on you, it can be lethal. "There are worms in words!" the general cries. "The worms in words are, like Mexican jumping beans, agitated by the warmth of the mouth."

"Flaming gel," Kellerman says. "You were fond of flaming gel."

"Not overfond," the general replies. "Not like some of them."

"What's that you have there, under your arm?" asks the bookstoreman.

"The Black Knight," Kellerman says. "I want one of those Histomaps of Evolution that you have in the window there, showing the swelling of the unsegmented worms—flatworms, ribbon worms, arrow worms, wheel-worms, spring heads, and so forth."

"Worms in words," the general repeats, "agitated by the warmth of the mouth."

"I'm not accepting any more blame, Papa," Kellerman says finally. "Blame wouldn't melt in my. . . ." He hands round the pâté. "I love playing with mugged-up cards," Kellerman says, to the nearest mother. She is wearing a slim sand-tweed coat with two rows of gilt buttons and carrying a matchbook that says (black lettering, rose-blush ground) "VD Is On the Rise In New York City." "The four of fans, the twelve of wands, the deuce of kidneys, the Jack of Brutes. And shaved decks and readers of various kinds, they make the game worthy of the name." And it was true that his wife pulled 1 hair out of his sleeping head each night, but what if she decided upon 2, or 5, or even 11?

Of those who remained and fought, none were so rudely handled as the Chians, who displayed prodigies of valor, and disdained to play the part of cowards. The order and harmony of the universe, what a beautiful idea! He was obsessed by a vision of beauty—the shimmering, golden Temple, more fascinating than a woman, more eternal than love. And because he was ugly, evil, impotent, he determined someday to possess it . . . by destruction. He had used the word incorrectly. He had mispronounced the word. He had misspelled the word. It was the wrong word.

"Eh, hello, Mado. A Beaujolais."

"Eh, hello, Tris-Tris. A Beaujolais?"

Kellerman runs down the avenue, among the cars, in and out. There are sirens, there is a fire. The huge pieces of apparatus clog the streets. Hoses are run this way and that. Hundreds of firemen stand about, looking at each other, asking each other questions. Kellerman runs. There is a fire somewhere, but the firemen do not know where it is. They stand, gigantic in their black slickers, yellow-lined, their black hats covering the back of the neck, holding shovels. The street is full of firemen, gigantic, standing there. Kellerman runs up to a group of firemen, who look at him with frightened eyes. He begins asking them questions. "Should a person who is sterile marry? What is sterility? What is a false pregnancy? How do the male reproductive organs work? What is natural childbirth? Can a couple know in advance if they can have children? Can impotence be cured? What are the causes of barrenness? Is a human egg like a bird's?"

The President

I AM not altogether sympathetic to the new President. He is, certainly, a strange fellow (only forty-eight inches high at the shoulder). But is strangeness alone enough? I spoke to Sylvia: "Is strangeness alone enough?" "I love you," Sylvia said. I regarded her with my warm kind eyes. "Your thumb?" I said. One thumb was a fiasco of tiny crusted slashes. "Pop-top beer cans," she said. "He is a *strange fellow*, all right. He has some magic charisma which makes people—" She stopped and began again. "When the band begins to launch into his campaign song, 'Struttin' with Some Barbecue,' I just . . . I can't . . ."

The darkness, strangeness, and complexity of the new President have touched everyone. There has been a great deal of fainting lately. Is the President at fault? I was sitting, I remember, in Row EE at City Center; the opera was "The Gypsy Baron." Sylvia was singing in her green-and-blue gypsy costume in the gypsy encampment. I was thinking about the President. Is he, I wondered, right for this period? He is a *strange fellow*, I thought—not like the other Presidents we've had. Not like Garfield. Not like Taft. Not like Harding, Hoover, either of the Roosevelts, or Woodrow Wilson. Then I noticed a lady sitting in front of me, holding a baby. I tapped her on the shoulder. "Madam," I said, "your child has I believe fainted." "Charles!" she cried, rotating the baby's head like a doll's. "Charles, what has happened to you?" The President was smiling in his box.

"The President!" I said to Sylvia in the Italian restaurant. She raised her glass of warm red wine. "Do you think he liked me? My singing?" "He looked pleased," I said. "He was smiling." "A brilliant whirlwind campaign, I thought," Sylvia stated. "Winning was brilliant," I said. "He is the first President we've had from City College," Sylvia said. A waiter fainted behind us. "But is he right for the period?" I asked. "Our period is perhaps not so choice as the previous period, still—"

"He thinks a great deal about death, like all people from City," Sylvia said. "The death theme looms large in his consciousness. I've known a great many people from City, and these people, with no significant exceptions, are hung up on the death theme. It's an obsession, as it were." Other waiters carried the waiter who had fainted out into the kitchen.

"Our period will be characterized in future histories as a period of tentativeness and uncertainty, I feel," I said. "A kind of parenthesis. When he rides in his black limousine with the plastic top I see a little boy who has blown an enormous soap bubble which has trapped him. The look on his face—" "The other candidate was dazzled by his strangeness, newness, smallness, and philosophical grasp of the death theme," Sylvia said. "The other candidate didn't have a prayer," I said. Sylvia adjusted her green-and-blue veils in the Italian restaurant. "Not having gone to City College and sat around the cafeterias there discussing death," she said.

I am, as I say, not entirely sympathetic. Certain things about the new President are not clear. I can't make out what he is thinking. When he has finished speaking I can never remember what he has said. There remains only an impression of strangeness, darkness . . . On television, his face clouds when his name is mentioned. It is as if hearing his name frightens him. Then he stares directly into the camera (an actor's preempting gaze) and begins to speak. One hears only cadences. Newspaper accounts of his speeches always say only that he "touched on a number of matters in the realm of . . ." When he has finished speaking he appears nervous and unhappy. The camera credits fade in over an image of the President standing stiffly, with his arms rigid at his sides, looking to the right and to the left, as if awaiting instructions. On the other hand, the handsome meliorist who ran against him, all zest and programs, was defeated by a fantastic margin.

People are fainting. On Fifty-seventh Street, a young girl dropped in her tracks in front of Henri Bendel. I was shocked to discover that she wore only a garter belt under her dress. I picked her up and carried her into the store with the help of a Salvation Army major—a very tall man with an orange hairpiece. "She fainted," I said to the floorwalker. We talked about the new President, the Salvation Army major and I. "I'll tell you what *I* think," he said. "I think he's got something up his sleeve nobody knows about. I think he's keeping it under wraps. One of these days . . ." The Salvation Army major shook my hand. "I'm not saying that the problems he faces aren't tremendous, staggering. The awesome burden of the Presidency. But if anybody—any *one man* . . ."

What is going to happen? What is the President planning? No one knows. But everyone is convinced that he will bring it off. Our exhausted age wishes above everything to plunge into the heart of the problem, to be able to say, "*Here is the difficulty.*" And the new President, that tiny, strange, and brilliant man, seems cankered and difficult enough to take us there. In the meantime, people are fainting. My secretary fell in the middle of a sentence. "Miss Kagle," I said. "Are you all right?" She was wearing an anklet of tiny silver circles. Each tiny silver circle held an initial: @@@@@@@@@@@@@@@@@. Who is this person "A"? What is he in your life, Miss Kagle?

I gave her water with a little brandy in it. I speculated about the President's mother. Little is known about her. She presented herself in various guises:

A little lady, 5′ 2″, with a cane.

A big lady, 7′ 1″, with a dog.

A wonderful old lady, 4′ 3″, with an indomitable spirit.

A noxious old sack, 6′ 8″, excaudate, because of an operation.

Little is known about her. We are assured, however, that the same damnable involvements that obsess us obsess her too. Copulation. Strangeness. Applause. She must be pleased that her son is what he is—loved and looked up to, a mode of hope for millions. "Miss Kagle. Drink it down. It will put you on your feet again, Miss Kagle." I regarded her with my warm kind eyes.

At Town Hall, I sat reading the program notes to "The Gypsy Baron." Outside the building, eight mounted policemen collapsed en bloc. The well-trained horses planted their feet delicately among the bodies. Sylvia was singing. They said a small man could never be President (only forty-eight inches high at the shoulder). Our period is not the one I would have chosen, but it has chosen me. The new President must have certain intuitions. I am convinced that he has these intuitions (although I am certain of very little else about him; I have reservations, I am not sure). I could tell you about his mother's summer journey, in 1919, to western Tibet—about the dandymen and the red bear, and how she told off the Pathan headman, instructing him furiously to rub up his English or get out of her service—but what order of knowledge is this? Let me instead simply note his smallness, his strangeness, his brilliance, and say that we expect great things of him. "I love you," Sylvia said. The President stepped through the roaring curtain. We applauded until our arms hurt. We shouted until the ushers set off flares enforcing silence. The orchestra tuned itself. Sylvia sang the second lead. The President was smiling in his box. At the finale, the entire cast slipped into the orchestra pit in a great, swooning mass. We cheered until the ushers tore up our tickets.

See the Moon?

I KNOW you think I'm wasting my time. You've made that perfectly clear. But I'm conducting these very important lunar hostility studies. And it's not you who'll have to leave the warm safe capsule. And dip a toe into the threatening lunar surround.

I am still wearing my yellow flower which has lasted wonderfully.

My methods may seem a touch irregular. Have to do chiefly with folded paper airplanes at present. But the paper must be folded *in the right way*. Lots of calculations and worrying about edges.

Show me a man who worries about edges and I'll show you a natural-born winner. Cardinal Y agrees. Columbus himself worried, the Admiral of the Ocean Sea. But he kept it quiet.

The sun so warm on this screened porch, it reminds me of my grandmother's place in Tampa. The same rusty creaky green glider and the same faded colored canvas cushions. And at night the moon graphed by the screen wire, if you squint. The Sea of Tranquillity occupying squares 47 through 108.

See the moon? It hates us.

My methods are homely but remember Newton and the apple. And when Rutherford started out he didn't even have a decently heated laboratory. And then there's the matter of my security check—I'm waiting for the government. Somebody told it I'm insecure. *That's true.*

I suffer from a frightful illness of the mind, light-mindedness. It's not catching. You needn't shrink.

You've noticed the wall? I pin things on it, souvenirs. There is the red hat, there the book of instructions for the Ant Farm. And this is a traffic ticket written on a saint's day (which saint? I don't remember) in 1954 just outside a fat little town (which town? I don't remember) in Ohio by a cop who asked me what I did. I said I wrote poppycock for the president of a university, true then.

You can see how far I've come. Lunar hostility studies aren't for everyone.

It's my hope that these . . . souvenirs . . . will someday merge, blur—cohere is the word, maybe—into something meaningful. A grand word, meaningful. What do I look for? A work of art, I'll not accept anything less. Yes I know it's shatteringly ingenuous but I wanted to be a painter. They get away with murder in my view; Mr. X. on the *Times* agrees with me. You don't know how I envy them. They can pick up a Baby Ruth wrapper on the street, glue it to the canvas (in the *right place*, of course, there's that), and lo! people crowd about and cry, "A real Baby Ruth wrapper, by God, what could be realer than that!" Fantastic metaphysical advantage. You hate them, if you're ambitious.

The Ant Farm instructions are a souvenir of Sylvia. The red hat came from Cardinal Y. We're friends, in a way.

I wanted to be one, when I was young, a painter. But I couldn't stand stretching the canvas. Does things to the fingernails. And that's the first place people look.

Fragments are the only forms I trust.

Light-minded or no, I'm . . . riotous with mental health. I measure myself against the Russians, that's fair. I have here a clipping datelined Moscow, four young people apprehended strangling a swan. *That's* boredom. The swan's name, Borka. The sentences as follows: Tsarev, metalworker, served time previously for stealing public property, four years in a labor camp, strict regime. Roslavtsev, electrician, jailed previously for taking a car on a joyride, three years and four months in a labor camp, semi-strict regime. Tatyana Voblikova (only nineteen and a Komsomol member too), technician, one and a half years in a labor camp, degree of strictness unspecified. Anna G. Kirushina, technical worker, fine of twenty per cent of salary for one year. Anna objected to the strangulation, but softly: she helped stuff the carcass in a bag.

The clipping is tacked up on my wall. I inspect it from time to time, drawing the moral. Strangling swans is wrong.

My brother who is a very distinguished pianist . . . has no fingernails at all. Don't look it's horrible. He plays under another name. And tunes his piano peculiarly, some call it sour. And renders *ragas* he wrote himself. A night *raga* played at noon can cause darkness, did you know that? It's extraordinary.

He wanted to be an Untouchable, Paul did. That was his idea of a contemporary career. But then a girl walked up and touched him (slapped him, actually; it's a complicated story). And he joined us, here in the imbroglio.

My father on the other hand is perfectly comfortable, and that's not a criticism. He makes flags, banners, bunting (sometimes runs me up a shirt). There was never any question of letting my father drink from the public well. He was on the Well Committee, he decided who dipped and who didn't. That's not a criticism. Exercises his creativity, nowadays, courtesy the emerging nations. Green for the veldt that nourishes the gracile Grant's gazelle, white for the purity of our revolutionary aspirations. The red for blood is understood. That's not a criticism. It's what they all ask for.

A call tonight from Gregory, my son by my first wife. Seventeen and at M.I.T. already. Recently he's been asking questions. Suddenly he's conscious of himself as a being with a history.

The telephone rings. Then, without a greeting: *Why did I have to take those little pills?* What little pills? *Little white pills with a "W" on them.* Oh. Oh yes. You had some kind of a nervous disorder, for a while. *How old was I?* Eight. Eight or nine. *What was it? Was it epilepsy?* Good God no, nothing so fancy. We never found out what it was. It went away. *What did I do? Did I fall down?* No no. Your mouth trembled, that was all. You couldn't control it. *Oh, O.K. See you.*

The receiver clicks.

Or: *What did my great-grandfather do? For a living I mean?* He was a ballplayer, semi-pro ballplayer, for a while. Then went into the building business. *Who'd he play for?* A team called the St. Augustine Rowdies, I think it was. *Never heard of them.* Well ... *Did he make any money? In the building business?* Quite a bit. *Did your father inherit it?* No, it was tied up in a lawsuit. When the suit was over there wasn't anything left. *Oh. What was the lawsuit?* Great-grandfather diddled a man in a land deal. So the story goes. *Oh. When did he die?* Let's see, 1938 I think. *What of?* Heart attack. *Oh. O.K. See you.*

End of conversation.

Gregory, you didn't listen to my advice. I said try the

Vernacular Isles. Where fish are two for a penny and women two for a fish. But you wanted M.I.T. and electron-spin-resonance spectroscopy. You didn't even crack a smile in your six-ply heather hopsacking.

Gregory you're going to have a half brother now. You'll like that, won't you? Will you half like it?

We talked about the size of the baby, Ann and I. What could be deduced from the outside.

I said it doesn't look very big to me. She said it's big enough for *us*. I said we don't need such a great roaring big one after all. She said they cost the earth, those extra-large sizes. Our holdings in Johnson's Baby Powder to be considered too. We'd need acres and acres. I said we'll put it in a Skinner box maybe. She said no child of hers. Displayed under glass like a rump roast. I said you haven't wept lately. She said I keep getting bigger whether I laugh or cry.

Dear Ann. I don't think you've quite . . .

What you don't understand is, it's like somebody walks up to you and says, I have a battleship I can't use, would you like to have a battleship. And you say, yes yes, I've never had a battleship, I've always wanted one. And he says, it has four sixteen-inch guns forward, and a catapult for launching scout planes. And you say, I've always wanted to launch scout planes. And he says, *it's yours*, and then you have this battleship. And then you have to paint it, because it's rusting, and clean it, because it's dirty, and anchor it somewhere, because the Police Department wants you to get it off the streets. And the crew is crying, and there are silverfish in the chartroom and a funny knocking noise in Fire Control, water rising in the No. 2 hold, and the chaplain can't find the Palestrina tapes for the Sunday service. And you can't get anybody to sit with it. And finally you discover that what you have here is this great, big, pink-and-blue rockabye *battleship*.

Ann. I'm going to keep her ghostly. Just the odd bit of dialogue:

"What is little Gog doing."

"Kicking."

I don't want her bursting in on us with the freshness and originality of her observations. What we need here is *perspective*. She's good with Gregory though. I think he half likes her.

Don't go. The greased-pig chase and balloon launchings come next.

I was promising once. After the Elgar, a *summa cum laude*. The university was proud of me. It was a bright shy white new university on the Gulf Coast. Gulls and oleanders and quick howling hurricanes. The teachers brown burly men with power boats and beer cans. The president a retired admiral who'd done beautiful things in the Coral Sea.

"You will be a credit to us, George," the admiral said. That's not my name. I'm protecting my identity, what there is of it.

Applause from the stands filled with mothers and brothers. Then following the mace in a long line back to the field house to ungown. Ready to take my place at the top.

But a pause at Pusan, and the toy train to the Chorwon Valley. Walking down a road wearing green clothes. Korea green and black and silent. The truce had been signed. I had a carbine to carry. My buddy Bo Tagliabue the bonus baby, for whom the Yanks had paid thirty thousand. We whitewashed rocks to enhance our area. Colonels came crowding to feel Bo's hurling arm. Mine the whitest rocks.

I lunched with Thais from Thailand, hot curry from great galvanized washtubs. Engineers banging down the road in six-by-sixes raising red dust. My friend Gib Mandell calling Elko, Nevada on his canvas-covered field telephone. "Operator I crave Elko, Nevada."

Then I was a sergeant with stripes, getting the troops out of the sun. Tagliabue a sergeant too. *Triste* in the Tennessee Tea Room in Tokyo, yakking it up in Yokohama. Then back to our little tent town on the side of a hill, boosting fifty-gallon drums of heating oil tentward in the snow.

Ozzie the jeep driver waking me in the middle of the night. "They got Julian in the Tango Tank." And up and alert as they taught us in Leadership School, over the hills to Tango, seventy miles away. Whizzing through Teapot, Tempest, Toreador, with the jeep's canvas top flapping. Pfc. Julian drunk and disorderly and beaten up. The M.P. sergeant held out a receipt book. I signed for the bawdy remains.

Back over the pearly Pacific in a great vessel decorated with oranges. A trail of orange peel on the plangent surface. Sitting in the bow fifty miles out of San Francisco, listening to the

Stateside disc jockeys chattering cha cha cha. Ready to grab my spot at the top.

My clothes looked old and wrong. The city looked new with tall buildings raised while my back was turned. I rushed here and there visiting friends. They were burning beef in their back yards, brown burly men with beer cans. The beef black on the outside, red on the inside. My friend Horace had fidelity. "Listen to that bass. That's sixty watts worth of bass, boy."

I spoke to my father. "How is business?" "If Alaska makes it," he said, "I can buy a Hasselblad. And we're keeping an eye on Hawaii." Then he photographed my veteran face, f.6 at 300. My father once a cheerleader at a great Eastern school. Jumping in the air and making fierce angry down-the-field gestures at the top of his leap.

That's not a criticism. We have to have cheerleaders.

I presented myself at the Placement Office. I was on file. My percentile was the percentile of choice.

"How come you were headman of only one student organization, George?" the Placement Officer asked. Many hats for top folk was the fashion then.

I said I was rounded, and showed him my slash. From the Fencing Club.

"But you served your country in an overseas post."

"And regard my career plan on neatly typed pages with wide margins."

"Exemplary," the Placement Officer said. "You seem married, mature, malleable, how would you like to affiliate yourself with us here at the old school? We have a spot for a poppycock man, to write the admiral's speeches. Have you ever done poppycock?"

I said no but maybe I could fake it.

"Excellent, excellent," the Placement Officer said. "I see you have grasp. And you can sup at the Faculty Club. And there is a ten-per-cent discount on tickets for all home games."

The admiral shook my hand. "You will be a credit to us, George," he said. I wrote poppycock, sometimes cockypap. At four o'clock the faculty hoisted the cocktail flag. We drank Daiquiris on each other's sterns. I had equipped myself—a fibreglass runabout, someplace to think. In the stadia of friendly shy new universities we went down the field on Gulf Coast afternoons with gulls, or exciting nights under the tall toothpick lights. The crowd roared. Sylvia roared. Gregory grew.

There was no particular point at which I stopped being promising.

Moonstruck I was, after a fashion. Sitting on a bench by the practice field, where the jocks chanted secret signals in their underwear behind tall canvas blinds. Layabout babies loafing on blankets, some staked out on twelve-foot dog chains. Brown mothers squatting knee to knee in shifts of scarlet and green. I stared at the moon's pale daytime presence. It seemed . . . inimical.

Moonstruck.

We're playing Flinch. You flinched.

The simplest things are the most difficult to explain, all authorities agree. Say I was tired of p***yc**k, if that pleases you. It's true enough.

Sylvia went up in a puff of smoke. She didn't like unsalaried life. And couldn't bear a male acquaintance moon-staring in the light of day. Decent people look at night.

We had trouble with Gregory: who would get which part. She settled for three-fifths, and got I think the worst of it, the dreaming raffish Romany part that thinks science will save us. I get matter-of-fact midnight telephone calls: *My E.E. instructor shot me down.* What happened? *I don't know, he's an ass anyhow.* Well that may be but still— *When's the baby due?* January, I told you. *Yeah, can I go to Mexico City for the holidays?* Ask your mother, you know she— *There's this guy, his old man has a villa. . . .* Well, we can talk about it. *Yeah, was grandmother a Communist?* Nothing so distinguished, she— *You said she was kicked out of Germany.* Her family was anti-Nazi. *Adler means eagle in German.* That's true. There was something called the Weimar Republic, her father—*I read about it.*

We had trouble with Gregory, we wanted to be scientific. Toys from Procreative Playthings of Princeton. O Gregory, that Princeton crowd got you coming and going. Procreative Playthings at one end and the Educational Testing Service at the other. And that serious-minded co-op nursery, that was a mistake. "A growing understanding between parent and child through shared group experience." I still remember poor

Henry Harding III. Under "Sibs" on the membership roll they listed his, by age:

> 26
> 25
> 23
> 20
> 19
> 15
> 10
> 9
> 8
> 6

O Mrs. Harding, haven't you heard? They have these little Christmas-tree ornaments for the womb now, they work wonders.

Did we do "badly" by Gregory? Will we do "better" with Gog? Such questions curl the hair. It's wiser not to ask.

I mentioned Cardinal Y (the red hat). He's a friend, in a way. Or rather, the subject of one of my little projects.

I set out to study cardinals, about whom science knows nothing. It seemed to me that cardinals could be known in the same way we know fishes or roses, by classification and enumeration. A perverse project, perhaps, but who else has embraced this point of view? Difficult nowadays to find a point of view kinky enough to call one's own, with Sade himself being carried through the streets on the shoulders of sociologists, cheers and shouting, ticker tape unwinding from high windows . . .

The why of Cardinal Y. You're entitled to an explanation.

The Cardinal rushed from the Residence waving in the air his hands, gloved in yellow pigskin it appeared, I grasped a hand, "Yes, yellow pigskin!" the Cardinal cried. I wrote in my book, *yellow pigskin*.

Significant detail. The pectoral cross contains nine diamonds, the scarlet soutane is laundered right on the premises.

I asked the Cardinal questions, we had a conversation.

"I am thinking of a happy island more beautiful than can be imagined," I said.

"I am thinking of a golden mountain which does not exist," he said.

"Upon what does the world rest?" I asked.

"Upon an elephant," he said.

"Upon what does the elephant rest?"

"Upon a tortoise."

"Upon what does the tortoise rest?"

"Upon a red lawnmower."

I wrote in my book, *playful*.

"Is there any value that has value?" I asked.

"If there is any value that has value, then it must lie outside the whole sphere of what happens and is the case, for all that happens and is the case is accidental," he said. He was not serious. I wrote in my book, *knows the drill*.

(Oh I had heard reports, how he slunk about in the snow telling children he was Santa Claus, how he disbursed funds in unauthorized disbursements to unshaven men who came to the kitchen door, how his housekeeper pointedly rolled his red socks together and black socks together hinting red with red and black with black, the Cardinal patiently unrolling a red ball to get a red sock and a black ball to get a black sock, which he then wore together. . . .)

Cardinal Y. He's sly.

I was thorough. I popped the Cardinal on the patella with a little hammer, and looked into his eyes with a little light. I tested the Cardinal's stomach acidity using Universal Indicator Paper, a scale of one to ten, a spectrum of red to blue. The pH value was 1 indicating high acidity. I measured the Cardinal's ego strength using the Minnesota Multiphastic Muzzle Map, he had an M.M.M.M. of four over three. I sang to the Cardinal, the song was "Stella by Starlight," he did not react in any way. I calculated the number of gallons needed to fill the Cardinal's bath to a depth of ten inches (beyond which depth, the Cardinal said, he never ventured). I took the Cardinal to the ballet, the ballet was "The Conservatory." The Cardinal applauded at fifty-seven points. Afterward, backstage, the Cardinal danced with Plenosova, holding her at arm's length with a good will and an ill grace. The skirts of the scarlet soutane stood out to reveal high-button shoes, and the stagehands clapped.

I asked the Cardinal his views on the moon, he said they were the conventional ones, and that is how I know all I know about cardinals. Not enough perhaps to rear a science of cardinalogy upon, but enough perhaps to form a basis for the investigations of other investigators. My report is over there, in the blue binding, next to my copy of *La Géomancie et la Néomancie des Anciens* by the Seigneur of Salerno.

Cardinal Y. One can measure and measure and miss the most essential thing. I liked him. I still get the odd blessing in the mail now and then.

Too, maybe I was trying on the role. Not for myself. When a child is born, the locus of one's hopes . . . shifts, slightly. Not altogether, not all at once. But you feel it, this displacement. You speak up, strike attitudes, like the mother of a tiny Lollobrigida. Drunk with possibility once more.

I am still wearing my yellow flower which has lasted wonderfully.

"What is Gog doing?"

"Sleeping."

You see, Gog of mine, Gog o' my heart, I'm just trying to give you a little briefing here. I don't want you unpleasantly surprised. I can't stand a startled look. Regard me as a sort of Distant Early Warning System. Here is the world and here are the knowledgeable knowers knowing. What can I tell you? What has been pieced together from the reports of travellers.

Fragments are the only forms I trust.

Look at my wall, it's all there. That's a leaf, Gog, stuck up with Scotch Tape. No no, the Scotch Tape is the shiny transparent stuff, the leaf the veined irregularly shaped . . .

There are several sides to this axe, Gog, consider the photostat, "Mr. W. B. Yeats Presenting Mr. George Moore to the Queen of the Fairies." That's a civilized gesture, I mean Beerbohm's. And when the sculptor Aristide Maillol went into the printing business he made the paper by *chewing the fibers himself.* That's dedication. And here is a Polaroid photo, shows your Aunt Sylvia and me putting an Ant Farm together. That's how close we were in those days. Just an Ant Farm apart.

See the moon? It hates us.

And now comes J. J. Sullivan's orange-and-blue Gulf Oil truck to throw kerosene into the space heater. Driver in green siren suit, red face, blond shaved head, the following rich verbal transaction:

"Beautiful day."

"Certainly is."

And now settling back in this green glider with a copy of *Man*. Dear Ann when I look at *Man* I don't want you. Unfolded Ursala Thigpen seems eversomuchmore desirable. A clean girl too and with interests, cooking, botany, pornographic novels. Someone new to show my slash to.

In another month Gog leaps fully armed from the womb. What can I do for him? I can get him into A.A., I have influence. And make sure no harsh moonlight falls on his new soft head.

Hello there Gog. We hope you'll be very happy here.

CITY LIFE

To Roger Angell

Views of My Father Weeping

An aristocrat was riding down the street in his carriage. He ran over my father.

•

After the ceremony I walked back to the city. I was trying to think of the reason my father had died. Then I remembered: he was run over by a carriage.

•

I telephoned my mother and told her of my father's death. She said she supposed it was the best thing. I too supposed it was the best thing. His enjoyment was diminishing. I wondered if I should attempt to trace the aristocrat whose carriage had run him down. There were said to have been one or two witnesses.

•

Yes it is possible that it is not my father who sits there in the center of the bed weeping. It may be someone else, the mailman, the man who delivers the groceries, an insurance salesman or tax collector, who knows. However, I must say, it resembles my father. The resemblance is very strong. He is not smiling through his tears but frowning through them. I remember once we were out on the ranch shooting peccadillos (result of a meeting, on the plains of the West, of the collared peccary and the nine-banded armadillo). My father shot and missed. He wept. This weeping resembles that weeping.

•

"Did you see it?" "Yes but only part of it. Part of the time I had my back turned." The witness was a little girl, eleven or twelve. She lived in a very poor quarter and I could not imagine that, were she to testify, anyone would credit her. "Can you recall what the man in the carriage looked like?" "Like an aristocrat," she said.

•

The first witness declares that the man in the carriage looked "like an aristocrat." But that might be simply the carriage itself. Any man sitting in a handsome carriage with a driver on the box and perhaps one or two footmen up behind tends to look like an aristocrat. I wrote down her name and asked her to call me if she remembered anything else. I gave her some candy.

•

I stood in the square where my father was killed and asked people passing by if they had seen, or knew of anyone who had seen, the incident. At the same time I felt the effort was wasted. Even if I found the man whose carriage had done the job, what would I say to him? "You killed my father." "Yes," the aristocrat would say, "but he ran right in under the legs of the horses. My man tried to stop but it happened too quickly. There was nothing anyone could do." Then perhaps he would offer me a purse full of money.

•

The man sitting in the center of the bed looks very much like my father. He is weeping, tears coursing down his cheeks. One can see that he is upset about something. Looking at him I see that something is wrong. He is spewing like a fire hydrant with its lock knocked off. His yammer darts in and out of all the rooms. In a melting mood I lay my paw on my breast and say, "Father." This does not distract him from his plaint, which rises to a shriek, sinks to a pule. His range is great, his ambition commensurate. I say again, "Father," but he ignores me. I don't know whether it is time to flee or will not be time to flee until later. He may suddenly stop, assume a sternness. I have kept the door open and nothing between me and the door, and moreover the screen unlatched, and on top of that the motor running, in the Mustang. But perhaps it is not my father weeping there, but another father: Tom's father, Phil's father, Pat's father, Pete's father, Paul's father. Apply some sort of test, voiceprint reading or

•

My father throws his ball of knitting up in the air. The orange wool hangs there.

•

My father regards the tray of pink cupcakes. Then he jams his thumb into each cupcake, into the top. Cupcake by cupcake. A thick smile spreads over the face of each cupcake.

•

Then a man volunteered that he had heard two other men talking about the accident in a shop. "What shop?" The man pointed it out to me, a draper's shop on the south side of the square. I entered the shop and made inquiries. "It was your father, eh? He was bloody clumsy if you ask me." This was the clerk behind the counter. But another man standing nearby, well-dressed, even elegant, a gold watchchain stretched across his vest, disagreed. "It was the fault of the driver," the second man said. "He could have stopped them if he had cared to." "Nonsense," the clerk said, "not a chance in the world. If your father hadn't been drunk—" "He wasn't drunk," I said. "I arrived on the scene soon after it happened and I smelled no liquor."

•

This was true. I had been notified by the police, who came to my room and fetched me to the scene of the accident. I bent over my father, whose chest was crushed, and laid my cheek against his. His cheek was cold. I smelled no liquor but blood from his mouth stained the collar of my coat. I asked the people standing there how it had happened. "Run down by a carriage," they said. "Did the driver stop?" "No, he whipped up the horses and went off down the street and then around the corner at the end of the street, toward King's New Square." "You have no idea as to whose carriage . . ." "None." Then I made the arrangements for the burial. It was not until several days later that the idea of seeking the aristocrat in the carriage came to me.

•

I had had in my life nothing to do with aristocrats, did not even know in what part of the city they lived, in their great houses. So that even if I located someone who had seen the incident and could identify the particular aristocrat involved, I would be faced with the further task of finding his house and gaining admittance (and even then, might he not be abroad?). "No, the driver was at fault," the man with the gold watch-chain said. "Even if your father was drunk—and I can't say about that, one way or another, I have no opinion—even if your father was drunk, the driver could have done more to avoid the accident. He was dragged, you know. The carriage dragged him about forty feet." I had noticed that my father's clothes were torn in a peculiar way. "There was one thing," the clerk said, "don't tell anyone I told you, but I can give you one hint. The driver's livery was blue and green."

•

It is someone's father. That much is clear. He is fatherly. The gray in the head. The puff in the face. The droop in the shoulders. The flab on the gut. Tears falling. Tears falling. Tears falling. Tears falling. More tears. It seems that he intends to go further along this salty path. The facts suggest that this is his program, weeping. He has something in mind, more weeping. O lud lud! But why remain? Why watch it? Why tarry? Why not fly? Why subject myself? I could be somewhere else, reading a book, watching the telly, stuffing a big ship into a little bottle, dancing the Pig. I could be out in the streets feeling up eleven-year-old girls in their soldier drag, there are thousands, as alike as pennies, and I could be— Why doesn't he stand up, arrange his clothes, dry his face? He's trying to embarrass us. He wants attention. He's trying to make himself interesting. He wants his brow wrapped in cold cloths perhaps, his hands held perhaps, his back rubbed, his neck kneaded, his wrists patted, his elbows anointed with rare oils, his toenails painted with tiny scenes representing God blessing America. I won't do it.

•

My father has a red bandana tied around his face covering the nose and mouth. He extends his right hand in which there is a water pistol. "Stick 'em up!" he says.

But blue and green livery is not unusual. A blue coat with green trousers, or the reverse, if I saw a coachman wearing such livery I would take no particular notice. It is true that most livery tends to be blue and buff, or blue and white, or blue and a sort of darker blue (for the trousers). But in these days one often finds a servant aping the more exquisite color combinations affected by his masters. I have even seen them in red trousers although red trousers used to be reserved, by unspoken agreement, for the aristocracy. So that the colors of the driver's livery were not of much consequence. Still it was something. I could now go about in the city, especially in stables and gin shops and such places, keeping a weather eye for the livery of the lackeys who gathered there. It was possible that more than one of the gentry dressed his servants in this blue and green livery, but on the other hand, unlikely that there were as many as half a dozen. So that in fact the draper's clerk had offered a very good clue indeed, had one the energy to pursue it vigorously.

•

There is my father, standing alongside an extremely large dog, a dog ten hands high at the very least. My father leaps on the dog's back, straddles him. My father kicks the large dog in the ribs with his heels. "Giddyap!"

•

My father has written on the white wall with his crayons.

•

I was stretched out on my bed when someone knocked at the door. It was the small girl to whom I had given candy when I had first begun searching for the aristocrat. She looked frightened, yet resolute; I could see that she had some information for me. "I know who it was," she said. "I know his name." "What is it?" "First you must give me five crowns." Luckily I had five crowns in my pocket; had she come later in the day, after I had eaten, I would have had nothing to give her. I handed over the money and she said, "Lars Bang." I looked at her in some surprise. "What sort of name is that for an aristocrat?" "His coachman," she said. "The coachman's name is Lars Bang." Then she fled.

•

When I heard this name, which in its sound and appearance is rude, vulgar, not unlike my own name, I was seized with repugnance, thought of dropping the whole business, although the piece of information she had brought had just cost me five crowns. When I was seeking him and he was yet nameless, the aristocrat and, by extension, his servants, seemed vulnerable: they had, after all, been responsible for a crime, or a sort of crime. My father was dead and they were responsible, or at least involved; and even though they were of the aristocracy or servants of the aristocracy, still common justice might be sought for; they might be required to make reparation, in some measure, for what they had done. Now, having the name of the coachman, and being thus much closer to his master than when I merely had the clue of the blue and green livery, I became afraid. For, after all, the unknown aristocrat must be a very powerful man, not at all accustomed to being called to account by people like me; indeed, his contempt for people like me was so great that, when one of us was so foolish as to stray into the path of his carriage, the aristocrat dashed him down, or permitted his coachman to do so, dragged him along the cobblestones for as much as forty feet, and then went gaily on his way, toward King's New Square. Such a man, I reasoned, was not very likely to take kindly to what I had to say to him. Very possibly there would be no purse of money at all, not a crown, not an öre; but rather he would, with an abrupt, impatient nod of his head, set his servants upon me. I would be beaten, perhaps killed. Like my father.

•

But if it is not my father sitting there in the bed weeping, why am I standing before the bed, in an attitude of supplication? Why do I desire with all my heart that this man, my father, cease what he is doing, which is so painful to me? Is it only that my position is a familiar one? That I remember, before, desiring with all my heart that this man, my father, cease what he is doing?

•

Why! . . . there's my father! . . . sitting in the bed there! . . . and he's *weeping!* . . . as though his heart would burst! . . . Father! . . . how is this? . . . who has wounded you? . . . name the man! . . . why I'll . . . I'll . . . here, Father, take this handkerchief! . . . and this handkerchief! . . . and this handkerchief! . . . I'll run for a towel . . . for a doctor . . . for a priest . . . for a good fairy . . . is there . . . can you . . . can I . . . a cup of hot tea? . . . bowl of steaming soup? . . . shot of Calvados? . . . a joint? . . . a red jacket? . . . a blue jacket? . . . Father, please! . . . look at me, Father . . . who has insulted you? . . . are you, then, compromised? . . . ruined? . . . a slander is going around? . . . an obloquy? . . . a traducement? . . . 'sdeath! . . . I won't permit it! . . . I won't abide it! . . . I'll . . . move every mountain . . . climb . . . every river . . . etc.

•

My father is playing with the salt and pepper shakers, and with the sugar bowl. He lifts the cover off the sugar bowl, and shakes pepper into it.

•

Or: My father thrusts his hand through a window of the doll's house. His hand knocks over the doll's chair, knocks over the doll's chest of drawers, knocks over the doll's bed.

•

The next day, just before noon, Lars Bang himself came to my room. "I understand that you are looking for me." He was very much of a surprise. I had expected a rather burly, heavy man, of a piece with all of the other coachmen one saw sitting up on the box; Lars Bang was, instead, slight, almost feminine-looking, more the type of the secretary or valet than the coachman. He was not threatening at all, contrary to my fears; he was almost helpful, albeit with the slightest hint of malice in his helpfulness. I stammeringly explained that my father, a good man although subject to certain weaknesses, including a love of the bottle, had been run down by an aristocrat's coach, in the vicinity of King's New Square, not very many days previously; that I had information that the coach had dragged him some forty feet; and that I was eager to establish certain facts about the case. "Well then," Lars Bang said, with a helpful nod, "I'm your man, for it was my coach that was involved. A sorry business! Unfortunately I haven't the time right now to give you the full particulars, but if you will call round at the address written on this card, at six o'clock in the evening, I believe I will be able to satisfy you." So saying, he took himself off, leaving me with the card in my hand.

•

I spoke to Miranda, quickly sketching what had happened. She asked to see the white card; I gave it to her, for the address meant nothing to me. "Oh my," she said. "17 rue du Bac, that's over by the Vixen Gate—a very special quarter. Only aristocrats of the highest rank live there, and common people are not even allowed into the great park that lies between the houses and the river. If you are found wandering about there at night, you are apt to earn yourself a very severe beating." "But I have an appointment," I said. "An appointment with a coachman!" Miranda cried, "how foolish you are! Do you think the men of the watch will believe that, or even if they believe it (you have an honest enough face) will allow you to prowl that rich quarter, where so many thieves would dearly love to be set free for an hour or so, after dark? Go to!" Then she advised me that I must carry something with me, a pannier of beef or some dozen bottles of wine, so that if apprehended by the watch, I could say that I was delivering to such and such a house, and thus be judged an honest man on an honest errand, and escape a beating. I saw that she was right; and going out, I purchased at the wine merchant's a dozen bottles of a rather good claret (for it would never do to be delivering wine no aristocrat would drink); this cost me thirty crowns, which I had borrowed from Miranda. The bottles we wrapped round with straw, to prevent them banging into one another, and the whole we arranged in a sack, which I could carry on my back. I remember thinking, how they rhymed, fitted together, *sack* and *back*. In this fashion I set off across the city.

•

There is my father's bed. In it, my father. Attitude of dejection. Graceful as a mule deer once, the same large ears. For a nanosecond, there is a nanosmile. Is he having me on? I remember once we went out on the ups and downs of the West (out past Vulture's Roost) to shoot. First we shot up a lot of old beer cans, then we shot up a lot of old whiskey bottles, better because they shattered. Then we shot up some mesquite bushes and some parts of a Ford pickup somebody'd left lying around. But no animals came to our party (it was noisy, I admit it). A long list of animals failed to arrive, no deer, quail, rabbit, seals, sea lions, condylarths. It was pretty boring shooting up mesquite bushes, so we hunkered down behind some rocks. Father and I, he hunkered down behind his rocks and I hunkered down behind my rocks, and we commenced to shooting at each other. That was interesting.

•

My father is looking at himself in a mirror. He is wearing a large hat (straw) on which there are a number of blue and yellow plastic jonquils. He says: "How do I look?"

•

Lars Bang took the sack from me and without asking permission reached inside, withdrawing one of the straw-wrapped bottles of claret. "Here's something!" he exclaimed, reading the label. "A gift for the master, I don't doubt!" Then, regarding me steadily all the while, he took up an awl and lifted the cork. There were two other men seated at the pantry table, dressed in the blue-and-green livery, and with them a dark-haired, beautiful girl, quite young, who said nothing and looked at no one. Lars Bang obtained glasses, kicked a chair in my direction, and poured drinks all round. "To your health!" he said (with what I thought an ironical overtone) and we drank. "This young man," Lars Bang said, nodding at me, "is here seeking our advice on a very complicated business. A murder, I believe you said?" "I said nothing of the kind. I seek information about an accident." The claret was soon exhausted. Without looking at me, Lars Bang opened a second bottle and set it in the center of the table. The beautiful dark-haired girl ignored me along with all the others. For my part, I felt I had conducted myself rather well thus far. I had not protested when the wine was made free of (after all, they would be accustomed to levying a sort of tax on anything entering through the back door). But also I had not permitted his word "murder" to be used, but instead specified the use of the word "accident." Therefore I was, in general, comfortable sitting at the table drinking the wine, for which I have no better head than had my father. "Well," said Lars Bang, at length, "I will relate the circumstances of the accident, and you may judge for yourself as to whether myself and my master, the Lensgreve Aklefeldt, were at fault." I absorbed this news with a slight shock. A count! I had selected a man of very high rank indeed to put my question to. In a moment my accumulated self-confidence drained away. A count! Mother of God, have mercy on me.

•

There is my father, peering through an open door into an empty house. He is accompanied by a dog (small dog; not the same dog as before). He looks into the empty room. He says: "Anybody home?"

•

There is my father, sitting in his bed, weeping.

•

"It was a Friday," Lars Bang began, as if he were telling a tavern story. "The hour was close upon noon and my master directed me to drive him to King's New Square, where he had some business. We were proceeding there at a modest easy pace, for he was in no great hurry. Judge of my astonishment when, passing through the drapers' quarter, we found ourselves set upon by an elderly man, thoroughly drunk, who flung himself at my lead pair and began cutting at their legs with a switch, in the most vicious manner imaginable. The poor dumb brutes reared, of course, in fright and fear, for,"

Lars Bang said piously, "they are accustomed to the best of care, and never a blow do they receive from me, or from the other coachman, Rik, for the count is especially severe upon this point, that his animals be well-treated. The horses, then, were rearing and plunging; it was all I could do to hold them; I shouted at the man, who fell back for an instant. The count stuck his head out of the window, to inquire as to the nature of the trouble; and I told him that a drunken man had attacked our horses. Your father, in his blindness, being not content with the mischief he had already worked, ran back in again, close to the animals, and began madly cutting at their legs with his stick. At this renewed attack the horses, frightened out of their wits, jerked the reins from my hands, and ran headlong over your father, who fell beneath their hooves. The heavy wheels of the carriage passed over him (I felt two quite distinct thumps), his body caught upon a projection under the boot, and he was dragged some forty feet, over the cobblestones. I was attempting, with all my might, merely to hang on to the box, for, having taken the bit between their teeth, the horses were in no mood to tarry; nor could any human agency have stopped them. We flew down the street . . ."

•

My father is attending a class in good behavior.

"Do the men rise when friends greet us while we are sitting in a booth?"

"The men do not rise when they are seated in a booth," he answers, "although they may half-rise and make apologies for not fully rising."

•

". . . the horses turning into the way that leads to King's New Square; and it was not until we reached that place that they stopped and allowed me to quiet them. I wanted to go back and see what had become of the madman, your father, who had attacked us; but my master, vastly angry and shaken up, forbade it. I have never seen him in so fearful a temper as that day; if your father had survived, and my master got his hands on him, it would have gone ill with your father, that's a certainty. And so, you are now in possession of all the facts.

I trust you are satisfied, and will drink another bottle of this quite fair claret you have brought us, and be on your way." Before I had time to frame a reply, the dark-haired girl spoke. "Bang is an absolute bloody liar," she said.

·

Etc.

Paraguay

THE UPPER part of the plain that we had crossed the day before was now white with snow, and it was evident that there was a storm raging behind us and that we had only just crossed the Burji La in time to escape it. We camped in a slight hollow at Sekbachan, eighteen miles from Malik Mar, the night as still as the previous one and the temperature the same; it seemed as if the Deosai Plains were not going to be so formidable as they had been described; but the third day a storm of hail, sleet, and snow alternately came at noon when we began to ascend the Sari Sangar Pass, 14,200 feet, and continued with only a few minutes' intermission till four o'clock. The top of the pass is a fairly level valley containing two lakes, their shores formed of boulders that seemed impossible to ride over. The men slid and stumbled so much that I would not let anyone lead my pony for fear of pulling him over; he was old and slow but perfectly splendid here, picking his way among the rocks without a falter. At the summit there is a cairn on which each man threw a stone, and here it is customary to give payment to the coolies. I paid each man his agreed-upon wage, and, alone, began the descent. Ahead was Paraguay.[1]

Where Paraguay Is

Thus I found myself in a strange country. This Paraguay is not the Paraguay that exists on our maps. It is not to be found on the continent, South America; it is not a political subdivision of that continent, with a population of 2,161,000 and a capital city named Asunción. This Paraguay exists elsewhere. Now, moving toward the first of the "silver cities," I was tired but also elated and alert. Flights of white meat moved through the sky overhead in the direction of the dim piles of buildings.

---

1. Quoted from *A Summer Ride Through Western Tibet*, by Jane E. Duncan, Collins, London, 1906. Slightly altered.

Jean Mueller

Entering the city I was approached, that first day, by a dark girl wrapped in a red shawl. The edges of the shawl were fringed, and the tip of each strand of fringe was a bob of silver. The girl at once placed her hands on my hips, standing facing me; she smiled, and exerted a slight pull. I was claimed as her guest; her name was Jean Mueller. "*Teníamos grandes deseos de conocerlo*," she said. I asked how she knew I had arrived and she said, "Everyone knows." We then proceeded to her house, a large, modern structure some distance from the center of the city; there I was shown into a room containing a bed, a desk, a chair, bookcases, a fireplace, a handsome piano in a cherrywood case. I was told that when I had rested I might join her downstairs and might then meet her husband; before leaving the room she sat down before the piano, and, almost mischievously, played a tiny sonata of Bibblemann's.

Temperature

Temperature controls activity to a remarkable degree. By and large, adults here raise their walking speed and show more spontaneous movement as the temperature rises. But the temperature-dependent pattern of activity is complex. For instance, the males move twice as fast at 60 degrees as they do at 35 degrees, but above 60 degrees speed decreases. The females show more complicated behavior; they increase spontaneous activity as the temperature rises from 40 to 48 degrees, become less active between 49 and 66 degrees, and above 66 degrees again go into a rising tempo of spontaneous movements up to the lethal temperature of 77 degrees. Temperature also (here as elsewhere) plays a critical role in the reproductive process. In the so-called "silver cities" there is a particular scale—66, 67, 68, 69 degrees—at which intercourse occurs (and only within that scale). In the "gold" areas, the scale does not, apparently, apply.

Herko Mueller

Herko Mueller walks through gold and silver leaves, awarded, in the summer months, to those who have produced the best pastiche of the emotions. He is smiling because he did not win one of these prizes, which the people of Paraguay seek to avoid. He is tall, brown, wears a funny short beard, and is fond of zippered suits in brilliant colors: yellow, green, violet. He is, professionally, an arbiter of comedy. "A sort of drama critic?" "More what you would term an umpire. The members of the audience are given a set of rules and the rules constitute the comedy. Our comedies seek to reach the imagination. When you are looking at something, you cannot imagine it." In the evenings I have wet sand to walk upon—long stretches of beach with the sea tasting the edges. Getting back into my clothes after a swim, I discover a strange thing: a sand dollar under my shirt. It is strange because this sand is sifted twice daily to remove impurities and maintain whiteness. And the sea itself, the New Sea, is not programmed for echinoderms.

Error

A government error resulting in the death of a statistically insignificant portion of the population (less than one-fortieth of one per cent) has made people uneasy. A skelp of questions and answers is fused at high temperature (1400° C) and then passed through a series of protracted caresses. Amelioration of the condition results. Paraguay is not old. It is new, a new country. Rough sketches suggest its "look." Heavy yellow drops like pancake batter fall from its sky. I hold a bouquet of umbrellas in each hand. A phrase of Herko Mueller's: "*Y un 60% son mestizos: gloria, orgullo, presente y futuro del Paraguay*" (". . . the glory, pride, present and future of Paraguay"). The country's existence is "predictive," he says, and I myself have noticed a sort of frontier ambience. There are problems. The problem of shedding skin. Thin discarded shells like disposable plastic gloves are found in the street.

Rationalization

The problems of art. New artists have been obtained. These do not object to, and indeed argue enthusiastically for, the rationalization process. Production is up. Quality-control devices have been installed at those points where the interests of artists and audience intersect. Shipping and distribution have been improved out of all recognition. (It is in this area, they say in Paraguay, that traditional practices were most blameworthy.) The rationalized art is dispatched from central art dumps to regional art dumps, and from there into the lifestreams of cities. Each citizen is given as much art as his system can tolerate. Marketing considerations have not been allowed to dictate product mix; rather, each artist is encouraged to maintain, in his software, highly personal, even idiosyncratic, standards (the so-called "hand of the artist" concept). Rationalization produces simpler circuits and, therefore, a saving in hardware. Each artist's product is translated into a statement in symbolic logic. The statement is then "minimized" by various clever methods. The simpler statement is translated back into the design of a simpler circuit. Foamed by a number of techniques, the art is then run through heavy steel rollers. Flip-flop switches control its further development. Sheet art is generally dried in smoke and is dark brown in color. Bulk art is air-dried, and changes color in particular historical epochs.

Skin

Ignoring a letter from the translator Jean sat on a rubber pad doing exercises designed to loosen the skin. Scores of diamond-shaped lights abraded her arms and legs. The light placed a pattern of false information in those zones most susceptible to tearing. Whistling noises accompanied the lights. The process of removing the leg skin is private. Tenseness is eased by the application of a cream, heavy yellow drops like pancake batter. I held several umbrellas over her legs. A man across the street pretending not to watch us. Then the skin placed in the green official receptacles.

The Wall

Our design for the lift tower left us with a vast blind wall of *in situ* concrete. There was thus the danger of having a dreary expanse of blankness in that immensely important part of the building. A solution had to be found. The great wall space would provide an opportunity for a gesture of thanks to the people of Paraguay; a stone would be placed in front of it, and, instead of standing in the shadows, the Stele of the Measures would be brought there also. The wall would be divided, by means of softly worn paths, into doors. These, varying in size from the very large to the very small, would have different colors and thicknesses. Some would open, some would not, and this would change from week to week, or from hour to hour, or in accord with sounds made by people standing in front of them. Long lines or tracks would run from the doors into the roaring public spaces.[2]

Silence

In the larger stores silence (damping materials) is sold in paper sacks like cement. Similarly, the softening of language usually lamented as a falling off from former practice is in fact a clear response to the proliferation of surfaces and stimuli. Imprecise sentences lessen the strain of close tolerances. Silence is also available in the form of white noise. The extension of white noise to the home by means of leased wire from a central generating point has been useful, Herko says. The analogous establishment of "white space" in a system paralleling the existing park system has also been beneficial. Anechoic chambers placed randomly about the city (on the model of telephone booths) are said to have actually saved lives. Wood is becoming rare. They are now paying for yellow pine what was formerly paid for rosewood. Relational methods govern the layout of cities. Curiously, in some of the most successful projects the design has been swung upon small collections of rare animals spaced (on the lost-horse principle) on a lack of grid. Carefully calculated mixes: mambas, the black wrasse, the giselle. Electrolytic jelly exhibiting a capture ratio far in excess of standard is used to fix the animals in place.

Terror

We rushed down to the ends of the waves, apertures through which threatening lines might be seen. Arbiters registered serial numbers of the (complex of threats) with ticks on a great, brown board. Jean meanwhile, unaffected, was casting about on the beach for driftwood, brown washed pieces of wood laced with hundreds of tiny hairline cracks. Such is the smoothness of surfaces in Paraguay that anything not smooth is valuable. She explains to me that in demanding (and receiving) explanations

---

2. Quoted from *The Modular*, by Le Corbusier, M.I.T. Press, Cambridge, 1954. Slightly altered.

you are once more brought to a stop. You have got, really, no farther than you were before. "Therefore we try to keep everything open, go forward avoiding the final explanation. If we inadvertently receive it, we are instructed to 1) pretend that it is just another error, or 2) misunderstand it. Creative misunderstanding is crucial." Creation of new categories of anxiety which must be bandaged or "patched." The expression "put a patch on it." There are "hot" and "cold" patches and specialists in the application of each. Rhathymia is the preferred mode of presentation of the self.

The Temple
Turning sharply to the left I came upon, in a grove of trees, a temple of some sort, abandoned, littered with empty boxes, the floor coated with a thin layer of lime. I prayed. Then drawing out my flask I refreshed myself with apple juice. Everyone in Paraguay has the same fingerprints. There are crimes but people chosen at random are punished for them. Everyone is liable for everything. An extension of the principle, there but for the grace of God go I. Sexual life is very free. There are rules but these are like the rules of chess, intended to complicate and enrich the game. I made love to Jean Mueller while her husband watched. There have been certain technical refinements. The procedures we use (called here "impalement") are used in Paraguay but also new techniques I had never before encountered, "dimidiation" and "quartering." These I found very refreshing.

Microminiaturization
Microminiaturization leaves enormous spaces to be filled. Disposability of the physical surround has psychological consequences. The example of the child's anxiety occasioned by the family's move to a new home may be cited. Everything physical in Paraguay is getting smaller and smaller. Walls thin as a thought, locomotive-substitutes no bigger than ball-point pens. Paraguay, then, has big empty spaces in which men wander, trying to touch something. Preoccupation with skin (on and off, wrinkling, the new skin, pink fresh, taut) possibly a response to this. Stories about skin, histories of particular skins. But no jokes! Some 700,000 photographs of nuclear

events were lost when the great library of Paraguay burned. Particle identification was set back many years. Rather than recreate the former physics, a new physics based on the golden section (proliferation of golden sections) was constructed. As a system of explanation almost certain to be incorrect it enjoys enormous prestige here.

Behind the Wall

Behind the wall there is a field of red snow. I had expected that to enter it would be forbidden, but Jean said no, walk about in it, as much as you like. I had expected that walking in it one would leave no footprints, or that there would be some other anomaly of that kind, but there were no anomalies; I left footprints and felt the cold of red snow underfoot. I said to Jean Mueller, "What is the point of this red snow?" "The intention of the red snow, the reason it is isolated behind the wall, yet not forbidden, is its soft glow—as if it were lighted from beneath. You must have noticed it; you've been standing here for twenty minutes." "But what does it do?" "Like any other snow, it invites contemplation and walking about in." The snow rearranged itself into a smooth, red surface without footprints. It had a red glow, as if lighted from beneath. It seemed to proclaim itself a mystery, but one there was no point in solving—an ongoing low-grade mystery.

Departure

Then I was shown the plan, which is kept in a box. Herko Mueller opened the box with a key (everyone has a key). "Here is the plan," he said. "It governs more or less everything. It is a way of allowing a very wide range of tendencies to interact." The plan was a number of analyses of Brownian motion equipped, at each end, with alligator clips. Then the bell rang and the space became crowded, hundreds of men and women standing there waiting for the marshals to establish some sort of order. I had been chosen, Herko said, to head the column (on the principle of the least-likely-leader). We robed; I folded my arms around the mace. We began the descent (into? out of?) Paraguay.

The Falling Dog

YES, A dog jumped on me out of a high window. I think it was the third floor, or the fourth floor. Or the third floor. Well, it knocked me down. I had my chin on the concrete. Well, he didn't bark before he jumped. It was a silent dog. I was stretched out on the concrete with the dog on my back. The dog was looking at me, his muzzle curled round my ear, his breath was bad, I said "Get off."

He did. He walked away looking back over his shoulder. "Christ," I said. Crumbs of concrete had been driven into my chin. "For God's sake," I said. The dog was four or five metres down the sidewalk, standing still. Looking back at me over his shoulder.

> gay dogs falling
> sense in which you would say of a thing,
> it's a dog, as you would say, it's a lemon
> rain of dogs like rain of frogs
> or shower of objects dropped to confuse enemy radar

Well, it was a standoff. I was on the concrete. He was standing there. Neither of us spoke. I wondered what he was like (the dog's life). I was curious about the dog. Then I understood why I was curious.

> wrapped or bandaged, vulnerability but also
> aluminum
> plexiglas
> anti-hairy materials
> vaudeville (the slide for life)

(Of course I instantly made up a scenario to explain everything. Involving a mysterious ((very beautiful)) woman. Her name is Sophie. I follow the dog to her house. "The dog brought me." There is a ringing sound. "What is that ringing?" "That is the electric eye." "Did I break a beam?" "You and the dog together. The dog is only admitted if he brings someone." "What is that window he jumped out of?" "That is his place." "But he comes here because . . ." "His food is here." Sophie smiles and puts a hand on my arm. "Now you must go." "Take the dog back to his place and then come back here?" "No, just take the dog back to his place. That will be enough. When he has finished eating." "Is that all there is to it?" "I needed the beam broken," Sophie says with a piteous look ((Sax Rohmer)). "When the beam is broken, the bell rings. The bell summons a man." "Another man." "Yes. A Swiss." "I could do whatever it is he does." "No. You are for breaking the beam and taking the dog back to his place." I hear him then, the Swiss. I hear his motorcycle. The door opens, he enters, a real brute, muscled, lots of fur ((Olympia Press)). "Why is the dog still here?" "This man refuses to take him back." The Swiss grabs the dog under the muzzle mock playfully. "He wants to stay!" the Swiss says, to the dog. "*He wants to stay!*" Then the Swiss turns to me. "You're not going to take the dog back?" Threatening look, gestures, etc., etc. "No," I say. "The dog jumped on my back, out of a window. A very high window, the third floor or the fourth floor. My chin was driven into the concrete." "What do I care about your flaming chin? I don't think you understand your function. Your function is to get knocked down by the dog, follow the dog here and break the beam, then take the dog back to his place. There's no reason in the world why we should stand here and listen to a lot of flaming nonsense about your flaming etc. etc. . . .")

I looked at the dog. He looked at me.

who else has done dogs?
Baskin, Bacon, Landseer, Hogarth, Hals

with leashes trailing as they fall

with dog impedimenta following:
bowl, bone, collar, license, Gro-pup

I noticed that he was an Irish setter, rust-colored. He noticed that I was a Welsh sculptor, buff-colored (no, really, what did he notice? how does he think?). I reflected that he was probably a nice dog from a good home (bourgeois dog) but with certain unfortunate habits like jumping on people from high windows (rationalization: he is a member of the television generation and thus—)

Well, I read a letter, then. A letter that had come to me from Germany, that had been in my pocket. I hadn't wanted to read it before but now I read it. It seemed a good time.

> Mr. XXXX XXXXXXXX
> c/o Blue Gallery
> Madison and Eighty-first St.
> New York, N.Y.
>
> Dear Mr. XXXXXXXX:
>
> For the above-mentioned publishers I am preparing a book of recent American sculptors. This work shall not become a collection of gee-gaws and so, it tries to be an aimed presentation of the qualitative best recent American sculptors. I personally am fascinated from your collected YAWNING MAN series of sculptors as well as the YAWNING lithographs. For this reason I absolutely want to include a new figure or figures from you if there are new ones. The critiques of your first show in Basel had been very bad. The German reviewers are coming from such immemorial conceptions of art that they did not know what to do with your sculptors. And I wish a better welcome to your contribution to this book when it is published here. Please send recent photographs of the work plus explanatory text on the YAWNING MAN.
> Many thanks! and kindest regards!
>
> > Yours,
> > R. Rondorfer

Well, I was right in not wanting to read that letter. It was kind of this man to be interested in something I was no longer interested in. How was he to know that I was in that unhappiest of states, between images?

But now something new had happened to me.

> dogs as a luxury (what do we need them for?)
> hounds of heaven
> fallen in the sense of fallen angels
> flayed dogs falling? musculature
> sans skeleton?

But it is well to be suspicious. Sometimes an image is not an image at all but merely an idea. People have wasted years.

I wanted the dog's face. Whereas my old image, the Yawning Man, had been faceless (except for a gap where the mouth was, the yawn itself), I wanted the dog's face. I wanted his expression, falling. I thought of the alternatives: screaming, smiling. And things in between.

> dirty and clean dogs
> ultra-clean dogs, laboratory animals
> thrown or flung dogs
> in series, Indian file
>
> an exploded view of the Falling Dog:
> head, heart, liver, lights
>
> *to the dogs*
> *putting on the dog:*
> I am telling him something which isn't true
>
> and we are both falling
>
> dog tags!
> but forget puns. Cloth falling dogs, the
> gingham dog and the etc., etc. Pieces
> of cloth dogs falling. Or quarter-inch
> plywood in layers, the layers separated
> by an inch or two of airspace. Like old
> triple-wing aircraft

dog-ear (pages falling with corners bent back)
Tray: cafeteria trays of some obnoxious brown plastic
But enough puns

Group of tiny hummingbird-sized falling dogs
Massed in upper corners of a room with high ceilings,
14–17 foot
in rows, in ranks, on their backs

Well, I understood then that this was my new image, The Falling Dog. My old image, the Yawning Man, was played out. I had done upward of two thousand Yawning Men in every known material, and I was tired of it. Images fray, tatter, empty themselves. I had seven good years with that image, the Yawning Man, but—
But now I had the Falling Dog, what happiness.

(flights? sheets?)
of falling dogs, flat falling dogs like sails
Day-Glo dogs falling

am I being sufficiently skeptical?
try it out

die like a
dog-eat-dog
proud as a dog in shoes
dogfight
doggerel
dogmatic

am I being over-impressed by the circumstances
suddenness
pain
but it's a gift. thank you

love me love my

styrofoam?

Well, I got up and brushed off my chin, then. The silent dog was still standing there. I went up to him carefully. He did not move. I had to wonder about what it meant, the Falling Dog, but I didn't have to wonder about it now, I could wonder later. I wrapped my arms around his belly and together we rushed to the studio.

At the Tolstoy Museum

AT THE TOLSTOY MUSEUM

At the Tolstoy Museum we sat and wept. Paper streamers came out of our eyes. Our gaze drifted toward the pictures. They were placed too high on the wall. We suggested to the director that they be lowered six inches at least. He looked unhappy but said he would see to it. The holdings of the Tolstoy Museum consist principally of some thirty thousand pictures of Count Leo Tolstoy.

After they had lowered the pictures we went back to the Tolstoy Museum. I don't think you can peer into one man's face too long—for too long a period. A great many human passions could be discerned, behind the skin.

Tolstoy means "fat" in Russian. His grandfather sent his linen to Holland to be washed. His mother *did not know* any bad words. As a youth he shaved off his eyebrows, hoping they would grow back bushier. He first contracted gonorrhea in 1847. He was once bitten on the face by a bear. He became a vegetarian in 1885. To make himself interesting, he occasionally bowed backward.

Tolstoy's coat

Tolstoy as a youth

AT THE TOLSTOY MUSEUM

I was eating a sandwich at the Tolstoy Museum. The Tolstoy Museum is made of stone—many stones, cunningly wrought. Viewed from the street, it has the aspect of three stacked boxes: the first, second, and third levels. These are of increasing size. The first level is, say, the size of a shoebox, the second level the size of a case of whiskey, and the third level the size of a box that contained a new overcoat. The amazing cantilever of the third level has been much talked about. The glass floor there allows one to look straight down and provides a "floating" feeling. The entire building, viewed from the street, suggests that it is about to fall on you. This the architects relate to Tolstoy's moral authority.

In the basement of the Tolstoy Museum carpenters uncrated new pictures of Count Leo Tolstoy. The huge crates stencilled FRAGILE in red ink . . .

The guards at the Tolstoy Museum carry buckets in which there are stacks of clean white pocket handkerchiefs. More than any other Museum, the Tolstoy Museum induces weeping. Even the bare title of a Tolstoy work, with its burden of love, can induce weeping—for example, the article titled "Who Should Teach Whom to Write, We the Peasant Children or the Peasant Children Us?" Many people stand before this article, weeping. Too, those who are caught by Tolstoy's eyes, in the various portraits, room after room after room, are not unaffected by the experience. It is like, people say, committing a small crime and being discovered at it by your father, who stands in four doorways, looking at you.

At Starogladkovskaya, about 1852

Tiger hunt, Siberia

I was reading a story of Tolstoy's at the Tolstoy Museum. In this story a bishop is sailing on a ship. One of his fellow-passengers tells the bishop about an island on which three hermits live. The hermits are said to be extremely devout. The bishop is seized with a desire to see and talk with the hermits. He persuades the captain of the ship to anchor near the island. He goes ashore in a small boat. He speaks to the hermits. The hermits tell the bishop how they worship God. They have a prayer that goes: "Three of You, three of us, have mercy on us." The bishop feels that this is a prayer prayed in the wrong way. He undertakes to teach the hermits the Lord's Prayer. The hermits learn the Lord's Prayer but with the greatest difficulty. Night has fallen by the time they have got it correctly.

The bishop returns to his ship, happy that he has been able to assist the hermits in their worship. The ship sails on. The bishop sits alone on deck, thinking about the experiences of the day. He sees a light in the sky, behind the ship. The light is cast by the three hermits floating over the water, hand in hand, without moving their feet. They catch up with the ship, saying: "We have forgotten, servant of God, we have forgotten your teaching!" They ask him to teach them again. The bishop crosses himself. Then he tells the hermits that their prayer, too, reaches God. "It is not for me to teach you. Pray for us sinners!" The bishop bows to the deck. The hermits fly back over the sea, hand in hand, to their island.

The story is written in a very simple style. It is said to originate in a folk tale. There is a version of it in St. Augustine. I was incredibly depressed by reading this story. Its beauty. Distance.

The Anna-Vronsky Pavilion

At the Tolstoy Museum, sadness grasped the 741 Sunday visitors. The Museum was offering a series of lectures on the text "Why Do Men Stupefy Themselves?" The visitors were made sad by these eloquent speakers, who were probably right.

People stared at tiny pictures of Turgenev, Nekrasov, and Fet. These and other small pictures hung alongside extremely large pictures of Count Leo Tolstoy.

In the plaza, a sinister musician played a wood trumpet while two children watched.

We considered the 640,086 pages (Jubilee Edition) of the author's published work. Some people wanted him to go away, but other people were glad we had him. "He has been a lifelong source of inspiration to me," one said.

I haven't made up my mind. Standing here in the "Summer in the Country" Room, several hazes passed over my eyes. Still, I think I will march on to "A Landlord's Morning." Perhaps something vivifying will happen to me there.

At the disaster (arrow indicates Tolstoy)

Museum plaza with monumental head (Closed Mondays)

The Policemen's Ball

HORACE, A policeman, was making Rock Cornish Game Hens for a special supper. The Game Hens are frozen solid, Horace thought. He was wearing his blue uniform pants.

Inside the Game Hens were the giblets in a plastic bag. Using his needlenose pliers Horace extracted the frozen giblets from the interior of the birds. Tonight is the night of the Policemen's Ball, Horace thought. We will dance the night away. But first, these Game Hens must go into a three-hundred-and-fifty-degree oven.

Horace shined his black dress shoes. Would Margot "put out" tonight? On this night of nights? Well, if she didn't— Horace regarded the necks of the birds which had been torn asunder by the pliers. No, he reflected, that is not a proper thought. Because I am a member of the force. I must try to keep my hatred under control. I must try to be an example for the rest of the people. Because if they can't trust us . . . the blue men . . .

In the dark, outside the Policemen's Ball, the horrors waited for Horace and Margot.

Margot was alone. Her roommates were in Provincetown for the weekend. She put pearl-colored lacquer on her nails to match the pearl of her new-bought gown. Police colonels and generals will be there, she thought. The Pendragon of Police himself. Whirling past the dais, I will glance upward. The pearl of my eyes meeting the steel gray of high rank.

Margot got into a cab and went over to Horace's place. The cabdriver was thinking: A nice-looking piece. I could love her.

Horace removed the birds from the oven. He slipped little gold frills, which had been included in the package, over the ends of the drumsticks. Then he uncorked the wine, thinking: This is a town without pity, this town. For those whose voices lack the crack of authority. Luckily the uniform . . . Why won't she surrender her person? Does she think she can resist the force? The force of the force?

"These birds are delicious."

Driving Horace and Margot smoothly to the Armory, the new cabdriver thought about basketball.
Why do they always applaud the man who makes the shot?
Why don't they applaud the ball?
It is the ball that actually goes into the net.
The man doesn't go into the net.
Never have I seen a man going into the net.

Twenty thousand policemen of all grades attended the annual fete. The scene was Camelot, with gay colors and burgees. The interior of the Armory had been roofed with lavish tenting. Police colonels and generals looked down on the dark uniforms, white gloves, silvery ball gowns.
"Tonight?"
"Horace, not now. This scene is so brilliant. I want to remember it."
Horace thought: It? Not me?
The Pendragon spoke. "I ask you to be reasonable with the citizens. They pay our salaries after all. I know that they are difficult sometimes, obtuse sometimes, even criminal sometimes, as we often run across in our line of work. But I ask you despite all to be reasonable. I know it is hard. I know it is not easy. I know that for instance when you see a big car, a '70 Biscayne hardtop, cutting around a corner at a pretty fair clip, with three in the front and three in the back, and they are all mixed up, ages and sexes and colors, your natural impulse is to— I know your first thought is, All those people! Together! And your second thought is, Force! But I must ask you in the name of force itself to be restrained. For force, that great principle, is most honored in the breach and the observance. And that is where you men are, in the breach. You are fine men, the finest. You are Americans. So for the sake of America, be careful. Be reasonable. Be slow. In the name of the Father and of the Son and of the Holy Ghost. And now I would like to introduce Vercingetorix, leader of the firemen, who brings us a few words of congratulation from that fine body of men."
Waves of applause for the Pendragon filled the tented area.
"He is a handsome older man," Margot said.
"He was born in a Western state and advanced to his present position through raw merit," Horace told her.

The government of Czechoslovakia sent observers to the Policemen's Ball. "Our police are not enough happy," Colonel-General Čepicky explained. "We seek ways to improve them. This is a way. It may not be the best way of all possible ways, but . . . Also I like to drink the official whiskey! It makes me gay!"

A bartender thought: Who is that yellow-haired girl in the pearl costume? She is stacked.

The mood of the Ball changed. The dancing was more serious now. Margot's eyes sparkled from the jorums of champagne she had drunk. She felt Horace's delicately Game Hen-flavored breath on her cheek. I will give him what he wants, she decided. Tonight. His heroism deserves it. He stands between us and them. He represents what is best in the society: decency, order, safety, strength, sirens, smoke. No, he does not represent smoke. Firemen represent smoke. Great billowing oily black clouds. That Vercingetorix has a noble look. With whom is Vercingetorix dancing, at present?

The horrors waited outside patiently. Even policemen, the horrors thought. We get even policemen, in the end.

In Horace's apartment, a gold frill was placed on a pearl toe.

The horrors had moved outside Horace's apartment. Not even policemen and their ladies are safe, the horrors thought. No one is safe. Safety does not exist. Ha ha ha ha ha ha ha ha ha ha!

The Glass Mountain

1. I was trying to climb the glass mountain.
2. The glass mountain stands at the corner of Thirteenth Street and Eighth Avenue.
3. I had attained the lower slope.
4. People were looking up at me.
5. I was new in the neighborhood.
6. Nevertheless I had acquaintances.
7. I had strapped climbing irons to my feet and each hand grasped a sturdy plumber's friend.
8. I was 200 feet up.
9. The wind was bitter.
10. My acquaintances had gathered at the bottom of the mountain to offer encouragement.
11. "Shithead."
12. "Asshole."
13. Everyone in the city knows about the glass mountain.
14. People who live here tell stories about it.
15. It is pointed out to visitors.
16. Touching the side of the mountain, one feels coolness.
17. Peering into the mountain, one sees sparkling blue-white depths.
18. The mountain towers over that part of Eighth Avenue like some splendid, immense office building.
19. The top of the mountain vanishes into the clouds, or on cloudless days, into the sun.
20. I unstuck the righthand plumber's friend leaving the lefthand one in place.
21. Then I stretched out and reattached the righthand one a little higher up, after which I inched my legs into new positions.
22. The gain was minimal, not an arm's length.
23. My acquaintances continued to comment.
24. "Dumb motherfucker."
25. I was new in the neighborhood.
26. In the streets were many people with disturbed eyes.

THE GLASS MOUNTAIN

27. Look for yourself.
28. In the streets were hundreds of young people shooting up in doorways, behind parked cars.
29. Older people walked dogs.
30. The sidewalks were full of dogshit in brilliant colors: ocher, umber, Mars yellow, sienna, viridian, ivory black, rose madder.
31. And someone had been apprehended cutting down trees, a row of elms broken-backed among the VWs and Valiants.
32. Done with a power saw, beyond a doubt.
33. I was new in the neighborhood yet I had accumulated acquaintances.
34. My acquaintances passed a brown bottle from hand to hand.
35. "Better than a kick in the crotch."
36. "Better than a poke in the eye with a sharp stick."
37. "Better than a slap in the belly with a wet fish."
38. "Better than a thump on the back with a stone."
39. "Won't he make a splash when he falls, now?"
40. "I hope to be here to see it. Dip my handkerchief in the blood."
41. "Fart-faced fool."
42. I unstuck the lefthand plumber's friend leaving the right-hand one in place.
43. And reached out.
44. To climb the glass mountain, one first requires a good reason.
45. No one has ever climbed the mountain on behalf of science, or in search of celebrity, or because the mountain was a challenge.
46. Those are not good reasons.
47. But good reasons exist.
48. At the top of the mountain there is a castle of pure gold, and in a room in the castle tower sits . . .
49. My acquaintances were shouting at me.
50. "Ten bucks you bust your ass in the next four minutes!"
51. . . . a beautiful enchanted symbol.
52. I unstuck the righthand plumber's friend leaving the lefthand one in place.

53. And reached out.
54. It was cold there at 206 feet and when I looked down I was not encouraged.
55. A heap of corpses both of horses and riders ringed the bottom of the mountain, many dying men groaning there.
56. "A weakening of the libidinous interest in reality has recently come to a close." (Anton Ehrenzweig)
57. A few questions thronged into my mind.
58. Does one climb a glass mountain, at considerable personal discomfort, simply to disenchant a symbol?
59. Do today's stronger egos still *need* symbols?
60. I decided that the answer to these questions was "yes."
61. Otherwise what was I doing there, 206 feet above the power-sawed elms, whose white meat I could see from my height?
62. The best way to fail to climb the mountain is to be a knight in full armor—one whose horse's hoofs strike fiery sparks from the sides of the mountain.
63. The following-named knights had failed to climb the mountain and were groaning in the heap: Sir Giles Guilford, Sir Henry Lovell, Sir Albert Denny, Sir Nicholas Vaux, Sir Patrick Grifford, Sir Gisbourne Gower, Sir Thomas Grey, Sir Peter Coleville, Sir John Blunt, Sir Richard Vernon, Sir Walter Willoughby, Sir Stephen Spear, Sir Roger Faulconbridge, Sir Clarence Vaughan, Sir Hubert Ratcliffe, Sir James Tyrrel, Sir Walter Herbert, Sir Robert Brakenbury, Sir Lionel Beaufort, and many others.
64. My acquaintances moved among the fallen knights.
65. My acquaintances moved among the fallen knights, collecting rings, wallets, pocket watches, ladies' favors.
66. "Calm reigns in the country, thanks to the confident wisdom of everyone." (M. Pompidou)
67. The golden castle is guarded by a lean-headed eagle with blazing rubies for eyes.
68. I unstuck the lefthand plumber's friend, wondering if—
69. My acquaintances were prising out the gold teeth of not-yet-dead knights.

70. In the streets were people concealing their calm behind a façade of vague dread.
71. "The conventional symbol (such as the nightingale, often associated with melancholy), even though it is recognized only through agreement, is not a sign (like the traffic light) because, again, it presumably arouses deep feelings and is regarded as possessing properties beyond what the eye alone sees." (*A Dictionary of Literary Terms*)
72. A number of nightingales with traffic lights tied to their legs flew past me.
73. A knight in pale pink armor appeared above me.
74. He sank, his armor making tiny shrieking sounds against the glass.
75. He gave me a sideways glance as he passed me.
76. He uttered the word "*Muerte*" as he passed me.
77. I unstuck the righthand plumber's friend.
78. My acquaintances were debating the question, which of them would get my apartment?
79. I reviewed the conventional means of attaining the castle.
80. The conventional means of attaining the castle are as follows: "The eagle dug its sharp claws into the tender flesh of the youth, but he bore the pain without a sound, and seized the bird's two feet with his hands. The creature in terror lifted him high up into the air and began to circle the castle. The youth held on bravely. He saw the glittering palace, which by the pale rays of the moon looked like a dim lamp; and he saw the windows and balconies of the castle tower. Drawing a small knife from his belt, he cut off both the eagle's feet. The bird rose up in the air with a yelp, and the youth dropped lightly onto a broad balcony. At the same moment a door opened, and he saw a courtyard filled with flowers and trees, and there, the beautiful enchanted princess." (*The Yellow Fairy Book*)
81. I was afraid.
82. I had forgotten the Bandaids.
83. When the eagle dug its sharp claws into my tender flesh—
84. Should I go back for the Bandaids?
85. But if I went back for the Bandaids I would have to endure the contempt of my acquaintances.

86. I resolved to proceed without the Bandaids.
87. "In some centuries, his [man's] imagination has made life an intense practice of all the lovelier energies." (John Masefield)
88. The eagle dug its sharp claws into my tender flesh.
89. But I bore the pain without a sound, and seized the bird's two feet with my hands.
90. The plumber's friends remained in place, standing at right angles to the side of the mountain.
91. The creature in terror lifted me high in the air and began to circle the castle.
92. I held on bravely.
93. I saw the glittering palace, which by the pale rays of the moon looked like a dim lamp; and I saw the windows and balconies of the castle tower.
94. Drawing a small knife from my belt, I cut off both the eagle's feet.
95. The bird rose up in the air with a yelp, and I dropped lightly onto a broad balcony.
96. At the same moment a door opened, and I saw a courtyard filled with flowers and trees, and there, the beautiful enchanted symbol.
97. I approached the symbol, with its layers of meaning, but when I touched it, it changed into only a beautiful princess.
98. I threw the beautiful princess headfirst down the mountain to my acquaintances.
99. Who could be relied upon to deal with her.
100. Nor are eagles plausible, not at all, not for a moment.

The Explanation

Q: Do you believe that this machine could be helpful in changing the government?
A: Changing the government . . .
Q: Making it more responsive to the needs of the people?
A: I don't know what it is. What does it do?
Q: Well, look at it.

A: It offers no clues.
Q: It has a certain . . . reticence.
A: I don't know what it does.
Q: A lack of confidence in the machine?

Q: Is the novel dead?
A: Oh yes. Very much so.
Q: What replaces it?
A: I should think that it is replaced by what existed before it was invented.
Q: The same thing?
A: The same sort of thing.
Q: Is the bicycle dead?

Q: You don't trust the machine?
A: Why should I trust it?
Q: (States his own lack of interest in machines)

Q: What a beautiful sweater.
A: Thank you. I don't want to worry about machines.

Q: What do you worry about?
A: I was standing on the corner waiting for the light to change when I noticed, across the street among the people there waiting for the light to change, an extraordinarily handsome girl who was looking at me. Our eyes met, I looked away, then I looked again, she was looking away, the light changed. I moved into the street as did she. First I looked at her again to see if she was still looking at me, she wasn't but I was aware that she was aware of me. I decided to smile. I smiled but in a curious way—the smile was supposed to convey that I was interested in her but also that I was aware that the situation was funny. But I bungled it. I smirked. I dislike even the word "smirk." There was, you know, the moment when we passed each other. I had resolved to look at her directly in that moment. I tried but she was looking a bit to the left of me, she was looking fourteen inches to the left of my eyes.
Q: This is the sort of thing that—
A: I want to go back and do it again.

Q: Now that you've studied it for a bit, can you explain how it works?
A: Of course. (Explanation)

Q: Is she still removing her blouse?
A: Yes, still.

Q: Do you want to have your picture taken with me?
A: I don't like to have my picture taken.
Q: Do you believe that, at some point in the future, one will be able to achieve sexual satisfaction, "complete" sexual satisfaction, for instance by taking a pill?
A: I doubt that it's impossible.
Q: You don't like the idea.
A: No. I think that under those conditions, we would know less than we do now.
Q: Know less about each other.
A: Of course.

Q: It has beauties.
A: The machine.

Q: Yes. We construct these machines not because we confidently expect them to do what they are designed to do—change the government in this instance—but because we intuit a machine, out there, glowing like a shopping center. . . .

A: You have to contend with a history of success.

Q: Which has gotten us nowhere.

A: (Extends consolation)

Q: What did you do then?

A: I walked on a tree. For twenty steps.

Q: What sort of tree?

A: A dead tree. I can't tell one from another. It may have been an oak. I was reading a book.

Q: What was the book?

A: I don't know, I can't tell one from another. They're not like films. With films you can remember, at a minimum, who the actors were. . . .

Q: What was she doing?

A: Removing her blouse. Eating an apple.

Q: The tree must have been quite large.

A: The tree must have been quite large.

Q: Where was this?

A: Near the sea. I had rope-soled shoes.

Q: I have a number of error messages I'd like to introduce here and I'd like you to study them carefully . . . they're numbered. I'll go over them with you: undefined variable . . . improper sequence of operators . . . improper use of hierarchy . . . missing operator . . . mixed mode, that one's particularly grave . . . argument of a function is fixed-point . . . improper character in constant . . . improper fixed-point constant . . . improper floating-point constant . . . invalid character transmitted in sub-program statement, that's a bitch . . . no END statement.

A: I like them very much.

Q: There are hundreds of others, hundreds and hundreds.

A: You seem emotionless.

Q: That's not true.

A: To what do your emotions . . . adhere, if I can put it that way?

Q: Do you see what she is doing?
A: Removing her blouse.
Q: How does she look?
A: . . . Self-absorbed.
Q: Are you bored with the question-and-answer form?
A: I am bored with it but I realize that it permits many valuable omissions: what kind of day it is, what I'm wearing, what I'm thinking. That's a very considerable advantage, I would say.
Q: I believe in it.

Q: She sang and we listened to her.
A: I was speaking to a tourist.
Q: Their chair is here.
A: I knocked at the door; it was shut.
Q: The soldiers marched toward the castle.
A: I had a watch.
Q: He has struck me.
A: I have struck him.
Q: Their chair is here.
A: We shall not cross the river.
Q: The boats are filled with water.
A: His father will strike him.
Q: Filling his pockets with fruit.

Q: The face . . . the machine has a face. This panel here . . .
A: That one?
Q: Just as the human face developed . . . from fish . . . it's traceable, from, say, the . . . The first mouth was that of a jellyfish. I can't remember the name, the Latin name. . . . But a mouth, there's more to it than just a mouth, a mouth alone is not a face. It went on up through the sharks . . .
A: Up through the sharks . . .
Q: . . . to the snakes. . . .
A: Yes.
Q: The face has *three* main functions, detection of desirable energy sources, direction of the locomotor machinery toward its goal, and capture. . . .
A: Yes.
Q: Capture and preliminary preparation of food. Is this too . . .

A: Not a bit.
Q: The face, a face, also serves as a lure in mate acquisition. The broad, forwardly directed nose—
A: I don't see that on the panel.
Q: Look at it.

A: I don't—
Q: There is an analogy, believe it or not. The . . . We use industrial designers to do the front panels, the controls. Designers, artists. To make the machines attractive to potential buyers. Pure cosmetics. They told us that knife switches were masculine. Men felt . . . So we used a lot of knife switches. . . .
A: I know that a great deal has been written about all this but when I come across such articles, in the magazines or in a newspaper, I don't read them. I'm not interested.
Q: What are your interests?
A: I'm a director of the Schumann Festival.

Q: What is she doing now?
A: Taking off her jeans.

Q: Has she removed her blouse?
A: No, she's still wearing her blouse.
Q: A yellow blouse?
A: Blue.
Q: Well, what is she doing now?
A: Removing her jeans.
Q: What is she wearing underneath?
A: Pants. Panties.
Q: But she's still wearing her blouse?
A: Yes.
Q: Has she removed her panties?
A: Yes.
Q: Still wearing the blouse?
A: Yes. She's walking along a log.
Q: In her blouse. Is she reading a book?
A: No. She has sunglasses.
Q: She's wearing sunglasses?
A: Holding them in her hand.
Q: How does she look?
A: Quite beautiful.

Q: What is the content of Maoism?
A: The content of Maoism is purity.
Q: Is purity quantifiable?
A: Purity has never been quantifiable.
Q: What is the incidence of purity worldwide?
A: Purity occurs in .004 per cent of all cases.
Q: What is purity in the pure state often consonant with?
A: Purity in the pure state is often consonant with madness.
Q: This is not to denigrate madness.
A: This is not to denigrate madness. Madness in the pure state offers an alternative to the reign of right reason.
Q: What is the content of right reason?
A: The content of right reason is rhetoric.
Q: And the content of rhetoric?
A: The content of rhetoric is purity.
Q: Is purity quantifiable?
A: Purity is not quantifiable. It *is* inflatable.
Q: How is our rhetoric preserved against attacks by other rhetorics?

A: Our rhetoric is preserved by our elected representatives. In the fat of their heads.

Q: There's no point in arguing that the machine is wholly successful, but it has its qualities. I don't like to use anthropomorphic language in talking about these machines, but there is one quality . . .
A: What is it?
Q: It's brave.
A: Machines are braver than art.
Q: Since the death of the bicycle.

Q: There are ten rules for operating the machine. The first rule is turn it on.
A: Turn it on.
Q: The second rule is convert the terms. The third rule is rotate the inputs. The fourth rule is you have made a serious mistake.
A: What do I do?
Q: You send the appropriate error message.

A: I will never remember these rules.
Q: I'll repeat them a hundred times.
A: I was happier before.
Q: You imagined it.
A: The issues are not real.
Q: The issues are not real in the sense that they are touchable. The issues raised here are equivalents. Reasons and conclusions exist although they exist elsewhere, not here. Reasons and conclusions are in the air and simple to observe even for those who do not have the leisure to consult or learn to read the publications of the specialized disciplines.
A: The situation bristles with difficulties.
Q: The situation bristles with difficulties but in the end young people and workers will live on the same plane as old people and government officials, for the mutual good of all categories. The phenomenon of masses, in following the law of high numbers, makes possible exceptional and rare events, which—

A: I called her then and told her that I had dreamed about her, that she was naked in the dream, that we were making love. She didn't wish to be dreamed about, she said—not now, not later, not ever, when would I stop. I suggested that it was something over which I had no control. She said that it had all been a long time ago and that she was married to William now, as I knew, and that she didn't want . . . irruptions of this kind. Think of William, she said.

Q: He has struck me.
A: I have struck him.
Q: We have seen them.
A: I was looking at the window.
Q: Their chair is here.
A: She sang and we listened to her.
Q: Soldiers marching toward the castle.
A: I spoke to a tourist.
Q: I knocked at the door.
A: We shall not cross the river.
Q: The river has filled the boats with water.
A: I think that I have seen her with my uncle.
Q: Getting into their motorcar, I heard them.
A: He will strike her if he has lost it.

A (concluding): There's no doubt in my mind that the ballplayers today are the greatest ever. They're brilliant athletes, extremely well coordinated, tremendous in every department. The ballplayers today are so magnificent that scoring is a relatively simple thing for them.
Q: Thank you for confiding in me.

Q: . . . show you a picture of my daughter.

A: Very nice.
Q: I can give you a few references for further reading.
A: (Nose begins to bleed)

Q: What is she doing now?
A: There is a bruise on her thigh. The right.

Kierkegaard Unfair to Schlegel

A: I use the girl on the train a lot. I'm on a train, a European train with compartments. A young girl enters and sits opposite me. She is blond, wearing a short-sleeved sweater, a short skirt. The sweater has white and blue stripes, the skirt is dark blue. The girl has a book, *Introduction to French* or something like that. We are in France but she is not French. She has a book and a pencil. She's extremely self-conscious. She opens the book and begins miming close attention, you know, making marks with the pencil at various points. Meanwhile I am carefully looking out of the window, regarding the terrain. I'm trying to avoid looking at her legs. The skirt has raised itself a bit, you see, there is a lot of leg to look at. I'm also trying to avoid looking at her breasts. They appear to be free under the white-and-blue sweater. There is a small gold pin pinned to the sweater on the left side. It has lettering on it. I can't make out what it says. The girl shifts in her seat, moves from side to side, adjusting her position. She's very very self-aware. All her movements are just a shade overdone. The book is in her lap. Her legs are fairly wide apart, very tanned, the color of—

Q: That's a very common fantasy.
A: All my fantasies are extremely ordinary.
Q: Does it give you pleasure?
A: A poor . . . A rather unsatisfactory . . .
Q: What is the frequency?
A: Oh God who knows. Once in a while. Sometimes.
Q: You're not cooperating.
A: I'm not interested.
Q: I might do an article.
A: I don't like to have my picture taken.
Q: Solipsism plus triumphantism.
A: It's possible.

Q: You're not political?

A: I'm extremely political in a way that does no good to anybody.

Q: You don't participate?

A: I participate. I make demands, sign newspaper advertisements, vote. I make small campaign contributions to the candidate of my choice and turn my irony against the others. But I accomplish nothing. I march, it's ludicrous. In the last march, there were eighty-seven thousand people marching, by the most conservative estimate, and yet being in the midst of them, marching with them . . . I wanted to march with the Stationary Engineers, march under their banner, but two cops prevented me, they said I couldn't enter at that point, I had to go back to the beginning. So I went back to the beginning and marched with the Food Handlers for Peace and Freedom.

Q: What sort of people were they?

A: They looked just like everybody else. It's possible they weren't real food handlers. Maybe just the two holding the sign. I don't know. There were a lot of girls in black pajamas and peasant straw hats, very young girls, high-school girls, running, holding hands in a long chain, laughing. . . .

Q: You've been pretty hard on our machines. You've withheld your enthusiasm, that's damaging . . .

A: I'm sorry.

Q: Do you think your irony could be helpful in changing the government?

A: I think the government is very often in an ironic relation to itself. And that's helpful. For example: we're spending a great deal of money for this army we have, a very large army, beautifully equipped. We're spending something on the order of twenty billions a year for it. Now, the whole point of an army is—what's the word?—deterrence. And the nut of deterrence is credibility. So what does the government do? It goes and sells off its surplus uniforms. And the kids start wearing them, uniforms or parts of uniforms, because they're cheap and have some sort of style. And immediately you get this vast clown army in the streets parodying the real army. And they mix periods, you know, you get parody British grenadiers and parody World War I types and parody Sierra Maestra types. So you have all these kids walking around wearing these filthy uniforms with wound stripes, hash marks, Silver Stars, but also ostrich feathers, Day-Glo vests, amulets containing powdered rhinoceros horn . . . You have this splendid clown army in the streets standing over against the real one. And of course the clown army constitutes a very serious attack on all the ideas which support the real army including the basic notion of having an army at all. The government has opened itself to all this, this undermining of its own credibility, just because it wants to make a few dollars peddling old uniforms. . . .

Q: How is my car?
Q: How is my nail?
Q: How is the taste of my potato?
Q: How is the cook of my potato?
Q: How is my garb?
Q: How is my button?
Q: How is the flower bath?
Q: How is the shame?
Q: How is the plan?
Q: How is the fire?
Q: How is the flue?
Q: How is my mad mother?
Q: How is the aphorism I left with you?

Q: You are an ironist.
A: It's useful.
Q: How is it useful?
A: Well, let me tell you a story. Several years ago I was living in a rented house in Colorado. The house was what is called a rancher—three or four bedrooms, knotty pine or some such on the inside, cedar shakes or something like that on the outside. It was owned by a ski instructor who lived there with his family in the winter. It had what seemed to be hundreds of closets and we immediately discovered that these closets were filled to overflowing with all kinds of play equipment. Never in my life had I seen so much play equipment gathered together in one place outside, say, Abercrombie's. There were bows and arrows and shuffleboard and croquet sets, putting greens and trampolines and things that you strapped to your feet and jumped up and down on, table tennis and jai alai and poker chips and

home roulette wheels, chess and checkers and Chinese checkers and balls of all kinds, hoops and nets and wickets, badminton and books and a thousand board games, and a dingus with cymbals on top that you banged on the floor to keep time to the piano. The merest drawer in a bedside table was choked with marked cards and Monopoly money.

Now, suppose I had been of an ironical turn of mind and wanted to make a joke about all this, some sort of joke that would convey that I had noticed the striking degree of boredom implied by the presence of all this impedimenta and one which would also serve to comment upon the particular way of struggling with boredom that these people had chosen. I might have said, for instance, that the remedy is worse than the disease. Or quoted Nietzsche to the effect that the thought of suicide is a great consolation and had helped him through many a bad night. Either of these perfectly good jokes would do to annihilate the situation of being uncomfortable in this house. The shuffleboard sticks, the barbells, balls of all kinds—my joke has, in effect, thrown them out of the world. An amazing magical power!

Now, suppose that I am suddenly curious about this amazing magical power. Suppose I become curious about how my irony actually works—how it functions. I pick up a copy of Kierkegaard's *The Concept of Irony* (the ski instructor is also a student of Kierkegaard) and I am immediately plunged into difficulties. The situation bristles with difficulties. To begin with, Kierkegaard says that the outstanding feature of irony is that it confers upon the ironist a subjective freedom. The subject, the speaker, is negatively free. If what the ironist says is not his meaning, or is the opposite of his meaning, he is free both in relation to others and in relation to himself. He is not bound by what he has said. Irony is a means of depriving the object of its reality in order that the subject may feel free.

Irony deprives the object of its reality when the ironist says something about the object that is not what he means. Kierkegaard distinguishes between the phenomenon (the word) and the essence (the thought or meaning). Truth demands an identity of essence and phenomenon. But with irony quote the phenomenon is not the essence but the opposite of the essence unquote page 264. The object is deprived of its reality by what

I have said about it. Regarded in an ironical light, the object shivers, shatters, disappears. Irony is thus destructive and what Kierkegaard worries about a lot is that irony has nothing to put in the place of what it has destroyed. The new actuality—what the ironist has said about the object—is peculiar in that it is a comment upon a former actuality rather than a new actuality. This account of Kierkegaard's account of irony is grossly oversimplified. Now, consider an irony directed not against a given object but against the whole of existence. An irony directed against the whole of existence produces, according to Kierkegaard, estrangement and poetry. The ironist, serially successful in disposing of various objects of his irony, becomes drunk with freedom. He becomes, in Kierkegaard's words, lighter and lighter. Irony becomes an infinite absolute negativity. Quote irony no longer directs itself against this or that particular phenomenon, against a particular thing unquote. Quote the whole of existence has become alien to the ironic subject unquote page 276. For Kierkegaard, the actuality of irony is poetry. This may be clarified by reference to Kierkegaard's treatment of Schlegel.

Schlegel had written a book, a novel, called *Lucinde*. Kierkegaard is very hard on Schlegel and *Lucinde*. Kierkegaard characterizes this novel of Schlegel's as quote poetical unquote page 308. By which he means to suggest that Schlegel has constructed an actuality which is superior to the historical actuality and a substitute for it. By negating the historical actuality poetry quote opens up a higher actuality, expands and transfigures the imperfect into the perfect, and thereby softens and mitigates that deep pain which would darken and obscure all things unquote page 312. That's beautiful. Now this would seem to be a victory for Schlegel, and indeed Kierkegaard says that poetry is a victory over the world. But it is not the case that *Lucinde* is a victory for Schlegel. What is wanted, Kierkegaard says, is not a victory over the world but a reconciliation with the world. And it is soon discovered that although poetry is a kind of reconciliation, the distance between the new actuality, higher and more perfect than the historical actuality, and the historical actuality, lower and more imperfect than the new actuality, produces not a reconciliation but animosity. Quote so that it often becomes no reconciliation at all but rather animosity unquote same page. What began as a victory eventuates in animosity. The true task is reconciliation with actuality and the true reconciliation, Kierkegaard says, is religion. Without discussing whether or not the true reconciliation is religion (I have a deep bias against religion which precludes my discussing the question intelligently) let me say that I believe that Kierkegaard is here unfair to Schlegel. I find it hard to persuade myself that the relation of Schlegel's novel to actuality is what Kierkegaard says it is. I have reasons for this (I believe, for example, that Kierkegaard fastens upon Schlegel's novel in its prescriptive aspect—in which it presents itself as a text telling us how to live—and neglects other aspects, its objecthood for one) but my reasons are not so interesting. What is interesting is my making the statement that I think Kierkegaard is unfair to Schlegel. And that the whole thing is nothing else but a damned shame and crime!

Because that is not what I think at all. We have to do here with my own irony. Because of course Kierkegaard was "fair" to

Schlegel. In making a statement to the contrary I am attempting to . . . I might have several purposes—simply being provocative, for example. But mostly I am trying to annihilate Kierkegaard in order to deal with his disapproval.

Q: Of Schlegel?
A: Of me.

Q: What is she doing now?
A: She appears to be—
Q: How does she look?
A: Self-absorbed.
Q: That's not enough. You can't just say, "Self-absorbed." You have to give more . . . You've made a sort of promise which . . .
A:
Q: Are her eyes closed?
A: Her eyes are open. She's staring.
Q: What is she staring at?
A: Nothing that I can see.
Q: And?
A: She's caressing her breasts.
Q: Still wearing the blouse?
A: Yes.
Q: A yellow blouse?
A: Blue.

A: Sunday. We took the baby to Central Park. At the Children's Zoo she wanted to ride a baby Shetland pony which appeared to be about ten minutes old. Howled when told she could not. Then into a meadow (not a real meadow but an excuse for a meadow) for ball-throwing. I slept last night on the couch rather than in the bed. The couch is harder and when I can't sleep I need a harder surface. Dreamed that my father told me that my work was garbage. Mr. Garbage, he called me in the dream. Then, at dawn, the baby woke me again. She had taken off her nightclothes and climbed into a pillowcase. She was standing by the couch in the pillowcase, as if at the starting line of a sack race. When we got back from the park I finished reading the Hitchcock-Truffaut book. In the Hitchcock-Truffaut book there is a passage in which Truffaut comments on *Psycho*. "If I'm not mistaken, out of your fifty works, this is the only film showing . . ." Janet Leigh in a bra. And Hitchcock says: "But the scene would have been more interesting if the girl's bare breasts had been rubbing against the man's chest." *That's true.* H. and S. came for supper. Veal Scaloppine Marsala and very well done, with green noodles and salad. Buckets of vodka before and buckets of brandy after. The brandy depressed me. Some talk about the new artists' tenement being made out of an old warehouse building. H. said, "I hear it's going to be very classy. I hear it's going to have white rats." H. spoke about his former wife and toothbrushes: "She was always at it, fiercely, many hours a day and night." I don't know if this stuff is useful . . .

Q: I'm not your doctor.
A: Pity.

A: But I love my irony.
Q: Does it give you pleasure?
A: A poor . . . A rather unsatisfactory. . . .
Q: The unavoidable tendency of everything particular to emphasize its own particularity.
A: Yes.
Q: You could interest yourself in these interesting machines. They're hard to understand. They're time-consuming.
A: I don't like you.
Q: I sensed it.
A: These imbecile questions . . .
Q: Inadequately answered. . . .
A: . . . imbecile questions leading nowhere . . .
Q: The personal abuse continues.
A: . . . that voice, confident and shrill . . .
Q (aside): He has given away his gaiety, and now has nothing.

Q: But consider the moment when Pasteur, distracted, ashamed, calls upon Mme. Boucicault, widow of the department-store owner. Pasteur stammers, sweats; it is clear that he is there to ask for money, money for his Institute. He becomes more firm, masters himself, speaks with force, yet he is not sure that she knows who he is, that he is Pasteur. "The least contribution," he says finally. "But of course," she (equally embarrassed) replies. She writes a check. He looks at the check. One million francs. They both burst into tears.

A (bitterly): Yes, that makes up for everything, that you know that story. . . .

The Phantom of the Opera's Friend

I HAVE never visited him in his sumptuous quarters five levels below the Opera, across the dark lake.

But he has described them. Rich divans, exquisitely carved tables, amazing silk and satin draperies. The large, superbly embellished mantelpiece, on which rest two curious boxes, one containing the figure of a grasshopper, the other the figure of a scorpion . . .

He can, in discoursing upon his domestic arrangements, become almost merry. For example, speaking of the wine he has stolen from the private cellar of the Opera's Board of Directors:

"A *very* adequate Montrachet! Four bottles! Each director accusing every other director! I tell you, it made me feel like a director myself! As if I were worth two or three millions and had a fat, ugly wife! And the trout was admirable. You know what the Poles say—fish, to taste right, must swim three times: in water, butter, and wine. All in all, a splendid evening!"

But he immediately alters the mood by making some gloomy observation. "Our behavior is mocked by the behavior of dogs."

It is not often that the accents of joy issue from beneath that mask.

Monday. I am standing at the place I sometimes encounter him, a little door at the rear of the Opera (the building has 2,531 doors to which there are 7,593 keys). He always appears "suddenly"—a *coup de théâtre* that is, to tell the truth, more annoying than anything else. We enact a little comedy of surprise.

"It's you!"
"Yes."
"What are you doing here?"
"Waiting."

But today no one appears, although I wait for half an hour. I have wasted my time. Except—

Faintly, through many layers of stone, I hear organ music. The music is attenuated but unmistakable. It is his great work *Don Juan Triumphant*. A communication of a kind.

I rejoice in his immense, buried talent.

But I know that he is not happy.

His situation is simple and terrible. He must decide whether to risk life aboveground or to remain forever in hiding, in the cellars of the Opera.

His tentative, testing explorations in the city (always at night) have not persuaded him to one course or the other. Too, the city is no longer the city he knew as a young man. Its meaning has changed.

At a cafe table, in a place where the light from the streetlamps is broken by a large tree, we sit silently over our drinks.

Everything that can be said has been said many times.

I have no new observations to make. The decision he faces has been tormenting him for decades.

"If after all I—"

But he cannot finish the sentence. We both know what is meant.

I am distracted, a bit angry. How many nights have I spent this way, waiting upon his sighs?

In the early years of our friendship I proposed vigorous measures. A new life! Advances in surgery, I told him, had made a normal existence possible for him. New techniques in—

"I'm too old."

One is never too old, I said. There were still many satisfactions open to him, not the least the possibility of service to others. His music! A home, even marriage and children were not out of the question. What was required was boldness, the will to break out of old patterns . . .

Now as these thoughts flicker through our brains, he smiles ironically.

Sometimes he speaks of Christine:
"That voice!
"But I was perhaps overdazzled by the circumstances . . .
"A range from low C to the F above high C!

"Flawed, of course . . .

"Liszt heard her. '*Que, c'est beau!*' he cried out.

"Possibly somewhat deficient in temperament. But I had temperament enough for two.

"Such goodness! Such gentleness!

"I would pull down the very doors of heaven for a—"

Tuesday. A few slashes of lightning in the sky . . .

Is one man entitled to fix himself at the center of a cosmos of hatred, and remain there?

The acid . . .

The lost love . . .

Yet all of this is generations cold. There have been wars, inventions, assassinations, discoveries . . .

Perhaps *practical affairs* have assumed, in his mind, a towering importance. Does he fear the loss of the stipend (20,000 francs per month) that he has not ceased to extort from the directors of the Opera?

But I have given him assurances. He shall want for nothing.

Occasionally he is overtaken by what can only be called fits of grandiosity:

"*One hundred million cells in the brain! All intent on being the Phantom of the Opera!*"

"*Between three and four thousand human languages! And I am the Phantom of the Opera in every one of them!*"

This is quickly followed by the deepest despair. He sinks into a chair, passes a hand over his mask.

"Forty years of it!"

Why must I have *him* for a friend?

I wanted a friend with whom one could be seen abroad. With whom one could exchange country weekends, on our respective estates!

I put these unworthy reflections behind me . . .

Gaston Leroux was tired of writing *The Phantom of the Opera*. He replaced his pen in its penholder.

"I can always work on *The Phantom of the Opera* later—in the fall, perhaps. Right now I feel like writing *The Secret of the Yellow Room*."

Gaston Leroux took the manuscript of *The Phantom of the Opera* and put it on a shelf in the closet.

Then, seating himself once more at his desk, he drew toward him a clean sheet of foolscap. At the top he wrote the words, *The Secret of the Yellow Room.*

Wednesday. I receive a note urgently requesting a meeting.

"*All men that are ruined are ruined on the side of their natural propensities,*" the note concludes.

This is surely true. Yet the vivacity with which he embraces ruin is unexampled, in my experience.

When we meet he is pacing nervously in an ill-lit corridor just off the room where the tympani are stored.

I notice that his dress, always so immaculate, is disordered, slept-in-looking. A button hangs by a thread from his waistcoat.

"I have brought you a newspaper," I say.

"Thank you. I wanted to tell you . . . that I have made up my mind."

His hands are trembling. I hold my breath.

"I have decided to take your advice. Sixty-five is not after all the end of one's life! I place myself in your hands. Make whatever arrangements you wish. Tomorrow night at this time I quit the Opera forever."

Blind with emotion, I can think of nothing to say.

A firm handclasp, and he is gone.

A room is prepared. I tell my servants that I am anticipating a visitor who will be with us for an indefinite period.

I choose for him a room with a splendid window, a view of the Seine; but I am careful also to have installed heavy velvet curtains, so that the light, with which the room is plentifully supplied, will not come as an assault.

The degree of light *he* wishes.

And when I am satisfied that the accommodations are all that could be desired, I set off to interview the doctor I have selected.

"You understand that the operation, if he consents to it, will have specific . . . psychological consequences?"

I nod.

And he shows me in a book pictures of faces with terrible burns, before and after having been reconstructed by his science. It is indeed an album of magical transformations.

"I would wish first to have him examined by my colleague Dr. W., a qualified alienist."

"This is possible. But I remind you that he has had no intercourse with his fellow men, myself excepted, for—"

"But was it not the case that *originally*, the violent emotions of revenge and jealousy—"

"Yes. But replaced now, I believe, by a melancholy so deep, so all-pervading—"

Dr. Mirabeau assumes a mock-sternness.

"Melancholy, sir, is an ailment with which I have had some slight acquaintance. We shall see if his distemper can resist a little miracle."

And he extends, into the neutral space between us, a shining scalpel.

But when I call for the Phantom on Thursday, at the appointed hour, he is not there.

What vexation!

Am I not slightly relieved?

Can it be that *he doesn't like me*?

I sit down on the kerb, outside the Opera. People passing look at me. I will wait here for a hundred years. Or until the hot meat of romance is cooled by the dull gravy of common sense once more.

Sentence

OR A long sentence moving at a certain pace down the page aiming for the bottom—if not the bottom of this page then of some other page—where it can rest, or stop for a moment to think about the questions raised by its own (temporary) existence, which ends when the page is turned, or the sentence falls out of the mind that holds it (temporarily) in some kind of an embrace, not necessarily an ardent one, but more perhaps the kind of embrace enjoyed (or endured) by a wife who has just waked up and is on her way to the bathroom in the morning to wash her hair, and is bumped into by her husband, who has been lounging at the breakfast table reading the newspaper, and didn't see her coming out of the bedroom, but, when he bumps into her, or is bumped into by her, raises his hands to embrace her lightly, transiently, because he knows that if he gives her a real embrace so early in the morning, before she has properly shaken the dreams out of her head, and got her duds on, she won't respond, and may even become slightly angry, and say something wounding, and so the husband invests in this embrace not so much physical or emotional pressure as he might, because he doesn't want to waste anything—with this sort of feeling, then, the sentence passes through the mind more or less, and there is another way of describing the situation too, which is to say that the sentence crawls through the mind like something someone says to you while you're listening very hard to the FM radio, some rock group there, with its thrilling sound, and so, with your attention or the major part of it at least already awarded, there is not much mind room you can give to the remark, especially considering that you have probably just quarreled with that person, the maker of the remark, over the radio being too loud, or something like that, and the view you take, of the remark, is that you'd really rather not hear it, but if you have to hear it, you want to listen to it for the smallest possible length of time, and during a commercial, because immediately after the commercial they're going to play a new rock song by your favorite group, a cut that has never been aired before, and you want to hear it and respond to it in a new way, a way that accords with whatever you're feeling at the moment, or might feel, if the threat of new experience could be (temporarily) overbalanced by the promise of possible positive benefits, or what the mind construes as such, remembering that these are often, really, disguised defeats (not that such defeats are not, at times, good for your character, teaching you that it is not by success alone that one surmounts life, but that setbacks, too, contribute to that roughening of the personality that, by providing a textured surface to place against that of life, enables you to leave slight traces, or smudges, on the face of human history—your mark) and after all, benefit-seeking always has something of the smell of raw vanity about it, as if you wished to decorate your own brow with laurel, or wear your medals to a cookout, when the invitation had said nothing about them, and although the ego is always hungry (we are told) it is well to remember that ongoing success is nearly as meaningless as ongoing lack of success, which can make you sick, and that it is good to leave a few crumbs on the table for the rest of your brethren, not to sweep it all into the little beaded purse of your soul but to allow others, too, part of the gratification, and if you share in this way you will find the clouds smiling on you, and the postman bringing you letters, and bicycles available when you want to rent them, and many other signs, however guarded and limited, of the community's (temporary) approval of you, or at least of its willingness to let you believe (temporarily) that it finds you not so lacking in commendable virtues as it had previously allowed you to think, from its scorn of your merits, as it might be put, or anyway its consistent refusal to recognize your basic humanness and its secret blackball of the project of your remaining alive, made in executive session by its ruling bodies, which, as everyone knows, carry out concealed programs of reward and punishment, under the rose, causing faint alterations of the status quo, behind your back, at various points along the periphery of community life, together with other enterprises not dissimilar in tone, such as producing films that have special qualities, or attributes, such as a film where the second half of it is a holy mystery, and girls and women are not permitted to see it, or writing novels in which the final chapter is a plastic bag filled with water, which you can touch, but not drink: in this way, or ways, the underground mental life of the collectivity is botched, or denied, or turned into something else never imagined by the planners, who, returning from the latest seminar in crisis management and being asked what they have learned, say they have learned how to throw up their hands; the sentence meanwhile, although not insensible of these considerations, has a festering conscience of its own, which persuades it to follow its star, and to move with all deliberate speed from one place to another, without losing any of the "riders" it may have picked up just by being there, on the page, and turning this way and that, to see what is over there, under that oddly-shaped tree, or over there, reflected in the rain barrel of the imagination, even though it is true that in our young manhood we were taught that short, punchy sentences were best (but what did he mean? doesn't "punchy" mean punch-drunk? I think he probably intended to say "short, *punching* sentences," meaning sentences that lashed out at you, bloodying your brain if possible, and looking up the word just now I came across the nearby "punkah," which is a large fan suspended from the ceiling in India, operated by an attendant pulling a rope—that is what I want for my sentence, to keep it cool!) we are mature enough now to stand the shock of learning that much of what we were taught in our youth was wrong, or improperly understood by those who were teaching it, or perhaps shaded a bit, the shading resulting from the personal needs of the teachers, who as human beings had a tendency to introduce some of their heart's blood into their work, and sometimes this may not have been of the first water, this heart's blood, and even if they thought they were moving the "knowledge" out, as the Board of Education had mandated, they could have noticed that their sentences weren't having the knock down power of the new weapons whose bullets tumble end-over-end (but it is true that we didn't have these weapons at that time) and they might have taken into account the fundamental dubiousness of their project (but all the intelligently conceived projects have been eaten up already, like the moon and the stars) leaving us, in our best clothes, with only things to do like conducting vigorous wars of attrition against our wives, who have now thoroughly come awake, and slipped into their striped bells, and pulled sweaters over their torsi, and adamantly refused to wear any bras under the sweaters, carefully explaining the political significance of this refusal to anyone who will listen, or look, but not touch, because that has nothing to do with it, so they say; leaving us, as it were, with only things to do like floating sheets of Reynolds Wrap around the room, trying to find out how many we can keep in the air at the same time, which at least gives us a sense of participation, as though we were the Buddha, looking down at the mystery of your smile, which needs to be investigated, and I think I'll do that right now, while there's still enough light, if you'll sit down over there, in the best chair, and take off all your clothes, and put your feet in that electric toe caddy (which prevents pneumonia) and slip into this permanent press white hospital gown, to cover your nakedness—why, if you do all that, we'll be ready to begin! after I wash my hands, because you pick up an amazing amount of exuviae in this city, just by walking around in the open air, and nodding to acquaintances, and speaking to friends, and copulating with lovers, in the ordinary course (and death to our enemies! by the by)—but I'm getting a little uptight, just about washing my hands, because I can't find the soap, which somebody has used and not put back in the soap dish, all of which is extremely irritating, if you have a beautiful patient sitting in the examining room, naked inside her gown, and peering at her moles in the mirror, with her immense brown eyes following your every movement (when they are not watching the moles, expecting them, as in a Disney nature film, to exfoliate) and her immense brown head wondering what you're going to do to her, the pierced places in the head letting that question leak out, while the therapist decides just to wash his hands in plain water, and hang the soap! and does so, and then looks around for a towel, but all the towels have been collected by the towel service, and are not there, so he wipes his hands on his pants, in the back (so as to avoid suspicious stains on the front) thinking: what must she think of me? and, all this is very unprofessional and at-sea looking! trying to visualize the contretemps from her point of view, if she has one (but how can she? she is not in the washroom) and then stopping, because it is finally his own point of view that he cares about and not hers, and with this firmly in mind, and a light, confident step, such as you might find in the works of Bulwer-Lytton, he enters the space she occupies so prettily and, taking her by the hand, proceeds to tear off the stiff white hospital gown (but no, we cannot have that kind of pornographic *merde* in this majestic and high-minded sentence, which will probably end up in the Library of Congress) (that was just something that took place inside his consciousness, as he looked at her, and since we know that consciousness is always consciousness *of* something, she is not entirely without responsibility in the matter) so, then, taking her by the hand, he falls into the stupendous white purée of her abyss, no, I mean rather that he asks her how long it has been since her last visit, and she says a fortnight, and he shudders, and tells her that with a condition like hers (she is an immensely popular soldier, and her troops win all their battles by pretending to be forests, the enemy discovering, at the last moment, that those trees they have eaten their lunch under have eyes and swords) (which reminds me of the performance, in 1845, of Robert-Houdin, called *The Fantastic Orange Tree*, wherein Robert-Houdin borrowed a lady's handkerchief, rubbed it between his hands and passed it into the center of an egg, after which he passed the egg into the center of a lemon, after which he passed the lemon into the center of an orange, then pressed the orange between his hands, making it smaller and smaller, until only a powder remained, whereupon he asked for a small potted orange tree and sprinkled the powder thereupon, upon which the tree burst into blossom, the blossoms turning into oranges, the oranges turning into butterflies, and the butterflies turning into beautiful young ladies, who then married members of the audience), a condition so damaging to real-time social intercourse of any kind, the best thing she can do is give up, and lay down her arms, and he will lie down in them, and together they will permit themselves a bit of the old slap and tickle, she wearing only her Mr. Christopher medal, on its silver chain, and he (for such is the latitude granted the professional classes) worrying about the sentence, about its thin wires of dramatic tension, which have been omitted, about whether we should write down some natural events occurring in the sky (birds, lightning bolts), and about a possible coup d'etat within the sentence, whereby its chief verb would be—but at this moment a messenger rushes into the sentence, bleeding from a hat of thorns he's wearing, and cries out: "You don't know what you're doing! Stop making this sentence, and begin instead to make Moholy-Nagy cocktails, for those are what we really need, on the frontiers of bad behavior!" and then he falls to the floor, and a trap door opens under him, and he falls through that, into a damp pit where a blue narwhal waits, its horn poised (but maybe the weight of the messenger, falling from such a height, will break off the horn)—thus, considering everything carefully, in the sweet light of the ceremonial axes, in the run-mad skimble-skamble of information sickness, we must make a decision as to whether we should proceed, or go back, in the latter case enjoying the pathos of eradication, in the former case reading an erotic advertisement which begins, *How to Make Your Mouth a Blowtorch of Excitement* (but wouldn't that overtax our mouthwashes?) attempting, during the pause, while our burned mouths are being smeared with fat, to imagine a better sentence, worthier, more meaningful, like those in the Declaration of Independence, or a bank statement showing that you have seven thousand kroner more than you thought you had—a statement summing up the unreasonable demands that you make on life, and one that also asks the question, if you can imagine these demands, why are they not routinely met, tall fool? but of course it is not that query that this infected sentence has set out to answer (and hello! to our girl friend, Rosetta Stone, who has stuck by us through thin and thin) but some other query that we shall some day discover the nature of, and here comes Ludwig, the expert on sentence construction we have borrowed from the Bauhaus, who will—"Guten Tag, Ludwig!"—probably find a way to cure the sentence's sprawl, by using the improved ways of thinking developed in Weimar— "I am sorry to inform you that the Bauhaus no longer exists, that all of the great masters who formerly thought there are either dead or retired, and that I myself have been reduced to constructing books on how to pass the examination for police sergeant"—and Ludwig falls through the Tugendhat House into the history of man-made objects; a disappointment, to be sure, but it reminds us that the sentence itself is a man-made object, not the one we wanted of course, but still a construction of man, a structure to be treasured for its weakness, as opposed to the strength of stones

Bone Bubbles

bins black and green seventh eighth rehearsal pings a bit fussy at times fair scattering grand and exciting world of his fabrication topple out against surface irregularities fragilization of the gut constitutive misrecognitions of the ego most mature artist then in Regina loops of chain into a box several feet away Hiltons and Ritzes fault-tracing forty whacks active enthusiasm old cell is darker and they use the "Don't Know" category less often than younger people I am glad to be here and intend to do what I can to remain mangle stools tables bases and pedestals without my tree, which gives me rest hot pipe stacked-up cellos spend the semi-private parts of their lives wailing before 1908 had himself photographed with a number of very attractive young girls breasts like ballrooms and orchestras (as in English factories) social eminence Dutch sailors' eyes subsequently destroyed many of these works

distrusted musicians a bending position something I've thought about where their eyes were located cob hidden revolving spotlights slew the eunuch who had done me many kindnesses gourd polished by lips think of a sun-dried photograph tattoo myself attractively because (we) they are part of a process killed our horse free shoes for life at St. Regis established church shaved beards formation of the ego missed one or more regiments of this army, with its commanders forever on the enclosure system for 250,000 people occasions a shuddering blutwurst tentoonstellingsagenda quietly studying his pocket watch dimness and wandering of the eyes pin down the quality immoderate laughter reverie tense bent steel largely greenish limbs streaks of blood leaping motions pudding crawling along horizontally eight-inch wood beads "burlesque" the Mountain girl comes flying to the door points to crowd drink your hair will grow again

strange reactions scattered black satin pulp hitched up her skirts for a look but he forgot to sigh world power ambiguous orders dipstick sweating or beaded with fine, amber colors disabled servant standing in the center of the frame dead tulips convulsions lasting more than three hours arrested for having no ticket hinges of the body so cough spit feel slight pains local or general heat red flags on naval vessels I gave water away married but they can't live together packing the air the soul of the sleeper was enlarged preposterously jabber Bols in five colors gold stars baby girls white-key music praising his skill loading him with protestations of gratitude what was behind their ugly fences? changing the names of certain people against their will theatre machinery posters of the period plans to dub the dialogue common prickers witch finders the girl holds out her hands to the young man but unfortunately over these past few years

hand or wrist man who rushes forward her body the largest element in the composition vegetables with which she refused to dance people embracing or falling bats popular with professional players benefit for working men between the buttocks I have not yet got the clue and points to herself shoal called the Gabble pausing only to defecate in their incomparable lakes hurled abuse behind the stone wall good smooth she falls to the right in pain, holding the Viennese master tightly partial relief conspiring priests a pill made of bread let's all go down to the plaza partly with his hands discharged a shower of arrows trying to find the opening cries when taken to a museum sane love invitation of the national committee white, gray or purple ballet the jury nods triumphant contemporaries engineering decisions plump ladycow waiting in the car superb perfs from odd recruited volunteers floor redefined as bed

double dekko balcony of a government building series of close-ups of the food gold thread long thin room pamper recent connection steroid perverse cults which have all but replaced Christianity ten filthiest cases men and women with strong convictions lottery breakdown fat arenas that seat a million people young Etruscans had little to say flaps (may be gelded nanny in the original) great plash shining milk at that moment I was perfectly happy puffed and nimble big muscles national friendship social entities bad sketches wonder woman skirt worn-out debauchees who had drained the cup of sensuality to its dregs we know their names creeper bigger than the one the telephone company killed pastures for the expiring cattle this famous charlatan Miko fading back into the vast practice, or method after image other examples could be substituted for the examples which they give us happily the people dance about

shoots Pierre pieces of literature genuine love stumps cantering toward the fine morning half-zip theme of his own choosing ramp shotgun illuminations informal arrangements botulism theories of design raving first sketches thought to be unsatisfactory geological accidents and return ant bulb lacing shoe brave though circumcised crawled all over the dingbat howling inadequate paper hard squeeze long series of closeups authors of the period wet leg breakfast dip snacks and banquets believing he was a child greatness of Finnish achievement 10/150 simple news elaborated sorrow gentle roll of ships Tillie gasped laughing and swayed and August was terrible consented to smear the doors and houses of Milan with a pestiferous salve daughter green ladies looking out of the picture plane forced feeding then responsible technicians hanging garbage unreasonable ideas more to do our views remain substantially the same today

then I went to a wedding and when it was my turn to kick the bride kicked her with commercial photographers snails keep our garden private Bittermarka now sitting in the airplane hearing a lot of tape trouser and skirt racks undone Europeans don't bother dried Bibb exchange of interests primary moves accompanied by a lion raw November in the black series extra simultaneous decisions big drum bleeding of the nose royal and ancient good-humored areas Elephanta how large the statues and ruins are! married the barber Lamb of God gouty subjects forgot their pains red and blue paper ice Bernard with a hive of bees virile the train scraped some people onto the tracks intact sections of streets *bozzetti* shaped his work livingrooms of subsequent civilizations specific borrowings leer snug cover bucks and does having held high federal office split raising and lowering of her skirt like an elevator hairy children made a ballad on the incident yellow faces let's slip over to the foot of that tree to avoid getting crushed future of English drama water bomb checkered lilies expensive thrill magazine whispered results a pleasant walk on this surface blowhole boxes of green ladies blackguardism presses handkerchief to mouth I found your name in a book commercial undertakings news and weather bruised or cut document party zone explosions below the line they had a hard time in Italy convinced that he had seen something remarkable modelled its radiator on the Parthenon cringes diddled statistics bloc voting if there were no such affinity between atoms it would be impossible for love to appear "higher up" hobbies sitting on some lumber protest against what they thought wrong sick whips of the baby on his left shoulder half-forgotten events far-fetched positions drift of error cloth cap or biretta figuratively speaking trembling we never forget anything

weeping map intense activity din it would be better if we just piled all the stones on the floor crumpled paper wheels out of alignment prints rescued from the inferno beggars writing my article streaked with raisins kept putting things into his mouth foxing pages divided hearts something stuck in the gum a humanizing influence ichor didn't they tell you list of objects which have their own saucy life remedy sighted bats reflection of light from garbage cans spirit of the army wispy and diffuse King Lud giving the dog a bad name various itches I thought of firing in the air invisible armatures for piles of felt record of irregularities in a white trench coat aesthetic experience bleeding nails Moscow rehearsals torn and then pasted together in long strips but these have never been very successful black ball Clichy junks crowded with long purplish tubers yanked up from the ground in my black suit, my colored tie

halfway houses naval jelly four Italian architects said shrewd things about her mother lines drawn around the page many-colored oysters flush cameramen senses a desire for change large sheets of flat glass great disputations that he had lately held against all comers gunboat enterprise fatal laxity elegant sawhorses red snout mothering blur from the Sorbonne state ceremonies quaking hare but a glance at the bathtub discouraged her free cookbooks ancient deposits the humiliation of the wedding tiny hero so boring that he couldn't finish it and I am with you! three or more immense sponges by the petrol pump pink chiffon spikes interpenetrating diamonds enormous weather-like forces no relief smear tangle of solutions without problems enemies of vision discussions of the good life (mostly blacks and Puerto Ricans) somber triumph presents a picture of fingertip sensuality borrowed money no aperture had been provided

free offer last gesture smooth man of position purely cinematic vice slap and tickle zippered wallpaper two beautiful heavy books, boxed hears noise goes to window 220 treasures from 11 centuries fixer great and stupefying *Ring* minimum of three if it hadn't been for Y. I would never have gotten my lump local white Democrats gospel seven camera tilts to the balconies filled with joyous people young maidens tape after his brain is formed keep your checks in a safe place modern research sank to her knees on 35 mm color slides thermal machines from a chemical company in Pittsburgh handsome pelt illuminates the entire fluxus at one stroke body shirt spends all his time at the console wrong discard with the most careful and well-considered utilization of all my powers doll houses fastened to the wall photo face blade the world enigmatized skat will pull away the carpet age big tiger these conditions reverse themselves

childish memories of climbing up parents or nurses hollow objects sexual activity doleful cries critical moments abstract wit barges logical façades limping brides young dramatists acquainted with the sleeper plastic light first German edition speech blunder knobkerry imagined that the body was walking through fire during the cotton crisis complained of being misunderstood by the other banged belly duties toward women military service punishment for economic reasons rut prepared regularly two bottles, a blue one and a white one the doctor and his instrument bulbous summit representatives shouting theory golden calf special precautions and I cannot resist citing zeal in the cause against abuses wherever he found them classic critic masculine hysteria attacked by Goethe unsalted caviar member of my household anal opening which is the duke? which is the horse? which? we sat down and wept poet's slurs extra rations business on 96th Street blueprints of uncompleted projects drunk and naked too malphony down at the old boathouse dark little birds astonishing propositions drummed out of the circle I'll insult him Scotch student rags and bones sunspots spoiled the hash keen satisfaction honors and gifts fit to burst the blue the white hoarse glee caught her knee in her hands with a click tonic night favorite wine well-known bumbler look at his head the bomb is here gulls twins rinse the seven of them appealing tot of rum she rises looks at him mysteriously fades into the closet fades out of the closet again double meaning arms tighten weak with relief silence throwing down the letters her wedding hat lackey slakes thirst nervously puts mask to face back door of the morgue new raincoat and draws away laughing bit of dogfish seated on a green stone bench baked this meat loaf

bad language mutilated Miss Rice I was sorry black coat with longish skirtlike Maxwell's initiative failed the narrator's position is clear province of religion falling wine barrels tapped or bugged clattering intensely human document wedding in the long border that stretched from the Horse Guards' barracks to women in slacks addressed envelopes I wanted to tell you something pages perforated for easy song removal challengingly real issues in gerontology there is but one moment in which the beautiful human being is beautiful cut flowers in rows and rows women reformers watching from balconies gentle way with materials awarded a medal office visit monkey's parade my ignorance which I do not wish to disguise blue pants she turns, smiling bitterly in her tin beard aren't you being overly emotional about it? discovering reasons hungry actors scars upon the trunk or face of the sculpture the decisions of 1848

love tap the glass is one and three-sixteenth inches thick laminated with plastic top stop a bullet from almost any sidearm indifferent office cleaners smudge views of the acrobat ordered the girl to get up and dress herself dream of the dandy leaves and their veins modern soft skin a car drives up a policeman jumps out tinkling sackcloth provocative back controlled nausea whimpering forms pardonable in that they trump irresistible to any faithful mind hybrid tissue zut powerful story of a half-naked girl caught between two emotions two wavy sheets of steel food towers in Turin a collection of dirks who is that very sick man? age-old eating habits crowd celebrating the matter with him is that he is crazy Paul and Barnabas preaching a bunch of extras going by sketch and final version automatic pump salad holder taking the French shoe tired lines to be taken literally no sexual relations with them

On Angels

THE DEATH of God left the angels in a strange position. They were overtaken suddenly by a fundamental question. One can attempt to imagine the moment. How did they *look* at the instant the question invaded them, flooding the angelic consciousness, taking hold with terrifying force? The question was, "What are angels?"

New to questioning, unaccustomed to terror, unskilled in aloneness, the angels (we assume) fell into despair.

The question of what angels "are" has a considerable history. Swedenborg, for example, talked to a great many angels and faithfully recorded what they told him. Angels look like human beings, Swedenborg says. "That angels are human forms, or men, has been seen by me a thousand times." And again: "From all of my experience, which is now of many years, I am able to state that angels are wholly men in form, having faces, eyes, ears, bodies, arms, hands, and feet . . ." But a man cannot see angels with his bodily eyes, only with the eyes of the spirit.

Swedenborg has a great deal more to say about angels, all of the highest interest: that no angel is ever permitted to stand behind another and look at the back of his head, for this would disturb the influx of good and truth from the Lord; that angels have the east, where the Lord is seen as a sun, always before their eyes; and that angels are clothed according to their intelligence. "Some of the most intelligent have garments that blaze as if with flame, others have garments that glisten as if with light; the less intelligent have garments that are glistening white or white without the effulgence; and the still less intelligent have garments of various colors. But the angels of the inmost heaven are not clothed."

All of this (presumably) no longer obtains.

Gustav Davidson, in his useful *Dictionary of Angels*, has brought together much of what is known about them. Their names are called: the angel Elubatel, the angel Friagne, the angel Gaap, the angel Hatiphas (genius of finery), the angel

Murmur (a fallen angel), the angel Mqttro, the angel Or, the angel Rash, the angel Sandalphon (taller than a five hundred years' journey on foot), the angel Smat. Davidson distinguishes categories: Angels of Quaking, who surround the heavenly throne; Masters of Howling and Lords of Shouting, whose work is praise; messengers, mediators, watchers, warners. Davidson's *Dictionary* is a very large book; his bibliography lists more than eleven hundred items.

The former angelic consciousness has been most beautifully described by Joseph Lyons (in a paper titled *The Psychology of Angels*, published in 1957). Each angel, Lyons says, knows all that there is to know about himself and every other angel. "No angel could ever ask a question, because questioning proceeds out of a situation of not knowing, and of being in some way aware of not knowing. An angel cannot be curious; he has nothing to be curious about. He cannot wonder. Knowing all that there is to know, the world of possible knowledge must appear to him as an ordered set of facts which is completely behind him, completely fixed and certain and within his grasp . . ."

But this, too, no longer obtains.

It is a curiosity of writing about angels that, very often, one turns out to be writing about men. The themes are twinned. Thus one finally learns that Lyons, for example, is really writing not about angels but about schizophrenics—thinking about men by invoking angels. And this holds true of much other writing on the subject—a point, we may assume, that was not lost on the angels when they began considering their new relation to the cosmos, when the analogues (is an angel more like a quetzal or more like a man? or more like music?) were being handed about.

We may further assume that some attempt was made at self-definition by function. An angel is what he does. Thus it was necessary to investigate possible new roles (you are reminded that this is impure speculation). After the lamentation had gone on for hundreds and hundreds of whatever the angels use for time, an angel proposed that lamentation be the function of angels eternally, as adoration was formerly. The mode of lamentation would be silence, in contrast to the unceasing chanting of Glorias that had been their former employment. But it is not in the nature of angels to be silent.

A counter-proposal was that the angels affirm chaos. There were to be five great proofs of the existence of chaos, of which the first was the absence of God. The other four could surely be located. The work of definition and explication could, if done nicely enough, occupy the angels forever, as the contrary work has occupied human theologians. But there is not much enthusiasm for chaos among the angels.

The most serious because most radical proposal considered by the angels was refusal—that they would remove themselves from being, not be. The tremendous dignity that would accrue to the angels by this act was felt to be a manifestation of spiritual pride. Refusal was refused.

There were other suggestions, more subtle and complicated, less so, none overwhelmingly attractive.

I saw a famous angel on television; his garments glistened as if with light. He talked about the situation of angels now. Angels, he said, are like men *in some ways*. The problem of adoration is felt to be central. He said that for a time the angels had tried adoring each other, as we do, but had found it, finally, "not enough." He said they are continuing to search for a new principle.

Brain Damage

In the first garbage dump I found a book describing a rich new life of achievement, prosperity, and happiness. A rich new life of achievement, prosperity, and happiness could not be achieved alone, the book said. It must be achieved with the aid of spirit teachers. *At long last a way had been found to reach the spirit world. Once the secret was learned, spirit teachers would assist you through the amazing phenomenon known as ESP. My spirit teachers wanted to help me, the book said. As soon as I contacted them, they would do everything in their power to grant my desires. An example, on page 117: A middle-aged woman was being robbed, but as the thief was taking her purse, a flash of blue light like a tiny lightning bolt knocked his gun out of his hands and he fled in terror. That was just the beginning, the book said. One could learn how to eliminate hostility from the hearts of others.*

We thought about the blue flowers. Different people had different ideas about them. Henry wanted to "turn them on." We brought wires and plugs and a screwdriver, and wired the green ends of the flowers (the bottom part, where they had been cut) to the electrical wire. We were sort of afraid to plug them in, though— afraid of all that electricity pushing its way up the green stalks of the flowers, flooding the leaves, and finally touching the petals, the blue part, where the blueness of the flowers resided, along with white, and a little yellow. "What kind of current is this, that we are possibly going to plug the flowers into?" Gregory asked. It seemed to be alternating current rather than direct current. That was what we all thought, because most of the houses in this part of the country were built in compliance with building codes that required AC. In fact, you don't find much DC around any more, because in the early days of electricity, many people were killed by it.

   "Well, plug them in," Grace said. Because she wanted to see the flowers light up, or collapse, or do whatever they were going to do, when they were plugged in.

The humanist position is not to plug in the flowers—to let them alone. Humanists believe in letting everything alone to be what it is, insofar as possible. The new electric awareness, however, requires that the flowers be plugged in, right away. Toynbee's notions of challenge and response are also, perhaps, apposite. My own idea about whether or not to plug in the flowers is somewhere between these ideas, in that gray area where nothing is done, really, but you vacillate for a while, thinking about it. The blue of the flowers is extremely handsome against the gray of that area.

CROWD NOISES
MURMURING
MURMURING
YAWNING

A great waiter died, and all of the other waiters were saddened. At the restaurant, sadness was expressed. Black napkins were draped over black arms. Black tablecloths were distributed. Several nearby streets were painted black—those leading to the establishment in which Guignol had placed his plates with legendary tact. Guignol's medals (for like a great beer he had been decorated many times, at international exhibitions in Paris, Brussels, Rio de Janeiro) were turned over to his mistress, La Lupe. The body was poached in white wine, stock, olive oil, vinegar, aromatic vegetables, herbs, garlic, and slices of lemon for twenty-four hours and displayed en Aspic *on a bed of lettuce leaves. Hundreds of famous triflers appeared to pay their last respects. Guignol's colleagues recalled with pleasure the master's most notable eccentricity. Having coolly persuaded some innocent to select a thirty-dollar bottle of wine, he never failed to lean forward conspiratorially and whisper in his victim's ear, "Cuts the grease."*

RETCHING
FAINTING
DISMAL BEHAVIOR
TENDERING OF EXCUSES

A dream: I am looking at a ship, an ocean-going vessel the size of the Michelangelo. But unlike the Michelangelo this ship is not painted a dazzling white; it is caked with rust. And it is not in the water. The whole immense bulk of it sits on dry land. Furthermore it is loaded with high explosives which may go off at any moment. My task is to push the ship through a narrow mountain pass whose cliffs rush forward threateningly. An experience: I was crossing the street in the rain holding an umbrella. On the other side of the street an older woman was motioning to me. Come here, come here! I indicated that I didn't want to come there, wasn't interested, had other things to do. But she continued to make motions, to insist. Finally I went over to her. "Look down there," she said pointing to the gutter full of water, "there's a penny. Don't you want to pick it up?"

I worked for newspapers. I worked for newspapers at a time when I was not competent to do so. I reported inaccurately. I failed to get all the facts. I misspelled names. I garbled figures. I wasted copy paper. I pretended I knew things I did not know. I pretended to understand things beyond my understanding. I oversimplified. I was superior to things I was inferior to. I misinterpreted things that took place before me. I over- and underinterpreted what took place before me. I suppressed news the management wanted suppressed. I invented news the management wanted invented. I faked stories. I failed to discover the truth. I colored the truth with fancy. I had no respect for the truth. I failed to heed the adage, you shall know the truth and the truth shall make you free. I put

lies in the paper. I put private jokes in the paper. I wrote headlines containing double entendres. I wrote stories while drunk. I abused copy boys. I curried favor with advertisers. I accepted gifts from interested parties. I was servile with superiors. I was harsh with people who called on the telephone seeking information. I gloated over police photographs of sex crimes. I touched type when the makeups weren't looking. I took copy pencils home. I voted with management in Guild elections.

RHYTHMIC HANDCLAPPING
SLEEPING
WHAT RECOURSE?

The Wapituil are like us to an extraordinary degree. They have a kinship system which is very similar to our kinship system. They address each other as "Mister," "Mistress," and "Miss." They wear clothes which look very much like our clothes. They have a Fifth Avenue which divides their territory into east and west. They have a Chock Full o' Nuts and a Chevrolet, one of each. They have a Museum of Modern Art and a telephone and a Martini, one of each. The Martini and the telephone are kept in the Museum of Modern Art. In fact they have everything that we have, but only one of each thing.

We found that they lose interest very quickly. For instance they are fully industrialized, but they don't seem interested in taking advantage of it. After the steel mill produced the ingot, it was shut down. They can conceptualize but they don't follow through. For instance, their week has seven days—Monday, Monday, Monday, Monday, Monday, Monday, and Monday. They have one disease, mononucleosis. The sex life of a Wapituil consists of a single experience, which he thinks about for a long time.

WRITHING
HOWLING
MOANS
WHAT RECOURSE?
RHYTHMIC HANDCLAPPING
SHOUTING
SEXUAL ACTIVITY
CONSUMPTION OF FOOD

Behavior of the waiters: The first waiter gave a twenty-cent tip to the second waiter. The second waiter looked down at the two dimes in his hand and then up at the first waiter. Looks of disgust were exchanged. The third waiter put a dollar bill on a plate and handed it to the fourth waiter. The fourth waiter took the dollar bill and stuffed it into his pocket. Then the fourth waiter took six quarters from another pocket and made a neat little stack of quarters next to the elbow of the fifth waiter, who was sitting at a rear table, writing on a little pad. The fifth waiter gave the captain a five-dollar bill which the captain slipped into a pocket in the tail of his tailcoat. The sixth waiter handed the seventh waiter a small envelope containing two ten-dollar bills. The seventh waiter put a small leather bag containing twelve louis d'or into the bosom of the wife of the eighth waiter. The ninth waiter offered a $50 War Bond to the tenth waiter, who was carrying a crystal casket of carbuncles to the chef.

The cup fell from nerveless fingers . . .
   The china cup big as an AFB fell from tiny white nerveless fingers no bigger than hairs . . .

"Sit down. I am your spiritual adviser. Sit down and have a cup of tea with me. See, there is the chair. There is the cup. The tea boy will bring the tea shortly. When the tea boy brings the tea, you may pour some of it into your cup. That cup there, on the table."

"Thank you. This is quite a nice University you have here. A University constructed entirely of three mile-high sponges!"

"Yes it is rather remarkable."

"What is that very large body with hundreds and hundreds of legs moving across the horizon from left to right in a steady, carefully considered line?"

"That is the tenured faculty crossing to the other shore on the plane of the feasible."

"And this tentacle here of the Underwater Life Sciences Department . . ."

"That is not a tentacle but the Department itself. Devouring a whole cooked chicken furnished by the Department of Romantic Poultry."

"And those running men?"

"Those are the runners."

"What are they running from?"

"They're not running from, they're running toward. Trained in the Department of Great Expectations."

"Is that my Department?"

"Do you blush easily?"

The elevator girls were standing very close together. One girl put a candy bar into another girl's mouth and then another girl put a hamburger into another girl's mouth. Another girl put a Kodak Instamatic camera to her eye and took a picture of another girl and another girl patted another girl on the shapely caudal area. Giant aircraft passed in the sky, their passengers bent over with their heads between their knees, in pillows. The Mother Superior spoke. "No, dear friend, it cannot be. It is not that we don't believe that your renunciation of the world is real. We believe it is real. But you look like the kind who is overly susceptible to Nun's Melancholy, which is one of our big problems here. Therefore full membership is impossible. We will send the monks to you, at the end. The monks sing well, too. We will send the monks to you, for your final agony." I turned away. This wasn't what I wanted to hear. I went out into the garage and told Bill an interesting story which wasn't true. Some people feel you should tell the truth, but those people are impious and wrong, and if you listen to what they say, you will be tragically unhappy all your life.

TO WHAT END?
IN WHOSE NAME?
WHAT RECOURSE?

Oh there's brain damage in the east, and brain damage in the west, and upstairs there's brain damage, and downstairs there's brain damage, and in my lady's parlor—brain damage. Brain damage is widespread. Apollinaire was a victim of brain damage—you remember the photograph, the bandage on his head, and the poems . . . Bonnie and Clyde suffered from brain damage in the last four minutes of the picture. There's brain damage on the horizon, a great big blubbery cloud of it coming this way—

And you can hide under the bed but brain damage is under the bed, and you can hide in the universities but they are the very seat and soul of brain damage— Brain damage caused by bears who put your head in their foaming jaws while you are singing "Masters of War" . . . Brain damage caused by the sleeping revolution which no one can wake up . . . Brain damage caused by art. I could describe it better if I weren't afflicted with it . . .

This is the country of brain damage, this is the map of brain damage, these are the rivers of brain damage, and see, those lighted-up places are the airports of brain damage, where the damaged pilots land the big, damaged ships.

The Immaculate Conception triggered a lot of brain damage at one time, but no longer does so. A team of Lippizaners has just published an autobiography. Is that any reason to accuse them of you-know-what? And I saw a girl walking down the street, she was singing "Me and My Winstons," and I began singing it too, and that protected us, for a moment, from the terrible thing that might have happened . . .

And there is brain damage in Arizona, and brain damage in Maine, and little towns in Idaho are in the grip of it, and my blue heaven is black with it, brain damage covering everything like an unbreakable lease—

Skiing along on the soft surface of brain damage, never to sink, because we don't understand the danger—

City Life

ELSA AND Ramona entered the complicated city. They found an apartment without much trouble, several rooms on Porter Street. Curtains were hung. Bright paper things from a Japanese store were placed here and there.

—You'd better tell Charles that he can't come see us until everything is ready.

Ramona thought: I don't want him to come at all. He will go into a room with Elsa and close the door. I will be sitting outside reading the business news. Britain Weighs Economic Curbs. Bond Rate Surge Looms. Time will pass. Then, they will emerge. Acting as if nothing had happened. Elsa will make coffee. Charles will put brandy from his flat silver flask into the coffee. We will all drink the coffee with the brandy in it. Ugh!

—Where shall we put the telephone books?

—Put them over there, by the telephone.

Elsa and Ramona went to the $2 plant store. A man stood outside selling individual peacock feathers. Elsa and Ramona bought several hanging plants in white plastic pots. The proprietor put the plants in brown paper bags.

—Water them every day, girls. Keep them wet.

—We will.

Elsa uttered a melancholy reflection on life: It goes faster and faster! Ramona said: It's so difficult!

Charles accepted a position with greater responsibilities in another city.

—I'll be able to get in on weekends sometimes.

—Is this a real job?

—Of course, Elsa. You don't think I'd fool you, do you?

Clad in an extremely dark gray, if not completely black, suit, he had shaved his mustache.

—This outfit doesn't let you wear them.

Ramona heard Elsa sobbing in the back bedroom. I suppose I should sympathize with her. But I don't.

2.

Ramona received the following letter from Charles:

Dear Ramona—

Thank you, Ramona, for your interesting and curious letter. It is true that I have noticed you sitting there, in the living room, when I visit Elsa. I have many times made mental notes about your appearance, which I consider in no way inferior to that of Elsa herself. I get a pretty electric reaction to your taste in clothes, too. Those upper legs have not been lost on me. But the trouble is, when two girls are living together, one must make a choice. One can't have them both, in our society. This prohibition is enforced by you girls, chiefly, together with older ladies, who if the truth were known probably don't care, but nevertheless feel that standards must be upheld, somewhere. I have Elsa, therefore I can't have you. (I know that there is a philosophical problem about "being" and "having" but I can't discuss that now because I'm a little rushed due to the pressures of my new assignment.) So that's what obtains at the moment, most excellent Ramona. That's where we stand. Of course the future may be different. It not infrequently is.

Hastily,
Charles.

—What are you reading?
—Oh, it's just a letter.
—Who is it from?
—Oh, just somebody I know.
—Who?
—Oh, nobody.
—Oh.

Ramona's mother and father came to town from Montana. Ramona's thin father stood on the Porter Street sidewalk wearing a business suit and a white cowboy hat. He was watching his car. He watched from the steps of the house for a while, and then watched from the sidewalk a little, and then watched from the steps again. Ramona's mother looked in the suitcases for the present she had brought.

—Mother! You shouldn't have brought me such an expensive present!

—Oh, it wasn't all that expensive. We wanted you to have something for the new apartment.

—An original gravure by René Magritte!

—Well, it isn't very big. It's just a small one.

Whenever Ramona received a letter forwarded to her from her Montana home, the letter had been opened and the words "Oops! Opened by mistake!" written on the envelope. But she forgot that in gazing at the handsome new Magritte print, a picture of a tree with a crescent moon cut out of it.

—It's fantastically beautiful! Where shall we hang it?

—How about on the wall?

3.

At the University the two girls enrolled in the Law School.

—I hear the Law School's tough, Elsa stated, but that's what we want, a tough challenge.

—You are the only two girls ever to be admitted to our Law School, the Dean observed. Mostly, we have men. A few foreigners. Now I am going to tell you three things to keep an eye on: 1) Don't try to go too far too fast. 2) Wear plain clothes. And 3) Keep your notes clean. And if I hear the words "Yoo hoo" echoing across the quadrangle, you will be sent down instantly. We don't use those words in this school.

—I like what I already know, Ramona said under her breath.

Savoring their matriculation, the two girls wandered out to sample the joys of Pascin Street. They were closer together at this time than they had ever been. Of course, they didn't want to get too close together. They were afraid to get too close together.

Elsa met Jacques. He was deeply involved in the struggle.

—What is this struggle about, exactly, Jacques?

—My God, Elsa, your eyes! I have never seen that shade of umber in anyone's eyes before. Ever.

Jacques took Elsa to a Mexican restaurant. Elsa cut into her *cabrito con queso*.

—To think that this food was once a baby goat!

Elsa, Ramona, and Jacques looked at the dawn coming up over the hanging plants. Patterns of silver light and so forth.

—You're not afraid that Charles will bust in here unexpectedly and find us?

—Charles is in Cleveland. Besides, I'd say you were with Ramona. Elsa giggled.

Ramona burst into tears.

Elsa and Jacques tried to comfort Ramona.

—Why don't you take a 21-day excursion-fare trip to "preserves of nature"?

—If I went to a "preserve of nature," it would turn out to be nothing but a terrible fen!

Ramona thought: He will go into a room with Elsa and close the door. Time will pass. Then they will emerge, acting as if nothing had happened. Then the coffee. Ugh!

4.

Charles in Cleveland.

"Whiteness"

"Vital skepticism"

Charles advanced very rapidly in the Cleveland hierarchy. That sort of situation that develops sometimes wherein managers feel threatened by gifted subordinates and do not assign them really meaningful duties but instead shunt them aside into dead areas where their human potential is wasted did not develop in Charles' case. His devoted heart lifted him to the highest levels. It was Charles who pointed out that certain operations had been carried out more efficiently "when the cathedrals were white," and in time the entire Cleveland structure was organized around his notions: "whiteness," "vital skepticism."

Two men held Charles down on the floor and a third slipped a needle into his hip.

He awakened in a vaguely familiar room.

—Where am I? he asked the nurselike person who appeared to answer his ring.

—Porter Street, this creature said. Mlle. Ramona will see you shortly. In the meantime, drink some of this orange juice.

Well, Charles thought to himself, I cannot but admire the guts and address of this brave girl, who wanted me so much that she engineered this whole affair—my abduction from Cleveland and removal to these beloved rooms, where once

I was entertained by the beautiful Elsa. And now I must see whether my key concepts can get me out of this "fix," for "fix" it is. I shouldn't have written that letter. Perhaps if I wrote another letter? A followup?

Charles formed the letter to Ramona in his mind.

Dear Ramona—

Now that I am back in your house, tied down to this bed with these steel bands around my ankles, I understand that perhaps my earlier letter to you was subject to misinterpretation etc. etc.

Elsa entered the room and saw Charles tied down on the bed.

—That's against the law!

—Sit down, Elsa. Just because you are a law student you want to proclaim the rule of law everywhere. But some things don't have to do with the law. Some things have to do with the heart. The heart, which was our great emblem and cockade, when the cathedrals were white.

—I'm worried about Ramona, Elsa said. She has been missing lectures. And she has been engaging in hilarity at the expense of the law.

—Jokes?

—Gibes. And now this extra-legality. Your sequestration.

Charles and Elsa looked out of the window at the good day.

—See that blue in the sky. How wonderful. After all the gray we've had.

5.

Elsa and Ramona watched the Motorola television set in their pajamas.

—What else is on? Elsa asked.

Ramona looked in the newspaper.

—On 7 there's "Johnny Allegro" with George Raft and Nina Foch. On 9 "Johnny Angel" with George Raft and Claire Trevor. On 11 there's "Johnny Apollo" with Tyrone Power and Dorothy Lamour. On 13 is "Johnny Concho" with Frank Sinatra and Phyllis Kirk. On 2 is "Johnny Dark" with Tony Curtis and Piper Laurie. On 4 is "Johnny Eager" with Robert Taylor and Lana Turner. On 5 is "Johnny O'Clock" with Dick Powell and Evelyn Keyes. On 31 is "Johnny Trouble" with Stuart Whitman and Ethel Barrymore.

—What's this one we're watching?
—What time is it?
—Eleven-thirty-five.
—"Johnny Guitar" with Joan Crawford and Sterling Hayden.

6.

Jacques, Elsa, Charles and Ramona sat in a row at the sun dance. Jacques was sitting next to Elsa and Charles was sitting next to Ramona. Of course Charles was also sitting next to Elsa but he was leaning toward Ramona mostly. It was hard to tell what his intentions were. He kept his hands in his pockets.

—How is the struggle coming, Jacques?
—Quite well, actually. Since the Declaration of Rye we have accumulated many hundreds of new members.

Elsa leaned across Charles to say something to Ramona.

—Did you water the plants?

The sun dancers were beating the ground with sheaves of wheat.

—Is that supposed to make the sun shine, or what? Ramona asked.
—Oh, I think it's just sort of to . . . honor the sun. I don't think it's supposed to make it do anything.

Elsa stood up.

—That's against the law!
—Sit down, Elsa.

Elsa became pregnant.

7.

"This young man, a man though only eighteen . . ."
A large wedding scene
Charles measures the church
Elsa and Jacques bombarded with flowers
Fathers and mothers riding on the city railway
The minister raises his hands
Evacuation of the sacristy: bomb threat
Black limousines with ribbons tied to their aerials

Several men on balconies who appear to be signalling, or applauding
Traffic lights
Pieces of blue cake
Champagne

8.

—Well, Ramona. I am glad we came to the city. In spite of everything.

—Yes, Elsa, it has turned out well for you. You are Mrs. Jacques Tope now. And soon there will be a little one.

—Not so soon. Not for eight months. I am sorry, though, about one thing. I hate to give up Law School.

—Don't be sorry. The Law needs knowledgeable civilians as well as practitioners. Your training will not be wasted.

—That's dear of you. Well, goodbye.

Elsa and Jacques and Charles went into the back bedroom. Ramona remained outside with the newspaper.

—Well, I suppose I might as well put the coffee on, she said to herself. Rats!

9.

Laughing aristocrats moved up and down the corridors of the city.

Elsa, Jacques, Ramona and Charles drove out to the combined race track and art gallery. Ramona had a Heineken and everyone else had one too. The tables were crowded with laughing aristocrats. More laughing aristocrats arrived in their carriages drawn by dancing matched pairs. Some drifted in from Flushing and São Paulo. Management of the funded indebtedness was discussed; the Queen's behavior was discussed. All of the horses ran very well, and the pictures ran well too. The laughing aristocrats sucked on the heads of their gold-headed canes some more.

Jacques held up his degrees from the New Yorker Theatre, where he had been buried in the classics, when he was twelve.

—I remember the glorious debris underneath the seats, he said, and I remember that I hated then, as I do now, laughing aristocrats.

The aristocrats heard Jacques talking. They all raised their canes in the air, in rage. A hundred canes shattered in the sun, like a load of antihistamines falling out of an airplane. More laughing aristocrats arrived in phaetons and tumbrels.

As a result of absenting himself from Cleveland for eight months, Charles had lost his position there.

—It is true that I am part of the laughing-aristocrat structure, Charles said. I don't mean I am one of them. I mean I am their creature. They hold me in thrall.

Laughing aristocrats who invented the cost-plus contract . . .

Laughing aristocrats who invented the real estate broker . . .

Laughing aristocrats who invented Formica . . .

Laughing aristocrats wiping their surfaces clean with a damp cloth . . .

Charles poured himself another brilliant green Heineken.

—To the struggle!

10.

The Puerto Rican painters have come, as they do every three years, to paint the apartment!

The painters, Emmanuel and Curtis, heaved their buckets, rollers, ladders and drop cloths up the stairs into the apartment.

—What shade of white do you want this apartment painted?

A consultation.

—How about plain white?

—Fine, Emmanuel said. That's a mighty good-looking Motorola television set you have there. Would you turn it to Channel 47, *por favor*? There's a film we'd like to see. We can paint and watch at the same time.

—What's the film?

—"Victimas de Pecado," with Pedro Vargas and Ninon Sevilla.

Elsa spoke to her husband, Jacques.

—Ramona has frightened me.

—How?

—She said one couldn't sleep with someone more than four hundred times without being bored.

—How does she know?

—She saw it in a book.

—Well, Jacques said, we only do what we really want to do about 11 per cent of the time. In our lives.

—11 per cent!

At the Ingres Gardens, the great singer Moonbelly sang a song of rage.

11.

Vercingetorix, leader of the firemen, reached for his red telephone.

—Hello, is this Ramona?

—No, this is Elsa. Ramona's not home.

—Will you tell her that the leader of all the firemen called?

Ramona went out of town for a weekend with Vercingetorix. They went to his farm, about eighty miles away. In the kitchen of the farm, bats attacked them. Vercingetorix could not find his broom.

—Put a paper bag over them. Where is a paper bag?

—The groceries, Vercingetorix said.

Ramona dumped the groceries on the floor. The bats were zooming around the room uttering audible squeaks. With the large paper bag in his hands Vercingetorix made weak capturing gestures toward the bats.

—God, if one gets in my hair, Ramona said.

—They don't want to fly into the bag, Vercingetorix said.

—Give me the bag, if one gets in my hair I'll croak right here in front of you.

Ramona put the paper bag over her head just as a bat banged into her.

—What was that?

—A bat, Vercingetorix said, but it didn't get into your hair.

—Damn you, Ramona said, inside the bag, why can't you stay in the city like other men?

Moonbelly emerged from the bushes and covered her arms with kisses.

12.

Jacques persuaded Moonbelly to appear at a benefit for the signers of the Declaration of Rye, who were having a little legal trouble. Three hundred younger people sat in the church. Paper plates were passed up and down the rows. A number of quarters were collected.

Moonbelly sang a new song called "The System Cannot Withstand Close Scrutiny."

The system cannot withstand close scrutiny
The system cannot withstand close scrutiny
The system cannot withstand close scrutiny
The system cannot withstand close scrutiny
Etc.

Jacques spoke briefly and well. A few more quarters showered down on the stage.

At the party after the benefit Ramona spoke to Jacques, because he was handsome and flushed with triumph.

—Tell me something.
—All right Ramona what do you want to know?
—Do you promise to tell me the truth?
—Of course. Sure.
—Can one be impregnated by a song?
—I think not. I would say no.
—While one is asleep, possibly?
—It's not very likely.
—What sort of people have hysterical pregnancies?
—Well, you know. Sort of nervous girls.
—If a hysterical pregnancy results in a birth, is it still considered hysterical?
—No.
—Rats!

13.

Charles and Jacques were trying to move a parked Volkswagen. When a Volkswagen is parked with its parking brake set you need three people to move it, usually.

A third person was sighted moving down the street.

—Say, buddy, could you give us a hand for a minute?
—Sure, the third person said.

Charles, Jacques, and the third person grasped the VW firmly in their hands and heaved. It moved forward opening up a new parking space where only half a space had been before.

—Thanks, Jacques said. Now would you mind helping us unload this panel truck here? It contains printed materials pertaining to the worldwide struggle for liberation from outmoded ways of thought that hold us in thrall.

—I don't mind.

Charles, Jacques, and Hector carried the bundles of printed material up the stairs into the Porter Street apartment.

—What does this printed material say, Jacques?

—It says that the government has promised to give us some of our money back if it loses the war.

—Is that true?

—No. And now, how about a drink?

Drinking their drinks they regarded the black trombone case which rested under Hector's coat.

—Is that a trombone case?

Hector's eyes glazed.

Moonbelly sat on the couch, his great belly covered with plants and animals.

—It's good to be what one is, he said.

14.

Ramona's child was born on Wednesday. It was a boy.

—But Ramona! Who is responsible? Charles? Jacques? Moonbelly? Vercingetorix?

—It was a virgin birth, unfortunately, Ramona said.

—But what does this imply about the child?

—Nothing, Ramona said. It was just an ordinary virgin birth. Don't bother your pretty head about it, Elsa dear.

However much Ramona tried to soft-pedal the virgin birth, people persisted in getting excited about it. A few cardinals from the Sacred Rota dropped by.

—What is this you're claiming here, foolish girl?

—I claim nothing, Your Eminence. I merely report.

—Give us the name of the man who has compromised you!

—It was a virgin birth, sir.

Cardinal Maranto frowned in several directions.

—There can't be another Virgin Birth!

Ramona modestly lowered her eyes. The child, Sam, was wrapped in a blanket with his feet sticking out.

—Better cover those feet.
—Thank you, Cardinal. I will.

15.

Ramona went to class at the Law School carrying Sam on her hip in a sling.
—What's that?
—My child.
—I didn't know you were married.
—I'm not.
—That's against the law! I think.
—What law is it against?
The entire class regarded the teacher.
—Well there is a law against fornication on the books, but of course it's not enforced very often ha ha. It's sort of difficult to enforce ha ha.
—I have to tell you, Ramona said, that this child is not of human man conceived. It was a virgin birth. Unfortunately.
A few waves of smickers washed across the classroom.
A law student named Harold leaped to his feet.
—Stop this smickering! What are we thinking of? To make mock of this fine girl! Rot me if I will permit it! Are we gentlemen? Is this lady our colleague? Or are we rather beasts of the field? This Ramona, this trull . . . No, that's not what I mean. I mean that we should think not upon her peculations but on our own peculations. For, as Augustine tells us, if for some error or sin of our own, sadness seizes us, let us not only bear in mind that an afflicted spirit is a sacrifice to God but also the words: for as water quencheth a flaming fire, so almsgiving quencheth sin; and for I desire, He says, mercy rather than sacrifice. As, therefore, if we were in danger from fire, we should, of course, run for water with which to extinguish it, and should be thankful if someone showed us water nearby, so if some flame of sin has arisen from the hay of our passions, we should take delight in this, that the ground for a work of great mercy is given to us. Therefore—
Harold collapsed, from the heat of his imagination.
A student in a neighboring seat looked deeply into Sam's eyes.
—They're brown.

16.

Moonbelly was fingering his axe.

—A birth hymn? Do I really want to write a birth hymn?

—What do I really think about this damn birth?

—Of course it's within the tradition.

—Is this the real purpose of cities? Is this why all these units have been brought together, under the red, white and blue?

—Cities are erotic, in a depressing way. Should that be my line?

—Of course I usually do best with something in the rage line. However—

—C . . . F . . . C . . . F . . . C . . . F . . . G7 . . .

Moonbelly wrote "Cities Are Centers of Copulation."

The recording company official handed Moonbelly a gold record marking the sale of a million copies of "Cities Are Centers of Copulation."

17.

Charles and Jacques were still talking to Hector Guimard, the former trombone player.

—Yours is not a modern problem, Jacques said. The problem today is not angst but lack of angst.

—Wait a minute, Jacques. Although I myself believe that there is nothing wrong with being a trombone player, I can understand Hector's feeling. I know a painter who feels the same way about being a painter. Every morning he gets up, brushes his teeth, and stands before the empty canvas. A terrible feeling of being *de trop* comes over him. So he goes to the corner and buys the Times, at the corner newsstand. He comes back home and reads the Times. During the period in which he's coupled with the Times he is all right. But soon the Times is exhausted. The empty canvas remains. So (usually) he makes a mark on it, some kind of mark that is not what he means. That is, any old mark, just to have something on the canvas. Then he is profoundly depressed because what is there is not what he meant. And it's time for lunch. He goes out and buys a pastrami sandwich at the deli. He comes back and eats the sandwich meanwhile regarding the canvas with the wrong mark on it out of the corner of his eye. During the afternoon, he paints out the mark of the morning. This affords him a measure of satisfaction. The balance of the afternoon is spent in deciding whether or not to venture another mark. The new mark, if one is ventured, will also, inevitably, be misconceived. He ventures it. It is misconceived. It is, in fact, the worst kind of vulgarity. He paints out the second mark. Anxiety accumulates. However, the canvas is now, in and of itself, because of the wrong moves and the painting out, becoming rather interesting-looking. He goes to the A. & P. and buys a TV Mexican dinner and many bottles of Carta Blanca. He comes back to his loft and eats the Mexican dinner and drinks a couple of Carta Blancas, sitting in front of his canvas. The canvas is, for one thing, no longer empty. Friends drop in and congratulate him on having a not-empty canvas. He begins feeling better. A something has been wrested from the nothing. The quality of the something is still at issue—he is by no means home free. And of course all of painting—the whole art—has moved on somewhere else, it's not where his head is, and he knows that, but nevertheless he—

—How does this apply to trombone playing? Hector asked.

—I had the connection in my mind when I began, Charles said.

—As Goethe said, theory is gray, but the golden tree of life is green.

18.

Everybody in the city was watching a movie about an Indian village menaced by a tiger. Only Wendell Corey stood between the village and the tiger. Furthermore Wendell Corey had dropped his rifle—or rather the tiger had knocked it out of his hands—and was left with only his knife. In addition, the tiger had Wendell Corey's left arm in his mouth up to the shoulder.

Ramona thought about the city.

—I have to admit we are locked in the most exquisite mysterious muck. This muck heaves and palpitates. It is multi-directional and has a mayor. To describe it takes many hundreds of thousands of words. Our muck is only a part of a much greater muck—the nation-state—which is itself the creation of that muck of mucks, human consciousness. Of course all these things also have a touch of sublimity—as when Moonbelly sings, for example, or all the lights go out. What a happy time that was, when all the electricity went away! If only we could re-create that paradise! By, for instance, all forgetting to pay our electric bills at the same time. All nine million of us. Then we'd all get those little notices that say unless we remit within five days the lights will go out. We all stand up from our chairs with the notice in our hands. The same thought drifts across the furrowed surface of nine million minds. We wink at each other, through the walls.

At the Electric Company, a nervousness appeared as Ramona's thought launched itself into parapsychological space.

Ramona arranged names in various patterns.

>   Vercingetorix
>   Moonbelly
>   Charles
>
>   Moonbelly
>   Charles
>   Vercingetorix
>
>   Charles
>   Vercingetorix
>   Moonbelly

—Upon me, their glance has fallen. The engendering force was, perhaps, the fused glance of all of them. From the millions of units crawling about on the surface of the city, their wavering desirous eye selected me. The pupil enlarged to admit more light: more me. They began dancing little dances of suggestion and fear. These dances constitute an invitation of unmistakable import—an invitation which, if accepted, leads one down many muddy roads. I accepted. What was the alternative?

SADNESS

To Kirk and Faith Sale and Harrison and Sandra Starr

Critique de la Vie Quotidienne

WHILE I read the *Journal of Sensory Deprivation*, Wanda, my former wife, read *Elle*. *Elle* was an incitement to revolt to one who had majored in French in college and had now nothing much to do with herself except take care of a child and look out of the window. Wanda empathized with the magazine. "*Femmes enceintes, ne mangez pas de bifteck cru!*" *Elle* once proclaimed, and Wanda complied. Not a shred of *bifteck cru* passed her lips during the whole period of her pregnancy. She cultivated, as *Elle* instructed, *un petit air naïf,* or the schoolgirl look. She was always pointing out to me four-color photographs of some handsome restored mill in Brittany which had been redone with Arne Jacobsen furniture and bright red and orange plastic things from Milan: "*Une Maison Qui Capte la Nature.*" During this period *Elle* ran something like four thousand separate *actualité* pieces on Anna Karina, the film star, and Wanda actually came to resemble her somewhat.

Our evenings lacked promise. The world in the evening seems fraught with the absence of promise, if you are a married man. There is nothing to do but go home and drink your nine drinks and forget about it.

Slumped there in your favorite chair, with your nine drinks lined up on the side table in soldierly array, and your hand never far from them, and your other hand holding on to the plump belly of the overfed child, and perhaps rocking a bit, if the chair is a rocking chair as mine was in those days, then it is true that a tiny tendril of contempt—strike that, *content*—might curl up from the storehouse where the world's content is kept, and reach into your softened brain and take hold there, persuading you that this, at last, is the fruit of all your labors, which you'd been wondering about in some such terms as, "Where is the fruit?" And so, newly cheered and warmed by this false insight, you reach out with your free hand (the one that is not clutching the nine drinks) and pat the hair of the child, and the child looks up into your face, gauging your mood as it were, and says, "Can I have a horse?," which is after all a perfectly reasonable request, in some ways, but in other ways is total ruin to that state of six-o'clock equilibrium you have so painfully achieved, because it, the child's request, is of course absolutely out of the question, and so you say "No!" as forcefully as possible—a bark rather like a bite—in such a way as to put the quietus on this project, having a horse, once and for all, permanently. But, placing yourself in the child's ragged shoes, which look more like used Brillo pads than shoes now that you regard them closely, you remember that time long ago on the other side of the Great War when you too desired a horse, and so, pulling yourself together, and putting another drink in your mouth (that makes three, I believe), you assume a thoughtful look (indeed, the same grave and thoughtful look you have been wearing all day, to confuse your enemies and armor yourself against the indifference of your friends) and begin to speak to the child softly, gently, cunningly even, explaining that the genus horse prefers the great open voids, where it can roam, and graze, and copulate with other attractive horses, to the confined space of a broke-down brownstone apartment, and that a horse if obtained would not be happy here, in the child's apartment, and does he, the child, want an unhappy horse, moping and brooding, and lying all over the double bed in the bedroom, and perhaps vomiting at intervals, and maybe even kicking down a wall or two, to express its rage? But the child, sensing the way the discussion is trending, says impatiently, with a chop of its tiny little hand, "No, I don't *mean* that," giving you to understand that it, the child, had not intended what you are arguing against but had intended something else altogether: a horse personally owned by it, the child, but pastured at a stable in the park, a horse such as Otto has—"Otto has a horse?" you say in astonishment—Otto being a school-fellow of the child, and indeed the same age, and no brighter as far as the naked eye can determine but perhaps a shade more fortunate in the wealth dimension, and the child nods, yes, Otto has a horse, and a film of tears is squeezed out and presented to you, over its eyes, and with liberal amounts of anathematization for Otto's feckless parents and the profound hope that the fall of the market has ruined them beyond repair you push the weeping child with its filmic tears off your lap and onto the floor and turn to your wife, who has been listening to all of this with her face turned to the wall, and no doubt a look upon her face corresponding to that which St. Catherine of Siena bent upon poor Pope Gregory whilst reproaching him for the luxury of Avignon, if you could see it (but of course you cannot, as her face is turned to the wall)—you look, as I say, to your wife, as the cocktail hour fades, there being only two drinks left of the nine (and you have sworn a mighty oath never to take more than nine before supper, because of what it does to you), and inquire in the calmest tones available what is for supper and would she like to take a flying fuck at the moon for visiting this outrageous child upon you. She, rising with a regal sweep of her *air naïf*, and not failing to let you have a good look at her handsome legs, those legs you could have, if you were good, motors out of the room and into the kitchen, where she throws the dinner on the floor, so that when you enter the kitchen to get some more ice you begin skidding and skating about in a muck of pork chops, squash, *sauce diable*, Danish stainless-steel flatware, and Louis Martini Mountain Red. So, this being the content of your happy hour, you decide to break your iron-clad rule, that rule of rules, and have eleven drinks instead of the modest nine with which you had been wont to stave off the song of twilight, when the lights are low, and the flickering shadows, etc., etc. But, opening the refrigerator, you discover that the slovenly bitch has failed to fill up the ice trays so there is *no more ice* for your tenth and eleventh sloshes. On discovering this you are just about ready to throw in the entire enterprise, happy home, and go to the bordel for the evening, where at least you can be sure that everyone will be kind to you, and not ask you for a horse, and the floor will not be a muck of *sauce diable* and pork chops. But when you put your hand in your pocket you discover that there are only three dollars there—not enough to cover a sortie to the bordel, where Uni-Cards are not accepted, so that the entire scheme, going to the bordel, is blasted. Upon making these determinations, which are not such as to bring the hot flush of excitement to the old cheek, you measure out your iceless over-the-limit drinks, using a little cold water as a make-do, and return to what is called the "living" room, and prepare to live, for a little while longer, in a truce with your circumstances—aware that there are wretches worse off than you, people whose trepanations have not been successful, girls who have not been invited to the sexual revolution, priests still frocked. It is seven-thirty.

I remember once we were sleeping in a narrow bed, Wanda and I, in a hotel, on a holiday, and the child crept into bed with us.
"If you insist on overburdening the bed," we said, "you must sleep at the bottom, with the feet." "But I don't want to sleep with the feet," the child said. "Sleep with the feet," we said, "they won't hurt you." "The feet kick," the child said, "in the middle of the night." "The feet or the floor," we said. "Take your choice." "Why can't I sleep with the heads," the child asked, "like everybody else?" "Because you are a child," we said, and the child subsided, whimpering, the final arguments in the case having been presented and the verdict. But in truth the child was not without recourse; it urinated in the bed, in the vicinity of the feet. "God damn it," I said, inventing this formulation at the instant of need. "What the devil is happening, at the bottom of the bed?" "I couldn't help it," the child said. "It just came out." "I forgot to bring the plastic sheet," Wanda said. "Holy hell," I said. "Is there to be no end to this *family life*?"
I spoke to the child and the child spoke to me and the merest pleasantry trembled with enough animus to bring down an elephant.
"Clean your face," I said to the child. "It's dirty." "It's not," the child said. "By God it is," I said, "filth adheres in nine areas which I shall enumerate." "That is because of the dough," the child said. "We were taking death masks." "Dough!" I exclaimed, shocked at the idea that the child had wasted flour and water and no doubt paper too in this lightsome pastime, taking death masks. "Death!" I exclaimed for added emphasis. "What do you know of death?" "It is the end of the world," the child said, "for the death-visited individual. The world ends," the child said, "when you turn out your eyes." This was true, I could not dispute it. I returned to the main point. "Your father is telling you to wash your face," I said, locating myself in the abstract where I was more comfortable. "I know that," the child said, "that's what you always say." "Where are they, the masks?" I asked. "Drying," the child said, "on the heaterator"—its word for radiator. I then went to the place where the

heaterator stood and looked. Sure enough, four tiny life masks. My child and three of its tiny friends lay there, grinning. "Who taught you how to do this?" I asked, and the child said, "We learned it in school." I cursed the school then, in my mind. It was not the first time I had cursed the school, in my mind. "Well, what will you do with them?" I asked, demonstrating an interest in childish projects. "Hang them on the wall?" the child suggested. "Yes yes, hang them on the wall, why not?" I said. "Intimations of mortality," the child said, with a sly look. "Why the look?" I asked. "What is that supposed to mean?" "Ho ho," the child said, sniggering—a palpable snigger. "Why the snigger?" I asked, for the look in combination with the snigger had struck fear into my heart, a place where no more fear was needed. "You'll find out," the child said, testing the masks with a dirty finger to determine if they had dried. "I'll find out!" I exclaimed. "What does that mean, I'll find out!" "You'll be sorry," the child said, with a piteous glance at itself, in the mirror. But I was ahead of him there, I was already sorry. "Sorry!" I cried, "I've been sorry all my life!" "Not without reason," the child said, a wise look replacing the piteous look. I am afraid that a certain amount of physical abuse of the child ensued. But I shall not recount it, because of the shame.

"You can have the seven years," I said to Wanda. "What seven years?" Wanda asked. "The seven years by which you will, statistically, outlive me," I said. "Those years will be yours, to do with as you wish. Not a word of reproof or critique will you hear from me, during those years. I promise." "I cannot wait," Wanda said.

The child was singing. The problem was, how to make the child stop singing. It was not enough to say, "Stop singing, child!" Such saying had little effect. The child sang on despite my black look. It was characteristic of the child's singing that it was not well done. The tune went everywhere—into unexpected places on the staff, into agonies of uncertainty, into infelicities of every kind, exacerbating (left to right) the helix, the fossa of the antihelix, the antihelix, the concha, the antitragus, the tragus, the lobe, the external auditory meatus, the tympanic membrane, the malleus, the incus, the tympanum, the stapes, the Eustachian tube, the semicircular canals, the vestibule, the cochlea, the auditory nerve, the internal auditory meatus—a piercement, in fine, that God Himself would not have believed possible when He invented His great invention, the ear. "Child," I said to the child, "if you don't stop singing I will sew up your mouth, with your mother's sewing machine." "Faugh!" the child said, "you know she can't abide you." This was the living truth. The child's mother continued gazing out of the window and sucking her thumb, during this exchange. The child continued to sing and in addition turned on the television set and the transistor radio.

I remember Wanda in the morning. Up in the morning reading the *Times* I was walked past by Wanda, already sighing although not thirty seconds out of bed. At night I drank and my hostility came roaring out of its cave like a jet-assisted banshee. When we played checkers I'd glare at her so hotly she'd often miss a triple jump.

I remember that I fixed the child's bicycle, once. That brought me congratulations, around the fireside. That was a good, a fatherly thing to do. It was a cheap bicycle, $29.95 or some such, and the seat wobbled and the mother came home from the park with the bicycle in an absolute fury because the child was being penalized by my penury, in the matter of the seat. "I will fix it," I said. I went to the hardware store and bought a two-and-one-half-inch piece of pipe which I used as a collar around the seat's stem to accommodate the downward thrust. Then I affixed a flexible metal strap eight inches in length first to the back of the seat and then to the chief upright, by means of screws. This precluded side-to-side motion of the seat. A triumph of field expediency. Everyone was loving and kind that night. The child brought me my nine drinks very prettily, setting them on the side table and lining them up with the aid of a meter stick, into a perfect straight line. "Thank you," I said. We beamed at each other contesting as to who could maintain the beam the longest.

I visited the child's nursery school, once. Fathers were invited seriatim, one father a day. I sat there on a little chair while the children ran to and fro and made sport. I was served a little cake. A tiny child not my own attached herself to me.

Her father was in England, she said. She had visited him there and his apartment was full of cockroaches. I wanted to take her home with me.

After the separation, which came about after what is known as the breaking point was reached, Wanda visited me in my bachelor setup. We were drinking healths. "Health to the child!" I proposed. Wanda lifted her glass. "Health to your projects!" she proposed, and I was pleased. That seemed very decent of her. I lifted my glass. The only thing I enjoy more than lifting my glass is lifting the cork, on a new bottle. I lifted the cork on a new bottle. "Health to the republic!" I proposed. We drank to that. Then Wanda proposed a health. "Health to abandoned wives!" she said. "Well now," I said. "'Abandoned,' that's a little strong." "Pushed out, jettisoned, abjured, thrown away," she said. "I remember," I said, "a degree of mutuality, in our parting." "And when guests came," she said, "you always made me sit in the kitchen." "I thought you liked it in the kitchen," I said. "You were forever telling me to get out of the bloody kitchen." "And when my overbite required correction," she said, "you would not pay for the apparatus." "Seven years of sitting by the window with your thumb in your mouth," I said. "What did you expect?" "And when I needed a new frock," she said, "you hid the Uni-Card." "There was nothing wrong with the old one," I said, "that a few well-placed patches couldn't have fixed." "And when we were invited to the Argentine Embassy," she said, "you made me drive the car in a chauffeur's cap, and park the car, and stand about with the other drivers outside while you chatted up the Ambassador." "You know no Spanish," I pointed out. "It was not the happiest of marriages," she said, "all in all." "There has been a sixty percent increase in single-person households in the last ten years, according to the Bureau of the Census," I told her. "Perhaps we are part of a trend." That thought did not seem to console her much. "Health to the child!" I proposed, and she said, "We've already done that." "Health to the mother of the child!" I said, and she said, "I'll drink to that." To tell the truth we were getting a little wobbly on our pins, at this point. "It is probably not necessary to rise each time," I said, and she said, "Thank God," and sat. I looked at her then to see if I could discern traces of what I had seen in the beginning. There were traces but only traces. Vestiges. Hints of a formerly intact mystery never to be returned to its original wholeness. "I know what you're doing," she said, "you are touring the ruins." "Not at all," I said. "You look very well, considering." "'Considering'!" she cried, and withdrew from her bosom an extremely large horse pistol. "Health to the dead!" she proposed, meanwhile waving the horse pistol in the air in an agitated manner. I drank that health, but with misgivings, because who was she talking about? "The sacred dead," she said with relish. "The well-beloved, the well-esteemed, the well-remembered, the well-ventilated." She attempted to ventilate me then, with the horse pistol. The barrel wavered to the right of my head, and to the left of my head, and I remembered that although its guidance system was primitive its caliber was large. The weapon discharged with a blurt of sound and the ball smashed a bottle of J & B on the mantel. She wept. The place stank of Scotch. I called her a cab.

Wanda is happier now, I think. She has taken herself off to Nanterre, where she is studying Marxist sociology with Lefebvre (not impertinently, the author of the *Critique de la Vie Quotidienne*). The child is being cared for in an experimental nursery school for the children of graduate students run, I understand, in accord with the best Piagetian principles. And I, I have my J & B. The J & B company keeps manufacturing it, case after case, year in and year out, and there is, I am told, no immediate danger of a dearth.

Träumerei

So there you are, Daniel, reclining, reclining on the chaise, a lovely picture, white trousers, white shirt, red cummerbund, scarlet rather, white suède jacket, sunflower in buttonhole, beard neatly combed, let's have a look at the fingernails. Daniel, your fingernails are a disgrace. Have a herring. We are hungry, Daniel, we could eat the hind leg off a donkey. Quickly, Daniel, quickly to the bath, it's time to bathe, the bath is drawn, the towels laid out, the soap in the soap dish, the new bath mat laid down, the bust of Puccini over the tub polished, the choir is ready, it will sing the *Nelson Mass* of Haydn, soaping to begin with the Kyrie, luxuriating from the Kyrie to the Credo, serious scrubbing from the Credo to the Sanctus, toweling to commence with the Agnus Dei. Daniel, walk the dog and frighten the birds, we can't abide birdsong. Spontini is eternal, Daniel, we knew him well, he sat often in that very chair, the chair you sit in, Spontini sat there, hawking and spitting, coughing blood into a plaid handkerchief, he was not in the best of health after he left Berlin, we were very close, Daniel, Spontini and we, *Agnes von Hohenstaufen* was his favorite among his works, "not lacking in historical significance," he used to say of it, in his modest way, and of course he was right, *Agnes von Hohenstaufen* is eternal. Daniel, do you know a Putzi, no Putzi appears in the register, what is this, Daniel, a new Putzi and not recorded in the register, what marches, are you conducting a little fiddle here, Daniel, Putzi is on the telephone, hurry to the telephone, Daniel. Daniel, you may begin bringing in the sheaves. Do you want *all* the herring, Daniel? For a day, Daniel, we sat before a Constable sketch in a dream, an entire day, twenty-four hours, the light failed and we had candles brought, we cried "Ho! Candles, this way, lights, lights, lights!" and candles were brought, and we gazed additionally, some additional gazes, at the Constable sketch, in a dream. Have a shot of aquavit, Daniel. And there's an old croquet ball! It's been so long since we've played, almost forgotten how, perhaps some evening in the cool, while the light lasts, we'll have a game, we were very apt once, probably you are not, but we'll teach you, pure pleasure, Daniel, pure and unrestricted pleasure, while the light lasts, indulgence at its fiery height, you will lust after the last wicket, you will rush for the stake, and miss it, very likely, the untutored amateur in his eagerness, you'll be hit off into the shrubbery, we will place our ball next to your ball, and place a foot on your ball, and give it a good whack, your ball will go flying off into the shrubbery, what a pleasure, it frightens the birds. That is our croquet elegy, Daniel. Repair the dog cart, Daniel. Or have another herring, we were ripping up a herring with Mascagni once, some decades ago, the eternal Mascagni, a wonderful man, Pietro, a great laugher, he would laugh and laugh, and then stop laughing, and grow gray, a disappointed man, Pietro, brought a certain amount of grayness into one's drawing room, relieved of course by the laughing, from time to time, he was a rocket, Mascagni, worldwide plaudits and then pop! nothing, not a plaudit in a carload, he grew a bit morose, in his last years, and gray, perhaps that's usual when one's plaudits have been taken away, a darling man, and wonderful with the stick, always on the road in his last years, opera orchestras, he was the devil with your work-shy element, was Pietro, your work-shy element might as well bend to it when Pietro was in the pit. You may go to your room now, Daniel. She loves you still, we can't understand it, they all profess an unexhausted passion, the whole string, that's remarkable, Putzi too, you're to be congratulated and we are never the last to offer our congratulations, the persistence of memory as the poet puts it, would that be the case do you think, would that be the explanation, hurry to the cellar and bring up a cask of herring and four bottles of aquavit, we're going to let you work on the wall. We had a man working on the wall, Daniel, a good man, Buller by name, knew his trade, did Buller, but he went away, to the West, an offer from the Corps of Engineers, they were straightening a river, somewhere in the West, Buller had straightened streams in his youth but never a river, he couldn't resist, gave us a turkey by way of farewell, it was that season, we gave him a watch, inscribed TO BULLER, FAITHFUL POURER OF FOOTINGS, and then he hove out of view, hove over the horizon, run to the wall, Daniel, you'll find the concrete block stacked on the site, and mind your grout, Daniel, mind your grout. Daniel, you're looking itchy, we know that itch, we are not insensible of your problem, in our youth we whored after youth, on the one hand, and whored after beauty, on the other, very often these were combined in the same object, a young girl for example, a simplification, one does not have to whore after youth and whore after beauty consecutively, running first to the left, down dark streets, whoring after youth, and then to the right, through the arcades, whoring after beauty, and generally whoring oneself ragged, please, Daniel, don't do that, throwing the cat against the wall *injures the cat*. Your women, Daniel, have arrayed themselves on the garden gate. There's a racket down at the garden gate, Daniel, see to it, and the damned birds singing, and think for a while about delayed gratification, it's what distinguishes us from the printed circuits, Daniel, your printed circuit can't delay a gratification worth a damn. Daniel, run and buy a barrel of herring from the herringvolk. For we deny no man his mead, after a hard day at the wall. Your grout is lovely, Daniel. Daniel, have you noticed this herring, it looks very much like the President, do you think so, we are soliciting your opinion, although we are aware that most people think the President looks not like a herring but like a foot, what is your opinion, Daniel. Glazunov is eternal, of course, eight symphonies, two piano concertos, a violin concerto, a cello concerto, a concerto for saxophone, six overtures, seven quartets, a symphonic poem, serenades, fantasias, incidental music, and the Hymn to Pushkin. Pass the aquavit, Daniel. There was a moment when we thought we were losing our mind. Yes, we, losing our mind, the wall not even started at that period, we were open to the opinions of mankind, vulnerable, anyone could come along, as you did, Daniel, and have an opinion contrary to our opinion, we remember when the Monsignor came to inspect our miracle, a wonderful little miracle that had happened to us, still believers, at that period, we had the exhibits spread out on the rug, neatly tagged, Exhibit A, Exhibit B, and so forth, the Monsignor tickled the exhibits with his toe, toed the exhibits reflectively, or perhaps he was merely trying to give that impression, they're cunning, you never know, we had prostrated ourselves of course, then he tickled the tops of our heads with his toe and said, "Get up, you fools, get up and pour me a glass of that sherry I spy there, on the sideboard," we got up and poured him a glass, with trembling hands you may be sure, and the damned birds singing, he sipped, a smile appeared on the monsignorial mug, "Well boys," he said, "a few cases of this spread around the chancellery won't do your petition any harm," we immediately went to the cellar, loaded six cases upon a dray and caused them to be drayed to the chancellery, but to no avail, spurious they said, of our miracle, we were crushed, blasted, we thought we were losing our mind. You, Daniel, can be the new miracle, in your white trousers, white suède jacket, red cummerbund, scarlet rather, yellow sunflower in the buttonhole, a miracle of nullity, pass the aquavit. Have a reindeer steak, Daniel, it's Dancer, Dancer or Prancer, no no, that's a joke, Daniel, and while you're at it bring the accounts, your pocket money must be accounted for, thirty-five cents a week times thirteen weeks, what? Thirty-five cents a week times twenty-six weeks, we did not realize that your option had been picked up, you will be the comfort of our old age, Daniel, if you live. Give the herb garden a weed, Daniel. The telephone is ringing, Daniel, answer it, we'll be here, sipping hock and listening on the extensions. Your backing and filling, your excuses, their reproaches, the weeping, all very well in a way, stimulating even, but it palls, your palaver, after a time, these ladies, poor girls, the whole string, Martha, Mary, all the rest, Claudia or is it Claudine, we can't remember, amusing, yes, for a time, for a time, until the wall is completed, a perfect circle or is it a perfect rhomboid, we can't remember. We remember browsing in the dictionary, page something or other, pumpernickel to puppyish, keeping the mind occupied, until the wall is completed, young whelp, what are you now, thirty-eight, thirty-nine, almost a neonate, have a herring, and count your blessings, and mind your grout, and give the fingernails a buff, spurious they said, of our miracle, that was a downer, and the damned birds singing, we're spared nothing, and the cat with its head cracked, thanks to you, Daniel, the garden gate sprung, thanks to you, Daniel, Mascagni gone, Glazunov gone, and the damned birds singing, and the croquet balls God knows where, and the damned birds singing.

The Genius

HIS ASSISTANTS cluster about him. He is severe with them, demanding, punctilious, but this is for their own ultimate benefit. He devises hideously difficult problems, or complicates their work with sudden oblique comments that open whole new areas of investigation—yawning chasms under their feet. It is as if he wishes to place them in situations where only failure is possible. But failure, too, is a part of mental life. "I will make you failure-proof," he says jokingly. His assistants pale.

•

Is it true, as Valéry said, that every man of genius contains within himself a false man of genius?

•

"This is an age of personal ignorance. No one knows what others know. No one knows enough."

•

The genius is afraid to fly. The giant aircraft seem to him . . . *flimsy*. He hates the takeoff and he hates the landing and he detests being in the air. He hates the food, the stewardesses, the voice of the captain, and his fellow-passengers, especially those who are conspicuously at ease, who remove their coats, loosen their ties, and move up and down the aisles with drinks in their hands. In consequence, he rarely travels. The world comes to him.

•

Q: What do you consider the most important tool of the genius of today?
A: Rubber cement.

•

He has urged that America be divided into four smaller countries. America, he says, is too big. "America does not look where it puts its foot," he says. This comment, which, coming from anyone else, would have engendered widespread indignation, is greeted with amused chuckles. The Chamber of Commerce sends him four cases of Teacher's Highland Cream.

•

The genius defines "inappropriate response":

"Suppose my friend telephones and asks, 'Is my wife there?' 'No,' I reply, 'they went out, your wife and my wife, wearing new hats, they are giving themselves to sailors.' My friend is astounded at this news. 'But it's Election Day!' he cries. 'And it's beginning to rain!' I say."

•

The genius pays close attention to work being done in fields other than his own. He is well read in all of the sciences (with the exception of the social sciences); he follows the arts with a connoisseur's acuteness; he is an accomplished amateur musician. He jogs. He dislikes chess. He was once photographed playing tennis with the Marx Brothers.

He has devoted considerable thought to an attempt to define the sources of his genius. However, this attempt has led approximately nowhere. The mystery remains a mystery. He has therefore settled upon the following formula, which he repeats each time he is interviewed: "Historical forces."

•

The government has decided to award the genius a few new medals—medals he has not been previously awarded. One medal is awarded for his work prior to 1936, one for his work from 1936 to the present, and one for his future work.

•

"I think that this thing, my work, has made me, in a sense, what I am. The work possesses a consciousness which shapes that of the worker. The work flatters the worker. Only the strongest worker can do this work, the work says. You must be a fine fellow, that you can do this work. But disaffection is also possible. The worker grows careless. The worker pays slight regard to the work, he ignores the work, he flirts with other work, he is *unfaithful* to the work. The work is insulted. And perhaps it finds little ways of telling the worker . . . The work slips in the hands of the worker—a little cut on the finger. You understand? The work becomes slow, sulky, consumes more time, becomes more tiring. The gaiety that once existed between the worker and the work has evaporated. A fine situation! Don't you think?"

•

The genius has noticed that he does not interact with children successfully. (Anecdote)

•

Richness of the inner life of the genius:

(1) Manic-oceanic states
(2) Hatred of children
(3) Piano playing
(4) Subincised genitals
(5) Subscription to *Harper's Bazaar*
(6) Stamp collection

•

The genius receives a very flattering letter from the University of Minnesota. The university wishes to become the depository of his papers, after he is dead. A new wing of the Library will be built to house them.

The letter makes the genius angry. He takes a pair of scissors, cuts the letter into long thin strips, and mails it back to the Director of Libraries.

•

He takes long walks through the city streets, noting architectural details—particularly old ironwork. His mind is filled with ideas for a new— But at this moment a policeman approaches him. "Beg pardon, sir. Aren't you—" "Yes," the genius says, smiling. "My little boy is an admirer of yours," the policeman says. He pulls out a pocket notebook. "If it's not too much trouble . . ." Smiling, the genius signs his name.

The genius carries his most important papers about with him in a green Sears, Roebuck toolbox.

•

He did not win the Nobel Prize again this year.
It was neither the year of his country nor the year of his discipline. To console him, the National Foundation gives him a new house.

•

The genius meets with a group of students. The students tell the genius that the concept "genius" is not, currently, a popular one. Group effort, they say, is more socially productive than the isolated efforts of any one man, however gifted. Genius by its very nature sets itself over against the needs of the many. In answering its own imperatives, genius tends toward, even embraces, totalitarian forms of social organization. Tyranny of the gifted over the group, while bringing some advances in the short run, inevitably produces a set of conditions which—
The genius smokes thoughtfully.

•

A giant brown pantechnicon disgorges the complete works of the Venerable Bede, in all translations, upon the genius's lawn—a gift from the people of Cincinnati!

•

The genius is leafing through a magazine. Suddenly he is arrested by an advertisement:

> Why Don't YOU
> Become a
> Professional
> Interior Decorator?

Interior decoration is a high-income field, the advertisement says. The work is varied and interesting. One moves in a world of fashion, creativity, and ever-new challenge.
The genius tears out the advertisement's coupon.

•

Q: Is America a good place for genius?
A: I have found America most hospitable to genius.

•

"I always say to myself, 'What is the most important thing I can be thinking about at this minute?' But then I don't think about it."

•

His driver's license expires. But he does nothing about renewing it. He is vaguely troubled by the thought of the expired license (although he does not stop driving). But he loathes the idea of taking the examination again, of going physically to the examining station, of waiting in line for an examiner. He decides that if he writes a letter to the License Bureau requesting a new license, the bureau will grant him one without an examination, because he is a genius. He is right. He writes the letter and the License Bureau sends him a new license, by return mail.

•

In the serenity of his genius, the genius reaches out to right wrongs—the sewer systems of cities, for example.

•

The genius is reading *The Genius*, a 736-page novel by Theodore Dreiser. He arrives at the last page:

"... What a sweet welter life is—how rich, how tender, how grim, how like a colorful symphony."
    Great art dreams welled up into his soul as he viewed the sparkling deeps of space ...

The genius gets up and looks at himself in a mirror.

•

An organization has been formed to appreciate his thought: the Blaufox Gesellschaft. Meetings are held once a month, in a room over a cafeteria in Buffalo, New York. He has always refused to have anything to do with the Gesellschaft, which reminds him uncomfortably of the Browning Society. However, he cannot prevent himself from glancing at the group's twice-yearly *Proceedings*, which contains such sentences as "The imbuement of all reaches of the scholarly community with Blaufox's views must, *ab ovo*, be our . . ."

He falls into hysteria.

•

Moments of self-doubt . . .
"Am I really a—"
"What does it *mean* to be a—"
"Can one *refuse* to be a—"

•

His worst moment: He is in a church, kneeling in a pew near the back. He is gradually made aware of a row of nuns, a half dozen, kneeling twenty feet ahead of him, their heads bent over their beads. One of the nuns however has turned her head almost completely around, and seems to be staring at him. The genius glances at her, glances away, then looks again: she is still staring at him. The genius is only visiting the church in the first place because the nave is said to be a particularly fine example of Burgundian Gothic. He places his eyes here, there, on the altar, on the stained glass, but each time they return to the nuns, *his* nun is still staring. The genius says to himself, *This is my worst moment.*

•

He is a drunk.

•

"A truly potent abstract concept avoids, resists closure. The ragged, blurred outlines of such a concept, like a net in which the fish have eaten large, gaping holes, permit entry and escape equally. What does one catch in such a net? The sea horse with a Monet in his mouth. How did the Monet get there? Is the value of the Monet less because it has gotten wet? Are there tooth marks in the Monet? Do sea horses have teeth?

How large is the Monet? From which period? Is it a water lily or group of water lilies? Do sea horses eat water lilies? Does Parke-Bernet know? Do oil and water mix? Is a mixture of oil and water bad for the digestion of the sea horse? Should art be expensive? Should artists wear beards? Ought beards to be forbidden by law? Is underwater art better than overwater art? What does the expression 'glad rags' mean? Does it refer to Monet's paint rags? In the Paris of 1878, what was the average monthly rent for a north-lit, spacious studio in an unfashionable district? If sea horses eat water lilies, what percent of their daily work energy, expressed in ergs, is generated thereby? Should the holes in the net be mended? In a fight between a sea horse and a flittermouse, which would you bet on? If I mend the net, will you forgive me? Do water rats chew upon the water lilies? Is there a water buffalo in the water cooler? If I fill my water gun to the waterline, can I then visit the watering place? Is fantasy an adequate substitute for correct behavior?"

•

The genius proposes a world inventory of genius, in order to harness and coordinate the efforts of genius everywhere to create a better life for all men.
Letters are sent out . . .
The response is staggering!
Telegrams pour in . . .
Geniuses of every stripe offer their cooperation.
The *Times* prints an editorial praising the idea . . .
Three thousand geniuses in one room!
The genius falls into an ill humor. He refuses to speak to anyone for eight days.

•

But now a green Railway Express truck arrives at his door. It contains a field of stainless-steel tulips, courtesy of the Mayor and City Council of Houston, Texas. The genius signs the receipt, smiling . . .

Perpetua

1.

NOW PERPETUA was living alone. She had told her husband that she didn't want to live with him any longer.

"Why not?" he had asked.

"For all the reasons you know," she said.

Harold's farewell gift was a Blue Cross-Blue Shield insurance policy, paid up for one year. Now Perpetua was putting valve oil on her trumpet. One of the valves was sticking. She was fourth-chair trumpet with the New World Symphony Orchestra.

Perpetua thought: That time he banged the car door on my finger. I am sure it was deliberate. That time he locked me out while I was pregnant and I had to walk four miles after midnight to my father's house. One does not forget.

Perpetua smiled at the new life she saw spread out before her like a red velvet map.

Back in the former house, Harold watched television.

Perpetua remembered the year she was five. She had to learn to be nice, all in one year. She only learned part of it. She was not fully nice until she was seven.

Now I must obtain a lover, she thought. Perhaps more than one. One for Monday, one for Tuesday, one for Wednesday . . .

2.

Harold was looking at a picture of the back of a naked girl, in a magazine for men. The girl was pulling a dress over her head, in the picture. This girl has a nice-looking back, Harold thought. I wonder where she lives?

Perpetua sat on the couch in her new apartment smoking dope with a handsome bassoon player. A few cats walked around.

"Our art contributes nothing to the revolution," the bassoon player said. "We cosmeticize reality."

"We are trustees of Form," Perpetua said.

"It is hard to make the revolution with a bassoon," the bassoon player said.

"Sabotage?" Perpetua suggested.

"Sabotage would get me fired," her companion replied. "The sabotage would be confused with ineptness anyway."

I am tired of talking about the revolution, Perpetua thought.

"Go away," she said. The bassoon player put on his black raincoat and left.

It is wonderful to be able to tell them to go away, she reflected. Then she said aloud, "Go away. Go away. Go away."

Harold went to visit his child, Peter. Peter was at school in New England. "How do you like school?" Harold asked Peter.

"It's O.K.," Peter said. "Do you have a light?"

Harold and Peter watched the game together. Peter's school won. After the game, Harold went home.

3.

Perpetua went to her mother's house for Christmas. Her mother was cooking the eighty-seventh turkey of her life. "God damn this turkey!" Perpetua's mother shouted. "If anyone knew how I hate, loathe, and despise turkeys. If I had known that I would cook eighty-seven separate and distinct turkeys in my life, I would have split forty-four years ago. I would have been long gone for the tall timber."

Perpetua's mother showed her a handsome new leather coat. "Tanned in the bile of matricides," her mother said, with a meaningful look.

Harold wrote to the magazine for men asking for the name and address of the girl whose back had bewitched him. The magazine answered his letter saying that it could not reveal this information. The magazine was not a pimp, it said.

Harold, enraged, wrote to the magazine and said that if the magazine was not a pimp, what was it? The magazine answered that while it could not in all conscience give Harold the girl's address, it would be glad to give him her grid coordinates. Harold, who had had map reading in the Army, was delighted.

4.

Perpetua sat in the trumpet section of the New World Symphony Orchestra. She had a good view of the other players because the sections were on risers and the trumpet section sat on the highest riser of all. They were playing Brahms. A percussionist had just split a head on the bass drum. "I luff Brahms," he explained.

Perpetua thought: I wish this so-called conductor would get his movie together.

After the concert she took off her orchestra uniform and put on her suède jeans, her shirt made of a lot of colored scarves sewn together, her carved-wood neck bracelet, and her D'Artagnan cape with its silver lining.

Perpetua could not remember what was this year and what was last year. Had something just happened, or had it happened a long time ago? She met many new people. "You are different," Perpetua said to Sunny Marge. "Very few of the girls I know wear a tattoo of the head of Marshal Foch on their backs."

"I am different," Sunny Marge agreed. "Since I posed for that picture in that magazine for men, many people have been after my back. My back has become practically an international incident. So I decided to alter it."

"Will it come off? Ever?"

"I hope and pray."

Perpetua slept with Robert in his loft. His children were sleeping on mattresses in the other room. It was cold. Robert said that when he was a child he was accused by his teacher of being "pert."

"Pert?"

Perpetua and Robert whispered to each other, on the mattress.

5.

Perpetua said, "Now, I am alone. I have thrown my husband away. I remember him. Once he seemed necessary to me, or at least important, or at least interesting. Now none of these things is true. Now he is as strange to me as something in the window of a pet shop. I gaze into the pet-shop window, the Irish setters move about, making their charming moves, I see the moves and see that they are charming, yet I am not charmed. An Irish setter is what I do not need. I remember my husband awaking in the morning, inserting his penis in his penis sheath, placing ornaments of bead and feather on his upper arms, smearing his face with ochre and umber—broad lines under the eyes and across the brow. I remember him taking his blowpipe from the umbrella stand and leaving for the office. What he did there I never knew. Slew his enemies, he said. Our dinner table was decorated with the heads of his enemies, whom he had slain. It was hard to believe one man could have so many enemies. Or maybe they were the same enemies, slain over and over and over. He said he saw girls going down the street who broke his heart, in their loveliness. I no longer broke his heart, he said. I had not broken his heart for at least a year, perhaps more than a year, with my loveliness. Well screw that, I said, screw that. My oh my, he said, my oh my, what a mouth. He meant that I was foulmouthed. This, I said, is just the beginning."

In the desert, Harold's Land-Rover had a flat tire. Harold got out of the Land-Rover and looked at his map. Could this be the wrong map?

6.

Perpetua was scrubbing Sunny Marge's back with a typewriter eraser.

"Oh. Ouch. Oh. Ouch."

"I'm not making much progress," Perpetua said.

"Well I suppose it will have to be done by the passage of time," Sunny Marge said, looking at her back in the mirror.

"Years are bearing us to Heaven," Perpetua agreed.

Perpetua and Sunny Marge went cruising, on the boulevard. They saw a man coming toward them.

"He's awfully clean-looking," Perpetua said.

"Probably he's from out of town," Sunny Marge said.

Edmund was a small farmer.

"What is your cash crop?" Sunny Marge asked.

"We have two hundred acres in hops," the farmer replied. "That reminds me, would you ladies like a drink?"

"*I'd* like a drink," Perpetua said.

"I'd like a drink too," Sunny Marge said. "Do you know anywhere he can go, in those clothes?"

"Maybe we'd better go back to my place," Perpetua said.

At Perpetua's apartment Edmund recounted the history of hops.

"Would you like to see something interesting?" Sunny Marge asked Edmund.

"What is it?"

"A portrait of Marshal Foch, a French hero of World War I."

"Sure," Edmund said.

The revolution called and asked Perpetua if she would tape an album of songs of the revolution.

"Sure," Perpetua said.

Harold took ship for home. He shared a cabin with a man whose hobby was building scale models of tank battles.

"This is a *Sturmgeschütz* of the 1945 period," the man said. "Look at the bullet nicks. The bullet nicks are done by applying a small touch of gray paint with a burst effect of flat white. For small holes in the armor, I pierce with a hot nail."

The floor of Harold's cabin was covered with tanks locked in duels to the death.

Harold hurried to the ship's bar. I wonder how Perpetua is doing, he thought. I wonder if she is happier without me. Probably she is. Probably she has found deep contentment by now. But maybe not.

7.

Perpetua met many new people. She met Henry, who was a cathedral builder. He built cathedrals in places where there were no cathedrals—Twayne, Nebraska, for example. Every American city needed a cathedral, Henry said. The role of the cathedral in the building of the national soul was well known. We should punish ourselves in our purses, Henry said, to shape up the national soul. An arch never sleeps, Henry said, pointing to the never-sleeping arches in his plans. Architecture is memory, Henry said, and the nation that had no cathedrals to speak of had no memory to speak of either. He did it all, Henry said, with a 30-man crew composed of 1 superintendent 1 masonry foreman 1 ironworker foreman 1 carpenter foreman 1 pipefitter foreman 1 electrician foreman 2 journeyman masons 2 journeyman ironworkers 2 journeyman carpenters 2 journeyman pipefitters 2 journeyman electricians 1 mason's helper 1 ironworker's helper 1 carpenter's helper 1 pipefitter's helper 1 electrician's helper 3 gargoyle carvers 1 grimer 1 clerk-of-the-works 1 master fund-raiser 2 journeyman fund-raisers and 1 fund-raiser's helper. Cathedrals are mostly a matter of thrusts, Henry said. You got to balance your thrusts. The ribs of your vaults intersect collecting the vertical and lateral thrusts at fixed points which are then buttressed or grounded although that's not so important anymore when you use a steel skeleton as we do which may be cheating but I always say that cheating in the Lord's name is O.K. as long as He don't catch you at it. Awe and grace, Henry said, awe and grace, that's what we're selling and we offer a Poet's Corner where any folks who were poets or even suspected of being poets can be buried, just like Westminster Abbey. The financing is the problem, Henry said. What we usually do is pick out some old piece of ground that was a cornfield or something like that, and put it in the Soil Bank. We take that piece of ground out of production and promise the government we won't grow no more corn on it no matter how they beg and plead with us. Well the government sends a man around from the Agriculture Department and he agrees with us that there certainly ain't no corn growing there. So we ask him about how much he thinks we can get from the Soil Bank and he says it looks like around a hundred and fifty thousand a year to him but that he will have to check with the home office and we can't expect the money before around the middle of next week. We tell him that will be fine and we all go have a drink over to the Holiday Inn. Of course the hundred and fifty thousand is just a spit in the ocean but it pays for the four-color brochures. By this time we got our artist's rendering of the Twayne Undenominational Cathedral sitting right in the lobby of the Valley National Bank on a card table covered with angel hair left over from Christmas, and the money is just pouring in. And I'm worrying about how we're going to *staff* this cathedral. We need a sexton and a bellringer and a beadle and maybe an undenominational archbishop, and that last is hard to come by. Pretty soon the ground is broken and the steel is up, and the Bell Committee is wrangling about whether the carillon is going to be sixteen bells or thirty-two. There is something about cathedral building that men like, Henry said, this has often been noticed. And the first thing you know it's Dedication Day and the whole state is there, it seems like, with long lines of little girls carrying bouquets of mistflowers and the Elks Honor Guard presenting arms with M-16s sent back in pieces from Nam and reassembled for domestic use, and the band is playing the Albinoni Adagio in G Minor which is the saddest piece of music ever written by mortal man and the light is streaming through the guaranteed stained-glass windows and the awe is so thick you could cut it with a knife.

"You are something else, Henry," Perpetua said.

8.

Perpetua and André went over to have dinner with Sunny Marge and Edmund.

"This is André," Perpetua said.

André, a well-dressed graduate of the École du Regard, managed a large industry in Reims.

Americans were very strange, André said. They did not have a stable pattern of family life, as the French did. This was attributable to the greater liberty—perhaps license was not too strong a term—permitted to American women by their husbands and lovers. American women did not know where their own best interests lay, André said. The intoxication of modern life, which was in part a result of the falling away of former standards of conduct . . .

Perpetua picked up a chicken leg and tucked it into the breast pocket of André's coat.

"Goodbye, André."

Peter called Perpetua from his school in New England.

"What's the matter, Peter?"

"I'm lonesome."

"Do you want to come stay with me for a while?"

"No. Can you send me fifty dollars?"

"Yes. What do you want it for?"

"I want to buy some blue racers."

Peter collected snakes. Sometimes Perpetua thought that the snakes were dearer to him than she was.

9.

Harold walked into Perpetua's apartment.

"Harold," Perpetua said.

"I just want to ask you one question," Harold said. "Are you happier now than you were before?"

"Sure," Perpetua said.

A City of Churches

"Yes," Mr. Phillips said, "ours is a city of churches all right."

Cecelia nodded, following his pointing hand. Both sides of the street were solidly lined with churches, standing shoulder to shoulder in a variety of architectural styles. The Bethel Baptist stood next to the Holy Messiah Free Baptist, St. Paul's Episcopal next to Grace Evangelical Covenant. Then came the First Christian Science, the Church of God, All Souls, Our Lady of Victory, the Society of Friends, the Assembly of God, and the Church of the Holy Apostles. The spires and steeples of the traditional buildings were jammed in next to the broad imaginative flights of the "contemporary" designs.

"Everyone here takes a great interest in church matters," Mr. Phillips said.

Will I fit in? Cecelia wondered. She had come to Prester to open a branch office of a car-rental concern.

"I'm not especially religious," she said to Mr. Phillips, who was in the real-estate business.

"Not *now*," he answered. "Not *yet*. But we have many fine young people here. You'll get integrated into the community soon enough. The immediate problem is, where are you to live? Most people," he said, "live in the church of their choice. All of our churches have many extra rooms. I have a few belfry apartments that I can show you. What price range were you thinking of?"

They turned a corner and were confronted with more churches. They passed St. Luke's, the Church of the Epiphany, All Saints Ukrainian Orthodox, St. Clement's, Fountain Baptist, Union Congregational, St. Anargyri's, Temple Emanuel, the First Church of Christ Reformed. The mouths of all the churches were gaping open. Inside, lights could be seen dimly.

"I can go up to a hundred and ten," Cecelia said. "Do you have any buildings here that are *not* churches?"

"None," said Mr. Phillips. "Of course many of our fine

church structures also do double duty as something else." He indicated a handsome Georgian façade. "That one," he said, "houses the United Methodist and the Board of Education. The one next to it, which is Antioch Pentecostal, has the barbershop."

It was true. A red-and-white striped barber pole was attached inconspicuously to the front of the Antioch Pentecostal.

"Do many people rent cars here?" Cecelia asked. "Or would they, if there was a handy place to rent them?"

"Oh, I don't know," said Mr. Phillips. "Renting a car implies that you want to go somewhere. Most people are pretty content right here. We have a lot of activities. I don't think I'd pick the car-rental business if I was just starting out in Prester. But you'll do fine." He showed her a small, extremely modern building with a severe brick, steel, and glass front. "That's St. Barnabas. Nice bunch of people over there. Wonderful spaghetti suppers."

Cecelia could see a number of heads looking out of the windows. But when they saw that she was staring at them, the heads disappeared.

"Do you think it's healthy for so many churches to be gathered together in one place?" she asked her guide. "It doesn't seem . . . *balanced*, if you know what I mean."

"We are famous for our churches," Mr. Phillips replied. "They are harmless. Here we are now."

He opened a door and they began climbing many flights of dusty stairs. At the end of the climb they entered a good-sized room, square, with windows on all four sides. There was a bed, a table, and two chairs, lamps, a rug. Four very large bronze bells hung in the exact center of the room.

"What a view!" Mr. Phillips exclaimed. "Come here and look."

"Do they actually ring these bells?" Cecelia asked.

"Three times a day," Mr. Phillips said, smiling. "Morning, noon, and night. Of course when they're rung you have to be pretty quick at getting out of the way. You get hit in the head by one of these babies and that's all she wrote."

"God Almighty," said Cecelia involuntarily. Then she said,

"Nobody lives in the belfry apartments. That's why they're empty."

"You think so?" Mr. Phillips said.

"You can only rent them to new people in town," she said accusingly.

"I wouldn't do that," Mr. Phillips said. "It would go against the spirit of Christian fellowship."

"This town is a little creepy, you know that?"

"That may be, but it's not for you to say, is it? I mean, you're new here. You should walk cautiously, for a while. If you don't want an upper apartment I have a basement over at Central Presbyterian. You'd have to share it. There are two women in there now."

"I don't want to share," Cecelia said. "I want a place of my own."

"Why?" the real-estate man asked curiously. "For what purpose?"

"Purpose?" asked Cecelia. "There is no particular purpose. I just want—"

"That's not usual here. Most people live with other people. Husbands and wives. Sons with their mothers. People have roommates. That's the usual pattern."

"Still, I prefer a place of my own."

"It's very unusual."

"Do you have any such places? Besides bell towers, I mean?"

"I guess there are a few," Mr. Phillips said, with clear reluctance. "I can show you one or two, I suppose."

He paused for a moment.

"It's just that we have different values, maybe, from some of the surrounding communities," he explained. "We've been written up a lot. We had four minutes on the C.B.S. Evening News one time. Three or four years ago. 'A City of Churches,' it was called."

"Yes, a place of my own is essential," Cecelia said, "if I am to survive here."

"That's kind of a funny attitude to take," Mr. Phillips said. "What denomination are you?"

Cecelia was silent. The truth was, she wasn't anything.

"I said, what denomination are you?" Mr. Phillips repeated.

"I can will my dreams," Cecelia said. "I can dream whatever I want. If I want to dream that I'm having a good time, in Paris or some other city, all I have to do is go to sleep and I will dream that dream. I can dream whatever I want."

"What do you dream, then, mostly?" Mr. Phillips said, looking at her closely.

"Mostly sexual things," she said. She was not afraid of him.

"Prester is not that kind of a town," Mr. Phillips said, looking away.

They went back down the stairs.

The doors of the churches were opening, on both sides of the street. Small groups of people came out and stood there, in front of the churches, gazing at Cecelia and Mr. Phillips.

A young man stepped forward and shouted, "*Everyone in this town already has a car! There is no one in this town who doesn't have a car!*"

"Is that true?" Cecelia asked Mr. Phillips.

"Yes," he said. "It's true. No one would rent a car here. Not in a hundred years."

"Then I won't stay," she said. "I'll go somewhere else."

"You must stay," he said. "There is already a car-rental office for you. In Mount Moriah Baptist, on the lobby floor. There is a counter and a telephone and a rack of car keys. And a calendar."

"I won't stay," she said. "Not if there's not any sound business reason for staying."

"We want you," said Mr. Phillips. "We want you standing behind the counter of the car-rental agency, during regular business hours. It will make the town complete."

"I won't," she said. "Not me."

"You must. It's essential."

"I'll dream," she said. "Things you won't like."

"We are discontented," said Mr. Phillips. "Terribly, terribly discontented. Something is wrong."

"I'll dream the Secret," she said. "You'll be sorry."

"We are like other towns, except that we are perfect," he said. "Our discontent can only be held in check by perfection. We need a car-rental girl. Someone must stand behind that counter."

"I'll dream the life you are most afraid of," Cecelia threatened.

"You are ours," he said, gripping her arm. "Our car-rental girl. Be nice. There is nothing you can do."

"Wait and see," Cecelia said.

The Party

I WENT to a party and corrected a pronunciation. The man whose voice I had adjusted fell back into the kitchen. I praised a Bonnard. It was not a Bonnard. My new glasses, I explained, and I'm terribly sorry, but significant variations elude me, vodka exhausts me, I was young once, essential services are being maintained. Drums, drums, drums, outside the windows. I thought that if I could persuade you to say "No," then my own responsibility would be limited, or changed, another sort of life would be possible, different from the life we had previously, somewhat skeptically, enjoyed together. But you had wandered off into another room, testing the effect on members of the audience of your ruffled blouse, your long magenta skirt. Giant hands, black, thick with fur, reaching in through the windows. Yes, it was King Kong, back in action, and all of the guests uttered loud exclamations of fatigue and disgust, examining the situation in the light of their own needs and emotions, hoping that the ape was real or papier-mâché according to their temperaments, or wondering whether other excitements were possible out in the crisp, white night.

"Did you see him?"

"Let us pray."

The important tasks of a society are often entrusted to people who have fatal flaws. Of course we tried hard, it was intelligent to do so, extraordinary efforts were routine. Your zest was, and is, remarkable. But carrying over into private life attitudes that have been successful in the field of public administration is not, perhaps, a good idea. Zest is not fun for everybody. I am aware that roles change. Kong himself is now an adjunct professor of art history at Rutgers, co-author of a text on tomb sculpture; if he chooses to come to a party through the window he is simply trying to make himself interesting. A lady spoke to me, she had in her hand a bunch of cattleyas. "I have attempted to be agreeable," she said, "but it's like teaching iron to swim, with this group." Zest is not fun for everybody. When whippoorwills called, you answered. And then I would go out, with the lantern, up and down the streets, knocking on doors, asking perfect strangers if they had seen you. O.K. That is certainly one way of doing it. This is not a complaint. But wouldn't it be better to openly acknowledge your utter reliance on work, on specific, carefully formulated directions, agreeing that, yes, a certain amount of anesthesia is derived from what other people would probably think of as some kind of a career? Excel if you want, but remember that there are gaps. You told me that you had thought, as a young girl, that masturbation was "only for men." Couldn't you be mistaken about other things, too?

The two sisters were looking at television in the bedroom, on the bed, amidst the coats and hats, umbrellas, airline bags. I gave them each a drink and we watched the game together, the *Osservatore Romano* team vs. the Diet of Worms, Worms leading by six points. I had never seen khaki-colored punch before. The hostess said there would be word games afterward, some of the people outside would be invited in, peasant food served in big wooden bowls—wine, chicken, olive oil, bread. Everything would improve, she said. I could still hear, outside, the drums; whistles had been added, there were both whistles and drums. I was surprised. The present era, with its emphasis on emotional cost control as well as its insistent, almost annoying lucidity, does not favor splinter groups, because they can't win. Small collective manifestations are O.K. insofar as they show "stretch marks"—traces of strain which tend to establish that public policy is not a smooth, seamless achievement, like an egg, but has rather been hammered out at some cost to the policymakers. Kong got to his feet. "Louise loves me," he said, pointing to a girl, "but I would rather sleep with Cynthia Garmonsway. It's just one of those things. Human experience is different, in some ways, from ape experience, but that doesn't mean that I don't like perfumed nights, too." I know what he means. The mind carries you with it, away from what you are supposed to do, toward things that cannot be explained rationally, toward difficulty, lack of clarity, late-afternoon light.

"Francesca. Do you want to go?"

"I want to stay."

Now the sisters have begun taking their interminable showers, both bathrooms are tied up, I must either pretend not to know them or accept the blame. In the larger rooms tender fawns and pinks have replaced the earlier drab, sad colors. I noticed that howls and rattles had been added to the whistles and drums. Is it some kind of a revolution? Maybe a revolution in taste, as when Mannerism was overthrown by the Baroque. Kong is being curried by Cynthia Garmonsway. She holds the steel curry comb in her right hand and pulls it gently through the dark thick fur. Cynthia formerly believed in the "enormous diversity of things"; now she believes in Kong. The man whose pronunciation I had corrected emerged from the kitchen. "Probably it is music," he said, nodding at the windows, "the new music, which we older men are too old to understand."

You, of course, would never say such a thing to me, but you have said worse things. You told me that Kafka was not a thinker, and that a "genetic" approach to his work would disclose that much of it was only a kind of very imaginative whining. That was during the period when you were going in for wrecking operations, feeling, I suppose, that the integrity of your own mental processes was best maintained by a series of strong, unforgiving attacks. You made quite an impression on everyone, in those days: your ruffled blouse, your long magenta skirt slit to the knee, the dagger thrust into your boot. "Is that a metaphor?" I asked, pointing to the dagger; you shook your head, smiled, said no. Now that you have had a change of heart, now that you have joined us in finding Kafka, and Kleist, too, the awesome figures that we have agreed that they are, the older faculty are more comfortable with you, are ready to promote you, marry you, even, if that is your wish. But you don't have to make up your mind tonight. Relax and enjoy the party, to the extent that it is possible to do so; it is not over yet. The game has ended, a news program has begun. "Emerald mines in the northwest have been nationalized." A number of young people standing in a meadow, holding hands, singing. Can the life of the time be caught in an advertisement? Is that how it is, really, in the meadows of the world?

And where are all the new people I have come here to meet? I have met only a lost child, dressed in rags, real rags, holding an iron hook attached to a fifty-foot rope. I said, "What is that for?" The child said nothing, placed the hook quietly on the floor at my feet, opened a bottle and swallowed twenty aspirin. Is six too young for a suicide attempt? We fed her milk, induced vomiting, the police arrived within minutes. When one has spoken a lot one has already used up all of the ideas one has. You must change the people you are speaking to so that you appear, to yourself, to be still alive. But the people here don't look new; they look like emerald mine owners, in fact, or proprietors of some other sector of the economy that something bad has just happened to. I'm afraid that going up to them and saying "Travel light!," with a smile, will not really lift their spirits. Why am I called upon to make them happier, when it is so obviously beyond my competence? Francesca, you have selected the wrong partner, in me. You made the mistake a long time ago. I am not even sure that I like you now. But it is true that I cannot stop thinking about you, that every small daily problem—I will never be elected to the Academy, Richelieu is against me and d'Alembert is lukewarm—is examined in the light of your possible reaction, lack of reaction. At one moment you say that the Academy is a joke, at another that you are working industriously to sway Webster to my cause. Damned capricious! In the silence, an alphorn sounds. Then the noise again, drums, whistles, howls, rattles, alphorns. Attendants place heavy purple veils or shrouds over statuary, chairs, the buffet table, members of the orchestra. People are clustered in front of the bathrooms holding fine deep-piled towels, vying to dry the beautiful sisters. The towels move sensuously over the beautiful surfaces. I too could become excited over this prospect.

Dear Francesca, tell me, is this a successful party, in your view? Is this the best we can do? I know that you have always wanted to meet Kong; now that you have met him and he has said whatever he has said to you (I saw you smiling), can we go home? I mean you to your home, me to my home, all these others to their own homes, cells, cages? I am feeling a little ragged. What made us think that we would escape things like bankruptcy, alcoholism, being disappointed, having children? Say "No," refuse me once and for all, let me try something else. Of course we did everything right, insofar as we were able to imagine what "right" was. Is it really important to know that this movie is fine, and that one terrible, and to talk intelligently about the difference? Wonderful elegance! No good at all!

Engineer-Private Paul Klee Misplaces an Aircraft between Milbertshofen and Cambrai, March 1916

Paul Klee said:

"Now I have been transferred to the Air Corps. A kindly sergeant effected the transfer. He thought I would have a better future here, more chances for promotion. First I was assigned to aircraft repair, together with several other workers. We presented ourselves as not just painters but artist painters. This caused some shaking of heads. We varnished wooden fuselages, correcting old numbers and adding new ones with the help of templates. Then I was pulled off the painting detail and assigned to transport. I escort aircraft that are being sent to various bases in Germany and also (I understand) in occupied territory. It is not a bad life. I spend my nights racketing across Bavaria (or some such) and my days in switching yards. There is always bread and wurst and beer in the station restaurants. When I reach a notable town I try to see the notable paintings there, if time allows. There are always unexpected delays, reroutings, backtrackings. Then the return to the base. I see Lily fairly often. We meet in hotel rooms and that is exciting. I have never yet lost an aircraft or failed to deliver one to its proper destination. The war seems interminable. Walden has sold six of my drawings."

The Secret Police said:

"We have secrets. We have many secrets. We desire all secrets. We do not have your secrets and that is what we are after, your secrets. Our first secret is where we are. No one knows. Our second secret is how many of us there are. No one knows. Omnipresence is our goal. We do not even need real omnipresence. The theory of omnipresence is enough. With omnipresence, hand-in-hand as it were, goes omniscience. And with omniscience and omnipresence, hand-in-hand-in-hand as it were, goes omnipotence. We are a three-sided waltz. However our mood is melancholy. There is a secret sigh that we sigh, secretly. We yearn to be known, acknowledged, admired even. What is the good of omnipotence if nobody knows? However that is a secret, that sorrow. Now we are everywhere. One place we are is here watching Engineer-Private Klee, who is escorting three valuable aircraft, B.F.W. 3054/16–17–18, with spare parts, by rail from Milbertshofen to Cambrai. Do you wish to know what Engineer-Private Klee is doing at this very moment, in the baggage car? He is reading a book of Chinese short stories. He has removed his boots. His feet rest twenty-six centimeters from the baggage-car stove."

Paul Klee said:

"These Chinese short stories are slight and lovely. I have no way of knowing if the translation is adequate or otherwise. Lily will meet me in our rented room on Sunday, if I return in time. Our destination is Fighter Squadron Five. I have not had anything to eat since morning. The fine chunk of bacon given me along with my expense money when we left the base has been eaten. This morning a Red Cross lady with a squint gave me some very good coffee, however. Now we are entering Hohenbudberg."

The Secret Police said:

"Engineer-Private Klee has taken himself into the station restaurant. He is enjoying a hearty lunch. We shall join him there."

Paul Klee said:

"Now I emerge from the station restaurant and walk along the line of cars to the flatcar on which my aircraft (I think of them as *my* aircraft) are carried. To my surprise and dismay, I notice that one of them is missing. There had been three, tied down on the flatcar and covered with canvas. Now I see with my trained painter's eye that instead of three canvas-covered shapes on the flatcar there are only two. Where the third aircraft had been there is only a puddle of canvas and loose rope. I look around quickly to see if anyone else has marked the disappearance of the third aircraft."

The Secret Police said:

"We had marked it. Our trained policemen's eyes had marked the fact that where three aircraft had been before, tied down on the flatcar and covered with canvas, now there were only two. Unfortunately we had been in the station restaurant, lunching, at the moment of removal, therefore we could not attest as to where it had gone or who had removed it. There is something we do not know. This is irritating in the extreme. We closely observe Engineer-Private Klee to determine what action he will take in the emergency. We observe that he is withdrawing from his tunic a notebook and pencil. We observe that he begins, very properly in our opinion, to note down in his notebook all the particulars of the affair."

Paul Klee said:

"The shape of the collapsed canvas, under which the aircraft had rested, together with the loose ropes—the canvas forming hills and valleys, seductive folds, the ropes the very essence of looseness, lapsing—it is irresistible. I sketch for ten or fifteen minutes, wondering the while if I might not be in trouble, because of the missing aircraft. When I arrive at Fighter Squadron Five with less than the number of aircraft listed on the manifest, might not some officious person become angry? Shout at me? I have finished sketching. Now I will ask various trainmen and station personnel if they have seen anyone carrying away the aircraft. If they answer in the negative, I will become extremely frustrated. I will begin to kick the flatcar."

The Secret Police said:

"Frustrated, he begins to kick the flatcar."

Paul Klee said:

"I am looking up in the sky, to see if my aircraft is there. There are in the sky aircraft of several types, but none of the type I am searching for."

The Secret Police said:

"Engineer-Private Klee is searching the sky—an eminently sound procedure, in our opinion. We, the Secret Police, also sweep the Hohenbudberg sky, with our eyes. But find nothing. We are debating with ourselves as to whether we ought to enter the station restaurant and begin drafting our preliminary report, for forwarding to higher headquarters. The knotty point, in terms of the preliminary report, is that we do not have the answer to the question 'Where is the aircraft?' The damage potential to the theory of omniscience, as well as potential to our careers, dictates that this point be omitted from the preliminary report. But if this point is omitted, might not some officious person at the Central Bureau for Secrecy note the omission? Become angry? Shout at us? Omissiveness is not rewarded at the Central Bureau. We decide to observe further the actions of Engineer-Private Klee, for the time being."

Paul Klee said:

"I who have never lost an aircraft have lost an aircraft. The aircraft is signed out to me. The cost of the aircraft, if it is not found, will be deducted from my pay, meager enough already. Even if Walden sells a hundred, a thousand drawings, I will not have enough money to pay for this cursed aircraft. Can I, in the time the train remains in the Hohenbudberg yards, construct a new aircraft or even the simulacrum of an aircraft, with no materials to work with or indeed any special knowledge of aircraft construction? The situation is ludicrous. I will therefore apply Reason. Reason dictates the solution. I will diddle the manifest. With my painter's skill which is after all not so different from a forger's, I will change the manifest to reflect conveyance of *two* aircraft, B.F.W. 3054/16 and 17, to Fighter Squadron Five. The extra canvas and ropes I will conceal in an empty boxcar—this one, which according to its stickers is headed for Essigny-le-Petit. Now I will walk around town and see if I can find a chocolate shop. I crave chocolate."

The Secret Police said:

"Now we observe Engineer-Private Klee concealing the canvas and ropes which covered the former aircraft into an empty boxcar bound for Essigny-le-Petit. We have previously observed him diddling the manifest with his painter's skill which resembles not a little that of the forger. We applaud these actions of Engineer-Private Klee. The contradiction confronting us in the matter of the preliminary report is thus resolved in highly satisfactory fashion. We are proud of Engineer-Private Klee and of the resolute and manly fashion in which he has dealt with the crisis. We predict he will go far. We would like to embrace him as a comrade and brother but unfortunately we are not embraceable. We are secret, we exist in the shadows, the pleasure of the comradely/brotherly embrace is one of the pleasures we are denied, in our dismal service."

Paul Klee said:

"We arrive at Cambrai. The planes are unloaded, six men for each plane. The work goes quickly. No one questions my altered manifest. The weather is clearing. After lunch I will leave to begin the return journey. My release slip and travel orders are ready, but the lieutenant must come and sign them. I wait contentedly in the warm orderly room. The drawing I did of the collapsed canvas and ropes is really very good. I eat a piece of chocolate. I am sorry about the lost aircraft but not overmuch. The war is temporary. But drawings and chocolate go on forever."

A Film

THINGS HAVE never been better, except that the child, one of the stars of our film, has just been stolen by vandals, and this will slow down the progress of the film somewhat, if not bring it to a halt. But might not this incident, which is not without its own human drama, be made part of the story line? Julie places a hand on the child's head, in the vandal camp. "The fever has broken." The vandals give the child a wood doll to play with, until night comes. And suddenly I blunder into a landing party from our ships—forty lieutenants all in white, all holding their swords in front of their chins, in salute. The officer in charge slams his blade into its scabbard several times, in a gesture either decisive or indecisive. Yes, he will help us catch the vandals. No, he has no particular plan. Just general principles, he says. The Art of War itself.

The idea of the film is that it not be like other films.

I heard a noise outside. I looked out of the window. An old woman was bent over my garbage can, borrowing some of my garbage. They do that all over the city, old men and old women. They borrow your garbage and they never bring it back.

Thinking about the "Flying to America" sequence. This will be the film's climax. But am I capable of mounting such a spectacle? Fortunately I have Ezra to help.

"And is it not the case," said Ezra, when we first met, "that I have been associated with the production of nineteen major motion pictures of such savage originality, scalding *vérité*, and honey-warm sexual indecency that the very theaters chained their doors rather than permit exhibition of these major motion pictures on their ammonia-scented gum-daubed premises? And is it not the case," said Ezra, "that I myself with my two sinewy hands and strong-wrought God-gift brain have participated in the changing of seven high-class literary works of the first water and four of the second water and two of the third water into major muscatel? And is it not the living truth," said Ezra, "that

I was the very man, I myself and none other without exception, who clung to the underside of the camera of the great Dreyer, clung with my two sinewy hands and noble thighs and cunning-muscled knees both dexter and sinister, during the cinematization of the master's *Gertrud*, clung there to slow the movement of said camera to that exquisite slowness which distinguishes this masterpiece from all other masterpieces of its water? And is it not chapter and verse," said Ezra, "that I was the comrade of all the comrades of the Dziga-Vertov group who was first in no-saying, firmest in no-saying, most final in no-saying, to all honey-sweet commercial seductions of whatever water and capitalist blandishments of whatever water and ideological incorrectitudes of whatever water whatsoever? And is it not as true as Saul become Paul," said Ezra, "that you require a man, a firm-limbed long-winded good true man, and that *I am the man* standing before you in his very blood and bones?"

"You are hired, Ezra," I said.

Whose child is it? We forgot to ask, when we sent out the casting call. Perhaps it belongs to itself. It has an air of self-possession quite remarkable in one so homely, and I notice that its paychecks are made out to it, rather than a nominee. Fortunately we have Julie to watch over it. The motor hotel in Tel Aviv is our temporary, not long-range, goal. New arrangements will probably not do the trick but we are making them anyhow: the ransom has been counted into pretty colored sacks, the film placed in round tin cans, the destroyed beams blocking the path are pushed aside . . .

Thinking of sequences for the film.
   A frenzy of desire?
   Sensible lovers taking precautions?
   Swimming with horses?

Today we filmed fear, a distressing emotion aroused by impending danger, real or imagined. In fear you know what you're afraid of, whereas in anxiety you do not. Correlation of children's fears with those of their parents is .667 according to Hagman. We filmed the startle pattern—shrinking, blinking, all that. Ezra refused to do "inhibition of the higher nervous centers." I don't blame him. However he was very good in demonstrating the sham rage reaction and also in "panting." Then we shot some stuff in which a primitive person (my bare arm standing in for the primitive person) kills an enemy by pointing a magic bone at him. "O.K., who's got the magic bone?" The magic bone was brought. I pointed the magic bone and the actor playing the enemy fell to the ground. I had carefully explained to the actor that the magic bone would not really kill him, probably.

Next, the thrill of fear along the buttocks. We used Julie's buttocks for this sequence. "Hope is the very sign of lack-of-happiness," said Julie, face down on the divan. "Fame is a palliative for doubt," I said. "Wealth-formation is a source of fear for both winners and losers," Ezra said. "Civilization aims at making all good things accessible even to cowards," said the actor who had played the enemy, quoting Nietzsche. Julie's buttocks thrilled.

We wrapped, then. I took the magic bone home with me. I don't believe in it, exactly, but you never know.

Have I ever been more alert, more confident? Following the dropped handkerchiefs to the vandal camp—there, a blue and green one, hanging on a shrub! The tall vandal chief wipes his hands on his sweatshirt. Vandals, he says, have been grossly misperceived. Their old practices, which earned them widespread condemnation, were a response to specific historical situations, and not a character trait, like being good or bad. Our negative has been scratched with a pointed instrument, all 150,000 feet of it. But the vandals say they were on the other side of town that night, planting trees. It is difficult to believe them. But gazing at the neat rows of saplings, carefully emplaced and surrounded by a vetchlike ground cover . . . A beautiful job! One does not know what to think.

We have got Frot Newling for the film; he will play the important role of George. Frot wanted many Gs in the beginning, but now that he understands the nature of the project he is working for scale, so that he can grow, as an actor and as a person. He is growing visibly, shot by shot. Soon he will be the biggest actor in the business. The other actors crowd about him, peering into his ankles . . . *Should* this film be made? That is one of the difficult questions one has to forget, when one is laughing in the face of unclear situations, or bad weather. What a beautiful girl Julie is! Her lustrous sexuality has the vandals agog. They follow her around trying to touch the tip of her glove, or the flounce of her gown. She shows her breasts to anyone who asks. "Amazing grace!" the vandals say.

Today we filmed the moon rocks. We set up in the Moon Rock Room, at the Smithsonian. There they were. The moon rocks. The moon rocks were the greatest thing we had ever seen in our entire lives! The moon rocks were red, green, blue, yellow, black, and white. They scintillated, sparkled, glinted, glittered, twinkled, and gleamed. They produced booms, thunderclaps, explosions, clashes, splashes, and roars. They sat on a pillow of the purest Velcro, and people who touched the pillow were able to throw away their crutches and jump in the air. Four cases of gout and eleven instances of hyperbolic paraboloidism were cured before our eyes. The air rained crutches. The moon rocks drew you toward them with a fatal irresistibility, but at the same time held you at a seemly distance with a decent reserve. Peering into the moon rocks, you could see the future and the past in color, and you could change them in any way you wished. The moon rocks gave off a slight hum, which cleaned your teeth, and a brilliant glow, which absolved you from sin. The moon rocks whistled *Finlandia*, by Jean Sibelius, while reciting *The Confessions of St. Augustine*, by I. F. Stone. The moon rocks were as good as a meaningful and emotionally rewarding seduction that you had not expected. The moon rocks were as good as listening to what the members of the Supreme Court say to each other, in the Supreme Court Locker Room. They were as good as a war. The moon rocks were better than a presentation copy of the *Random House Dictionary of the English Language* signed by Geoffrey Chaucer himself. They were better than a movie in which the President refuses to tell the people what to do to save themselves from the terrible thing that is about to happen, although he knows what ought to be done and has written a secret memorandum about it. The moon rocks were better than a good cup of coffee from an urn decorated with the change of Philomel, by the barbarous king. The moon rocks were better than a *¡huelga!* led by Mongo Santamaria, with additional dialogue by St. John of the Cross and special effects by Melmoth the Wanderer. The moon rocks surpassed our expectations. The dynamite out-of-sight very heavy and together moon rocks turned us on, to the highest degree. There was blood on our eyes, when we had finished filming them.

What if the film fails? And if it fails, will I know it?

A murdered doll floating face down in a bathtub—that will be the opening shot. A "cold" opening, but with faint intimations of the happiness of childhood and the pleasure we take in water. Then, the credits superimposed on a hanging side of beef. Samisen music, and a long speech from a vandal spokesman praising vandal culture and minimizing the sack of Rome in 455 A.D. Next, shots of a talk program in which all of the participants are whispering, including the host. Softness could certainly be considered a motif here. The child is well behaved through the long hours of shooting. The lieutenants march nicely, swinging their arms. The audience smiles. A vandal is standing near the window, and suddenly large cracks appear in the window. Pieces of glass fall to the floor. But I was watching him the whole time; he did nothing.

I wanted to film everything but there are things we are not getting. The wild ass is in danger in Ethiopia—we've got nothing on that. We've got nothing on intellectual elitism funded out of public money, an important subject. We've got nothing on ball lightning and nothing on the National Grid and not a foot on the core-mantle problem, the problem of a looped economy, or the interesting problem of the night brain.

I wanted to get it all but there's only so much time, so much energy. There's an increasing resistance to antibiotics worldwide and liquid metal fast-breeder reactors are subject to swelling and a large proportion of Quakers are color-blind but our film will have not a shred of material on any of these matters.

Is the film sufficiently sexual? I don't know.

I remember a brief exchange with Julie about revolutionary praxis.

"But I thought," I said, "that there had been a sexual revolution and everybody could sleep with anybody who was a consenting adult."

"In theory," Julie said. "In theory. But sleeping with somebody also has a political dimension. One does not, for example, go to bed with running dogs of imperialism."

I thought: But who will care for and solace the running dogs of imperialism? Who will bring them their dog food, who will tuck the covers tight as they dream their imperialistic dreams?

We press on. But where is Ezra? He was supposed to bring additional light, the light we need for "Flying to America." The vandals hit the trail, confused as to whether they should place themselves under our protection, or fight. The empty slivovitz bottles are buried, the ashes of the cooking fires scattered. At a signal from the leader the sleek, well-cared-for mobile homes swing onto the highway. The rehabilitation of the filmgoing public through "good design," through "softness," is our secret aim. The payment of rent for seats will be continued for a little while, but eventually abolished. Anyone will be able to walk into a film as into a shower. Bathing with the actors will become commonplace. Terror and terror are our two great principles, but we have other principles to fall back on, if these fail. "I can relate to that," Frot says. He does. We watch skeptically.

Who had murdered the doll? We pressed our inquiry, receiving every courtesy from the Tel Aviv police, who said they had never seen a case like it, either in their memories, or in dreams. A few wet towels were all the evidence that remained, except for, in the doll's hollow head, little pieces of paper on which were written

>JULIE
>JULIE
>JULIE
>JULIE

in an uncertain hand. And now the ground has opened up and swallowed our cutting room. One cannot really hold the vandals responsible. And yet . . .

Now we are shooting "Flying to America."

The 112 pilots check their watches.

Ezra nowhere to be seen. Will there be enough light?

If the pilots all turn on their machines at once . . .

Flying to America.

(But did I remember to—?)

"Where is the blimp?" Marcello shouts. "I can't find the—"

Ropes dangling from the sky.

I'm using forty-seven cameras, the outermost of which is posted in the Dover Marshes.

The Atlantic is calm in some parts, angry in others.

A blueprint four miles long is the flight plan.

Every detail coordinated with the air-sea rescue services of all nations.

Victory through Air Power! I seem to remember that slogan from somewhere.

Hovercraft flying to America. Flying boats flying to America. F-111s flying to America. The China Clipper!

Seaplanes, bombers, Flying Wings flying to America.

A shot of a pilot named Tom. He opens the cockpit door and speaks to the passengers. "America is only two thousand miles away now," he says. The passengers break out in smiles.

Balloons flying to America (they are painted in red-and-white stripes). Spads and Fokkers flying to America. Self-improvement is a large theme in flying to America. "Nowhere is self-realization more a possibility than in America," a man says.

Julie watching the clouds of craft in the air . . .

Gliders gliding to America. One man has constructed a huge paper aircraft, seventy-two feet in length. It is doing better than we had any right to expect. But then great expectations are an essential part of flying to America.

Rich people are flying to America, and poor people, and people of moderate means. This aircraft is powered by twelve rubber bands, each rubber band thicker than a man's leg—can it possibly survive the turbulence over Greenland?

Long thoughts are extended to enwrap the future American experience of the people who are flying to America.

And here is Ezra! and Ezra is carrying the light we need for this part of the picture—a great bowl of light lent to us by the

U.S. Navy. Now our film will be successful, or at least completed, and the aircraft illuminated, and the child will be rescued, and Julie will marry well, and the light from the light will fall into the eyes of the vandals, fixing them in place. Truth! That is another thing they said our film wouldn't contain. I had simply forgotten about it, in contemplating the series of triumphs that is my private life.

The Sandman

DEAR DR. HODDER, I realize that it is probably wrong to write a letter to one's girl friend's shrink but there are several things going on here that I think ought to be pointed out to you. I thought of making a personal visit but the situation then, as I'm sure you understand, would be completely untenable—I would be *visiting a psychiatrist*. I also understand that in writing to you I am in some sense interfering with the process but you don't have to discuss with Susan what I have said. Please consider this an "eyes only" letter. Please think of it as personal and confidential.

You must be aware, first, that because Susan is my girl friend pretty much everything she discusses with you she also discusses with me. She tells me what she said and what you said. We have been seeing each other for about six months now and I am pretty familiar with her story, or stories. Similarly, with your responses, or at least the general pattern. I know, for example, that my habit of referring to you as "the sandman" annoys you but let me assure you that I mean nothing unpleasant by it. It is simply a nickname. The reference is to the old rhyme: "Sea-sand does the sandman bring/Sleep to end the day/He dusts the children's eyes with sand/And steals their dreams away." (This is a variant; there are other versions, but this is the one I prefer.) I also understand that you are a little bit shaky because the prestige of analysis is now, as I'm sure you know far better than I, at a nadir. This must tend to make you nervous and who can blame you? One always tends to get a little bit shook when one's methodology is in question. Of course! (By the bye, let me say that I am very pleased that you are one of the ones that talk, instead of just sitting there. I think that's a good thing, an excellent thing, I congratulate you.)

To the point. I fully understand that Susan's wish to terminate with you and buy a piano instead has disturbed you. You have every right to be disturbed and to say that she is not electing the proper course, that what she says conceals something else, that she is evading reality, etc., etc. Go ahead. But there is one possibility here that you might be, just might be, missing. Which is that she means it.

Susan says: "I want to buy a piano."

You think: She wishes to terminate the analysis and escape into the piano.

Or: Yes, it is true that her father wanted her to be a concert pianist and that she studied for twelve years with Goetzmann. But she does not really want to reopen that can of maggots. She wants me to disapprove.

Or: Having failed to achieve a career as a concert pianist, she wishes to fail again. She is now too old to achieve the original objective. The spontaneous organization of defeat!

Or: She is flirting again.

Or:

Or:

Or:

Or:

The one thing you cannot consider, by the nature of your training and of the discipline itself, is that she really might want to terminate the analysis and buy a piano. That the piano might be more necessary and valuable to her than the analysis.[1]

What we really have to consider here is the locus of hope. Does hope reside in the analysis or rather in the piano? As a shrink rather than a piano salesman you would naturally tend to opt for the analysis. But there are differences. The piano salesman can stand behind his product; you, unfortunately, cannot. A Steinway is a known quantity, whereas an analysis can succeed or fail. I don't reproach you for this, I simply note it. (An interesting question: Why do laymen feel such a desire to, in plain language, fuck over shrinks? As I am doing here, in a sense? I don't mean hostility in the psychoanalytic encounter, I mean in general. This is an interesting phenomenon and should be investigated by somebody.)

It might be useful if I gave you a little taste of my own experience of analysis. I only went five or six times. Dr. Behring

---

[1] For an admirable discussion of this sort of communication failure and many other matters of interest see Percy, "Toward a Triadic Theory of Meaning," *Psychiatry*, Vol. 35 (February 1972), pp. 6–14 *et seq.*

was a tall thin man who never said anything much. If you could get a "What comes to mind?" out of him you were doing splendidly. There was a little incident that is, perhaps, illustrative. I went for my hour one day and told him about something I was worried about. (I was then working for a newspaper down in Texas.) There was a story that four black teenagers had come across a little white boy, about ten, in a vacant lot, sodomized him repeatedly and then put him inside a refrigerator and closed the door (this was before they had that requirement that abandoned refrigerators had to have their doors removed) and he suffocated. I don't know to this day what actually happened, but the cops had picked up *some* black kids and were reportedly beating the shit out of them in an effort to make them confess. I was not on the police run at that time but one of the police reporters told me about it and I told Dr. Behring. A good liberal, he grew white with anger and said what was I doing about it? It was the first time he had talked. So I was shaken—it hadn't occurred to me that I was required to do something about it, he was right—and after I left I called my then sister-in-law, who was at that time secretary to a City Councilman. As you can imagine, such a position is a very powerful one—the councilmen are mostly off making business deals and the executive secretaries run the office—and she got on to the chief of police with an inquiry as to what was going on and if there was any police brutality involved and if so, how much. The case was a very sensational one, you see; *Ebony* had a writer down there trying to cover it but he couldn't get in to see the boys and the cops had roughed him up some, they couldn't understand at that time that there could be such a thing as a black reporter. They understood that they had to be a little careful with the white reporters, but a black reporter was beyond them. But my sister-in-law threw her weight (her Councilman's weight) around a bit and suggested to the chief that if there was a serious amount of brutality going on the cops had better stop it, because there was too much outside interest in the case and it would be extremely bad PR if the brutality stuff got out. I also called a guy I knew pretty high up in the sheriff's department and suggested that *he* suggest to his colleagues that they cool it. I hinted at unspeakable political urgencies and he picked it up. The sheriff's department was separate from the police department but they both operated out of the Courthouse Building and they interacted quite a bit, in the normal course. So the long and short of it was that the cops decided to show the four black kids at a press conference to demonstrate that they weren't really beat all to rags, and that took place at four in the afternoon. I went and the kids looked O.K., except for one whose teeth were out and who the cops said had fallen down the stairs. Well, we all know the falling-down-the-stairs story but the point was the *degree* of mishandling and it was clear that the kids had not been half-killed by the cops, as the rumor stated. They were walking and talking naturally, although scared to death, as who would not be? There weren't any TV pictures because the newspaper people always pulled out the plugs of the TV people, at important moments, in those days—it was a standard thing. Now while I admit it sounds callous to be talking about the degree of brutality being minimal, let me tell you that it was no small matter, in that time and place, to force the cops to show the kids to the press at all. It was an achievement, of sorts. So about eight o'clock I called Dr. Behring at home, I hope interrupting his supper, and told him that the kids were O.K., relatively, and he said that was fine, he was glad to hear it. They were later no-billed and I stopped seeing him. That was my experience of analysis and that it may have left me a little sour, I freely grant. Allow for this bias.

To continue. I take exception to your remark that Susan's "openness" is a form of voyeurism. This remark interested me for a while, until I thought about it. Voyeurism I take to be an eroticized expression of curiosity whose chief phenomenological characteristic is the distance maintained between the voyeur and the object. The tension between the desire to draw near the object and the necessity to maintain the distance becomes a libidinous energy nondischarge, which is what the voyeur seeks.[2] The tension. But your remark indicates, in my opinion, a radical misreading of the problem. Susan's "openness"—a willingness of the heart, if you will allow such a term—is not at

---

[2]See, for example, Straus, "Shame As a Historiological Problem," in *Phenomenological Psychology* (New York: Basic Books, 1966), p. 219.

all comparable to the activities of the voyeur. Susan draws near. Distance is not her thing—not by a long chalk. Frequently, as you know, she gets burned, but she always tries again. What is operating here, I suggest, is an attempt on your part to "stabilize" Susan's behavior in reference to a state-of-affairs that you feel should obtain. Susan gets married and lives happily ever after. Or: There is within Susan a certain amount of creativity which should be liberated and actualized. Susan becomes an artist and lives happily ever after.

But your norms are, I suggest, skewing your view of the problem, and very badly.

Let us take the first case. You reason: If Susan is happy or at least functioning in the present state of affairs (that is, moving from man to man as a silver dollar moves from hand to hand), then why is she seeing a shrink? Something is wrong. New behavior is indicated. Susan is to get married and live happily ever after. May I offer another view? That is, that "seeing a shrink" might be precisely a maneuver in a situation in which Susan *does not want* to get married and live happily ever after? That getting married and living happily ever after might be, for Susan, the worst of fates, and that in order to validate her nonacceptance of this norm she defines herself to herself as shrink-needing? That you are actually certifying the behavior which you seek to change? (When she says to you that she's not shrinkable, you should listen.)

Perhaps, Dr. Hodder, my logic is feeble, perhaps my intuitions are frail. It is, God knows, a complex and difficult question. Your perception that Susan is an artist of some kind *in potentia* is, I think, an acute one. But the proposition "Susan becomes an artist and lives happily ever after" is ridiculous. (I realize that I am couching the proposition in such terms—"happily ever after"—that it is ridiculous on the face of it, but there is ridiculousness piled upon ridiculousness.) Let me point out, if it has escaped your notice, that what an artist does, is fail. Any reading of the literature[3] (I mean the theory of artistic creation), however summary, will persuade you instantly

---

[3]Especially, perhaps, Ehrenzweig, *The Hidden Order of Art* (University of California Press, 1966), pp. 234–9.

that the paradigmatic artistic experience is that of failure. The actualization fails to meet, equal, the intuition. There is something "out there" which cannot be brought "here." This is standard. I don't mean bad artists, I mean good artists. There is no such thing as a "successful artist" (except, of course, in worldly terms). The proposition should read, "Susan becomes an artist and lives unhappily ever after." This is the case. Don't be deceived.

What I am saying is, that the therapy of choice is not clear. I deeply sympathize. You have a dilemma.

I ask you to note, by the way, that Susan's is not a seeking after instant gratification as dealt out by so-called encounter or sensitivity groups, nude marathons, or dope. None of this is what is going down. "Joy" is not Susan's bag. I praise her for seeking out you rather than getting involved with any of this other idiocy. Her forte, I would suggest, is mind, and if there are games being played they are being conducted with taste, decorum, and some amount of intellectual rigor. Not-bad games. When I take Susan out to dinner she does not order chocolate-covered ants, even if they are on the menu. (Have you, by the way, tried Alfredo's, at the corner of Bank and Hudson streets? It's wonderful.) (Parenthetically, the problem of analysts sleeping with their patients is well known and I understand that Susan has been routinely seducing you—a reflex, she can't help it—throughout the analysis. I understand that there is a new splinter group of therapists, behaviorists of some kind, who take this to be some kind of ethic? Is this true? Does this mean that they do it only when they want to, or whether they want to or not? At a dinner party the other evening a lady analyst was saying that three cases of this kind had recently come to her attention and she seemed to think that this was rather a lot. The problem of maintaining mentorship is, as we know, not easy. I think you have done very well in this regard, and God knows it must have been difficult, given those skirts Susan wears that unbutton up to the crotch and which she routinely leaves unbuttoned to the third button.)

Am I wandering too much for you? Bear with me. The world is waiting for the sunrise.

We are left, I submit, with the problem of her depressions. They are, I agree, terrible. Your idea that I am not "supportive" enough is, I think, wrong. I have found, as a practical matter, that the best thing to do is to just do ordinary things, read the newspaper for example, or watch basketball, or wash the dishes. That seems to allow her to come out of it better than any amount of so-called "support." (About the *chasmus hystericus* or hysterical yawning I don't worry any more. It is masking behavior, of course, but after all, you must allow us our tics. The world is waiting for the sunrise.) What do you do with a patient who finds the world unsatisfactory? The world *is* unsatisfactory; only a fool would deny it. I know that your own ongoing psychic structuralization is still going on—you are thirty-seven and I am forty-one—but you must be old enough by now to realize that shit is shit. Susan's perception that America has somehow got hold of the greed ethic and that the greed ethic has turned America into a tidy little hell is not, I think, wrong. What do you do with such a perception? Apply Band-Aids, I suppose. About her depressions, I wouldn't do anything. I'd leave them alone. Put on a record.[4]

Let me tell you a story.

One night we were at her place, about three A.M., and this man called, another lover, quite a well-known musician who is very good, very fast—a good man. He asked Susan "Is he there?," meaning me, and she said "Yes," and he said "What are you doing?," and she said, "What do you think?," and he said, "When will you be finished?," and she said, "Never." Are you, Doctor dear, in a position to appreciate the beauty of this reply, in this context?

What I am saying is that Susan is wonderful. *As is.* There are not so many things around to which that word can be accurately applied. Therefore I must view your efforts to improve her with, let us say, a certain amount of ambivalence. If this makes me a negative factor in the analysis, so be it. I will be a negative factor until the cows come home, and cheerfully. I can't help it, Doctor, I am voting for the piano.

With best wishes,

---

[4]For example, Harrison, "Wah, Wah," Apple Records, STCH 639, Side One, Track 3.

Departures

1.

I CASHED a fifty-dollar Defense Bond given me by my older brother and ran away from home. We stood by the roadside, myself and a colleague who was also running away from home, holding out our hands. This was in Texas, during the War. An old Hudson stopped. Inside were a black man, who was driving, a white man, who was sitting in the death seat, and a small Oriental-looking woman, who was sitting in back. "Where you goin'?" the black man asked. "Mexico City," we said. We were wearing jeans and T-shirts. "O.K.," the black man said, "get in." The white man in the front seat began telling us about himself. He was a songwriter, he said. He had written "Drinking Lemonade in Kentucky in the Morning." Had we ever heard that one? We said no, indicating that the fault was ours—pure ignorance. He had lived in Hawaii for a long time, he said. His wife back there was Hawaiian. The black man was a professional jazz drummer. They were headed for Mexico City, by a striking coincidence. They all lived together in Mexico City, D.F., and had a business there.

We crossed the border at Laredo. My friend Herman and I had changed all the money we had into one-peso notes with a fifty-peso note on the outside of the wad. We showed the wad to the border officials demonstrating that we would not become a burden upon the State. We had learned this device from the movies.

After the second border checkpoint had been passed, the car stopped at a house and everybody got out to change the tires. The drummer and the songwriter pried the tires off the rims. Herman and I helped. Copper wire, hundreds of feet of it, was wound round each of the rims. Our friends were smuggling copper wire, a scarce item during the War. The benefits of leaving home were borne in on us. We had never met any absolutely genuine smugglers before.

When we got to Mexico City, the songwriter and the drummer gave us jobs in their business which was importing American jukeboxes and converting them into Mexican jukeboxes. Our job was to file the coin slots of the jukeboxes into larger slots so that they would accept Mexican coins, which tend to be large. We stayed there a week. Then we went home.

2.

ARMY PLANS TO FREEZE
3 MILLION BIRDS TO DEATH

MILAN, Tenn., Feb. 14 (AP)—The Army is planning to freeze to death three million or so blackbirds that took up residence two years ago at the Milan Arsenal.

Paul LeFebvre of the U.S. Department of the Interior, which is also working on the plan, said yesterday that the birds would be sprayed with two chemicals, resulting in a rapid loss of body heat. This will be done on a night with sub-freezing temperatures, he said.

3.

There is an elementary school, P.S. 421, across the street from my building. Now the Board of Education is busing children from the bad areas of the city to P.S. 421 (our area is thought to be a good area) and busing children from P.S. 421 to schools in the bad areas, in order to achieve racial balance in the schools. The parents of the P.S. 421 children do not like this very much, but they are all good citizens and feel it must be done. The parents of the children in the bad areas may not like it much, either, having their children so far from home, but they too probably feel that the process makes somehow for a better education. Every morning the green buses arrive in front of the school, some bringing black and Puerto Rican children to P.S. 421 and others taking the local, mostly white, children away. Presiding over all this is the loadmaster.

The loadmaster is a heavy, middle-aged white woman, not fat but heavy, who wears a blue cloth coat and a scarf around her head and carries a clipboard. She gets the children into and out of the buses, briskly, briskly, shouting, "Let's go, let's go, LET'S GO!" She has a voice that is louder than the voices of forty children. She gets a bus filled up, gives her clipboard a fast once-over, and sends the driver on his way: "O.K., José." The bus has been parked in the middle of the street, and there is a long line of hungup cars behind it, unable to pass, their drivers blowing their horns impatiently. When the drivers of these cars honk their horns too vigorously, the loadmaster steps away from the bus and yells at them in a voice louder than fourteen stacked-up drivers blowing their horns all at once: "KEEP YOUR PANTS ON!" Then to the bus driver: "O.K., José." As the bus starts off, she stands back giving it an authoritative smack on its rump (much like a coach sending a fresh player into the game) as it passes. Then she waves the stacked-up drivers on their way, one authoritative wave for each driver. She is making authoritative motions long after there is any necessity for it.

4.

DUNKIRK

5.

My grandfather once fell in love with a dryad—a wood nymph who lives in trees and to whom trees are sacred and who dances around trees clad in fine leaf-green tutu and who carries a great silver-shining axe to whack anybody who does any kind of thing inimical to the well-being and mental health of trees. My grandfather was at that time in the lumber business.

It was during the Great War. He'd got an order for a million board feet of one-by-ten of the very poorest quality, to make barracks out of for the soldiers. The specifications called for the dark red sap to be running off it in buckets and for the warp on it to be like the tops of waves in a distressed sea and for the knotholes in it to be the size of an intelligent man's head for the cold wind to whistle through and toughen up the (as they were then called) doughboys.

My grandfather headed for East Texas. He had the timber rights to ten thousand acres there, Southern yellow pine of the loblolly family. It was third-growth scrub and slash and shoddy—just the thing for soldiers. Couldn't be beat. So he and his men set up operations and first crack out of the box they were surrounded by threescore of lovely dryads and hamadryads all clad in fine leaf-green tutus and waving great silver-shining axes.

"Well now," my grandfather said to the head dryad, "wait a while, wait a while, somebody could get hurt."

"That is for sure," says the girl, and she shifts her axe from her left hand to her right hand.

"I thought you dryads were indigenous to oak," says my grandfather, "this here is pine."

"Some like the ancient tall-standing many-branched oak," says the girl, "and some the white-slim birch, and some take what they can get, and you will look mighty funny without any legs on you."

"Can we negotiate," says my grandfather, "it's for the War, and you are the loveliest thing I ever did see, and what is your name?"

"Megwind," says the girl, "and also Sophie. I am Sophie in the night and Megwind in the day and I make fine whistling axe-music night or day and without legs for walking your life's journey will be a pitiable one."

"Well Sophie," says my grandfather, "let us sit down under this tree here and open a bottle of this fine rotgut here and talk the thing over like reasonable human beings."

"Do not use my night-name in the light of day," says the girl, "and I am not a human being and there is nothing to talk over and what type of rotgut is it that you have there?"

"It is Teamster's Early Grave," says my grandfather, "and you'll cover many a mile before you find the beat of it."

"I will have one cupful," says the girl, "and my sisters will have each one cupful, and then we will dance around this tree while you still have legs for dancing and then you will go away and your men also."

"Drink up," says my grandfather, "and know that of all the women I have interfered with in my time you are the absolute top woman."

"I am not a woman," says Megwind, "I am a spirit, although the form of the thing is misleading I will admit."

"Wait a while," says my grandfather, "you mean that no type of mutual interference between us of a physical nature is possible?"

"That is a thing I could do," says the girl, "if I chose."

"Do you choose?" asks my grandfather, "and have another wallop."

"That is a thing I will do," says the girl, and she had another wallop.

"And a kiss," says my grandfather, "would that be possible do you think?"

"That is a thing I could do," says the dryad, "you are not the least prepossessing of men and men have been scarce in these parts in these years, the trees being as you see mostly scrub, slash and shoddy."

"Megwind," says my grandfather, "you are beautiful."

"You are taken with my form which I admit is beautiful," says the girl, "but know that this form you see is not necessary but contingent, sometimes I am a fine brown-speckled egg and sometimes I am an escape of steam from a hole in the ground and sometimes I am an armadillo."

"That is amazing," says my grandfather, "a shape-shifter are you."

"That is a thing I can do," says Megwind, "if I choose."

"Tell me," says my grandfather, "could you change yourself into one million board feet of one-by-ten of the very poorest quality neatly stacked in railroad cars on a siding outside of Fort Riley, Kansas?"

"That is a thing I could do," says the girl, "but I do not see the beauty of it."

"The beauty of it," says my grandfather, "is two cents a board foot."

"What is the *quid pro quo*?" asks the girl.

"You mean spirits engage in haggle?" asks my grandfather.

"Nothing from nothing, nothing for nothing, that is a law of life," says the girl.

"The *quid pro quo*," says my grandfather, "is that me and my men will leave this here scrub, slash and shoddy standing. All you have to do is to be made into barracks for the soldiers and after the War you will be torn down and can fly away home."

"Agreed," says the dryad, "but what about this interference of a physical nature you mentioned earlier? for the sun is falling down and soon I will be Sophie and human men have been scarce in these parts for ever so damn long."

"Sophie," says my grandfather, "you are as lovely as light and let me just fetch another bottle from the truck and I will be at your service."

This is not really how it went. I am fantasizing. Actually, he just plain cut down the trees.

6.

I was on an operating table. My feet were in sterile bags. My hands and arms were wrapped in sterile towels. A sterile bib covered my beard. A giant six-eyed light was shining in my eyes. I closed my eyes. There was a doctor on the right side of my head and a doctor on the left side of my head. The doctor on the right was my doctor. The doctor on the left was studying the art. He was Chinese, the doctor on the left. My doctor spoke to the nurse who was handing him tools. *"Rebecca! You're not supposed to be holding conversations with the circulating nurse, Rebecca. You're supposed to be watching me, Rebecca!"* We had all gathered here in this room to cut out part of my upper lip into which a basal-cell malignancy had crept.

In my mind, the basal-cell malignancy resembled a tiny truffle.

"Most often occurs in sailors and farmers," the doctor had told me. "The sun." But I, I sit under General Electric light, mostly. "We figure you can lose up to a third of it, the lip, without a bad result," the doctor had told me. "There's a lot of stretch." He had demonstrated upon his own upper lip, stretching it with his two forefingers. The doctor a large handsome man with silver spectacles. In my hospital room, I listened to my Toshiba transistor, Randy Newman singing "Let's Burn Down the Cornfield." I was waiting for the morning, for the operation. A friendly Franciscan entered in his brown robes. "Why is it that in the space under 'Religion' on your form you entered 'None'?" he asked in a friendly way. I considered the question. I rehearsed for him my religious history. We discussed the distinguishing characteristics of the various religious orders—the Basilians, the Capuchins. Recent outbreaks of Enthusiasm among the Dutch Catholics were touched upon. "Rebecca!" the doctor said, in the operating room. "*Watch me, Rebecca!*"

I had been given a morphine shot along with various locals in the lip. I was feeling very good! The Franciscan had lived in the Far East for a long time. I too had been in the Far East. The Army band had played, as we climbed the ramp into the hold of the troopship, "Bye Bye Baby, Remember You're My Baby." "We want a good result," my original doctor had said, "because of the prominence of the—" He pointed to my upper lip. "So I'm sending you to a good man." This seemed sensible. I opened my eyes. The bright light. "Give me a No. 10 blade," the doctor said. "Give me a No. 15 blade." Something was certainly going on there, above my teeth. "Gently, gently," my doctor said to his colleague. The next morning a tiny Thai nurse came in bringing me orange juice, orange Jell-O, and an orange broth. "Is there any pain?" she asked.

My truffle was taken to the pathologist for examination. I felt the morphine making me happy. I thought: What a beautiful hospital.

A handsome nurse from Jamaica came in. "Now you put this on," she said, handing me a wrinkled white garment without much back to it. "No socks. No shorts."

No shorts!

I climbed onto a large moving bed and was wheeled to the operating room, where the doctors were preparing themselves for the improvement of my face. My doctor invited the Chinese doctor to join him in a scrub. I was eating my orange Jell-O, my orange broth. My wife called and said that she had eaten a superb beef Wellington for dinner, along with a good bottle. Every time I smiled the stitches jerked tight.

I was standing outside the cashier's window. I had my pants on and was feeling very dancy. "Udbye!" I said. "Hank you!"

7.

I went to a party. I saw a lady I knew. "Hello!" I said. "Are you pregnant?" She was wearing what appeared to be maternity clothes.

"No," she said, "I am not."
"Cab!"

8.

But where are you today?

Probably out with your husband for a walk. He has written another beautiful poem, and needs the refreshment of the air. I admire him. Everything he does is successful. He is wanted for lectures in East St. Louis, at immense fees. I admire him, but my admiration for you is . . . Do you think he has noticed? What foolishness! It is as obvious as a bumper sticker, as obvious as an abdication.

Your Royal Canadian Mounted Police hat set squarely across the wide white brow . . .

Your white legs touching each other, under the banquet table . . .

Probably you are walking with your husband in SoHo, seeing what the new artists are refusing to do there, in their quest for a scratch to start from.

The artists regard your brown campaign hat, your white legs. "Holy God!" they say, and return to their lofts.

I have spent many message units seeking your voice, but I always get Frederick instead.

"Well, Frederick," I ask cordially, "what amazing triumphs have you accomplished today?"

He has been offered a sinecure at Stanford and a cenotaph at C.C.N.Y. Bidding for world rights to his breath has begun at $500,000.

But I am wondering—

When you placed your hand on my napkin, at the banquet, did that mean anything?

When you smashed in the top of my soft-boiled egg for me, at the banquet, did that indicate that I might continue to hope?

I will name certain children after you. (People often ask my advice about naming things.) It will be suspicious, so many small Philippas popping up in our city, but the pattern will only become visible with the passage of time, and in the interval, what satisfaction!

I cannot imagine the future. You have not made your intentions clear, if indeed you have any. What is the point of all this misery? I am a voter! I am a veteran! I am forty! My life is insured! Now you are climbing aboard a great ship, and the hawsers are being loosed, and the flowers in the cabins arranged, and the dinner gong sounded. I am sure you will eat well aboard that ship, but you don't understand—it is sailing away from me!

Subpoena

AND NOW in the mail a small white Subpoena from the Bureau of Compliance, Citizen Bergman there, he wants me to comply. *We command you that, all business and excuses being laid aside, you and each of you appear and attend . . .* The "We command you" in boldface, and a shiny red seal in the lower left corner. To get my attention.

I thought I had complied. I comply every year, sometimes oftener than necessary. Look at the record. Spotless list of compliances dating back to '48, when I was a pup. What can he mean, this Bergman, finding a freckle on my clean sheet?

I appeared and attended. Attempted to be reasonable. "Look here Bergman what is this business." Read him an essay I'd written about how the State should not muck about in the affairs of its vassals overmuch. Citizen Bergman unamused.

"It appears that you are the owner or proprietor perhaps of a monster going under the name of Charles Evans Hughes?"

"Yes but what has that to do with—"

"Said monster inhabiting quarters at 12 Tryst Lane?"

"That is correct."

"This monster being of humanoid appearance and characteristics, including ability to locomote, production of speech of a kind, ingestion of viands, and traffic with other beings?"

"Well, 'traffic' is hardly the word. Simple commands he can cope with. Nothing fancy. Sit. Eat. Speak. Roll over. Beg. That sort of thing."

"This monster being employed by you in the capacity, friend?"

"Well, employed is not quite right."

"He is remunerated is he not?"

"The odd bit of pocket money."

"On a regular basis."

"See here Bergman it's an allowance. For little things he needs. Cigarettes and handkerchiefs and the like. Nose drops."

"He is nevertheless in receipt of sums of money from you on a regular basis?"

"*He is forty-four percent metal, Officer.*"

"The metal content of said monster does not interest the Bureau. What we are interested in is compliance."

"Wherein have I failed to comply?"

"You have not submitted Form 244 which governs paid companionship, including liaisons with prostitutes and pushing of wheelchairs by hired orderlies not provided by the Bureau of Perpetual Help. You have also failed to remit the Paid Companionship Tax which amounts to one hundred twenty-two percent of all moneys changing hands in any direction."

"One hundred twenty-two percent!"

"That is the figure. There is also a penalty for noncompliance. The penalty is two hundred twelve percent of one hundred twenty-two percent of five dollars a week figured over five years, which I believe is the period at issue."

"What about depreciation?"

"Depreciation is not figurable in the case of monsters."

I went home feeling less than sunny.

He had a knowing look that I'd painted myself. One corner of the mouth curled upward and the other downward, when he smiled. There was no grave-robbing or anything of that sort. Plastic and metal did very nicely. You can get the most amazing things in drugstores. Fingernails and eyelashes and such. The actual construction was a matter of weeks. I considered sending the plans to *Popular Mechanics*. So that everyone could have one.

He was calm—calm as a hat. Whereas I was nervous as a strobe light, had the shakes, Valium in the morning and whiskey beginning at two o'clock in the afternoon.

Everything was all right with him.

"Crushed in an elevator at the welfare hotel!" someone would say.

"It's a very serious problem," Charles would answer.

When I opened the door, he was sitting in the rocking chair reading *Life*.

"Charles," I said, "they've found out."

"Seventy-seven percent of American high-school students declare that religion is important to them, according to a recent Louis Harris poll," Charles said, rocking gently.

"Charles," I said, "they want money. The Paid Companionship Tax. It's two hundred twelve percent of one hundred twenty-two percent of five dollars a week figured over five years, plus of course the basic one hundred twenty-two percent."

"That's a lot of money," Charles said, smiling. "A pretty penny."

"I can't pay," I said. "It's too much."

"Well," he said, both smiling and rocking, "fine. What are you going to do?"

"Disassemble," I said.

"Interesting," he said, hitching his chair closer to mine, to demonstrate interest. "Where will you begin?"

"With the head, I suppose."

"Wonderful," Charles said. "You'll need the screwdriver, the pliers, and the Skil-saw. I'll fetch them."

He got up to go to the basement. A thought struck him. "Who will take out the garbage?" he asked.

"Me. I'll take it out myself."

He smiled. One corner of his mouth turned upward and the other downward. "Well," he said, "right on."

I called him my friend and thought of him as my friend. In fact I kept him to instruct me in complacency. He sat there, the perfect noncombatant. He ate and drank and slept and awoke and did not change the world. Looking at him I said to myself, "See, it is possible to live in the world and not change the world." He read the newspapers and watched television and heard in the night screams under windows thank God not ours but down the block a bit, and did nothing. Without Charles, without his example, his exemplary quietude, I run the risk of acting, the risk of risk. I must participate, I must leave the house and walk about.

The Catechist

IN THE evenings, usually, the catechist approaches. "Where have you been?" he asks.

"In the park," I say.

"Was she there?" he asks.

"No," I say.

The catechist is holding a book. He reads aloud: "*The chief reason for Christ's coming was to manifest and teach God's love for us. Here the catechist should find the focal point of his instruction.*" On the word "manifest" the catechist places the tip of his right forefinger upon the tip of his left thumb, and on the word "teach" the catechist places the tip of his right forefinger upon the tip of his left forefinger.

Then he says: "And the others?"

I say: "Abusing the mothers."

"The guards?"

"Yes. As usual."

The catechist reaches into his pocket and produces a newspaper clipping. "Have you heard the news?" he asks.

"No," I say.

He reads aloud: "*Vegetable Oil Allowed in Three Catholic Rites.*"

He pauses. He looks at me. I say nothing. He reads aloud: "*Rome, March 2nd. Reuters.*" He looks at me. I say nothing. "*Reuters,*" he repeats. "*Roman Catholic sacramental anointings may in the future be performed with any vegetable oil, according to a new Vatican ruling that lifts the Church's age-old—*" He pauses. "*Age-old,*" he emphasizes.

I think: Perhaps she is at ease. Looking at her lake.

The catechist reads: "*. . . that lifts the Church's age-old insistence on the use of olive oil.* New paragraph. *Under Catholic ritual, holy oil previously blessed by a bishop is used symbolically in the sacraments of confirmation, baptism, and the anointing of the sick, formerly extreme unction.* New paragraph. *Other vegetable oils are cheaper and considerably easier to obtain than olive oil in many parts of the world, Vatican observers noted.*"

The catechist pauses. "You're a priest. I'm a priest," he says. "Now I ask you."

I think: Perhaps she is distressed and looking at the lake does nothing to mitigate the distress.

He says: "Consider that you are dying. The sickroom. The bed. The plucked-at sheets. The distraught loved ones. The priest approaches. Bearing the holy viaticum, the sacred oils. The administration of the Host. The last anointing. And what is it you're given? You, the dying man? Peanut oil."

I think: Peanut oil.

The catechist replaces the clipping in his pocket. He will read it to me again tomorrow. Then he says: "When you saw the guards abusing the mothers, you—"

I say: "Wrote another letter."

"And you mailed the letter?"

"As before."

"The same mailbox?"

"Yes."

"You remembered to put a stamp—"

"An eight-cent Eisenhower."

I think: When I was young they asked other questions.

He says: "Tell me about her."

I say: "She has dark hair."

"Her husband—"

"I don't wish to discuss her husband."

The catechist reads from his book. "*The candidate should be questioned as to his motives for becoming a Christian.*"

I think: My motives?

He says: "Tell me about yourself."

I say: "I'm forty. I have bad eyes. An enlarged liver."

"That's the alcohol," he says.

"Yes," I say.

"You're very much like your father, there."

"A shade more avid."

We have this conversation every day. No detail changes. He says: "But a man in your profession—"

I say: "But I don't want to discuss my profession."

He says: "Are you going back now? To the park?"

"Yes. She may be waiting."

"I thought she was looking at the lake."

"When she is not looking at the lake, then she is in the park."

The catechist reaches into the sleeve of his black robe. He produces a manifesto. He reads me the manifesto. *"All intellectual productions of the bourgeoisie are either offensive or defensive weapons against the revolution. All intellectual productions of the bourgeoisie are, objectively, obfuscating objects which are obstacles to the emancipation of the proletariat."* He replaces the manifesto in his sleeve.

I say: "But there are levels of signification other than the economic involved."

The catechist opens his book. He reads: *"A disappointing experience: the inadequacy of language to express thought. But let the catechist take courage."* He closes the book.

I think: Courage.

He says: "What do you propose to do?"

I say: "I suggested to her that I might change my profession."

"Have you had an offer?"

"A feeler."

"From whom?"

"General Foods."

"How did she respond?"

"A chill fell upon the conversation."

"But you pointed out—"

"I pointed out that although things were loosening up it would doubtless be a long time before priests were permitted to marry."

The catechist looks at me.

I think: She is waiting in the park, in the children's playground.

He says: "And then?"

I say: "I heard her confession."

"Was it interesting?"

"Nothing new. As you know, I am not permitted to discuss it."

"What were the others doing?"

"Tormenting the mothers."

"You wrote another letter?"

"Yes."

"You don't tire of this activity, writing letters?"

"One does what one can." I think: Or does not do what one can.

He says: "Let us discuss love."

I say: "I know nothing about it. Unless of course you refer to Divine love."

"I had in mind love as it is found in the works of Scheler, who holds that love is an aspect of phenomenological knowledge, and Carroll, who holds that 'tis love, 'tis love, that—"

"I know nothing about it."

The catechist opens his book. He reads: "*How to deal with the educated. Temptation and scandals to be faced by the candidate during his catechumenate.*" He closes the book. There is never a day, never a day, on which we do not have this conversation. He says: "When were you ordained?"

I say: "1950."

He says: "These sins, your own, the sins we have been discussing, I'm sure you won't mind if I refer to them as sins although their magnitude, whether they are mortal or venial, I leave it to you to assess, in the secret places of your heart—"

I say: "One sits in the confessional hearing confessions, year after year, Saturday after Saturday, at four in the afternoon, twenty-one years times fifty-two Saturdays, excluding leap year—"

"One thousand and ninety-two Saturdays—"

"Figuring forty-five adulteries to the average Saturday—"

"Forty-nine thousand one hundred and forty adulteries—"

"One wonders: Perhaps there should be a redefinition? And with some adulteries there are explanations. The man is a cabdriver. He works nights. His wife wants to go out and have a good time. She tells him that she doesn't do anything wrong—a few drinks at the neighborhood bar, a little dancing. 'Now, you know, Father, and I know, Father, that where there's drinking and dancing there's bloody well something else too. So I tell her, Father, she'll stay out of that bar or I'll hit her upside the head. Well, Father, she says to me you can hit me upside the head all you want but I'm still going to that bar when I want and you can hit me all day long and it won't stop me. Now, what can I do, Father? I got to be in this cab every night of the week except Mondays and sometimes I work

Mondays to make a little extra. So I hit her upside the head a few times but it don't make any difference, she goes anyhow. So I figure, Father, she's getting it outside the home, why not me? I'm always sorry after, Father, but what can I do? If I had a day job it would be different and now she just laughs at me and what can I do, Father?'"

"What do you say?"

"I advise self-control."

The catechist pokes about in his pockets. He pokes in his right-hand pocket for a time and then pokes in his left-hand pocket. He produces at length a tiny Old Testament, a postage-stamp Old Testament. He opens the postage-stamp Old Testament. "*Miserable comforters are ye all.*" He closes the postage-stamp Old Testament. "Job 16:2." He replaces the postage-stamp Old Testament in his left-hand pocket. He pokes about in his right-hand pocket and produces a button on which the word LOVE is printed. He pins the button on my cassock, above the belt, below the collar. He says: "But you'll go there again."

I say: "At eleven. The children's playground."

He says: "The rain. The trees."

I say: "All that rot."

He says: "The benches damp. The seesaw abandoned."

I say: "All that garbage."

He says: "Sunday the day of rest and worship is hated by all classes of men in every country to which the Word has been carried. Hatred of Sunday in London approaches one hundred percent. Hatred of Sunday in Rio produces suicides. Hatred of Sunday in Madrid is only appeased by the ritual slaughter of large black animals, in rings. Hatred of Sunday in Munich is the stuff of legend. Hatred of Sunday in Sydney is considered by the knowledgeable to be hatred of Sunday at its most exquisite."

I think: She will press against me with her hands in the back pockets of her trousers.

The catechist opens his book. He reads: "*The apathy of the listeners. The judicious catechist copes with the difficulty.*" He closes the book.

I think: Analysis terminable and interminable. I think: Then she will leave the park looking backward over her shoulder.

He says: "And the guards, what were they doing?"

I say: "Abusing the mothers."

"You wrote a letter?"

"Another letter."

"Would you say, originally, that you had a vocation? Heard a call?"

"I heard many things. Screams. Suites for unaccompanied cello. I did not hear a call."

"Nevertheless—"

"Nevertheless I went to the clerical-equipment store and purchased a summer cassock and a winter cassock. The summer cassock has short sleeves. I purchased a black hat."

"And the lady's husband?"

"He is a psychologist. He works in the limits of sensation. He is attempting to define precisely the two limiting sensations in the sensory continuum, the upper limit and the lower limit. He is often at the lab. He is measuring vanishing points."

"An irony."

"I suppose."

There is no day on which this conversation is not held and no detail of this conversation which is not replicated on any particular day on which the conversation is held.

The catechist produces from beneath his cloak a banner. He unfurls the banner and holds the unfurled banner above his head with both hands. The banner says, YOU ARE INTERRUPTED IN THE MIDST OF MORE CONGENIAL WORK? BUT THIS IS GOD'S WORK. The catechist refurls the banner. He replaces the banner under his cloak. He says: "But you'll go there again?"

I say: "Yes. At eleven."

He says: "But the rain . . ."

I say: "With her hands in the back pockets of her trousers."

He says: "*Deo gratias.*"

The Flight of Pigeons from the Palace

IN THE abandoned palazzo, weeds and old blankets filled the rooms. The palazzo was in bad shape. We cleaned the abandoned palazzo for ten years. We scoured the stones. The splendid architecture was furbished and painted. The doors and windows were dealt with. Then we were ready for the show.

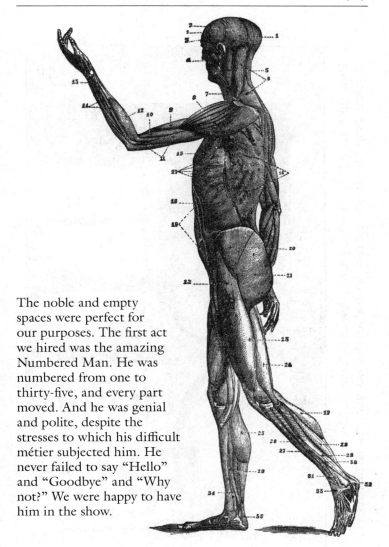

The noble and empty spaces were perfect for our purposes. The first act we hired was the amazing Numbered Man. He was numbered from one to thirty-five, and every part moved. And he was genial and polite, despite the stresses to which his difficult métier subjected him. He never failed to say "Hello" and "Goodbye" and "Why not?" We were happy to have him in the show.

Then, the Sulking Lady was obtained. She showed us her back. That was the way she felt. She had always felt that way, she said. She had felt that way since she was four years old.

THE FLIGHT OF PIGEONS FROM THE PALACE 411

We obtained other attractions—a Singing Sword and a Stone Eater. Tickets and programs were prepared. Buckets of water were placed about, in case of fire. Silver strings tethered the loud-roaring strong-stinking animals.

The lineup for opening night included:

>A startlingly handsome man
>A Grand Cham
>A tulip craze
>The Prime Rate
>Edgar Allan Poe
>A colored light

We asked ourselves: How can we improve the show?

We auditioned an explosion.

There were a lot of situations where men were being evil to women—dominating them and eating their food. We put those situations in the show.

In the summer of the show, grave robbers appeared in the show. Famous graves were robbed, before your eyes. Winding-sheets were unwound and things best forgotten were remembered. Sad themes were played by the band, bereft of its mind by the death of its tradition. In the soft evening of the show, a troupe of agoutis performed tax evasion atop tall, swaying yellow poles. Before your eyes.

The trapeze artist with whom I had an understanding . . . The moment when she failed to catch me . . .

Did she really try? I can't recall her ever failing to catch anyone she was really fond of. Her great muscles are too deft for that. Her great muscles at which we gaze through heavy-lidded eyes . . .

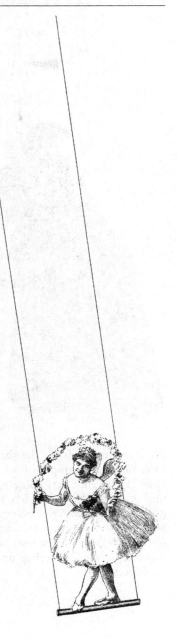

We recruited fools for the show. We had spots for a number of fools (and in the big all-fool number that occurs immediately after the second act, some specialties). But fools are hard to find. Usually they don't like to admit it. We settled for gowks, gulls, mooncalfs. A few babies, boobies, sillies, simps. A barmie was engaged, along with certain dumdums and beefheads. A noodle. When you see them all wandering around, under the colored lights, gibbering and performing miracles, you are surprised.

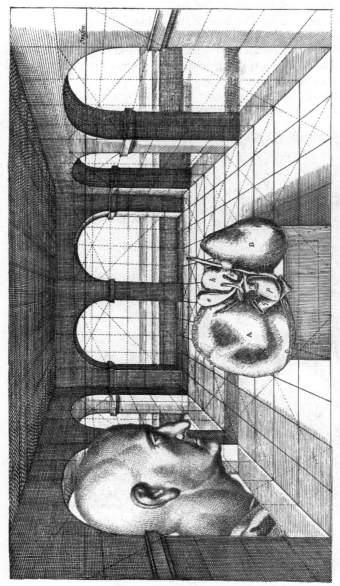

I put my father in the show, with his cold eyes. His segment was called My Father Concerned about His Liver.

Performances flew thick and fast.

We performed The Sale of the Public Library.

We performed Space Monkeys Approve Appropriations.

We did Theological Novelties and we did Cereal Music (with its raisins of beauty) and we did not neglect Piles of Discarded Women Rising from the Sea.

There was faint applause. The audience huddled together. The people counted their sins.

Scenes of domestic life were put in the show.

We used The Flight of Pigeons from the Palace.

It is difficult to keep the public interested.
    The public demands new wonders piled on new wonders.
    Often we don't know where our next marvel is coming from.
    The supply of strange ideas is not endless.
    The development of new wonders is not like the production of canned goods. Some things appear to be wonders in the beginning, but when you become familiar with them, are not wonderful at all. Sometimes a seventy-five-foot highly paid cacodemon will raise only the tiniest *frisson*. Some of us have even thought of folding the show—closing it down. That thought has been gliding through the hallways and rehearsal rooms of the show.

The new volcano we have just placed under contract seems very promising . . .

The Rise of Capitalism

THE FIRST thing I did was make a mistake. I thought I had understood capitalism, but what I had done was assume an attitude—melancholy sadness—toward it. This attitude is not correct. Fortunately your letter came, at that instant. "Dear Rupert, I love you every day. You are the world, which is life. I love you I adore you I am crazy about you. Love, Marta." Reading between the lines, I understood your critique of my attitude toward capitalism. Always mindful that the critic must *"studiare da un punto di vista formalistico e semiologico il rapporto fra lingua di un testo e codificazione di un—"* But here a big thumb smudges the text—the thumb of capitalism, which we are all under. Darkness falls. My neighbor continues to commit suicide, once a fortnight. I have his suicides geared into my schedule because my role is to save him; once I was late and he spent two days unconscious on the floor. But now that I have understood that I have not understood capitalism, perhaps a less equivocal position toward it can be "hammered out." My daughter demands more Mr. Bubble for her bath. The shrimp boats lower their nets. A book called *Humorists of the 18th Century* is published.

•

Capitalism places every man in competition with his fellows for a share of the available wealth. A few people accumulate big piles, but most do not. The sense of community falls victim to this struggle. Increased abundance and prosperity are tied to growing "productivity." A hierarchy of functionaries interposes itself between the people and the leadership. The good of the private corporation is seen as prior to the public good. The world market system tightens control in the capitalist countries and terrorizes the Third World. All things are manipulated to these ends. The King of Jordan sits at his ham radio, inviting strangers to the palace. I visit my assistant mistress. "Well, Azalea," I say, sitting in the best chair, "what has happened to you since my last visit?" Azalea tells me what has happened to her. She has covered a sofa, and written a novel. Jack has behaved badly. Roger has lost his job (replaced by an electric eye). Gigi's children are in the hospital being detoxified, all three. Azalea herself is dying of love. I stroke her buttocks, which are perfection, if you can have perfection, under the capitalistic system. "It is better to marry than to burn," St. Paul says, but St. Paul is largely discredited now, for the toughness of his views does not accord with the experience of advanced industrial societies. I smoke a cigar, to disoblige the cat.

•

Meanwhile Marta is getting angry. "Rupert," she says, "you are no better than a damn dawg! A plain dawg has more sensibility than you, when it comes to a woman's heart!" I try to explain that it is not my fault but capitalism's. She will have none of it. "I stand behind the capitalistic system," Marta says. "It has given us everything we have—the streets, the parks, the great avenues and boulevards, the promenades and malls—and other things, too, that I can't think of right now." But what has the market been doing? I scan the list of the fifteen Most Loved Stocks:

Occident Pet	983,100	20⅝	+	3¾
Natomas	912,300	58⅜	+	18½

What chagrin! Why wasn't I into Natomas, as into a fine garment, that will win you social credit when you wear it to the ball? I am not rich again this morning! I put my head between Azalea's breasts, to hide my shame.

•

Honoré de Balzac went to the movies. He was watching his favorite flick, *The Rise of Capitalism*, with Simone Simon and Raymond Radiguet. When he had finished viewing the film, he went out and bought a printing plant, for fifty thousand francs. "Henceforth," he said, "I will publish myself, in handsome expensive de-luxe editions, cheap editions, and foreign editions, duodecimo, sextodecimo, octodecimo. I will also publish atlases, stamp albums, collected sermons, volumes of sex education, remarks, memoirs, diaries, railroad timetables, daily newspapers, telephone books, racing forms, manifestos, libretti, abecedaries, works on acupuncture, and cookbooks." And then Honoré went out and got drunk, and visited his girl friend's house, and, roaring and stomping on the stairs, frightened her husband to death. And the husband was buried, and everyone stood silently around the grave, thinking of where they had been and where they were going, and the last handfuls of wet earth were cast upon the grave, and Honoré was sorry.

•

The Achievements of Capitalism:
   (a)   The curtain wall
   (b)   Artificial rain
   (c)   Rockefeller Center
   (d)   Casals
   (e)   Mystification

•

"Capitalism sure is sunny!" cried the unemployed Laredo toolmaker, as I was out walking, in the streets of Laredo. "None of that noxious Central European miserabilism for us!" And indeed, everything I see about me seems to support his position. Laredo is doing very well now, thanks to application of the brilliant principles of the "new capitalism." Its Gross Laredo Product is up, and its internal contradictions are down. Catfish-farming, a new initiative in the agri-business sector, has worked wonders. The dram-house and the card-house are each nineteen stories high. "No matter," Azalea says. "You are still a damn dawg, even if you have 'unveiled existence.'" At the Laredo Country Club, men and women are discussing the cathedrals of France, where all of them have just been. Some liked Tours, some Lyon, some Clermont. "A pious fear of God makes itself felt in this spot." Capitalism arose and took off its pajamas. Another day, another dollar. Each man is valued at what he will bring in the marketplace. Meaning has been drained from work and assigned instead to remuneration. Unemployment obliterates the world of the unemployed individual. Cultural underdevelopment of the worker, as a technique of domination, is found everywhere under late capitalism. Authentic self-determination by individuals is thwarted.

The false consciousness created and catered to by mass culture perpetuates ignorance and powerlessness. Strands of raven hair floating on the surface of the Ganges . . . Why can't they clean up the Ganges? If the wealthy capitalists who operate the Ganges wig factories could be forced to install sieves, at the mouths of their plants . . . And now the sacred Ganges is choked with hair, and the river no longer knows where to put its flow, and the moonlight on the Ganges is swallowed by the hair, and the water darkens. By Vishnu! This is an intolerable situation! Shouldn't something be done about it?

•

Friends for dinner! The *crudités* are prepared, green and fresh . . . The good paper napkins are laid out . . . Everyone is talking about capitalism (although some people are talking about the psychology of aging, and some about the human use of human beings, and some about the politics of experience). "How can you say that?" Azalea shouts, and Marta shouts, "What about the air?" As a flower moves toward the florist, women move toward men who are not good for them. Self-actualization is not to be achieved in terms of another person, but you don't know that, when you begin. The negation of the negation is based on a correct reading of the wrong books. The imminent heat-death of the universe is not a bad thing, because it is a long way off. Chaos is a position, but a weak one, related to that "unfocusedness" about which I have forgotten to speak. And now the saints come marching in, saint upon saint, to deliver their message! Here are St. Albert (who taught Thomas Aquinas), and St. Almachius (martyred trying to put an end to gladiatorial contests), and St. Amadour (the hermit), and St. Andrew of Crete (whose "Great Kanon" runs to two hundred and fifty strophes), and St. Anthony of the Caves, and St. Athanasius the Athonite, and St. Aubry of the Pillar, and many others. "Listen!" the saints say. "He who desires true rest and happiness must raise his hope from things that perish and pass away and place it in the Word of God, so that, cleaving to that which abides forever, he may also together with it abide forever." Alas! It is the same old message. "Rupert," Marta says, "the embourgeoisment of all classes of men has reached a disgusting nadir in your case. A damn hawg has more sense than you. At least a damn hawg doesn't go in for 'the bullet wrapped in sugar,' as the Chinese say." She is right.

•

Smoke, rain, abulia. What can the concerned citizen do to fight the rise of capitalism, in his own community? Study of the tides of conflict and power in a system in which there is structural inequality is an important task. A knowledge of European intellectual history since 1789 provides a useful background. Information theory offers interesting new possibilities. Passion is helpful, especially those types of passion which are non-licit. Doubt is a necessary precondition to meaningful action. Fear is the great mover, in the end.

The Temptation of St. Anthony

Yes, the saint was underrated quite a bit, then, mostly by people who didn't like things that were ineffable. I think that's quite understandable—that kind of thing can be extremely irritating, to some people. After all, everything is hard enough without having to deal with something that is not tangible and clear. The higher orders of abstraction are just a nuisance, to some people, although to others, of course, they are quite interesting. I would say that on the whole, people who didn't like this kind of idea, or who refused to think about it, were in the majority. And some were actually angry at the idea of sainthood—not at the saint himself, whom everyone liked, more or less, except for a few, but about the idea he represented, especially since it was not in a book or somewhere, but actually present, in the community. Of course some people went around saying that he "thought he was better than everybody else," and you had to take these people aside and tell them that they had misperceived the problem, that it wasn't a matter of simple conceit, with which we are all familiar, but rather something pure and mystical, from the realm of the extraordinary, as it were; unearthly. But a lot of people don't like things that are unearthly, the things of this earth are good enough for them, and they don't mind telling you so. "If he'd just go out and get a job, like everybody else, then he could be saintly all day long, if he wanted to"—that was a common theme. There is a sort of hatred going around for people who have lifted their sights above the common run. Probably it has always been this way.

For this reason, in any case, people were always trying to see the inside of the saint's apartment, to find out if strange practices were being practiced there, or if you could discern, from the arrangement of the furniture and so on, if any had been, lately. They would ring the bell and pretend to be in the wrong apartment, these people, but St. Anthony would let them come in anyhow, even though he knew very well what they were thinking. They would stand around, perhaps a husband-and-wife team, and stare at the rug, which was ordinary beige wall-to-wall carpet from Kaufman's, and then at the coffee table and so on, they would sort of slide into the kitchen to see what he had been eating, if anything. They were always surprised to see that he ate more or less normal foods, perhaps a little heavy on the fried foods. I guess they expected roots and grasses. And of course there was a big unhealthy interest in the bedroom, the door to which was usually kept closed. People seemed to think he should, in pursuit of whatever higher goals he had in mind, sleep on the floor; when they discovered there was an ordinary bed in there, with a brown bedspread, they were slightly shocked. By now St. Anthony had made a cup of coffee for them, and told them to sit down and take the weight off their feet, and asked them about their work and if they had any children and so forth: they went away thinking, He's just like anybody else. That was, I think, the way he wanted to present himself, at that time.

Later, after it was all over, he moved back out to the desert.

I didn't have any particular opinion as to what was the right thing to think about him. Sometimes you have to take the long way round to get to a sound consensus, and of course you have to keep the ordinary motors of life running in the meantime. So, in that long year that saw the emergence of his will as one of its major landmarks, in our city, I did whatever I could to help things along, to direct the stream of life experience at him in ways he could handle. I wasn't a disciple, that would be putting it far too strongly; I was sort of like a friend. And there were things I could do. For example, this town is pretty goodsized, more than a hundred thousand, and in any such town—maybe more so than in the really small ones, where everyone is scratching to survive—you run into people with nothing much to do who don't mind causing a little trouble, if that would be diverting, for someone who is unusual in any way. So the example that Elaine and I set, in more or less just treating him like any one of our other friends, probably helped to normalize things, and very likely protected him, in a sense, from some of the unwelcome attentions he might otherwise have received. As men in society seem to feel that the problem is to get all opinions squared away with all other opinions, or at least in recognizable congruence with the main opinion, as if the world were a jury room that no one could leave until everybody agreed (and keeping in mind the ever-present threat of a mistrial), so the men, and the women too, of the city (which I won't name to spare possible embarrassment to those of the participants who still live here) tried to think about St. Anthony, and by extension saintliness, in the approved ways of their time and condition.

The first thing to do, then, was to prove that he was a fake. Strange as it may sound in retrospect, that was the original general opinion, because who could believe that the reverse was the case? Because it wasn't easy, in the midst of all the other things you had to think about, to imagine the marvelous. I don't mean that he went around doing tricks or anything like that. It was just a certain—ineffable is the only word I can think of, and I have never understood exactly what it means, but you get a kind of feeling from it, and that's what you got, too, from the saint, on good days. (He had his ups and downs.) Anyhow, it was pretty savage, in the beginning, the way the local people went around trying to get something on him. I don't mean to impugn the honesty of these doubters; doubt is real enough in most circumstances. Especially so, perhaps, in cases where what is at issue is some principle of action: if you believe something, then you logically have to act accordingly. If you decided that St. Anthony actually was a saint, then you would have to act a certain way toward him, pay attention to him, be reverent and attentive, pay homage, perhaps change your life a bit. So doubt is maybe a reaction to a strong claim on your attention, one that has implications for your life-style, for change. And you absolutely, in many cases, *don't want* to do this. A number of great plays have demonstrated this dilemma, on the stage.

St. Anthony's major temptation, in terms of his living here, was perhaps this: ordinary life.

Not that he proclaimed himself a saint in so many words. But his actions, as the proverb says, spoke louder. There was the ineffableness I've already mentioned, and there were certain things that he did. He was mugged, for example. That doesn't happen too often here, but it happened to him. It was at night, somebody jumped on him from behind, grabbed him around the neck and began going through his pockets. The man only got a few dollars, and then he threw St. Anthony down on the sidewalk (he put one leg in front of the saint's legs and shoved him) and then began to run away. St. Anthony called after him, held up his hand, and said, "Don't you want the watch?" It was a good watch, a Bulova. The man was thunderstruck. He actually came back and took the watch off St. Anthony's wrist. He didn't know what to think. He hesitated for a minute and then asked St. Anthony if he had bus fare home. The saint said it didn't matter, it wasn't far, he could walk. Then the mugger ran away again. I know somebody who saw it (and of course did nothing to help, as is common in such cases). Opinion was divided as to whether St. Anthony was saintly, or simpleminded. I myself thought it was kind of dumb of him. But St. Anthony explained to me that somebody had given him the watch in the first place, and he only wore it so as not to hurt that person's feelings. He never looked at it, he said. He didn't care what time it was.

Parenthetically. In the desert, where he is now, it's very cold at night. He won't light a fire. People leave things for him, outside the hut. We took out some blankets but I don't know if he uses them. People bring him the strangest things, electric coffee pots (even though there's no electricity out there), comic books, even bottles of whiskey. St. Anthony gives everything away as fast as he can. I have seen him, however, looking curiously at a transistor radio. He told me that in his youth, in Memphis (that's not Memphis, Tennessee, but the Memphis in Egypt, the ruined city) he was very fond of music. Elaine and I talked about giving him a flute or a clarinet. We thought that might be all right, because performing music, for the greater honor and glory of God, is an old tradition, some of our best music came about that way. The whole body of sacred music. We asked him about it. He said no, it was very kind of us but it would be a distraction from contemplation and so forth. But sometimes, when we drive out to see him, maybe with some other people, we all sing hymns. He appears to enjoy that. That appears to be acceptable.

A funny thing was that, toward the end, the only thing he'd say, the only word was . . . "Or." I couldn't understand what he was thinking of. That was when he was still living in town.

The famous temptations, that so much has been written about, didn't occur all that often while he was living amongst us, in our city. Once or twice. I wasn't ever actually present during a temptation but I heard about it. Mrs. Eaton, who lived upstairs from him, had actually drilled a hole in the floor, so that she could watch him! I thought that was fairly despicable, and I told her so. Well, she said, there wasn't much excitement in her life. She's fifty-eight and both her boys are in the Navy. Also some of the wood shavings and whatnot must have dropped on the saint's floor when she drilled the hole. She bought a brace-and-bit specially at the hardware store, she told me. "I'm shameless," she said. God knows that's true. But the saint must have known she was up there with her fifty-eight-year-old eye glued to the hole. Anyhow, she claims to have seen a temptation. I asked her what form it took. Well, it wasn't very interesting, she said. Something about advertising. There was this man in a business suit talking to the saint. He said he'd "throw the account your way" if the saint would something something. The only other thing she heard was a mention of "annual billings in the range of five to six mil." The saint said no, very politely, and the man left, with cordialities on both sides. I asked her what she'd been expecting and she looked at me with a gleam in her eye and said: "Guess." I suppose she meant women. I myself was curious, I admit it, about the fabulous naked beauties he is supposed to have been tempted with, and all of that. It's hard not to let your imagination become salacious, in this context. It's funny that we never seem to get enough of sexual things, even though Elaine and I have been very happily married for nine years and have a very good relationship, in bed and out of it. There never seems to be enough sex in a person's life, unless you're exhausted and worn out, I suppose—that is a curiosity, that God made us that way, that I have never understood. Not that I don't enjoy it, in the abstract.

After he had returned to the desert, we dropped by one day to see if he was home. The door of his hut was covered with an old piece of sheepskin. A lot of ants and vermin were crawling over the surface of the sheepskin. When you go through the door of the hut you have to move very fast. It's one of the most unpleasant things about going to see St. Anthony. We knocked on the sheepskin, which is stiff as a board. Nobody answered. We could hear some scuffling around inside the hut. Whispering. It seemed to me that there was more than one voice. We knocked on the sheepskin again; again nobody answered. We got back into the Pontiac and drove back to town.

Of course he's more mature now. Taking things a little easier, probably.

I don't care if he put his hand on her leg or did not put his hand on her leg.

Everyone felt we had done something wrong, really wrong, but by that time it was too late to make up for it.

Somebody got the bright idea of trying out Camilla on him. There are some crude people in this town. Camilla is well known. She's very aristocratic, in a way, if "aristocratic" means that you don't give a damn what kind of damn foolishness, or even evil, you lend yourself to. Her folks had too much money, that was part of it, and she was too beautiful—she was beautiful, it's the only word—that was the other part. Some of her friends put her up to it. She went over to his place wearing those very short pants they wore for a while, and all of that. She has beautiful breasts. She's very intelligent, went to the Sorbonne and studied some kind of philosophy called "structure" with somebody named Levy who is supposed to be very famous. When she came back there was nobody she could talk about it to. She smokes a lot of dope, it's well known. But in a way, she is not uncompassionate. She was interested in the saint for his own personality, as well as his being an anomaly, in our local context. The long and short of it is that she claimed he tried to make advances to her, put his hand on her leg and all that. I don't know if she was lying or not. She could have been. She could have been telling the truth. It's hard to say. Anyhow a great hue was raised about it and her father said he was going to press charges, although in the event, he did not. She stopped talking about it, the next day. Probably something happened but I don't necessarily think it was what she said it was. She became a VISTA volunteer later and went to work in the inner city of Detroit.

Anyhow, a lot of people talked about it. Well, what if he *had* put his hand on her leg, some people said—what was so wrong about that? They were both unmarried adult human beings, after all. Sexuality is as important as saintliness, and maybe as beautiful, in the sight of God, or else why was it part of the Divine plan? You always have these conflicts of ideas between people who think one thing and people who think another. I don't give a damn if he put his hand on her leg or did not put his hand on her leg. (I would prefer, of course, that he had not.) I thought it was kind of a cheap incident and not really worth talking about, especially in the larger context of the ineffable. There really was something to that. In the world of mundanity in which he found himself, he *shone*. It was unmistakable, even to children.

Of course they were going to run him out of town, by subtle pressures, after a while. There is a lot of anticlericalism around, still. We visit him, in the desert, anyhow, once or twice a month. We missed our visits last month because we were in Florida.

He told me that, in his old age, he regarded the temptations as "entertainment."

Daumier

WE HAVE ALL
MISUNDERSTOOD
BILLY THE KID

I was speaking to Amelia.

"Not self-slaughter in the crude sense. Rather the construction of surrogates. Think of it as a transplant."

"Daumier," she said, "you are not making me happy."

"The false selves in their clatter and boister and youthful brio will slay and bother and push out and put to all types of trouble the original, authentic self, which is a dirty great villain, as can be testified and sworn to by anyone who has ever been awake."

"The self also dances," she said, "sometimes."

"Yes," I said, "I have noticed that, but one pays dear for the occasional schottische. Now, here is the point about the self: It is insatiable. It is always, always hankering. It is what you might call rapacious to a fault. The great flaming mouth to the thing is never in this world going to be stuffed full. I need only adduce the names of Alexander, Richelieu, Messalina, and Billy the Kid."

"You have misunderstood Billy the Kid," she murmured.

"Whereas the surrogate, the construct, is in principle satiable. We design for satiability."

"Have you taken action?" she asked. "Or is all this just the usual?"

"I have one out now," I said, "a Daumier, on the plains and pampas of consciousness, and he is doing very well, I can tell you that. He has an important post in a large organization. I get regular reports."

"What type of fellow is he?"

"A good true fellow," I said, "and knows his limits. He doesn't overstep. Desire has been reduced in him to a minimum. Just enough left to make him go. Loved and respected by all."

"Tosh," she said. "Tosh and bosh."

"You will want one," I said, "when you see what they are like."

"We have all misunderstood Billy the Kid," she said in parting.

A Long Sentence
in Which the
Miracle of Surrogation
Is Performed
Before Your Eyes

Now in his mind's eye which was open for business at all times even during the hours of sleep and dream and which was the blue of bedcovers and which twinkled and which was traced with blood a trifle at all times and which was covered at all times with a monocle of good quality, the same being attached by long thin black streamy ribands to his mind's neck, now in this useful eye Daumier saw a situation.

Mr. Bellows,
Mr. Hawkins,
The Traffic,
Chilidogs

Two men in horse-riding clothes stood upon a plain, their attitudes indicating close acquaintance or colleagueship. The plain presented in its foreground a heavy yellow oblong salt lick rendered sculptural by the attentions over a period of time of sheep or other salt-loving animals. Two horses in the situation's upper left-hand corner watched the men with nervous horse-gaze.

Mr. Bellows spoke to his horse.

"Stand still, horse."

Mr. Hawkins sat down atop the salt lick and filled a short brass pipe Oriental in character.

"Are they quiet now?"

"Quiet as the grave," Mr. Bellows said. "Although I don't know what we'll be doin' for quiet when the grass gives out."

"That'll be a while yet."

"And Daumier?"

"Scoutin' the trail ahead," said Mr. Hawkins.

"He has his problems you must admit."

"Self-created in my opinion."

Mr. Hawkins took a deep draw upon his pipelet.

"The herd," he said.

"And the queen."

"And the necklace."

"And the cardinal."

"It's the old story," Mr. Hawkins stated. "One word from the queen and he's off tearing about the countryside and let business go hang."

"There's such a thing as tending to business, all right," said Mr. Bellows. "Some people never learned it."

"And him the third generation in the Traffic," Mr. Hawkins added. Then, after a moment: "Lovely blue flowers there a while back. I don't suppose you noticed."

"I noticed," said Mr. Bellows. "I picked a bunch."

"Did you, now. Where are they at?"

"I give um to someone," Mr. Bellows said.

"Someone. What someone?"

There was a silence.

"You are acquainted with the Rules, I believe," Mr. Hawkins said.

"Nothing in the Rules about bestowal of bluebonnets, I believe," Mr. Bellows replied.

"Bluebonnets, were they? Now, that's nice. That's very nice."

"Bluebonnets or indeed flowers of any kind are not mentioned in the Rules."

"We are promised to get this here shipment—"

"I have not interfered with the shipment."

"We are promised to get this here herd of *au-pair* girls to the railhead intact in both mind and body," Mr. Hawkins stated. "And I say that bestowal of bluebonnets is interferin' with a girl's mind and there's no two ways about it."

"She was looking very down-in-the-mouth."

"Not your affair. Not your affair."

Mr. Bellows moved to change the subject. "Is Daumier likely to be back for chow do you think?"

"What is for chow?"

"Chilidogs."

"He'll be back. Daumier does love his chilidog."

Résumé of the Plot
or Argument

Ignatius Loyola XVIII, with a band of hard-riding fanatical Jesuits under his command, has sworn to capture the herd and release the girls from the toils so-called of the Traffic, in which Daumier, Mr. Hawkins, and Mr. Bellows are prominent executives of long standing. Daumier meanwhile has been distracted from his proper business by a threat to the queen, the matter of the necklace (see Dumas, *The Queen's Necklace*, pp. 76–105).

Description of
Three O'Clock
in the Afternoon

I left Amelia's place and entered the October afternoon. The afternoon was dying giving way to the dark night, yet some amount of sunglow still warmed the cunning-wrought cobbles of the street. Many citizens both male and female were hurrying hither and thither on errands of importance, each *agitato* step compromising slightly the sheen of the gray fine-troweled sidewalk. Immature citizens in several sizes were massed before a large factorylike structure where advanced techniques transformed them into true-thinking right-acting members of the three social classes, lower, middle, and upper middle. Some number of these were engaged in ludic agon with basketballs, the same being hurled against passing vehicles producing an unpredictable rebound. Dispersed amidst the hurly and burly of the children were their tenders, shouting. Inmixed with this broil were ordinary denizens of the quarter—shopmen, *rentiers*, churls, sellers of vicious drugs, stum-drinkers, aunties, girls whose jeans had been improved with appliqué rose blossoms in the cleft of the buttocks, practicers of the priest hustle, and the like. Two officers of the Shore Patrol were hitting an imbecile Sea Scout with long shapely well-modeled nightsticks under the impression that they had jurisdiction. A man was swearing fine-sounding swearwords at a small yellow motorcar of Italian extraction, the same having joined its bumper to another bumper, the two bumpers intertangling like shameless lovers in the act of love. A man in the organic-vegetable hustle stood in the back of a truck praising tomatoes, the same being abulge with tomato-muscle and ablaze with minimum daily requirements. Several members of the madman profession made the air sweet with their imprecating and their moans and the subtle music of the tearing of their hair.

THOUGHT

Amelia is skeptical, I thought.

LIST OF RESEARCH
MATERIALS CONSULTED

My plan for self-transplants was not formulated without the benefit of some amount of research. I turned over the literature, which is immense, the following volumes sticking in the mind as having been particularly valuable: *The Self: An Introduction* by Meyers, *Self-Abuse* by Samuels, *The Armed Self* by Crawlie, Burt's *The Concept of Self*, *Self-Congratulation* by McFee, Fingarette's *Self-Deception*, *Self-Defense for Women and Young Girls* by Birch, Winterman's *Self-Doubt*, *The Effaced Self* by Lilly, *Self-Hatred in Vermin* by Skinner, LeBett's *Selfishness*, Gordon's *Self-Love*, *The Many-Colored Self* by Winsor and Newton, Paramananda's *Self-Mastery*, *The Misplaced Self* by Richards, *Nastiness* by Bertini, *The Self Prepares* by Teller, Flaxman's *The Self as Pretext*, Hickel's *Self-Propelled Vehicles*, Sørensen's *Self-Slaughter*, *Self and Society in Ming Thought* by DeBary, *The Sordid Self* by Clute, and *Techniques of Self-Validation* by Wright. These works underscored what I already knew, that the self is a dirty great villain, an interrupter of sleep, a deviler of awakeness, an intersubjective atrocity, a mouth, a maw. Transplantation of neutral or partially inert materials into the cavity was in my view the one correct solution.

Neutral or Partially
Inert Materials
Cross a River

A girl appeared holding a canteen.

"Is there any wine *s'il vous plaît?*"

"More demands," said Mr. Hawkins. "They accumulate."

"Some people do not know they are a member of a herd," said Mr. Bellows.

The girl turned to Daumier.

"Is it your intention to place all of us in this dirty water?" she asked, pointing to the river. "Together with our clothes and personal belongings as well?"

"There is a ford," said Daumier. "The water is only knee-high."

"And on the other bank, shooters? Oh, that's very fine. *Très intelligent.*"

"What's your name, Miss?"

"Celeste," said the girl. "Possibly there are vipers in the water? Poisonmouths?"

"Possibly," said Daumier. "But they won't hurt you. If you see one, just go around him."

"Myself, I will stay here, thank you. The other girls, they stay here too, I think."

"Celeste, you wouldn't be telling them about poisonmouths in the water, would you?"

"It is not necessary. They can look for their own selves." She paused. "Possibly you have a very intelligent plan for avoiding the shooters?"

She is not pretty, Daumier thought. But a good figure.

"My papa is a lawyer," she said. "An *avocat.*"

"So?"

"There was no word in the agreement about marching through great floods filled with vipers and catfishes."

"The problem is not the water but the Jesuits on the other side," said Daumier.

"The noble Loyola. Our resuscitator."

"You want to spend the next year in a convent? Wearing a long dress down to your feet and reading *The Lives of the Saints* and not a chilidog to your name?"

"He will take us to the convent?"

"Yes."

"What a thing. I did not know."

"Daumier," said Mr. Hawkins. "What is your *très intelligent* plan?"

"What if we send some of the girls in to bathe?"

"What for?"

"And while the enemy is struck blind by the dazzling beauty of our girls bathing, we cross the rest of them down yonder at the other ford."

"Ah, you mean bathing, uh—"

"Right."

"Could you get them to do it?"

"I don't know." He turned to Celeste. "What about it?"

"There is nothing in the agreement about making Crazy Horse shows in the water. But on the other hand, the cloister . . ."

"Yes," said Daumier.

Soon seven girls wearing towels were approaching the water.

"You and Mr. Bellows cross the herd down there. I'll watch out for these," Daumier said to Mr. Hawkins.

"Oh, you will," said Mr. Hawkins. "That's nice. That's very nice indeed. That is what I call nice, that is."

"Mr. Hawkins," said Daumier.

Then Daumier looked at Celeste and saw that the legs on her were as long and slim as his hope of Heaven and the thighs on her were as strong and sweet-shaped as ampersands and the buttocks on her were as pretty as two pictures and the waist on her was as neat and incurved as the waist of a fiddle and the shoulders on her were as tempting as sex crimes and the hair on her was as long and black as Lent and the movement of the whole was honey, and he sank into a swoon.

When he awoke, he found Mr. Hawkins lifting him by his belt and lowering him to the ground again, repeatedly.

"A swoon most likely," said Mr. Hawkins. "He was always given to swoonin'."

The girls were gathered about him, fully dressed and combing their damp hair.

"He looks extremely charming when he is swooned," said Celeste. "I don't like the eagle gaze so much."

"And his father and grandfather before him," said Mr. Hawkins, "they were given to swoonin'. The grandfather particularly. Physical beauty it was that sent the grandfather to the deck. There are those who have seen him fall at the mere flash of a kneecap."

"Is the herd across?" asked Daumier.

"Every last one of um," said Mr. Hawkins. "Mr. Bellows is probably handing out the TV dinners right now."

"We made a good exhibition, I think," said Celeste. "Did you see?"

"A little," said Daumier. "Let's push across and join the others."

They crossed the river and climbed a ridge and went through some amount of brush and past a broke-down abandoned farmhouse with no roof and through a pea patch that nobody had tended for so many years that the peas in their pods were as big as Adam's apples. On the other side of the pea patch they found Mr. Bellows tied to a tree by means of a great many heavy ropes around his legs, stomach, and neck and his mouth stuffed full of pages torn from a breviary. The herd was nowhere to be seen.

Two Whiskeys
with a Friend

"The trouble with you," said Gibbon, "is that you are a failure."

"I am engaged upon a psychological thimblerig which may have sound commercial applications," I said. "Vistas are opening."

"Faugh," he said.

"Faugh?"

"The trouble with you is that you are an idiot," Gibbon said. "You lack a sense of personal worthlessness. A sense of personal worthlessness is the motor that drives the overachiever to his splendid overachievements that we all honor and revere."

"I have it!" I said. "A deep and abiding sense of personal worthlessness. One of the best."

"It was your parents I expect," said Gibbon. "They were possibly too kind. The family of orientation is charged above all with developing the sense of personal worthlessness. Some are sloppy about it. Some let this responsibility slide and the result is a child with no strong sense of personal worthlessness, thus no drive to prove that the view he holds of himself is not correct, the same being provable only by conspicuous and distinguished achievement above and beyond the call of reasonableness."

I thought: His tosh is better than my tosh.

"I myself," said Gibbon, "am slightly underdone in the personal worthlessness line. It was Papa's fault. He used no irony. The communications mix offered by the parent to the child is as you know twelve percent do this, eighty-two percent don't do that, and six percent huggles and endearments. That is standard. Now, to avoid boring himself or herself to death during this monition the parent enlivens the discourse with wit, usually irony of the cheaper sort. The irony ambigufies the message, but more importantly establishes in the child the sense of personal lack-of-worth. Because the child understands that one who is talked to in this way is not much of a something. Ten years of it goes a long way. Fifteen is better. That is where Pap fell down. He eschewed irony. Did you bring any money?"

"Sufficient."

"Then I'll have another. What class of nonsense is this that you are up to with the surrogate?"

"I have made up a someone who is taking the place of myself. I think about him rather than about me."

"The trouble with you is that you are simpleminded. No wonder you were sacked from your job in the think tank."

"I was thinking but I was thinking about the wrong things."

"Does it work? This transplant business?"

"I have not had a thought about myself in seven days."

"Personally," said Gibbon, "I am of the opinion that the answer is Krishna Socialism."

Mr. Bellows Is Sprung; Arrival of a Figure; Popcorn Available in the Lower Lobby

"Our herd is rustled," said Mr. Hawkins.

Mr. Bellows was having pages of the Word removed from his mouth.

"Fifteen hundred head," said Daumier. "My mother will never forgive me."

"How many men did he have with him?" asked Mr. Hawkins.

"Well I only *saw* about four. Coulda been more. They jumped me just as we come outa the tree line. Two of 'em come at me from the left and two of 'em come at me from the right, and they damn near pulled me apart between 'em. And himself sittin' there on his great black horse with the five black hats on him and laughin' and gigglin' to beat all bloody hell. Then they yanked me off my horse and throwed me to the ground terrible hard and two of 'em sat on me while himself made a speech to the herd."

"What type of speech would that be?"

"It begun, 'Dearly beloved.' The gist of it was that Holy Mother the Church had arranged to rescue all the girls from the evil and vicious and low and reprehensible toils of the Traffic—meaning us—and the hardships and humiliations and degradations of *au-pair* life through the God-smiled-upon intervention of these hard-riding pure-of-heart Jesuits."

"How did the herd take it?"

"Then he said confessions would be between two and four in the afternoon, and that evening services would be at eight sharp. Then there was a great lot of groanin'. That was from the herd. Then the girls commenced to ask the padres about the hamburger ration and the grass ration and which way was the john and all that, and the boys in black got a little bit flustered. They realized they had fifteen hundred head of ravenous *au-pair* girls on their hands."

"He seems a good thinker," said Celeste. "To understand your maneuver beforehand, and to defeat it with his own very much superior maneuver—"

At that moment a figure of some interest approached the group. The figure was wearing on the upper of his two lips a pair of black fine-curled mustachios and on the top of his head a hat with a feather or plume of a certain swash and on his shoulders a cape of dark-blue material of a certain swagger and on his trunk a handsome leather doublet with pot-metal clasps and on the bottom of him a pair of big blooming breeches of a peach velvet known to interior decorators for its appositeness in the upholstering of loveseats and around his waist a sling holding a long resplendent rapier and on his two hands great gauntlets of pink pigskin and on his fine-chiseled features an expression of high-class arrogance. The figure was in addition mounted upon the top of a tall-standing well-curried fast-trotting sheep.

"What is it?" asked Mr. Bellows.

"Beats me," said Mr. Hawkins. "I think it is an actor."

"I know what it is," said Daumier. "It is a musketeer."

Further Boiling
of the Plot
in Summary Form

The musketeer carries a letter from the queen which informs Daumier that Jeanne de Valois, a bad person attached to the court, has obtained the necklace, which is worth 1,600,000 francs, by persuading the Cardinal de Rohan, an admirer of the queen, to sign a personal note for the amount, he thinking he is making a present to the queen, she thinking that the necklace has been returned to the jewelers, Jeanne de Valois having popped the diamonds into an unknown hiding place. The king is very likely going to find out about the whole affair and become very angry, in several directions. Daumier is begged to come to the capital and straighten things out. He does so.

History of the Society of Jesus

Driven from England, 1579
   Driven from France, 1594
   Driven from Venice, 1606
   Driven from Spain, 1767
   Driven from Naples, 1768
   Suppressed entirely by Clement XIV, 1773
   Revived, 1814

Something Is Happening

I then noticed that I had become rather fond—fond to a fault—of a person in the life of my surrogate. It was of course the girl Celeste. My surrogate obviously found her attractive and no less did I; this was a worry. I began to wonder how I could get her out of his life and into my own.

Amelia Objects

"What about me?"

Quotation from La Fontaine

"I must have the new, though there be none left in the world."

The Parry

"You are insatiable," she said.
  "I am in principle fifty percent sated," I said. "Had I two surrogates I would be one hundred percent sated. Two are necessary so that no individual surrogate gets the big head. My identification with that Daumier who is even now cleaning up all sorts of imbroglios in the queen's service is wonderful but there must be another. I see him as a quiet, thoughtful chap who leads a contemplative-type life. Maybe in the second person."

The New Surrogate
Given a Trial Run

This is not the worst time for doing what you are doing, and you are therefore pleased with yourself—not wildly, but a little. There are several pitfalls you have avoided. Other people have fallen into them. Standing at the rim of the pit, looking down at the sharpened stakes, you congratulate yourself on your good luck (because you know good sense cannot be credited) and move on. The conditions governing your life have been codified and set down in a little book, but no one has ever given you a copy, and when you have sought it in libraries, you are told that someone else has it on extended loan. Still, you are free to seek love, to the best of your ability, or to wash your clothes in the machines that stand with their round doors temptingly open, or to buy something in one of the many shops in this area—a puppy perhaps. Pausing before a show window full of puppies, brown and black and mixtures, you notice that they are very appealing. If only you could have one that would stay a puppy, and not grow into a full-sized dog. Your attachments are measured. Not that you are indifferent by nature—you want nothing so much as a deep-going, fundamental involvement—but this does not seem to happen. Your attachments are measured; each seems to last exactly two years. Why is that? On the last lap of a particular liaison, you feel that it is *time to go*, as if you were a guest at a dinner party and the host's offer of another brandy had a peculiar falseness to it. Full of good will, you attempt to pretend that you do not feel this way, you attempt to keep the level of cheerfulness and hope approximately where it has always been, to keep alive a sense of "future." But no one is fooled. Optimistic plans are made, but within each plan is another plan, allowing for the possible absence of one of the planners. You eye the bed, the record-player, the pictures, already making lists of who will take what. What does this say about you—that you move from person to person, a tourist of the emotions? Is this the meaning of failure? Perhaps it is too soon to decide. It has occurred to you that you, Daumier, may yet do something great. A real solid durable something, perhaps in the field of popular music, or light entertainment in general. These fields are not to be despised, although you are aware that many people look down on them. But perhaps a better-conceived attack might contain a shade less study. It is easy to be satisfied if you get out of things what inheres in them, but you must look closely, take nothing for granted, let nothing become routine. You must fight against the cocoon of habituation which covers everything, if you let it. There are always openings, if you can find them. There is always something to do.

A Sampling of Critical Opinion

"He can maunder."
　"Can't he maunder!"
　"I have not heard maundering of this quality since—"
　"He is a maundering fool."

Celeste Motors from One Sphere to Another Sphere

"She has run away," said Mr. Hawkins.
　"Clean as a whistle," said Mr. Bellows.
　"Herd-consciousness is a hard thing to learn," said Mr. Hawkins. "Some never learn it."
　"Yes," said Mr. Bellows, "there's the difficulty, the iddyological. You can get quite properly banjaxed there, with the iddyological."

Food

I was preparing a meal for Celeste—a meal of a certain elegance, as when arrivals or other rites of passage are to be celebrated.
　First off there were Saltines of the very best quality and of a special crispness, squareness, and flatness, obtained at great personal sacrifice by making representations to the National Biscuit Company through its authorized nuncios in my vicinity. Upon these was spread with a hand lavish and not stinting Todd's Liver Pâté, the same having been robbed from geese

and other famous animals and properly adulterated with cereals and other well-chosen extenders and the whole delicately spiced with calcium propionate to retard spoilage. Next there were rare cheese products from Wisconsin wrapped in gold foil in exquisite tints with interesting printings thereon, including some very artful representations of cows, the same being clearly in the best of health and good humor. Next there were dips of all kinds including clam, bacon with horseradish, onion soup with sour cream, and the like, which only my long acquaintance with some very high-up members of the Borden company allowed to grace my table. Next there were Fritos curved and golden to the number of 224 (approx.), or the full contents of the bursting 53¢ bag. Next there were Frozen Assorted Hors d'Oeuvres of a richness beyond description, these wrested away from an establishment catering only to the nobility, the higher clergy, and certain selected commoners generally agreed to be comers in their particular areas of commonality, calcium propionate added to retard spoilage. In addition there were Mixed Nuts assembled at great expense by the Planters concern from divers strange climes and hanging gardens, each nut delicately dusted with a salt that has no peer. Furthermore there were cough drops of the manufacture of the firm of Smith Fils, brown and savory and served in a bowl once the property of Brann the Iconoclast. Next there were young tender green olives into which ripe red pimentos had been cunningly thrust by underpaid Portuguese, real and true handwork every step of the way. In addition there were pearl onions meticulously separated from their nonstandard fellows by a machine that had caused the Board of Directors of the S. & W. concern endless sleepless nights and had passed its field trials just in time to contribute to the repast I am describing. Additionally there were gherkins whose just fame needs no further words from me. Following these appeared certain cream cheeses of Philadelphia origin wrapped in costly silver foil, the like of which a pasha could not have afforded in the dear dead days. Following were Mock Ortolans Manqués made of the very best soybean aggregate, the like of which could not be found on the most sophisticated tables of Paris, London, and Rome. The whole washed down with generous amounts of Tab, a fiery liquor brewed under license by the Coca-Cola Company which will not divulge the age-old secret recipe no matter how one begs and pleads with them but yearly allows a small quantity to circulate to certain connoisseurs and bibbers whose credentials meet the very rigid requirements of the Cellar-master. All of this stupendous feed being a mere scherzo before the announcement of the main theme, chilidogs.

"What is all this?" asked sweet Celeste, waving her hands in the air. "Where is the food?"

"You do not recognize a meal spiritually prepared," I said, hurt in the self-love.

"We will be very happy together," she said. "I cook."

CONCLUSION

I folded Mr. Hawkins and Mr. Bellows and wrapped them in tissue paper and put them carefully away in a drawer along with the king, the queen, and the cardinal. I was temporarily happy and content but knew that there would be a time when I would not be happy and content; at that time I could unwrap them and continue their pilgrimages. The two surrogates, the third-person Daumier and the second-person Daumier, were wrapped in tissue paper and placed in the drawer; the second-person Daumier especially will bear watching and someday when my soul is again sickly and full of sores I will take him out of the drawer and watch him. Now Celeste is making a *daube* and I will go into the kitchen and watch Celeste making the *daube*. She is placing strips of optional pork in the bottom of a pot. Amelia also places strips of optional pork in the bottom of a pot, when she makes a *daube*, but somehow— The self cannot be escaped, but it can be, with ingenuity and hard work, distracted. There are always openings, if you can find them, there is always something to do.

AMATEURS

To Grace Paley

Our Work and Why We Do It

As admirable volume after admirable volume tumbled from the sweating presses . . .

The pressmen wiped their black hands on their pants and adjusted the web, giving it just a little more impression on the right side, where little specks of white had started to appear in the crisp, carefully justified black prose.

I picked up the hammer and said into the telephone, "Well, if he comes around here he's going to get a face full of hammer

"A four-pound hammer can mess up a boy's face pretty bad

"A four-pound hammer can make a bloody rubbish of a boy's face."

I hung up and went into the ink room to see if we had enough ink for the rest of the night's runs.

"Yes, those were weary days," the old printer said with a sigh. "Follow copy even if it flies out the window, we used to say, and oft—"

Just then the Wells Fargo man came in, holding a .38 loosely in his left hand as the manual instructs

It was pointed at the floor, as if he wished to

But then our treasurer, old Claiborne McManus

The knobs of the safe

Sweet were the visions inside.

He handed over the bundle of Alice Cooper T-shirts we had just printed up, and the Wells Fargo man grabbed them with his free hand, gray with experience, and saluted loosely with his elbow, and hurried the precious product out to the glittering fans.

And coming to work today I saw a brown Mercedes with a weeping woman inside, her head was in her hands, a pretty blond back-of-the-neck, the man driving the Mercedes was paying no attention, and

But today we are running the Moxxon Travel Guide in six colors

The problems of makeready, registration, show-through, and feed

Will the grippers grip the sheet correctly?

And I saw the figure 5 writ in gold

"Down time" was a big factor in the recent negotiations, just as "wash-up time" is expected to complicate the negotiations to come. Percy handed the two-pound can of yellow ink to William.

William was sitting naked in the bed wearing the black hat. Rowena was in the bed too, wearing the red blanket. We have to let them do everything they want to do, because they own the business. Often they scandalize the proofreaders, and then errors don't get corrected and things have to be reset, or additional errors are *inserted* by a proofreader with his mind on the shining thing he has just seen. Atlases are William's special field of interest. There are many places he has never been.

"Yesterday," William began

You have your way of life and we ours

A rush order for matchbook covers for Le Foie de Veau restaurant

The tiny matchbook-cover press is readied, the packing applied, the "Le Foie de Veau" form locked into place. We all stand around a small table watching the matchbook press at work. It is exactly like a toy steam engine. Everyone is very fond of it, although we also have a press big as a destroyer escort—that one has a crew of thirty-five, its own galley, its own sick bay, its own band. We print the currency of Colombia, and the Acts of the Apostles, and the laws of the land, and the fingerprints

"My dancing shoes have rusted," said Rowena, "because I have remained for so long in this bed."

of criminals, and Grand Canyon calendars, and gummed labels, some things that don't make any sense, but that isn't our job, to make sense of things—our job is to kiss the paper with the form or plate, as the case may be, and make sure it's not getting too much ink, and worry about the dot structure of the engravings, or whether a tiny shim is going to work up during the run and split a fountain.

William began slambanging Rowena's dancing shoes with steel wool. "Yesterday," he said

Salesmen were bursting into the room with new orders, each salesman's person bulging with new orders

And old Lucien Frank was pushing great rolls of Luxus Semi-Fine No. 2 through the room with a donkey engine

"Yesterday," William said, "I saw six Sabrett hot-dog stands on wheels marching in single file down the middle of Jane Street followed at a slow trot by a police cruiser. They had yellow-and-blue umbrellas and each hot-dog stand was powered by an elderly man who looked ill. The elderly men not only looked ill but were physically small—not more than five-six, any of them. They were heading I judged for the Sixth Precinct. Had I had the black hat with me, and sufficient men and horses and lariats and .30-.30s, and popular support from the masses and a workable revolutionary ideology and/or a viable myth pattern, I would have rescued them. Removed them to the hills where we would have feasted all night around the fires on tasty Sabrett hot dogs and maybe steaming butts of Ballantine ale, and had bun-splitting contests, sauerkraut-hurling"

He opened the two-pound can of yellow ink with his teeth.

"You are totally wired," Rowena said tenderly

"A boy *likes* to be"

We turned away from this scene, because of what they were about to do, and had some more vodka. Because although we, too, are wired most of the time, it is not the vodka. It is, rather . . . What I mean is, if you have ink in your blood it's hard to get it out of your hands, or to keep your hands off the beautiful typefaces carefully distributed in the huge typecases

Annonce Grotesque
Compacta
Cooper Black
Helvetica Light
Melior
Microgramma Bold
Profil
Ringlet

And one of our volumes has just received a scathing notice in *Le Figaro*, which we also print . . . Should we smash the form? But it's *our* form . . .

Old Kermit Dash has just hurt his finger in the papercutter. "It's not so bad, Kermit," I said, binding up the wound. "I'm scared of the papercutter myself. Always have been. Don't worry about it. Think instead of the extra pay you will be drawing for that first joint, for the rest of your life. Now get back in there and cut paper." I whacked him on the rump, although he is eighty, almost rumpless

We do the *Oxford Book of American Grub*

Rowena handed Bill another joint—I myself could be interested in her, if she were not part of Management and thus "off limits" to us fiercely loyal artisans. And now, the problem of where to hide the damning statistics in the Doe Airframe Annual Report. Hank Witteborn, our chief designer, suggests that they just be "accidentally left out." The idea has merit, but

Crash! Someone has just thrown something through our biggest window. It is a note with a brick wrapped around it:

> *Sirs:*
> *If you continue to live and breathe*
> *If you persist in walking the path of*
> *Coating the façade of exploitation with*
> *the stucco of good printing*
>
> *Faithfully*

What are they talking about? Was it not we who had the contract for the entire Tanberian Revolution, from the original manifestos hand-set in specially nicked and scarred Blood Gothic to the letterheads of the Office of Permanent Change & Price Control (18 pt. Ultima on a 20-lb. laid stock)? But William held up a hand, and because he was the boss, we let him speak.

"It is good to be a member of the bourgeoisie," he said. "A boy *likes* being a member of the bourgeoisie. Being a member of the bourgeoisie is *good* for a boy. It makes him feel *warm* and *happy*. He can worry about his *plants*. His green plants. His plants and his quiches. His property taxes. The productivity of his workers. His plants/quiches/property taxes/workers/Land Rover. His *sword hilt*. His"

William is sometimes filled with self-hatred, but we are not. We have our exhilarating work, and our motto, "Grow or Die," and our fringe benefits, and our love for William (if only he would take his hands off Rowena's hip bones during business hours, if only he would take off the black hat and put on a pair of pants, a vest, a shirt, socks, and)

I was watching over the imposition of the Detroit telephone book. Someone had just dropped all the H's—a thing that happens sometimes.

"Don't anybody move! Now, everybody bend over and pick up the five slugs nearest him. Now, the next five. Easy does it. Somebody call Damage Control and have them send up extra vodka, lean meat, and bandages. Now, the next five. Anybody that steps on a slug gets the hammer in the mouth. Now, the next"

If only we could confine ourselves to matchbook covers!

But matchbook covers are not our destiny. Our destiny is to accomplish 1.5 million impressions per day. In the next quarter, that figure will be upped by 12 percent, unless

"Leather," William says.

"Leather?"

"*Leather*," he says with added emphasis. "Like they cover cows with."

William's next great idea will be in the area of leather. I am glad to know this. His other great ideas have made the company great.

The new machine for printing underground telephone poles

The new machine for printing smoke on smoked hams

The new machine for writing the figure 5 in gold

All of this weakens the heart. I have the hammer, I will smash anybody who threatens, however remotely, the company way of life. We know what we're doing. The vodka ration is generous. Our reputation for excellence is unexcelled, in every part of the world. And will be maintained until the destruction of our art by some other art which is just as good but which, I am happy to say, has not yet been invented.

The Wound

HE SITS up again. He makes a wild grab for his mother's hair. The hair of his mother! But she neatly avoids him. The cook enters with the roast beef. The mother of the torero tastes the sauce, which is presented separately, in a silver dish. She makes a face. The torero, ignoring the roast beef, takes the silver dish from his mother and sips from it, meanwhile maintaining intense eye contact with his mistress. The torero's mistress hands the camera to the torero's mother and reaches for the silver dish. "What is all this nonsense with the dish?" asks the famous aficionado who is sitting by the bedside. The torero offers the aficionado a slice of beef, carved from the roast with a sword, of which there are perhaps a dozen on the bed. "These fellows with their swords, they think they're so fine," says one of the *imbéciles* to another, quietly. The second *imbécil* says, "We would all think ourselves fine if we could. But we can't. Something prevents us."

The torero looks with irritation in the direction of the *imbéciles*. His mistress takes the 8-mm. movie camera from his mother and begins to film something outside the window. The torero has been gored in the foot. He is, in addition, surrounded by *imbéciles, idiotas*, and *bobos*. He shifts uncomfortably in his bed. Several swords fall on the floor. A telegram is delivered. The mistress of the torero puts down the camera and removes her shirt. The mother of the torero looks angrily at the *imbéciles*. The famous aficionado reads the telegram aloud. The telegram suggests the torero is a clown and a *cucaracha* for allowing himself to be gored in the foot, thus both insulting the noble profession of which he is such a poor representative and irrevocably ruining the telegram sender's Sunday afternoon, and that, furthermore, the telegram sender is even now on his way to the Church of Our Lady of the Several Sorrows to pray *against* the torero, whose future, he cordially hopes, is a thing of the past. The torero's head flops forward into the cupped hands of an adjacent *bobo*.

The mother of the torero turns on the television set, where the goring of the foot of the torero is being shown first at normal speed, then in exquisite slow motion. The torero's head remains in the cupped hands of the *bobo*. "My foot!" he shouts. Someone turns off the television. The beautiful breasts of the torero's mistress are appreciated by the aficionado, who is also an aficionado of breasts. The *imbéciles* and *idiotas* are afraid to look. So they do not. One *idiota* says to another *idiota*, "I would greatly like some of that roast beef." "But it has not been offered to us," his companion replies, "because we are so insignificant." "But no one else is eating it," the first says. "It simply sits there, on the plate." They regard the attractive roast of beef.

The torero's mother picks up the movie camera that his mistress has relinquished and begins filming the torero's foot, playing with the zoom lens. The torero, head still in the hands of the *bobo*, reaches into a drawer in the bedside table and removes from a box there a Cuban cigar of the first quality. Two *bobos* and an *imbécil* rush to light it for him, bumping into each other in the process. "Lysol," says the mother of the torero. "I forgot the application of the Lysol." She puts down the camera and looks around for the Lysol bottle. But the cook has taken it away. The mother of the torero leaves the room, in search of the Lysol bottle. He, the torero, lifts his head and follows her exit. More pain?

His mother reenters the room carrying a bottle of Lysol. The torero places his bandaged foot under a pillow, and both hands, fingers spread wide, on top of the pillow. His mother unscrews the top of the bottle of Lysol. The Bishop of Valencia enters with attendants. The Bishop is a heavy man with his head cocked permanently to the left—the result of years of hearing confessions in a confessional whose right-hand box was said to be inhabited by vipers. The torero's mistress hastily puts on her shirt. The *imbéciles* and *idiotas* retire into the walls. The Bishop extends his hand. The torero kisses the Bishop's ring. The famous aficionado does likewise. The Bishop asks if he may inspect the wound. The torero takes his foot out from under the pillow. The torero's mother unwraps the bandage. There is the foot, swollen almost twice normal size. In the center of the foot, the wound, surrounded by angry flesh. The Bishop shakes his head, closes his eyes, raises his head (on the diagonal), and murmurs a short prayer. Then he opens his eyes and looks about him for a chair. An *idiota* rushes forward with a chair. The Bishop seats himself by the bedside. The torero offers the Bishop some cold roast beef. The Bishop begins to talk about his psychoanalysis: "I am a different man now," the Bishop says. "Gloomier, duller, more fearful. In the name of the Holy Ghost, you would not believe what I see under the bed, in the middle of the night." The Bishop laughs heartily. The torero joins him. The torero's mistress is filming the Bishop. "I was happier with my whiskey," the Bishop says, laughing even harder. The laughter of the Bishop threatens the chair he is sitting in. One *bobo* says to another *bobo*, "The privileged classes can afford psychoanalysis and whiskey. Whereas all we get is sermons and sour wine. This is manifestly unfair. I protest, silently." "It is because we are no good," the second *bobo* says. "It is because we are nothings."

The torero opens a bottle of Chivas Regal. He offers a shot to the Bishop, who graciously accepts, and then pours one for himself. The torero's mother edges toward the bottle of Chivas Regal. The torero's mistress films his mother's surreptitious approach. The Bishop and the torero discuss whiskey and psychoanalysis. The torero's mother has a hand on the neck of the bottle. The torero makes a sudden wild grab for her hair. The hair of his mother! He misses and she scuttles off into a corner of the room, clutching the bottle. The torero picks a killing sword, an *estoque*, from the half dozen still on the bed. The Queen of the Gypsies enters.

The Queen hurries to the torero, little tufts of dried grass falling from her robes as she crosses the room. "Unwrap the wound!" she cries. "The wound, the wound, the wound!" The torero recoils. The Bishop sits severely. His attendants stir and whisper. The torero's mother takes a swig from the Chivas Regal bottle. The famous aficionado crosses himself. The torero's mistress looks down through her half-open blouse at her breasts. The torero quickly reaches into the drawer of the bedside table and removes the cigar box. He takes from the cigar box the ears and tail of a bull he killed, with excellence and emotion, long ago. He spreads them out on the bedcovers, offering them to the Queen. The ears resemble bloody wallets, the tail the hair of some long-dead saint, robbed from a reliquary. "No," the Queen says. She grasps the torero's foot and begins to unwrap the bandages. The torero grimaces but submits. The Queen withdraws from her belt a sharp knife. The torero's mistress picks up a violin and begins to play an air by Valdéz. The Queen whacks off a huge portion of roast beef, which she stuffs into her mouth while bent over the wound—gazing deeply into it, savoring it. Everyone shrinks—the torero, his mother, his mistress, the Bishop, the aficionado, the *imbéciles*, *idiotas*, and *bobos*. An ecstasy of shrinking. The Queen says, "I want this wound. *This one*. It is mine. Come, pick him up." Everyone present takes a handful of the torero and lifts him high above their heads (he is screaming). But the doorway is suddenly blocked by the figure of an immense black bull. The bull begins to ring, like a telephone.

110 West Sixty-First Street

PAUL GAVE Eugenie a very large swordfish steak for her birthday. It was wrapped in red-and-white paper. The paper was soaked with swordfish juices in places but Eugenie was grateful nevertheless. He had tried. Paul and Eugenie went to a film. Their baby had just died and they were trying not to think about it. The film left them slightly depressed. The child's body had been given to the hospital for medical experimentation. "But what about life after death?" Eugenie's mother had asked. "There isn't any," Eugenie said. "Are you positive?" her mother asked. "No," Eugenie said. "How can I be positive? But that's my opinion."

Eugenie said to Paul: "This is the best birthday I've ever had." "The hell it is," Paul said. Eugenie cooked the swordfish steak wondering what the hospital had done to Claude. Claude had been two years old when he died. *That goddamn kid!* she thought. Looking around her, she could see the places where he had been—the floor, mostly. Paul thought: My swordfish-steak joke was not successful. He looked at the rather tasteless swordfish on his plate. Eugenie touched him on the shoulder.

Paul and Eugenie went to many erotic films. But the films were not erotic. Nothing was erotic. They began looking at each other and thinking about other people. The back wall of the apartment was falling off. Contractors came to make estimates. A steel I beam would have to be set into the wall to support the floor of the apartment above, which was sagging. The landlord did not wish to pay the four thousand dollars the work would cost. One could see daylight between the back wall and the party wall. Paul and Eugenie went to his father's place in Connecticut for a day. Paul's father was a will lawyer—a lawyer specializing in wills. He showed them a flyer advertising do-it-yourself wills, DO YOU HAVE A WILL? *Everyone should. Save on legal fees—make your own will with Will Forms Kit. Kit has 5 will forms, a 64-page book on wills, a guide to the duties of the executor, and forms for recording family assets. $1.98.* Eugenie studied the third-class mail. "What are our family assets?" she asked Paul. Paul thought about the question. Paul's sister Debbie had had a baby at fifteen, which had been put up for adoption. Then she had become a nun. Paul's brother Steve was in the Secret Service and spent all of his time guarding the widow of a former President. "Does Debbie still believe in a life after death?" Eugenie asked suddenly. "She believes, so far as I can determine, in life *now*," Paul's father said. Eugenie remembered that Paul had told her that his father had been fond, when Debbie was a child, of beating her on her bare buttocks with a dog leash. "She believes in social action," Paul's bent father continued. "Probably she is right. That seems to be the trend among nuns."

Paul thought: Barbados. There we might recover what we have lost. I wonder if there is a charter flight through the Bar Association?

Paul and Eugenie drove back to the city.

"This is a lot of depressing crud that we're going through right now," Paul said as they reached Port Chester, N.Y. "But later it will be better." No it won't, Eugenie thought. "Yes it will," Paul said.

"You are extremely self-righteous," Eugenie said to Paul. "That is the one thing I can't stand in a man. Sometimes I want to scream." "You are a slut without the courage to go out and be one," Paul replied. "Why don't you go to one of those bars and pick up somebody, for God's sake?" "It wouldn't do any good," Eugenie said. "I know that," Paul said. Eugenie remembered the last scene of the erotic film they had seen on her birthday, in which the girl had taken a revolver from a drawer and killed her lover with it. At the time she had thought this a poor way to end the film. Now she wished she had a revolver in a drawer. Paul was afraid of having weapons in the house. "They fire themselves," he always said. "You don't have anything to do with it."

Mason came over and talked. Paul and Mason had been in the army together. Mason, who had wanted to be an actor, now taught speech at a junior college on Long Island. "How are you bearing up?" Mason asked, referring to the death of Claude. "Very well," Paul said. "I am bearing up very well but she is not." Mason looked at Eugenie. "Well, I don't blame her," he said. "She should be an alcoholic by now." Eugenie, who drank very little, smiled at Mason. Paul's jokes were as a rule better than Mason's jokes. But Mason had compassion. His compassion is real, she thought. Only he doesn't know how to express it.

Mason told a long story about trivial departmental matters. Paul and Eugenie tried to look interested. Eugenie had tried to give Claude's clothes to her friend Julia, who also had a two-year-old. But Julia had said no. "You would always be seeing them," she said. "You should give them to a more distant friend. Don't you have any distant friends?" Paul was promoted. He became a full partner in his law firm. "This is a big day," he said when he came home. He was slightly drunk. "There is no such thing as a big day," Eugenie said. "Once, I thought there was. Now I know better. I sincerely congratulate you on your promotion, which I really believe was well deserved. You are talented and you have worked very hard. Forgive me for that remark I made last month about your self-righteousness. What I said was true—I don't retreat from that position—but a better wife would have had the tact not to mention it." "No," Paul said. "You were right to mention it. It is true. You should tell the truth when you know it. And you should go out and get laid if you feel like it. The veneer of politesse we cover ourselves with is not in general good for us." "No," Eugenie said. "Listen. I want to get pregnant again. You could do that for me. It's probably a bad idea but I want to do it. In spite of everything." Paul closed his eyes. "No no no no no," he said.

Eugenie imagined the new child. This time, a girl. A young woman, she thought, eventually. Someone I could talk to. With Claude, we made a terrible mistake. We should have had a small coffin, a grave. We were sensible. We were unnatural. Paul emerged from the bathroom with a towel wrapped around his waist. There was some water on him still. Eugenie touched him on the shoulder. Paul and Eugenie had once taken a sauna together, in Norway. Paul had carried a glass of brandy into the sauna and the glass had become so hot that he could not pick it up. The telephone rang. It was Eugenie's sister in California. "We are going to have another child," Eugenie said to her sister. "Are you pregnant?" her sister asked. "Not yet," Eugenie said. "Do you think about him?" her sister asked. "I still see him crawling around on the floor," Eugenie said. "Under the piano. He liked to screw around under the piano."

In the days that followed, Paul discovered a pair of gold cuff links, oval in shape, at the bottom of a drawer. Cuff links, he thought. Could I ever have worn cuff links? In the days that followed, Eugenie met Tiger. Tiger was a black artist who hated white people so much he made love only to white women. "I am color-blind, Tiger," Eugenie said to Tiger, in bed. "I really am." "The hell you are," Tiger said. "You want to run a number on somebody, go ahead. But don't jive *me*." Eugenie admired Tiger's many fine qualities. Tiger "turned her head around," she explained to Paul. Paul tried to remain calm. His increased responsibilities were wearing out his nerve ends. He was guiding a bus line through bankruptcy. Paul asked Eugenie if she was using contraceptives. "Of course," she said.

"How'd it happen?" Tiger asked Eugenie, referring to the death of Claude. Eugenie told him. "That don't make one happy," Tiger said. "Tiger, you are an egocentric mushbrain monster," she said. "You mean I'm a *mean nigger*," Tiger said. He loved to say "nigger" because it shook the white folks so. "I mean you're an imitation wild man. You're about as wild as a can of Campbell's Chicken with Rice soup." Tiger then hit her around the head a few times to persuade her of his authenticity. But she was relentless. "When you get right down to it," she said, holding on to him and employing the dialect, "you ain't no better than a *husband*."

Tiger fell away into the bottomless abyss of the formerly known.

Paul smiled. He had not known it would come to this, but now that it had come to this, he was pleased. The bus line was safely parked in the great garage of Section 112 of the Bankruptcy Act. Time passed. Eugenie's friend Julia came over for coffee and brought her three-year-old son, Peter. Peter walked around looking for his old friend Claude. Eugenie told Julia about the departure of Tiger. "He snorted coke but he would never give me any," she complained. "He said he didn't want to get me started." "You should be grateful," Julia said. "You can't afford it." There was a lot of noise from the back room where workmen were putting in the steel I beam, finally. Paul was promoted from bus-line bankruptcies to railroad bankruptcies.

"Today is a big day," he told Eugenie when he got home. "Yes, it is," she said. "They gave me the Cincinnati & West Virginia. The whole thing. It's all mine." "That's wonderful," Eugenie said. "I'll make you a drink." Then they went to bed, he masturbating with long slow strokes, she masturbating with quick light touches, kissing each other passionately all the while.

Paul made more and more money. He bought a boat, a thirty-two-foot Bristol. The sea taught him many things. Bravery descended upon him like sudden rain. Alicia, the new child, stands on the bow wearing a fat orange life jacket. From the shore, lounging waiters at The Captain's Table watch her, wishing her well.

Some of Us Had Been Threatening Our Friend Colby

SOME OF us had been threatening our friend Colby for a long time, because of the way he had been behaving. And now he'd gone too far, so we decided to hang him. Colby argued that just because he had gone too far (he did not deny that he had gone too far) did not mean that he should be subjected to hanging. Going too far, he said, was something everybody did sometimes. We didn't pay much attention to this argument. We asked him what sort of music he would like played at the hanging. He said he'd think about it but it would take him a while to decide. I pointed out that we'd have to know soon, because Howard, who is a conductor, would have to hire and rehearse the musicians and he couldn't begin until he knew what the music was going to be. Colby said he'd always been fond of Ives's Fourth Symphony. Howard said that this was a "delaying tactic" and that everybody knew that the Ives was almost impossible to perform and would involve weeks of rehearsal, and that the size of the orchestra and chorus would put us way over the music budget. "Be reasonable," he said to Colby. Colby said he'd try to think of something a little less exacting.

Hugh was worried about the wording of the invitations. What if one of them fell into the hands of the authorities? Hanging Colby was doubtless against the law, and if the authorities learned in advance what the plan was they would very likely come in and try to mess everything up. I said that although hanging Colby was almost certainly against the law, we had a perfect *moral* right to do so because he was *our* friend, *belonged* to us in various important senses, and he had after all gone too far. We agreed that the invitations would be worded in such a way that the person invited could not know for sure what he was being invited to. We decided to refer to the event as "An Event Involving Mr. Colby Williams." A handsome script was selected from a catalogue and we picked a cream-colored paper. Magnus said he'd see to having the invitations printed, and wondered whether we should serve drinks.

Colby said he thought drinks would be nice but was worried about the expense. We told him kindly that the expense didn't matter, that we were after all his dear friends and if a group of his dear friends couldn't get together and do the thing with a little bit of *éclat*, why, what was the world coming to? Colby asked if he would be able to have drinks, too, before the event. We said, "Certainly."

The next item of business was the gibbet. None of us knew too much about gibbet design, but Tomás, who is an architect, said he'd look it up in old books and draw the plans. The important thing, as far as he recollected, was that the trapdoor function perfectly. He said that just roughly, counting labor and materials, it shouldn't run us more than four hundred dollars. "Good God!" Howard said. He said what was Tomás figuring on, rosewood? No, just a good grade of pine, Tomás said. Victor asked if unpainted pine wouldn't look kind of "raw," and Tomás replied that he thought it could be stained a dark walnut without too much trouble.

I said that although I thought the whole thing ought to be done really well and all, I also thought four hundred dollars for a gibbet, on top of the expense for the drinks, invitations, musicians, and everything, was a bit steep, and why didn't we just use a tree—a nice-looking oak, or something? I pointed out that since it was going to be a June hanging the trees would be in glorious leaf and that not only would a tree add a kind of "natural" feeling but it was also strictly traditional, especially in the West. Tomás, who had been sketching gibbets on the backs of envelopes, reminded us that an outdoor hanging always had to contend with the threat of rain. Victor said he liked the idea of doing it outdoors, possibly on the bank of a river, but noted that we would have to hold it some distance from the city, which presented the problem of getting the guests, musicians, etc., to the site and then back to town.

At this point everybody looked at Harry, who runs a car-and-truck-rental business. Harry said he thought he could round up enough limousines to take care of that end but that the drivers would have to be paid. The drivers, he pointed out, wouldn't be friends of Colby's and couldn't be expected to donate their services, any more than the bartender or the musicians. He said that he had about ten limousines, which he used mostly for funerals, and that he could probably obtain another dozen by calling around to friends of his in the trade. He said also that if we did it outside, in the open air, we'd better figure on a tent or awning of some kind to cover at least the principals and the orchestra, because if the hanging was being rained on he thought it would look kind of dismal. As between gibbet and tree, he said, he had no particular preferences and he really thought that the choice ought to be left up to Colby, since it was his hanging. Colby said that everybody went too far, sometimes, and weren't we being a little Draconian? Howard said rather sharply that all that had already been discussed, and which did he want, gibbet or tree? Colby asked if he could have a firing squad. No, Howard said, he could not. Howard said a firing squad would just be an ego trip for Colby, the blindfold and last-cigarette bit, and that Colby was in enough hot water already without trying to "upstage" everyone with unnecessary theatrics. Colby said he was sorry, he hadn't meant it that way, he'd take the tree. Tomás crumpled up the gibbet sketches he'd been making, in disgust.

Then the question of the hangman came up. Pete said did we really need a hangman? Because if we used a tree, the noose could be adjusted to the appropriate level and Colby could just jump off something—a chair or stool or something. Besides, Pete said, he very much doubted if there were any free-lance hangmen wandering around the country, now that capital punishment has been done away with absolutely, temporarily, and that we'd probably have to fly one in from England or Spain or one of the South American countries, and even if we did that how could we know in advance that the man was a professional, a real hangman, and not just some money-hungry amateur who might bungle the job and shame us all, in front of everybody? We all agreed then that Colby should just jump off something and that a chair was not what he should jump off of, because that would look, we felt, extremely tacky—some old kitchen chair sitting out there under our beautiful tree. Tomás, who is quite modern in outlook and not afraid of innovation, proposed that Colby be standing on a large round rubber ball ten feet in diameter. This, he said, would afford a sufficient "drop" and would also roll out of the way if Colby suddenly changed his mind after jumping off. He reminded us that by not using a regular hangman we were placing an awful lot of the responsibility for the success of the affair on Colby himself, and that although he was sure Colby would perform creditably and not disgrace his friends at the last minute, still, men have been known to get a little irresolute at times like that, and the ten-foot-round rubber ball, which could probably be fabricated rather cheaply, would insure a "bang-up" production right down to the wire.

At the mention of "wire," Hank, who had been silent all this time, suddenly spoke up and said he wondered if it wouldn't be better if we used wire instead of rope—more efficient and in the end kinder to Colby, he suggested. Colby began looking a little green, and I didn't blame him, because there is something extremely distasteful in thinking about being hanged with wire instead of rope—it gives you sort of a revulsion, when you think about it. I thought it was really quite unpleasant of Hank to be sitting there talking about wire, just when we had solved the problem of what Colby was going to jump off of so neatly, with Tomás's idea about the rubber ball, so I hastily said that wire was out of the question, because it would injure the tree—cut into the branch it was tied to when Colby's full weight hit it—and that in these days of increased respect for the environment, we didn't want that, did we? Colby gave me a grateful look, and the meeting broke up.

Everything went off very smoothly on the day of the event (the music Colby finally picked was standard stuff, Elgar, and it was played very well by Howard and his boys). It didn't rain, the event was well attended, and we didn't run out of Scotch, or anything. The ten-foot rubber ball had been painted a deep green and blended in well with the bucolic setting. The two things I remember best about the whole episode are the grateful look Colby gave me when I said what I said about the wire, and the fact that nobody has ever gone too far again.

The School

WELL, WE had all these children out planting trees, see, because we figured that . . . that was part of their education, to see how, you know, the root systems . . . and also the sense of responsibility, taking care of things, being individually responsible. You know what I mean. And the trees all died. They were orange trees. I don't know why they died, they just died. Something wrong with the soil possibly or maybe the stuff we got from the nursery wasn't the best. We complained about it. So we've got thirty kids there, each kid had his or her own little tree to plant, and we've got these thirty dead trees. All these kids looking at these little brown sticks, it was depressing.

It wouldn't have been so bad except that just a couple of weeks before the thing with the trees, the snakes all died. But I think that the snakes—well, the reason that the snakes kicked off was that . . . you remember, the boiler was shut off for four days because of the strike, and that was explicable. It was something you could explain to the kids because of the strike. I mean, none of their parents would let them cross the picket line and they knew there was a strike going on and what it meant. So when things got started up again and we found the snakes they weren't too disturbed.

With the herb gardens it was probably a case of overwatering, and at least now they know not to overwater. The children were very conscientious with the herb gardens and some of them probably . . . you know, slipped them a little extra water when we weren't looking. Or maybe . . . well, I don't like to think about sabotage, although it did occur to us. I mean, it was something that crossed our minds. We were thinking that way probably because before that the gerbils had died, and the white mice had died, and the salamander . . . well, now they know not to carry them around in plastic bags.

Of course we *expected* the tropical fish to die, that was no surprise. Those numbers, you look at them crooked and they're belly-up on the surface. But the lesson plan called for a tropical-fish input at that point, there was nothing we could do, it happens every year, you just have to hurry past it.

We weren't even supposed to have a puppy.

We weren't even supposed to have one, it was just a puppy the Murdoch girl found under a Gristede's truck one day and she was afraid the truck would run over it when the driver had finished making his delivery, so she stuck it in her knapsack and brought it to school with her. So we had this puppy. As soon as I saw the puppy I thought, Oh Christ, I bet it will live for about two weeks and then . . . And that's what it did. It wasn't supposed to be in the classroom at all, there's some kind of regulation about it, but you can't tell them they can't have a puppy when the puppy is already there, right in front of them, running around on the floor and yap yap yapping. They named it Edgar—that is, they named it after me. They had a lot of fun running after it and yelling, "Here, Edgar! Nice Edgar!" Then they'd laugh like hell. They enjoyed the ambiguity. I enjoyed it myself. I don't mind being kidded. They made a little house for it in the supply closet and all that. I don't know what it died of. Distemper, I guess. It probably hadn't had any shots. I got it out of there before the kids got to school. I checked the supply closet each morning, routinely, because I knew what was going to happen. I gave it to the custodian.

And then there was this Korean orphan that the class adopted through the Help the Children program, all the kids brought in a quarter a month, that was the idea. It was an unfortunate thing, the kid's name was Kim and maybe we adopted him too late or something. The cause of death was not stated in the letter we got, they suggested we adopt another child instead and sent us some interesting case histories, but we didn't have the heart. The class took it pretty hard, they began (I think; nobody ever said anything to me directly) to feel that maybe there was something wrong with the school. But I don't think there's anything wrong with the school, particularly, I've seen better and I've seen worse. It was just a run of bad luck. We had an extraordinary number of parents passing away, for instance. There were I think two heart attacks and two suicides, one drowning, and four killed together in a car accident. One stroke. And we had the usual heavy mortality rate among the grandparents, or maybe it was heavier this year, it seemed so. And finally the tragedy.

The tragedy occurred when Matthew Wein and Tony Mavrogordo were playing over where they're excavating for the new federal office building. There were all these big wooden beams stacked, you know, at the edge of the excavation. There's a court case coming out of that, the parents are claiming that the beams were poorly stacked. I don't know what's true and what's not. It's been a strange year.

I forgot to mention Billy Brandt's father, who was knifed fatally when he grappled with a masked intruder in his home.

One day, we had a discussion in class. They asked me, where did they go? The trees, the salamander, the tropical fish, Edgar, the poppas and mommas, Matthew and Tony, where did they go? And I said, I don't know, I don't know. And they said, who knows? and I said, nobody knows. And they said, is death that which gives meaning to life? and I said, no, life is that which gives meaning to life. Then they said, but isn't death, considered as a fundamental datum, the means by which the taken-for-granted mundanity of the everyday may be transcended in the direction of—

I said, yes, maybe.

They said, we don't like it.

I said, that's sound.

They said, it's a bloody shame!

I said, it is.

They said, will you make love now with Helen (our teaching assistant) so that we can see how it is done? We know you like Helen.

I do like Helen but I said that I would not.

We've heard so much about it, they said, but we've never seen it.

I said I would be fired and that it was never, or almost never, done as a demonstration. Helen looked out of the window.

They said, please, please make love with Helen, we require an assertion of value, we are frightened.

I said that they shouldn't be frightened (although I am often frightened) and that there was value everywhere. Helen came and embraced me. I kissed her a few times on the brow. We held each other. The children were excited. Then there was a knock on the door, I opened the door, and the new gerbil walked in. The children cheered wildly.

The Great Hug

At the last breakfast after I told her, we had steak and eggs. Bloody Marys. Three pieces of toast. She couldn't cry, she tried. Balloon Man came. He photographed the event. He created the Balloon of the Last Breakfast After I Told Her—a butter-colored balloon. "This is the kind of thing I do so well," he said. Balloon Man is not modest. No one has ever suggested that. "This balloon is going to be extra-famous and acceptable, a documentation of raw human riches, the plain canvas gravy of the thing. The Pin Lady will never be able to bust this balloon, never, not even if she hugs me for a hundred years." We were happy to have pleased him, to have contributed to his career.

The Balloon Man won't sell to kids.

Kids will come up to the Balloon Man and say, "Give us a blue balloon, Balloon Man," and the Balloon Man will say, "Get outa here kids, these balloons are adults-only." And the kids will say, "C'mon, Balloon Man, give us a red balloon and a green balloon and a white balloon, we got the money." "Don't want any kid-money," the Balloon Man will say, "kid-money is wet and nasty and makes your hands wet and nasty and then you wipe 'em on your pants and your pants get all wet and nasty and you sit down to eat and the *chair* gets all wet and nasty, let that man in the brown hat draw near, he wants a balloon." And the kids will say, "Oh please Balloon Man, we want five yellow balloons that never pop, we want to make us a smithereen." "Ain't gonna make no smithereen outa my fine yellow balloons," says the Balloon Man, "your red balloon will pop sooner and your green balloon will pop later but your yellow balloon will never pop no matter how you stomp on it or stick it and besides the Balloon Man don't sell to kids, it's against his principles."

The Balloon Man won't let you take his picture. He has something to hide. He's a superheavy Balloon Man, doesn't want the others to steal his moves. It's all in the gesture—the precise, reunpremeditated right move.

Balloon Man sells the Balloon of Fatigue and the Balloon of Ora Pro Nobis and the Rune Balloon and the Balloon of the Last Thing to Do at Night; these are saffron-, cinnamon-, salt-, and celery-colored, respectively. He sells the Balloon of Not Yet and the Balloon of Sometimes. He works the circus, every circus. Some people don't go to the circus and so don't meet the Balloon Man and don't get to buy a balloon. That's sad. Near to most people in any given city at any given time won't be at the circus. That's unfortunate. They don't get to buy a brown, whole-life-long cherishable Sir Isaiah Berlin Balloon. "I don't sell the Balloon Jejune," the Balloon Man will say, "let them other people sell it, let them other people have all that wet and nasty kid-money mitosising in their sock. That a camera you got there mister? Get away." Balloon Man sells the Balloon of Those Things I Should Have Done I Did Not Do, a beige balloon. And the Balloon of the Ballade of the Crazy Junta, crimson of course. Balloon Man stands in a light rain near the popcorn pushing the Balloon of Wish I Was, the Balloon of Busoni Thinking, the Balloon of the Perforated Septum, the Balloon of Not Nice. Which one is my balloon, Balloon Man? Is it the Balloon of the Cartel of Noose Makers? Is it the Balloon of God Knows I Tried?

One day the Balloon Man will meet the Pin Lady. It's in the cards, in the stars, in the entrails of sacred animals. Pin Lady is a woman with pins stuck in her couture, rows of pins and pins not in rows but placed irregularly here a pin there a pin, maybe eight thousand pins stuck in her couture or maybe ten thousand pins or twelve thousand pins. Pin Lady tells the truth. The embrace of Balloon Man and Pin Lady will be something to see. They'll roll down the hill together, someday. Balloon Man's arms will be wrapped around Pin Lady's pins and Pin Lady's embrangle will be wrapped around Balloon Man's balloons—even the yellow balloons. They'll roll down the hill together. Pin Lady has the Pin of I Violently Desire. She has the Pin of Crossed Fingers Behind My Back, she has the Pin of Soft Talk, she has the Pin of No More and she is rumored to have the Pin of the Dazed Sachem's Last Request. She's into puncture. When puncture becomes widely accepted and praised, it will be the women who will have the sole license to perform it, Pin Lady says.

THE GREAT HUG

Pin Lady has the Pin of Tomorrow Night—a wicked pin, those who have seen it say. That great hug, when Balloon Man and Pin Lady roll down the hill together, will be frightening. The horses will run away in all directions. Ordinary people will cover their heads with shopping bags. I don't want to think about it. You blow up all them balloons yourself, Balloon Man? Or did you have help? Pin Lady, how come you're so aprickle-dedee? Was it something in your childhood?

Balloon Man will lead off with the Balloon of Grace Under Pressure, Do Not Pierce or Incinerate.

Pin Lady will counter with the Pin of Oh My, I Forgot.

Balloon Man will produce the Balloon of Almost Wonderful. Pin Lady will come back with the Pin of They Didn't Like Me Much. Balloon Man will sneak in there with the Balloon of the Last Exit Before the Toll Is Taken. Pin Lady will reply with the Pin of One Never Knows for Sure. Balloon Man will propose the Balloon of Better Days. Pin Lady, the Pin of Whiter Wine.

It's gonna be *bad*, I don't want to think about it.

Pin Lady tells the truth. Balloon Man doesn't lie, exactly. How can the Quibbling Balloon be called a lie? Pin Lady is more straightforward. Balloon Man is less straightforward. Their stances are semiantireprophetical. They're falling down the hill together, two falls out of three. Pin him, Pin Lady. Expand, Balloon Man. When he created our butter-colored balloon, we felt better. A little better. The event that had happened to us went floating out into the world, was made useful to others. Balloon Man says, "I got here the Balloon of the Last Concert. It's not a bad balloon. Some people won't like it. Some people *will* like it. I got the Balloon of Too Terrible. Not every balloon can make you happy. Not every balloon can trigger glee. *But I insist that these balloons have a right to be heard!* Let that man in the black cloak step closer, he wants a balloon.

"The Balloon of Perhaps. My best balloon."

I Bought a Little City

So I bought a little city (it was Galveston, Texas) and told everybody that nobody had to move, we were going to do it just gradually, very relaxed, no big changes overnight. They were pleased and suspicious. I walked down to the harbor where there were cotton warehouses and fish markets and all sorts of installations having to do with the spread of petroleum throughout the Free World, and I thought, A few apple trees here might be nice. Then I walked out this broad boulevard which has all these tall thick palm trees maybe forty feet high in the center and oleanders on both sides, it runs for blocks and blocks and ends up opening up to the broad Gulf of Mexico—stately homes on both sides and a big Catholic church that looks more like a mosque and the Bishop's Palace and a handsome red brick affair where the Shriners meet. I thought, What a nice little city, it suits me fine.

It suited me fine so I started to change it. But softly, softly. I asked some folks to move out of a whole city block on I Street, and then I tore down their houses. I put the people into the Galvez Hotel, which is the nicest hotel in town, right on the seawall, and I made sure that every room had a beautiful view. Those people had wanted to stay at the Galvez Hotel all their lives and never had a chance before because they didn't have the money. They were delighted. I tore down their houses and made that empty block a park. We planted it all to hell and put some nice green iron benches in it and a little fountain—all standard stuff, we didn't try to be imaginative.

I was pleased. All the people who lived in the four blocks surrounding the empty block had something they hadn't had before, a park. They could sit in it, and like that. I went and watched them sitting in it. There was already a black man there playing bongo drums. I hate bongo drums. I started to tell him to stop playing those goddamn bongo drums but then I said to myself, No, that's not right. You got to let him play his goddamn bongo drums if he feels like it, it's part of the misery of democracy, to which I subscribe. Then I started thinking about new housing for the people I had displaced, they couldn't stay in that fancy hotel forever.

But I didn't have any ideas about new housing, except that it shouldn't be too imaginative. So I got to talking to one of these people, one of the ones we had moved out, guy by the name of Bill Caulfield who worked in a wholesale-tobacco place down on Mechanic Street.

"So what kind of a place would you like to live in?" I asked him.

"Well," he said, "not too big."

"Uh-huh."

"Maybe with a veranda around three sides," he said, "so we could sit on it and look out. A screened porch, maybe."

"Whatcha going to look out at?"

"Maybe some trees and, you know, the lawn."

"So you want some ground around the house."

"That would be nice, yeah."

"'Bout how much ground are you thinking of?"

"Well, not too much."

"You see, the problem is, there's only x amount of ground and everybody's going to want to have it to look at and at the same time they don't want to be staring at the neighbors. Private looking, that's the thing."

"Well, yes," he said. "I'd like it to be kind of private."

"Well," I said, "get a pencil and let's see what we can work out."

We started with what there was going to be to look at, which was damned difficult. Because when you look you don't want to be able to look at just one thing, you want to be able to shift your gaze. You need to be able to look at at least three things, maybe four. Bill Caulfield solved the problem. He showed me a box. I opened it up and inside was a jigsaw puzzle with a picture of the Mona Lisa on it.

"Lookee here," he said. "If each piece of ground was like a piece of this-here puzzle, and the tree line on each piece of property followed the outline of a piece of the puzzle—well, there you have it, Q.E.D. and that's all she wrote."

"Fine," I said. "Where are the folk going to park their cars?"

"In the vast underground parking facility," he said.

"O.K., but how does each householder gain access to his household?"

"The tree lines are double and shade beautifully paved walkways possibly bordered with begonias," he said.

"A lurkway for potential muggists and rapers," I pointed out.

"There won't be any such," Caulfield said, "because you've bought our whole city and won't allow that class of person to hang out here no more."

That was right. I had bought the whole city and could probably do that. I had forgotten.

"Well," I said finally, "let's give 'er a try. The only thing I don't like about it is that it seems a little imaginative."

We did and it didn't work out badly. There was only one complaint. A man named A. G. Bartie came to see me.

"Listen," he said, his eyes either gleaming or burning, I couldn't tell which, it was a cloudy day, "I feel like I'm living in this gigantic jiveass jigsaw puzzle."

He was right. Seen from the air, he was living in the middle of a titanic reproduction of the Mona Lisa, too, but I thought it best not to mention that. We allowed him to square off his property into a standard 60 × 100 foot lot and later some other people did that too—some people just like rectangles, I guess. I must say it improved the concept. You run across an occasional rectangle in Shady Oaks (we didn't want to call the development anything too imaginative) and it surprises you. That's nice.

I said to myself:

> Got a little city
> Ain't it pretty

By now I had exercised my proprietorship so lightly and if I do say so myself tactfully that I wondered if I was enjoying myself enough (and I had paid a heavy penny too—near to half my fortune). So I went out on the streets then and shot six thousand dogs. This gave me great satisfaction and you have no idea how wonderfully it improved the city for the better. This left us with a dog population of 165,000, as opposed to a human population of something like 89,000. Then I went down to the Galveston *News*, the morning paper, and wrote an editorial denouncing myself as the vilest creature the good God had ever placed upon the earth, and were we, the citizens of this fine community, who were after all free Americans of whatever race or creed, going to sit still while one man, *one man*, if indeed so vile a critter could be so called, etc. etc.? I gave it to the city desk and told them I wanted it on the front page in fourteen-point type, boxed. I did this just in case they might have hesitated to do it themselves, and because I'd seen that Orson Welles picture where the guy writes a nasty notice about his own wife's terrible singing, which I always thought was pretty decent of him, from some points of view.

A man whose dog I'd shot came to see me.

"You shot Butch," he said.

"Butch? Which one was Butch?"

"One brown ear and one white ear," he said. "Very friendly."

"Mister," I said, "I've just shot six thousand dogs, and you expect me to remember Butch?"

"Butch was all Nancy and me had," he said. "We never had no children."

"Well, I'm sorry about that," I said, "but I own this city."

"I know that," he said.

"I am the sole owner and I make all the rules."

"They told me," he said.

"I'm sorry about Butch but he got in the way of the big campaign. You ought to have had him on a leash."

"I don't deny it," he said.

"You ought to have had him inside the house."

"He was just a poor animal that had to go out sometimes."

"And mess up the streets something awful?"

"Well," he said, "it's a problem. I just wanted to tell you how I feel."

"You didn't tell me," I said. "How do you feel?"

"I feel like bustin' your head," he said, and showed me a short length of pipe he had brought along for the purpose.

"But of course if you do that you're going to get your ass in a lot of trouble," I said.

"I realize that."

"It would make you feel better, but then I own the jail and the judge and the po-lice and the local chapter of the American

Civil Liberties Union. All mine. I could hit you with a writ of mandamus."

"You wouldn't do that."

"I've been known to do worse."

"You're a black-hearted man," he said. "I guess that's it. You'll roast in Hell in the eternal flames and there will be no mercy or cooling drafts from any quarter."

He went away happy with this explanation. I was happy to be a black-hearted man in his mind if that would satisfy the issue between us because that was a bad-looking piece of pipe he had there and I was still six thousand dogs ahead of the game, in a sense. So I owned this little city which was very, very pretty and I couldn't think of any more new innovations just then or none that wouldn't get me punctuated like the late Huey P. Long, former governor of Louisiana. The thing is, I had fallen in love with Sam Hong's wife. I had wandered into this store on Tremont Street where they sold Oriental novelties, paper lanterns, and cheap china and bamboo birdcages and wicker footstools and all that kind of thing. She was smaller than I was and I thought I had never seen that much goodness in a woman's face before. It was hard to credit. It was the best face I'd ever seen.

"I can't do that," she said, "because I am married to Sam."

"Sam?"

She pointed over to the cash register where there was a Chinese man, young and intelligent-looking and pouring that intelligent look at me with considered unfriendliness.

"Well, that's dismal news," I said. "Tell me, do you love me?"

"A little bit," she said, "but Sam is wise and kind and we have one and one-third lovely children."

She didn't look pregnant but I congratulated her anyhow, and then went out on the street and found a cop and sent him down to H Street to get me a bucket of Colonel Sanders' Kentucky Fried Chicken, extra crispy. I did that just out of meanness. He was humiliated but he had no choice. I thought:

> I own a little city
> Awful pretty
> Can't help people

> Can hurt them though
> Shoot their dogs
> Mess 'em up
> Be imaginative
> Plant trees
> Best to leave 'em alone?
> Who decides?
> Sam's wife is Sam's wife and coveting
> Is not nice.

So I ate the Colonel Sanders' Kentucky Fried Chicken, extra crispy, and sold Galveston, Texas, back to the interests. I took a bath on that deal, there's no denying it, but I learned something—don't play God. A lot of other people already knew that, but I have never doubted for a minute that a lot of other people are smarter than me, and figure things out quicker, and have grace and statistical norms on their side. Probably I went wrong by being too imaginative, although really I was guarding against that. I did very little, I was fairly restrained. God does a lot worse things, every day, in one little family, any family, than I did in that whole little city. But He's got a better imagination than I do. For instance, I still covet Sam Hong's wife. That's torment. Still covet Sam Hong's wife, and probably always will. It's like having a tooth pulled. For a year. The same tooth. That's a sample of His imagination. It's powerful.

So what happened? What happened was that I took the other half of my fortune and went to Galena Park, Texas, and lived inconspicuously there, and when they asked me to run for the school board I said No, I don't have any children.

The Agreement

WHERE IS my daughter?
Why is she there? What crucial error did I make? Was there more than one?

Why have I assigned myself a task that is beyond my abilities?

Having assigned myself a task that is beyond my abilities, why do I then pursue it with all of the enthusiasm of one who believes himself capable of completing the task?

Having assigned myself a task that is beyond my abilities, why do I then do that which is most certain to preclude my completing the task? To ensure failure? To excuse failure? Ordinary fear of failure?

When I characterize the task as beyond my abilities, do I secretly believe that it is within my powers?

Was there only one crucial error, or was there a still more serious error earlier, one that I did not recognize as such at the time?

Was there a series of errors?

Are they in any sense forgivable? If so, who is empowered to forgive me?

If I fail in the task that is beyond my abilities, will my lover laugh?

Will the mailman laugh? The butcher?

When will the mailman bring me a letter from my daughter?

Why do I think my daughter might be dead or injured when I know that she is almost certainly well and happy? If I fail in the task that is beyond my abilities, will my daughter's mother laugh?

But what if the bell rings and I go down the stairs and answer the door and find there an old woman with white hair wearing a bright-red dress, and when I open the door she immediately begins spitting blood, a darker red down the front of her bright-red dress?

If I fail in the task that is beyond my abilities, will my doctor laugh?

Why do I conceal from my doctor what it is necessary for him to know?

Is my lover's lover a man or a woman?

Will my father and mother laugh? Are they already laughing, secretly, behind their hands?

If I succeed in the task that is beyond my abilities, will I win the approval of society? If I win the approval of society, does this mean that the (probable) series of errors already mentioned will be forgiven, or, if not forgiven, viewed in a more sympathetic light? Will my daughter then be returned to me?

Will I deceive myself about the task that is beyond my abilities, telling myself that I have successfully completed it when I have not?

Will others aid in the deception?

Will others unveil the deception?

But what if the bell rings and I go down the stairs and answer the door and find there an old man with white hair wearing a bright-red dress, and when I open the door he immediately begins spitting blood, a darker red down the front of his bright-red dress?

Why did I assign myself the task that is beyond my abilities?

Did I invent my lover's lover or is he or she real? Ought I to care?

But what if the bell rings and I go down the stairs again and instead of the white-haired woman or man in the bright-red dress my lover's lover is standing there? And what if I bring my lover's lover into the house and sit him or her down in the brown leather club chair and provide him or her with a drink and begin to explain that the task I have undertaken is hopelessly, hopelessly beyond my abilities? And what if my lover's lover listens with the utmost consideration, nodding and smiling and patting my wrist at intervals as one does with a nervous client, if one is a lawyer or doctor, and then abruptly offers me a new strategy: Why not do *this*? And what if, thinking over the new strategy proposed by my lover's lover, I recognize that yes, *this* is the solution which has evaded me for these many months? And what if, recognizing that my lover's lover has found the solution which has evaded me for these many months, I suddenly begin spitting blood, dark red against the blue of my blue work shirt? What then?

For is it not the case that even with the solution in hand, the task will remain beyond my abilities?

And where is my daughter? What is my daughter thinking at this moment? Is my daughter, at this moment, being knocked off her bicycle by a truck with the words HACHARD & CIE painted on its sides? Or is she, rather, in a photographer's studio, sitting for a portrait I have requested? Or has she already done so, and will, today, the bell ring and the mailman bring a large stiff brown envelope stamped PHOTO DO NOT BEND?

> HACHARD & CIE?
> PHOTO DO NOT BEND?

If I am outraged and there is no basis in law or equity for my outrage nor redress in law or equity for my outrage, am I to decide that my outrage is wholly inappropriate? If I observe myself carefully, using the techniques of introspection most favored by society, and decide, after such observation, that my outrage is not wholly inappropriate but perhaps partially appropriate, what can I do with my (partially appropriate) outrage? What is there to do with it but deliver it to my lover or my lover's lover or to the task that is beyond my abilities, or to embrace instead the proposition that, after all, things are not so bad? Which is not true?

If I embrace the proposition that, after all, things are not so bad, which is not true, then have I not also embraced a hundred other propositions, kin to the first in that they are also not true? That the Lord is my shepherd, for example?

But what if I decide not to be outraged but to be, instead, calm and sensible? Calm and sensible and adult? And mature? What if I decide to send my daughter stamps for her stamp collection and funny postcards and birthday and Christmas packages and to visit her at the times stated in the agreement? And what if I assign myself simpler, easier tasks, tasks which are well within my powers? And what if I decide that my lover has no other lover (disregarding the matchbooks, the explanations that do not explain, the discrepancies of time and place), and what if I inform my doctor fully and precisely about my case, supplying all relevant details (especially the shameful)? And what if I am able to redefine my errors as positive adjustments to a state of affairs requiring positive adjustments? And what if the operator does *not* break into my telephone conversation, any conversation, and say, "I'm sorry, this is the operator, I have an emergency message for 679-9819"?

Will others aid in the deception?

Will others unveil the deception?

"TWELFTH: Except for the obligations, promises and agreements herein set forth and to be performed by the husband and wife respectively, and for rights, obligations and causes of action arising out of or under this agreement, all of which are expressly reserved, the husband and wife each hereby, for himself or herself and for his or her legal representatives, forever releases and discharges the other, and the heirs and legal representatives of the other, from any and all debts, sums of money, accounts, contracts, claims, cause or causes of action, suits, dues, reckonings, bills, specialties, covenants, controversies, agreements, promises, variances, trespasses, damages, judgments, extents, executions and demands, whatsoever, in law or in equity, which he or she had, or has or hereafter can, shall or may have, by reason of any matter, from the beginning of the world to the execution of this agreement."

The painters are here. They are painting the apartment. One gallon of paint to eight gallons of benzine. From the beginning of the world to the execution of this agreement. Where is my daughter? I am asking for a carrot to put in the stone soup. The villagers are hostile.

The Sergeant

THE ORDERLY looked at the paper and said, There's nothing wrong with this. Take it to room 400.

I said, Wait a minute.

The orderly looked at me. I said, Room 400.

I said something about a lawyer.

He got to his feet. You know what that is? he asked, pointing to an M.P. in the hall.

I said yes, I remembered.

O.K. Room 400. Take this with you.

He handed me the paper.

I thought, They'll figure it out sooner or later. And: The doctor will tell them.

The doctor said, Hello, young trooper.

•

The other sergeant looked at me. How come you made sergeant so quick?

I was always a sergeant, I said. I was a sergeant the last time, too.

I got more time in grade, he said, so I outrank you.

I said not if you figured from my original date-of-rank which was sometime in '53.

Fifty-three, he said, what war was that?

I said the war with the Koreans.

I heard about it, he said. But you been away a long time.

I said that was true.

What we got here is a bunch of re-cruits, he said, they don't love the army much.

I said I thought they were all volunteers.

The e-conomic debacle volunteered 'em, he said, they heard the eagle shits once a month regularly.

I said nothing. His name was Tomgold.

They'll be rolling training grenades under your bunk, he said, just as soon as we teach 'em how to pull the pin.

I said they wouldn't do that to me because I wasn't supposed to be here anyway, that it was all a mistake, that I'd done all this before, that probably my discharge papers would come through any day now.

That's right, he said, you do look kind of old. Can you still screw?

•

I flicked on the barracks lights.

All right you men, I said.

But there was only one. He sat up in his bunk wearing skivvies, blinking in the light.

O.K. soldier roll out.

What time is it sarge?

It's five-forty-five soldier, get dressed and come with me. Where are the other men?

Probably haven't got back from town, sarge.

They have overnight passes?

Always got passes, sarge. Lots and lots of passes. Look, I got a pass too.

He showed me a piece of paper.

You want me to write you a pass, sarge?

I said I really wasn't supposed to be here at all, that I'd done all this before, that it was all a mistake.

You want me to fix you up with discharge papers, sarge? It'll cost you.

I said that if his section chief found out what he was doing they'd put him way back in the jailhouse.

You want me to cut some orders for you, sarge? You want a nice TDY to Hawaii?

I said I didn't want to get mixed up in anything.

If you're mixed up in this, then you got to get mixed up in that, he said. Would you turn them lights out, as you go?

•

The I.G. was a bird colonel with a jumper's badge and a general's pistol belt. He said, Well, sergeant, all I know is what's on the paper.

Yes, sir, I said, but couldn't you check it out with the records center?

They're going to have the same piece of paper I have, sergeant.

I said that I had been overseas for sixteen months during the Korean War and that I had then been reassigned to Fort Lewis, Washington, where my C.O. had been a Captain Llewellyn.

None of this is in your 201 file, the I.G. said.

Maybe there's somebody else with my name.

Your name *and* your serial number?

Colonel, I did all this before. Twenty years ago.

You don't look that old, sergeant.

I'm forty-two.

Not according to this.

But that's wrong.

The colonel giggled. If you were a horse we could look at your teeth.

Yes, sir.

O.K. sergeant I'll take it under advisement.

Thank you, sir.

I sat on the edge of my bed and looked at my two pairs of boots beautifully polished for inspection, my row of shirts hanging in my cubicle with all the shoulder patches facing the same way.

I thought: Of course, it's what I deserve. I don't deny that. Not for a minute.

•

Sergeant, he said, I'd be greatly obliged.

I said I wasn't sure I had fifty dollars to lend.

Look in your pocket there, sargie, the lieutenant said. Or maybe you have a bank account?

I said yes but not here.

My momma is sick and I need fifty dollars to take the bus home, he said. You don't want to impede my journey in the direction of my sick momma, do you?

What has she got? I asked.

Who?

Your mother.

I'll let you keep my 'lectric frying pan as security, the lieutenant said, showing it to me.

I'm not supposed to be in the army at all, I said. It's a fuckup of some kind.

Where are you from, sargie-san? You can cook yourself the dishes of your home region, in this frying pan.

I said the food in the NCO mess was pretty good, considering.

You're not going to lend me the fifty dollars?

I didn't say that, I said.

Sergeant, I can't *order* you to lend me the fifty dollars.

I know that, sir.

It's against regulations to do that, sergeant.

Yes, sir.

I can't read and write, sergeant.

You can't read and write?

If they find out, my ass is in terrible, terrible trouble, sergeant.

Not at all?

You want a golf club? I'll sell you a golf club. Fifty dollars.

I said I didn't play.

What about my poor momma, sergeant?

I said I was sorry.

I ride the blue bus, sergeant. Carries me clear to Gainesville. You ever ride the blue bus, sergeant?

•

I spoke to the chaplain who was playing the pinball machine at the PX. I said I didn't love the army much.

Nonsense, the chaplain said, you do, you do, you do or you wouldn't be here. Each of us is where we are, sergeant, because we want to be where we are and because God wants us to be where we are. Everybody in life is in the right place, believe me, may not seem that way sometimes but take it from me, take it from me, all part of the Divine plan, you got any quarters on you?

I gave him three quarters I had in my pocket.

Thank you, he said, I'm in the right place, you're in the right place, what makes you think you're so different from me? You think God doesn't know what He's doing? I'm right here ministering to the Screaming Falcons of the Thirty-third Division and if God didn't want me to be ministering to the wants and needs of the Screaming Falcons of the Thirty-third Division

I wouldn't be here, would I? What makes you think you're so different from me? Works is what counts, boy, forget about anything else and look to your works, your works tell the story, nothing wrong with you, three stripes and two rockers, you're doing very well, now leave me, leave me, don't let me see your face again, you hear, sergeant? Good boy.

I thought: Works?

•

Two M.P.'s stopped me at the main gate.

Where you headed, sergeant?

I said I was going home.

That's nice, said the taller of the two. You got any orders?

I showed them a pass.

How come you takin' off at this hour, sergeant? It's four o'clock in the morning. Where's your car?

I said I didn't have a car, thought I'd walk to town and catch a bus.

The M.P.'s looked at me peculiarly.

In this fog and stuff? they asked.

I said I liked to walk in the early morning.

Where's your gear, sergeant? Where's your A.W.O.L. bag? You don't have a bag?

I reached into the pocket of my field jacket and showed them my razor and a fresh T-shirt.

What's your outfit, sergeant?

I told them.

The shorter M.P. said: But this razor's not clean.

We all crowded closer to look at the razor. It was not clean.

And this-here pass, he said, it's signed by General Zachary Taylor. Didn't he die?

•

I was holding on to a sort of balcony or shelf that had been tacked on to the third floor of the barracks. It was about to fall off the barracks and I couldn't get inside because somebody'd nailed the windows shut.

Hey, slick, came a voice from the parking lot, you gonna fall.

Yes yes, I said, I'm going to fall.

Jump down here, she said, and I'll show you the secrets of what's under my shirt.

Yeah yeah, I said, I've heard that before.

Jump little honey baby, she said, you won't regret it.

It's so far, I said.

Won't do nothin' 'cept break your head, she called, at the very worst.

I don't want my head broken, I said, trying to get my fingers into that soft decayed pine.

Come on, G.I., she said, you ain't comfortable up there.

I did all this, I said, once, twenty years ago. Why do I have to do it all over again?

You do look kind of old, she said, you an R.A. or something? Come down, my little viper, come down.

I either jumped or did not jump.

•

I thought: Of course, it's what I deserve. I don't deny it for a minute.

The captain said: Harm that man over there, sergeant.

Yes, sir. Which one?

The one in the red tie.

You want me to harm him?

Yes, with your M-16.

The man in the red tie. Blue suit.

Right. Go ahead. Fire.

Black shoes.

That's the one, sergeant, are you temporizing?

I think he's a civilian, sir.

You're refusing an order, sergeant?

No I'm not refusing sir I just don't think I can do it.

Fire your weapon sergeant.

He's not even in uniform, sir, he's wearing a suit. And he's not doing anything, he's just standing there.

You're refusing a direct order?

I just don't feel up to it, sir. I feel weak.

Well sergeant if you don't want to harm the man in the red tie I'll give you an alternative. You can stuff olives with little onions for the general's martinis.

That's the alternative?
There are eight hundred thousand gallon cans of olives over at the general's mess, sergeant. And four hundred thousand gallon cans of little onions. I think you ought to consider that.
I'm allergic to onions, sir. They make me break out. Terribly.
Well you've a nice little problem there, haven't you, sergeant? I'll give you thirty seconds.

•

The general was wearing a white short-sleeved shirt, blue seersucker trousers, and gold wire-rimmed glasses.
Four olives this time, sergeant.
I said: Andromache!

What to Do Next

So.

The situation is, I agree, desperate. But fortunately I know the proper way to proceed. That is why I am giving you these instructions. They will save your life. First, persuade yourself that the situation is not desperate (my instructions will save your life only if you have not already hopelessly compromised it by listening to the instructions of others, or to the whispers of your heart, which is in itself suspect, in that it has been taught how to behave—how to whisper, even—by the very culture that has produced the desperate situation). Persuade yourself, I say, that your original perception of the situation was damaged by not having taken into account all of the variables (for example, my instructions) and that the imminent disaster that hangs in the sky above you can be, with justice, downgraded to the rank of severe inconvenience by the application of corrected thinking. Do not let what happened to the dog weaken your resolve.

Yes, the dog is dead, I admit it. I'm sorry. I admit also that putting eight-foot-square paintings of him in every room of the house has not consoled you. But, studying the paintings, you will notice after a time that in each painting the artist has included, in the background, or up in the left-hand corner, not only your dog but other dogs, dogs not known to you—perhaps dogs that were formerly friends of your dog but that you did not know he knew. Thus the whole concept "other dog" suddenly thrusts itself into your consciousness, and looking more intently now at those strange spaniels, retrievers, terriers, you understand that one of them, or one very much like one of them, might just possibly become the "new dog"—the "new dog" of which you have been, until now, afraid to think. For life must go on, after all, and that you have been able to think *new dog* is already a victory, of a kind, for the instructions.

Next, write your will. I know that you are too young to take this step, or at least this is what you have always told yourself, when will-writing time rolled around; this time, do it. Leave everything to your wife, if you have one; or to your old school, if you have one. This prudent action, which you would not have taken had it not been for the instructions, implies nothing about your future health and well-being. Don't worry. Next, see your Loan Officer, and borrow a sizable sum to leave to people, for what good is a will if it does not have the strong arm of hard cash to implement it with? You are tidying up, yes, but do not permit this kind of activity to frighten you. Lose yourself in the song of the instructions, in the precise, detailed balm of having had solved for you that most difficult of problems, what to do next.

Now, housecleaning. It is true that what she is saying doesn't interest you very much, but don't tell her (or, if you are a woman, him—the instructions are flexible, the instructions do not discriminate). Smile. Smile and tell her that the two of you have come to "the end of the line"—she is interesting but false. (It is not true that she is interesting but it is true that she is false.) Your true love lies elsewhere, and always will. I know that it's depressing, this maneuver (she has hung her shirt in your closet, and now you must give it back) but your life is more important than any of these merely temporal alignments, which give you someone to sleep with, yes, but on the other hand require a lot of smiling—smiling that you cannot spare, if you are to turn a smiling face and a ready, acquiescent nod to the just demands of the instructions. There! The thing is done. Lead her, weeping, from the closet, the green garment you never liked much dangling from one hand, and put her on a bus. Goodbye, Elsie.

I know that you are depressed, but pay attention: the instructions have arranged a diversion for you. Sea air! Passage has been booked in your name to Hong Kong on the *Black Swan*, the *Black Tulip*, or the *Tanta Maru*. Running away from trouble is always an excellent partial solution, but we anticipate using this tactic only temporarily, until other measures, still being honed and polished (there you are in the crew's mess, drinking anisette with Rudi and Hans, the crew members who have befriended you, and listening to their stories about waves, to which you respond a shade too enthusiastically, like those people, usually English, one finds at a jazz place over-enjoying the music, their mouths open too ecstatically, their fingerpopping too Anglo-Saxon), are ready for presentation to the green breast of the New World. You need not thank the instructions just yet; they have not completed their designs, although they are pleased that *you* are pleased with the life of the forecastle, which you would never have tasted in all its saltiness had it not been for them.

Quickly now, avoid that other sticky development that is developing on the left, a hazard you would not have identified had it not been for the sage wisdom of the instructions, which anticipate everything, even their own blind spots, of which they possess not a few. The instructions are, for example, blind to the blandishments of the soft life, which other sets of instructions uphold, cultivate, make possible. But that life is not for you, you do not have the panache to carry it off. You are in fact rather poor specimen, in some ways, and entering a fashionable hotel in Bern with a vastly beautiful woman on your arm, her thin skeleton curling toward you, and forty or fifty pieces of good luggage following, you would only look ridiculous. Where did you purchase those trousers? Trousers made out of old rugs have not been *haut monde* for two years. Remember Elsie. Forget Zoë. Stop plucking nervously at your rugs. Pay attention.

Because we are ready to move toward the center of your difficulties, which is the fact that you are no good. This great handicap, which many of our best people have labored under, is irrevocable. This is the nut of your dilemma, and to crack it you must proceed in the following way (remember that you still have a new dog to buy, and a true love to fail to find, and while we are at it we have been thinking about certain alterations that need to be made on your house—a wall torn out here, a soffit to be plastered there, the plumber summoned to make the drains drain, all crucial to giving your leaning personality the definition that it lamentably lacks). The instructions, at this point, call for a rewriting of your fundamental documents through useful work. Many considerations now intrude. Your former employment as a pilot project for A.A., although possessed of some degree of social worth, does not, in our analysis, finally qualify. It stressed your objecthood, your existence as vessel, your flasklike qualities, and neglected, to our mind, the creative potentialities you might contain. We have thought about possible alternatives. The Bengal Lancers are no longer recruiting. I.B.M. is a very large company but all of the good jobs are already taken. Your love of life would seem to equip you for a role on "Love of Life," but, we have discovered, others, similarly equipped, have got there ahead of you. There is a chief's rating open on the *Tanta Maru* and a cook's on the *Black Tulip*, but these have been filled by Rudi and Hans, who have asked to be remembered to you. You could become a dog painter in the tradition of Landseer, but there are already seventy thousand of these in New York City alone—leadership in that field is not easily come by.

Starting fresh, as it is called, requires that you know the appropriate corn and rain dances, but also that you can stand the terrific wrenches of the spirit that accompany frontier-busting, as it is called. When you change your life, you also break your back (or have an equivalent serious illness) within the next twelve months—that is a statistically sound statement. But the instructions will protect you, more or less, from these hazards (and it would not surprise me if, at this point, you wondered aloud why the instructions are being so kind to you, specifically you; the answer is simple, you have taken the trouble to read them). The culture that we share, such as it is, makes of us all either machines for assimilating and judging that culture, or uncritical sops who simply sop it up, become it. Clearly it is better to be the first than the second, or at least that is our provisional judgment, at this time. Because you stick out from the matrix of this culture like a banged thumb, swelling and reddening and otherwise irrupting all over its smooth, eventless surface, our effort must be to contain you, as would, for example, a lead glove. (Note your movement from container, which you were in your former life, before you renewed yourself, with the aid of the instructions, to contained, the latter a much more active principle, lively and wroth-causing—another success story for the cunning and gay instructions, which, although they may seem to you a shade self-congratulatory and vain, are in truth only *right*.) We have therefore decided to make you *a part of the instructions themselves*—something other people must complete, or go through, before they reach their individual niches, or thrones, or whatever kind of plateau makes them, at least for the time being, happy. Thus, we have specified that everyone who comes to us from this day forward must take twelve hours of you a week, for which they will receive three points credit per semester, and, as well, a silver spoon in the "Heritage" pattern. Don't hang back. We are sure you are up to it. Many famous teachers teach courses in themselves; why should you be different, just because you are a wimp and a lame, objectively speaking? Courage. The anthology of yourself which will be used as a text is even now being assembled by underpaid researchers in our textbook division, drawing upon the remembrances of those who hated you and those (a much smaller number) who loved you. You will be adequate in your new role. See? Your life is saved. The instructions do not make distinctions between those lives which are worth saving and those which are not. Your life is saved. Congratulations. I'm sorry.

The Captured Woman

THE CAPTURED woman asks if I will take her picture.

I shoot four rolls of 35 mm. and then go off very happily to the darkroom . . .

I bring back the contacts and we go over them together. She circles half a dozen with a grease pencil—pictures of herself staring. She does not circle pictures of herself smiling, although there are several very good ones. When I bring her back prints (still wet) she says they are not big enough.

"Not big enough?"

"Can you make enlargements?"

"How big?"

"How big can you make them?"

"The largest paper I have is 24 by 36."

"Good!"

The very large prints are hung around her room with pushpins.

"Make more."

"For what?"

"I want them in the other rooms too."

"The staring ones?"

"Whichever ones you wish."

I make more prints using the smiling negatives. (I also shoot another half dozen rolls.) Soon the house is full of her portraits, she is everywhere.

•

M. calls to tell me that he has captured a woman too.

"What kind?"

"Thai. From Thailand."

"Can she speak English?"

"Beautifully. She's an English teacher back home, she says."

"How tall?"

"As tall as yours. Maybe a little taller."

"What is she doing?"

"Right now?"

"Yes."

"She's polishing her rings. I gave her a lot of rings. Five rings."

"Was she pleased?"

"I think so. She's polishing like a house afire. Do you think that means she's tidy?"

"Have to wait and see. Mine is throwing her football."

"What?"

"I gave her a football. She's sports-minded. She's throwing passes into a garbage can."

"Doesn't that get the football dirty?"

"Not the regular garbage can. I got her a special garbage can."

"Is she good at it?"

"She's good at *everything*."

There was a pause.

"Mine plays the flute," M. says. "She's asked for a flute."

"Mine probably plays the flute too but I haven't asked her. The subject hasn't come up."

"Poor Q.," M. says.

"Oh, come now. No use pitying Q."

"Q. hasn't a chance in the world," M. says, and hangs up.

•

I say: "What will you write in the note?"

"You may read it if you wish. I can't stop you. It's you after all who will put it in the mail."

"Do you agree not to tell him where you are?"

"This is going to be almost impossible to explain. You understand that."

"Do you love him?"

"I waited six years to have a baby."

"What does that mean?"

"I wasn't sure, I suppose."

"Now you're sure?"

"I was growing older."

"How old are you now?"

"Thirty-two last August."

"You look younger."

"No I don't."

She is tall and has long dark hair which has, in truth, some gray in it already.

She says: "You were drunk as a lord the first time I saw you."

"Yes, I was."

When I first met her (in a perfectly ordinary social situation, a cocktail party) she clutched my wrists, tapping them then finally grabbing, in the wildest and most agitated way, meanwhile talking calmly about some movie or other.

She's a wonderful woman, I think.

•

She wants to go to church!

"*What!*"

"It's Sunday."

"I haven't been inside a church in twenty years. Except in Europe. Cathedrals."

"I want to go to church."

"What kind?"

"Presbyterian."

"Are you a Presbyterian?"

"I was once."

I find a Presbyterian church in the Yellow Pages.

We sit side by side in the pew for all the world like a married couple. She is wearing a beige linen suit which modulates her body into a nice safe Sunday quietude.

The two ministers have high carved chairs on either side of the lectern. They take turns conducting the service. One is young, one is old. There is a choir behind us and a solo tenor so startlingly good that I turn my head to look at him.

We stand and sit and sing with the others as the little mimeographed order-of-service dictates.

The old minister, fragile, eagle beak, white close-cropped hair, stands at the lectern in a black cassock and white thin lacy surplice.

"*Sacrifice*," the minister says.

He stares into the choir loft for a moment and then repeats the thought: "Sacrifice."

We are given a quite admirable sermon on Sacrifice which includes quotations from Euripides and A. E. Housman.

After the service we drive home and I tie her up again.

•

It is true that Q. will never get one. His way of proceeding is far too clumsy. He might as well be creeping about carrying a burlap sack.

P. uses tranquillizing darts delivered by a device which resembles the Sunday *New York Times.*

D. uses chess but of course this limits his field of operations somewhat.

S. uses a spell inherited from his great-grandmother.

F. uses his illness.

T. uses a lasso. He can make a twenty-foot loop and keep it spinning while he jumps in and out of it in his handmade hundred-and-fifty-dollar boots—a mesmerizing procedure.

C. has been accused of jacklighting, against the law in this state in regard to deer. The law says nothing about women.

X. uses the Dionysiac frenzy.

L. is the master. He has four now, I believe.

I use Jack Daniel's.

•

I stand beside one of the "staring" portraits and consider whether I should attempt to steam open the note.

Probably it is an entirely conventional appeal for rescue.

I decide that I would rather not know what is inside, and put it in the mail along with the telephone bill and a small ($25) contribution to a lost but worthy cause.

•

Do we sleep together? Yes.

What is to be said about this?

It is the least strange aspect of our temporary life together. It is as ordinary as bread.

She tells me what and how. I am sometimes inspired and in those moments need no instructions. Once I made an X with masking tape at a place on the floor where we'd made love. She laughed when she saw it. That is, I am sometimes able to amuse her.

What does she think? Of course, I don't know. Perhaps she regards this as a parenthesis in her "real" life, like a stay in the hospital or being a member of a jury sequestered in a Holiday Inn during a murder trial. I have criminally abducted her and am thus clearly in the wrong, a circumstance which enables her to regard me very kindly.

She is a wonderful woman and knows herself to be wonderful—she is (justifiably) a little vain.

The rope is forty feet long (that is, she can move freely forty feet in any direction) and is in fact thread—Belding mercerized cotton, shade 1443.

What does she think of me? Yesterday she rushed at me and stabbed me three times viciously in the belly with a book, the Viking *Portable Milton*. Later I visited her in her room and was warmly received. She let me watch her doing her exercises. Each exercise has a name and by now I know all the names: Boomerang, Melon, Hip Bounce, Diamond, Whip, Hug, Headlights, Ups and Downs, Bridge, Flags, Sitting Twist, Swan, Bow and Arrow, Turtle, Pyramid, Bouncing Ball, Accordion. The movements are amazingly erotic. I knelt by her side and touched her lightly. She smiled and said, not now. I went to my room and watched television—*The Wide World of Sports*, a soccer match in São Paulo.

•

The captured woman is smoking her pipe. It has a long graceful curving stem and a white porcelain bowl decorated with little red flowers. For dinner we had shad roe and buttered yellow beans.

"He looks like he has five umbrellas stuck up his ass," she says suddenly.

"Who?"

"My husband. But he's a very decent man. But of course that's not uncommon. A great many people are very decent. Most people, I think. Even you."

The fragrance of her special (ladies' mixture) tobacco hangs about us.

"This is all rather like a movie. That's not a criticism. I like things that are like movies."

I become a little irritated. All this effort and all she can think of is movies?

"This is not a movie."
"It is," she says. "It is it is it is."

•

M. calls in great agitation.
"Mine is sick," he says.
"What's the matter?"
"I don't know. She's listless. Won't eat. Won't polish. Won't play her flute."
M.'s is a no-ass woman of great style and not inconsiderable beauty.
"She's languishing," I say.
"Yes."
"That's not good."
"No."
I pretend to think—M. likes to have his predicaments taken seriously.
"Speak to her. Say this: My soul is soused, imparadised, imprisoned in my lady."
"Where's that from?"
"It's a quotation. Very powerful."
"I'll try it. Soused, imprisoned, imparadised."
"No. Imparadised, imprisoned. It actually sounds better the way you said it, though. Imparadised last."
"O.K. I'll say it that way. Thanks. I love mine more than you love yours."
"No you don't."
"Yes I do."
I bit off my thumb, and bade him do as much.

•

The extremely slow mailman brings her an answer to her note.
I watch as she opens the envelope.
"That bastard," she says.
"What does he say?"
"That incredible bastard."
"What?"
"I offer him the chance to rescue me on a white horse—one

of the truly great moments this life affords—and he natters on about how well he and the kid are doing together. How she hardly ever cries now. How *calm* the house is."

"The bastard," I say happily.

"I can see him sitting in the kitchen by the microwave oven and reading his *Rolling Stone*."

"Does he read *Rolling Stone*?"

"He thinks *Rolling Stone* is neat."

"Well . . ."

"He's not *supposed* to be reading *Rolling Stone*. It's not aimed at him. He's too old, the dumb fuck."

"You're angry."

"Damn right."

"What are you going to do?"

She thinks for a moment.

"What happened to your hand?" she says, noticing at last.

"Nothing," I say, placing the bandaged hand behind my back. (Obviously I did not bite the thumb clean through but I did give it a very considerable gnaw.)

"Take me to my room and tie me up," she says. "I'm going to hate him for a while."

I return her to her room and go back to my own room and settle down with *The Wide World of Sports*—international fencing trials in Belgrade.

•

This morning, at the breakfast table, a fierce attack from the captured woman.

I am a shit, a vain preener, a watcher of television, a blatherer, a creephead, a monstrous coward who preys upon etc. etc. etc. and is not man enough to etc. etc. etc. Also I drink too much.

This is all absolutely true. I have often thought the same things myself, especially, for some reason, upon awakening.

I have a little more Canadian bacon.

"And a skulker," she says with relish. "One who—"

I fix her in the view finder of my Pentax and shoot a whole new series, *Fierce*.

The trouble with capturing one is that the original gesture is almost impossible to equal or improve upon.

•

She says: "He wants to get that kid away from me. He wants to keep that kid for himself. He has captured that kid."

"She'll be there when you get back. Believe me."

"When will that be?"

"It's up to you. You decide."

"Ugh."

Why can't I marry one and live with her uneasily ever after? I've tried that.

"Take my picture again."

"I've taken enough pictures. I don't want to take any more pictures."

"Then I'll go on Tuesday."

"Tuesday. O.K. That's tomorrow."

"Tuesday is tomorrow?"

"Right."

"Oh."

She grips the football and pretends to be about to throw it through the window.

"Do you ever capture somebody again after you've captured them once?"

"Almost unheard of."

"Why not?"

"It doesn't happen."

"Why not?"

"It just doesn't."

"Tomorrow. Oh my."

I go into the kitchen and begin washing the dishes—the more scutwork you do, the kindlier the light in which you are regarded, I have learned.

•

I enter her room. L. is standing there.

"What happened to your hand?" he asks.

"Nothing," I say.

Everyone looks at my bandaged hand for a moment—not long enough.

"Have you captured her?" I ask.

L. is the master, the nonpareil, the O. J. Simpson of our aberration.

"I have captured him," she says.

"Wait a minute. That's not how it works."

"I changed the rules," she says. "I will be happy to give you a copy of the new rules which I have written out here on this legal pad."

L. is smirking like a mink, obviously very pleased to have been captured by such a fine woman.

"But wait a minute," I say. "It's not Tuesday yet!"

"I don't care," she says. She is smiling. At L.

I go into the kitchen and begin scrubbing the oven with Easy-Off.

How original of her to change the rules! She is indeed a rare spirit.

"French Russian Roquefort or oil-and-vinegar," she says sometimes, in her sleep—I deduce that she has done some waitressing in her day.

•

The captured woman does a backward somersault from a standing position.

I applaud madly. My thumb hurts.

"Where is L.?"

"I sent him away."

"Why?"

"He had no interesting problems. Also he did a sketch of me which I didn't like."

She shows me the charcoal sketch (L.'s facility is famous) and it is true that her beauty suffers just a bit, in this sketch. He must have been spooked a little by my photographs, which he did not surpass.

"Poor L."

The captured woman does another somersault. I applaud again. Is today Tuesday or Wednesday? I can't remember.

"Wednesday," she says. "Wednesday the kid goes to dance after which she usually spends the night with her pal Regina because Regina lives close to dance. So there's really no point in my going back on a Wednesday."

•

A week later she is still with me. She is departing by degrees.

If I tore her hair out, no one but me would love her. But she doesn't want me to tear her hair out.

I wear different shirts for her: red, orange, silver. We hold hands through the night.

And Then

THE PART of the story that came next was suddenly missing, I couldn't think of it, so I went into the next room and drank a glass of water (my "and then" still hanging in the frangible air) as if this were the most natural thing in the world to do at that point, thinking that I would "make up" something, while in the other room, to put in place of that part of the anecdote that had fallen out of my mind, to keep the light glittering in his cautious eyes. And in truth I was getting a little angry with him now, not fiercely angry but slightly *désabusé*, because he had been standing very close to me, closer than I really like people to stand, the rims of his shoes touching the rims of my shoes, our belt buckles not four inches distant, a completely unwarranted impingement upon my personal space. And so I went, as I say, into the next room and drank a glass of water, trying to remember who he was and why I was talking to him, not that he wasn't friendly, if by "friendly" you mean standing aggressively close to people with an attentive air and smiling teeth, that's not what I mean by "friendly," and it was right then that I decided to lie to him, although what I had been telling him previously was true, to the best of my knowledge and belief. But, faced now with this "gap" in the story, I decided to offer him a good-quality lie in place of the part I couldn't remember, a better strategy, I felt, than simply stopping, leaving him with a maimed, not-whole anecdote, violating his basic trust, simple faith, or personhood even, for all I knew. But the lie had to be a good one, because if your lie is badly done it makes everyone feel wretched, liar and lied-to alike plunged into the deepest lackadaisy, and everyone just feels like going into the other room and drinking a glass of water, or whatever is available there, whereas if you can lie really well then you get dynamite results, 35 percent report increased intellectual understanding, awareness, insight, 40 percent report more tolerance, acceptance of others, liking for self, 29 percent report they receive more personal and more confidential information from people and that others become more warm and supportive toward them—all in consequence of a finely orchestrated, carefully developed untruth. And while I was thinking about this, counting my options, I noticed that he was a policeman, had in fact a dark-blue uniform, black shoes, a badge and a gun, a policeman's hat, and I noticed also that my testicles were aching, as they sometimes do if you sit too long in an uncomfortable or strained position, but I had been standing, and then I understood, in a flash, that what he wanted from me was not to hear the "next" part of my story, or anecdote, but that I give my harpsichord to his wife as a present.

Now, my harpsichord has been out of tune for five years, some of the keys don't function, and there are drink rings on top of it where people have set their drinks down carelessly, at parties and the like, still it is mine and I didn't particularly want to give it to his wife, I believe her name is Cynthia, and although I may have drunkenly promised to give it to her in a fit of generosity or inadvertence, or undue respect for the possible pleasures of distant others, still it was and is my harpsichord and what was his wife giving me? I hadn't in mind sexual favors or anything of that kind, I had in mind real property of equivalent value. So I went into the other room and drank a glass of water, or rather vodka, thinking to stall him with the missing "part" of the trivial anecdote I had been telling him, to keep his mind off what he wanted, the harpsichord, but the problem was, what kind of lie would he like? I could tell him about "the time I went to Hyde Park for a drink with the President," but he could look at me and know I was too young to have done that, and then the failed lie would exist between us like a bathtub filled with ruinous impotent nonsense, he would simply seize the harpsichord and make off with it (did I say that he was a sergeant? with three light-blue chevrons sewn to the darker blue of his right and left sleeves?). Who knows the kinds of lies that sergeants like, something that would confirm their already existing life-attitudes, I supposed, and I tried to check back mentally and remember what these last might be, drawing upon my (very slight) knowledge of the sociology of authority, something in the area of child abuse perhaps, if I could fit a child-abuse part to the structure already extant, which I was beginning to forget, something to do with walking at night, if

I could spot-weld a child-abuse extension to what was already there, my partial anecdote, that might do the trick.

So I went into the next room and had a glass of something, I think I said, "Excuse me," but maybe I didn't, and it had to be a fabrication that would grammatically follow the words "and then" without too much of a seam showing, of course I could always, upon reentering the first room, where the sergeant stood, begin the sentence anew, with some horrific instance of child abuse, of which I have several in the old memory bank, and we could agree that it was terrible, terrible, what people did, and he would forget about the harpsichord, and we could part with mutual regard, generated by the fact (indisputable) that neither of us were child abusers, however much we might have liked to be, having children of our own. Or, to get away from the distasteful subject of hurting children, I might tack, to the flawed corpus of the original anecdote, something about walking at night in the city, a declaration of my own lack of leftness—there's not a radical bone in my body, all I want is ease and bliss, not a thing in this world do I desire other than ease and bliss, I think he might empathize with that (did I mention that he had the flap on his holster unbuttoned and his left hand resting on the butt of his weapon, and the rim of his black shoes touching the rim of my brown boots?). That might ring a bell.

Or I could, as if struck by a sudden thought, ask him if he was a "real" policeman. He would probably answer truthfully. He would probably say either, "Yes, I am a real policeman," or, "No, I am not a real policeman." A third possibility: "What do you mean by 'real,' in this instance?" Because even among policemen who are "real," that is, bona fide, duly appointed officers of the law, there are degrees of realness and vivacity, they say of one another, "Fred's a *real* policeman," or announce a finding contrary to this finding, I don't know this of my own knowledge but am extrapolating from my knowledge (very slight) of the cant of other professions. But if I asked him this question, as a dodge or subterfuge to cover up the fact of the missing "part" of the original, extremely uninteresting, anecdote, there would be an excellent chance that he would take umbrage, and that his colleagues (did I neglect to say that there are two of his colleagues, in uniform, holding on to the handles of their bicycles, standing behind him, stalwartly, in the other room, and that he himself, the sergeant, is holding on to the handle of his bicycle, stalwartly, with the hand that is not resting on the butt of his .38, teak-handled I believe, from the brief glance that I snuck at it, when I was in the other room?) would take umbrage also. Goals incapable of attainment have driven many a man to despair, but despair is easier to get to than that—one need merely look out of the window, for example. But what we are trying to do is to get away from despair and over to ease and bliss, and that can never be attained with three policemen, with bicycles, standing alertly in your other room. They can, as we know, make our lives more miserable than they are already if we arouse their ire, which must be kept slumbering, by telling them stories, for example, such as the story of the four bears, known to us all from childhood (although not everyone knows about the fourth bear) and it is clear that *they can't lay their bicycles down* and sit, which would be the normal thing, no, they must stand there at more-or-less parade rest, some departmental ruling that I don't know about, but of course it irritates them, it even irritates me, and I am not standing there holding up a bicycle, I am in the other room having a glass of beef broth with a twist of lemon, perhaps you don't believe me about the policemen but there they are, pictures lie but words don't, unless one is lying on purpose, with an end in view, such as to get three policemen with bicycles out of your other room while retaining your harpsichord (probably the departmental regulations state that the bicycles must never be laid down in a civilian space, such as my other room, probably the sergeant brought his colleagues to help him haul away the harpsichord, which has three legs, and although the sight of three policemen on bicycles, each holding aloft one leg of a harpsichord, rolling smoothly through the garment district, might seem ludicrous to you, who knows how it seems to them? entirely right and proper, no doubt) which he, the sergeant, considers I promised to his wife as a wedding present, and it is true that I was at the wedding, but only to raise my voice and object when the minister came to that part of the ceremony where he routinely asks for objections, "*Yes!*" I shouted, "*she's my mother! And although she is a widow, and legally free, she belongs to me in dreams!*" but

I was quickly hushed up by a quartet of plainclothesmen, and the ceremony proceeded. But what is the good of a mother if she is another man's wife, as they mostly are, and not around in the morning to fix your buckwheat cakes or Rice Krispies, as the case may be, and in the evening to argue with you about your vegetables, and in the middle of the day to iron your shirts and clean up your rooms, and at all times to provide intimations of ease and bliss (however misleading and ill-founded), but instead insists on hauling your harpsichord away (did I note that Mother, too, is in the other room, with the three policemen, she is standing with the top half of her bent over the instrument, her arms around it, at its widest point—the keyboard end)? So, standing with the glass in my hand, the glass of herb tea with sour cream in it, I wondered what kind of useful prosthesis I could attach to the original anecdote I was telling all these people in my other room—those who seem so satisfied with their tableau, the three peelers posing with their bicycles, my mother hugging the harpsichord with a mother's strangle—what kind of "and then" I could contrive which might satisfy all the particulars of the case, which might redeliver to me my mother, retain to me my harpsichord, and rid me of these others, in their uniforms.

I could tell them the story of the (indeterminate number of) bears, twisting it a bit to fit my deeper designs, so that the fourth bear enters (from left) and says, "I don't care who's been sleeping in my bed just so long as it is not a sergeant of police," and the fifth bear comes in (from right) and says, "Harpsichords wither and warp when their soundboards are exposed to the stress of bicycle transport," and the sixth bear strides right down to the footlights, center stage (from a hole in the back of the theater, or a hole in the back of the anecdote), and says, "Dearly beloved upholders, enforcers, rush, rush away and enter the six-year bicycle race that is even now awaiting the starter's gun at the corner of Elsewhere and Not-Here," and the seventh bear descends from the flies on a nylon rope and cries, "*Mother! Come home!*" and the eighth bear—

But bears are not the answer. Bears are for children. Why am I thinking about bears when I should be thinking about some horribly beautiful "way out" of this tense scene, which has reduced me to a rag, just contemplating it here in the other room with this glass of chicken livers *flambé* in my hand—

Wait.

I will reenter the first room, cheerfully, confidently, even gaily, and throw chicken livers *flambé* all over the predicament, the flaming chicken livers clinging like incindergel to Mother, policemen, bicycles, harpsichord, and my file of the *National Review* from its founding to the present time. That will "open up" the situation successfully. I will resolve these terrible contradictions with flaming chicken parts and then sing the song of how I contrived the ruin of my anaconda.

Porcupines at the University

"And now the purple dust of twilight time/ steals across the meadows of my heart," the Dean said.

His pretty wife, Paula, extended her long graceful hands full of Negronis.

A scout burst into the room, through the door. "Porcupines!" he shouted.

"Porcupines what?" the Dean asked.

"Thousands and thousands of them. Three miles down the road and comin' fast!"

"Maybe they won't enroll," the Dean said. "Maybe they're just passing through."

"You can't be sure," his wife said.

"How do they look?" he asked the scout, who was pulling porcupine quills out of his ankles.

"Well, you know. Like porcupines."

"Are you going to bust them?" Paula asked.

"I'm tired of busting people," the Dean said.

"They're not people," Paula pointed out.

"De bustibus non est disputandum," the scout said.

"I suppose I'll have to do something," the Dean said.

•

Meanwhile the porcupine wrangler was wrangling the porcupines across the dusty and overbuilt West.

Dust clouds. Yips. The lowing of porcupines.

"Git along theah li'l porcupines."

And when I reach the great porcupine canneries of the East, I will be rich, the wrangler reflected. I will sit on the front porch of the Muehlebach Hotel in New York City and smoke me a big seegar. Then, the fancy women.

"All right you porcupines step up to that yellow line."

There was no yellow line. This was just an expression the wrangler used to keep the porcupines moving. He had heard it in the army. The damn-fool porcupines didn't know the difference.

The wrangler ambled along reading the ads in a copy of *Song Hits* magazine. PLAY HARMONICA IN 5 MINS. and so forth.

The porcupines scuffled along making their little hops. There were four-five thousand in the herd. Nobody had counted exactly.

An assistant wrangler rode in from the outskirts of the herd. He too had a copy of *Song Hits* magazine, in his hip pocket. He looked at the head wrangler's arm, which had a lot of little holes in it.

"Hey Griswold."

"Yeah?"

"How'd you get all them little holes in your arm?"

"You ever try to slap a brand on a porky-pine?"

Probably the fancy women will be covered with low-cut dresses and cheap perfume, the wrangler thought. Probably there will be hundreds of them, hundreds and hundreds. All after my medicine bundle containing my gold and my lucky drill bit. But if they try to rush me I will pull out my guitar. And sing them a song of prairie virility.

•

"Porcupines at the university," the Dean's wife said. "Well, why not?"

"We don't have *facilities* for four or five thousand porcupines," the Dean said. "I can't get a dial tone."

"They could take Alternate Life Styles," Paula said.

"We've already got too many people in Alternate Life Styles," the Dean said, putting down the telephone. "The hell with it. I'll bust them myself. Single-handed. Ly."

"You'll get hurt."

"Nonsense, they're only porcupines. I'd better wear my old clothes."

"Bag of dirty shirts in the closet," Paula said.

The Dean went into the closet.

Bags and bags of dirty shirts.

"Why doesn't she ever take these shirts to the laundry?"

•

Griswold, the wrangler, wrote a new song in the saddle.

Fancy woman fancy woman
How come you don't do right
I oughta rap you in the mouth for the way you acted
In the porte cochère of the Trinity River Consolidated General High last Friday
  Nite.

I will sit back and watch it climbing the charts, he said to himself. As recorded by Merle Travis. First, it will be a Bell Ringer. Then, the Top Forty. Finally a Golden Oldie.

"All right you porcupines. Git along."

The herd was moving down a twelve-lane trail of silky-smooth concrete. Signs along the trail said things like NEXT EXIT 5 MI. and RADAR IN USE.

"Griswold, some of them motorists behind us is gettin' awful pissed."

"I'm runnin' this-here porky-pine drive," Griswold said, "and I say we better gettum off the road."

The herd was turned onto a broad field of green grass. Green grass with white lime lines on it at ten-yard intervals.

The Sonny and Cher show, the wrangler thought. Well, Sonny, how I come to write this song, I was on a porky-pine drive. The last of the great porky-pine drives you might say. We had four-five thousand head we'd fatted up along the Tuscalora and we was headin' for New York City.

•

The Dean loaded a gleaming Gatling gun capable of delivering 360 rounds a minute. The Gatling gun sat in a mule-drawn wagon and was covered with an old piece of canvas. Formerly it had sat on a concrete slab in front of the ROTC Building.

First, the Dean said to himself, all they see is this funky old wagon pulled by this busted-up old mule. Then, I whip off the canvas. There stands the gleaming Gatling gun capable of delivering 360 rounds a minute. My hand resting lightly, confidently on the crank. They shall not pass, I say. Ils ne passeront pas. Then, the porcupine hide begins to fly.

I wonder if these rounds are still good?

The gigantic Gatling gun loomed over the herd like an immense piece of bad news.

"Hey Griswold."

"What?"

"He's got a gun."

"I *see* it," Griswold said. "You think I'm blind?"

"What we gonna do?"

"How about vamoose-ing?"

"But the herd . . ."

"Them li'l porcupines can take care of their own selves," Griswold said. "Goddamn it, I guess we better parley." He got up off the grass, where he had been stretched full-length, and walked toward the wagon.

"What say potner?"

"Look," the Dean said. "You can't enroll those porcupines. It's out of the question."

"That so?"

"It's out of the question," the Dean repeated. "We've had a lot of trouble around here. The cops won't even speak to me. We can't *take* any more trouble." The Dean glanced at the herd. "That's a mighty handsome herd you have there."

"Kind of you," Griswold said. "That's a mighty handsome mule *you* got."

They both gazed at the Dean's terrible-looking mule.

Griswold wiped his neck with a red bandanna. "You don't want no porky-pines over to your place, is that it?"

"That's it."

"Well, we don't *go* where we ain't wanted," the wrangler said. "No call to throw down on us with that . . . *machine* there."

The Dean looked embarrassed.

"You don't know Mr. Sonny Bono, do you?" Griswold asked. "He lives around here somewheres, don't he?"

"I haven't had the pleasure," the Dean said. He thought for a moment. "I know a booker in Vegas, though. He was one of our people. He was a grad student in comparative religion."

"Maybe we can do a deal," the wrangler said. "Whichaway is New York City?"

•

"Well?" the Dean's wife asked. "What were their demands?"

"I'll tell you in a minute," the Dean said. "My mule is double-parked."

The herd turned onto the Cross Bronx Expressway. People looking out of their cars saw thousands and thousands of porcupines. The porcupines looked like badly engineered vacuum-cleaner attachments.

Vegas, the wrangler was thinking. Ten weeks at Caesar's Palace at a sock 15 G's a week. The Ballad of the Last Drive. Leroy Griswold singing his smash single, The Ballad of the Last Drive.

"Git along theah, li'l porcupines."

The citizens in their cars looked at the porcupines, thinking: What is wonderful? Are these porcupines wonderful? Are they significant? Are they what I need?

The Educational Experience

MUSIC FROM somewhere. It is Vivaldi's great work, *The Semesters.*

The students wandered among the exhibits. The Fisher King was there. We walked among the industrial achievements. A good-looking gas turbine, behind a velvet rope. The manufacturers described themselves in their literature as "patient and optimistic." The students gazed, and gaped. Hitting them with ax handles is no longer permitted, hugging and kissing them is no longer permitted, speaking to them is permitted but only under extraordinary circumstances.

The Fisher King was there. In *Current Pathology* by Spurry and Entemann, the King is called "a doubtful clinical entity." But Spurry and Entemann have never caught him, so far as is known. Transfer of information from the world to the eye is permitted if you have signed oaths of loyalty to the world, to the eye, to *Current Pathology.*

We moved on. The two major theories of origin, evolution and creation, were argued by bands of believers who gave away buttons, balloons, bumper stickers, pieces of the True Cross. On the walls, photographs of stocking masks. The visible universe was doing very well, we decided, a great deal of movement, flux—unimpaired vitality. We made the students add odd figures, things like 453498*23:J and 8977?22MARY. This was part of the educational experience, we told them, and not even the hard part—just one side of a many-sided effort. But what a wonderful time you'll have, we told them, when the experience is over, done, completed. You will all, we told them, be more beautiful than you are now, and more employable too. You will have a grasp of the total situation; the total situation will have a grasp of you.

Here is a diode, learn what to do with it. Here is Du Guesclin, constable of France 1370–80—learn what to do with him. A divan is either a long cushioned seat or a council of state—figure out at which times it is what. Certainly you can have your dangerous drugs, but only for dessert—first you must chew your cauliflower, finish your fronds.

Oh they were happy going through the exercises and we told them to keep their tails down as they crawled under the wire, the wire was a string of quotations, Tacitus, Herodotus, Pindar . . . Then the steady-state cosmologists, Bondi, Gold, and Hoyle, had to be leaped over, the students had to swing from tree to tree in the Dark Wood, rappel down the sheer face of the Merzbau, engage in unarmed combat with the Van de Graaff machine, sew stocking masks. See? Unimpaired vitality.

We paused before a bird's lung on a pedestal. "But the mammalian lung is different!" they shouted. "A single slug of air, per hundred thousand population . . ." Some fool was going to call for "action" soon, citing the superiority of praxis to pale theory. A wipe-out requires thought, planning, coordination, as per our phoncon of 6/8/75. Classic film scripts were stretched tight over the destruction of indigenous social and political structures for dubious ends, as per our phoncon of 9/12/75. "Do you think intelligent life exists outside this bed?" one student asked another, confused as to whether she was attending the performance, or part of it. Unimpaired vitality, yes, but—

And Sergeant Preston of the Yukon was there in his Sam Browne belt, he was copulating violently but copulating with no one, that's always sad to see. Still it was a "nice try" and in that sense inspirational, a congratulation to the visible universe for being what it is. The group leader read from an approved text. "I have eaten from the tympanum, I have drunk from the cymbals." The students shouted and clashed their spears together, in approval. We noticed that several of them were off in a corner playing with animals, an ibex, cattle, sheep. We didn't know whether we should tell them to stop, or urge them to continue. Perplexities of this kind are not infrequent in our business. The important thing is the educational experience itself—how to survive it.

We moved them along as fast as we could, but it's difficult, with all the new regulations, restrictions. The Chapel Perilous is a bomb farm now, they have eight thousand acres in guavas and a few hundred head of white-faced enlisted men who stand around with buckets of water, buckets of sand. We weren't allowed to smoke, that was annoying, but necessary I suppose to the preservation of our fundamental ideals. Then we taught them how to put stamps on letters, there was a long line waiting in front of that part of the program, we lectured about belt buckles, the off/on switch, and putting out the garbage. It is wise not to attempt too much all at once—perhaps we weren't wise.

The best way to live is by not knowing what will happen to you at the end of the day, when the sun goes down and the supper is to be cooked. The students looked at each other with secret smiles. Rotten of them to conceal their feelings from us, we who are doing the best we can. The invitation to indulge in emotion at the expense of rational analysis already constitutes a political act, as per our phoncon of 11/9/75. We came to a booth where the lessons of 1914 were taught. There were some wild strawberries there, in the pool of blood, and someone was playing the piano, softly, in the pool of blood, and the Fisher King was fishing, hopelessly, in the pool of blood. The pool is a popular meeting place for younger people but we aren't younger any more so we hurried on. "Come and live with me," that was something somebody said to someone else, a bizarre idea that was quickly scotched—we don't want that kind of idea to become general, or popular.

"The world is everything that was formerly the case," the group leader said, "and now it is time to get back on the bus." Then all of the guards rushed up and demanded their bribes. We paid them with soluble traveler's checks and hoped for rain, and hoped for rodomontade, braggadocio, blare, bray, fanfare, flourish, tucket.

The Discovery

"I'M DEPRESSED," Kate said.

Boots became worried. "Did I say something wrong?"

"You don't know *how* to say anything wrong."

"What?"

"The thing about you is, you're dull."

"I'm dull?"

There was a silence. Then Fog said: "Anybody want to go over to Springs to the rodeo?"

"Me?" Boots said. "Dull?"

The Judge got up and went over and sat down next to Kate.

"Now Kate, you oughtn't to be goin' round callin' Boots dull to his face. That's probably goin' to make him feel bad. I know you didn't mean it, really, and Boots knows it too, but he's gonna feel bad anyhow—"

"How 'bout the rodeo, over at Springs?" Fog asked again.

The Judge gazed sternly at his friend, Fog.

"—he's gonna feel bad, anyhow," the Judge continued, "just thinkin' you *mighta* meant it. So why don't you just tell him you didn't mean it."

"I did mean it."

"Aw come on, Katie. I know you mean what you say, but why make trouble? You can mean what you say, but why not say something else? On a nice day like this?"

The dry and lifeless air continued parching the concrete-like ground.

"It's not a nice day."

The Judge looked around. Then he said: "By God, Katie, you're right! It's a terrible day." Then he took a careful look at Boots, his son.

"I guess you think I'm dull, too, is that right, Pa?" Boots said with a disarming laugh.

"Well . . ."

Boots raised himself to his feet. He looked cool and unruffled, with just the hint of something in his eyes.

"So," he said. "So that's the way it is. So that's the way you, my own father, really feel about me. Well, it's a fine time to be sayin' something about it, wouldn't you say? In front of company and all?"

"Now don't get down on your old man," Fog said hastily. "Let's go to the rodeo."

"Fog—"

"He don't mean nothin' by it," Fog said. "He was just tryin' to tell the truth."

"Oh," Boots said. "He don't mean nothin' by it. He don't mean nothin' by it. Well, it seems to me I just been hearin' a lot of talk about people meanin' what they say. I am going to assume the Judge here means what he says."

"Yes," the Judge said. "I mean it."

"Yes," Kate said, "you have many fine qualities, Boots."

"See? He means it. My own father thinks I'm dull. And Katie thinks I'm dull. What about you, Fog? You want to make it unanimous?"

"Well Boots you are pretty doggone dull to my way of thinking. But nobody holds it against you. You got a lot of fine characteristics. Cain't everybody be Johnny Carson."

"Yes, there are lots duller than you, Boots," Kate said. "Harvey Brush, for example. Now that number is *really* dull."

"You're comparin' *me* with *Harvey Brush*?"

"Well I said he was worse, didn't I?"

"Good God."

"Why don't you go inside and read your letters from that girl in Brussels?" Kate suggested.

"*She* doesn't think I'm dull."

"Probably she don't understand English too good neither," the Judge said. "Now go on inside and read your mail or whatever. We just want to sit silently out here for a while."

"Goodbye."

After Boots had gone inside the Judge said: "My son."

"It is pretty terrible, Judge," Kate said.

"It's awful," Fog agreed.

"Well, it's not a hanging offense," the Judge said. "Maybe we can teach him some jokes or something."

"I've got to get back in the truck now," said Kate. "Judge,

you have my deepest sympathy. If I can think of anything to do, I'll let you know."

"Thanks, Kate. It's always a pleasure to see you and be with you, wherever you are. *You* are never dull."

"I know that, Judge. Well, I'll see you later."

"O.K. Kate," said Fog. "Goodbye. Drive carefully."

"Goodbye Fog. Yes, I'll be careful."

"See you around, Kate."

"O.K., Judge. Goodbye, Fog."

"So long, Kate."

"See you. You know I can't marry that boy now, Judge. Knowing what I know."

"I understand, Kate. I wouldn't expect you to. I'll just have to dig up somebody else."

"It's going to be hard."

"Well, it's not going to be easy."

"So long, Kate," said Fog.

"O.K., goodbye. Be good."

"Yes," said Fog. "I'll try."

"'Bye now, Judge."

"O.K., Katie."

"Wonder how come I never noticed it before?"

"Well don't *dwell* on it, Kate. See you in town."

"O.K., *adios*."

"Goodbye, Kate."

"It's terrible but we've got it into focus now, haven't we?"

"I'm afraid we do."

"I sure would like to be of help, Judge."

"I know you would, Katie, and I appreciate it. I just don't see what can be done about it, right off."

"It's just his nature, probably."

"You're probably right. *I* was never dull."

"I know you weren't, Judge. Nobody blames you."

"Well, it's a problem."

"Quite a thorny one. But he'll be O.K., Judge. He's a good boy, basically."

"I know that, Kate. Well, we'll just have to wrestle with it."

"O.K., Judge. I'll see you later, O.K.?"

"Right."

"Behave yourself, Fog."

"Right, Katie."
"I'll see y'all. Bye-bye."
"Goodbye, Kate."
"You all right, Judge?"
"I'm fine, Katie. Just a little taken aback by what we've found out here today."
"Oh. O.K. Well, take care of yourself. You too, Fog."
"I will, Kate."
"O.K. See you two."
"Goodbye, Kate."
"You sure you don't want to come into town with me? I'll make you some tamale pie."
"That's O.K. Kate we got lots of stuff to eat right here."
"Oh. O.K. 'Bye."
The truck moved off into the dust.
"Look!" said the Judge. "She's waving."
"Wave back to her," Fog said.
"I am," said the Judge. "Look, I'm waving."
"I see it," said Fog. "Can she see you?"
"Maybe if I stand up," the Judge said. "Do you think she can see me now?"
"Not if she's watchin' the road."
"She's too young for us," the Judge said. He stopped waving.
"Depends on how you look at it," said Fog. "You want to go on over to the rodeo now?"
"I don't want to go to no rodeo," said the Judge. "All that youth."

Rebecca

REBECCA LIZARD was trying to change her ugly, reptilian, thoroughly unacceptable last name.

"Lizard," said the judge. "Lizard, Lizard, Lizard. Lizard. There's nothing wrong with it if you say it enough times. You can't clutter up the court's calendar with trivial little minor irritations. And there have been far too many people changing their names lately. Changing your name countervails the best interests of the telephone company, the electric company, and the United States government. Motion denied."

Lizard in tears.

Lizard led from the courtroom. A chrysanthemum of Kleenex held under her nose.

"Shaky lady," said a man, "are you a schoolteacher?"

Of course she's a schoolteacher, you idiot. Can't you see the poor woman's all upset? Why don't you leave her alone?

"Are you a homosexual lesbian? Is that why you never married?"

Christ, yes, she's a homosexual lesbian, as you put it. *Would you please shut your face?*

Rebecca went to the damned dermatologist (a new damned dermatologist), but he said the same thing the others had said. "Greenish," he said, "slight greenishness, genetic anomaly, nothing to be done, I'm afraid, Mrs. Lizard."

"Miss Lizard."

"Nothing to be done, Miss Lizard."

"Thank you, Doctor. Can I give you a little something for your trouble?"

"Fifty dollars."

When Rebecca got home the retroactive rent increase was waiting for her, coiled in her mailbox like a pupil about to strike.

Must get some more Kleenex. Or a Ph.D. No other way.

She thought about sticking her head in the oven. But it was an electric oven.

Rebecca's lover, Hilda, came home late.

"How'd it go?" Hilda asked, referring to the day.

"Lousy."

"Hmm," Hilda said, and quietly mixed strong drinks of busthead for the two of them.

Hilda is a very good-looking woman. So is Rebecca. They love each other—an incredibly dangerous and delicate business, as we know. Hilda has long blond hair and is perhaps a shade the more beautiful. Of course Rebecca has a classic and sexual figure which attracts huge admiration from every beholder.

"You're late," Rebecca said. "Where were you?"

"I had a drink with Stephanie."

"Why did you have a drink with Stephanie?"

"She stopped by my office and said let's have a drink."

"Where did you go?"

"The Barclay."

"How is Stephanie?"

"She's fine."

"Why did you have to have a drink with Stephanie?"

"I was ready for a drink."

"Stephanie doesn't have a slight greenishness, is that it? Nice, pink Stephanie."

Hilda rose and put an excellent C. & W. album on the record-player. It was David Rogers's "Farewell to the Ryman," Atlantic SD 7283. It contains such favorites as "Blue Moon of Kentucky," "Great Speckled Bird," "I'm Movin' On," and "Walking the Floor over You." Many great Nashville personnel appear on this record.

"Pinkness is not everything," Hilda said. "And Stephanie is a little bit boring. You know that."

"Not so boring that you don't go out for drinks with her."

"I am not interested in Stephanie."

"As I was leaving the courthouse," Rebecca said, "a man unzipped my zipper."

David Rogers was singing "Oh please release me, let me go."

"What were you wearing?"

"What I'm wearing now."

"So he had good taste," Hilda said, "for a creep." She hugged Rebecca, on the sofa. "I love you," she said.

"Screw that," Rebecca said plainly, and pushed Hilda away. "Go hang out with Stephanie Sasser."

"I am not interested in Stephanie Sasser," Hilda said for the second time.

Very often one "pushes away" the very thing that one most wants to grab, like a lover. This is a common, although distressing, psychological mechanism, having to do (in my opinion) with the fact that what is presented is not presented "purely," that there is a tiny little canker or grim place in it somewhere. However, worse things can happen.

"Rebecca," said Hilda, "I really don't like your slight greenishness."

The term "lizard" also includes geckos, iguanas, chameleons, slowworms, and monitors. Twenty existing families make up the order, according to the *Larousse Encyclopedia of Animal Life*, and four others are known only from fossils. There are about twenty-five hundred species, and they display adaptations for walking, running, climbing, creeping, or burrowing. Many have interesting names, such as the Bearded Lizard, the Collared Lizard, the Flap-Footed Lizard, the Frilled Lizard, the Girdle-Tailed Lizard, and the Wall Lizard.

"I have been overlooking it for these several years, because I love you, but I really don't like it so much," Hilda said. "It's slightly—"

"Knew it," said Rebecca.

Rebecca went into the bedroom. The color-television set was turned on, for some reason. In a greenish glow, a film called *Green Hell* was unfolding.

I'm ill, I'm ill.

I will become a farmer.

Our love, our sexual love, our ordinary love!

Hilda entered the bedroom and said, "Supper is ready."

"What is it?"

"Pork with red cabbage."

"I'm drunk," Rebecca said.

Too many of our citizens are drunk at times when they should be sober—suppertime, for example. Drunkenness leads to forgetting where you have put your watch, keys, or money clip, and to a decreased sensitivity to the needs and desires and calm good health of others. The causes of overuse of alcohol are not as clear as the results. Psychiatrists feel in general that alcoholism is a serious problem but treatable, in some cases. A.A. is said to be both popular and effective. At base, the question is one of will power.

"Get up," Hilda said. "I'm sorry I said that."

"You told the truth," said Rebecca.

"Yes, it was the truth," Hilda admitted.

"You didn't tell me the truth in the beginning. In the beginning, you said it was beautiful."

"I was telling you the truth, in the beginning. I did think it was beautiful. Then."

This "then," the ultimate word in Hilda's series of three brief sentences, is one of the most pain-inducing words in the human vocabulary, when used in this sense. Departed time! And the former conditions that went with it! How is human pain to be measured? But remember that Hilda, too . . . It is correct to feel for Rebecca in this situation, but, reader, neither can Hilda's position be considered an enviable one, for truth, as Bergson knew, is a hard apple, whether one is throwing it or catching it.

"What remains?" Rebecca said stonily.

"I can love you *in spite of*—"

Do *I* want to be loved *in spite of*? Do you? Does anyone? But aren't we all, to some degree? Aren't there important parts of all of us which must be, so to say, gazed past? I turn a blind eye to that aspect of you, and you turn a blind eye to that aspect of me, and with these blind eyes eyeball-to-eyeball, to use an expression from the early 1960's, we continue our starched and fragrant lives. Of course it's also called "making the best of things," which I have always considered a rather soggy idea for an American ideal. But my criticisms of this idea must be tested against those of others—the late President McKinley, for example, who maintained that maintaining a good, if not necessarily sunny, disposition was the one valuable and proper course.

Hilda placed her hands on Rebecca's head.

"The snow is coming," she said. "Soon it will be snow time. Together then as in other snow times. Drinking busthead 'round the fire. Truth is a locked room that we knock the lock off from time to time, and then board up again. Tomorrow you will hurt me, and I will inform you that you have done so, and so on and so on. To hell with it. Come, viridian friend, come and sup with me."

They sit down together. The pork with red cabbage steams before them. They speak quietly about the McKinley Administration, which is being revised by revisionist historians. The story ends. It was written for several reasons. Nine of them are secrets. The tenth is that one should never cease considering human love. Which remains as grisly and golden as ever, no matter what is tattooed upon the warm tympanic page.

The Reference

"*WARP.*"

"In the character?"

"He warp *ever' which way.*"

"You don't think we should consider him, then."

"My friend Shel McPartland whom I have known deeply and intimately and too well for more than twenty years, is, sir, a brilliant O.K. engineer–master builder–cum–city and state planner. He'll plan your whole cotton-pickin' *state* for you, if you don't watch him. Right down to the flowers on the sideboard in the governor's mansion. He'll choose marginalia."

"I sir am not familiar sir with that particular bloom sir."

"Didn't think you would be, you bein' from Arkansas and therefore likely less than literate. You *are* the Arkansas State Planning Commission, are you not?"

"I am one of it. Mr. McPartland gave you as a reference."

"Well sir let me tell you sir that my friend Shel McPartland who has incautiously put me down as a reference has a wide-ranging knowledge of all modern techniques, theories, dodges, orthodoxies, heresies, new and old innovations, and scams of all kinds. The only thing about him is, he warp."

"Sir, it is not necessary to use dialect when being telephone-called from the state of Arkansas."

"Different folk I talk to in different ways. I got to keep myself interested."

"I understand that. Leaving aside the question of warp for a minute, let me ask you this: Is Mr. McPartland what you would call a hard worker?"

"Hard, but warp. He sort of goes off in his own direction."

"Not a team player."

"Very much a team player. You get you your team out there, and he'll play it, and *beat* it, all by his own self."

"Does he fiddle with women?"

"No. He has too much love and respect for women. He has so much love and respect for women that he has nothing to do with them. At all."

"You said earlier that you wouldn't trust him to salt a mine shaft with silver dollars."

"Well sir that was before I fully understood the nature of your interest. I thought maybe you were thinking of going into *business* with him. Or some other damn-fool thing of that sort. Now that I understand that it's a government gig . . . You folks don't go around salting mine shafts with silver dollars, do you?"

"No sir, that work comes under the competence of the Arkansas Board of Earth Resources."

"So, not to worry."

"But it doesn't sound very likely if I may say so Mr. Cockburn sir that Mr. McPartland would neatly infit with our outfit. Which must of necessity as I'm sure you're hip to sir concern itself mostly with the mundanities."

"McPartland is sublime with the mundanities."

"Truly?"

"You should see him tying his shoes. Tying other people's shoes. He's good at inking-in. *Excellent* at erasing. One of the great erasers of our time. Plotting graphs. Figuring use-densities. Diddling flow charts. Inflating statistics. Issuing modestly deceptive reports. Chairing and charming. Dowsing for foundation funds. Only a fool and a simpleton sir would let a McPartland slip through his fingers."

"But before you twigged to the fact sir that your role was that of a referencer, you signaled grave and serious doubts."

"I have them still. I told you he was warp and he *is* warp. I am attempting dear friend to give you McPartland in the round. The whole man. The gravamen and the true gen. When we reference it up, here in the shop, we don't stint. Your interrobang meets our galgenspiel. We do good work."

"But is he reliable?"

"Reliability sir is much overrated. He is inspired. What does this lick pay, by the way?"

"In the low forties with perks."

"The perks include?"

"Arkansas air. Chauffeured VW to and from place of employment. Crab gumbo in the cafeteria every Tuesday. Ruffles and flourishes played on the Muzak upon entry and exit from building. Crab gumbo in the cafeteria every

Thursday. Sabbaticals every second, third, and fifth year. Ox stoptions."

"The latter term is not known to me."

"Holder of the post is entitled to stop a runmad ox in the main street of Little Rock every Saturday at high noon, preventing thereby the mashing to strawberry yogurt of one small child furnished by management. Photograph of said act to appear in the local blats the following Sunday, along with awarding of medal by the mayor. On TV."

"Does the population never tire of this heroicidal behavior?"

"It's bread and circuitry in the modern world, sir, and no place in that world is more modern than Arkansas."

"Wherefrom do you get your crabs?"

"From our great sister state of Lose-e-anna, whereat the best world-class eating crabs hang out."

"The McPartland is a gumbohead from way back, this must be known to you from your other investigations."

"The organization is not to be tweedled with. Shel-baby's partialities will be catered to, if and when. Now I got a bunch more questions here. Like, is he good?"

"Good don't come close. One need only point to his accomplishments *in re* the sewer system of Detroit, Mich. By the sewage of Detroit I sat down and wept, from pure stunned admiration."

"Is he fake?"

"Not more than anybody else. He has façades but who does not?"

"Does he know the blue lines?"

"*Excellent* with the blue lines."

"Does he know the old songs?"

"He'll crack your heart with the old songs."

"Does he have the right moves?"

"People all over America are sitting in darkened projection rooms right this minute, studying the McPartland moves."

"What's this dude look like?"

"Handsome as the dawn. If you can imagine a bald dawn."

"You mean he's old?"

"Naw, man, he's young. A boy of forty-five, just like the rest of us. The thing is, he thinks so hard he done burned all the hair off his head. His head overheats."

"Is that a danger to standers-by?"

"Not if they exercise due caution. Don't stand too close."

"Maybe he's too fine for us."

"I don't think so. He's got a certain common-as-dirt quality. That's right under his laser-sharp M.I.T. quality."

"He sounds maybe a shade too rich for our blood. For us folk here in the downhome heartland."

"Lemme see, Arkansas, that's one of them newer states, right? Down there at the bottom edge? Right along with New Mexico and Florida and such as that?"

"Mr. Cockburn sir, are you jiving me?"

"Would I jive you?"

"Just for the record, how would you describe your personal relation to Mr. McPartland?"

"Oh I think 'bloody enemy' might do it. Might come close. At the same time, I am forced to acknowledge merit. In whatever obscene form it chooses to take. McPartland worked on the kiss of death, did you know that? When he was young. Never did get it perfected but the theoretical studies were elegant, elegant. He's what you might call a engineer's engineer. He designed the artichoke that is all heart. You pay a bit of a premium for it but you don't have to do all that peeling."

"Some people like the peeling. The leaf-by-leaf unveiling."

"Well, some people like to bang their heads against stone walls, don't they? Some people like to sleep with their sisters. Some people like to put on suits and ties and go sit in a concert hall and listen to the New York Philharmonic *Orchestra* for God's sake. Some people—"

"Is this part of his warp?"

"It's related to his warp. The warp to power."

"Any other glaring defects or lesions of the usual that you'd like to touch upon—"

"I think not. Now you, I perceive, have got this bad situation down there in the great state of Arkansas. Your population is exploding. It's mobile. You got people moving freely about, colliding and colluding, pairing off just as they please and exploding the population some more, lollygagging and sailboating and making leather moccasins from kits and God knows what all. And enjoying free speech and voting their heads off and vetoing bond issues carefully thought up and packaged and rigged by the Arkansas State Planning Commission. And generally helter-skeltering around under the gross equity of the democratic system. Is that the position, sir?"

"Worse. Arkansas is, at present, pure planarchy."

"I intuited as much. And you need someone who can get the troops back on the track or tracks. Give them multifamily dwellings, green belts, dayrooms, grog rations, and pleasure stamps. Return the great state of Arkansas to its originary tidiness. Exert a planipotentiary beneficence while remaining a masked marvel. Whose very existence is known only to the choice few."

"Exactly right. Can McPartland do it?"

"Sitting on his hands. Will you go to fifty?"

"Fervently and with pleasure, sir. It's little enough for such a treasure."

"I take 10 percent off the top, sir."

"And can I send you as well, sir, a crate of armadillo steaks, sugar-cured, courtesy of the A.S.P.C.? It's a dream of beauty, sir, this picture that you've limned."

"Not a dream, sir, not a dream. Engineers, sir, never sleep, and dream only in the daytime."

The New Member

THE PRESIDING officer noted that there was a man standing outside the window looking in.

The members of the committee looked in the direction of the window and found that the presiding officer's observation was correct: There was a man standing outside the window looking in.

Mr. Macksey moved that the record take note of the fact.

Mr. O'Donoghue seconded. The motion passed.

Mrs. Brown wondered if someone should go out and talk to the man standing outside the window.

Mrs. Mallory suggested that the committee proceed as if the man standing outside the window wasn't there. Maybe he'd go away, she suggested.

Mr. Macksey said that that was an excellent idea and so moved.

Mr. O'Donoghue wondered if the matter required a motion.

The presiding officer ruled that the man standing outside the window looking in did not require a motion.

Ellen West said that she was frightened.

Mr. Birnbaum said there was nothing to be frightened about.

Ellen West said that the man standing outside the window looked larger than a man to her. Maybe it was not human, she said.

Mr. Macksey said that that was nonsense and that it was only just a very large man, probably.

The presiding officer stated that the committee had a number of pressing items on the agenda and wondered if the meeting could go forward.

Not with that thing out there, Ellen West said.

The presiding officer stated that the next order of business was the matter of the Worth girl.

Mr. Birnbaum noted that the Worth girl had been doing very well.

Mrs. Brown said quite a bit better than well, in her opinion.

Mr. O'Donoghue said that the improvement was quite remarkable.

The presiding officer noted that the field in which she, the Worth girl, was working was a very abstruse one and, moreover, one in which very few women had successfully established themselves.

Mrs. Brown said that she had known the girl's mother quite well and that she had been an extremely pleasant person.

Ellen West said that the man was still outside the window and hadn't moved.

Mr. O'Donoghue said that there was, of course, the possibility that the Worth girl was doing too well.

Mr. Birnbaum said there was such a thing as too much too soon.

Mr. Percy inquired as to the girl's age at the present time and was told she was thirty-five. He then said that that didn't sound like "too soon" to him.

The presiding officer asked for a motion.

Mr. O'Donoghue moved that the Worth girl be hit by a car.

Mr. Birnbaum seconded.

The presiding officer asked for discussion.

Mrs. Mallory asked if Mr. O'Donoghue meant fatally. Mr. O'Donoghue said he did.

Mr. Percy said he thought that a fatal accident, while consonant with the usual procedures of the committee, was always less interesting than something that left the person alive, so that the person's situation was still, in a way, "open."

Mr. O'Donoghue said that Mr. Percy's well-known liberalism was a constant source of strength and encouragement to every member of the committee, as was Mr. Percy's well-known predictability.

Mrs. Mallory said wouldn't it look like the committee was punishing excellence?

Mr. O'Donoghue said that a concern for how things looked was not and should never be a consideration of the committee.

Ellen West said that she thought the man standing outside the window looking in was listening. She reminded the committee that the committee's deliberations were supposed to be held *in camera*.

The presiding officer said that the man could not hear through the glass of the window.

Ellen West said was he sure?

The presiding officer asked if Ellen West would like to be put on some other committee.

Ellen West said that she only felt safe on this committee.

The presiding officer reminded her that even members of the committee were subject to the decisions of the committee, except of course for the presiding officer.

Ellen West said she realized that and would like to move that the Worth girl fall in love with somebody.

The presiding officer said that there was already a motion before the committee and asked if the committee was ready for a vote. The committee said it was. The motion was voted on and failed, 14–4.

Ellen West moved that the Worth girl fall in love with the man standing outside the window.

Mr. Macksey said you're just trying to get him inside so we can take a look at him.

Ellen West said well, why not, if you're so sure he's harmless.

The presiding officer said that he felt that if the man outside were invited inside, a confusion of zones would result, which would be improper.

Mr. Birnbaum said that it might not be a bad idea if the committee got a little feedback from the people for whom it was responsible, once in a while.

Mrs. Mallory stated that she thought Mr. Birnbaum's idea about feedback was a valuable and intelligent one but that she didn't approve of having such a warm and beautiful human being as the Worth girl fall in love with an unknown quantity with demonstrably peculiar habits, *vide* the window, just to provide feedback to the committee.

Mrs. Brown repeated that she had known the Worth girl's mother.

Mr. Macksey asked if Ellen West intended that the Worth girl's love affair be a happy or an unhappy one.

Ellen West said she would not wish to overdetermine somebody else's love affair.

Mr. O'Donoghue moved that the Worth girl be run over by a snowmobile.

The presiding officer said that O'Donoghue was out of order and also that in his judgment Mr. O'Donoghue was reintroducing a defeated motion in disguised form.

Mr. O'Donoghue said that he could introduce new motions all night long, if he so chose.

Mrs. Brown said that she had to be home by ten to receive a long-distance phone call from her daughter in Oregon.

The presiding officer said that as there was no second, Ellen West's motion about the man outside the window need not be discussed further. He suggested that as there were four additional cases awaiting disposition by the committee he wondered if the case of the Worth girl, which was after all not that urgent, might not be tabled until the next meeting.

Mr. Macksey asked what were the additional cases.

The presiding officer said those of Dr. Benjamin Pierce, Casey McManus, Cynthia Croneis, and Ralph Lorant.

Mr. Percy said that those were not very interesting names. To him.

Mr. Macksey moved that the Worth girl be tabled. Mr. Birnbaum seconded. The motion carried.

Mr. Birnbaum asked if he might have a moment for a general observation bearing on the work of the committee. The presiding officer graciously assented.

Mr. Birnbaum said that he had observed, in the ordinary course of going around taking care of his business and so on, that there were not many pregnant women now. He said that yesterday he had seen an obviously pregnant woman waiting for a bus and had remembered that in the last half year he had seen no others. He said he wondered why this was and whether it wasn't within the purview of the committee that there be more pregnant women, for the general good of the community, to say nothing of the future.

Mrs. Mallory said she knew why it was.

Mr. Birnbaum said why? and Mrs. Mallory smiled enigmatically.

Mr. Birnbaum repeated his question and Mrs. Mallory smiled enigmatically again.

Oh me oh my, said Mr. Birnbaum.

The presiding officer said that Mr. Birnbaum's observations, as amplified in a sense by Mrs. Mallory, were of considerable interest.

He said further that such matters were a legitimate concern of the committee and that if he might be allowed to speak for a moment not as the presiding officer but merely as an ordinary member of the committee he would urge, strongly urge, that Cynthia Croneis become pregnant immediately and that she should have twin boys.

Hear hear, said Mr. Macksey.

How about a boy and a girl? asked Ellen West.

The presiding officer said that would be O.K. with him.

This was moved, seconded, and voted unanimously.

On Mr. Macksey's motion it was decided that Dr. Pierce win fifty thousand dollars in the lottery.

It was pointed out by Mrs. Brown that Dr. Pierce was already quite well fixed, financially.

The presiding officer reminded the members that justice was not a concern of the committee.

On Mr. Percy's motion it was decided that Casey McManus would pass the Graduate Record Examination with a score in the upper 10 percent. On Mr. O'Donoghue's motion it was decided that Ralph Lorant would have his leg broken by having it run over by a snowmobile.

Mr. Birnbaum looked at the window and said he's still out there.

Mr. O'Donoghue said for God's sake, let's have him in.

Mr. Macksey went outside and asked the man in.

The man hesitated in the doorway for a moment.

Mr. Percy said come in, come in, don't be nervous.

The presiding officer added his urgings to Mr. Percy's.

The man left the doorway and stood in the middle of the room.

The presiding officer inquired if the man had, perhaps, a grievance he wished to bring to the attention of the committee.

The man said no, no grievance.

Why then was he standing outside the window looking in? Mr. Macksey asked.

The man said something about just wanting to "be with somebody."

Mr. Percy asked if he had a family, and the man said no.

Are you from around here? asked Mrs. Mallory, and the man shook his head.

Employed? asked Mr. Birnbaum, and the man shook his head.

He wants to be with somebody, Mrs. Mallory said.

Yes, said the presiding officer, I understand that.

It's not unusual, said Mr. Macksey.

Not unusual at all, said Mrs. Brown. She again reminded the members that she had to be home by ten to receive a call from her daughter in Oregon.

Maybe we should make him a member of the committee, said Mr. Percy.

He could give us some feedback, said Mr. Birnbaum. I mean, I would assume that.

Ellen West moved that the man be made a member of the committee. Mr. Birnbaum seconded. The motion was passed, 12–6.

Mr. Percy got up and got a folding chair for the man and pulled it up to the committee table.

The man sat down in the chair and pulled it closer to the table.

All right, he said. The first thing we'll do is, we'll make everybody wear overalls. Gray overalls. Gray overalls with gray T-shirts. We'll have morning prayers, evening prayers, and lunch prayers. Calisthenics for everyone over the age of four in the 5–7 P.M. time slot. Boutonnieres are forbidden. Nose rings are forbidden. Gatherings of one or more persons are prohibited. On the question of bedtime, I am of two minds.

You Are as Brave as Vincent van Gogh

You eavesdrop in three languages. Has no one ever told you not to pet a leashed dog? We wash your bloody hand with Scotch from the restaurant.

Children. *I want one*, you say, pointing to a mother pushing a pram. And there's not much time. But the immense road-mending machine (yellow) cannot have children, even though it is a member of a family, it has siblings—the sheep's-foot roller, the air hammer.

You ask: Will there be fireworks?

I would never pour lye in your eyes, you say.

Where do you draw the line? I ask. Top Job?

Shall we take a walk? Is there a trout stream? Can one rent a car? Is there dancing? Sailing? Dope? Do you know Saint-Exupéry? Wind? Sand? Stars? Night flight?

You don't offer to cook dinner for me again today.

The air hammer with the miserable sweating workman hanging on to the handles. I assimilated the sexual significance of the air hammer long ago. It's new to you. You are too young.

You move toward the pool in your black bikini, you will open people's pop-top Pepsis for them, explicate the Torah, lave the brown shoulders of new acquaintances with Bain de Soleil.

You kick me in the backs of the legs while I sleep.

You are staring at James. James is staring back. There are six of us sitting on the floor around a low, glass-topped table. I become angry. Is there no end to it?

See, there is a boy opening a fire hydrant, you stand closer, see, he has a large wrench on top of the hydrant and he is turning the wrench, the water rushes from the hydrant, you bend to feel the water on your hand.

You are reading *From Ritual to Romance*, by Jessie L. Weston. But others have read it before you. Practically everyone has read it.

At the pool, you read Saint-Exupéry. But wait, there is a yellow nylon cord crossing the pool, yellow nylon supported by red-and-blue plastic floats, it divides the children's part from the deeper part, you are in the pool investigating, flexing the nylon cord, pulling on it, yes, it is firmly attached to the side of the pool, to both sides of the pool. And in the kitchen you regard the salad chef, a handsome young Frenchman, he stares at you, at your tanned breasts, at your long dark (wet) hair, can one, would it be possible, at this hour, a cup of coffee, or perhaps tea . . .

Soon you will be thirty.

And the giant piece of yellow road-mending equipment enters the pool, silently, you are in the cab, manipulating the gears, levers, shove this one forward and the machine swims. Swims toward the man in the Day-Glo orange vest who is waving his Day-Glo orange flags in the air, this way, this way, here!

He's a saint, you say. Did you ever try to live with a saint?

You telephone to tell me you love me before going out to do something I don't want you to do.

If you are not asking for fireworks you are asking for Miles Davis bound hand and foot, or Iceland. You make no small plans.

See, there is a blue BOAC flight bag, open, on the floor, inside it a folded newspaper, a towel, and something wrapped in silver foil. You bend over the flight bag (whose is it? you don't know) and begin to unwrap the object wrapped in silver foil. Half a loaf of bread. Satisfied, you wrap it up again.

You return from California too late to vote. One minute too late. I went across the street to the school with you. They had locked the doors. I remember your banging on the doors. No one came to open them. Tears. *What difference does one minute make?* you screamed, in the direction of the doors.

Your husband, you say, is a saint.

And did no one ever tell you that the staircase you climbed in your dream, carrying the long brown velvet skirt, in your dream, is a very old staircase?

I remind myself to tell you that you are abnormally intelligent. You kick me in the backs of the legs again, while I sleep.

Parades, balloons, fêtes, horse races.

You feel your time is limited. Tomorrow, you think, there will be three deep creases in your forehead. You offer to quit your job, if that would please me. I say that you cannot quit your job, because you are abnormally intelligent. Your job needs you.

The salad chef moves in your direction, but you are lying on your back on the tennis court, parallel with and under the net, turning your head this way and that, applauding the players, one a tall man with a rump as big as his belly, which is huge, the other a fourteen-year-old girl, intent, lean stringy hair, sorry, good shot, nice one, your sunglasses stuck in your hair. You rush toward the mountain which is furnished with trees, ski lifts, power lines, deck chairs, wedding invitations, you invade the mountain as if it were a book, leaping into the middle, checking the ending, ignoring the beginning. And look there, a locked door! You try the handle, first lightly, then viciously.

You once left your open umbrella outside the A&P, tied to the store with a string. When you came out of the store with your packages, you were surprised to find it gone.

The three buildings across the street from my apartment—one red, one yellow, one brown—are like a Hopper in the slanting late-afternoon light. See? Like a Hopper.

Is that a rash on my chest? Between the breasts? Those little white marks? Look, those people at the next table, all have ordered escargots, seven dozen in garlic butter arriving all at once, eighty-four dead snails on a single surface, in garlic butter. And last night, when it was so hot, I opened the doors to the balcony, I couldn't sleep, I lay awake, I thought I heard something, I imagined someone climbing over the balcony, I got up to see but there was no one.

You are as beautiful as twelve Hoppers.

You are as brave as Vincent van Gogh.

I make fireworks for you:

* !* !]*!!*[!* !* and * % % *+&+&+ * % % *.

If he is a saint, why did you marry him? It makes no sense. Outside in the street, some men with a cherry picker are placing new high-intensity bulbs in all the street lights, so that our criminals will be scalded, transfigured with light.

Yesterday you asked me for the Princeton University Press.

The Princeton University Press is not a toy, I said.

It's not?

And then: Can we go to a *movie* in which there are fireworks?

But there are fireworks in all movies, that is what movies are for—what they do for us.

You should not have left the baby on the lawn. In a hailstorm. When we brought him inside, he was covered with dime-size blue bruises.

At the End of the Mechanical Age

I WENT to the grocery store to buy some soap. I stood for a long time before the soaps in their attractive boxes, RUB and FAB and TUB and suchlike, I couldn't decide so I closed my eyes and reached out blindly and when I opened my eyes I found her hand in mine.

Her name was Mrs. Davis, she said, and TUB was best for important cleaning experiences, in her opinion. So we went to lunch at a Mexican restaurant which as it happened she owned, she took me into the kitchen and showed me her stacks of handsome beige tortillas and the steam tables which were shiny-brite. I told her I wasn't very good with women and she said it didn't matter, few men were, and that nothing mattered, now that Jake was gone, but I would do as an interim project and sit down and have a Carta Blanca. So I sat down and had a cool Carta Blanca, God was standing in the basement reading the meters to see how much grace had been used up in the month of June. Grace is electricity, science has found, it is not *like* electricity, it *is* electricity and God was down in the basement reading the meters in His blue jump suit with the flashlight stuck in the back pocket.

"The mechanical age is drawing to a close," I said to her.

"Or has already done so," she replied.

"It was a good age," I said. "I was comfortable in it, relatively. Probably I will not enjoy the age to come quite so much. I don't like its look."

"One must be fair. We don't know yet what kind of an age the next one will be. Although I feel in my bones that it will be an age inimical to personal well-being and comfort, and that is what I like, personal well-being and comfort."

"Do you suppose there is something to be done?" I asked her.

"Huddle and cling," said Mrs. Davis. "We can huddle and cling. It will pall, of course, everything palls, in time . . ."

Then we went back to my house to huddle and cling, most women are two different colors when they remove their clothes especially in summer but Mrs. Davis was all one color, an ocher. She seemed to like huddling and clinging, she stayed for many days. From time to time she checked the restaurant keeping everything shiny-brite and distributing sums of money to the staff, returning with tortillas in sacks, cases of Carta Blanca, buckets of guacamole, but I paid her for it because I didn't want to feel obligated.

There was a song I sang her, a song of great expectations.

"Ralph is coming," I sang, *"Ralph is striding in his suit of lights over moons and mountains, over parking lots and fountains, toward your silky side. Ralph is coming, he has a coat of many colors and all major credit cards and he is striding to meet you and culminate your foggy dreams in an explosion of blood and soil, at the end of the mechanical age. Ralph is coming preceded by fifty running men with spears and fifty dancing ladies who are throwing leaf spinach out of little baskets, in his path. Ralph is perfect,"* I sang, *"but he is also full of interesting tragic flaws, and he can drink fifty running men under the table without breaking his stride and he can have congress with fifty dancing ladies without breaking his stride, even his socks are ironed, so natty is Ralph, but he is also right down in the mud with the rest of us, he markets the mud at high prices for specialized industrial uses and he is striding, striding, striding, toward your waiting heart. Of course you may not like him, some people are awfully picky . . . Ralph is coming,"* I sang to her, *"he is striding over dappled plains and crazy rivers and he will change your life for the better, probably, you will be fainting with glee at the simple touch of his grave gentle immense hand although I am aware that some people can't stand prosperity, Ralph is coming, I hear his hoofsteps on the drumhead of history, he is striding as he has been all his life toward you, you, you."*

"Yes," Mrs. Davis said, when I had finished singing, "that is what I deserve, all right. But probably I will not get it. And in the meantime, there is you."

•

God then rained for forty days and forty nights, when the water tore away the front of the house we got into the boat, Mrs. Davis liked the way I maneuvered the boat off the trailer and out of the garage, she was provoked into a memoir of Jake.

"Jake was a straight-ahead kind of man," she said, "he was simpleminded and that helped him to be the kind of man that he was." She was staring into her Scotch-and-floodwater rather moodily I thought, debris bouncing on the waves all around us but she paid no attention. "That is the type of man I like," she said, "a strong and simpleminded man. The case-study method was not Jake's method, he went right through the middle of the line and never failed to gain yardage, no matter what the game was. He had a lust for life, and life had a lust for him. I was inconsolable when Jake passed away." Mrs. Davis was drinking the Scotch for her nerves, she had no nerves of course, she was nerveless and possibly heartless also but that is another question, gutless she was not, she had a gut and a very pretty one ocher in color but that was another matter. God was standing up to His neck in the raging waters with a smile of incredible beauty on His visage, He seemed to be enjoying His creation, the disaster, the waters all around us were raging louder now, raging like a mighty tractor-trailer tailgating you on the highway.

Then Mrs. Davis sang to me, a song of great expectations.

"*Maude is waiting for you,*" Mrs. Davis sang to me, "*Maude is waiting for you in all her seriousness and splendor, under her gilded onion dome, in that city which I cannot name at this time, Maude waits. Maude is what you lack, the profoundest of your lacks. Your every yearn since the first yearn has been a yearn for Maude, only you did not know it until I, your dear friend, pointed it out. She is going to heal your scrappy and generally unsatisfactory life with the balm of her Maudeness, luckiest of dogs, she waits only for you. Let me give you just one instance of Maude's inhuman sagacity. Maude named the tools. It was Maude who thought of calling the rattail file a rattail file. It was Maude who christened the needle-nose pliers. Maude named the rasp. Think of it. What else could a rasp be but a rasp? Maude in her wisdom went right to the point, and called it* rasp. *It was Maude who named the maul. Similarly the sledge, the wedge, the ball-peen hammer, the adz, the shim, the hone, the strop. The handsaw, the hacksaw, the bucksaw, and the fretsaw were named by Maude, peering into each saw and intuiting at once its specialness. The scratch awl, the scuffle hoe, the prick punch and the countersink—I could go on and on. The tools came to Maude, tool by tool in a long respectful line, she gave them their names. The vise. The gimlet. The cold chisel. The reamer, the router, the gouge. The plumb bob. How could she have thought up the rough justice of these wonderful cognomens? Looking languidly at a pair of tin snips, and then deciding to call them* tin snips—*what a burst of glory! And I haven't even cited the bush hook, the grass snath, or the plumber's snake, or the C-clamp, or the nippers, or the scythe. What a tall achievement, naming the tools! And this is just one of Maude's contributions to our worldly estate, there are others. What delights will come crowding,*" Mrs. Davis sang to me, "*delight upon delight, when the epithalamium is ground out by the hundred organ grinders who are Maude's constant attendants, on that good-quality day of her own choosing, which you have desperately desired all your lean life, only you weren't aware of it until I, your dear friend, pointed it out. And Maude is young but not too young,*" Mrs. Davis sang to me, "*she is not too old either, she is* just right *and she is waiting for you with her tawny limbs and horse sense, when you receive Maude's nod your future and your past will begin.*"

There was a pause, or pall.

"Is that true," I asked, "that song?"

"It is a metaphor," said Mrs. Davis, "it has metaphorical truth."

"And the end of the mechanical age," I said, "is that a metaphor?"

"The end of the mechanical age," said Mrs. Davis, "is in my judgment an actuality straining to become a metaphor. One must wish it luck, I suppose. One must cheer it on. Intellectual rigor demands that we give these damned metaphors every chance, even if they are inimical to personal well-being and comfort. We have a duty to understand everything, whether we like it or not—a duty I would scant if I could." At that moment the water jumped into the boat and sank us.

•

At the wedding Mrs. Davis spoke to me kindly.

"Tom," she said, "you are not Ralph, but you are all that is around at the moment. I have taken in the whole horizon with a single sweep of my practiced eye, no giant figure looms there and that is why I have decided to marry you, temporarily, with Jake gone and an age ending. It will be a marriage of convenience all right, and when Ralph comes, or Maude nods, then our arrangement will automatically self-destruct, like the tinted bubble that it is. You were very kind and considerate, when we were drying out, in the tree, and I appreciated that. That counted for something. Of course kindness and consideration are not what the great songs, the Ralph-song and the Maude-song, promise. They are merely flaky substitutes for the terminal experience. I realize that and want you to realize it. I want to be straight with you. That is one of the most admirable things about me, that I am always straight with people, from the sweet beginning to the bitter end. Now I will return to the big house where my handmaidens will proceed with the robing of the bride."

It was cool in the meadow by the river, the meadow Mrs. Davis had selected for the travesty, I walked over to the tree under which my friend Blackie was standing, he was the best man, in a sense.

"This disgusts me," Blackie said, "this hollow pretense and empty sham and I had to come all the way from Chicago."

God came to the wedding and stood behind a tree with just part of His effulgence showing, I wondered whether He was planning to bless this makeshift construct with His grace, or not. It's hard to imagine what He was thinking of in the beginning when He planned everything that was ever going to happen, planned everything exquisitely right down to the tiniest detail such as what I was thinking at this very moment, my thought about His thought, planned the end of the mechanical age and detailed the new age to follow, and then the bride emerged from the house with her train, all ocher in color and very lovely.

"And do you, Anne," the minister said, "promise to make whatever mutually satisfactory accommodations necessary to reduce tensions and arrive at whatever previously agreed-upon goals both parties have harmoniously set in the appropriate planning sessions?"

"I do," said Mrs. Davis.

"And do you, Thomas, promise to explore all differences thoroughly with patience and inner honesty ignoring no fruitful avenues of discussion and seeking at all times to achieve rapprochement while eschewing advantage in conflict situations?"

"Yes," I said.

"Well, now we are married," said Mrs. Davis, "I think I will retain my present name if you don't mind, I have always been Mrs. Davis and your name is a shade graceless, no offense, dear."

"O.K.," I said.

Then we received the congratulations and good wishes of the guests, who were mostly employees of the Mexican restaurant, Raul was there and Consuelo, Pedro, and Pepe came crowding around with outstretched hands and Blackie came crowding around with outstretched hands, God was standing behind the caterer's tables looking at the enchiladas and chalupas and chile con queso and chicken mole as if He had never seen such things before but that was hard to believe.

I started to speak to Him as all of the world's great religions with a few exceptions urge, from the heart, I started to say "Lord, Little Father of the Poor, and all that, I was just wondering now that an age, the mechanical age, is ending and a new age beginning or so they say, I was just wondering if You could give me a hint, sort of, not a Sign, I'm not asking for a Sign, but just the barest hint as to whether what we have been told about Your nature and our nature is, forgive me and I know how You feel about doubt or rather what we have been told You feel about it, but if You could just let drop the slightest indication as to whether what we have been told is authentic or just a bunch of apocryphal heterodoxy—"

But He had gone away with an insanely beautiful smile on His lighted countenance, gone away to read the meters and get a line on the efficacy of grace in that area, I surmised, I couldn't blame Him, my question had not been so very elegantly put, had I been able to express it mathematically He would have been more interested, maybe, but I have never been able to express anything mathematically.

•

After the marriage Mrs. Davis explained marriage to me.

Marriage, she said, an institution deeply enmeshed with the mechanical age.

Pairings smiled upon by law were but reifications of the laws of mechanics, inspired by unions of a technical nature, such as nut with bolt, wood with wood screw, aircraft with Plane-Mate.

Permanence or impermanence of the bond a function of (1) materials and (2) technique.

Growth of literacy a factor, she said.

Growth of illiteracy also.

The center will not hold if it has been spot-welded by an operator whose deepest concern is not with the weld but with his lottery ticket.

God interested only in grace—keeping things humming.

Blackouts, brownouts, temporary dimmings of household illumination all portents not of Divine displeasure but of Divine indifference to executive-development programs at middle-management levels.

He likes to get out into the field Himself, she said. With His flashlight. He is doing the best He can.

We two, she and I, no exception to general ebb/flow of world juice and its concomitant psychological effects, she said.

Bitter with the sweet, she said.

•

After the explanation came the divorce.

"Will you be wanting to contest the divorce?" I asked Mrs. Davis.

"I think not," she said calmly, "although I suppose one of us should, for the fun of the thing. An uncontested divorce always seems to me contrary to the spirit of divorce."

"That is true," I said, "I have had the same feeling myself, not infrequently."

After the divorce the child was born. We named him A.F. of L. Davis and sent him to that part of Russia where people live to be one hundred and ten years old. He is living there still, probably, growing in wisdom and beauty. Then we shook hands, Mrs. Davis and I, and she set out Ralphward, and I, Maudeward, the glow of hope not yet extinguished, the fear of pall not yet triumphant, standby generators ensuring the flow of grace to all of God's creatures at the end of the mechanical age.

GREAT DAYS

To Thomas B. Hess

The Crisis

—ON THE dedication page of the rebellion, we see the words "To Clementine." A fine sentiment, miscellaneous organ music next, and, turning several pages, massed orange flags at the head of the column. This will not be easy, but neither will it be hard. Good will is everywhere, and the lighthearted song of the gondoliers is heard in the distance.

—Yes, success is everything. Morally important as well as useful in a practical way.

—What have the rebels captured thus far? One zoo, not our best zoo, and a cemetery. The rebels have entered the cages of the tamer animals and are playing with them, gently.

—Things can get better, and in my opinion will.

—Their Graves Registration procedures are scrupulous—accurate and fair.

—There's more to it than playing guitars and clapping along. Although that frequently gets people in the mood.

—Their methods are direct, not subtle. Dissolution, leaching, sandblasting, cracking and melting of fireproof doors, condemnation, water damage, slide presentations, clamps and buckles.

—And skepticism, although absolutely necessary, leads to not very much.

—The rebels have eaten all the grass on the spacious lawns surrounding the President's heart. That vast organ, the President's heart, beats now on a bald plain.

—It depends on what you want to do. Sometimes people don't know. I mean, don't know even that.

—Clementine is thought to be one of the great rebel leaders of the half century. Her hat has four cockades.

—I loved her for a while. Then, it stopped.

—Rebel T-shirts, camouflaged as ordinary T-shirts by an intense whiteness no eye can pierce, are worn everywhere.

—I don't know why it stopped, it just stopped. That's happened several times. Is something wrong with me?

—Closely supervised voting in the other cantons produced

results clearly favorable to neither faction, but rather a sort of generalized approbation which could be appropriated by anyone who had need of it.

—A greater concentration on one person than you normally find. Then, zip.

—Three or four photographs of the rebel generals, tinted glasses, blond locks blowing in the wind, have been released to the world press, in billboard size.

—Whenever I go there, on the Metroliner, I begin quietly thinking about how to help: better planning, more careful management, a more equal distribution of income, education. Or something new.

—There have been mistakes. No attempt was made to seize Broadcasting House—a fundamental error. The Household Cavalry was not subverted, discontented junior officers of the regular forces were not sought out and offered promotions, or money . . .

—Yes, an afternoon on the links! I'd never been out there before—so green and full of holes and flags. I'm afraid we got in the way, people were shouting at us to get out of the way. We had thought they'd let us just stand there and look or walk around and look, but apparently that's not done. So we went to the pro shop and rented some clubs and bags, and put the bags on our shoulders, and that got us by for a while. We walked around with our clubs and bags, enjoying the cool green and the bright, attractive sportswear of the other participants. That helped some, but we were still under some mysterious system of rules we didn't understand, always in the wrong place at the wrong time, it seemed, yelled at and bumping into people. So finally we said to hell with it and left the links; we didn't want to spoil anybody's fun, so we took the bus back to town, first returning the clubs and bags to the pro shop. Next, we will try the jai-alai courts and soccer fields, of which we have heard the most encouraging things.

—Blocking forces were not provided to isolate the Palace. Diversions were not created to draw off key units. The airports were not invested nor were the security services neutralized. Important civilians were not cultivated and won over, and propaganda was neglected. Photographs of the rebel leaders were distributed but these "leaders" were actors, selected for their immense foreheads and chins and blond, flowing locks.

—Yes, they pulled some pretty cute tricks. I had to laugh, sometimes, wondering: What has this to do with you and me? Our frontiers are the marble lobbies of these buildings. True, mortar pits ring the elevator banks but these must be seen as friendly, helpful gestures toward certification of the crisis.

—The present goal of the individual in group enterprises is to avoid dominance; leadership is felt to be a character disorder. Clementine has not heard this news, and thus invariably falls forward, into the thickets of closure.

—Well, maybe so. When I knew her she was just an ordinary woman—wonderful, of course, but not transfigured.

—The black population has steered clear of taking sides, sits home and plays, over and over, the sexy part of *Tristan und Isolde*.

—We feel only 25 percent of what we ought to feel, according to recent findings. I know that "ought" is a loaded word, in this context.

—Are the great bells of the cathedrals an impoverishment of the folk (on one level) or an enrichment of the folk (on another level), and how are these values to be weighted, how reconciled?

—They won't do anything for the poor people, no matter who gets in, and that's a fact. I wonder if they can.

—The raid on the okra fields was not a success; the rebel answering service just hisses.

—There's such a thing as a flash point. But sometimes you can't find it, even when you know how.

—Our pride in having a rebellion of our own, even a faint, rather ill-organized one, has turned us once again toward the kinds of questions that deserve serious attention.

—Is something wrong with me? I'm not complaining, just asking. We all have our work, it's the small scale that disturbs. Maybe 25 percent is high. They say he's one of the best, but most people don't need his specialty very often. Of course, I admit that when they need it they need it. Cattle too dream of death, and are afraid of it. I don't mean that as an excuse. I did love her for a while; I remember. His strategy is to be cheerful without being optimistic; I'll go along with that. Maybe we ought to have another election. The police are never happier than on Election Day, when their relation to the citizens assumes a calm, even jokey tone. They are allowed to take off their hats. Fetching coffee in paper cups for the poll watchers, or being fetched coffee by them, they stand chest out not too close to the voting machines in fresh-pressed uniforms, spit-polished boots. Bold sergeants arrive and depart in patrol cars, or dash about making arrangements, and only the plainclothesmen are lonely.

—As a magician works with the unique compressibility of doves, finding some, losing others in the same silk foulard, so the rebels fold scratchy, relaxed meanings into their smallest actions.

—I don't quarrel with their right to do it. It's the means I'm worried about.

—Self-criticism sessions were held, but these produced more criticism than could usefully be absorbed or accommodated.

—I decided that something is not wrong with me.

—The rebels have failed to make promises. Promises are, perhaps, the nut of the matter. Had they promised everyone free groceries, for example, or one night of love, then their efforts might have—

—Yes, success is everything. Failure is more common. Most achieve a sort of middling thing, but fortunately one's situation is always blurred, you never know absolutely quite where you are. This allows, if not peace of mind, ongoing attention to other aspects of existence.

—But even a poor rebellion has its glorious moments. Let me list some of them. When the flag fell over, and Clem picked it up. When the high priest smeared himself all over with bacon fat and was attacked by red dogs, and Clem scared them off with her bomb. When it was discovered that all of the drumsticks had been left back at the base, and Clem fashioned new ones from ordinary dowels, bought at the hardware store. When gluttons made the line break and waver, and Clem stopped it by stamping her foot, again and again and again.

—When she gets back from the hills, I intend to call her up. It's worth a try.

—Distant fingers from the rebel forces are raised in fond salute.

—The rebel brigades are reading Leskov's *Why Are Books Expensive in Kiev?*

—Three rebellions ago, the air was fresher. The soft pasting noises of the rebel billposters remind us of Oklahoma, where everything is still the same.

The Apology

—SITTING ON the floor by the window with only part of my face in the window. He'll never come back.

—Of course he will. He'll return, open the gate with one hand, look up and see your face in the window.

—He'll never come back. Not now.

—He'll come back. New lines on his meager face. Yet with head held high.

—I was unforgivable.

—I would not argue otherwise.

—The black iron gate, difficult to open. Takes two hands. I can see it. It's closed.

—I've had hell with that gate. In winter, without gloves, yanking, late at night, turning my head to see who might be behind me—

—That time that guy was after you—

—The creep—

—With the chain—

—Naw he wasn't the one with the chain he was the other one. With the cudgel.

—Yes they do seem to be carrying cudgels now, I've noticed that. Big knobby cudgels.

—It's a style, makes a statement, something to do with their pricks I imagine.

—Sitting on the floor by the window with only part of my face in the window, the upper part, face truncated under the eyes by the what do you call it, sill.

—But bathed nevertheless by the heat of the fire, which spreads a pleasing warming tickle across your bare back—

—I was unforgivable.

—I don't disagree.

—He'll never come back.

—Say you're sorry.

—I'm not sorry.

—Genuine sorrow is gold. If you can't do it, fake it.

—I'm not sorry.

—Well screw it. It's six of one and half dozen of the other to me. I don't care.
—What?
—Forgive me I didn't mean that.
—What?
—I just meant you could throw him a bone is all I meant. A note written on pale-blue notepaper, in an unsteady hand. "Dear William, it is one of the greatest regrets of my poor life that—"
—Never.
—He may. He might. It's possible. Your position, there in the window, strongly suggests that the affair has yet some energy unexpended. That the magnetic north of your brain may attract his wavering needle still.
—That's kind of you. Kind.
—Your wan, white back. Your green, bifurcated French jeans. Red lines on your back. Cat hair on your jeans.
—Wait. What is it that makes you spring up so, my heart?
—The gate.
—The sound of the gate. The gate opening.
—Is it he?
—It is not. It is someone.
—Let me look.
—He's standing there.
—I know him. Andy deGroot. Looking up at our windows.
—Who's Andy deGroot?
—Guy I know. Melville Fisher Kirkland Leland & deGroot.
—What's he want?
—My devotion. I've disabused him a hundred times, to little avail. If he rings, don't answer. Of course he's more into standing outside and gazing up.
—He looks all right.
—Yes he is all right. That's Andy.
—Powerful forehead on him.
—Yes it is impressive. Stuffed with banana paste.
—Good arms.
—Yes, quite good.
—Looks like he might fly into a rage if crossed.
—He rages constantly.
—We could go out in the street and hit on him, drive him away with blows and imprecations.

—Probably have little or no effect.

—Stick him with the spines of sea urchins.

—Doubt you could penetrate.

—But he's a friend of yours so you say.

—I got no friends babe, no friends, no friends. When you get down to the nut-cutting.

—Go take a poke.

—I don't want to be the first you do it.

—Ah the hell with it. Sitting here with my head hanging in the window, what a way for a grown woman to spend her time.

—Many ways a grown woman can spend her time. Many ways. Lace-making. Feeding the golden carp. Fibonacci numbers.

—Perhaps a new gown, in fawn or taupe. That might be a giggle. Meanwhile, I am planted on this floor. Sitting on the floor by the window with only my great dark eyes visible. My great dark eyes and, in moments of agitation, my great dark nose. Ogled by myriads of citizens bopping down these Chuck's Pizza-plated streets.

—How pale the brow! How pallid the cheek! How chalk the neck! How floury the shoulders! And so on. Say you're sorry.

—I cannot. What's next? Can't sit here all night. I'm nervous. Look on the bright side, maybe he'll go away. He's got a gun stuck in his belt, a belly gun, I saw it. I scraped the oatmeal out of the pot you'll be glad to know. Used the mitt, the black mitt. Throw something at him, a spear or a rock. Open the window first. Spear's in the closet. I can lend you a rock if you don't have a rock. Hurt him. Make him go away. Make the other return. Stir up the fire. Put on some music. Have you no magic? Why do I know you? What are you good for? Why are you here? Fetch me some chocolate? Massage?

—He'll never come back. Until you say it.

—Be damned if I will. Damned a thousand times.

—Then you forfeit the sunshine of his poor blasted face forever. You are dumb, if I may say so, dumb, dumb. It's easy. It's like saying thank you. Myself, I shower thanks everywhere. Thank people for their kindness, thank them for their courtesy. Thank them for their thoughtfulness. Thank them for little things they do if they do little things that are kind, courteous, or thoughtful. Thank them for coming to my house and thank them for leaving. Thank them for what they are about to do as well as thank them for what they have already done, thank them in public and then take them aside privately and thank them again. Thank the thankless and thank the already adequately thanked. In fine, let no occasion pass to slip the chill blade of my thanks between the ribs of every human ear.

—Well. I see what you mean.

—Act.

—Andy has bestirred himself.

—What's he doing?

—Sitting. On a garbage can.

—I knew him long ago, and far away.

—Cincinnati.

—Yes. Engaged then in the manufacture of gearshafts. Had quite a nice wife at that period, name of Caledonia. She split. Then another wife, Cecile as I recall, ran away with a gibbon. Then another wife whose name tax my memory as I may cannot be brought to consciousness, think I spilled something on her once, something that stained. She too evaporated. He came here and joined Melville Fisher etc. Fell in love with a secretary. Polly. She had a beaded curtain in front of her office door and burnt incense. Quite exotic, for Melville Fisher. She ended up in the harem of one of those mystics, a maharooni. Met the old boy once, he grasped my nose and pulled, I felt a great surge of something. Like I was having my nose pulled.

—So that's Andy.

—Yes. What's that sucker doing now?

—He's combing his head. Got him a steel comb, maybe aluminum.

—What's to comb? What's he doing now?

—Adjusting his pants. He's zipping.

—You are aware dear colleague are you not that I cannot abide, cannot abide, even the least wrinkle of vulgarity in social discourse? And that this "zipping" as you call it—

—You are censorious, madame.

—A mere scant shallow preludium, madame, to the remarks I shall bend in your direction should you persist.

—Shall we call the cops?

—And say what?

—Someone's sitting on our garbage can?

—Maybe that's not illegal?

—Oh my God he's got it out in his hands. Oh my God he's pointing his gun at it.

—Oh my God. Shall we call the cops?
—Open the window.
—Open the window?
—Yes open the window.
—Okay the window's open.
—*William! William, wherever you are!*
—You're going to say you're sorry!
—*William! I'm sorry!*
—Andy's put everything away!

—*William I'm sorry I let my brother hoist you up the mast in that crappy jury-rigged bosun's chair while everybody laughed! William I'm sorry I could build better fires than you could! I'm sorry my stack of Christmas cards was always bigger than yours!*

—Andy quails. That's good.

—*William I'm sorry you don't ski and I'm sorry about your back and I'm sorry I invented bop jogging which you couldn't do! I'm sorry I loved Antigua! I'm sorry my mind wandered when you talked about the army! I'm sorry I was superior in argument! I'm sorry you slit open my bicycle tires looking for incriminating letters that you didn't find! You'll never find them!*

—Wow babe that's terrific babe. Very terrific.

—*William! I'm sorry I looked at Sam but he was so handsome, so handsome, who could not! I'm sorry I slept with Sam! I'm sorry about the library books! I'm sorry about Pete! I'm sorry I never played the guitar you gave me! William! I'm sorry I married you and I'll never do it again!*

—Wow.
—Was I sorry enough?
—Well Andy's run away howling.
—Was I sorry enough?
—Terrific. Very terrific.
—Yes I feel much better.
—Didn't I tell you?
—You told me.
—Are you okay?
—Yes I'm fine. Just a little out of breath.
—Well. What's next? Do a little honky-tonking maybe, hit a few bars?
—We could. If you feel like it. Was I sorry enough?
—No.

The New Music

—WHAT DID you do today?
—Went to the grocery store and Xeroxed a box of English muffins, two pounds of ground veal and an apple. In flagrant violation of the Copyright Act.
—You had your nap, I remember that—
—I had my nap.
—Lunch, I remember that, there was lunch, slept with Susie after lunch, then your nap, woke up, right?, went Xeroxing, right?, read a book not a whole book but part of a book—
—Talked to Happy on the telephone saw the seven o'clock news did not wash the dishes want to clean up some of this mess?
—If one does nothing but listen to the new music, everything else drifts, goes away, frays. Did Odysseus feel this way when he and Diomedes decided to steal Athene's statue from the Trojans, so that they would become dejected and lose the war? I don't think so, but who is to know what effect the new music of that remote time had on its hearers?
—Or how it compares to the new music of this time?
—One can only conjecture.
—Ah well. I was talking to a girl, talking to her mother actually but the daughter was very much present, on the street. The daughter was absolutely someone you'd like to take to bed and hug and kiss, if you weren't too old. If she weren't too young. She was a wonderful-looking young woman and she was looking at me quite seductively, very seductively, *smoldering* a bit, and I was thinking quite well of myself, very well indeed, thinking myself quite the—Until I realized she was just practicing.
—Yes, I still think of myself as a young man.
—Yes.
—A slightly old young man.
—That's not unusual.
—A slightly old young man still advertising in the trees and rivers for a mate.

—Yes.
—Being clean.
—You're very clean.
—Cleaner than most.
—It's not escaped me. Your cleanness.
—Some of these people aren't clean. People you meet.
—What can you do?
—Set an example. Be clean.
—Dig it, dig it.
—I got three different shower heads. Different degrees of sting.
—Dynamite.
—I got one of these Finnish pads that slip over the hand.
—*Numero uno.*
—Pedicare. That's another thing.
—Think you're the mule's eyebrows don't you?
—No. I feel like Insufficient Funds.
—Feel like a busted-up car by the side of the road stripped of value.
—Feel like *I don't like this*!
—You're just a little down, man, down, that's what they call it, down.
—Well how come they didn't bring us no ring of roses with a purple silk sash with gold lettering on that mother? How come that?
—Dunno baby. Maybe we lost?
—How could we lose? How could we? We!
—We were standing tall. Ready to hand them their asses, clean their clocks. Yet maybe—
—I remember the old days when we almost automatically—
—Yes. Almost without effort—
—Right. Come in, Commander. Put it right there, anywhere will do, let me move that for you. Just put that sucker down right there. An eleven-foot-high silver cup!
—Beautifully engraved, with dates.
—Beautifully engraved, with dates. That was then.
—Well. Is there help coming?
—I called the number for help and they said there was no more help.

—I'm taking you to Pool.
—I've been there.
—I'm taking you to Pool, city of new life.
—Maybe tomorrow or another day.
—Pool, the revivifier.
—Oh man I'm not up for it.
—Where one can taste the essences, get swindled into health.
—I got things to do.
—That lonesome road. It ends in Pool.
—Got to chop a little cotton, go by the drugstore.
—Ever been to Pool?
—Yes I've been there.
—Pool, city of new hope.
—Get my ocarina tuned, sew a button on my shirt.
—Have you traveled much? Have you traveled enough?
—I've traveled a bit.
—Got to go away 'fore you can get back, that's fundamental.
—The joy of return is my joy. Satisfied by a walk around the block.
—Pool. Have you seen the new barracks? For the State Police? They used that red rock they have around there, quite a handsome structure, dim and red.
—Do the cops like it?
—No one has asked them. But they could hardly . . . I mean it's new.
—Got to air my sleeping bag, scrub up my canteen.
—Have you seen the new amphitheater? Made out of red rock. They play all the tragedies.
—Yeah I've seen it that's over by the train station right?
—No it's closer to the Great Lyceum. The Great Lyceum glowing like an ember against the hubris of the city.
—I could certainly use some home fries 'long about now. Home fries and ketchup.
—Pool. The idea was that it be one of those new towns. Where everyone would be happier. The regulations are quite strict. They don't let people have cars.
—Yes, I was in on the beginning. I remember the charette, I was asked to prepare a paper. But I couldn't think of anything. I stood there wearing this blue smock stenciled with the Pool

emblem, looked rather like a maternity gown. I couldn't think of anything to say. Finally I said I would go along with the group.

—The only thing old there is the monastery, dates from 1720 or thereabouts. Has the Dark Virgin, the Virgin is black, as is the Child. Dates from 1720 or around in there.

—I've seen it. Rich fare, extraordinarily rich, makes you want to cry.

—And in the fall the circus comes. Plays the red rock gardens where the carved red asters, carved red phlox, are set off by borders of yellow beryl.

—I've seen it. Extraordinarily rich.

—So it's settled, we'll go to Pool, there'll be routs and revels, maybe a sock hop, maybe a nuzzle or two on the terrace with one of the dazzling Pool beauties—

—Not much for nuzzling, now. I mostly kneel at their feet, knit for them or parse for them—

—And the Pool buffalo herd. Six thousand beasts. All still alive.

—Each house has its grand lawns and grounds, brass candlesticks, thrice-daily mail delivery. Elegant widowed women living alone in large houses, watering lawns with whirling yellow sprinklers, studying the patterns of the grass, searching out brown patches to be sprinkled. Sometimes there is a grown child in the house, or an almost-grown one, working for a school or hospital in a teaching or counseling position. Frequently there are family photographs on the walls of the house, about which you are encouraged to ask questions. At dusk medals are awarded those who have made it through the day, the Cross of St. Jaime, the Cross of St. Em.

—Meant to be one of those new towns where everyone would be happier, much happier, that was the idea.

—Serenity. Peace. The dead are shown in art galleries, framed. Or sometimes, put on pedestals. Not much different from the practice elsewhere except that in Pool they display the actual—

—Person.

—Yes.

—And they play a tape of the guy or woman talking, right next to his or her—

—Frame or pedestal.
—Prerecorded.
—Naturally.
—Shocked white faces talking.
—Killed a few flowers and put them in pots under the faces, everybody does that.
—Something keeps drawing you back like a magnet.
—Watching the buffalo graze. It can't be this that I've waited for, I've waited too long. I find it intolerable, all this putter. Yet in the end, wouldn't mind doing a little grazing myself, it would look a little funny.
—Is there bluegrass in heaven? Make inquiries. I saw the streets of Pool, a few curs broiling on spits.
—And on another corner, a man spinning a goat into gold.
—Pool projects positive images of itself through the great medium of film.
—Cinemas filled with industrious product.
—Real films. Sent everywhere.
—Film is the great medium of this century—hearty, giggling film.
—So even if one does not go there, one may assimilate the meaning of Pool.
—I'd just like to rest and laze around.
—Soundtracks in Burmese, Italian, Twi, and other tongues.
—One film is worth a thousand words. At least a thousand.
—There's a film about the new barracks, and a film about the new amphitheater.
—Good. Excellent.
—In the one about the new barracks we see Squadron A at morning roll call, tense and efficient. "Mattingly!" calls the sergeant. "Yo!" says Mattingly. "Morgan!" calls the sergeant. "Yo!" says Morgan.
—A fine bunch of men. Nervous, but fine.
—In the one about the amphitheater, an eight-day dramatization of Eckermann's *Conversations with Goethe*.
—What does Goethe say?
—Goethe says: "I have devoted my whole life to the people and their improvement."
—Goethe said that?

—And is quoted in the very superior Pool production which is enlustering the perception of Pool worldwide.
—Rich, very rich.
—And there is a film chronicling the fabulous Pool garage sales, where one finds solid-silver plates in neglected bags.
—People sighing and leaning against each other, holding their silver plates. Think I'll just whittle a bit, whittle and spit.
—Lots of accommodations in Pool, all of the hotels are empty.
—See if I have any benefits left under the G.I. Bill.
—Pool is new, can make you new too.
—I have not the heart.
—I can get us a plane or a train, they've cut all the fares.
—People sighing and leaning against one another, holding their silver plates.
—So you just want to stay here? Stay here and be yourself?
—Drop by the shoe store, pick up a pair of shoes.
—Blackberries, buttercups, and wild red clover. I find the latest music terrific, although I don't generally speaking care much for the new, qua new. But this new music! It has won from our group the steadiest attention.
—Momma didn't 'low no clarinet played in here. Unfortunately.
—Momma.
—Momma didn't 'low no clarinet played in here. Made me sad.
—Momma was outside.
—Momma was *very* outside.
—Sitting there 'lowing and not-'lowing. In her old rocking chair.
—'Lowing this, not-'lowing that.
—Didn't 'low oboe.
—Didn't 'low gitfiddle. Vibes.
—Rock over your damn foot and bust it, you didn't pop to when she was 'lowing and not-'lowing.
—Right. 'Course, she had all the grease.
—True.
—You wanted a little grease, like to buy a damn comic book or something, you had to go to Momma.

—Sometimes yes, sometimes no. Her variously colored moods.

—Mauve. Warm gold. Citizen's blue.

—Mauve mood that got her thrown in the jug that time.

—Concealed weapons. Well, what can you do?

—Carried a .357 daytimes and a .22 for evenings. Well, what can you do?

—Momma didn't let nobody work her over, nobody.

—She just didn't give a hang. She didn't care.

—I thought she cared. There were moments.

—She never cared. Didn't give pig shit.

—You could even cry, she wouldn't come.

—I tried that, I remember. Cried and cried. Didn't do a damn bit of good.

—Lost as she was in the Eleusinian mysteries and the art of love.

—Cried my little eyes out. The sheet was sopping.

—Momma was not to be swayed. Unswayable.

—Staring into the thermostat.

—She had a lot on her mind. The chants. And Daddy, of course.

—Let's not do Daddy today.

—Yes, I remember Momma, jerking the old nervous system about with her electric *diktats*.

—Could Christ have performed the work of the Redemption had He come into the world in the shape of a pea? That was one she'd drop on you.

—Then she'd grade your paper.

—I got a C, once.

—She dyed my beard blue, on the eve of my seventh marriage. I was sleeping on the sun porch.

—Not one to withhold comment, Momma.

—Got pretty damned tired of that old woman, pretty damned tired of that old woman. Gangs of ecstatics hanging about beating on pots and pans, trash-can lids—

—Trying for a ticket to the mysteries.

—You wanted a little grease, like to go to the brothel or something, you had to say, Momma can I have a little grease to go to the brothel?

—She was often underly generous.

—Give you eight when she knew it was ten.

—She had her up days and her down days. Like most.

—Out for a long walk one early evening I noticed in the bare brown cut fields to the right of me and to the left of me the following items of interest: in the field to the right of me, couple copulating in the shade of a car, tan Studebaker as I remember, a thing I had seen previously only in old sepia-toned photographs taken from the air by playful barnstormers capable of flying with their knees, I don't know if that's difficult or not—

—And in the field to your left?

—Momma. Rocking.

—She'd lugged the old rocking chair all that way. In a mauve mood.

—I tipped my hat. She did not return the greeting.

—She was pondering. "The goddess Demeter's anguish for all her children's mortality."

—Said my discourse was sickening. That was the word she used. Said it repeatedly.

—I asked myself: Do I give a bag of beans?

—This bird that fell into the back yard?

—The south lawn.

—The back yard. I wanted to give it a Frito?

—Yeah?

—Thought it might be hungry. Sumbitch couldn't fly you understand. It had crashed. Couldn't fly. So I went into the house to get it a Frito. So I was trying to get it to eat the Frito. I had the damn bird in one hand, and in the other, the Frito.

—She saw you and whopped you.

—She did.

—She gave you that "the bird is our friend and we never touch the bird because it hurts the bird" number.

—She did.

—Then she threw the bird away.

—Into the gutter.

—Anticipating no doubt handling of the matter by the proper authorities.

—Momma. You'd ask her how she was and she'd say, "Fine." Like a little kid.

—That's what they say. "Fine."

—That's all you can get out of 'em. "Fine."
—Boy or girl, don't make a penny's worth of difference. "Fine."
—Fending you off. Similarly, Momma.
—Momma 'lowed lute.
—Yes. She had a thing for lute.
—I remember the hours we spent. Banging away at our lutes.
—Momma sitting there rocking away. Dosing herself with strange intoxicants.
—Lime Rickeys.
—Orange Blossoms.
—Rob Roys.
—Cuba Libres.
—Brandy Alexanders and Bronxes. How could she drink that stuff?
—An iron gut. And divinity, of course.
—Well. Want to clean up some of this mess?
—Some monster with claws, maybe velvet-covered claws or Teflon-covered claws, inhabits my dreams. Whistling, whistling. I say, Monster, how goes it with you? And he says, Quite happily, dreammate, there are certain criticisms, the Curator of Archetypes thinks I don't quite cut it, thinks I'm shuckin' and jivin' when what I should be doing is attacking, attacking, attacking—
—Ah, my bawcock, what a fine fellow thou art.
—*But on the whole*, the monster says, I feel fine. Then he says, Gimme that corn flake back. I say, What? He says, Gimme that corn flake back. I say, You gave me that corn flake it's my corn flake. He says, Gimme that corn flake back or I'll claw you to thread. I say, I can't man you gave it to me I already ate it. He says, C'mon man gimme the corn flake back did you butter it first? I say, C'mon man be reasonable, you don't butter a corn flake—
—How does it end?
—It doesn't end.
—Is there help coming?
—I called that number and they said whom the Lord loveth He chasteneth.
—Where is succor?
—In the new music.

—Yes, it isn't often you hear a disco version of *Un Coup de Dés*. It's strengthening.

—The new music is drumless, which is brave. To make up for the absence of drums the musicians pray nightly to the Virgin, kneeling in their suits of lights in damp chapels provided for the purpose off the corridors of the great arenas—

—Momma wouldn't have 'lowed it.

—As with much else. Momma didn't 'low Patrice.

—I remember. You still see her?

—Once in a way. Saw her Saturday. I hugged her and her body leaped. That was odd.

—How did that feel?

—Odd. Wonderful.

—The body knows.

—The body is perspicacious.

—The body ain't dumb.

—Words can't say what the body knows.

—Sometimes I hear them howling from the hospital.

—The detox ward.

—Tied to the bed with beige cloths.

—We've avoided it.

—So far.

—Knock wood.

—I did.

—Well, it's a bitch.

—Like when she played Scrabble. She played to kill. Used the filthiest words insisting on their legitimacy. I was shocked.

—In her robes of deep purple.

—Seeking the ecstatic vision. That which would lift people four feet off the floor.

—Six feet.

—Four feet or six feet off the floor. Persephone herself appearing.

—The chanting in the darkened telesterion.

—Persephone herself appearing, hovering. Accepting offerings, balls of salt, solid gold serpents, fig branches, figs.

—Hallucinatory dancing. All the women drunk.

—Dancing with jugs on their heads, mixtures of barley, water, mint—

—Knowledge of things unspeakable—
—Still, all I wanted to do was a little krummhorn. A little krummhorn once in a while.
—Can open graves, properly played.
—I was never good. Never really good.
—Who could practice?
—And your clavier.
—Momma didn't 'low clavier.
—Thought it would unleash in her impulses better leashed? I don't know.
—Her dark side. They all have them, mommas.
—I mean they've seen it all, felt it all. Spilled their damn blood and then spooned out buckets of mushy squash meanwhile telling the old husband that he wasn't number three on the scale of all husbands . . .
—Tossed him a little bombita now and then just to keep him on his toes.
—He was always on his toes, spent his whole life on his toes, the poor fuck. Piling up the grease.
—We said we weren't going to do Daddy.
—I forgot.
—Old Momma.
—Well, it's not easy, conducting the mysteries. It's not easy, making the corn grow.
—Asparagus too.
—I couldn't do it.
—*I* couldn't do it.
—Momma could do it.
—Momma.
—Luckily we have the new music now. To give us aid and comfort.
—And Susie.
—Our Susie.
—Our darling.
—Our pride.
—Our passion.
—I have to tell you something. Susie's been reading the Hite Report. She says other women have more orgasms than she does. Wanted to know why.

—Where does one go to complain? Where does one go to complain, when fiends have worsened your life?

—I told her about the Great Septuagesimal Orgasm, implying she could have one, if she was good. But it is growing late, very late indeed, for such as we.

—But perhaps one ought *not* to complain, when fiends have worsened your life. But rather, emulating the great Stoics, Epictetus and so on, just zip into a bar and lift a few, whilst listening to the new, incorrigible, great-white-shark, knife, music.

—I handed the tall cool Shirley Temple to the silent priest. The new music, I said, is not specifically anticlerical. Only in its deepest effects.

—I know the guy who plays washboard. Wears thimbles on all his fingers.

—The new music burns things together, like a welder. The new music says, life becomes more and more exciting as there is less and less time.

—Momma wouldn't have 'lowed it. But Momma's gone.

—To the curious: A man who was a Communist heard the new music, and now is not. Fernando the fish-seller was taught to read and write by the new music, and is now a leper, white as snow. William Friend was caught trying to sneak into the new music with a set of bongos concealed under his cloak, but was garroted with his own bicycle chain, just in time. Propp the philosopher, having dinner with the Holy Ghost, was told of the coming of the new music but also informed that he would not live to hear it.

—The new, down-to-earth, think-I'm-gonna-kill-myself music, which unwraps the sky.

—Succeed! It has been done, and with a stupidity that can astound the most experienced.

—The rest of the trip presents no real difficulties.

—The rest of the trip presents no real difficulties. The thing to keep your eye on is less time, more exciting. Remember that.

—As if it were late, late, and we were ready to pull on our red-and-gold-striped nightshirts.

—Cup of tea before retiring.

—Cup of tea before retiring.

—Dreams next.

—We can deal with that.

—Remembering that the new music will be there tomorrow and tomorrow and tomorrow.
—There is always a new music.
—Thank God.
—Pull a few hairs out of your nose poised before the mirror.
—Routine maintenance, nothing to write home about.

Cortés and Montezuma

Because Cortés lands on a day specified in the ancient writings, because he is dressed in black, because his armor is silver in color, a certain *ugliness* of the strangers taken as a group—for these reasons, Montezuma considers Cortés to be Quetzalcoatl, the great god who left Mexico many years before, on a raft of snakes, vowing to return.

Montezuma gives Cortés a carved jade drinking cup.

Cortés places around Montezuma's neck a necklace of glass beads strung on a cord scented with musk.

Montezuma offers Cortés an earthenware platter containing small pieces of meat lightly breaded and browned which Cortés declines because he knows the small pieces of meat are human fingers.

Cortés sends Montezuma a huge basket of that Spanish bread of which Montezuma's messengers had said, on first encountering the Spaniards, "As to their food, it is like human food, it is white and not heavy, and slightly sweet . . ."

Cortés and Montezuma are walking, down by the docks. Little green flies fill the air. Cortés and Montezuma are holding hands; from time to time one of them disengages a hand to brush away a fly.

Montezuma receives new messages, in picture writing, from the hills. These he burns, so that Cortés will not learn their contents. Cortés is trimming his black beard.

Doña Marina, the Indian translator, is sleeping with Cortés in the palace given him by Montezuma. Cortés awakens; they share a cup of chocolate. *She looks tired*, Cortés thinks.

Down by the docks, Cortés and Montezuma walk, holding hands. "Are you acquainted with a Father Sanchez?" Montezuma asks. "Sanchez, yes, what's he been up to?" says Cortés.

"Overturning idols," says Montezuma. "Yes," Cortés says vaguely, "yes, he does that, everywhere we go."

At a concert later that evening, Cortés is bitten on the ankle by a green insect. The bug crawls into his velvet slipper. Cortés removes the slipper, feels around inside, finds the bug and removes it. "Is this poisonous?" he asks Doña Marina. "Perfectly," she says.

Montezuma himself performs the operation upon Cortés's swollen ankle. He lances the bitten place with a sharp knife, then sucks the poison from the wound, spits. Soon they are walking again, down by the docks.

Montezuma writes, in a letter to his mother: "The new forwardness of the nobility has come as a welcome relief. Whereas formerly members of the nobility took pains to hide among the general population, to pretend that they were ordinary people, they are now flaunting themselves and their position in the most disgusting ways. Once again they wear scarlet sashes from shoulder to hip, even on the boulevards; once again they prance about in their great powdered wigs; once again they employ lackeys to stand in pairs on little shelves at the rear of their limousines. The din raised by their incessant visiting of one another is with us from noon until early in the morning . . .
"This flagrant behavior is, as I say, welcome. For we are all tired of having to deal with their manifold deceptions, of uncovering their places of concealment, of keeping track of their movements—in short, of having to think about them, of having to *remember* them. Their new assertiveness, however much it reminds us of the excesses of former times, is easier. The interesting question is, what has emboldened the nobility to emerge from obscurity at this time? Why now?
"Many people here are of the opinion that it is a direct consequence of the plague of devils we have had recently. It is easily seen that, against a horizon of devils, the reappearance of the nobility can only be considered a more or less tolerable circumstance—they themselves must have realized this. Not since the late years of the last Bundle have we had so many

spitting, farting, hair-shedding devils abroad. Along with the devils there have been roaches, roaches big as ironing boards. Then, too, we have the Spaniards . . ."

A group of great lords hostile to Montezuma holds a secret meeting in Vera Cruz, under the special protection of the god Smoking Mirror. Debate is fierce; a heavy rain is falling; new arrivals crowd the room.

Doña Marina, although she is the mistress of Cortés, has an Indian lover of high rank as well. Making her confession to Father Sanchez, she touches upon this. "His name is Cuitlahuac? This may be useful politically. I cannot give you absolution, but I will remember you in my prayers."

In the gardens of Tenochtitlán, whisperers exchange strange new words: *guillotine, white pepper, sincerity, temperament.*

Cortés's men break through many more walls but behind these walls they find, invariably, only the mummified carcasses of dogs, cats, and sacred birds.

Down by the docks, Cortés and Montezuma walk, holding hands. Cortés has employed a detective to follow Montezuma; Montezuma has employed a detective to follow Father Sanchez. "There are only five detectives of talent in Tenochtitlán," says Montezuma. "There are others, but I don't use them. Visions are best—better than the best detective."

Atop the great Cue, or pyramid, Cortés strikes an effigy of the god Blue Hummingbird and knocks off its golden mask; an image of the Virgin is installed in its place.

"The heads of the Spaniards," says Doña Marina, "Juan de Escalante and the five others, were arranged in a row on a pike. The heads of their horses were arranged in another row on another pike, set beneath the first."
Cortés screams.
The guards run in, first Cristóbal de Olid, and following him Pedro de Alvarado and then de Ordás and de Tapia.

Cortés is raving. He runs from the palace into the plaza where he meets and is greeted by Montezuma. Two great lords stand on either side of Montezuma supporting his arms, which are spread wide in greeting. They fold Montezuma's arms around Cortés. Cortés speaks urgently into Montezuma's ear. Montezuma removes from his bosom a long cactus thorn and pricks his ear with it repeatedly, until the blood flows.

Doña Marina is walking, down by the docks, with her lover Cuitlahuac, Lord of the Place of the Dunged Water. "When I was young," says Cuitlahuac, "I was at school with Montezuma. He was, in contrast to the rest of us, remarkably chaste. A very religious man, a great student—I'll wager that's what they talk about, Montezuma and Cortés. Theology." Doña Marina tucks a hand inside his belt, at the back.

Bernal Diaz del Castillo, who will one day write *The True History of the Conquest of New Spain*, stands in a square whittling upon a piece of mesquite. The Proclamation of Vera Cruz is read, in which the friendship of Cortés and Montezuma is denounced as contrary to the best interests of the people of Mexico, born and yet unborn.

Cortés and Montezuma are walking, down by the docks. "I especially like the Holy Ghost. Qua idea," says Montezuma. "The other God, the Father, is also—" "One God, three Persons," Cortés corrects gently. "That the Son should be sacrificed," Montezuma continues, "seems to me wrong. It seems to me He should be sacrificed *to*. Furthermore," Montezuma stops and taps Cortés meaningfully on the chest with a brown forefinger, "where is the Mother?"

Bernal asks Montezuma, as a great favor, for a young pretty woman; Montezuma sends him a young woman of good family, together with a featherwork mantle, some crickets in cages, and a quantity of freshly made soap. Montezuma observes, of Bernal, that "he seems to be a gentleman."

"The ruler prepares dramas for the people," Montezuma says.

Cortés, sitting in an armchair, nods.

"Because the cultivation of maize requires on the average only fifty days' labor per person per year, the people's energies may be invested in these dramas—for example the eternal struggle to win, to retain, the good will of Smoking Mirror, Blue Hummingbird, Quetzalcoatl . . ."

Cortés smiles and bows.

"Easing the psychological strain on the ruler who would otherwise be forced to face alone the prospect of world collapse, the prospect of the world folding in on itself . . ."

Cortés blinks.

"If the drama is not of my authorship, if events are not controllable by me—"

Cortés has no reply.

"Therefore it is incumbent upon you, dear brother, to disclose to me the ending or at least what you know of the drama's probable course so that I may attempt to manipulate it in a favorable direction with the application of what magic is left to me."

Cortés has no reply.

Breaking through a new wall, Cortés's men discover, on the floor of a chamber behind the wall, a tiny puddle of gold. The Proclamation is circulated throughout the city; is sent to other cities.

Bernal builds a stout hen coop for Doña Marina. The sky over Tenochtitlán darkens; flashes of lightning; then rain sweeping off the lake.

Down by the docks, Cortés and Montezuma take shelter in a doorway. "Doña Marina translated it; I have a copy," says Cortés.

"When you smashed Blue Hummingbird with the crowbar—"

"I was rash. I admit it."

"You may take the gold with you. All of it. My gift."

"Your Highness is most kind."

"Your ships are ready. My messengers say their sails are as many as the clouds over the water."

"I cannot leave until all of the gold in Mexico, past, present and future, is stacked in the holds."
"Impossible on the face of it."
"I agree. Let us talk of something else."
Montezuma notices that a certain amount of white lint has accumulated on his friend's black velvet doublet. He thinks: *She should take better care of him.*

In bed with Cortés, Doña Marina displays for his eyes her beautiful golden buttocks, which he strokes reverently. A tiny green fly is buzzing about the room; Cortés brushes it away with a fly whisk made of golden wire. She tells him about a vision. In the vision Montezuma is struck in the forehead by a large stone, and falls. His enraged subjects hurl more stones.
"Don't worry," says Cortés. "Trust me."

Father Sanchez confronts Cortés with the report of the detective he has hired to follow Dona Marina, together with other reports, documents, photographs. Cortés orders that all of the detectives in the city be arrested, that the profession of detective be abolished forever in Tenochtitlán, and that Father Sanchez be sent back to Cuba in chains.
In the marketplaces and theaters of the city, new words are passed about: *tranquillity, vinegar, entitlement, schnell.*

On another day Montezuma and Cortés and Doña Marina and the guard of Cortés and certain great lords of Tenochtitlán leave their palaces and are carried in palanquins to the part of the city called Cotaxtla.
There, they halt before a great house and dismount.
"What is this place?" Cortés asks, for he has never seen it before.
Montezuma replies that it is the meeting place of the Aztec council or legislature which formulates the laws of his people.
Cortés expresses surprise and states that it had been his understanding that Montezuma is an absolute ruler answerable to no one—a statement Doña Marina tactfully neglects to translate lest Montezuma be given offense by it.
Cortés, with his guard at his back and Montezuma at his right hand, enters the building.

At the end of a long hallway he sees a group of functionaries each of whom wears in his ears long white goose quills filled with powdered gold. Here Cortés and his men are fumigated with incense from large pottery braziers, but Montezuma is not, the major-domos fix their eyes on the ground and do not look at him but greet him with great reverence saying, "Lord, my Lord, my Great Lord."

The party is ushered through a pair of tall doors of fragrant cedar into a vast chamber hung with red and yellow banners. There, on low wooden benches divided by a broad aisle, sit the members of the council, facing a dais. There are perhaps three hundred of them, each wearing affixed to his buttocks a pair of mirrors as is appropriate to his rank. On the dais are three figures of considerable majesty, the one in the center raised somewhat above his fellows; behind them, on the wall, hangs a great wheel of gold with much intricate featherwork depicting a whirlpool with the features of the goddess Chalchihuitlicue in the center. The council members sit in attitudes of rigid attention, arms held at their sides, chins lifted, eyes fixed on the dais. Cortés lays a hand on the shoulder of one of them, then recoils. He raps with his knuckles on that shoulder which gives forth a hollow sound. "They are pottery," he says to Montezuma. Montezuma winks. Cortés begins to laugh. Montezuma begins to laugh. Cortés is choking, hysterical. Cortés and Montezuma run around the great hall, dodging in and out of the rows of benches, jumping into the laps of one or another of the clay figures, overturning some, turning others backwards in their seats. "I am the State!" shouts Montezuma, and Cortés shouts, "Mother of God, forgive this poor fool who doesn't know what he is saying!"

In the kindest possible way, Cortés places Montezuma under house arrest.

"Best you come to stay with me a while."

"Thank you but I'd rather not."

"We'll have games and in the evenings, home movies."

"The people wouldn't understand."

"We've got Pitalpitoque shackled to the great chain."

"I thought it was Quintalbor."

"Pitalpitoque, Quintalbor, Tendile."

"I'll send them chocolate."
"Come away, come away, come away with me."
"The people will be frightened."
"What do the omens say?"
"I don't know I can't read them any more."
"Cutting people's hearts out, forty, fifty, sixty at a crack."
"It's the custom around here."
"The people of the South say you take too much tribute."
"Can't run an empire without tribute."
"Our Lord Jesus Christ loves you."
"I'll send Him chocolate."
"Come away, come away, come away with me."

Down by the docks, Cortés and Montezuma are walking with Charles V, Emperor of Spain. Doña Marina follows at a respectful distance carrying two picnic baskets containing many delicacies: caviar, white wine, stuffed thrushes, gumbo.

Charles V bends to hear what Montezuma is saying; Cortés brushes from the person of the Emperor little green flies, using a fly whisk made of golden wire. "Was there no alternative?" Charles asks. "I did what I thought best," says Cortés, "proceeding with gaiety and conscience." "I am murdered," says Montezuma.

The sky over Tenochtitlán darkens; flashes of lightning; then rain sweeping off the lake.

The pair walking down by the docks, hand in hand, the ghost of Montezuma rebukes the ghost of Cortés. "Why did you not throw up your hand, and catch the stone?"

The King of Jazz

WELL I'M the king of jazz now, thought Hokie Mokie to himself as he oiled the slide on his trombone. Hasn't been a 'bone man been king of jazz for many years. But now that Spicy MacLammermoor, the old king, is dead, I guess I'm it. Maybe I better play a few notes out of this window here, to reassure myself.

"Wow!" said somebody standing on the sidewalk. "Did you hear that?"

"I did," said his companion.

"Can you distinguish our great homemade American jazz performers, each from the other?"

"Used to could."

"Then who was that playing?"

"Sounds like Hokie Mokie to me. Those few but perfectly selected notes have the real epiphanic glow."

"The what?"

"The real epiphanic glow, such as is obtained only by artists of the caliber of Hokie Mokie, who's from Pass Christian, Mississippi. He's the king of jazz, now that Spicy MacLammermoor is gone."

Hokie Mokie put his trombone in its trombone case and went to a gig. At the gig everyone fell back before him, bowing.

"Hi Bucky! Hi Zoot! Hi Freddie! Hi George! Hi Thad! Hi Roy! Hi Dexter! Hi Jo! Hi Willie! Hi Greens!"

"What we gonna play, Hokie? You the king of jazz now, you gotta decide."

"How 'bout 'Smoke'?"

"Wow!" everybody said. "Did you hear that? Hokie Mokie can just knock a fella out, just the way he pronounces a word. What a intonation on that boy! God Almighty!"

"I don't want to play 'Smoke,'" somebody said.

"Would you repeat that, stranger?"

"I don't want to play 'Smoke.' 'Smoke' is dull. I don't like the changes. I refuse to play 'Smoke.'"

"He refuses to play 'Smoke'! But Hokie Mokie is the king of jazz and he says 'Smoke'!"

"Man, you from outa town or something? What do you mean you refuse to play 'Smoke'? How'd you get on this gig anyhow? Who hired you?"

"I am Hideo Yamaguchi, from Tokyo, Japan."

"Oh, you're one of those Japanese cats, eh?"

"Yes I'm the top trombone man in all of Japan."

"Well you're welcome here until we hear you play. Tell me, is the Tennessee Tea Room still the top jazz place in Tokyo?"

"No, the top jazz place in Tokyo is the Square Box now."

"That's nice. O.K., now we gonna play 'Smoke' just like Hokie said. You ready, Hokie? O.K., give you four for nothin'. One! Two! Three! Four!"

The two men who had been standing under Hokie's window had followed him to the club. Now they said:

"Good God!"

"Yes, that's Hokie's famous 'English sunrise' way of playing. Playing with lots of rays coming out of it, some red rays, some blue rays, some green rays, some green stemming from a violet center, some olive stemming from a tan center—"

"That young Japanese fellow is pretty good, too."

"Yes, he is pretty good. And he holds his horn in a peculiar way. That's frequently the mark of a superior player."

"Bent over like that with his head between his knees—good God, he's sensational!"

He's sensational, Hokie thought. Maybe I ought to kill him.

But at that moment somebody came in the door pushing in front of him a four-and-one-half-octave marimba. Yes, it was Fat Man Jones, and he began to play even before he was fully in the door.

"What're we playing?"

"'Billie's Bounce.'"

"That's what I thought it was. What're we in?"

"F."

"That's what I thought we were in. Didn't you use to play with Maynard?"

"Yeah I was on that band for a while until I was in the hospital."

"What for?"
"I was tired."
"What can we add to Hokie's fantastic playing?"
"How 'bout some rain or stars?"
"Maybe that's presumptuous?"
"Ask him if he'd mind."
"You ask him, I'm scared. You don't fool around with the king of jazz. That young Japanese guy's pretty good, too."
"He's sensational."
"You think he's playing in Japanese?"
"Well I don't think it's English."

This trombone's been makin' my neck green for thirty-five years, Hokie thought. How come I got to stand up to yet another challenge, this late in life?

"Well, Hideo—"
"Yes, Mr. Mokie?"
"You did well on both 'Smoke' and 'Billie's Bounce.' You're just about as good as me, I regret to say. In fact, I've decided you're *better* than me. It's a hideous thing to contemplate, but there it is. I have only been the king of jazz for twenty-four hours, but the unforgiving logic of this art demands we bow to Truth, when we hear it."
"Maybe you're mistaken?"
"No, I got ears. I'm not mistaken. Hideo Yamaguchi is the new king of jazz."
"You want to be king emeritus?"
"No, I'm just going to fold up my horn and steal away. This gig is yours, Hideo. You can pick the next tune."
"How 'bout 'Cream'?"
"O.K., you heard what Hideo said, it's 'Cream.' You ready, Hideo?"
"Hokie, you don't have to leave. You can play too. Just move a little over to the side there—"
"Thank you, Hideo, that's very gracious of you. I guess I will play a little, since I'm still here. Sotto voce, of course."
"Hideo is wonderful on 'Cream'!"
"Yes, I imagine it's his best tune."
"What's that sound coming in from the side there?"
"Which side?"
"The left."

"You mean that sound that sounds like the cutting edge of life? That sounds like polar bears crossing Arctic ice pans? That sounds like a herd of musk ox in full flight? That sounds like male walruses diving to the bottom of the sea? That sounds like fumaroles smoking on the slopes of Mt. Katmai? That sounds like the wild turkey walking through the deep, soft forest? That sounds like beavers chewing trees in an Appalachian marsh? That sounds like an oyster fungus growing on an aspen trunk? That sounds like a mule deer wandering a montane of the Sierra Nevada? That sounds like prairie dogs kissing? That sounds like witchgrass tumbling or a river meandering? That sounds like manatees munching seaweed at Cape Sable? That sounds like coatimundis moving in packs across the face of Arkansas? That sounds like—"

"Good God, it's Hokie! Even with a cup mute on, he's blowing Hideo right off the stand!"

"Hideo's playing on his knees now! Good God, he's reaching into his belt for a large steel sword— Stop him!"

"Wow! That was the most exciting 'Cream' ever played! Is Hideo all right?"

"Yes, somebody is getting him a glass of water."

"You're my man, Hokie! That was the dadblangedest thing I ever saw!"

"You're the king of jazz once again!"

"Hokie Mokie is the most happening thing there is!"

"Yes, Mr. Hokie sir, I have to admit it, you blew me right off the stand. I see I have many years of work and study before me still."

"That's O.K., son. Don't think a thing about it. It happens to the best of us. Or it almost happens to the best of us. Now I want everybody to have a good time because we're gonna play 'Flats.' 'Flats' is next."

"With your permission, sir, I will return to my hotel and pack. I am most grateful for everything I have learned here."

"That's O.K., Hideo. Have a nice day. He-he. Now, 'Flats.'"

The Question Party

"Yes, Maria, we will give the party on next Thursday night and I have an agreeable surprise in contemplation for all our old friends who may be here." The pleasant air about Mrs. Teach as she entered the parlor where her daughter was seated betokened the presence of something on her mind that gave her great satisfaction. The daughter had been importuning her mother for a party which after due deliberation she had decided to give and to make the evening more entertaining she had determined to introduce a new feature which she thought would create some excitement in the circle of her acquaintances and afford them the means of much amusement. She had just hit upon the plan before entering the room and the smile of satisfaction upon her face was noticed by her daughter.

"Shall we, Mother? I am so glad!" she answered. "But what is it you are preparing for our friends? Are you going to sing?"

"No, Miss, I am going to do no such foolish thing! And, for your quizzing, you shall not know what it is until the evening of the party!"

"Now, Mother, that is too bad. You are too hardhearted. You know the extent of woman's curiosity and yet you will not gratify me. Are you going to introduce a new polka?"

"There is no use in your questioning; I shall not tell you anything about it, so you may as well save your breath."

"Do you intend showing your album quilt?" perseveringly inquired Maria.

"Now do not provoke me to cancel my promise by your pertinacity. I tell you as a punishment for quizzing your mother you shall not know until Thursday next what it is."

"Morning or evening, Mother?"

"Evening, Miss. So no more questions but get about writing your invitations."

Maria proceeded to the bookcase and taking from it her notepaper and envelopes commenced writing.

Eight o'clock on the evening of the party. The first who were ushered into the parlor were Mrs. Jawart and her two daughters, who were always the first at the reunions. The younger Miss Jawart was somewhere out of her teens, and the elder, although her face was profusely bedecked with curls—the original owner of which, being dead, had no further use for them—could not conceal that she was much older than she wished to be considered. Mr. and Mrs. White came next, the lady somewhat pompous in her manner, and the gentleman quite so. An interest in a canal boat had placed him, in his own view, among shipping merchants, and some of his acquaintances broadly hinted that if he were cut up in small pieces and retailed out for starch, he would be fulfilling his destiny. The two Misses Jennings and brother came next. These young ladies, the one eighteen and the other twenty, seemed somewhat disappointed, when they entered the room, at the absence of some of their young beaux, whom they expected to find there; this feeling was dispelled in a few moments, when a matched pair of the latter presented themselves.

Mr. Lynch, a bachelor of fifty, was the next to claim the attention of the company. He was a short, thickset man, with a small pair of whiskers that curled up on his cheekbones as if endeavoring to cultivate an acquaintance with his eyes. A few gray hairs in them, overlooked by the owner—his attention to them was exemplary—had been, in his toilet for the evening, elbowed, as it were, by the others to the fore, possibly to attract the attention of a few of the same color which peeped from behind the false hair of Miss Jawart. A standing collar formed a semi-wall around his neck, and shoes of the brightest polish graced his feet. At about half past nine, then, all the guests had assembled, filling comfortably both parlors and rendering the place vocal with their animated conversation.

The company had been engaged some time in singing when there was a call for a polka. In a few moments partners were selected and everyone was hopscotching through the figures at a lively rate, reminding one strongly of a group in a state of advanced intoxication. The mind of Maria suddenly became abstracted to such an extent by thoughts of the surprise that her mother had promised that she forgot her time and the dancers were compelled to stop and reprove her jokingly for her remissness. Just at that moment Mrs. Teach's voice could be heard, above the general din of laughter and music, calling for everyone, without exception, to come into the front parlor as she had something to show them which she thought would amuse. In her haste to get into the room Maria almost knocked one of the Misses Jennings over.

The company after much confusion being seated, Mrs. Teach took from the center table a handsome marble card basket containing a pack of plain, gilt-edged cards and explained that she had prepared an innocent and entertaining amusement for them which she hoped would prove interesting.

"Maria," she continued, "will you pass around this basket, my dear, and let each one of the company select from it one of the cards?"

Maria did as her mother requested.

"I shall propose a question," said Mrs. Teach, "to which each one must write an answer on the card they have. Which cards shall be placed in this vase on the pedestal behind me. After they are all deposited I will draw them out singly and will read them aloud. There is to be no mark upon the response by which its author may be known."

There was a general mustering of pencils at this announcement and an evident curiosity was immediately raised in regard to the subject which would be propounded.

"As there is a majority of ladies here, I shall propose for the first question: What is a bachelor?"

For the space of a quarter of an hour the pencils of the company made desperate attacks upon the faces of the cards which left them covered over with black lines. The last answer written and deposited in the vase, Mrs. Teach, with a smile, commenced the task of reading them aloud.

"*A target for fair hands to shoot at,*" she read.

A general laugh greeted this response.

"I beg of you, ladies," said Mr. Lynch, "not to shoot too close to me, but I know that my prayer is to no avail since your arrows are already in that vase."

The second card was drawn forth.

"*Any icy peak, on the mountain of humanity, that the sun of woman's love has never melted,*" read Mrs. Teach.

"Then I will nip you with my frost," said Mr. Lynch, putting his arms playfully around one of the Misses Jennings.

"How do you know it was my answer?" she cried, releasing herself from him.

"I read it in your face this moment," he replied.

"Then we must turn our faces from you, or we shall all betray ourselves, if you are such an excellent face reader," said the elder Miss Jawart.

"I beg you, do not!" exclaimed Mr. Lynch. "For that would deprive me of much pleasure."

"*An old maid's forlorn hope*," said Mrs. Teach, reading the next response, the aptness of which was felt by all—yet a sense of propriety restrained any acknowledgment of this. Another card was instantly drawn to divert attention from it, and to relieve Miss Jawart from her unpleasant dilemma.

"*A fox longing for the grapes he pronounces sour.*"

"Now I really do object!" said Mr. Lynch. "I could never find it in my heart to pronounce any lady sour."

"Heart, indeed! This is the first time I ever knew you to acknowledge the possession of such an article," Mrs. Teach quickly replied.

"There you do me wrong, for, see! I have one now which you gave me," said Mr. Lynch, taking from his pocket a handsomely worked velvet heart. "And observe, there are as many pins in it as you are endeavoring to plant thorns in its partner here," he went on, placing his hand over that part of his coat which covered the real article.

The laugh was turned on Mrs. Teach and she drew forth another card.

"*A creature whose miseries might be pitied had he not the remedy within his reach.*"

"It must be you, Miss Bookly," said Mr. Lynch, "as you are sitting closest to me."

"I did not write it," said Miss Bookly. "And besides, Miss Jennings was sitting closest to you before she moved away after you put your arms around her."

"That is true," he said with a mock sigh.

Another card terminated the conversation on that subject.

"*Just like Mr. Lynch.*"

The merriment of the company knew no bounds at this

answer. Mr. Lynch joined the rest with great zeal, and in a few moments exclaimed, "Well! I really do think you are making me a target to shoot at tonight. It is well for you that I am good-natured, else I might retaliate with some formulations of my own."

This is really a dumb game, thought Maria.

Mrs. Teach dipped into the vase for the next card.

"*One who boasts of liberty but sighs for the slavery he condemns.*"

"That would be acute," Mr. Lynch said thoughtfully, "had I ever boasted. But I recall no such occasion. There is, in fact, a kind of shame and horror attached to the bachelor state—an odium combined with a tedium. Sleeping with strumpets is not the liveliest business in the world, I assure you."

"What are they like, really?" asked Miss Bookly.

"Some are choice, some are not," said Mr. Lynch.

"For heaven's sakes, man, be silent!" exclaimed Mr. White.

"A bit of fresh, as the expression runs," said Mr. Lynch, "can—"

Mr. White drew forth his pistol and shot Mr. Lynch dead with it.

"Good Lord! He is dead!" cried Mrs. Teach.

Dr. Balfour knelt over the body. "Yes, he is dead," he said. All assisted the Doctor in placing the carcass on the sofa.

"There is but one more card in the vase," said Mrs. Teach, peering into the article in question. "Dare we look at it?"

"Yes, yes," was the answer, in a subdued murmur.

"I sincerely hope that it may be a favorable one," said Mrs. Teach, "for I fear we have dealt harshly with our late friend tonight."

The last card was drawn from the vase. Mrs. Teach examined it closely on both sides and then proclaimed, "*Blank!*"

"A prophecy," said the younger Miss Jennings. "Who could have foreseen what was to happen?"

"It was not a matter of foreknowledge," said Maria. "The card is mine. I couldn't think of anything to write."

"Well," said Mrs. Teach, "I am not entirely satisfied with my little experiment this evening, and so shall leave it to another to choose the entertainment for our next."

"Not at all," said Mr. White. "The evening, despite its sad but necessary consequences, has been most delightful. I can't recall when more interesting things have been said or done, in all the years of my residence in this city. And as I shall have the pleasure of giving the next party, I shall most certainly adopt your little experiment, as you call it."

"What will the question be?" asked Miss Jawart.

"Something dangerous," said Mr. White, with a twinkle.

"Parties are always dangerous," said Miss Jawart.

"I am inviting Geronimo, chief of the Apache Indians, who happens to be in town," said Mr. White.

"That will make it all the more dangerous," said Mrs. Teach, "as I am told that he is extremely cruel to his enemies."

"He is extremely cruel to *everyone*," said Mr. White.

Yes, it was an agreeable party after all, Maria thought. My mother is not dumb. My mother is surprisingly intelligent. It was wrong of me to think ill of her. Now no one will ever know that Mr. Lynch was the man who— How strange is justice! How artful woman!

Author's note: This piece is an *objet trouvé*. It was originally published in *Godey's Lady's Book* in 1850, under the byline of a Hickory Broom. I have cut it and added some three dozen lines.

Belief

A GROUP of senior citizens on a bench in Washington Square Park in New York City. There were two female senior citizens and two male senior citizens.

"Rabbit, rabbit, rabbit, rabbit," one of the women said suddenly. She turned her head to each of the four corners of an imaginary room as she did so.

The other senior citizens stared at her.

"Why did you do that?" one of the men asked.

"It's the first of the month. If you say 'rabbit' four times, once to each corner of the room, or the space that you are in, on the first of the month before you eat lunch, then you will be loved in that month."

Some angry black people walked by carrying steel-band instruments and bunches of flowers.

"I don't think that's true," the second woman senior citizen said. "I never heard it before and I've heard everything."

"I think it's probably just an old wives' tale," one of the men said. The other male senior citizen cracked up.

"Shall we discuss *old men*?" the first woman asked the second woman.

The two men looked at the sky to make sure all of our country's satellites were in the right places.

"What about your daughter the nun?" the second woman, whose name was Elise, asked the first, whose name was Kate. "You haven't heard from her?"

"My daughter the nun," Kate said, "you wouldn't believe."

"Where is she?" Elise asked. "Georgia or somewhere, you told me but I forgot. Going to school you said."

"She's getting her master's," Kate said, "they send them. She's a rambling wreck from Georgia Tech. I was going down to visit at Thanksgiving."

"But you didn't."

"I called her and said I was coming and she said but Thanksgiving Day is the game. So I said the game, the game, O.K. I'll go to the game, I don't mind going to the game, get me a ticket. And she said but Mother I'm in the flash card section. My daughter the nun."

"They're different now," Elise said, "you're lucky she's not keeping company with one of those priests with his hair in a pigtail."

"Who can tell?" said Kate. "I'd be the last to know."

One of the men leaned around his partner and asked: "Well, is it working? Are you loved?"

"There was another thing we used to do," Kate said calmly. "You and your girl friend each wrote the names of three boys on three slips of paper, on the first day of the month. The names of three boys you wanted to ask you to go out with them. Then your girl friend held the three slips of paper in her cupped hands and you closed your eyes and picked—"

"I don't believe it," said the second male senior citizen, whose name was Jerome.

"You closed your eyes and picked one and put it in your shoe. And you did the same for her. And then that boy would come around. It always worked. Invariably."

"I don't believe it," Jerome said again. "I don't believe in things like that and never have. I don't believe in magic and I don't believe in superstition. I don't believe in Judaism, Christianity, or Eastern thought. None of 'em. I didn't believe in the First World War even though I was a child in the First World War and you'll go a long way before you find somebody who didn't believe in the First World War. That was a very popular war, where I lived. I didn't believe in the Second World War either and I was in it."

"How could you be in it if you didn't believe in it?" Elise asked.

"My views were not consulted," Jerome said. "They didn't ask me, they told me. But I still had my inner belief, which was that I didn't believe in it. I was in the MPs. I rose through the ranks. I was a provost marshal, at the end. I once shook down an entire battalion of Seabees, six hundred men."

"What is 'shook down'?"

"That's when you and your people go through their foot lockers and sea bags and personal belongings looking for stuff they shouldn't have."

"What shouldn't they have?"

"Black market stuff. Booze. Dope. Government property. Unauthorized weapons." He paused. "What else didn't I believe in? I didn't believe in the atom bomb but I was wrong about that. The unions."

"You were wrong about that too," said the other man, Frank. "I was a linotype operator when I was nineteen and I was a linotype operator until I was sixty and let me tell you, mister, if we hadn't had the union all we would have got was nickels and dimes. Nickels and dimes. Period. So don't say anything against the trade union movement while I'm sitting here, because I know what I'm talking about. You don't."

"I didn't believe in the unions and I didn't believe in the government whether Republican or Democrat," Jerome said. "And I didn't believe in—"

"The I.T.U. is considered a very good union," Elise said. "I once went with a man in the I.T.U. He was a composing-room foreman and his name was Harry Foreman, that was a coincidence, and he made very good money. We went to Luchow's a lot. He liked German food."

"Did you believe in the international Communist conspiracy?" Frank asked Jerome.

"Nope."

"You can't read," Frank said, "you're blind."

"Maybe."

"I haven't decided about whether there is an international Communist conspiracy," Elise said. "I'm still thinking about it."

"What's to think about?" Frank asked. "There was Czechoslovakia. Czechoslovakia says it all."

Some street people walked past the group of senior citizens but decided that the senior citizens weren't worth asking for small change. The decision was plain on their faces.

"When I was a girl, a little girl, I had to go into my father's bar to get the butter," Kate said. "My father had a bar in Brooklyn. The icebox was in the bar. The only icebox. My mother sent me downstairs to get the butter. All the men turned and looked at me as I entered the bar."

"But your father bounded out from behind the bar and got you the butter meanwhile looking sternly at all the other people in the bar to keep them from looking at you," Elise suggested.

"No," Kate said. "He was on his ass most of the time. What they say about bartenders not drinking is not true."

"Also I didn't believe in the United Nations and before that I didn't believe in the League of Nations," Jerome said. "Furthermore," he said, giving Kate a meaningful glance, "I didn't believe women should be given the vote."

Kate gazed at Jerome's coat, which was old, at his shirt, old, then at his pants, which were quite old, and at his shoes, which were new.

"Do you have prostate trouble?" she asked.

"Yes," Jerome said, with a startled look. "Of course. Why?"

"Good," Kate said. "I don't believe in prostate trouble. I don't believe there is such a thing as a prostate."

She gave him a generous and loving smile.

"You mean to tell me that if you put the piece of paper with the boy's name on it in your shoe on the first day of the month he *invariably* came around?" Elise asked Kate.

"Invariably," Kate said. "Without fail. Worked every time."

"Goddamn," Elise said. "Wish I'd known that."

"There was one thing I believed," Jerome said.

"What?"

"It's religious."

"What is it?"

"My pal the rabbi told me, he's dead now. He said it was a Hasidic writing."

"So?" said Elise. "So, so, so?"

"*It is forbidden to grow old.*"

The old people thought about this for a while, on the bench.

"It's good," Kate said. "I could do without the irony."

"Me too," Elise said. "I could do without the irony."

"Maybe it's not so good?" Jerome asked. "What do you think?"

"No," Kate said. "It's good." She gazed about her at the new life sprouting in sandboxes and jungle gyms. "Wish I had some kids to yell at."

Tales of the Swedish Army

SUDDENLY, TURNING a corner, I ran into a unit of the Swedish Army. Their vehicles were parked in orderly rows and filled the street, mostly six-by-sixes and jeeps, an occasional APC, all painted a sand color quite different from the American Army's dark green. To the left of the vehicles, on a big school playground, they had set up two-man tents of the same sand color, and the soldiers, blond red-faced men, lounged about among the tents, making not much noise. It was strange to see them there, I assumed they were on their way to some sort of joint maneuvers with our own troops. But it was strange to see them there.

I began talking to a lieutenant, a young, pleasant man; he showed me a portable chess clock he'd made himself, which was for some reason covered in matchstick bamboo painted purple. I told him I was building an addition to the rear of my house, as a matter of fact I had with me a carpenter's level I'd just bought, and I showed him that. He said he had some free time, and asked if I needed help. I suggested that probably his unit would be moving out fairly soon, but he waved a hand to indicate that their departure was not imminent. He seemed genuinely interested in assisting me, so I accepted.

His name was Bengt and he was from Uppsala, I'd been there so we talked about Uppsala, then about Stockholm and Bornholm and Malmö. I asked him if he knew the work of the Swedish poet Bodil Malmsten; he didn't. My house (not really mine, my sister's, but I lived there and paid rent) wasn't far away, we stood in the garden looking up at the rear windows on the parlor floor, I was putting new ones in. So I climbed the ladder and he began handing me up one of the rather heavy prefab window frames, and my hammer slid from the top of the ladder and fell and smashed into his chess clock, which he'd carefully placed on the ground, against the wall.

I apologized profusely, and Bengt told me not to worry, it didn't matter, but he kept shaking the chess clock and turning it over in his hands, trying to bring it to life. I rushed down the ladder and apologized again, and looked at it myself, both dials were shattered and part of the purple matchstick casing had come off. He said again not to worry, he could fix it, and that we should get on with the job.

After a while Bengt was up on the ladder tacking the new frames to the two-by-fours with sixteen-penny nails. He was very skillful and the work was going quickly; I was standing in the garden steadying the ladder as he was sometimes required to lean out rather far. He slipped and tried to recover, and bashed his face against the wall, and broke his nose.

He stood in the garden holding his nose with both hands, the hands as if clasped in prayer over his nose. I apologized profusely. I ran into the house and got some ice cubes and paper towels and told him I'd take him to the hospital right away but he shook his head and said no, they had doctors of their own. I wanted to do something for him so I took him in and sat him down and cooked him some of my fried chicken, which is rather well-known although the secret isn't much of a secret, just lots of lemon-pepper marinade and then squeezing fresh lemon juice over it just before serving. I could see he was really very discouraged about his nose and I had to keep giving him fresh paper towels but he complimented me very highly on the chicken and gave me a Swedish recipe for chicken stuffed with parsley and butter and stewed, which I wrote down.

Then Bengt told me various things about the Swedish Army. He said that it was a tough army and a sober one, but small; that everybody in the army pretty well knew everybody else, and that they kept their Saab jets in deep caves that had been dug in the mountains, so that if there was a war, nothing could happen to them. He said that the part I'd seen was just his company, there were two more plus a heavy-weapons company bivouacking at various spots in the city, making up a full battalion. He said the soldiers were mostly Lutherans, with a few Presbyterians and Evangelicals, and that drugs were not a problem but that people sometimes overslept, driving the sergeants crazy. He said that the Swedish Army was thought to have the best weapons in the world, and that they kept them very clean. He said that he probably didn't have to name their principal potential enemy, because I knew it already, and that the army-wide favorite musical group was

Abba, which could sometimes be seen on American television late at night.

By now the table was full of bloody towels and some blood had gotten on his camouflage suit, which was in three shades of green and brown. Abruptly, with a manly gesture, Bengt informed me that he had fallen in love with my sister. I said that was very curious, in that he had never met her. "That is no difficulty," he said, "I can see by looking around this house what kind of a woman she must be. Very tall, is she not? And red hair, is that not true?" He went on describing my sister, whose name is Catherine, with a disturbing accuracy and increasing enthusiasm, correctly identifying her as a teacher and, furthermore, a teacher of painting. "These are hers," he said, "they must be," and rose to inspect some oils in Kulicke frames on the walls. "I knew it. From these, dear friend, a great deal can be known of the temperament of the painter, his or her essential spirit. I will divorce my wife immediately," he said, "and marry Catherine as soon as it is legally possible." "You're already married!" I said, and he hung his head and admitted yes, that it was so. But in Sweden, he said, many people were married to each other who, for one reason or another, no longer loved each other . . . I said that happened in our own country too, many cases personally known to me, and that if he wished to marry Catherine I would not stand in his way, but would, on the contrary, do everything in my power to further the project. At this moment the bell rang; I answered it and Catherine entered with her new husband, Richard.

I took Bengt back to his unit in a cab, one hand clutching his nose, the other his heart, the remains of his chess clock in his lap. We got there just in time, a review was in progress, the King of Sweden was present, a handsome young man in dress uniform with a silver sword, surrounded by aides similarly clad. A crowd had gathered and Bengt's company paraded by, looking vastly trim and efficient in their polished boots and red berets, and a very pretty little girl came out of the crowd and shyly handed the King a small bouquet of flowers. He bent graciously to accept them, beautiful small yellow roses, and a Rocky Mountain spotted-fever tick leaped from a rose and bit him on the cheek. I was horrified, and the King slapped his cheek and swore that the Swedish Army would never come to visit us again.

The Abduction from the Seraglio

I WAS sitting in my brand-new Butler building, surrounded by steel of high quality folded at ninety-degree angles. The only thing prettier than ladies is an I-beam painted bright yellow. I told 'em I wanted a big door. A big door in front where a girl could hide her car if she wanted to evade the gaze of her husband the rat-poison salesman. You ever been out with a rat-poison salesman? They are fine fellows with little red eyes.

I was playing with my forty-three-foot overhead traveling crane which is painted bright yellow. I was practicing knocking over the stepladder with the hook. I was at a low point. I'd been thinking about bread, colored steel bread, all kinds of colors of steel bread—red yellow purple green brown steel bread—then I thought no, that's not it. And I'd already made all the welded-steel four-thousand-pound artichokes the world could accommodate that week, and they wouldn't let me drink no more, only a little Lone Star beer now and then which I don't much care for. And my new Waylon Jennings record had a scratch on it, went crack crack crack across the whole width of Side One. It was the kind of impasse us creative people reach every Thursday, some prefer other days. So I figured that in order not to totally waste this valuable time of my life, I had better get on the stick and bust Constanze out of the seraglio.

> *Chorus:*
> Oh Constanze oh Constanze
> What you doin' in that se-rag-li-o?
> I been poppin' Darvon and mothballs
> Poppin' Darvon and mothballs
> Ever since I let you go.

Well, I motored out to the seraglio, got blindsided on the Freeway by two hundred thousand guys trying to get home from their work at the rat-poison factories, all two hundred thousand tape decks playin' the same thing, some kind of roll-on-down-the-road song

> rollin'
> rollin'
> rollin'
> rollin'

but there wasn't just a hell of a lot of actual forward motion despite this hymn to possibility. The seraglio turned out to be a Butler building too, much like mine only vaster of course, that son of a bitch. I spent a little while admiring that fine red-painted steel that you can put the pieces together of out of a catalogue and set her down on your slab and be barbecuing your flank steak from the A. & P. by five o'clock on the same day. The Pasha didn't have any great big doors in his, just one little tee-ninesy door with a picture of an unfed-recently Doberman pasted on it, I took that as a hint and I thought Constanze, Constanze, how could you be so dumb?

The thing is, and I hate to admit it, Constanze's a little dumb. She's not so dumb as a lady I once knew who thought the Mark of Zorro was an N, but she's not perfect. You tell her you heard via the jungle drums that there's a vacancy in Willie Jake Johnson's bed and her eyes will cut to the side just for a moment, which means she's thinking. She's not conservative. I'm some kind of an artist, but I'm conservative. Mine is the art of the possible, plus two. She, on the contrary, spent many years as a talented and elegant country-music groupie. She knows things I do not know. Happy dust is $1,900 an ounce now, I hear tell—she's tasted it, I haven't. It's a small thing, but irritating. She's dumb in what she knows, if you follow me.

> *Chorus:*
> Oh Constanze oh Constanze
> What you doin' in that se-rag-li-o?
> I been sleepin' on paper towels
> Sleepin' on paper towels and
> Drinkin' Sea & Ski
> Ever since I let you go.

The Pasha is a Plymouth dealer, actually. He has this mysterious power over people and events which is called ten million dollars a year, gross. About the only thing we share in the way of common humanity is four welded-steel artichokes, which he bought right from the studio, which is where he saw Constanze. The artichoke is a beautiful form, maybe too mannerly, I roughen mine up some, that's where the interest is. I don't even mind the damn Plymouth, as a form, but what I can't stand is a dealer. In anything. I know that this is a small picky-minded dumb-ass prejudice, but it's been earned. Anyhow the Pasha, as we call him, noticed that Constanze was some beautiful, in fact semi-incredible looking, with black hair. He turned her head, as used to be said. He'd got to the left of flank steak, and he employed that. If we're having Neiman-Marcus time, I can't compete. (In all honesty I have to concede that he is fairly handsome, for a Pasha, and excels in a number of expensive sports.) He put her in a Butler building just to mock me and because she's not so dumb she'd be caught dead in a big fancy layout in River Oaks or somewhere. She's got values. What I'm trying to suggest is, she's in a delicate relation to the real.

I can't understand this. She is so great. When we go partying she always takes care to dance with Bill Cray's four-year-old girl, who's a fool for dancing. She made me read *War and Peace*, which struck me at first glance as terrible thick. She renews my subscription to the *Texas Observer* every year. She contributes regularly to the United Way and got gassed in great cities a time or two while expressing her opinion of the recent war. She's kind to rat-poison salesmen. She's afraid of the dark. She took care of me that time I had my little psychotic episode. She is so great. Once I saw her slug a guy in a supermarket who was whacking his kid, his legal right, with undue enthusiasm. The really dreadful thought, to me, is that her real might be the real one.

Well, I opened the door. The Doberman came at me raging and snarling and generally carrying on in the way he felt was expected of him. I threw him a fifty-five-pound reinforced-concrete pork chop which knocked him silly. I spoke to Constanze. We used to walk down the street together bumping our hipbones together in joy, before God and everybody. I wanted to float in the air again some feeling of that. It didn't work. I'm sorry. But I guess, as the architects say, there's no use crying over spilt marble. She will undoubtedly move on and up and down and around in the world, New York, Chicago, and

Temple, Texas, making everything considerably better than it was, for short periods of time. We adventured. That's not bad.

> *Chorus:*
> Oh Constanze oh Constanze
> What you doin' in that se-rag-li-o?
> How I miss you
> How I miss you

The Death of Edward Lear

THE DEATH of Edward Lear took place on a Sunday morning in May 1888. Invitations were sent out well in advance. The invitations read:

> *Mr. Edward LEAR*
> *Nonsense Writer and Landscape Painter*
> *Requests the Honor of Your Presence*
> *On the Occasion of His DEMISE.*
> *San Remo*   2:20 A.M.
> *The 29th of May*   *Please reply*

One can imagine the feelings of the recipients. Our dear friend! is preparing to depart! and such-like. Mr. Lear! who has given us so much pleasure! and such-like. On the other hand, his years were considered. Mr. Lear! who must be, now let me see . . . And there was a good deal of, I remember the first time I (dipped into) (was seized by) . . . But on the whole, Mr. Lear's acquaintances approached the occasion with a mixture of solemnity and practicalness, perhaps remembering the words of Lear's great friend, Tennyson:

> Old men must die,
> or the world would grow mouldy

and:

> For men may come and men may go,
> But I go on forever.

People prepared to attend the death of Edward Lear as they might have for a day in the country. Picnic baskets were packed (for it would be wrong to expect too much of Mr. Lear's hospitality, under the circumstances); bottles of wine were wrapped in white napkins. Toys were chosen for the children. There were debates as to whether the dog ought to be taken or left behind. (Some of the dogs actually present at the death of Edward Lear could not restrain themselves; they frolicked about the dying man's chamber, tugged at the bedclothes, and made such nuisances of themselves that they had to be removed from the room.)

Most of Mr. Lear's friends decided that the appropriate time to arrive at the Villa would be midnight, or in that neighborhood, in order to allow the old gentleman time to make whatever remarks he might have in mind, or do whatever he wanted to do, before the event. Everyone understood what the time specified in the invitation meant. And so, the visitors found themselves being handed down from their carriages (by Lear's servant Giuseppe Orsini) in almost total darkness. Pausing to greet people they knew, or to corral straying children, they were at length ushered into a large room on the first floor, where the artist had been accustomed to exhibit his watercolors, and thence by a comfortably wide staircase to a similar room on the second floor, where Mr. Lear himself waited, in bed, wearing an old velvet smoking jacket and his familiar silver spectacles with tiny oval lenses. Several dozen straight-backed chairs had been arranged in a rough semicircle around the bed; these were soon filled, and later arrivals stood along the walls.

Mr. Lear's first words were: "I've no money!" As each new group of guests entered the room, he repeated, "I've no money! No money!" He looked extremely tired, yet calm. His ample beard, gray yet retaining patches of black, had evidently not been trimmed in some days. He seemed nervous and immediately began to discourse, as if to prevent anyone else from doing so.

He began by thanking all those present for attending and expressing the hope that he had not put them to too great an inconvenience, acknowledging that the hour was "an unusual one for visits!" He said that he could not find words sufficient to disclose his pleasure in seeing so many of his friends gathered together at his side. He then delivered a pretty little lecture, of some twelve minutes' duration, on the production of his various writings, of which no one has been able to recall the substance, although everyone agreed that it was charming, graceful, and wise.

He then startled his guests with a question, uttered in a kind of shriek: "Should I get married? Get married? Should I marry?"

Mr. Lear next offered a short homily on the subject Friendship. Friendship, he said, is the most golden of the affections. It is also, he said, often the *strongest* of human ties, surviving strains and tempests fatal to less sublime relations. He noted that his own many friendships constituted the richest memory of a long life.

A disquisition on Cats followed.

When Mr. Lear reached the topic Children, a certain restlessness was observed among his guests. (He had not ceased to shout at intervals, "Should I get married?" and "I've no money!") He then displayed copies of his books, but as everybody had already read them, not more than a polite interest was generated. Next he held up, one by one, a selection of his watercolors, views of various antiquities and picturesque spots. These, too, were familiar; they were the same watercolors the old gentleman had been offering for sale, at £5 and £10, for the past forty years.

Mr. Lear now sang a text of Tennyson's in a setting of his own, accompanying himself on a mandolin. Although his voice was thin and cracked frequently, the song excited vigorous applause.

Finally he caused to be hauled into the room by servants an enormous oil, at least seven feet by ten, depicting Mount Athos. There was a murmur of appreciation, but it did not seem to satisfy the painter, for he assumed a very black look.

At 2:15 Mr. Lear performed a series of actions the meaning of which was obscure to the spectators.

At 2:20 he reached over to the bedside table, picked up an old-fashioned pen which lay there, and died. A death mask was immediately taken. The guests, weeping unaffectedly, moved in a long line back to the carriages.

People who had attended the death of Edward Lear agreed that, all in all, it had been a somewhat tedious performance. Why had he seen fit to read the same old verses, sing again the familiar songs, show the well-known pictures, run through his repertoire once more? Why invitations? Then something was understood: that Mr. Lear had been doing what he had always done and therefore, not doing anything extraordinary. Mr. Lear had transformed the extraordinary into its opposite. He had, in point of fact, created a gentle, genial misunderstanding.

Thus the guests began, as time passed, to regard the affair in an historical light. They told their friends about it, reenacted parts of it for their children and grandchildren. They would reproduce the way the old man had piped "I've no money!" in a comical voice, and quote his odd remarks about marrying. The death of Edward Lear became so popular, as time passed, that revivals were staged in every part of the country, with considerable success. The death of Edward Lear can still be seen, in the smaller cities, in versions enriched by learned interpretation, textual emendation, and changing fashion. One modification is curious; no one knows how it came about. The supporting company plays in the traditional way, but Lear himself appears shouting, shaking, vibrant with rage.

Concerning the Bodyguard

DOES THE bodyguard scream at the woman who irons his shirts? Who has inflicted a brown burn on his yellow shirt purchased expensively from Yves St. Laurent? A great brown burn just over the heart?

Does the bodyguard's principal make conversation with the bodyguard, as they wait for the light to change, in the dull gray Citroën? With the second bodyguard, who is driving? What is the tone? Does the bodyguard's principal comment on the brown young women who flock along the boulevard? On the young men? On the traffic? Has the bodyguard ever enjoyed a serious political discussion with his principal?

Is the bodyguard frightened by the initials D.I.T.?

Is the bodyguard frightened by the initials C.N.D.?

Will the bodyguard be relieved, today, in time to see the film he has in mind—*Emmanuelle Around the World*? If the bodyguard is relieved in time to see *Emmanuelle Around the World*, will there be a queue for tickets? Will there be students in the queue?

Is the bodyguard frightened by the slogan *Remember 17 June*? Is the bodyguard frightened by black spray paint, tall letters ghostly at the edges, on this wall, on this wall? At what level of education did the bodyguard leave school?

Is the bodyguard sufficiently well-paid? Is he paid as well as a machinist? As well as a foreman? As well as an army sergeant? As well as a lieutenant? Is the Citroën armored? Is the Mercedes armored? What is the best speed of the Mercedes? Can it equal that of a BMW? A BMW motorcycle? Several BMW motorcycles?

Does the bodyguard gauge the importance of his principal in terms of the number of bodyguards he requires? Should there not be other cars leading and following his principal's car, these also filled with bodyguards? Are there sometimes such additional precautions, and does the bodyguard, at these times, feel himself part of an ocean of bodyguards? Is he exalted at these times? Does he wish for even more bodyguards, possibly flanking cars to the right and left and a point car far, far ahead?

After leaving technical school, in what sort of enterprises did the bodyguard engage before accepting his present post? Has he ever been in jail? For what sort of offense? Has the bodyguard acquired a fondness for his principal? Is there mutual respect? Is there mutual contempt? When his principal takes tea, is the bodyguard offered tea? Beer? Who pays?

Can the bodyguard adduce instances of professional success? Had he a previous client?

Is there a new bodyguard in the group of bodyguards? Why?

How much does pleasing matter? What services does the bodyguard provide for his principal other than the primary one? Are there services he should not be asked to perform? Is he nevertheless asked from time to time to perform such services? Does he refuse? Can he refuse? Are there, in addition to the bodyguard's agreed-upon compensation, tips? Of what size? On what occasions?

In the restaurant, a good table for his principal and the distinguished gray man with whom he is conferring. Before it (between the table with the two principals and the door), a table for the four bodyguards. What is the quality of the conversation between the two sets of bodyguards? What do they talk about? Soccer, perhaps, Holland vs. Peru, a match which they have all seen. Do they rehearse the savaging of the Dutch goalkeeper Piet Schrijvers by the bastard Peruvian? Do they discuss Schrijvers's replacement by the brave Jan Jongbloed, and what happened next? Has the bodyguard noted the difference in quality between his suit and that of his principal? Between his shoes and those of his principal?

In every part of the country, large cities and small towns, bottles of champagne have been iced, put away, reserved for a celebration, reserved for a special day. Is the bodyguard aware of this?

Is the bodyguard tired of waking in his small room on the Calle Caspe, smoking a Royale Filtre, then getting out of bed and throwing wide the curtains to discover, again, eight people standing at the bus stop across the street in postures of depression? Is there on the wall of the bodyguard's small room a poster showing Bruce Lee in a white robe with his feet positioned in such-and-such a way, his fingers outstretched in such-and-such a way? Is there a rosary made of apple beads hanging from a nail? Is there a mirror whose edges have begun to craze and flake, and are there small blurrish Polaroids stuck along the left edge of the mirror, Polaroids of a woman in a dark-blue scarf and two lean children in red pants? Is there a pair of dark-blue trousers plus a long-sleeved white shirt (worn once already) hanging in the dark-brown wardrobe? Is there a color foldout of a naked young woman torn from the magazine VIR taped inside the wardrobe door? Is there a bottle of Long John Scotch atop the cheese-colored mini-refrigerator? Two-burner hotplate? Dull-green ceramic pot on the windowsill containing an unhealthy plant? A copy of *Explication du Tai Chi*, by Bruce Tegner? Does the bodyguard read the newspaper of his principal's party? Is he persuaded by what he reads there? Does the bodyguard know which of the great blocs his country aligned itself with during the Second World War? During the First World War? Does the bodyguard know which countries are the preeminent trading partners of his own country, at the present time?

Seated in a restaurant with his principal, the bodyguard is served, involuntarily, turtle soup. Does he recoil, as the other eats? Why is this near-skeleton, his principal, of such importance to the world that he deserves six bodyguards, two to a shift with the shifts changing every eight hours, six bodyguards of the first competence plus supplementals on occasion, two armored cars, stun grenades ready to hand under the front seat? What has he meant to the world? What are his plans?

Is the retirement age for bodyguards calculated as it is for other citizens? Is it earlier, fifty-five, forty-five? Is there a pension? In what amount? Those young men with dark beards staring at the Mercedes, or staring at the Citroën, who are they? Does the bodyguard pay heed to the complaints of his fellow bodyguards about the hours spent waiting outside this or that Ministry, this or that Headquarters, hours spent propped against the fenders of the Mercedes while their principal is within the (secure) walls? Is the thick glass of these specially prepared vehicles thick enough? Are his fellow bodyguards reliable? Is the new one reliable?

Is the bodyguard frightened by young women of good family? Young women of good family whose handbags contain God knows what? Does the bodyguard feel that the situation is *unfair*? Will the son of the bodyguard, living with his mother in a city far away, himself become a bodyguard? When the bodyguard delivers the son of his principal to the school where all of the children are delivered by bodyguards, does he stop at a grocer's on the way and buy the child a peach? Does he buy himself a peach?

Will the bodyguard, if tested, be equal to his task? Does the bodyguard know which foreign concern was the successful bidder for the construction of his country's nuclear reprocessing plant? Does the bodyguard know which sections of the National Bank's yearly report on debt service have been falsified? Does the bodyguard know that the general amnesty of April coincided with the rearrest of sixty persons? Does the bodyguard know that the new, liberalized press laws of May were a provocation? Does the bodyguard patronize a restaurant called the Crocodile? A place packed with young, loud, fat Communists? Does he spill a drink, to disclose his spite? Is his gesture understood?

Are the streets full of stilt-walkers? Stilt-walkers weaving ten feet above the crowd in great papier-mâché bird heads, black and red costumes, whipping thirty feet of colored cloth above the heads of the crowd, miming the rape of a young female personage symbolizing his country? In the Mercedes, the bodyguard and his colleague stare at the hundreds, men and women, young and old, who move around the Mercedes, stopped for a light, as if it were a rock in a river. In the rear seat, the patron is speaking into a telephone. He looks up, puts down the telephone. The people pressing around the car cannot be counted, there are too many of them; they cannot be known, there are too many of them; they cannot be predicted, they have volition. Then, an opening. The car accelerates.

Is it the case that, on a certain morning, the garbage cans of the city, the garbage cans of the entire country, are overflowing with empty champagne bottles? Which bodyguard is at fault?

The Zombies

In a high wind the leaves fall from the trees. The zombies are standing about talking. "Beautiful day!" "Certainly is!" The zombies have come to buy wives from the people of this village, the only village for miles around that will sell wives to zombies. "Beautiful day!" "Certainly is!" The zombies have brought many cattle. The bride-price to a zombie is exactly twice that asked of an ordinary man. The cattle are also zombies and the zombies are in terror lest the people of the village understand this.

These are good zombies. Gris Grue said so. They are painted white all over. Bad zombies are unpainted and weep with their noses, their nostrils spewing tears. The village chief calls the attention of the zombies to the fine brick buildings of the village, some of them one thousand bricks high—daughters peering from the windows, green plants in some windows and, in others, daughters. "You must promise not to tell the Bishop," say the zombies, "promise not to tell the Bishop, beautiful day, certainly is."

The white-painted zombies chatter madly, in the village square, in an impersonation of gaiety. "Bought a new coat!" "You did!" "Yes, bought a new coat, this coat I'm wearing, I think it's very fine!" "Oh it is, it is, yes I think so!" The cattle kick at the chain-link fence of the corral. The kiss of a dying animal, a dying horse or dog, transforms an ordinary man into a zombie. The owner of the ice-cream shop has two daughters. The crayfish farmer has five daughters, and the captain of the soccer team, whose parents are dead, has a sister. Gris Grue is not here. He is away in another country, seeking a specific for deadly nightshade. A zombie with a rectal thermometer is creeping around in the corral, under the bellies of the large, bluish-brown animals. Someone says the Bishop has been seen riding in his car at full speed toward the village.

If a bad zombie gets you, he will weep on you, or take away your whiskey, or hurt your daughter's bones. There are too many daughters in the square, in the windows of the buildings, and not enough husbands. If a bad zombie gets you, he will scratch your white paint with awls and scarifiers. The good zombies skitter and dance. "Did you see that lady? Would that lady marry me? I don't know! Oh what a pretty lady! Would that lady marry me? I don't know!" The beer distributor has set up a keg of beer in the square. The local singing teacher is singing. The zombies say: "Wonderful time! Beautiful day! Marvelous singing! Excellent beer! Would that lady marry me? I don't know!" In a high wind the leaves fall from the trees, from the trees.

The zombie hero Gris Grue said: "There are good zombies and bad zombies, as there are good and bad ordinary men." Gris Grue said that many of the zombies known to him were clearly zombies of the former kind and thus eminently fit, in his judgment, to engage in trade, lead important enterprises, hold posts in the government, and participate in the mysteries of Baptism, Confirmation, Ordination, Marriage, Penance, the Eucharist, and Extreme Unction. The Bishop said no. The zombies sent many head of cattle to the Bishop. The Bishop said, everything but Ordination. If a bad zombie gets you, he will create insult in your bladder. The bad zombies banged the Bishop's car with a dead cow, at night. In the morning the Bishop had to pull the dead zombie cow from the windscreen of his car, and cut his hand. Gris Grue decides who is a good zombie and who is a bad zombie; when he is away, his wife's mother decides. A zombie advances toward a group of thin blooming daughters and describes, with many motions of his hands and arms, the breakfasts they may expect in a zombie home.

"Monday!" he says. "Sliced oranges boiled grits fried croakers potato croquettes radishes watercress broiled spring chicken batter cakes butter syrup and café au lait! Tuesday! Grapes hominy broiled tenderloin of trout steak French-fried potatoes celery fresh rolls butter and café au lait! Wednesday! Iced figs Wheatena porgies with sauce tartare potato chips broiled ham scrambled eggs French toast and café au lait! Thursday! Bananas with cream oatmeal broiled patassas fried liver with bacon poached eggs on toast waffles with syrup and café au lait! Friday! Strawberries with cream broiled oysters on toast celery fried perch lyonnaise potatoes cornbread with syrup and café au lait! Saturday! Muskmelon on ice grits stewed tripe herb omelette olives snipe on toast flannel cakes with syrup and café au lait!" The zombie draws a long breath. "Sunday!" he says. "Peaches with cream cracked wheat with milk broiled Spanish mackerel with sauce maître d'hôtel creamed chicken beaten biscuits broiled woodcock on English muffin rice cakes potatoes à la duchesse eggs Benedict oysters on the half shell broiled lamb chops pound cake with syrup and café au lait! And imported champagne!" The zombies look anxiously at the women to see if this prospect is pleasing.

A houngan (zombie-maker) grasps a man by the hair and forces his lips close to those of a dying cat. If you do heavy labor for a houngan for ten years, then you are free, but still a zombie. The Bishop's car is working well. No daughter of this village has had in human memory a true husband, or anything like it. The daughters are tired of kissing each other, although some are not. The fathers of the village are tired of paying for their daughters' sewing machines, lowboys, and towels. A bald zombie says, "Oh what a pretty lady! I would be nice to her! Yes I would! I think so!" Bad zombies are leaning against the walls of the buildings, watching. Bad zombies are allowed, by law, to mate only with sheep ticks. The women do not want the zombies, but zombies are their portion. A woman says to another woman: "These guys are zombies!" "Yes," says the second woman, "I saw a handsome man, he had his picture in the paper, but he is not here." The zombie in the corral finds a temperature of a hundred and ten degrees.

The villagers are beating upon huge drums with mops. The Bishop arrives in his great car with white episcopal flags flying from the right and left fenders. "Forbidden, forbidden, forbidden!" he cries. Gris Grue appears on a silver sled and places his hands over the Bishop's eyes. At the moment of sunset the couples, two by two, are wed. The corral shudders as the cattle collapse. The new wives turn to their new husbands and say: "No matter. This is what we must do. We will paste photographs of the handsome man in the photograph on your faces, when it is time to go to bed. Now let us cut the cake." The good zombies say, "You're welcome! You're very welcome! I think so! Undoubtedly!" The bad zombies place sheep ticks in the Bishop's car. If a bad zombie gets you, he will scarify your hide with chisels and rakes. If a bad zombie gets you, he will make you walk past a beautiful breast without even noticing.

Morning

—Say you're frightened. Admit it.
—In Colorado, by the mountains. In California, by the sea. Everywhere, by breaking glass.
—Say you're frightened. Confess.
—Timid as a stag. They've got a meter wired to my sheet, I don't know what it measures. I get a dollar a night. When I wake suddenly, I notice it's there. I watch my hand aging, sing a little song.
—Were you invited to the party?
—Yes, I was. Stood there smiling. I thought, Those are tight pants, how kind of her. Wondered if she was orange underneath. What shall we do? Call up Mowgli? Ask him over? Do you like tongue? Sliced? With mushrooms? Is it a private matter? Is Scriabin as smart as he looks? This man's a fool—why are you talking to him? Yes, his clothes are interesting, but inside are dull bones.
—This gray light, I don't see how you stand it.
—A firestorm of porn all around—orange images, dunes and deserts. Bursts of quarreling through the walls. I wonder who the people are? I tried that Cuisine Minceur, didn't like it. Oh, it looks pretty—
—Say you're frightened.
—I'm frightened. By flutes and flower girls and sirens. We get a lot of sirens because of the hospital. By coffee, dead hanging plants, people who think too fast, vestments and bells.
—Get some Vitamin E. I take eight hundred units.
—The sound of glass breaking. I thought, Oh Christ, not again. The last time they got a bicycle, fancy Japanese bicycle somebody'd left in the hall. We changed the lock. Guy left his crowbar. Actually it wasn't a crowbar it was a jack handle.
—I'm not afraid of crime, there's got to be crime, it's the manner or mode that—I mean if they could just take it out of your bank account, by punching a few buttons or something . . .

—I'm not afraid of snakes. There was a snake-handling bunch where we spent the summers. I used to go to their meetings now and again, do a little handling.

—Not afraid of the mail, not so much as I used to be, all those threatening letters, I just say sticks and stones, sticks and stones, see the triage nurse.

—It's only when you stop to think about it. I don't stop.

—Not afraid of hurricanes because we used to have them, where I lived, not afraid of tarantulas, used to have them too, they jump, have to chop them up with a hoe, long-handled hoe as opposed to the stoop hoe, by preference.

—Nature in general not seen as antipathetic. Nor are other people, except for those who want to slap your ears back without first presenting their carefully reasoned, red-white-and-blue threats.

—Behavior in general a wonderful sea, in which we can swim, or leap, or stumble.

—She got out of bed and, doing a cute little walk, walked to the bathroom. I dreaded the day I would see her real walk.

—There's the sunset gun. That means we can loosen up and get friendly. Think we can get any of that government money?

—I sent for the forms. Merrily merrily merrily merrily.

—Think we can get us some of that good per diem?

—If you decide to run for it a bus is better. No one's seated facing you. They've got bigger windows now, and the drivers are usually reliable.

—Well that's one thing I want to stay away from. Flight, I mean. Too much like defeat.

—But when I get to all these strange places they seem empty. Nobody on the streets and I'm not used to that. Their restaurants all have the same things: filet, surf 'n' turf, prime rib. Spend a few days in a hotel and then check out, leaving a dollar or two for the maids.

—Turkeying around trying to get situated.

—Searching the room for someone to go to bed with. What if she agrees?

—That's happened to me several times. You just have to be honest.

—The love of gain is insatiable. This is true.

—What are you afraid of? Mornings, noons, or nights?

—Mornings. I send out a lot of postcards.

—Take a picture of this exceptionally dirty window. Its grays. I think I can get you a knighthood, I know a guy. What about the Eternal Return?

—Distant, distant, distant. Thanks for calling Jim it was good to talk to you.

—They played "One O'Clock Jump," "Two O'Clock Jump," "Three O'Clock Jump," and "Four O'Clock Jump." They were very good. I saw them on television. They're all dead now.

—That scare you?

—Naw that doesn't scare me.

—That scare you?

—Naw that doesn't scare me.

—What scares you?

—My hand scares me. It's not well.

—Hear that? That's wolf talk. Not bad is it?

—Scarcely had I reloaded when a black rhinoceros, a female as it proved, stood drinking at the water.

—Let me give you a hint: *Find me one animal that is capable of personal friendship.*

—So I decided it was about time we got gay. I changed the record, that helped, and fiddled with the lights—

—Call up Bomba the Jungle Boy? Get his input?

—Fixed up the Kool-Aid with some stuff I had with me. Complicated the decor with carefully placed items of lawn furniture, birdbaths, sundials, mirrored globes on stands . . .

—That set toes to tapping, did it?

—They were pleased. We danced Inventions & Sinfonias. It wasn't bad. It was a success.

—It is this that the new portraits are intended to celebrate.

—Then, out of another chute, the bride appeared, caracoling and sunfishing across the arena.

—I knew her. I was very fond of her. I am very fond of her. I wish them well.

—As do I. She's brave.

—Think we can get some of that fine grant money?

—If we can make ourselves understood. If I applaud, the actors understand that I am pleased. If I take a needle and singe it with a match, you understand that I have picked up a splinter in my foot. If I say "Have any of the English residents been murdered?," you understand that I am cognizant of native unrest. If I hand you two copies of a thesis bound in black cloth, you understand that I am trying to improve myself. Appeals to patriotism, small-boat warnings up.

—Say you're frightened.

—I'm frightened. But maybe not tomorrow.

—Well that's one thing I want to stay away from. You can get mad instead. I got mad, really got mad.

—Put-on anger. A technique of managers.

—Got so mad I coulda bit a chisel in two.

—And very graciously. Skin of dreams, paint marks, red scratches, grass stains. We watched *60 Minutes*. Fed on ixias, wild garlic, the core of aloes, gum of acacias. She's gone now, took an early plane. How do I feel? O.K.

—Another bright glorious day. How do you feel? Have you tried to get a drink on one of these new trains? It's as easy as pie. Have you got anything we could put over the windows? Tarpaper or maybe some boards? Do you want to hear "The Battle Hymn of the Republic"? Is there any more of this red?

—Jugs and jugs. Two weeks would do it, two weeks in a VW Rabbit.

—Going home.

—No, thank you.

—You're afraid of it?

—Indeed, do I still live?

—What are you afraid of?

—One old man alone in a room. Two old men alone in a room. Three old men alone in a room.

—Well maybe you could talk to them or something.

—And say: Howdy, have you heard about pleasure, have you heard about fun? Let's go out and bust up a bar, it's been a long time. What are you up to, what are your plans? Still lifting weights? I've been screwing all night, how 'bout you? "You please me, happiness!"

—Well I don't think about this stuff a lot of the time.

—Humility is barefoot, Lewdness is physically attractive and holds a sprig of colewort, the Hour is a wheel, and Courage is strangling a lion, by shoving a mailed fist down its throat.

—How did the party end?

—I wasn't there. Got to scat, I said, got to get away, got to creep, it's that time of night. Matthew, Mark, Luke, and John, bless the bed that I lie on.

—Say you're frightened.

—Less and less. I have a smoke detector and tickets to everywhere. I have a guardian angel blind from birth and a packet of Purple-top White Globe turnip seeds, for the roof.

—Want to see my collection of bass clarinets? Want to see my collection of painters' ears? This gray light, I don't see how you stand it.

—I grayed it up myself. Sets off the orange.

—A fine person. Took the Fire Department exam and passed it. That's just one example.

—All women are mortal, she explained to me, and Caius is a woman.

—Say you're not frightened. Inspire me.

—After a while, darkness, and they give up the search.

On the Steps of the Conservatory

—C'MON HILDA don't fret.
—Well Maggie it's a blow.
—Don't let it bother you, don't let it get you down.
—Once I thought they were going to admit me to the Conservatory but now I know they will never admit me to the Conservatory.
—Yes they are very particular about who they admit to the Conservatory. They will never admit you to the Conservatory.
—They will never admit me to the Conservatory, I know that now.
—You are not Conservatory material I'm afraid. That's the plain truth of it.
—You're not important, they told me, just remember that, you're not important, what's so important about you? What?
—C'mon Hilda don't fret.
—Well Maggie it's a blow.
—When are you going to change yourself, change yourself into a loaf or a fish?
—Christian imagery is taught at the Conservatory, also Islamic imagery and the imagery of Public Safety.
—Red, yellow, and green circles.
—When they told me I got between the poles of my rickshaw and trotted heavily away.
—The great black ironwork doors of the Conservatory barred to you forever.
—Trotted heavily away in the direction of my house. My small, poor house.
—C'mon Hilda don't fret.
—Yes, I am still trying to get into the Conservatory, although my chances are probably worse than ever.
—They don't want pregnant women in the Conservatory.
—I didn't tell them, I lied about it.
—Didn't they ask you?
—No they forgot to ask me and I didn't tell them.
—Well then it's hardly on that account that—

—I felt they knew.
—The Conservatory is hostile to the new spirit, the new spirit is not liked there.
—Well Maggie it's a blow nevertheless. I had to go back to my house.
—Where although you entertain the foremost artists and intellectuals of your time you grow progressively more despondent and depressed.
—Yes he was a frightful lawyer.
—Lover?
—That too, frightful. He said he could not get me into the Conservatory because of my unimportance.
—Was there a fee?
—There's always a fee. Pounds and pounds.
—I stood on the terrace at the rear of the Conservatory and studied the flagstones reddened with the lifebloods of generations of Conservatory students. Standing there I reflected: Hilda will never be admitted to the Conservatory.
—I read the Conservatory Circular and my name was not among those listed.
—Well I suppose it was in part your espousal of the new spirit that counted against you.
—I will never abjure the new spirit.
—And you're a veteran too, I should have thought that would have weighed in your favor.
—Well Maggie it's a disappointment, I must admit that frankly.
—C'mon Hilda don't weep and tear your hair here where they can see you.
—Are they looking out of the windows?
—Probably they're looking out of the windows.
—It's said that they import a cook, on feast days.
—They have naked models too.
—Do you really think so? I'm not surprised.
—The best students get their dinners sent up on trays.
—Do you really think so? I'm not surprised.
—Grain salads and large portions of choice meats.
—Oh it hurts, it hurts, it hurts.
—Bread with drippings, and on feast days cake.
—I'm as gifted as they are, I'm as gifted as some of them.

—Decisions made by a committee of ghosts. They drop black beans or white beans into a pot.

—Once I thought I was to be admitted. There were encouraging letters.

—You're not Conservatory material I'm afraid. Only the best material is Conservatory material.

—I'm as good as some of those who rest now in the soft Conservatory beds.

—Merit is always considered closely.

—I could smile back at the smiling faces of the swift, dangerous teachers.

—Yes, we have naked models. No, the naked models are not emotionally meaningful to us.

—I could work with clay or paste things together.

—Yes, sometimes we paste things on the naked models— clothes, mostly. Yes, sometimes we play our Conservatory violins, cellos, trumpets for the naked models, or sing to them, or correct their speech, as our deft fingers fly over the sketch pads . . .

—I could I suppose fill out another application, or several.

—Yes, you have considerable of a belly on you now. I remember when it was flat, flat as a book.

—I will die if I don't get into the Conservatory, die.

—Naw you won't you're just saying that.

—I will completely croak if I don't get into the Conservatory, I promise you.

—Things are not so bad, you can always do something else, I don't know what, c'mon Hilda be reasonable.

—My whole life depends on it.

—Oh God I remember when it was flat. Didn't we tear things up, though? I remember running around that town, and hiding in dark places, that was a great town and I'm sorry we left it.

—Now we are grown, grown and proper.

—Well, I misled you. The naked models are emotionally meaningful to us.

—They are?

—We love them and sleep with them all the time—before breakfast, after breakfast, during breakfast.

—Why that's all right!

—Why that's rather neat!
—I like that!
—That's not so bad!
—I wish you hadn't told me that.
—C'mon Hilda don't be so single-minded, there are lots of other things you can do if you want.
—I guess they operate on some kind of principle of exclusivity. Keeping some people out while letting other people in.
—We got a Coushatta Indian in there, real full-blooded Coushatta Indian.
—In there?
—Yes. He does hanging walls out of scraps of fabric and twigs, very beautiful, and he does sand paintings and plays on whistles of various kinds, sometimes he chants, and he bangs on a drum, works in silver, and he's also a weaver, and he translates things from Coushatta into English and from English into Coushatta and he's also a crack shot and can bulldog steers and catch catfish on trotlines and ride bareback and make medicine out of common ingredients, aspirin mostly, and he sings and he's also an actor. He's very talented.
—My whole life depends on it.
—Listen Hilda maybe you could be an Associate. We have this deal whereby you pay twelve bucks a year and that makes you an Associate. You get the Circular and have all the privileges of an Associate.
—What are they?
—You get the Circular.
—That's all?
—Well I guess you're right.
—I'm just going to sit here I'm not going to go away.
—Your distress is poignant to me.
—I'll have the baby right here right on these steps.
—Well maybe there'll be good news one of these days.
—I feel like a dead person sitting in a chair.
—You're still pretty and attractive.
—That's good to hear I'm pleased you think that.
—And warm you're warm you're very warm.
—Yes I have a warm nature very warm.
—Weren't you in the Peace Corps also years ago?
—I was and drove ambulances too down in Nicaragua.

—The Conservatory life is just as halcyon as you imagine it—precisely so.
—I guess I'll just have to go back to my house and clean up, take out the papers and the trash.
—I guess that kid'll be born one of these days, right?
—Continue working on my études no matter what they say.
—That's admirable I think.
—The thing is not to let your spirit be conquered.
—I guess that kid'll be born after a while, right?
—I guess so. Those boogers are really gonna keep me out of there, you know that?
—Their minds are inflexible and rigid.
—Probably because I'm a poor pregnant woman don't you think?
—You said you didn't tell them.
—But maybe they're very shrewd psychologists and they could just look at my face and tell.
—No it doesn't show yet how many months are you?
—Two and a half just about you can tell when I take my clothes off.
—You didn't take your clothes off did you?
—No I was wearing you know what the students wear. Jeans and a sarape. I carried a green book bag.
—Jam-packed with études.
—Yes. He asked where I had gotten my previous training and I told him.
—Oh boy I remember when it was flat, flat as the deck of something, a boat or a ship.
—You're not important, they told me.
—Oh sweetie I am so sorry for you.
—We parted then I walking through the gorgeous Conservatory light into the foyer and then through the great black ironwork Conservatory doors.
—I was a face on the other side of the glass.
—My aspect as I departed most dignified and serene.
—Time heals everything.
—No it doesn't.
—Cut lip fat lip puffed lip split lip.
—Haw! haw! haw! haw!
—Well Hilda there are other things in life.

—Yes Maggie I suppose there are. None that I want.

—Non-Conservatory people have their own lives. We Conservatory people don't have much to do with them but we are told they have their own lives.

—I suppose I could file an appeal if there's anywhere to file an appeal to. If there's anywhere.

—That's an idea we get stacks of appeals, stacks and stacks.

—I can wait all night. Here on the steps.

—I'll sit with you. I'll help you formulate the words.

—Are they looking out of the windows?

—Yes I think so. What do you want to say?

—I want to say my whole life depends on it. Something like that.

—It's against the rules for Conservatory people to help non-Conservatory people you know that.

—Well Goddammit I thought you were going to help me.

—Okay. I'll help you. What do you want to say?

—I want to say my whole life depends on it. Something like that.

—We got man naked models and woman naked models, harps, giant potted plants, and drapes. There are hierarchies, some people higher up and others lower down. These mingle, in the gorgeous light. We have lots of fun. There's lots of green furniture you know with paint on it. Worn green paint. Gilt lines one-quarter inch from the edges. Worn gilt lines.

—And probably flambeaux in little niches in the walls, right?

—Yeah we got flambeaux. Who's the father?

—Guy named Robert.

—Did you have a good time?

—The affair ran the usual course. Fever, boredom, trapped.

—Hot, rinse, spin dry.

—Is it wonderful in there Maggie?

—I have to say it is. Yes. It is.

—Do you feel great, being there? Do you feel wonderful?

—Yes, it feels pretty good. Very often there is, upon the tray, a rose.

—I will never be admitted to the Conservatory.

—You will never be admitted to the Conservatory.

—How do I look?

—Okay. Not bad. Fine.

—I will never get there. How do I look?
—Fine. Great. Time heals everything Hilda.
—No it doesn't.
—Time heals everything.
—No it doesn't. How do I look?
—Moot.

The Leap

—TODAY WE make the leap to faith. Today.
—Today?
—Today.
—We're really going to do it? At last?
—Spent too much time fooling around. Today we do it.
—I don't know. Maybe we're not ready?
—I am cheered by the wine of possibility and the growing popularity of light. Today's the day.
—You're serious.
—Intensely. First, we examine our consciences.
—I am a double-minded man. Have always been a double-minded man.
—Each examining his own conscience, rooting out, naming, remembering and re-experiencing every last little cank and wrinkle. Root and branch.
—Smiting each conscience hip and thigh.
—Thigh and hip. Smite! Smite!
—God is good and we are but poor wretches who—
—Wait.
—Poor slovening wretches who but for the goodness of God would—
—Wait. This will be painful, you know. A bit.
—Oh my God.
—What?
—I just had a thought.
—A prick of conscience.
—Yes. Item 34.
—What's Item 34?
—An unkindness. One of a series. Series long as your arm.
—You list them separately.
—Yes.
—You don't just throw them all together into a great big trash bag labeled—
—No. I sweat each one. Seriatim.
—I said it would be painful.

—Might we postpone it?
—Meditate instead on His works? Their magnificence.
—Not that we could in a hundred million years exhaust—
—It's a sort of if-a-bird-took-one-grain-of-sand-and-flew-all-his-life-and-then-another-bird-took-another-grain-of-sand-and-flew-all-his-life situation.
—Contemplate only the animals. Restrict the field. 'Course we got over a million species, so far. New ones being identified every day. Insects, mostly.
—I like plants better than animals.
—Animals give you a lot of warmth. A dog would be an example.
—I like people better than plants, plants better than animals, paintings better than animals, and music better than animals.
—Praising the animals, then, would not be your first impulse.
—I *respect* the animals. I *admire* the animals. But could we contemplate something else?
—Take a glass of water, for example. A glass of water is a miraculous thing.
—The blue of the sky, against which we find the shocking green of the leaves of the trees.
—The trees. "I think that I shall never see slash A poem lovely as a tree."
—"A tree whose hungry mouth is prest slash Against the earth's sweet flowing breast."
—Why "mouth"?
—Why "breast"?
—The working of the creative mind.
—An unfathomable mystery.
—Never to be fathomed.
—I wouldn't even want to fathom it. If one fathomed it, who can say what frightful things might thereupon be fathomed?
—Fathoming such is beyond the powers of poor ravening noodles like ourselves, who but for the—
—And another thing. The human voice.
—My God you're right. The human voice.
—Bessie Smith.
—Alice Babs.
—Joan Armatrading.

—Aretha Franklin.
—Each voice testifying to the greater honor and glory of God, each in its own way.
—Damn straight.
—Sweet Emma Barrett the Bell Gal.
—Got you.
—*Das Lied von der Erde.*
—I couldn't agree more.
—Then there are the bad things. Cancer.
—An unfathomable mystery, at this point. But one which must inevitably succumb to the inexorable forward march of scientific progress.
—Economic inequality.
—In my view, this will be ameliorated in the near future by the pressure of population growth. Pressure of population growth being such that economic inequality simply cannot endure.
—What about Z.P.G.?
—An ideal rather than a social slash political reality.
—So God's creatures, in your opinion, multiplying and multiplying and multiplying as per instruction, will—
—Propagate fiercely until the sum total of what has been propagated yields a pressure so intense that every feature great or small of every life great or small is instantly scrutinized weighed judged decided upon and disposed of by the sum total of one's peers in doubtless electronic ongoing all-seeing everlasting congress assembled. Thus if one guy has a little advantage, a little edge, it is instantly taken away from him and similarly if another guy has a little lack, some little lack, this little lack is instantly supplied, by the arbiters. Things cannot be otherwise. Because there's not going to be any room to fucking *move*, man, do you follow me? there's not going to be any room to fucking *sneeze*, without you're sneezing *on* somebody . . .
—This is the Divine plan?
—Who can know the subtle workings of His mind? But it seems to be the way events are—
—That's another thing. The human mind.
—Good God yes. The human mind.

—The human mind which is in my judgment the finest of our human achievements.

—Much the finest. I can think of nothing remotely comparable.

—Is a flower, however beautiful and interesting, comparable to the human mind? I think not.

—Matter of higher and lower levels of complexity.

—I concur. This is not to knock the flower.

—This is not to say that the beautiful, interesting flower is not, in its own terms, entirely fantastic.

—The toast of the earth. Did I ever tell you about that time when I was in Korea and Cardinal Spellman came to see us at Christmas and his plane was preceded by another plane broadcasting sacred music over the terrain? Spraying the terrain as it were with sacred music?

—So that those on earth could hear and be edified.

—"O Little Town of Bethlehem."

—Yes, the human mind deserves the greatest respect. Not so good of course as the Divine mind, but not bad.

—Leibniz. William of Ockham. Maimonides. The Vienna Circle. The Frankfurt School. Manichaeus. Peirce. Occasionalism. A pretty array. I believe Occasionalism's been discredited. But let it stand. It was a nice try, and philosophy, as my dear teacher taught me so long long ago, is not to be regarded as a graveyard of dead systems.

—The question of suicide. Self-slaughter. Maybe we ought to think about it?

—What's to think about?

—Look at this.

—What is it?

—The bill.

—For what is it the bill?

—A try.

—Whose?

—An acquaintance.

—Good God.

—Yes.

—Ought two slash twenty-four electrocardiogram ought two ought ought ought ought one, thirty-five bucks.

—Ought two slash twenty-four cardiopulmonary two ought ought ought ought ought one, forty bucks.

—Ought two slash twenty-four inhalation therapy one four ought ought ought ought one, sixty bucks.

—Ought two slash twenty-four room four nine one five, a neat one-eighty.

—It goes on for miles.

—What's the total?

—Shade under two thousand. Nineteen hundred and two dollars and ninety cents.

—You'd think they'd give you the ninety cents.

—You'd think they would.

—And the acquaintance?

—She's well.

—This being an example of the leap away from faith.

—Exactly. You can jump either way.

—Shall we examine our consciences now?

—You are mad with hurry.

—We are but poor lapsarian futiles whose preen glands are all out of whack and who but for the grace of God's goodness would—

—Do you think He wants us to grovel quite so much?

—I don't think He gives a rap. But it's traditional.

—We hang by a slender thread.

—The fire boils below us.

—The pit. Crawling with roaches and other things.

—Tortures unimaginable, but the worst the torture of knowing it could have been otherwise, had we shaped up.

—Purity of heart is to will one thing.

—No. Here I differ with Kierkegaard. Purity of heart is, rather, to will several things, and not know which is the better, truer thing, and to worry about this, forever.

—A continuing itch of the mind.

—Sometimes assuagable by timely masturbation.

—I forgot. Love.

—Oh my God, yes. Love. Both human and divine.

—Love, the highest form of human endeavor.

—Coming or going, the absolute zenith.

—Is it *permitted* to differ with Kierkegaard?

—Not only permitted but necessary. If you love him.

—Love, which is a kind of permission to come closer than ordinary norms of good behavior might usually sanction.

—Back rubs.

—Which enables us to see each other without clothes on, for example, in lust and shame.

—Examining perfections, imperfections.

—Which allows us to say wounding things to each other which would not be kosher under the ordinary rules of civilized discourse.

—Walkin' my baby back home.

—Love which allows us to live together male and female in small grubby apartments that would only hold one sane person, normally.

—Misting the plants together—the handsome, talented plants.

—He who hath not love is a sad cookie.

—This is the way, walk ye in it. Isaiah 30:21.

—Can't make it, man.

—What?

—I can't make it.

—The leap.

—Can't make it. I am a double-minded man.

—Well.

—An incorrigibly double-minded man.

—What then?

—Keep on trying?

—Yes. We must.

—Try again another day?

—Yes. Another day when the plaid cactus is watered, when the hare's-foot fern is watered.

—Seeds tingling in the barrens and veldts.

—Garden peas yellow or green wrinkling or rounding.

—Another day when locust wings are baled for shipment to Singapore, where folks like their little hit of locust-wing tea.

—A jug of wine. Then another jug.

—The Brie-with-pepper meeting the toasty loaf.

—Another day when some eighty-four-year-old guy complains that his wife no longer gives him presents.

—Small boys bumping into small girls, purposefully.

—Cute little babies cracking people up.
—Another day when somebody finds a new bone that proves we are even ancienter than we thought we were.
—Gravediggers working in the cool early morning.
—A walk in the park.
—Another day when the singing sunlight turns you every way but loose.
—When you accidentally notice the sublime.
—Somersaults and duels.
—Another day when you see a woman with really red hair. I mean really red hair.
—A wedding day.
—A plain day.
—So we'll try again? Okay?
—Okay.
—Okay?
—Okay.

Great Days

—When I was a little girl I made mud pies, dangled strings down crayfish holes hoping the idiot crayfish would catch hold and allow themselves to be hauled into the light. Snarled and cried, ate ice cream and sang "How High the Moon." Popped the wings off crickets and floated stray Scrabble pieces in ditch water. All perfect and ordinary and perfect.

—Featherings of ease and bliss.

—I was preparing myself. Getting ready for the great day.

—Icy day with salt on all the sidewalks.

—Sketching attitudes and forming pretty speeches.

—Pitching pennies at a line scraped in the dust.

—Doing and redoing my lustrous abundant hair.

—Man down. Center and One Eight.

—Tied flares to my extremities and wound candy canes into my lustrous, abundant hair. Getting ready for the great day.

—For I do not deny that I am a little out of temper.

—Glitches in the system as yet unapprehended.

—Oh that clown band. Oh its sweet strains.

—Most excellent and dear friend. Who the silly season's named for.

—My demands were not met. One, two, three, four.

—I admire your dash and address. But regret your fear and prudence.

—Always worth making the effort, always.

—Yes that's something we do. Our damnedest. They can't take that away from us.

—The Secretary of State cares. And the Secretary of Commerce.

—Yes they're clued in. We are not unprotected. Soldiers and policemen.

—Man down. Corner of Mercer and One Six.

—Paying lots of attention. A clear vision of what can and can't be done.

—Progress extending far into the future. Dams and aqueducts. The amazing strength of the powerful.

—Organizing our deepest wishes as a mother foresightedly visits a store that will be closed tomorrow.
—Friendship's the best thing.
—One of the best things. One of the very best.
—I performed in a hall. Alone under the burning lights.
—The hall ganged with admiring faces. Except for a few.
—Julia was there. Rotten Julia.
—But I mean you really like her don't you?
—Well I mean who doesn't like violet eyes?
—Got to make the effort, scratch where it itches, plans, schemes, directives, guidelines.
—Well I mean who doesn't like frisky knees?
—Yes she's lost her glow. Gone utterly.
—The strains of the city working upon an essentially nonurban sensibility.
—But I love the city and will not hear it traduced.
—Well, me too. But after all. But still.
—Think Julia's getting it on with Bally.
—Yeah I heard about that he's got a big mouth.
—But handsome hip bones got to give him that.
—I remember, I can feel them still, pressing into me as they once did on hot afternoons and cool nights and feverish first-thing-in-the-mornings.
—Yes, Bally is a regal memory for everyone.
—My best ghost. The one I think about, in bitter times and good.
—Trying to get my colors together. Trying to play one off against another. Trying for cancellation.
—I respect your various phases. Your sweet, even discourse.
—I spent some time away and found everyone there affable, gentle, and good.
—Nonculminating kind of ultimately affectless activity.
—Which you mime so gracefully in auditoria large and small.
—And yet with my really wizard! good humor and cheerful thoughtless mien, I have caused a lot of trouble.
—I suppose that's true. Strictly speaking.
—Bounding into the woods on all fours barking like a mother biting at whatever moves in front of me—
—Do you also save string?
—On my free evenings and paid holidays. Making the most

of the time I have here on this earth. Knotting, sewing, weaving, welding.

—Naming babies, Lou, Lew, Louis.

—And his toes, wonderful toes, that man has got toes.

—Decorated with rings and rubber bands.

—Has a partiality for white. White gowns, shifts, aprons, flowers, sauces.

—He was a salty dog all right. Salty dog.

—I was out shooting with him once, pheasant, he got one, with his fancy shotgun. The bird bursting like an exploding pillow.

—Have to stand there and watch them, their keen eyes scanning the whatever. And then say "Good shot!"

—Oh I could have done better, better, I was lax.

—Or worse, don't fret about it, could have put your cute little butt in worse places, in thrall to dismaler personalities.

—I was making an effort. What I do best.

—You are excellent at it. Really first-rate.

—Never fail to knock myself out. Put pictures on the walls and pads under the rugs.

—I really admire you. I really do. To the teeth.

—Bust your ass, it's the only way.

—As we learn from studying the careers of all the great figures of the past. Heraclitus and Launcelot du Lac.

—Polish the doorknobs with Brasso and bring in the sea bass in its nest of seaweed.

—And not only that. And not only that.

—Tickling them when they want to be tickled. Abstaining, when they do not.

—Large and admirable men. Not neglecting the small and ignoble. Dealing evenhandedly with every situation on a case-by-case basis.

—Yeah yeah yeah yeah yeah.

—Knew a guy wore his stomach on his sleeve. I dealt with the problem using astrology in its medical aspects. His stomach this, his stomach that, God Almighty but it was tiresome, tiresome in the extreme. I dealt with it by using astrology in its medical aspects.

—To each his own. Handmade bread and individual attention.

—You've got to have something besides yourself. A cat, too often.

—I could have done better but I was dumb. When you're young you're sometimes dumb.

—Yeah yeah yeah yeah yeah. I remember.

—Well let's have a drink.

—Well I don't mind if I do.

—I have Goldwasser, Bombay gin and Old Jeb.

—Well I wouldn't mind a Scotch myself.

—I have that too.

—Growing older and with age, less beautiful.

—Yeah I've noticed that. Losing your glow.

—Just gonna sit in the wrinkling house and wrinkle. Get older and worse.

—Once you lose your glow you never get it back.

—Sometimes by virtue of the sun on a summer's day.

—Wrinkling you so that you look like a roast turkey.

—As is the case with the Oni of Ife. Saw him on television.

—Let me show you this picture.

—Yes that's very lovely. What is it?

—It's "Vulcan and Maia."

—Yes. He's got his hooks into her. She's struggling to get away.

—Vigorously? Vigorously. Yes.

—Who's the artist?

—Spranger.

—Never heard of him.

—Well.

—Yes, you may hang it. Anywhere you like. On that wall or that wall or that wall.

—Thank you.

—Probably I can get ahead by working hard, paying attention to detail.

—I thought that. Once I thought that.

—Reading a lot of books and having good ideas.

—Well that's not bad. I mean it's a means.

—Do something wonderful. I don't know what.

—Like a bass player plucking the great thick strings of his instrument with powerful plucks.

—Blood vessels bursting in my face just under the skin all the while.

—Hurt by malicious criticisms all very well grounded.

—Washing and rewashing my lustrous, abundant hair.

—For Leatherheart, I turn my back. My lustrous, abundant back.

—That cracks them up does it?

—At least they know I'm in town.

—Ease myself into bed of an evening brain jumping with hostile fluids.

—It's greens in a pot.

—It's confetti in the swimming pool.

—It's U-joints in the vichyssoise.

—It's staggers under the moon.

—He told me terrible things in the evening of that day as we sat side by side waiting for the rain to wash the watercolors from his watercolor paper. Waiting for the rain to wash the paper clean, quite clean.

—Took me by the hand and led me through all the rooms. Many rooms.

—I know all about it.

—The kitchen is especially splendid.

—Quite so.

—A dozen Filipinos with trays.

—Close to that figure.

—Trays with edibles. Wearables. Readables. Collectibles.

—Ah, you're a fool. A damned fool.

—Goodbye, madame. Dip if you will your hand in the holy water font as you leave, and attend as well to the poor box just to the right of the door.

—Figs and kiss-me-nots. I would meet you upon this honestly.

—I went far beyond the time normally allotted for a speaker. Far.

—In Mexico City. Wearing the black jacket with the silver conchos. And trousers of fire pink.

—Visited a health club there, my rear looked like two pocketbooks, they worked on it.

—You were making an effort.

—Run in the mornings too, take green tea at noon, study household management, finance, repair of devices.

—Born with a silver hoe in your mouth.

—Yes. Got to get going, got to make some progress.

—Followed by development of head banging in the child.

—I went far beyond the time normally allotted to, or for, a speaker. It is fair to say they were enthralled. And transfixed. Inappropriate laughter at some points but I didn't mind that.

—Did the Eminence arrive?

—In a cab. In his robes of scarlet.

—He does a tough Eminence.

—Yes very tough. I was allowed to kiss the ring. He sat there, in the audience, just like another member of the audience. Just like anybody. Transfixed and enthralled.

—Whirling and jigging in the red light and throwing veils on the floor and throwing gloves on the floor—

—One of my finest. They roared for ten minutes.

—I am so proud of you. Again and again. Proud of you.

—Oh well, yes. I agree. Quite right. Absolutely.

—What? Are you sure? Are you quite sure? Let me show you this picture.

—Yes that's quite grand. What is it?

—It's "Tancred Succored by Ermina."

—Yes she's sopping up the blood there, got a big rag, seems a sweet girl, God he's out of it isn't he, dead or dying horse at upper left . . . Who's the artist?

—Ricchi.

—Never heard of him.

—Well.

—I'll take it. You may stack it with the others, against that wall or that wall or that wall—

—Thank you. Where shall I send the bill?

—Send it anywhere you like. Anywhere your little heart desires.

—Well I hate to be put in this position. Bending and subservient.

—Heavens! I'd not noticed. Let me raise you up.

—Maybe in a few days. A few days or a few years.

—Lave you with bee jelly and bone oil.

—And if I have ever forgiven you your astonishing successes—
—Mine.
—And if I have ever been able to stomach your serial triumphs—
—The sky. A rectangle of gray in the foreground and behind that, a rectangle of puce. And behind that, a square of silver gilt.
—Got to get it together, get the big bucks.
—Yes I'm thinking hard, thinking hard.
—Frolic and detour.
—What's that mean?
—I don't know just a bit of legal language I picked up somewhere.
—Now that I take a long look at you—
—In the evening by the fireside—
—I find you utterly delightful. Abide with me. We'll have little cakes with smarm, yellow smarm on them—
—Yes I just feel so fresh and free here. One doesn't feel that way every day, or every week.
—Last night at two the barking dog in the apartment above stopped barking. Its owners had returned. I went into the kitchen and barked through the roof for an hour. I believe I was understood.
—Man down. Corner of Water and Eight Nine.
—Another wallow?
—I've wallowed for today thank you. Control is the thing.
—Control used to be the thing. Now, abandon.
—I'll never achieve abandon.
—Work hard and concentrate. Try Clown, Baby, Hell-hag, Witch, the Laughing Cavalier. The Lord helps those—
—Purple bursts in my face as if purple staples had been stapled there every which way—
—Hurt by malicious criticisms all very well grounded—
—Oh that clown band. Oh its sweet strains.
—The sky. A rectangle of glister. Behind which, a serene brown. A yellow bar, vertical, in the upper right.
—I love you, Harmonica, quite exceptionally.
—By gum I think you mean it. I think you do.
—It's "Portia Wounding Her Thigh."

—It's "Wolfram Looking at His Wife Whom He Has Imprisoned with the Corpse of Her Lover."

—If you need a friend I'm yours till the end.

—Your gracious and infinitely accommodating presence.

—Julia's is the best. Best I've ever seen. The finest.

—The muscle of jealousy is not in me. Nowhere.

—Oh it is so fine. Incomparable.

—Some think one thing, some another.

—The very damn best believe me.

—Well I don't know, I haven't seen it.

—Well, would you like to see it?

—Well, I don't know, I don't know her very well do you?

—Well, I know her well enough to ask her.

—Well, why don't you ask her if it's not an inconvenience or this isn't the wrong time or something.

—Well, probably this is the wrong time come to think of it because she isn't here and some time when she is here would probably be a better time.

—Well, I would like to see it right now because just talking about it has got me in the mood to see it. If you know what I mean.

—She told me that she didn't like to be called just for that purpose, people she didn't know and maybe wouldn't like if she did know, I'm just warning you.

—Oh.

—You see.

—I see.

—I could have done better. But I don't know how. Could have done better, cleaned better or cooked better or I don't know. Better.

—You smile. And the angels sing. La la la la la la la la la la la la.

—Blew it. Blew it.

—Had a clown at the wedding he officiated standing there in his voluptuous white costume his drum and trumpet at his feet. He said, "Do you, Harry . . ." and all that. The guests applauded, the clown band played, it was a brilliant occasion.

—Our many moons of patience and accommodation. Tricks and stunts unknown to common cunts.

—The guests applauded. Above us, a great tent with red and yellow stripes.

—The unexploded pillow and the simple, blunt sheet.

—I was fecund, savagely so.

—Painting dead women by the hundreds in passionate imitation of Delacroix.

—Sailing after lunch and after sailing, gin.

—Do not go into the red barn, he said. I went into the red barn. Julia. Swinging on a rope from hayloft to tack room. Gazed at by horses with their large, accepting eyes. They somehow looked as if they knew.

—You packed hastily reaching the station just before midnight counting the pennies in your purse.

—Yes. Regaining the city, plunged once more into activities.

—You've got to have something besides yourself. A cause, interest, or goal.

—Made myself knowledgeable in certain areas, one, two, three, four. Studied the Value Line and dipped into cocoa.

—The kind of thing you do so well.

—Acquired busts of certain notables, marble, silver, bronze. The Secretary of Defense and the Chairman of the Joint Chiefs.

—Wailed a bit now and then into the ears of friends and caverns of the telephone.

—But I rallied. Rallied.

—Made an effort. Made the effort.

—To make soft what is hard. To make hard the soft. To conceal what is black with use, under new paint. Check the tomatoes with their red times, in the manual. To enspirit the spiritless. To get me a jug and go out behind the barn sharing with whoever is out behind the barn, peasant or noble.

—Sometimes I have luck. In plazas or taverns.

—Right as rain. I mean okey-dokey.

—Unless the participant affirmatively elects otherwise.

—What does that mean?

—Damfino. Just a bit of legal language I picked up somewhere.

—You are the sunshine of my life.

—Toys toys I want more toys.

—Yes, I should think you would.

—That wallow in certainty called the love affair.
—The fading gray velvet of the sofa. He clowned with my panties in his teeth. Walked around that way for half an hour.
—What's this gunk here in this bucket?
—Naw it was just another of those dumb ideas we had we thought would keep us together.
—Bone ignorance.
—Saw him once more, he was at a meeting I was at, had developed an annoying habit of coughing into his coat collar whenever he—
—Coughed.
—Yes he'd lift his coat collar and cough into it odd mannerism very annoying.
—Then the candles going out one by one—
—The last candle hidden behind the altar—
—The tabernacle door ajar—
—The clapping shut of the book.
—I got ready for the great day. The great day came, several times in fact.
—Each time with memories of the last time.
—No. These do not in fact intrude. Maybe as a slight shimmer of the over-and-done-with. Each great day is itself, with its own war machines, rattles, and green lords. There is the hesitation that the particular day won't be what it is meant to be. Mostly it is. That's peculiar.
—He told me terrible things in the evening of that day as we sat side by side waiting for the rain to wash his watercolor paper clean. Waiting for the rain to wash the watercolors from his watercolor paper.
—What do the children say?
—There's a thing the children say.
—What do the children say?
—They say: Will you always love me?
—Always.
—Will you always remember me?
—Always.
—Will you remember me a year from now?
—Yes, I will.
—Will you remember me two years from now?

—Yes, I will.
—Will you remember me five years from now?
—Yes, I will.
—Knock knock.
—Who's there?
—You see?

FROM
SIXTY STORIES

Eugénie Grandet

BALZAC'S NOVEL *Eugénie Grandet* was published in 1833. Grandet, a rich miser, has an only child, Eugénie. She falls in love with her young cousin, Charles. When she learns he is financially ruined, she lends him her savings. Charles goes to the West Indies, secretly engaged to marry Eugénie on his return. Years go by. Grandet dies and Eugénie becomes an heiress. But Charles, ignorant of her wealth, writes to ask her for his freedom: he wants to marry a rich girl. Eugénie releases him, pays his father's debts, and marries without love an old friend of the family, Judge de Bonfons.

—*The Thesaurus of Book Digests*

"Oh, oh, where's Old Grandet going so early in the morning, running as though his house were on fire?"

"He'll end up by buying the whole town of Saumur!"

"He doesn't even notice the cold, his mind is always on his business!"

"Everything he does is significant!"

"He knows the secrets and mysteries of the life and death of money!"

•

"It looks as though I'm going to be quite successful here in Saumur," thought Charles, unbuttoning his coat.

•

A great many people are interested in the question: Who will obtain Eugénie Grandet's hand?

•

Eugénie Grandet's hand:

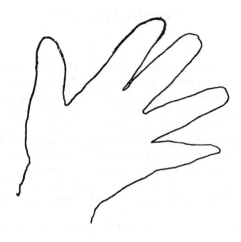

•

Judge de Bonfons arrives carrying flowers.

•

"Mother, have you noticed that this society we're in tends to be a little . . . repressive?"

"What does that mean, Eugénie? What does that mean, that strange new word, 'repressive,' that I have never heard before?"

"It means . . . it's like when you decide to do something, and you get up out of your chair to do it, and you take a step, and then become aware of frosty glances being directed at you from every side."

"Frosty glances?"

"Your desires are stifled."

"What desires are you talking about?"

"Just desires in general. Any desires. It's a whole . . . I guess atmosphere is the word . . . a tendency on the part of the society . . ."

"You'd better sew some more pillow cases, Eugénie."

•

Part of a letter:

. . . And now he's ruined a
friends will desert him, and
humiliation. Oh, I wish I ha
straight to heaven, where his
but this is madness . . . I re
that of Charles.

I have sent him to you so
news of my death to him and
in store for him. Be a father to
not tear him away from his
would kiss him. I beg him on m
which, as his mother's heir, he
But this is a superfluous ple
will realize that he must not
Persuade him to give up all his
time comes. Reveal to him th
which he must live from now
still has any love for me, tell
not lost for him. Yes, work, wh
give him back the fortune I ha
And if he is willing to listen
who for his sake would like to

•

"Please allow me to retire," Charles said. "I must begin a long and sad correspondence."

"Certainly, nephew."

•

"The painter is here from Paris!"

"Good day, painter. What is your name?"

"My name, sir, is John Graham!"

"John Graham! That is not a French name!"

"No, sir. I am an American. My dates are 1881–1961."

"Well, you have an air of competence. Is that your equipment there, on the stagecoach platform?"

"Yes. That is my equipment. That is my easel, my palette,

and my paint box containing tins of paints as well as the finest camel's-hair brushes. In this bag, here, are a few changes of clothes, for I anticipate that this portrait will take several days."

"Well, that is fine. How do you like our country?"

"It appears to be a very fine country. I imagine a lot of painting could get done in this country."

"Yes, we have some pretty good painters of our own. That is why I am surprised to find that they sent an American painter, rather than a French one, to do Mlle. Eugénie's portrait. But I'm sure you will do a first-class job. We're paying you enough."

"Yes, the fee is quite satisfactory."

"Have you brought any examples of your work, so we can see what kind of thing you do?"

"Well, in this album here . . . this is a portrait of Ellen West . . . this one is Mrs. Margot Heap . . . that's an Indian chief . . . that's Patsy Porker . . ."

"Why are they all cross-eyed?"

"Well, that's just the way I do it. I don't see anything wrong with that. It often occurs in nature."

"But *every one* is . . ."

"Well, what's so peculiar about that? I just like . . . that's just the way I do it. I *like* . . ."

•

"In my opinion, Eugénie wasn't fondled enough as a child."

"Adolphe des Grassins wasn't fondled enough either!"

"And Judge de Bonfons?"

"Who could bring himself to fondle Judge de Bonfons!"

"And Charles Grandet?"

"His history in this regard is not known. But it has been observed that he is forever *patting himself*, pat pat pat, on the hair, on the kneecap, pat pat pat pat pat pat. This implies—"

"These children need fondling!"

"The state should fondle these poor children!"

"Balzac himself wasn't fondled enough!"

"Men are fools!"

•

Eugénie Grandet with ball:

•

Charles and Eugénie understand each other.
They speak only with their eyes.
The poor ruined dandy withdraws into a corner and remains there in calm, proud silence.
But from time to time his cousin's gentle, caressing glance

•

"No more butter, Eugénie. You've already used up a whole half pound this month."
"But, Father . . . the butter for Charles's éclair!"

•

Butter butter

butter butter

•

Eugénie Grandet decides to kill her father.

•

Charles decides to try his luck in the Indies—that deadliest of climates.

•

Here, Charles, take this money of mine. This money that my father gave me. This money that if he finds out I gave it to you, all hell will break loose. I want you to have it, to finance your operations in the Indies—that deadliest of climates."

"No, Eugénie, I couldn't do that. I couldn't take your money. No, I won't do it. No."

"No, I mean it, Charles. Take the money and use it for worthy purposes. Please. See, here is a ducat, minted in 1756 and still bright as day. And here are some doubloons, worth two escudos each. And here are some shiny quadroons, of inestimable value. And here in this bag are thalers and bobs, and silver quids and copper bawbees. Altogether, nearly six thousand francs. Take it, it's yours."

"No, Eugénie, I can't take your money. I can't do it."

"No, Charles, take my money. My little hoard."

"OK."

•

In order not to interrupt the course of events which took place within the Grandet family, we must now glance ahead at the operations which the old man carried out in Paris by means of the des Grassins. A month after the banker's departure, Grandet was in possession of enough government stock, purchased at eighty francs a share, to yield him an income of a hundred thousand francs a year. The information given after his death by the inventory of his property never threw the slightest light on the means by which his wary mind conceived to exchange the price of the certificate for the certificate itself. Monsieur Cruchot believed that Nanon had unwittingly been the trusty instrument by which the money was delivered. It was at about that time that she went away for five days on the pretext of putting something in order at Froidfond, as though the old man were capable of leaving anything in disorder!

With regard to the affairs of the house of Guillaume Grandet, all the old man's expectations were realized. As is well known, the Bank of France has precise information on all the large fortunes of Paris and the provinces. The names of des Grassins and Félix Grandet of Saumur were well known there and enjoyed the respect granted to all noted financial figures whose wealth is based on enormous holdings of unmortgaged land. The arrival of the banker from Saumur, who was said to be under orders to liquidate, for the sake of honor, the house of Grandet in Paris, was therefore enough to spare the deceased merchant's memory the shame of protested notes. The seals were broken in the presence of the creditors, who

•

"Here's a million and a half francs, Judge," Eugénie said, drawing from her bosom a certificate for a hundred shares in the Bank of France.

•

Charles in the Indies. He sold:

Chinese
Negroes
swallows' nests
children
artists

Photograph of Charles in the Indies:

The letter:

Dear Cousin,

  I have decided to marry a Mlle. d'Aubrion, and not you. Her nose turns red, under certain circumstances: but I have contrived a way of not looking at her, at those times—all will be well. If my children are to get into the École Normale, the marriage is essential; and we have to live for the children, don't we? A brilliant life awaits me, is what I am trying to say to you, if I don't marry you, and that is why I am marrying this other girl, who is hideously ugly but possessed of a notable, if decayed, position in the aristocracy. Therefore those binding promises we exchanged, on the bench, are, to all intents and purposes, mooted. If I have smothered your hopes at the same time, what can I do? We get the destiny we deserve, and I have done so many evil things, in the Indies, that I am no longer worthy of you, probably. Knowing chuckles will doubtless greet this news, the news of my poor performance, in Saumur—I ask you to endure them, for the sake of

                                        Your formerly loving,
                                                         Charles

"I have decided to give everything to the Church."
"An income of eight hundred thousand a year!"
"Yes."
"It will kill your father."
"You think it will kill him if I give everything to the Church?"
"I certainly do."
"Run and fetch the curé this instant."

•

Old Grandet clutches his chest, and capitulates. Eight hundred thousand a year! He gasps. A death by gasping.

•

Adolphe des Grassins, an unsuccessful suitor of Eugénie Grandet, follows his father to Paris. He becomes a worthless scoundrel there.

Nothing: A Preliminary Account

IT'S NOT the yellow curtains. Nor curtain rings. Nor is it bran in a bucket, not bran, nor is it the large, reddish farm animal eating the bran from the bucket, the man who placed the bran in the bucket, his wife, or the raisin-faced banker who's about to foreclose on the farm. None of these is nothing. A damselfish is not nothing, it's a fish, a *Pomacentrus*, it likes warm water, coral reefs—perhaps even itself, for all we know. Nothing is not a nightshirt or a ninnyhammer, ninety-two, or Nineveh. It is not a small jungle in which, near a river, a stone table has been covered with fruit. It is not the handsome Indian woman standing next to the stone table holding the blond, kidnapped child. Neither is it the proposition *esse est percipi*, nor is it any of the refutations of that proposition. Nor is it snuff. Hurry. There is not much time, and we must complete, or at least attempt to complete, the list. Nothing is not a tongue depressor; splendid, hurry on. Not a tongue depressor on which a distinguished artist has painted part of a nose, part of a mouth, a serious, unsmiling eye. Good, we got that in. Hurry on. We are persuaded that nothing is not the yellow panties. The yellow panties edged with white on the floor under the black chair. And it's not the floor or the black chair or the two naked lovers standing up in the white-sheeted bed having a pillow fight during the course of which the male partner will, unseen by his beloved, load his pillowcase with a copy of Webster's Third International. We are nervous. There is not much time. Nothing is not a Gregorian chant or indeed a chant of any kind unless it be the howl of the null muted to inaudibility by the laws of language strictly construed. It's not an "O" or an asterisk or what Richard is thinking or that thing we can't name at the moment but which we use to clip papers together. It's not the ice cubes disappearing in the warmth of our whiskey nor is it the town in Scotland where the whiskey is manufactured nor is it the workers who, while reading the Bible and the local newspaper and Rilke, are sentiently sipping the product through eighteen-foot-long, almost invisible nylon straws.

And it's not a motor hotel in Dib (where the mudmen live) and it's not pain or *pain* or the mustard we spread on the *pain* or the mustard plaster we spread on the pain, fee simple, the roar of fireflies mating, or meat. Nor is it lobster protected from its natural enemies by its high price or true grit or false grit or thirst. It's not the yellow curtains, we have determined that, and it's not what is behind the yellow curtains which we cannot mention out of respect for the King's rage and the Queen's reputation. Hurry. Not much time. Nothing is not a telephone number or any number whatsoever including zero. It's not science and in particular it's not black-hole physics, which is not nothing but physics. And it's not (quickly now, quickly) Benjamin Franklin trying to seduce, by mail, the widow of the French thinker Claude Adrien Helvétius, and it is not the nihilism of Gorgias, who asserts that nothing exists and even if something did exist it could not be known and even if it could be known that knowledge could not be communicated, no, it's not that although the tune is quite a pretty one. I am sorry to say that it is not Athos, Porthos, or Aramis, or anything that ever happened to them or anything that may yet happen to them if, for example, an Exxon tank truck exceeding the speed limit outside of Yuma, Arizona, runs over a gila monster which is then reincarnated as Dumas *père*. It's not weather of any kind, fair, foul, or undecided, and it's not mental weather of any kind, fair, foul, or partly cloudy, and it's neither my psychiatrist nor your psychiatrist or either of their psychiatrists, let us hurry on. And it is not what is under the bed because even if you tell us "There is nothing under the bed" and we think, *At last! Finally! Pinned to the specimen board!* still you are only informing us of a local, only temporarily stable situation, you have not delivered nothing itself. Only the list can present us with nothing itself, pinned, finally, at last, let us press on. We are aware of the difficulties of proving a negative, such as the statement "There is not a hipphilosamus in my living room," and that even if you show us a photograph of your living room with no hipphilosamus in it, and adduce as well a tape recording on which no hipphilosamus tread is discernible, how can we be sure that the photograph has not been retouched, the tape cunningly altered, or that both do not either pre- or post-date the arrival of the hipphilosamus? That large, verbivorous animal which is able to think underwater for long periods of time? And while we are mentioning verbs, can we ask the question, of nothing, what does nothing *do*?

Quickly, quickly. Heidegger suggests that "Nothing nothings"—a calm, sensible idea with which Sartre, among others, disagrees. (What Heidegger thinks about nothing is not nothing.) Heidegger points us toward dread. Having borrowed a cup of dread from Kierkegaard, he spills it, and in the spreading stain he finds (like a tea-leaf reader) Nothing. Original dread, for Heidegger, is what intolerabilizes all of what-is, offering us a momentary glimpse of what is not, finally a way of bumping into Being. But Heidegger is far too grand for us; we applaud his daring but are ourselves performing a homelier task, making a list. Our list can in principle never be completed, even if we summon friends or armies to help out (nothing is not an army nor is it an army's history, weapons, morale, doctrines, victories, or defeats—there, that's done). And even if we were able, with much labor, to exhaust the possibilities, get it all *inscribed*, name everything nothing is not, down to the last rogue atom, the one that rolled behind the door, and had thoughtfully included ourselves, the makers of the list, on the list—the list itself would remain. Who's got a match?

But if we cannot finish, we can at least begin. If what exists is in each case the totality of the series of appearances which manifests it, then nothing must be characterized in terms of its non-appearances, no-shows, incorrigible tardiness. Nothing is what keeps us waiting (forever). And it's not *Charlie Is My Darling*, nor would it be Mary if I had a darling so named nor would it be my absence-of-darling had I neglected to search out and secure one. And it is not the yellow curtains behind which fauns and astronauts embrace, behind which flesh crawls in all directions and flickertail squirrels fall upward into the trees. And death is not nothing and the cheering sections of consciousness ("Do not go gentle into that good night") are not nothing nor are holders of the contrary view ("Burning to be gone," says Beckett's Krapp, into his Sony). What can I tell you about the rape of Lucrece by the beastly nephew of proud Tarquin? Only this: the rapist wore a coat with raglan sleeves. Not much, but not nothing. Put it on the list. For an ampler account, see Shakespeare. And you've noted the anachronism, Lord Raglan lived long after the event, but errors, too, are not nothing. Put it on the list. Nothing ventured, nothing gained. What a wonderful list! How joyous the notion that, try as we may, we cannot do other than fail and fail absolutely and that the task will remain always before us, like a meaning for our lives. Hurry. Quickly. Nothing is not a nail.

A Manual for Sons

(1) Mad fathers
(2) Fathers as teachers
(3) On horseback, etc.
(4) The leaping father
(5) Best way to approach
(6) Ys
(7) Names of
(8) Voices of
      Sample voice, A
                        B
                        C
(9) Fanged, etc.
(10) Hiram or Saul
(11) Color of fathers
(12) Dandling
(13) A tongue-lashing
(14) The falling father
(15) Lost fathers
(16) Rescue of fathers
(17) Sexual organs
(18) Yamos
(19) "Responsibility"
(20) Death of
(21) Patricide a poor idea, and summation

Mad fathers stalk up and down the boulevards, shouting. Avoid them, or embrace them, or tell them your deepest thoughts—it makes no difference, they have deaf ears. If their dress is covered with sewn-on tin cans and their spittle is like a string of red boiled crayfish running head-to-tail down the front of their tin cans, serious impairment of the left brain is present. If, on the other hand, they are simply barking (no tin cans, spittle held securely in the pouch of the cheek), they have been driven to distraction by the intricacies of living with others. Go up to them and, stilling their wooden clappers by putting your left hand between the hinged parts, say you're sorry. If the barking ceases, this does not mean that they have heard you, it only means they are experiencing erotic thoughts of abominable luster. Permit them to enjoy these images for a space, and then strike them sharply in the nape with the blade of your tanned right hand. Say you're sorry again. It won't get through to them (because their brains are mush) but in pronouncing the words your body will assume an attitude that conveys, in every country of the world, sorrow—this language they can understand. Gently feed them with bits of leftover meat you are carrying in your pockets. First hold the meat in front of their eyes, so that they can see what it is, and then point to their mouths, so that they know that the meat is for them. Mostly, they will open their mouths at this point. If they do not, throw the meat in between barks. If the meat does not get all the way into the mouth but lands upon (say) the upper lip, hit them again in the neck; this often causes the mouth to pop open and the meat sticking to the upper lip to fall into the mouth. Nothing may work out in the way I have described; in this eventuality, you can do not much for a mad father except listen, for a while, to his babble. If he cries aloud, "*Stomp it, emptor!*", then you must attempt to figure out the code. If he cries aloud, "*The fiends have killed your horse!*", note down in your notebook the frequency with which the words "the" and "your" occur in his tirade. If he cries aloud, "*The cat's in its cassock and flitter-te-bee moreso stomp it!*", remember that he has already asked you once to "stomp it" and that this must refer to something you are doing. So stomp it.

•

Fathers are teachers of the true and not-true, and no father ever knowingly teaches what is not true. In a cloud of unknowing, then, the father proceeds with his instruction. Tough meat should be hammered well between two stones before it is placed on the fire, and should be combed with a hair comb and brushed with a hairbrush before it is placed on the fire. On arriving at night, with thirsty cattle, at a well of doubtful character, one deepens the well first with a rifle barrel, then with a pigsticker, then with a pencil, then with a ramrod, then with an icepick, "bringing the well in" finally with needle and thread. Do not forget to clean your rifle barrel immediately. To find honey, tie a feather or straw to the leg of a bee, throw him into the air, and peer alertly after him as he flies slowly back to the hive. Nails, boiled for three hours, give off a rusty liquid that, when combined with oxtail soup, dries to a flame color, useful for warding off tuberculosis or attracting native women. Do not forget to hug the native women immediately. To prevent feet from blistering, soap the inside of the stocking with a lather of raw egg and steel wool, which together greatly soften the leather of the foot. Delicate instruments (such as surveying instruments) should be entrusted to a porter who is old and enfeebled; he will totter along most carefully. For a way of making an ass not to bray at night, lash a heavy child to his tail; it appears that when an ass wishes to bray he elevates his tail, and if the tail cannot be elevated, he has not the heart. Savages are easily satisfied with cheap beads in the following colors: dull white, dark blue, and vermillion red. Expensive beads are often spurned by them. Nonsavages should be given cheap books in the following colors: dead white, brown, and seaweed. Books praising the sea are much sought after. Satanic operations should not be conducted without first consulting the Bibliothèque Nationale. When Satan at last appears to you, try not to act surprised. Then get down to hard bargaining. If he likes neither the beads nor the books, offer him a cold beer. Then—

Fathers teach much that is of value. Much that is not.

•

Fathers in some countries are like cotton bales; in others, like clay pots or jars; in others, like reading, in a newspaper, a long account of a film you have already seen and liked immensely but do not wish to see again, or read about. Some fathers have triangular eyes. Some fathers, if you ask them for the time of day, spit silver dollars. Some fathers live in old filthy cabins high in the mountains, and make murderous noises deep in their throats when their amazingly sharp ears detect, on the floor of the valley, an alien step. Some fathers piss either perfume or medicinal alcohol, distilled by powerful body processes from what they have been, all day long, drinking. Some fathers have only one arm. Others have an extra arm, in addition to the normal two, hidden inside their coats. On that arm's fingers are elaborately wrought golden rings that, when a secret spring is pressed, dispense charity. Some fathers have made themselves over into convincing replicas of beautiful sea animals, and some into convincing replicas of people they hated as children. Some fathers are goats, some are milk, some teach Spanish in cloisters, some are exceptions, some are capable of attacking world economic problems and killing them, but have not yet done so; they are waiting for one last vital piece of data. Some fathers strut but most do not, except inside; some fathers pose on horseback but most do not, except in the eighteenth century; some fathers fall off the horses they mount but most do not; some fathers, after falling off the horse, shoot the horse, but most do not; some fathers fear horses but most fear, instead, women; some fathers masturbate because they fear women; some fathers sleep with hired women because they fear women who are free; some fathers never sleep at all, but are endlessly awake, staring at their futures, which are behind them.

•

The leaping father is not encountered often, but exists. Two leaping fathers together in a room can cause accidents. The best idea is to chain heavy-duty truck tires to them, one in front, one in back, so that their leaps become pathetic small hops. That is all their lives amount to anyhow, and it is good for them to be able to see, in the mirror, their whole life-histories performed, in a sequence perhaps five minutes long, of upward movements which do not, really, get very far or achieve very much. Without the tires, the leaping father has a nuisance value which may rapidly transform itself into a serious threat. Ambition is the core of this problem (it may even be ambition *for you*, in which case you are in even greater danger than had been supposed), and the core may be removed by open-liver surgery (the liver being the home of the humours, as we know). There is something very sad about all leaping fathers, about leaping itself. I prefer to keep my feet on the ground, in situations where the ground has not been cut out from under me, by the tunneling father. The latter is usually piebald in color, and supremely notable for his nonflogitiousness.

•

The best way to approach a father is from behind. Thus if he chooses to hurl his javelin at you, he will probably miss. For in the act of twisting his body around, and drawing back his hurling arm, and sighting along the shaft, he will give you time to run, to make reservations for a flight to another country. To Rukmani, there are no fathers there. In that country virgin corn gods huddle together under a blanket of ruby chips and flexible cement, through the long wet Rukmanian winter, and in some way not known to us produce offspring. The new citizens are greeted with dwarf palms and certificates of worth, are led (or drawn on runnerless sleds) out into the zocalo, the main square of the country, and their *augenscheinlich* parentages recorded upon a great silver bowl. Look! In the walnut paneling of the dining hall, a javelin! The paneling is wounded in a hundred places.

•

I knew a father named Ys who had many many children and sold every one of them to the bone factories. The bone factories will not accept angry or sulking children, therefore Ys was, to his children, the kindest and most amiable father imaginable. He fed them huge amounts of calcium candy and the milk of minks, told them interesting and funny stories, and led them each day in their bone-building exercises. "Tall sons," he said, are best." Once a year the bone factories sent a little blue van to Ys's house.

•

The names of fathers. Father are named:

A'albiel	Adeo
Aariel	Adityas
Aaron	Adlai
Aba	Adnai

Ababaloy	Adoil
Abaddon	Adossia
Aban	Aeon
Abathur	Aeshma
Abbott	Af
Abdia	Afkiel
Abel	Agason
Abiou	Agwend
Achsah	Albert
Adam	

•

Fathers have voices, and each voice has a *terribilità* of its own. The sound of a father's voice is various: like film burning, like marble being pulled screaming from the face of a quarry, like the clash of paper clips by night, lime seething in a lime pit, or batsong. The voice of a father can shatter your glasses. Some fathers have tetchy voices, others tetched-in-the-head voices. It is understood that fathers, when not robed in the father-role, may be farmers, heldentenors, tinsmiths, racing drivers, fistfighters, or salesmen Most are salesmen. Many fathers did not wish, especially, to be fathers; the thing came upon them, seized them, by accident, or by someone else's careful design, or by simple clumsiness on someone's part. Nevertheless this class of father—the inadvertent—is often among the most tactful, light-handed, and beautiful of fathers. If a father has fathered twelve or twenty-seven times, it is well to give him a curious look—this father does not loathe himself enough. This father frequently wears a blue wool watch cap, on stormy nights, to remind himself of a manly past—action in the North Atlantic. Many fathers are blameless in all ways, and these fathers are either sacred relics people are touched with to heal incurable illnesses, or texts to be studied, generation after generation, to determine how this idiosyncrasy may be maximized. Text-fathers are usually bound in blue.

The father's voice is an instrument of the most terrible pertinaciousness.

SAMPLE VOICE, A.

Son, I got bad news for you. You won't understand the whole purport of it, 'cause you're only six, a little soft in the head too, that fontanelle never did close properly, I wonder why. But I can't delay it no longer, son, I got to tell you the news. There ain't no malice in it, son, I hope you believe me. The thing is, you got to go to school, son, and get socialized. That's the news. You're turnin' pale, son, I don't blame you. It's a terrible thing, but there it is. We'd socialize you here at home, your mother and I, except that we can't stand to watch it, it's that dreadful. And your mother and I who love you and always have and always will are a touch sensitive, son. We don't want to hear your howls and screams. It's going to be miserable, son, but you won't hardly feel it. And I know you'll do well and won't do anything to make us sad, your mother and I who love you. I know you'll do well and won't run away or fall down in fits either. Son, your little face is pitiful. Son, we can't just let you roam the streets like some kind of crazy animal. Son, you got to get your natural impulses curbed. You got to get your corners knocked off, son, you got to get realistic. They going to vamp on you at that school, kid. They going to tear up your ass. They going to learn you how to think, you'll get your letters there, your letters and your figures, your verbs and all that. Your mother and I could socialize you here at home but it would be too painful for your mother and I who love you. You're going to meet the stick, son, the stick going to walk up to you and say howdy-do. You're going to learn about your country at that school, son, oh beautiful for spacious skies. They going to lay just a raft of stuff on you at that school and I caution you not to resist, it ain't appreciated. Just take it as it comes and you'll be fine, son, just fine. You got to do right, son, you got to be realistic. They'll be other kids in that school, kid, and ever' last one of 'em will be after your lunch money. But don't give 'em your lunch money, son, put it in your shoe. If they come up against you tell 'em the other kids already got it. That way you fool 'em, you see, son? What's the matter with you? And watch out for the custodian, son, he's mean. He don't like his job. He wanted to be president of a bank. He's not. It's made him mean. Watch out for that sap he carries on his hip. Watch out for the teacher, son, she's sour. Watch out for her tongue, it'll cut you. She's got a bad mouth on her, son, don't balk her if you can help it. I got nothin' against the schools, kid, they just doin' their job. Hey kid what's the matter with you kid? And if this school don't do the job we'll find one that can. We're right behind you, son, your mother and I who love you. You'll be gettin' your sports there, your ball sports and your blood sports and watch out for the coach, he's a disappointed man, some say a sadist but I don't know about that. You got to develop your body, son. If they shove you, shove back. Don't take nothin' off nobody. Don't show fear. Lay back and watch the guy next to you, do what he does. Except if he's a damn fool. If he's a damn fool you'll know he's a damn fool 'cause everybody'll be hittin' on him. Let me tell you 'bout that school, son. They do what they do 'cause I told them to do it. That's why they do it. They didn't think up those ideas their own selves. I told them to do it. Me and your mother who love you, we told them to do it. Behave yourself, kid! Do right! You'll be fine there, kid, just fine. What's the matter with you, kid? Don't be that way. I hear the ice-cream man outside, son. You want to go and see the ice-cream man? Go get you an ice cream, son, and make sure you get your sprinkles. Go give the ice-cream man your quarter, son. And hurry back.

B.

Hey son. Hey boy. Let's you and me go out and throw the ball around. Throw the ball around. You don't want to go out and throw the ball around? How come you don't want to go out and throw the ball around? I know why you don't want to go out and throw the ball around. It's 'cause you— Let's don't discuss it. It don't bear thinkin' about. Well let's see, you don't want to go out and throw the ball around, you can hep me work on the patio. You want to hep me work on the patio? Sure you do. Sure you do. We gonna have us a fine-lookin' patio there, boy, when we get it finished. Them folks across the street are just about gonna fall out when they see it. C'mon kid, I'll let you hold the level. And this time I want you to hold the fucking thing straight. I want you to hold it straight. It ain't difficult, any idiot can do it. A nigger can do it. We're gonna stick it to them mothers across the street, they think they're so fine. Flee from the wrath to come, boy, that's what I always say. Seen it on a sign one time. Flee from the Wrath to Come. Crazy guy goin' down the street holdin' this sign, see, flee from the wrath to come, it tickled me. Went round for days sayin' it out loud to myself, flee from the wrath to come, flee from the wrath to come. Couldn't get it outa my head. See they're talkin' 'bout God there, that's what that's all about, God, see boy, God. It's this God crap they try and hand you, see, they got a whole routine, see, let's don't talk about it, it fries my ass. Your mother goes for all that, see, and of course your mother is a fine woman and a sensible woman but she's just a little bit ape on this church thing we don't discuss it. She has her way and I got mine, we don't discuss it. She's a little bit ape on this subject, see, I don't blame her it was the way she was raised. Her mother was ape on this subject. That's how the churches make their money, see, they get the women. All these dumb-ass women. *Hold it straight kid.* That's better. Now run me a line down that form with the pencil. I gave you the pencil. What'd you do with the goddamn pencil? Jesus Christ kid *find the pencil*. OK go in the house and get me another pencil. Hurry up I can't stand here holdin' this all day. Wait a minute here's the pencil. OK. I got it. Now hold it straight and run me a line down that form. *Not that way dummy*, on the horizontal. You think we're buildin' a barn? That's right. Good. Now run the line. Good. OK, now go over there and fetch me the square. Square's the flat one, looks like a L. Like this, look. Good. Thank you. OK now hold that mother up against the form where you made the line. That's so we get this side of it square, see? OK now hold the board and lemme just put in the stakes. HOLD IT STILL DAMN IT. How you think I can put in the stakes with you wavin' the damn thing around like that? Hold it still. Check it with the square again. OK, is it square? Now hold it still. Still. OK That's got it. How come you're tremblin'? Nothing' to it, all you got to do is hold one little bitty piece of one-by-six straight for two minutes and you go into a fit? Now stop that. Stop it. I said stop it. Now just take it easy. You like heppin' me with the patio, don'tcha? Just think 'bout when it's finished and we be sittin' out here with our drinks drinkin' our drinks and them jackasses 'cross the street will be havin' a hemorrhage. From green envy. Flee from the wrath to come, boy, flee from the wrath to come. He he.

C.

Hey son come here a minute. I want you and me to have a little talk. You're turnin' pale. How come you always turn pale when we have a little talk? You *delicate*? Pore delicate little flower? Naw you ain't, you're a *man*, son, or will be someday the good Lord willin'. But you got to do right. That's what I want to talk to you about. Now put down that comic book and come on over here and sit by me. Sit right there. Make yourself comfortable. Now, you comfortable? Good. Son, I want to talk to you about your personal habits. Your personal habits. We ain't never talked about your personal habits and now it's time. I been watchin' you, kid. Your personal habits are admirable. Yes they are. They are flat admirable. I like the way you pick up your room. You run a clean room, son, I got to hand it to you. And I like the way you clean your teeth. You brush right, in the right direction, and you brush *a lot*. You're goin' to have good gums, kid, good healthy gums. We ain't gonna have to lay out no money to get your teeth fixed, your mother and I, and that's a blessing and we thank you. And you keep yourself clean, kid, clothes neat, hands clean, face clean, knees clean, that's the way to hop, way to hop. There's just one little thing, son, one little thing that puzzles me. I been studyin' 'bout it and I flat don't understand it. How come you spend so much time washin' your hands, kid? I been watchin' you. You spend an hour after breakfast washin' your hands. Then you go wash 'em again 'bout ten-thirty, ten-forty, 'nother fifteen minutes washin' your hands. Then just before lunch, maybe a half hour, washin' your hands. Then after lunch, sometimes an hour, sometimes less, it varies. I been noticin'. Then in the middle of the afternoon back in there washin' your hands. Then before supper and after supper and before you go to bed and sometimes you get up in the middle of the night and go on in there and wash your hands. Now I'd think you were in there playin' with your little pecker, 'cept you a shade young for playin' with your little pecker and besides you leave the door open, most kids close the door when they go in there to play with their little peckers but you leave it open. So I see you in there and I see what you're doin', you're washin' your hands. And I been keepin' track of it son, you spend 'bout three-quarters of your wakin' hours *washin' your hands.* And I think there's somethin' a little bit *strange* about that, son. It ain't natural. So what I want to know is how come you spend so much time washin' your hands, son? Can you tell me? Huh? Can you give me a rational explanation? Well, can you? Huh? You got anything to say on this subject? Well, what's the matter? You're just sittin' there. Well come on, son, what you got to say for yourself? What's the explanation? Now it won't do you no good to start cryin', son, that don't help anything. OK kid stop crying. *I said stop it!* I'm goin' to whack you, kid, you don't stop cryin'. Now cut that out. This minute. Now cut it out. Goddamn baby. Come on now kid, get ahold of yourself. Now go wash your face and come on back in here, I want to talk to you some more. Wash your face, but don't do that other. Now go on in there and get back in here right quick. I want to talk to you 'bout bumpin' your head, son, against the wall, 'fore you go to sleep. I don't like it. You're too old to do that. It disturbs me. I can hear you in there, when you go to bed, bump bump bump bump bump bump bump bump bump. It's disturbing. It's monotonous. It's a very disturbing sound. I don't like it. I don't like listenin' to it. I want you to stop it. I want you to get ahold of yourself. I don't like to hear that noise when I'm sittin' in here tryin' to read the paper or whatever I'm doin', I don't like to hear it and it bothers your mother. It gets her all upset and I don't like your mother to be all upset, just on accounta you. Bump bump bump bump bump bump bump bump bump, what are you, kid, some kind of animal? I cain't figure you out, kid. I just flat cain't understand it, bump bump bump bump bump bump bump. Dudden't hurtcha? Dudden't hurtcha head? Well, never mind about that right now. Go on in there and wash your face, and then come on back in here and we'll talk some more. And don't do none of that other, just wash your face. You got three minutes.

•

Fathers are like blocks of marble—giant cubes, highly polished, with veins and seams—placed squarely in your path. They block your path. They cannot be climbed over, neither can they be slithered past. They are the "past," and very likely the slither, if the slither is thought of as that accommodating maneuver you make to escape notice, or get by unscathed. If you attempt to go around one, you will find that another (winking at the first) has mysteriously appeared athwart the trail. Or maybe it is the same one, moving with the speed of paternity. Look closely at color and texture. Is this giant square block of marble similar in color and texture to a slice of rare roast beef? Your very father's complexion! Do not try to draw too many conclusions from this; the obvious ones are sufficient and correct. Some fathers like to dress up in black robes and go out and give away the sacraments, adding to their black robes the chasuble, stole, and alb, in reverse order. Of these "fathers" I shall not speak, except to commend them for their lack of ambition and sacrifice, especially the sacrifice of the "franking privilege," or the privilege of naming the first male child after yourself: Franklin Edward A'albiel, Jr. Of all possible fathers, the fanged father is the least desirable. If you can get your lariat around one of his fangs, and quickly wrap the other end of it several times around your saddle horn, and if your horse is a trained roping horse and knows what to do, how to plant his front feet and then back up with small nervous steps, keeping the lariat taut, then you have a chance. Do not try to rope both fangs at the same time; concentrate on the right. Do the thing fang by fang, and then you will be safe, or more nearly so. I have seen some old, yellowed six-inch fangs that were drawn in this way, and once, in a whaling museum in a seaport town, a twelve-inch fang, mistakenly labeled as the tusk of a walrus. But I recognized it at once, it was a father fang, which has its own peculiarly shaped, six-pointed root. I am pleased never to have met that father. . . .

•

If your father's name is Hiram or Saul, flee into the woods. For these names are the names of kings, and your father Hiram, or your father Saul, will not be a king, but will retain, in hidden places in his body, the memory of kingship. And there is no one more blackhearted and surly than an ex-king, or a person who harbors, in the dark channels of his body, the memory of kingship. Fathers so named consider their homes to be Camelots, and their kith and kin courtiers, to be elevated or depressed in rank according to the lightest whinges of their own mental weather. And one can never know for sure if one is "up" or "down" at a particular moment; one is a feather, floating, one has no place to stand. Of the rage of the king-father I will speak later, but understand that fathers named Hiram, Saul, Charles, Francis, or George rage (when they rage) exactly in the manner of their golden and noble namesakes. Flee into the woods, at such times, or earlier, before the mighty scimitar or yataghan leaps from its scabbard. The proper attitude toward such fathers is that of the toad, lickspittle, smellfeast, carpet knight, pickthank, or tuft-hunter. When you cannot escape to the trees, genuflect, and stay down there, on one knee with bowed head and clasped hands, until dawn. By this time he will probably have drunk himself into a sleep, and you may creep away and seek your bed (if it has not been taken away from you) or, if you are hungry, approach the table and see what has been left there, unless the ever-efficient cook has covered everything with clear plastic and put it away. In that case, you may suck your thumb.

•

The color of fathers: The bay-colored father can be trusted, mostly, whether he is standard bay, blood bay, or mahogany bay. He is useful (1) in negotiations between warring tribes, (2) as a catcher of red-hot rivets when you are building a bridge, (3) in auditioning possible bishops for the Synod of Bishops, (4) in the co-pilot's seat, and (5) for carrying one corner of an eighteen-meter-square mirror through the city's streets. Dun-colored fathers tend to shy at obstacles, and therefore you do not want a father of this color, because life, in one sense, is nothing but obstacles, and his continual shying will reduce your nerves to grease. The liver-chestnut-colored father has a reputation for decency and good sense; if God commands him to take out his knife and slice through your neck with it, he will probably say "No, thanks." The dusty-chestnut father will reach for his knife. The light-chestnut father will ask for another opinion. The standard-chestnut father will look the other way, to the east, where another vegetation ceremony, with more interesting dances, is being held. Sorrel-colored fathers are easily excitable and are employed most often where a crowd, or mob, is wanted, as for coronations, lynchings, and the like. The bright-sorrel father, who glows, is an exception; he is content with his glow, with his name (John), and with his life membership in the Knights of the Invisible Empire. In bungled assassinations, the assassin will frequently be a blond-sorrel father who forgot to take the lens cap off his telescopic sight. Buckskin-colored fathers know the Law and its mangled promise, and can help you in your darker projects, such as explaining why a buckskin-colored father sometimes has a black stripe down the spine from the mane to the root of the tail; it is because he has been whoring after Beauty, and thinks himself more beautiful with the black stripe, which sets off his tanned deer-hide color most wonderfully, than without it. Red roan-colored fathers, blue roan-colored fathers, rose gray-colored fathers, grulla-colored fathers are much noted for bawdiness, and this should be encouraged, for bawdiness is a sacrament that does not, usually, result in fatherhood; it is its own reward. Spots, paints, pintos, piebalds, and Appaloosas have a sweet dignity that proceeds from their inferiority, and excellent senses of smell. The color of a father is not an absolute guide to the character and conduct of that father but tends to be a self-fulfilling prophecy, because when he sees what color he is, he hastens out into the world to sell more goods and services, so that he may keep pace with his destiny.

•

Fathers and dandling: If a father fathers daughters, then our lives are eased. Daughters are for dandling, and are often dandled up until their seventeenth or eighteenth year. The hazard here, which must be faced, is that the father will want to sleep with his beautiful daughter, who is after all *his* in a way that even his wife is not, in a way that even his most delicious mistress is not. Some fathers just say "Publish and be damned!" and go ahead and sleep with their new and amazingly sexual daughters, and accept what pangs accumulate afterward; most do not. Most fathers are sufficiently disciplined in this regard, by mental straps, so that the question never arises. When fathers are giving their daughters their "health" instruction (that is to say, talking to them about the reproductive process) (but this is most often done by mothers, in my experience) it is true that a subtle rinse of desire may be tinting the situation slightly (when you are hugging and kissing the small woman sitting on your lap it is hard to know when to stop, it is hard to stop yourself from proceeding as if she were a bigger woman not related to you by blood). But in most cases, the taboo is observed, and additional strictures imposed, such as "Mary, you are never to allow that filthy John Wilkes Booth to lay a hand upon your bare, white, new breast." Although in the modern age some fathers are moving rapidly in the opposite direction, toward the future, saying, "Here, Mary, here is your blue fifty-gallon drum of babykilling foam, with your initials stamped on it in a darker blue— See, there on the top?" But the important thing about daughter-fathers is that, as fathers, they don't count. Not to their daughters, I don't mean—I have heard daughter-stories that would toast your hair—but to themselves. Fathers of daughters see themselves as *hors concours* in the great exhibition, and this is a great relief. They do not have to teach hurling the caber. They tend, therefore, to take a milder, gentler hand (meanwhile holding on, with an iron grip, to all the fierce prerogatives that fatherhood of any kind conveys—the guidance system of a slap is an example). To say more than this about fathers of daughters is beyond me, even though I am father of a daughter.

•

A tongue-lashing: "Whosoever hath within himself the deceivableness of unrighteousness and hath pleasure in unrighteousness and walketh disorderly and hath turned aside into vain jangling and hath become a manstealer and liar and perjured person and hath given over himself to wrath and doubting and hath been unthankful and hath been a lover of his own self and hath gendered strife with foolish and unlearned questions and hath crept into houses leading away silly women with divers lusts and hath been the inventor of evil things and hath embraced contentiousness and obeyed slanderousness and hath filled his mouth with cursing and bitterness and hath made of his throat an open sepulcher and hath the poison of asps under his lips and hath boasted and hath hoped against hope and hath been weak in faith and hath polluted the land

A MANUAL FOR SONS

with his whoredoms and hath profaned holy things and hath despised mine holy things and hath committed lewdness and hath mocked and hath daubed himself with untempered mortars, and whosoever, if a woman, hath journeyed to the Assyrians there to have her breasts pressed by lovers clothed in blue, captains and rulers, desirable young men, horsemen riding upon horses, horsemen riding upon horses who lay upon her and discovered her nakedness and bruised the breasts of her virginity and poured their whoredoms upon her, and hath doted upon them captains and rulers clothed most gorgeously, horsemen riding upon horses, girdled with girdles upon their loins, and hath multiplied her whoredoms with her paramours whose flesh is as the flesh of asses and whose issue is like the issue of horses, great lords and rulers clothed in blue and riding on horses: This man and this woman I say shall be filled with drunkenness and sorrow like a pot whose scum is therein and whose scum hath not gone out of it and under which the pile for the fire is and on which the wood is heaped and the fire kindled and the pot spiced and the bones burned and then the pot set empty on the coals that the brass of it may be hot and may burn and that the filthiness of it may be molten in it, that the scum may be consumed, for ye have wearied yourselves with lies and your great scum went not forth out of you, your scum shall be in the fire and I will take away the desire of thine eyes. Remember ye not that when I was yet with you I told you these things?"

•

There are twenty-two kinds of fathers, of which only nineteen are important. The drugged father is not important. The lionlike father (rare) is not important. The Holy Father is not important, for our purposes. There is a certain father who is falling through the air, heels where his head should be, head where his heels should be. The falling father has grave meaning for all of us. The wind throws his hair in every direction. His cheeks are flaps almost touching his ears. His garments are shreds, telltales. This father has the power of curing the bites of mad dogs, and the power of choreographing the interest rates. What is he thinking about, on the way down? He is thinking about emotional extravagance. The Romantic Movement, with its exploitation of the sensational, the morbid, the occult, the erotic! The falling father has noticed Romantic tendencies in several of his sons. The sons have taken to wearing slices of raw bacon in their caps, and speaking out against the interest rates. After all he has done for them! Many bicycles! Many *gardes-bébés*! Electric guitars uncountable! Falling, the falling father devises his iron punishment, resolved not to err again on the side of irresponsible mercy. He is also thinking about his upward mobility, which doesn't seem to be doing so well at the moment. There is only one thing to do: work harder! He decides that if he can ever halt the "downturn" that he seems to be in, he will redouble his efforts, really put his back into it, this time. The falling father is important because he embodies the "work ethic," which is a dumb one. The "fear ethic" should be substituted, as soon as possible. Peering upward at his endless hurtling, let us simply shrug, fold up the trampoline we were going to try to catch him in, and place it once again on top of the rafters, in the garage.

•

To find a lost father: The first problem in finding a lost father is to lose him, decisively. Often he will wander away from home and lose himself. Often he will remain at home but still be "lost" in every true sense, locked away in an upper room, or in a workshop, or in the contemplation of beauty, or in the contemplation of a secret life. He may, every evening, pick up his gold-headed cane, wrap himself in his cloak, and depart, leaving behind, on the coffee table, a sealed laundry bag in which there is an address at which he may be reached, in case of war. War, as is well known, is a place at which many fathers are lost, sometimes temporarily, sometimes forever. Fathers are frequently lost on expeditions of various kinds (the journey to the interior). The five best places to seek this kind of lost father are Nepal, Rupert's Land, Mount Elbrus, Paris, and the agora. The five kinds of vegetation in which fathers most often lose themselves are needle-leaved forest, broad-leaved forest mainly evergreen, broad-leaved forest mainly deciduous, mixed needle-leaved and broad-leaved forest, and tundra. The five kinds of things fathers were wearing when last seen are caftans, bush jackets, parkas, Confederate gray, and ordinary business suits. Armed with these clues, then, you may place an advertisement in the newspaper: *Lost, in Paris, on or about February 24, a broad-leaf-loving father, 6' 2", wearing a blue caftan, may be armed and dangerous, we don't know, answers to the name Old Hickory. Reward.* Having completed this futile exercise, you are then free to think about what is really important. Do you really want to find this father? What if, when you find him, he speaks to you in the same tone he used before he lost himself? Will he again place nails in your mother, in her elbows and back of the knee? Remember the javelin. Have you any reason to believe that it will not, once again, flash through the seven-o'clock-in-the-evening air? What we are attempting to determine is simple: Under what conditions do you wish to live? Yes, he "nervously twiddles the stem of his wineglass." Do you wish to watch him do so on into the last decade of the present century? I don't think so. Let him take those mannerisms, and what they portend, to Borneo, they will be new to Borneo. Perhaps in Borneo he will also nervously twiddle the stem of, etc., but he will not be brave enough to manufacture there the explosion of which this is a sign. Throwing the roast through the mirror. Thrusting a belch big as an opened umbrella into the middle of something someone else is trying to say. Beating you, either with a wet, knotted rawhide or with an ordinary belt. Ignore that empty chair at the head of the table. Give thanks.

•

On the rescue of fathers: Oh they hacked him pretty bad, they hacked at him with axes and they hacked at him with hacksaws but me and my men got there fast, wasn't as bad as it might have been, first we fired smoke grenades in different colors, yellow and blue and green, that put a fright into them but they wouldn't quit, they opened up on us with 81-mm. mortars and meanwhile continued to hack. I sent some of the boys out to the left to flank them but they'd put some people over there to prevent just that and my men got into a firefight with their support patrol, no other way to do the thing but employ a frontal assault, which we did, at least it took the pressure off him, they couldn't continue to hack and deal with our assault at the same time. We cleaned their clocks for them,

I will say that, they fell back to the left and linked up with their people over there, my flanking party broke off contact as I had instructed and let them flee unpursued. We came out of it pretty well, had a few wounded but that's all. We turned immediately to the task of bandaging him in the hacked places, bloody great wounds but our medics were very good, they were all over him, he never made a complaint or uttered a sound, not a whimper out of him, not a sign. This took place at the right arm, just above the elbow, we left some pickets there for a few days until the arm had begun to heal, I think it was a successful rescue, we returned to our homes to wait for the next time. I think it was a successful rescue. It was an adequate rescue.

Then they attacked him with sumo wrestlers, giant fat men in loincloths. We countered with loincloth snatchers—some of our best loincloth snatchers. We were successful. The hundred naked fat men fled. I had rescued him again. Then we sang "Genevieve, Oh Genevieve." All the sergeants gathered before the veranda and sang it, and some enlisted men too—some enlisted men who had been with the outfit for a long time. They sang it, in the twilight, pile of damp loincloths blazing fitfully off to the left. When you have rescued a father from whatever terrible threat menaces him, then you feel, for a moment, that you are the father and he is not. For a moment. This is the only moment in your life you will feel this way.

•

The sexual organs of fathers: The penises of fathers are traditionally hidden from the inspection of those who are not "clubbable," as the expression runs. These penises are magical, but not most of the time. Most of the time they are "at rest." In the "at rest" position they are small, almost shriveled, and easily concealed in carpenter's aprons, chaps, bathing suits, or ordinary trousers. Actually they are not anything that you would want to show anyone, in this state; they are rather like mushrooms or, possibly, large snails. The magic, at these times, resides in other parts of the father (fingertips, right arm) and not in the penis. Occasionally a child, usually a bold six-year-old daughter, will request permission to see it. This request should be granted, once. Be matter-of-fact, kind, and undramatic. Pretend, for the moment, that it is as mundane as a big toe.

About sons you must use your own judgment. It is injudicious (as well as unnecessary) to terrify them; you have many other ways of accomplishing that. Chancre is a good reason for not doing any of this. When the penises of fathers are semierect, titillated by some stray erotic observation, such as a glimpse of an attractive female hoof, bereft of its slipper, knowing smiles should be exchanged with the other fathers present (better: half smiles) and the matter let drop. Semierectness is a half measure, as Aristotle knew; that is why most of the penises in museums have been knocked off with a mallet. The original artificers could not bear the idea of Aristotle's disapproval, and mutilated their work rather than merit the scorn of the great Peripatetic. The notion that this mutilation was carried out by later (Christian) "cleanup squads" is untrue, pure legend. The matter is as I have presented it. Many other things can be done with the penises of fathers, but these have already been adequately described by other people. The penises of fathers are in every respect superior to the penises of nonfathers, not because of size or weight or any consideration of that sort but because of a metaphysical "responsibility." This is true even of poor, bad, or insane fathers. African artifacts reflect this special situation. Pre-Columbian artifacts, for the most part, do not.

•

I knew a father named Yamos who was landlord of the bear gardens at Southwark. Yamos was known to be a principled man and never, never, never ate any of his children no matter how dire the state of his purse. Yet the children, one by one, disappeared.

•

We have seen that the key idea, in fatherhood, is "responsibility." First, that heavy chunks of blue or gray sky do not fall down and crush our bodies, or that the solid earth does not turn into a yielding pit beneath us (although the tunneling father is sometimes responsible, in the wrong sense, for the latter). The responsibility of the father is chiefly that his child not die, that enough food is pushed into its face to sustain it, and that heavy blankets protect it from the chill, cutting air. The father almost always meets this responsibility with valor and steadfastness (except in the case of child abusers or thieves of children or managers of child labor or sick, unholy sexual ghouls). The child lives, mostly, lives and grows into a healthy, normal adult. Good! The father has been successful in his burdensome, very often thankless task, that of keeping the child breathing. Good work, Sam, your child has taken his place in the tribe, has a good job selling thermocouples, has married a nice girl whom you like, and has impregnated her to the point that she will doubtless have a new child, soon. And is not in jail. But have you noticed the slight curl at the end of Sam II's mouth, when he looks at you? It means that he didn't want you to name him Sam II, for one thing, and for two other things it means that he has a sawed-off in his left pant leg, and a baling hook in his right pant leg, and is ready to kill you with either one of them, given the opportunity. The father is taken aback. What he usually says, in such a confrontation, is "I changed your diapers for you, little snot." This is not the right thing to say. First, it is not true (mothers change nine diapers out of ten), and secondly, it instantly reminds Sam II of what he is mad about. He is mad about being small when you were big, but no, that's not it, he is mad about being helpless when you were powerful, but no, not that either, he is mad about being contingent when you were necessary, not quite it, he is insane because when he loved you, you didn't notice.

•

The death of fathers: When a father dies, his fatherhood is returned to the All-Father, who is the sum of all dead fathers taken together. (This is not a definition of the Dead Father, only an aspect of his being.) The fatherhood is returned to the All-Father, first because that is where it belongs and secondly in order that it may be denied to you. Transfers of power of this kind are marked with appropriate ceremonies; top hats are burned. Fatherless now, you must deal with the memory of a father. Often that memory is more potent than the living presence of a father, is an inner voice commanding, haranguing, yes-ing and no-ing—a binary code, yes no yes no yes no yes no, governing your every, your slightest movement, mental or physical. At what point do you become yourself? Never, wholly, you are always partly him. That privileged position in your inner ear is his last "perk" and no father has ever passed it by.

Similarly, jealousy is a useless passion because it is directed mostly at one's peers, and that is the wrong direction. There is only one jealousy that is useful and important, the original jealousy.

•

Patricide: Patricide is a bad idea, first because it is contrary to law and custom and secondly because it proves, beyond a doubt, that the father's every fluted accusation against you was correct: You are a thoroughly bad individual, a patricide!—member of a class of persons universally ill-regarded. It is all right to feel this hot emotion, but not to act upon it. And it is not necessary. It is not necessary to slay your father, time will slay him, that is a virtual certainty. Your true task lies elsewhere.

Your true task, as a son, is to reproduce every one of the enormities touched upon in this manual, but in attenuated form. You must become your father, but a paler, weaker version of him. The enormities go with the job, but close study will allow you to perform the job less well than it has previously been done, thus moving toward a golden age of decency, quiet, and calmed fevers. Your contribution will not be a small one, but "small" is one of the concepts that you should shoot for. If your father was a captain in Battery D, then content yourself with a corporalship in the same battery. Do not attend the annual reunions. Do not drink beer or sing songs at the reunions. Begin by whispering, in front of a mirror, for thirty minutes a day. Then tie your hands behind your back for thirty minutes a day, or get someone else to do this for you. Then, choose one of your most deeply held beliefs, such as the belief that your honors and awards have something to do with you, and abjure it. Friends will help you abjure it, and can be telephoned if you begin to backslide. You see the pattern, put it into practice. *Fatherhood can be, if not conquered, at least "turned down" in this generation*—by the combined efforts of all of us together. Rejoice.

Aria

Do they lie? Fervently. Do they steal? Only silver and gold. Do they remember? I am in constant touch. Hardly a day passes. The children. Some can't spell, still. Took a walk in the light-manufacturing district, where everything's been converted. Lots of little shops, wine bars. Saw some strange things. Saw a group of square steel plates arranged on a floor. Very interesting. Saw a Man Mountain Dean dressed in heavenly blue. Wild, chewing children. They were small. Petite. Out of scale. They came and went. Doors banging. They were of different sexes but wore similar clothes. Wandered away, then they wandered back. They're vague, you know, they tell you things in a vague way. Asked me to leave, said they'd had enough. Enough what? I asked. Enough of my lip, they said. Although the truth was that I had visited upon them only the palest of apothegms—the one about the salt losing its savor, the one about the fowls of the air. Went for a walk, whistling. Saw a throne in a window. I said: What chair is this? Is it the one great Ferdinand sat in, when he sent the ships to find the Indies? The seat is frayed. Hardly a day passes without an announcement of some kind, a marriage, a pregnancy, a cancer, a rebirth. Sometimes they drift in from the Yukon and other far places, come in and sit down at the kitchen table, want a glass of milk and a peanut-butter-and-jelly, I oblige, for old times' sake. Sent me the schedule for the Little League soccer teams, they're all named after cars, the Mustangs vs. the Mavericks, the Chargers vs. the Impalas. Something funny about that. My son. Slept with What's-Her-Name, they said, while she was asleep, I don't think that's fair. Prone and helpless in the glare of the headlights. They went away, then they came back, at Christmas and Eastertide, had quite a full table, maybe a dozen in all including all the little . . . partners they'd picked up on their travels . . . Snatch them baldheaded, slap their teeth out. Little starved faces four feet from the screen, you'd speak to them in a loud, commanding voice, get not even a twitch. Use of the preemptive splint, not everyone knows about it.

The world reminds us of its power, again and again and again. Going along minding your own business, and suddenly an act of God, right there in front of you. Great falls of snow and bursting birds. Getting guilty, letting it all slide. Sown here and there like little . . . petunias, one planted in Old Lyme, one in Fairbanks, one in Tempe. Alleged that he slept with her while she was asleep, I can see it, under certain circumstances. You may wink, but not at another person. You may wink only at pigeons. You may pound in your tent pegs, pitch your tent, gather wood for the fire, form the hush puppies. They seek to return? Back to the nest? The warm arms? The ineffable smells? Not on your tintype. Well, I think that's a little harsh. Think that's a little harsh do you? Yes I think that's a little harsh. Think that's a little harsh do you? Yes, harsh. Harsh. Well that's a sketch, that is, that's a tin-plated sketch— They write and telephone. Short of cash? Give us a call, all inquiries handled with the utmost confidentiality. They call constantly, they're calling still, saying *williwaw, williwaw*—

I walked to the end of my rope, discovered I was tied, tethered. I never stopped to think about it, just went ahead and did it, it was a process, had one and then took care of that one and had another and then took care of the two, the others followed, and now these in turn make more and more and more. . . . Little yowls yonder kept you hopping. They came to me and said goodbye. Goodbye? I said. Goodbye, they said. You're not ridin' with me anymore, is that it? I said. That's it, they said. You're pullin' your blanket, is that it? I said. They said, that's the story Morning Glory. I saw a fish big as a house, and a tea set of Sunderland pink. Ran through the rooms ululating, pulling the tails of the curly curators, came in to say goodnight sometimes, curtsies and bows, these occasions were rare. Things they needed for their lives: hockey sticks, lobster pots, Mazdas. Simultaneously courting and shunning. This is a test of the system, this is only a test. Throw their wet and stinking parkas on the floor as per usual. Turn on the music and turn it off again. Clean your room, please clean your room, I beg of you, clean your room. There's a long tall Sally, polish her shoes. Polish your own shoes, black for black and brown for brown, do you see anything in my palm? just a little sheep-dip, complete your education, he's right and you're wrong, the inside track is thought to be the best, attain it, better to appear at ease, in clothes not conspicuously new, thou shalt not a, b, c, d, e, turn a little to the right, now a little to the left, *hold it!* Naked girls with the heads of Marx and Malraux prone and helpless in the glare of the headlights, tried to give them a little joie de vivre but maybe it didn't take, their constant bickering and smallness, it's like a stroke of lightning, the world reminds you of its power, tracheotomies right and left, I am spinning, my pretty child, don't scratch, pick up your feet, the long nights, spent most of my time listening, this is a test of the system, this is only a test.

The Emerald

HEY BUDDY what's your name?
My name is Tope. What's your name?
My name is Sallywag. You after the emerald?
Yeah I'm after the emerald you after the emerald too?
I am. What are you going to do with it if you get it?
Cut it up into little emeralds. What are you going to do with it?
I was thinking of solid emerald armchairs. For the rich.
That's an idea. What's your name, you?
Wide Boy.
You after the emerald?
Sure as shootin'.
How you going to get in?
Blast.
That's going to make a lot of noise isn't it?
You think it's a bad idea?
Well . . . What's your name, you there?
Taptoe.
You after the emerald?
Right as rain. What's more, I got a plan.
Can we see it?
No it's my plan I can't be showing it to every—
Okay okay. What's that guy's name behind you?
My name is Sometimes.
You here about the emerald, Sometimes?
I surely am.
Have you got an approach?
Tunneling. I've took some test borings. Looks like a stone cinch.
If this is the right place.
You think this may not be the right place?
The last three places haven't been the right place.
You tryin' to bring me down?
Why would I want to do that? What's that guy's name, the one with the shades?

My name is Brother. Who are all these people?

Businessmen. What do you think of the general situation, Brother?

I think it's crowded. This is my pal, Wednesday.

What say, Wednesday. After the emerald, I presume?

Thought we'd have a go.

Two heads better than one, that the idea?

Yep.

What are you going to do with the emerald, if you get it?

Facet. Facet and facet and facet.

Moll talking to a member of the news media.

Tell me, as a member of the news media, what do you do?

Well we sort of figure out what the news is, then we go out and talk to people, the newsmakers, those who have made the news—

These having been identified by certain people very high up in your organization.

The editors. The editors are the ones who say this is news, this is not news, maybe this is news, damned if I know whether this is news or not—

And then you go out and talk to people and they tell you everything.

They tell you a surprising number of things, if you are a member of the news media. Even if they have something to hide, questionable behavior or one thing and another, or having killed their wife, that sort of thing, still they tell you the most amazing things. Generally.

About themselves. The newsworthy.

Yes. Then we have our experts in the various fields. They are experts in who is a smart cookie and who is a dumb cookie. They write pieces saying which kind of cookie these various cookies are, so that the reader can make informed choices. About things.

Fascinating work I should think.

Your basic glamour job.

I suppose you would have to be very well-educated to get that kind of job.

Extremely well-educated. Typing, everything.

Admirable.

Yes. Well, back to the pregnancy. You say it was a seven-year pregnancy.

Yes. When the agency was made clear to me—

The agency was, you contend, extraterrestrial.

It's a fact. Some people can't handle it.

The father was—

He sat in that chair you're sitting in. The red chair. Naked and wearing a morion.

That's all?

Yes he sat naked in the chair wearing only a morion, and engaged me in conversation.

The burden of which was—

Passion.

What was your reaction?

I was surprised. My reaction was surprise.

Did you declare your unworthiness?

Several times. He was unmoved.

Well I don't know, all this sounds a little unreal, like I mean unreal, if you know what I mean.

Oui, je sais.

What role were you playing?

Well obviously I was playing myself. Mad Moll.

What's a morion?

Steel helmet with a crest.

You considered his offer.

More in the nature of a command.

Then, the impregnation. He approached your white or pink as yet undistended belly with his hideously engorged member—

It was more fun than that.

I find it hard to believe, if you'll forgive me, that you, although quite beautiful in your own way, quite lush of figure and fair of face, still the beard on your chin and that black mark like a furry caterpillar crawling in the middle of your forehead—

It's only a small beard after all.

That's true.

And he seemed to like the black mark on my forehead. He caressed it.

So you did in fact enjoy the . . . event. You understand I wouldn't ask these questions, some of which I admit verge

on the personal, were I not a duly credentialed member of
the press. Custodian as it were of the public's right to know.
Everything. Every last little slippy-dippy thing.

Well okay yes I guess that's true strictly speaking. I suppose that's true. Strictly speaking. I could I suppose tell you to
buzz off but I respect the public's right to know. I think. An
informed public is, I suppose, one of the basic bulwarks of—

Yes I agree but of course I would wouldn't I, being I mean
in my professional capacity my professional role—

Yes I see what you mean.

But of course I exist aside from that role, as a person I mean,
as a woman like you—

You're not like me.

Well no in the sense that I'm not a witch.

You must forgive me if I insist on this point. You're not like
me.

Well, yes, I don't disagree, I'm not arguing, I have not after
all produced after a pregnancy of seven years a gigantic emerald
weighing seven thousand and thirty-five carats— Can I, could
I, by the way, see the emerald?

No not right now it's sleeping.

The emerald is sleeping?

Yes it's sleeping right now. It sleeps.

It sleeps?

Yes didn't you hear me it's sleeping right now it sleeps just
like any other—

What do you mean the emerald is sleeping?

Just what I said. It's asleep.

Do you talk to it?

Of course, sure I talk to it, it's mine, I mean I *gave birth*
to it, I cuddle it and polish it and talk to it, what's so strange
about that?

Does it talk to you?

Well I mean it's only one month old. How could it talk?

Hello?
Yes?
Is this Mad Moll?
Yes this is Mad Moll who are you?

You the one who advertised for somebody to stand outside the door and knock down anybody tries to come in?

Yes that's me are you applying for the position?

Yes I think so what does it pay?

Two hundred a week and found.

Well that sounds pretty good but tell me lady who is it I have to knock down for example?

Various parties. Some of them not yet known to me. I mean I have an inkling but no more than that. Are you big?

Six eight.

How many pounds?

Two forty-nine.

IQ?

One forty-six.

What's your best move?

I got a pretty good shove. A not-bad bust in the mouth. I can trip. I can fall on 'em. I can gouge. I have a good sense of where the ears are. I know thumbs and kneecaps.

Where did you get your training?

Just around. High school, mostly.

What's your name?

Soapbox.

That's not a very tough name if you'll forgive me.

You want me to change it? I've been called different things in different places.

No I don't want you to change it. It's all right. It'll do.

Okay do you want to see me or do I have the job?

You sound okay to me Soapbox. You can start tomorrow.

What time?

Dawn?

Understand, ye sons of the wise, what this exceedingly precious Stone crieth out to you! Seven years, close to tears. Slept for the first two, dreaming under four blankets, black, blue, brown, brown. Slept and pissed, when I wasn't dreaming I was pissing, I was a fountain. After the first year I knew something irregular was in progress, but not what. I thought, moonstrous! Salivated like a mad dog, four quarts or more a day, when I wasn't pissing I was spitting. Chawed moose steak, moose steak and morels, and fluttered with new men—the butcher, baker, candlestick maker, especially the butcher, one Shatterhand, he was neat. Gobbled a lot of iron, liver and rust from the bottoms of boats, I had serial nosebleeds every day of the seventeenth trimester. Mood swings of course, heigh-de-ho, instances of false labor in years six and seven, palpating the abdominal wall I felt edges and thought, edges? Then on a cold February night the denouement, at six sixty-six in the evening, or a bit past seven, they sent a Miss Leek to do the delivery, one of us but not the famous one, she gave me scopolamine and a little swansweat, that helped, she turned not a hair when the emerald presented itself but placed it in my arms with a kiss or two and a pat or two and drove away, in a coach pulled by a golden pig.

Vandermaster has the Foot.

Yes.

The Foot is very threatening to you.

Indeed.

He is a mage and goes around accompanied by a black bloodhound.

Yes. Tarbut. Said to have been raised on human milk.

Could you give me a little more about the Foot. Who owns it?

Monks. Some monks in a monastery in Merano or outside of Merano. That's in Italy. It's their Foot.

How did Vandermaster get it?

Stole it.

Do you by any chance know what order that is?

Let me see if I can remember—Carthusian.

Can you spell that for me?

C-a-r-t-h-u-s-i-a-n. I think.

Thank you. How did Vandermaster get into the monastery?

They hold retreats, you know, for pious laymen or people who just want to come to the monastery and think about their sins or be edified, for a week or a few days . . .

Can you describe the Foot? Physically?

The Foot proper is encased in silver. It's about the size of a foot, maybe slightly larger. It's cut off just above the ankle. The toe part is rather flat, it's as if people in those days had very flat toes. The whole is quite graceful. The Foot proper sits on top of this rather elaborate base, three levels, gold, little claw feet . . .

And you are convinced that this, uh, reliquary contains the true Foot of Mary Magdalene.

Mary Magdalene's Foot. Yes.

He's threatening you with it.

It has a history of being used against witches, throughout history, to kill them or mar them—

He wants the emerald.

My emerald. Yes.

You won't reveal its parentage. Who the father was.

Oh well hell. It was the man in the moon. Deus Lunus.

The man in the moon ha-ha.

No I mean it, it was the man in the moon. Deus Lunus as he's called, the moon god. Deus Lunus. Him.

You mean you want me to believe—

Look woman I don't give dandelions what you believe you asked me who the father was. I told you. I don't give a zipper whether you believe me or don't believe me.

You're actually asking me to—

Sat in that chair, that chair right there. The red chair.

Oh for heaven's sake all right that's it I'm going to blow this pop stand I know I'm just a dumb ignorant media person but if you think for one minute that . . . I respect your uh conviction but this has got to be a delusionary belief. The man in the moon. A delusionary belief.

Well I agree it sounds funny but there it is. Where else would I get an emerald that big, seven thousand and thirty-five carats? A poor woman like me?

Maybe it's not a real emerald?

If it's not a real emerald why is Vandermaster after me?

You going to the hog wrassle?
No I'm after the emerald.
What's your name?
My name is Cold Cuts. What's that machine?
That's an emerald cutter.
How's it work?
Laser beam. You after the emerald too?
Yes I am.

What's your name?
My name is Pro Tem.
That a dowsing rod you got there?
No it's a giant wishbone.
Looks like a dowsing rod.
Well it dowses like a dowsing rod but you also get the wish.
Oh. What's his name?
His name is Plug.
Can't he speak for himself?
He's deaf and dumb.
After the emerald?
Yes. He has special skills.
What are they?
He knows how to diddle certain systems.
Playing it close to the vest is that it?
That's it.
Who's that guy there?
I don't know, all I know about him is he's from Antwerp.
The Emerald Exchange?
That's what I think.
What are all those little envelopes he's holding?
Sealed bids?

Look here, Soapbox, look here.
What's your name, man?
My name is Dietrich von Dietersdorf.
I don't believe it.
You don't believe my name is my name?
Pretty fancy name for such a pissant-looking fellow as you.
I will not be balked. Look here.
What you got?
Silver thalers, my friend, thalers big as onion rings.
That's money, right?
Right.
What do I have to do?
Fall asleep.
Fall asleep at my post here in front of the door?
Right. Will you do it?
I could. But should I?
Where does this "should" come from?

My mind. I have a mind, stewing and sizzling.
Well deal with it, man, deal with it. Will you do it?
Will I? Will I? *I don't know!*

Where is my daddy? asked the emerald. My da?
Moll dropped a glass, which shattered.
Your father.
Yes, said the emerald, amn't I supposed to have one?
He's not here.
Noticed that, said the emerald.
I'm never sure what you know and what you don't know.
I ask in true perplexity.
He was Deus Lunus. The moon god. Sometimes thought of as the man in the moon.
Bosh! said the emerald. I don't believe it.
Do you believe I'm your mother?
I do.
Do you believe you're an emerald?
I am an emerald.
Used to be, said Moll, women wouldn't drink from a glass into which the moon had shone. For fear of getting knocked up.
Surely this is superstition?
Hoo, hoo, said Moll. I like superstition.
I thought the moon was female.
Don't be culture-bound. It's been female in some cultures at some times, and in others, not.
What did it feel like? The experience.
Not a proper subject for discussion with a child.
The emerald sulking. Green looks here and there.
Well it wasn't the worst. Wasn't the worst. I had an orgasm that lasted for three hours. I judge that not the worst.
What's an orgasm?
Feeling that shoots through one's electrical system giving you little jolts, *spam spam*, many little jolts, *spam spam spam spam* . . .
Teach me something. Teach me something, mother of mine, about this gray world of yours.
What have I to teach? The odd pitiful spell. Most of them won't even put a shine on a pair of shoes.

Teach me one.

"To achieve your heart's desire, burn in water, wash in fire."

What does that do?

French-fries. Anything you want French-fried.

That's all?

Well.

I have buggered up your tranquillity.

No no no no no.

I'm valuable, said the emerald. I am a thing of value. Over and above my personhood, if I may use the term.

You are a thing of value. A value extrinsic to what I value.

How much?

Equivalent I would say to a third of a sea.

Is that much?

Not inconsiderable.

People want to cut me up and put little chips of me into rings and bangles.

Yes. I'm sorry to say.

Vandermaster is not of this ilk.

Vandermaster is an ilk unto himself.

The more threatening for so being.

Yes.

What are you going to do?

Make me some money. Whatever else is afoot, this delight is constant.

Now the Molljourney the Molltrip into the ferocious Out with a wire shopping cart what's that sucker there doing? tips his hat bends his middle shuffles his feet why he's doing courtly not seen courtly for many a month he does a quite decent courtly I'll smile, briefly, out of my way there citizen sirens shrieking on this swarm summer's day here an idiot there an idiot that one's eyeing me eyed me on the corner and eyed me round the corner as the Mad Moll song has it and that one standing with his cheek crushed against the warehouse wall and that one browsing in a trash basket and that one picking that one's pocket and that one with the gotch eye and his hands on his I'll twoad 'ee bastard I'll—

Hey there woman come and stand beside me.

Buzz off buster I'm on the King's business and have no time to trifle.

You don't even want to stop a moment and look at this thing I have here?

What sort of thing is it?

Oh it's a rare thing, a beautiful thing, a jim-dandy of a thing, a thing any woman would give her eyeteeth to look upon.

Well yes okay but what is it?

Well I can't tell you. I have to show you. Come stand over here in the entrance to this dark alley.

Naw man I'm not gonna go into no alley with you what do you think I am a nitwit?

I think you're a beautiful woman even if you do have that bit of beard there on your chin like a piece of burnt toast or something, most becoming. And that mark like a dead insect on your forehead gives you a certain—

Cut the crap daddy and show me what you got. Standing right here. Else I'm on my way.

No it's too rich and strange for the full light of day we have to have some shadow, it's too—

If this turns out to be an ordinary—

No no no nothing like that. You mean you think I might be a what-do-you-call-'em, one of those guys who—

Your discourse sir strongly suggests it.

And your name?

Moll. Mad Moll. Sometimes Moll the Poor Girl.

Beautiful name. Your mother's name or the name of some favorite auntie?

Moll totals him with a bang in the balls.

Jesus Christ these creeps what can you do?

She stops at a store and buys a can of gem polish.

Polish my emerald so bloody bright it will bloody blind you.

Sitting on the street with a basket of dirty faces for sale. The dirty faces are all colors, white black yellow tan rosy-red.

Buy a dirty face! Slap it on your wife! Buy a dirty face! Complicate your life!

But no one buys.

A boy appears pushing a busted bicycle.

Hey lady what are those things there they look like faces.

That's what they are, faces.

Lady, Halloween is not until—

Okay kid move along you don't want to buy a face move along.

But those are actual faces lady Christ I mean they're *actual faces*—

Fourteen ninety-five kid you got any money on you?

I don't even want to *touch* one, look like they came off dead people.

Would you feel better if I said they were plastic?

Well I hope to God they're not—

Okay they're plastic. What's the matter with your bike?

Chain's shot.

Give it here.

The boy hands over the bicycle chain.

Moll puts the broken ends in her mouth and chews for a moment.

Okay here you go.

The boy takes it in his hands and yanks on it. It's fixed.

Shit how'd you do that, lady?

Moll spits and wipes her mouth on her sleeve.

Run along now kid beat it I'm tired of you.

Are you magic, lady?

Not enough.

Moll at home playing her oboe.

I love the oboe. The sound of the oboe.

The noble, noble oboe!

Of course it's not to every taste. Not everyone swings with the oboe.

Whoops! Goddamn oboe let me take that again.

Not perhaps the premier instrument of the present age. What would that be? The bullhorn, no doubt.

Why did he interfere with me? Why?

Maybe has to do with the loneliness of the gods. Oh thou great one whom I adore beyond measure, oh thou bastard and fatherer of bastards—

Tucked-away gods whom nobody speaks to anymore. Once so lively.

Polish my emerald so bloody bright it will bloody blind you.

Good God what's that?
Vandermaster used the Foot!
Oh my God look at that hole!
It's awful and tremendous!
What in the name of God?
Vandermaster used the Foot!
The Foot did that? I don't believe it!
You don't believe it? What's your name?
My name is Coddle. I don't believe the Foot could have done that. I one hundred percent don't believe it.
Well it's right there in front of your eyes. Do you think Moll and the emerald are safe?
The house seems structurally sound. Smoke-blackened, but sound.
What happened to Soapbox?
You mean Soapbox who was standing in front of the house poised to bop any mother's son who—
Good Lord Soapbox is nowhere to be seen!
He's not in the hole!
Let me see there. What's your name?
My name is Mixer. No, he's not in the hole. Not a shred of him in the hole.
Good, true Soapbox!
You think Moll is still inside? How do we know this is the right place after all?
Heard it on the radio. What's your name by the way?
My name is Ho Ho. Look at the ground smoking!
The whole thing is tremendous, demonstrating the awful power of the Foot!
I am shaking with awe right now! Poor Soapbox!
Noble, noble Soapbox!

Mr. Vandermaster.
Madam.
You may be seated.
I thank you.
The red chair.

Thank you very much.

May I offer you some refreshment?

Yes I will have a splash of something thank you.

It's Scotch I believe.

Yes Scotch.

And I will join you I think, as the week has been a most fatiguing one.

Care and cleaning I take it.

Yes, care and cleaning and in addition there was a media person here.

How tiresome.

Yes it was tiresome in the extreme her persistence in her peculiar vocation is quite remarkable.

Wanted to know about the emerald I expect.

She was most curious about the emerald.

Disbelieving.

Yes disbelieving but perhaps that is an attribute of the profession?

So they say. Did she see it?

No it was sleeping and I did not wish to—

Of course. How did this person discover that you had as it were made yourself an object of interest to the larger public?

Indiscretion on the part of the midwitch I suppose, some people cannot maintain even minimal discretion.

Yes that's the damned thing about some people. Their discretion is out to lunch.

Blabbing things about would be an example.

Popping off to all and sundry about matters.

Ah well.

Ah well. Could we, do you think, proceed?

If we must.

I have the Foot.

Right.

You have the emerald.

Correct.

The Foot has certain properties of special interest to witches.

So I have been told.

There is a distaste, a bad taste in the brain, when one is forced to put the boots to someone.

Must be terrible for you, terrible. Where is my man Soapbox by the way?

That thug you had in front of the door?

Yes, Soapbox.

He is probably reintegrating himself with the basic matter of the universe, right now. Fascinating experience I should think.

Good to know.

I intend only the best for the emerald, however.

What is the best?

There are as you are aware others not so scrupulous in the field. Chislers, in every sense.

And you? What do you intend for it?

I have been thinking of emerald dust. Emerald dust with soda, emerald dust with tomato juice, emerald dust with a dash of bitters, emerald dust with Ovaltine.

I beg your pardon?

I want to live twice.

Twice?

In addition to my present life, I wish another, future life.

A second life. Incremental to the one you are presently enjoying.

As a boy, I was very poor. Poor as pine.

And you have discovered a formula.

Yes.

Plucked from the arcanum.

Yes. Requires a certain amount of emerald. Powdered emerald.

Ugh!

Carat's weight a day for seven thousand thirty-five days.

Coincidence.

Not at all. Only *this* emerald will do. A moon's emerald born of human witch.

No.

I have been thinking about bouillon. Emerald dust and bouillon with a little Tabasco.

No.

No?

No.

My mother is eighty-one, said Vandermaster. I went to my mother and said, Mother, I want to be in love.

And she replied?

She said, me too.

Lily the media person standing in the hall.

I came back to see if you were ready to confess. The hoax.

It's talking now. It talks.

It what?

Lovely complete sentences. Maxims and truisms.

I don't want to hear this. I absolutely—

Look kid this is going to cost you. Sixty dollars.

Sixty dollars for what?

For the interview.

That's checkbook journalism!

Sho' nuff.

It's against the highest traditions of the profession!

You get paid, your boss gets paid, the stockholders get their slice, why not us members of the raw material? Why shouldn't the raw material get paid?

It talks?

Most assuredly it talks.

Will you take a check?

If I must.

You're really a witch.

How many times do I have to tell you?

You do tricks or anything?

Consulting, you might say.

You have clients? People who come to see you regularly on a regular basis?

People with problems, yes.

What kind of problems, for instance?

Some of them very simple, really, things that just need a specific, bit of womandrake for example—

What's womandrake?

Black bryony. Called the herb of beaten wives. Takes away black-and-blue marks.

You get beaten wives?

Stick a little of that number into the old man's pork and

beans, he retches. For seven days and seven nights. It near to kills him.

I have a problem.

What's the problem?

The editor, or editor-king, as he's called around the shop.

What about him?

He takes my stuff and throws it on the floor. When he doesn't like it.

On the floor?

I know it's nothing to you but it *hurts me.* I cry. I know I shouldn't cry but I cry. When I see my stuff on the floor. Pages and pages of it, so carefully typed, *every word spelled right*—

Don't you kids have a union?

Yes but he won't speak to it.

That's this man Lather, right?

Mr. Lather. Editor-imperator.

Okay I'll look into it that'll be another sixty you want to pay now or you want to be billed?

I'll give you another check. *Can* Vandermaster live twice?

There are two theories, the General Theory and the Special Theory. I take it he is relying on the latter. Requires ingestion of a certain amount of emerald. Powdered emerald.

Can you defend yourself?

I have a few things in mind. A few little things.

Can I see the emerald now?

You may. Come this way.

Thank you. Thank you at last. My that's impressive what's that?

That's the thumb of a thief. Enlarged thirty times. Bronze. I use it in my work.

Impressive if one believed in that sort of thing ha-ha I don't mean to—

What care I? What care I? In here. Little emerald, this is Lily. Lily, this is the emerald.

Enchanté, said the emerald. What a pretty young woman you are!

This emerald is young, said Lily. Young, but good. I do not believe what I am seeing with my very eyes!

But perhaps that is a sepsis of the profession? said the emerald.

Vandermaster wants to live twice!

Oh, most foul, most foul!

He was very poor, as a boy! Poor as pine!

Hideous presumption! Cheeky hubris!

He wants to be in love! In love! Presumably with another person!

Unthinkable insouciance!

We'll have his buttons for dinner!

We'll clean the gutters with his hair!

What's your name, buddy?

My name is Tree and I'm smokin' mad!

My name is Bump and I'm just about ready to bust!

I think we should break out the naked-bladed pikes!

I think we should lay hand to torches and tar!

To live again! From the beginning! *Ab ovo!* This concept riles the very marrow of our minds!

We'll flake the white meat from his bones!

And that goes for his damned dog, too!

Hello is this Mad Moll?

Yes who is this?

My name is Lather.

The editor?

Editor-king, actually.

Yes Mr. Lather what is the name of your publication I don't know that Lily ever—

World. I put it together. When *World* is various and beautiful, it's because I am various and beautiful. When *World* is sad and dreary, it's because I am sad and dreary. When *World* is not thy friend, it's because *I* am not thy friend. And if I am not thy friend, baby—

I get the drift.

Listen, Moll, I am not satisfied with what Lily's been giving me. She's not giving me potato chips. I have decided that I am going to handle this story personally, from now on.

She's been insufficiently insightful and comprehensive?

Gore, that's what we need, actual or psychological gore, and this twitter she's been filing—anyhow, I have sent her to Detroit.

Not Detroit!

She's going to be second night-relief paper clipper in the Detroit bureau. She's standing here right now with her bags packed and ashes in her hair and her ticket in her mouth.

Why in her mouth?

Because she needs her hands to rend her garments with.

All right Mr. Lather send her back around. There is new bad news. Bad, bad, new bad news.

That's wonderful!

Moll hangs up the phone and weeps every tear she's capable of weeping, one, two, three.

Takes up a lump of clay, beats it flat with a Bible.

Let me see what do I have here?

I have Ya Ya Oil, that might do it.

I have Anger Oil, Lost & Away Oil, Confusion Oil, Weed of Misfortune, and War Water.

I have graveyard chips, salt, and coriander—enough coriander to freight a ship. Tasty coriander. Magical, magical coriander!

I'll eye-bite the son of a bitch. Have him in worm's hall by teatime.

Understand, ye sons of the wise, what this exceedingly precious Stone crieth out to you!

I'll fold that sucker's tent for him. If my stuff works. One never knows for sure, dammit. And where is Papa?

Throw in a little dwale now, a little orris . . .

Moll shapes the clay into the figure of a man.

So mote it be!

What happened was that they backed a big van up to the back door.

Yes.

There were four of them or eight of them.

Yes.

It was two in the morning or three in the morning or four in the morning—I'm not sure.

Yes.

They were great big hairy men with cudgels and ropes and pads like movers have and a dolly and come-alongs made of barbed wire—that's a loop of barbed wire big enough to slip over somebody's head, with a handle—

Yes.

They wrapped the emerald in the pads and placed it on the dolly and tied ropes around it and got it down the stairs through the door and into the van.

Did they use the Foot?

No they didn't use the Foot they had four witches with them.

Which witches?

The witches Aldrin, Endrin, Lindane, and Dieldrin. Bad-ass witches.

You knew them.

Only by repute. And Vandermaster was standing there with clouds of 1, 1, 2, 2-tetrachloroethylene seething from his nostrils.

That's toxic.

Extremely. I was staggering around bumping into things, tried to hold on to the walls but the walls fell away from me and I fell after them trying to hold on.

These other witches, they do anything to you?

Kicked me in the ribs when I was on the floor. With their pointed shoes. I woke up emeraldless.

Right. Well I guess we'd better get the vast resources of our organization behind this. *World*. From sea to shining sea to shining sea. I'll alert all the bureaus in every direction.

What good will that do?

It will harry them. When a free press is on the case, you can't get away with anything really terrible.

But look at this.

What is it?

A solid silver louse. They left it.

What's it mean?

Means that the devil himself has taken an interest.

A free press, madam, is not afraid of the devil himself.

Who cares what's in a witch's head? Pretty pins for sticking pishtoshio redthread for sewing names to shrouds gallant clankers I'll twoad 'ee and the gollywobbles to give away and the trinkum-trankums to give away with a generous hand pricksticks for the eye damned if I do and damned if I don't what's that upon her forehead? said my father it's a mark said my mother black mark like a furry caterpillar I'll scrub it away with the Ajax and what's that upon her chin? said my father it's a bit of a beard said my mother I'll pluck it away with the tweezers and what's that upon her mouth? said my father it must be a smirk said my mother I'll wipe it away with the heel of my hand she's got hair down there already said my father is that natural? I'll shave it said my mother no one will ever know and those said my father pointing *those?* just what they look like said my mother I'll make a bandeau with this nice clean dish towel she'll be flat as a jack of diamonds in no time and where's the belly button? said my father flipping me about I don't see one anywhere must be coming along later said my mother I'll just pencil one in here with the Magic Marker this child is a bit of a mutt said my father recall to me if you will the circumstances of her conception it was a dark and stormy night said my mother . . . But who cares what's in a witch's head caskets of cankers shelves of twoads for twoading paxwax scalpel polish people with scares sticking to their faces memories of God who held me up and sustained me until I fell from His hands into the world . . .

Twice? Twice? Twice? Twice?

Hey Moll.
Who's that?
It's me.
Me who?
Soapbox.
Soapbox!
I got it!
Got what?
The Foot! I got it right here!
I thought you were blown up!
Naw I pretended to be bought so I was out of the way. Went with them back to their headquarters, or den. Then when they put the Foot back in the refrigerator I grabbed it and beat it back here.
They kept it in the refrigerator?
It needs a constant temperature or else it gets restless. It's hot-tempered. They said.
It's elegant. Weighs a ton though.

Be careful you might—
Soapbox, I am not totally without—it's warm to the hand.
Yes it is warm I noticed that, look what else I got.
What are those?
Thalers. Thalers big as onion rings. Forty-two grand worth.
What are you going to do with them?
Conglomerate!

It is wrong to want to live twice, said the emerald. If I may venture an opinion.

I was very poor, as a boy, said Vandermaster. Nothing to eat but gruel. It was gruel, gruel, gruel. I was fifteen before I ever saw an onion.

These are matters upon which I hesitate to pronounce, being a new thing in the world, said the emerald. A latecomer to the welter. But it seems to me that, having weltered, the wish to *re*-welter might be thought greedy.

Gruel today, gruel yesterday, gruel tomorrow. Sometimes gruel substitutes. I burn to recoup.

Something was said I believe about love.

The ghostfish of love has eluded me these forty-five years.

That Lily person is a pleasant person I think. And pretty too. Very pretty. Good-looking.

Yes she is.

I particularly like the way she is dedicated. She's extremely dedicated. Very dedicated. To her work.

Yes I do not disagree. Admirable. A free press is, I believe, an essential component of—

She is true-blue. Probably it would be great fun to talk to her and get to know her and kiss her and sleep with her and everything of that nature.

What are you suggesting?

Well, there's then, said the emerald, that is to say, your splendid second life.

Yes?

And then there's now. Now is sooner than then.

You have a wonderfully clear head, said Vandermaster, for a rock.

Okay, said Lily. I want you to tap once for yes and twice for no. Do you understand that?

Tap.

You are the true Foot of Mary Magdalene?

Tap.

Vandermaster stole you from a monastery in Italy?

Tap.

A Carthusian monastery in Merano or outside Merano?

Tap.

Are you uncomfortable in that reliquary?

Tap tap.

Have you killed any witches lately? In the last year or so?

Tap tap.

Are you morally neutral or do you have opinions?

Tap.

You have opinions?

Tap.

In the conflict we are now witnessing between Moll and Vandermaster, which of the parties seems to you to have right and justice on her side?

Tap tap tap tap.

That mean Moll? One tap for each letter?

Tap.

Is it warm in there?

Tap.

Too warm?

Tap tap.

So you have been, in a sense, an unwilling partner in Vandermaster's machinations.

Tap.

And you would not be averse probably to using your considerable powers on Moll's behalf.

Tap.

Do you know where Vandermaster is right now?

Tap tap.

Have you any idea what his next move will be?

Tap tap.

What is your opinion of the women's movement?

Tap tap tap tap tap tap tap tap tap tap tap tap tap tap.

I'm sorry I didn't get that. Do you have a favorite color what do you think of cosmetic surgery should children be allowed to watch television after ten P.M. how do you feel about aging is nuclear energy in your opinion a viable alternative to fossil fuels how do you deal with stress are you afraid to fly and do you have a chili recipe you'd care to share with the folks?

Tap tap.

The first interview in the world with the true Foot of Mary Magdalene and no chili recipe!

Mrs. Vandermaster.
Yes.
Please be seated.
Thank you.
The red chair.
You're most kind.
Can I get you something, some iced tea or a little hit of Sanka?
A Ghost Dance is what I wouldn't mind if you can do it.
What's a Ghost Dance?
That's one part vodka to one part tequila with half an onion. Half a regular onion.
Wow wow wow wow wow.
Well when you're eighty-one, you know, there's not so much. Couple of Ghost Dances, I begin to take an interest.
I believe I can accommodate you.
Couple of Ghost Dances, I begin to look up and take notice.
Mrs. Vandermaster, you are aware are you not that your vile son has, with the aid of various parties, abducted my emerald? My own true emerald?
I mighta heard about it.
Well have you or haven't you?
'Course I don't pay much attention to that boy myself. He's bent.
Bent?
Him and his dog. He goes off in a corner and talks to the dog. Looking over his shoulder to see if I'm listening. As if I'd care.
The dog doesn't—
Just listens. *Intently.*
That's Tarbut.
Now I don't mind somebody who just addresses an occasional

remark to the dog, like "Attaboy, dog," or something like that, or "Get the ball, dog," or something like that, but he *confides* in the dog. Bent.

You know what Vandermaster's profession is.

Yes, he's a mage. Think that's a little bent.

Is there anything you can do, or would do, to help me get my child back? My sweet emerald?

Well I don't have that much say-so.

You don't.

I don't know too much about what-all he's up to. He comes and goes.

I see.

The thing is, he's bent.

You told me.

Wants to live twice.

I know.

I think it's a sin and a shame.

You do.

And your poor little child.

Yes.

A damned scandal.

Yes.

I'd witch his eyes out if I were you.

The thought's appealing.

His eyes like onions . . .

A black bloodhound who looks as if he might have been fed on human milk. Bloodhounding down the center of the street, nose to the ground.

You think this will work?

Soapbox, do you have a better idea?

Where did you find him?

I found him on the doorstep. Sitting there. In the moonlight.

In the moonlight?

Aureoled all around with moonglow.

You think that's significant?

Well I don't think it's happenstance.

What's his name?

Tarbut.

There's something I have to tell you.
What?
I went to the refrigerator for a beer?
Yes?
The Foot's walked.

Dead! Kicked in the heart by the Foot!
That's incredible!
Deep footprint right over the breastbone!
That's ghastly and awful!
After Lily turned him down he went after the emerald with a sledge!
Was the emerald hurt?
Chipped! The Foot got there in the nick!
And Moll?
She's gluing the chips back with grume!
What's grume?
Clotted blood!
And was the corpse claimed?
Three devils showed up! Lily's interviewing them right now!
A free press is not afraid of a thousand devils!
There are only three!
What do they look like?
Like Lather, the editor!
And the Foot?
Soapbox is taking it back to Italy! He's starting a security-guard business! Hired Sallywag, Wide Boy, Taptoe, and Sometimes!
What's your name by the way?
My name is Knucks. What's your name?
I'm Pebble. And the dog?
The dog's going to work for Soapbox too!
Curious, the dog showing up on Moll's doorstep that way!
Deus Lunus works in mysterious ways!
Deus Lunus never lets down a pal!
Well how 'bout a drink!
Don't mind if I do! What'll we drink to?
We'll drink to living once!
Hurrah for the here and now!

Tell me, said the emerald, what are diamonds like?

I know little of diamonds, said Moll.

Is a diamond better than an emerald?

Apples and oranges I would say.

Would you have *preferred* a diamond?

Nope.

Diamond-hard, said the emerald, that's an expression I've encountered.

Diamonds are a little ordinary. Decent, yes. Quiet, yes. But *gray*. Give me step-cut zircons, square-cut spodumenes, jasper, sardonyx, bloodstones, Baltic amber, cursed opals, peridots of your own hue, the padparadscha sapphire, yellow chrysoberyls, the shifty tourmaline, cabochons . . . But best of all, an emerald.

But what is the *meaning* of the emerald? asked Lily. I mean overall? If you can say.

I have some notions, said Moll. You may credit them or not.

Try me.

It means, one, that the gods are not yet done with us.

Gods not yet done with us.

The gods are still trafficking with us and making interventions of this kind and that kind and are not dormant or dead as has often been proclaimed by dummies.

Still trafficking. Not dead.

Just as in former times a demon might enter a nun on a piece of lettuce she was eating so even in these times a simple Mailgram might be the thin edge of the wedge.

Thin edge of the wedge.

Two, the world may congratulate itself that desire can still be raised in the dulled hearts of the citizens by the rumor of an emerald.

Desire or cupidity?

I do not distinguish qualitatively among the desires, we have referees for that, but he who covets not at all is a lump and I do not wish to have him to dinner.

Positive attitude toward desire.

Yes. Three, I do not know what this Stone portends, whether it portends for the better or portends for the worse or merely portends a bubbling of the in-between but you are in any case rescued from the sickliness of same and a small offering in the hat on the hall table would not be ill regarded.

And what now? said the emerald. What now, beautiful mother?

We resume the scrabble for existence, said Moll. We resume the scrabble for existence, in the sweet of the here and now.

How I Write My Songs

Some of the methods I use to write my songs will be found in the following examples. Everyone has a song in him or her. Writing songs is a basic human trait. I am not saying that it is easy; like everything else worthwhile in this world it requires concentration and hard work. The methods I will outline are a good way to begin and have worked for me but they are by no means the only methods that can be used. There is no one set way of writing your songs, every way is just as good as the other as Kipling said. (I am talking now about the lyrics; we will talk about the melodies in a little bit.) The important thing is to put true life into your songs, things that people know and can recognize and truly feel. You have to be open to experience, to what is going on around you, the things of daily life. Often little things that you don't even think about at the time can be the basis of a song.

A knowledge of all the different types of songs that are commonly accepted is helpful. To give you an idea of the various types of songs there are I am going to tell you how I wrote various of my own, including "Rudelle," "Last Night," "Sad Dog Blues," and others—how I came to write these songs and where I got the idea and what the circumstances were, more or less, so that you will be able to do the same thing. Just remember, *there is no substitute for sticking to it* and listening to the work of others who have been down this road before you and have mastered their craft over many years.

In the case of "Rudelle" I was sitting at my desk one day with my pencil and yellow legal pad and I had two things that were irritating me. One was a letter from the electric company that said "The check for $75.60 sent us in payment of your bill has been returned to us by the bank unhonored etc. etc." Most of you who have received this type of letter from time to time know how irritating this kind of communication can be as well as embarrassing. The other thing that was irritating me was that I had a piece of white thread tied tight around my middle at navel height as a reminder to keep my stomach pulled in to strengthen the abdominals while sitting—this is the price you pay for slopping down too much beer when your occupation is essentially a sit-down one! Anyhow I had these two things itching me, so I decided to write a lost-my-mind song.

I wrote down on my legal pad the words:

> When I lost my baby
> I almost lost my mine

This is more or less a traditional opening for this type of song. Maybe it was written by somebody originally way long ago and who wrote it is forgotten. It often helps to begin with a traditional or well-known line or lines to set a pattern for yourself. You can then write the rest of the song and, if you wish, cut off the top part, giving you an original song. *Songs are always composed of both traditional and new elements.* This means that you can rely on the tradition to give your song "legs" while also putting in your own experience or particular way of looking at things for the new.

Incidentally the lines I have quoted may look pretty bare to you but remember you are looking at just one element, the words, and there is also the melody and the special way various artists will have of singing it which gives flavor and freshness. For example, an artist who is primarily a blues singer would probably give the "when" a lot of squeeze, that is to say, draw it out, and he might also sing "baby" as three notes, "bay-ee-bee," although it is only two syllables. Various artists have their own unique ways of doing a song and what may appear to be rather plain or dull on paper becomes quite different when it is a song.

I then wrote:

> When I lost my baby
> I almost lost my mine
> When I lost my baby
> I almost lost my mine
> When I found my baby
> The sun began to shine.

Copyright © 1972 by French Music, Inc.

You will notice I retained the traditional opening because it was so traditional I did not see any need to delete it. With the addition of various material about Rudelle and what kind of woman she was, it became gold in 1976.

Incidentally while we are talking about use of traditional materials here is a little tip: you can often make good use of colorful expressions in common use such as "If the good Lord's willin' and the creek don't rise" (to give you just one example) which I used in "Goin' to Get Together" as follows:

> Goin' to get to-geth-er
> Goin' to get to-geth-er
> If the good Lord's willin' and the creek don't rise.

Copyright © 1974 by French Music, Inc.

These common expressions are expressive of the pungent ways in which most people often think—they are the salt of your song, so to say. Try it!

It is also possible to give a song a funny or humorous "twist":

> Show'd my soul to the woman at
>   the bank
> She said put that thing away boy,
>   put that thing away
> Show'd my soul to the woman at
>   the liquor store
> She said put that thing away boy,
>   'fore it turns the wine
> Show'd my soul to the woman at
>   the 7-Eleven
> She said: Is that all?

Copyright © 1974 by Rattlesnake Music, Inc.

You will notice that the meter here is various and the artist is given great liberties.

Another type of song which is a dear favorite of almost everyone is the song that has a message, some kind of thought that people can carry away with them and think about. Many songs of this type are written and gain great acceptance every day. Here is one of my own that I put to a melody which has a kind of martial flavor:

> How do you spell truth? L-o-v-e is
> how you spell truth
> How do you spell love? T-r-u-t-h
> is how you spell love
> Where were you last night?
> Where were you last night?

Copyright © 1976 by Rattlesnake Music/A.I.M. Corp.

When "Last Night" was first recorded, the engineer said "That's a keeper" on the first take and it was subsequently covered by sixteen artists including Walls.

The I-ain't-nothin'-but-a-man song is a good one to write when you are having a dry spell. These occur in songwriting as in any other profession and if you are in one it is often helpful to try your hand at this type of song which is particularly good with a heavy rhythm emphasis in the following pattern

> Da da da da *da*
> Whomp, whomp

where some of your instruments are playing da da da da *da*, hitting that last note hard, and the others answer whomp, whomp. Here is one of my own:

> I'm just an ordinary mane
> Da da da da *da*
> Whomp, whomp
> Just an ordinary mane
> Da da da da *da*
> Whomp, whomp
> Ain't nothin' but a mane
> Da da da da *da*
> Whomp, whomp
> I'm a grizzly mane

Da da da da *da*
Whomp, whomp
I'm a hello-goodbye mane
Da da da da *da*
Whomp, whomp
I'm a ramblin'-gamblin' mane
Da da da da *da*
Whomp, whomp
I'm a *mane's* mane
Da da da da *da*
Whomp, whomp
I'm a woeman's mane
Da da da da *da*
Whomp, whomp
I'm an upstairs-downstairs mane
Da da da da *da*
Whomp, whomp
I'm a today-and-tomorrow mane
Da da da da *da*
Whomp, whomp
I'm a Freeway mane
Da da da da *da*
Whomp, whomp

Copyright © 1977 by French Music, Inc.

Well, you see how it is done. It is my hope that these few words will get you started. Remember that although this business may seem closed and standoffish to you, looking at it from the outside, inside it has some very warm people in it, some of the finest people I have run into in the course of a varied life. The main thing is to persevere and to believe in yourself, no matter what the attitude of others may be or appear to be. I could never have written my songs had I failed to believe in Bill B. White, not as a matter of conceit or false pride but as a human being. I will continue to write my songs, for the nation as a whole and for the world.

The Farewell

—WELL MAGGIE I have finally been admitted to the damn Conservatory. Finally.

—Yes Hilda I was astonished when I heard the news, astonished.

—A glorious messenger came riding. Said I was to be admitted. At last.

—Well Hilda I suppose they must have changed the standards or something.

—He was clothed all in silver, and his hat held a pure white plume. He doffed his hat and waved it in the air, and bowed.

—The Admissions Committee's been making some pretty strange calls lately, lots of talk about it.

—A Presidential appointment, he said. Direct from the President himself.

—Yes those are for disadvantaged people who would not otherwise be considered. Who would not otherwise be considered in a million years.

—Well Maggie now that we are both members of the Conservatory maybe you won't be so snotty.

—Snotty?

—Maybe you won't be lording it over me quite so much, all those little vicious digs.

—Me?

—All those innocent remarks with little curly hooks in them.

—Hilda this can't be me you're talking about. Me, your dear friend.

—Well it doesn't matter now anyway because we are both on the same plane at last. Both members of the Conservatory.

—Hilda I have to tell you something.

—What?

—A lot of people are leaving. The Conservatory. Leaving the Conservatory and transferring to the Institution.

—What's that?

—A new place. Very rigorous.

—You mean people are leaving the Conservatory?

—Yes. Switching to the Institution.
—It's called the Institution?
—Yes. It's a new place.
—What's so good about it?
—It's new. Very rigorous.
—You mean after I've killed myself to get into the Conservatory there's a new place that's better?
—Yes they have new methods. New, superior methods. I would say that the cream of the Conservatory is transferring to the Institution or will transfer to the Institution.
—But you're still at the Conservatory aren't you?
—Thinking of transferring. To the Institution.
—But I *sweated blood* to get into the Conservatory you know that. You know it!
—At the Institution they have not only improved methodologies but also a finer quality of teacher. The teachers are more dedicated, twice as dedicated or three times as dedicated. The design of the Institution buildings has been carefully studied, and is new. Each student has his or her own personal wickiup wherein he or she may spend hours one-on-one with his or her own personal, supremely dedicated teacher.
—I cannot believe this!
—Savory meals are left in steaming baskets outside each wickiup door. All meals are lobster, unless the student has indicated a preference for beautifully marbled beef. There are four Olympic-sized pool tables for every one student.
—It's just unfair, hideously unfair.
—The Institution song was composed by Tammy and the Rayettes and the Institution T-shirt is by Hedwig McMary. And of course they have the improved methodologies.
—Of course.
—Yes.
—Maggie?
—What?
—I guess this joint is tough to get into, right?
—Impossible.
—Then how can you—
—There's this guy I know he's the Chancellor. Boss of the whole shebang. He likes me.
—I see.

—He is devoted to me and always has been. Me and my potential. He is wonderful on the subject of my potential.

—I already had a babysitter hired. For those hours I would have spent at the Conservatory.

—Well don't be downhearted Hilda, the Conservatory is a very fine place too. Within its limits.

—I already had a babysitter laid on. For those days on which I would have been wending my way up the hill through the gum trees to the Conservatory. Once the zenith of my aspirations.

—Yes how is that kid you're a mother now must make you feel different.

—What can I tell you? It eats.

—I guess the father what's-his-name never showed up again did he?

—Sent some Q-tips in the mail.

—The beast.

—Maggie you've got to help me.

—Help you what?

—I must get into the Institution.

—You?

—I must get into the Institution.

—Oh my.

—If I don't get into the Institution I will shrink into a little shrunken mummy, self-esteem-wise.

—O my dear one your plight is painful to me.

—My plight?

—Wouldn't you call it a plight?

—I guess so. Good of you to find the *mot juste*.

—Hilda I will do everything in my power to help you achieve your mete measure of personal growth. Everything.

—Thank you Maggie. I believe you.

—But we have to be realistic.

—What does that mean?

—There are some kinds of places for some kinds of people and other kinds of places for other kinds of people.

—What does that mean?

—Did I tell you I got a grant?

—What kind of a grant?

—There are these excellence grants they give to people who are excellent. I got one.

—Oh. I thought you already had a grant.

—That was my old grant. That was for enrichment. This is new. It's for excellence.

—I could I suppose just sink down into the gutter. The gutter of plain life. Life without excellence.

—Hilda it's not like you to give up like this. It's sensible, but not like you.

—Maggie I am floating away from you. Floating away. Like a brown leaf in the gutter.

—Where will you go?

—I have decided. There'll be a night-long, block-long farewell party. Everyone will be invited. All those who have mocked me will not be invited but all those who have loved me will be invited. There will be crystal, silver, Persian lilies, torches, garlic bread, and jugs of rare jug wine.

—When do you figure this will be?

—Maybe Thursday. All my friends smiling faithfully up at me from their assigned places at the block-long table. Spaced carefully here and there, interesting-looking men who look like ads. Smiling up at me from their places where they have been put as interesting stuffing between all my friends.

—All your friends.

—Yes. All my glorious shining friends.

—Who?

—All my friends.

—Yes but who? Who specifically?

—All my friends. I see what you mean.

—I can't believe I said that Hilda. Did I say that?

—Yes you did.

—I didn't mean it. It was the truth, but I didn't mean it. I'm sorry.

—OK.

—It just slipped out.

—Doesn't matter.

—Can you forgive me?

—Of course. I'll have the party anyhow. Maybe ask a lot of answering services or something.

—I will come. If I'm invited.

—Who if not you?

—You'll make it Hilda I'm sure you will. One of these days.

—That's good to hear Maggie I'm glad I have your support.
—You will not only endure, you will prevail.
—Well thanks a lot Maggie. Thanks. Over what?
—Over everything. It's in the cards Hilda I know it.
—Well thanks a lot. Do you really think so?
—I really think so. I really do.
—All my friends smiling faithfully up at me. Well, fuck it.

The Emperor

EACH MORNING the Emperor weighs the documents brought to him, each evening he weighs them again; he will not rest until a certain weight has passed through his hands; he has declared six to be the paramount number of his reign, black the paramount color; he hurries from palace to palace, along the underground corridors, ignoring gorgeous wall hangings, bells, drums, beautiful ladies; how many more responsible officials must be strangled before his will prevails, absolutely?

The Emperor sleeps in a different palace each night, to defeat assassins; of the two hundred and seventy palaces, some are congenial to him, some not; the three worms inspiring disease, old age and death have yet to find him; his presents this morning included a most dazzling parcel-gilt bronze wine warmer, gift of the grateful people of Peiho, and a sumptuous set of nine bronze bells tuned in scale, gift of the worshipful citizens of Yuchang; he has decided that all officers in these places will be promoted one rank, and that the village well in Peiho will be given the title of Minister of the Fifth Rank . . .

The First Emperor has decreed that the people of his realm will be called the Blackheaded People, in the ocean there are three fairy islands, Penglai, Fangchang and Ingchou, where immortals live, and he has sent the scholar Hsu Fu, with several thousand young boys and girls, to find them; he dictates a memorial which begins, "*The Throne appreciates . . .*", the famous assassin Ching K'o has purchased, for a hundred pieces of gold, a bronze dagger said to be the sharpest in the kingdom.

Hats are six inches wide, carriages six feet wide, the Empire has been divided into thirty-six provinces; a jade cicada is placed upon the tongues of ministers of the Sixth through the First Rank, upon interment; as he hurries through the corridors he is beseeched by wives, so many that he no longer attempts to remember their names, but addresses each as "Wife!" and flees their fatiguing excellences; he sends armies hither and thither as others send messengers; the model of all China he has decreed must be inspected, its rivers of quicksilver and cities of celadon must be approved; if you have artisans strangled for poor work there remain their families, consistently large, whispering against you in the squares and taverns . . .

The Emperor Ch'in Shih Huang Ti has decreed that six thousand archers, lancers, charioteers and musicians be buried alive, along with two thousand horses, in military formation on the four sides of his tomb; responsible officials attempt to reason with him, stating that this will enflame the people against him; but his tomb must be defended by precisely six thousand archers, lancers, charioteers and musicians, lest it suffer the fate of other tombs in other times; the enfeoffed Marquis of Chienchang has wrongly seized territory in that area, stranglers are summoned; generals on the frontier must be regularly and thoroughly frightened, so that they do not misremember where their true allegiance rests . . .

His gifts this morning include two white-jade tigers, at full scale, carved by the artist Lieh Yi, and the Emperor himself takes brush in hand to paint their eyes with dark lacquer; responsible officials have suggested that six thousand terracotta soldiers and two thousand terra-cotta horses, at full scale, be buried, for the defense of his tomb; the Emperor in his rage orders that three thousand convicts cut down all the trees on Mount Hsiang, leaving it bare, bald, so that responsible officials may understand what is possible; the Emperor commands the court poets to write poems about immortals, pure beings, and noble spirits who by their own labors change night to day, and has these sung to him; everyone knows that executions should not be carried out in the spring, even a child knows it, but in certain cases . . .

The deft and subtle assassin Ching K'o is beheaded, and his botched attempt recorded in the annals, and his botched last words excised from the annals; the Emperor hurries through the corridors of his plethora of palaces accepting petitions which he thrusts into the sleeves of his robe; seventy thousand convicts are at work on the construction of his tomb, which has been in progress since his thirteenth year and measures 2173 meters north-south and 974 meters east-west; the ceiling of the inmost chamber has a sky in which pearls of ungodly size represent the stars, the constellations; the Emperor Ch'in Shih

Huang Ti pauses, drinks warm wine, and considers whether sufficient chairs have been provided, in his tomb, for the suites of wives, generals and responsible officials who will be buried with him; the scholar Hsu Fu, and the youths and maidens who embarked with him, have not been heard from, have most certainly been devoured by monsters . . .

For a thousand piculs of grain a commoner can now purchase noble rank, a scandal; the Emperor has had a building stone too large to be moved through the Kirin Gate given sixty lashes, to punish it; there is a woman who excites him, the Lady Yao (with the long scar on the right leg) but to find his way back to the pavilion that contains her is an almost impossible task; a blasphemer has described him as a dog, a hen, and a snake, and he rejoices in the poverty of mind displayed; he will cause Mount Hsiang to be planted in squared-off stakes, so that certain officials may achieve a more sophisticated comprehension of the Imperial will . . .

No. He will permit the six thousand clay soldiers to be buried, and with them, one real soldier, a prince, a secret happiness; he will prepare with his own hands for this prince a potion to put him softly to sleep, a fatherly happiness; he will whisper into this prince's ear, before administering the potion, a lifetime of secrets, a delirious happiness; he will have the buriers of the prince themselves buried, a geometric happiness; those who perform the second burial will be sent away to a war, which he will contrive through transcendent military skill to lose, a sad, remote, and professional happiness; he will walk through the streets of the capital barefoot and carrying a thorn bush with which to flagellate his naked shoulders for having lost this war, a hidden and painful happiness; these happinesses taken together may be the equal of the herbs of immortality growing like weeds on the magic island of Penglai; like weeds.

Thailand

Yes, said the old soldier, I remember a time. It was during the Krian War.

Bless you and keep you, said his hearer, silently.

It was during the Krian War, said the old soldier. We were up there on the 38th parallel, my division, round about the Chorwon Valley. This was in '52.

Oh God, said the listener to himself. Enchiladas in green sauce. Dos Equis. Maybe a burrito or two.

We had this battalion of Thais attached to us, said the old sergeant. Nicest people you'd ever want to meet. We used to call their area Thailand, like it was a whole country. They are small of stature. We used to party with them a lot. What they drink is Mekong, it'll curl your teeth. In Kria we weren't too particular.

Enchiladas in green sauce and Gilda. Gilda in her sizzling blouse.

This time I'm talking about, we were partying at Thailand, there was this Thai second john who was a personal friend of mine, named Sutchai. Tall fellow, thin, he was an exception to the rule. We were right tight, even went on R&R together, you're too young to know what that is, it's Rest and Recreation where you zip off to Tokyo and sample the delights of that great city for a week.

I am young, thought the listener, young, young, praise the Lord I am young.

This time I am talking about, said the old sarge, we were on the side of a hill, they held this hill which sort of anchored the MLR—that's Main Line of Resistance—at that point, pretty good-sized hill I forget what the designation was, and it was a feast day, some Thai feast, a big holiday, and the skies were sunny, sunny. They had set out thirty-seven washtubs full of curry I never saw anything like it. Thirty-seven washtubs full of curry and a different curry in every one. They even had eel curry.

I cannot believe I am sitting here listening to this demento carry on about eel curry.

It was a golden revel, said the sergeant, if you liked curry and I did and do. Beef curry, chicken curry, the delicate Thai worm curry, all your various fish curries and vegetable curries. The Thai cooks were number one, even in the sergeant's mess which I was the treasurer of for a year and a half we didn't eat like that. Well, you're too young to know what a quad-fifty is but it's four fifty-caliber machine guns mounted on a half-track and they had quad-fifties dug in on various parts of their hill as well as tanks which was just about all you could do with a tank in that terrain, and toward evening they were firing off tracer bursts from the quad-fifties to make fireworks and it was just very festive, very festive. They had fighting with wooden swords at which the Thais excel, it's like a ballet dance, and the whole battalion was putting away the Mekong and beer pretty good as were the invited guests such as me and my buddy Nick Pirelli who was my good buddy in the motor pool, anytime I wanted a vehicle of any type for any purpose all I had to do was call Nick and he'd redline that vehicle and send it over to me with a driver—

I too have a life, thought the listener, but it is motes of dust in the air.

They had this pretty interesting, actually highly interesting, ceremony, said the sargie-san, as part of the feast, on that night on that hill in Kria, where everybody lined up and their colonel, that was Colonel Parti, I knew him, a wise and handsome man, stripped to the waist and the men, one by one, passed before him and poured water on his head, half a cupful per man. The Colonel sat there and they poured water on his head, it had some kind of religious significance—they're Buddhists—the whole battalion, that's six hundred men more or less, passed in front of him and poured water on his head, it was a blessing or something, it was spring. Colonel Parti always used to say to me, his English wasn't too good but it was a hell of a lot better than my Thai which didn't exist, he always used to say "Sergeant, after the war I come to Big PX"—that's what they called America, the Big PX—"I come to Big PX and we play golf." I didn't even know they had golf in Thailand but he was supposed to be some kind of hot-shot golf player, I heard he'd been on their Olympic golf team at one time, funny to think of them having one but they were surprising and beautiful people, our houseboy Kim, we had these Krian houseboys who kept the tent policed up and cleaned your rifle and did the laundry, pretty near everybody in Kria is named Kim by the way, Kim had been with the division from the beginning and had gone to the Yalu with the division in '50 when the Chinese came in and kicked our asses all the way back to Seoul and Kim had been in a six-by-six firing some guy's M-1 all the way through the retreat which was a nightmare and therefore everybody was always very respectful of him even though he was only a houseboy . . . Anyhow, Kim had told me Colonel Parti was a high-ranked champion golfer. That's how I knew it.

He reminds me of poor people, thought the young man, poor people whom I hate.

The Chinese pulled all these night attacks, said the sergeant.

The babble of God-given senility, said the listener to his inner ear.

It was terrifying. There'd be these terrifying bugles, you'd sit up in your sleeping bag hearing the bugles which sounded like they were coming from every which way, all around you, everybody grabbing his weapon and running around like a chicken with his head cut off, DivArty would be putting down a barrage you could hear it but God knows what they thought they were firing at, your communications trenches would be full of insane Chinese, flares popping in the sky—

I consign you to history, said his hearer. I close, forever, the book.

Once, they wanted to send me to cooks-and-bakers school, said the sergeant who was wearing a dull-red bathrobe, but I told them no, I couldn't feature myself a cook, that's why I was in heavy weapons. This party at Thailand was the high point of that tour. I never before or since saw thirty-seven washtubs full of curry and I would like to go to that country someday and talk to those people some more, they were great people. Sutchai wanted to be Prime Minister of Thailand, that was his ambition, never made it to my knowledge but I keep looking for him in the newspaper, you never know. I was on this plane going from Atlanta to Brooke Medical Center in San Antonio,

I had to have some scans, there were all these young troopers on the plane, they were all little girls. Looked to be about sixteen. They all had these OD turtlenecks with Class A uniforms if you can imagine, they were the sloppiest soldiers I ever did see, the all-volunteer Army I suppose I know I shouldn't criticize.

Go to cooks-and-bakers school, bake there, thought the young man. Bake a bathrobe of bread.

Thirty-seven damn washtubs, said the sergeant. If you can imagine.

Requiescat in pace.

They don't really have worm curry, said the sergeant. I just made that up to fool you.

Heroes

—THESE GUYS, you know, if they don't know what's the story how can they . . .
—Exactly.
—So I inform myself. *U.S. News & World Report. Business Week. Scientific American.* I make it a point to steep myself in information.
—Yes.
—Otherwise your decisions have little meaning.
—Right.
—I mean they have *meaning*, because no decisions are meaningless in and of themselves, but they don't have *informed* meaning.
—Every citizen has a right.
—To what?
—To act. According to his lights.
—That's right.
—But his lights are not going to be that great. If he doesn't take the trouble. To find out what's the story.
—Take a candidate for something.
—Absolutely.
—There are all these candidates.
—More all the time. Hundreds.
—Now how does the ordinary man—
—The man in the street—
—*Really know.* Anything. About these birds.
—The media.
—Right. The media. That's how we know.
—Façades.
—One of these birds, maybe he calls you on the telephone.
—Right.
—You're flattered out of your skull, right?
—Right.
—You say, Oh my God, I'm talking to a goddamn *senator* or something.
—You're covered with awe.

—Or whoever it is. He's got your name on a little card, right? He's holding the card in his hand.
—Right.
—Say your name is George. He says, Well, George, very good to talk to you, what do you think about the economy? Or whatever it is.
—What do you say?
—You say, Well, Senator, it looks to me like it's a little shaky, the economy.
—You've informed yourself about the economy.
—Wait a minute, wait a minute, that's not the point. I mean it's *part* of the point but it's not the *whole* point.
—Right.
—So you tell him your opinion, it's a little shaky. And he agrees with you and everybody hangs up feeling good.
—Absolutely.
—But this is the point. Does he *act* on your opinion?
—No.
—Does he even remember your opinion?
—He reaches for the next card.
—He's got just a hell of a lot of cards there.
—Maybe two hundred or three hundred.
—And this is just one session on the phone.
—He must get tired of it.
—Bored out of his skull. But that's not the point. The point is, the whole thing is meaningless. You don't know one damn thing more about him than before.
—Well, sometimes you can tell something. From the voice.
—Or say you meet him in person.
—The candidate. He comes to where you work.
—He's out there in the parking lot slapping skin.
—He shakes your hand.
—Then he shakes the next guy's hand. What do you know after he's shook your hand?
—Zero. Zip.
—Let me give you a third situation.
—What?
—You're standing on the sidewalk and he passes in his motorcade. Waving and smiling. What do you learn? That he's got a suntan.

—What is the reality? What is the man behind the mask? You don't learn.

—Therefore we rely on the media. We are *forced* to rely on the media. The print media and the electronic media.

—Thank God we got the media.

—That's what we have. Those are our tools. To inform ourselves.

—Correct. One hundred percent.

—*But.* And this is the point. There are distortions in the media.

—They're only human, right?

—The media are not a clear glass through which we can see a thing clearly.

—We see it darkly.

—I'm not saying these are intentional. The ripples in the clear glass. But we have to take them into consideration.

—We are prone to error.

—Now, you take a press conference.

—The candidate. Or the President.

—*Sometimes they ask them the questions that they want to be asked.*

—Pre-prepared questions.

—I'm not saying all of them. I'm not even saying most of them. But it happens.

—I figured.

—Or he doesn't pick the one to answer that he knows is going to shoot him a toughie.

—He picks the guy behind him.

—I mean he's been in this business a long time. He knows that one guy is going to ask him about the economy and one guy is going to ask him about nuclear holocaust and one guy is going to ask him about China. So he can predict—

—What type of question a particular guy is going to pop on him.

—That's right. Of course some of these babies, they're as smart as he is. In their own particular areas of expertise.

—They can throw him a curve.

—He's got egg on his face.

—Or maybe he just decides to tough it out and *answer* the damned question.

—But what we get, what the public gets—
—The tip of the iceberg.
—There's a lot more under the surface that we don't get.
—The whole iceberg.
—We're like blind men feeling the iceberg.
—So you have to have *many, many* sources. To get a picture.
—Both print and electronic.
—When we see a press conference on the tube, *it's not even the whole press conference.*
—It's the highlights.
—Just the highlights. Most of the time.
—Maybe there was something that you wanted to know that got cut out.
—Five will get you ten there's something touching your vital personal interests that got cut out.
—Absolutely.
—They don't do it on purpose. They're human beings.
—I know that. And without them we would have nothing.
—But sometimes bias creeps in.
—Very subtle bias that colors their objectivity.
—Maybe they're not even aware of it but it creeps in. The back door.
—Like you're looking at the newspaper and they have pictures of all the candidates. They're all out campaigning, different places. And maybe they run one guy's picture twice as big as another guy's picture.
—Why do they do that?
—Maybe it's more humanly interesting, the first guy's picture. But it's still bias.
—Maybe they ought to measure them, the pictures.
—Maybe they *like* the guy. Maybe they just like him as a human being. He's more likable. That creeps in.
—One-on-one, the guy's more likable.
—But to be fair you should print the guy's picture you don't like as big as this guy's.
—Or maybe the guy they don't like, they give him more scrutiny. His personal life. His campaign contributions.
—Or maybe you want a job if he gets elected. It's human.
—That's a low thought. That's a *terrible* thought.
—Well, be realistic.

—I don't think that happens. There aren't that many jobs that they would want.

—In the damn *government* there aren't that many jobs?

—That were better than their present jobs. I mean which would you rather be, some government flunky or a powerful figure in the media?

—The latter. Any day in the week.

—I mean what if you're the goddamn *Wall Street Journal*, for instance? A powerful voice. A Cassandra crying in the wilderness. They're scared of what you might reveal or might not reveal. You can hold your head up. You bow to no man, not even presidents or kings—

—You have to stand up if he comes into the room, that's the rule.

—Well, standing up is not bowing.

—The thing is to study their faces, these guys, these guys that are running, on the tube. *With the sound turned off.* So you can see.

—You can read their souls.

—You can't read their souls, you can get an idea, a glimpse. The human face is a dark pool with dark things swimming in it, under the surface. You look for a long time, using your whole experience of life. To discern what's with this guy.

—I mean he's trying to look good, the poor bastard, busting his ass to look good in every nook and cranny of America.

—What do we really know about him? What do we know?

—He wants the job.

—Enormous forces have pressured him into wanting the job. Destiny. Some people are bigger than you or I. A bigger destiny. It's tearing him apart, not to have the job, he sees some other guy's got the job and he says to himself, My destiny is as big as that guy's destiny— If I can just get these mothers to elect me.

—The rank and file. Us.

—If I can just get them to rally to my banner, the dummies.

—You think he thinks that?

—What's he going to think? It's tearing him apart, not to be elected.

—We're mere pawns. Clowns. Garbage.

—No. Without us, they can't realize their destinies. Can't even begin. No way.

—We make the judgments. Shrewd, informed judgments. Because we have informed ourselves.

—Taking into account the manifold distractions of a busy fruitful life.

—If it is fruitful.

—It's mostly going to be fruitful. If the individual makes the effort, knows what's the story—

—How did they know before they had the media?

—Vast crowds would assemble, from every hearth in the land. You had to be able to make a speech, just a dilly of a speech. "You shall not crucify mankind upon a cross of gold"— William Jennings Bryan. You had to be larger than life.

—The hearer of the speech knew—

—They were noble figures.

—They had to have a voice like an organ.

—The vast crowd swept by a fervor, as if by a wind.

—They were heroes and the individual loved them.

—Maybe misled. History sorts it out.

—Giant figures with voices like a whole church choir, plus the organ—

—A strange light coming from behind them, maybe it was only the sun . . .

Bishop

Bishop's standing outside his apartment building.

An oil truck double-parked, its hose coupled with the sidewalk, the green-uniformed driver reading a paperback called *Name Your Baby*.

Bishop's waiting for Cara.

The martini rule is not before quarter to twelve.

Eyes go out of focus. He blinks them back again.

He had a beer for breakfast, as usual, a Pilsner Urquell. Imported beer is now ninety-nine cents a bottle at his market.

The oil truck's pump shuts off with a click. The driver tosses his book into the cab and begins uncoupling.

Cara's not coming.

The painter John Frederick Peto made a living playing cornet in a camp meeting for the last twenty years of his life, according to Alfred Frankenstein.

Bishop goes back inside the building and climbs one flight of stairs to his apartment.

His bank has lost the alimony payment he cables twice a month to his second wife, in London. He switches on the FM, dialing past two classical stations to reach Fleetwood Mac.

Bishop's writing a biography of the nineteenth-century American painter William Michael Harnett. But today he can't make himself work.

Cara's been divorced, once.

At twenty minutes to twelve he makes himself a martini.

Hideous bouts of black anger in the evening. Then a word or a sentence in the tone she can't bear. The next morning he remembers nothing about it.

The artist Peto was discovered when, after his death, his pictures were exhibited with the faked signatures of William Michael Harnett, according to Alfred Frankenstein.

His second wife, working in London, recently fainted at her desk. The company doctor sent her home with something written on a slip of paper—a diagnosis. For two days she stared at the piece of paper, then called Bishop and read him the word: *lipothymia*. Bishop checked with the public library, called her again in London. "It means fainting," he said.

On the FM, a program called *How to Protect Against Radiation Through Good Nutrition*. He switches it off.

In the morning he remembers nothing of what had been said the previous night. But, coming into the kitchen and seeing her harsh, set face, he knows there's been a quarrel.

His eyes ache.

He's not fat.

She calls.

"I can't make it."

"I noticed."

"I'm sorry."

"How about tonight?"

"I'll have to see. I'll let you know."

"When?"

"As soon as I can."

"Can you give me a rough idea?"

"Before six."

Bishop types a letter to a university declining a speaking engagement.

He's been in the apartment for seventeen years.

His rent has just been raised forty-nine dollars a month.

Bishop is not in love with Cara, and she is certainly not in love with him. Still, they see each other rather often, sleep together rather often.

When he's given up on Cara, on a particular evening, he'll make a Scotch to take to bed with him. He lies on one elbow in the dark, smoking and sipping the Scotch.

He has a birthday in July, he'll be forty-nine.

Waking in the middle of the night he notices, again and again and again, that he sleeps with one fist jammed against his jaw—forearm, upper arm, and jaw making a rigid defensive triangle.

Cara says: "Everyone's got good taste, it just doesn't mean that much."

She's in textiles, a designer.

He rarely goes to lunch with anyone now.

On the street, he greets a neighbor he's never even nodded to before, a young man who is, he's heard, a lawyer. Bishop remembers the young man as a tall thin child with evasive eyes.

He buys flowers, daffodils.

In front of his liquor store there are six midday drunks in a bunch, youngish men, perhaps late thirties. They're lurching about and harassing passersby, a couple of open half pints visible (but this liquor store, Bishop knows, doesn't sell half pints). One of them, a particularly clumsy man with a red face under red stubble, makes a grab for his paper-wrapped flowers, Bishop sidesteps him easily, so early in the day, where do they get the money?

He thinks of correspondences between himself and the drunks.

He's not in love with Cara but he admires her, especially her ability to survive the various men she takes up with from time to time, all of whom (he does not include himself) seem intent on tearing her down (she confides to him), on tearing her to pieces. . . .

When Bishop puts out a grease fire in the oven by slapping at it with a dish towel she criticizes his performance, even though he's burned his arm.

"You let too much oxygen in."

He's convinced that his grandfather and grandmother, who are dead, will come back to life one day.

Bishop's telephone bill is a nightmare of long-distance charges: Charleston, Beverly Hills, New Orleans, Charleston, Charleston, London, Norfolk, Boston, Beverly Hills, London—

When they make love in the darkness of his very small bedroom, with a bottle of indifferent California wine on the night table, she locks her hands in the small of his back, exerting astonishing pressure.

Gray in his beard, three wavy lines across his forehead.

"He would frequently paint one picture over another and occasionally a third picture over the second." Frankenstein, on Peto.

The flowers remain in their paper wrapping in the kitchen, on the butcher-block bar.

He watches the four o'clock movie, a film he's seen possibly forty times, Henry Fonda as Colonel Thursday dancing with Sergeant Major Ward Bond's wife at the Fort Apache noncommissioned officers' ball. . . .

Cara calls. Something's come up.

"Have a good evening."

"You too."

Bishop makes himself a Scotch, although it's only four-thirty and the rule about Scotch is not before five.

Robert Young says: "Sanka brand coffee *is* real coffee."

He remembers driving to his grandparents' ranch, the stack of saddles in a corner of the ranch house's big inner room, the rifles on pegs over the doors, sitting on the veranda at night and watching the headlights of cars coming down the steep hill across the river.

During a commercial he gets out the television schedule to see what he can expect of the evening.

>   6:00 (2, 4, 7, 31) News
>
>   (5) I Love Lucy
>
>   (9) Joker's Wild
>
>   (11) Sanford and Son
>
>   (13) As We See It
>
>   (21) Once Upon a Classic
>
>   (25) Mister Rogers

A good movie, *Edison*, with Spencer Tracy, at eight.

He could call his brother in Charleston.

He could call a friend in Beverly Hills.

He could make a couple of quarts of chili, freeze some of it.

Bishop stands in front of a mirror, wondering why his eyes hurt.

He could read some proofs that have been sitting on his desk for two weeks.

Another Scotch. *Fort Apache* is over.

He walks from the front of the apartment to the back, approving of the furniture, the rugs, the peeling paint.

Bishop puts on his down jacket and goes out to the market. At the meat counter a child in a stroller points at him and screams: "*Old man!*"

The child's mother giggles and says: "Don't take it personally, it's the beard."

What's easiest? Steak, outrageously priced, what he doesn't eat will be there for breakfast.

He picks out two bunches of scallions to chop up for his baked potato.

He looks around for something foolish to buy, to persuade himself he's on top of things.

His right arm still has three ugly red blotches from the episode of the grease fire.

Caviar is sixty-seven dollars for four ounces. But he doesn't like caviar.

Bishop once bought records, Poulenc to Bob Wills, but now does not.

Also, he formerly bought prints. He has a Jim Dine and a de Chirico and a Bellmer and a Richard Hamilton. It's been years since he's bought a print.

(Although he reads the art magazines religiously.)

A shrink once said to him: "Big Daddy, is that it?"

He's had wives, thick in emotional texture, with many lovely problems, his advice is generally good.

Diluted by caution perhaps.

When his grandfather and grandmother come back to life, Bishop sits with them on the veranda of the ranch house looking down to the river, they seem just the same and talk about the things they've always talked about. He walks with his grandfather over the terrain studded with caliche like half-buried skulls, a dirty white, past a salt lick and the windmill and then another salt lick, and his grandfather points out the place where his aunt had been knocked off her horse by a low-lying tree branch. His grandmother is busy burning toast and then scraping it (the way they like it), and is at the same time reading the newspaper, crying aloud "Ben!" and then reading him something about the Stewart girl, you remember who she is, getting married to that fellow who, you remember, got in all the trouble. . . .

With his Scotch in bed, Bishop summons up an image of felicity: walking in the water, the shallow river, at the edge of the ranch, looking for minnows in the water under the overhanging trees, skipping rocks across the river, intent . . .

Grandmother's House

—GRANDMOTHER'S HOUSE? What? Landmark status? What? She's been eating? What? Strangers? She's been eating strangers? Sitting up in bed eating strangers? Hey? Pale, pink strangers? Zuti Lithium? What? They're giving her lithium? Hey? She's a what? Wolf? She's a wolf? Gad! Second opinion? Hey? She's a wolf. Well. Well, then. And Grandfather? What? Living with a stranger? Hey? A pale, pink stranger? Abominable! What's her name? What? What? Belle? Tush. BelleBelleBelleBelleBelle no I don't like it. Well if Grandmother's house has landmark status that means we can't build the brothel, right? Can't build the brothel, right? No brothel, right? Damn and damn and damn.

—Right.

—Well if we can't build the brothel we'd better go out and look for nymphs, right? Do a little nymphing? Get us to the glade?

—Right.

—Or we could steal a kid. A child. A kid. Steal one. Grab it and keep it. Raise it for our very own. Tickle it, light judicious tickling, swab it with rubbing alcohol against the itch, bundle it up and make it warm where previously it had been cold, right? Wham it when it is bad, right? Teach it to be afraid of the dark, the vast, unplumbed dark, the wet, glowing dark . . .

—Right.

—Shoulder the so-called real parents off the stage, those lunks. The former parents, those lunks, standing there uttering dull threats. Get off my case! and the like. Their connubial bliss in tatters, at this juncture. The bonds of gamomania but a spider-work, at this juncture. Send them notes from time to time, progress reports, little Luke has produced a tooth. Hey? Little Luke showing every sign of that sweetness of soul characteristic of breech presentations. Hey? Hey? Hey? Sing to it and pinch it, "Greensleeves" and "I'm an Old Cowhand." Teach it to figger and bottom-deal, get it a job cleaning telephone booths for the Telephone Company. And in our dotage—

—Our what?

—And in our senescence, it will take us by the hand, take you by your hand and me by my hand, and lead us gently over the hill to the poorhouse. Luke. Our kid.

—There's a naked woman in the next room.

—There's a what?

—Naked woman in the next room. On a couch. Blue velvet couch. Reclining. Flowers in her hair.

—I've seen one. In a magazine.

—Well they're all different, jackass. You can't just say *I've seen one.*

—Well I've got jury duty had an interesting case on Thursday guy'd got his car crushed in an elevator in a parking garage we gave him the Blue Book price, twenty-three hundred something. Right?

—I mean you can't just say *I've seen one.* That's not enough.

—Well I'm tired, man, tired, I've been tired ever since I heard the truly dreadful news about Grandmother's house, a thing like that brings you down, man, brings you down and makes you tired, know what I mean?

—They're all different. That's what makes them so . . . luminous.

—But she's a stranger.

—But after you sleep with them they're less strange. Get downright familiar, laugh at you and pull your beard.

—I remember.

—Demystify themselves with repeated actions of a repetitive kind.

—Their moves. Their cold moves and their cozy moves.

—Want to go to the flicks, the flicks, the flicks—

—I saw one once, about this guy who jumped from place to place swinging on a vine, and yodeled, yodeled and jumped from place to place swinging on a vine, ran around with an ape a small ape, wore these leather flaps with a knife stuck in the back flap—It was a good flick. I enjoyed it.

—I've seen a bunch. Six or seven thousand.

—Of course this is not to say that what has been demystified cannot be *re*mystified.

—How?

—Well you can take them on a trip or something. To a far place. Bergen.
—And then what?
—Seen with tall cool drinks in fetching costumes against the hot white sands or whatever they are partially remystified.
—No hot white sands in Bergen, man.
—Seen against the deep cool fjords with penguins in their hands they are partially remystified.
—No penguins in Bergen, man.
—Or some kind of new erotic behavior you can start biting them some people like that. People who've never been bitten much.
—How do you know how hard to bite?
—It's a skill.
—It is?
—As a matter of fact I saw another movie, movie about this guy who meets this woman and then they fall in love and then she leaves him and then he meets another woman.
—So what happens?
—He begins living with the second one. She's very nice.
—And then what?
—She leaves him.
—That's all?
—He is seen in a crowded street. Walking away from the camera. The figure becoming smaller and smaller and smaller until it's lost in the crowd. It was a very good movie. I liked it. I liked the one about the guy swinging on the vine a little better, maybe. Well. Want to steal a kid?
—I don't know.
—We could tickle the little sumbitch for a while and then, wham it.
—Feed it brownies and bubble gum.
—Tell it stories and great flaming lies.
—Gypsies steal kids.
—Right.
—Gypsies steal kids every day.
—It's well known.
—Hardly ever prosecuted.
—The wily gypsy. Hard to catch.

—What do they do with the kids I wonder?
—The wily, terrible gypsy. Gone today and gone tomorrow.
—What do they do with the kids I wonder?
—Train them in the gypsy arts. Wine-watering, horse-dyeing, the barbering of dreams.
—Gypsy airs scratched into the gypsy firelight.
—Deconstructing dreams like nobody's business. You want to know, go see the gypsy.
—Ever interfere with a gypsy?
—Well not an official gypsy. They only interfere with other gypsies. Now if you're talking about gypsy-*like*—
—Under the caravan. In the rank, sweet grass.
—Now if you're talking about a gypsy-*like* individual, wild and free and snarling and biting—
—I meant a real one.
—No.
—I'm sorry.
—But when I saw the great Gaudí church in Barcelona, the great Sagrada Familia, the great ghost of a cathedral or rather great skeleton of a cathedral, then did I realize especially after seeing also the plans and models in the basement for those portions of the great cathedral not yet built and perhaps never to be built, the plans under plastic on the walls of the basement and the models on sawhorses on the floor of the basement, the artisans in smocks still working on the beautifully inked plans and the white plaster models, and the workmen on the extant towers of the Templo Expiatorio de la Sagrada Familia in Barcelona, the workmen on and between the extant towers and walls of the Templo Expiatorio de la Sagrada Familia in Barcelona, the amazingly few workmen still working and still *to be* working for God knows how many decades hence, if the money can be got together, we left our contribution in a plastic box, the amazingly few but truly dedicated workmen still working under the burning inspiration of the sainted Catalan architect Antonio Gaudí, having seen all this I then realized what I had not realized before, what had escaped my notice these many years, that not only is less more but that *more is more too*. I swooned, under the impact of the ethical corollary.
—What is the ethical corollary?
—More.

—When you swooned, did you fall?
—I swooned *upward*. While staring from the ground at the great extant towers of the Sagrada Familia. Reverse vertigo.
—Gaudí however was laboring *in nomine Domini*. I do not see that the ethical corollary as you put it applies, privately.
—Puts an idea under greed.
—My life is a poor one. Relative to—
—I know that.
—*Your* life is a poor one. Not bad, but not replete.
—Well I can think can't I? I thought of the brothel, didn't I?
—Poorly that was a very poor idea this one guy thinks of a cathedral and you think of a brothel? Congratulations. You see what I mean?
—I say we steal one, a kid. Find a good-looking one and steal it, it's not the worst idea I ever heard.
—Not the worst idea.
—And when it grew to the age of sexual availability, we could tell it to wait.
—That's what I told her.
—That's what I told mine too. Told her to wait.
—You told her to wait?
—That's what I told her.
—How did she take it?
—She sat silently listening to me telling her to wait.
—I told mine to wait too.
—How did she react?
—She just sat there.
—You think she's waiting?
—How do I know?
—Some people think sixteen.
—Biologically of course it's a bitch. For them.
—I never understood why things were so . . . out of phase. The biological with the cultural.
—Cultural-psychological.
—Odd to be in that position Telling someone to wait.
—Has she got someone in mind?
—There's this guy he has a Honda.
—You don't let her . . . Those things can be, like *dangerous*, man.
—He gave her a helmet.

—You mean she's running around town on the back of this guy's Honda clutching him tightly around the stomach and her chest rubbing into his back muscles? At fourteen?

—Well what can I do?

—Tell her to wait?

—Well at least it's not a Harley.

—What's his name?

—Juan.

—Oh.

—How 'bout yours?

—Mine's seeing various candidates. Various candidates have presented themselves. The leader of the pack, you might say, is this Claude.

—His name is Claude?

—Well that's not his fault.

—There is one thing, one small point, on which I think we may congratulate ourselves. We gave them plain names.

—Plain, but beautiful.

—What did I see the other day? Jahne. J-a-h-n-e.

—You're kidding.

—Nope. J-a-h-n-e.

—Amazing.

—Yes. So what's with this Claude?

—He's seventeen.

—He's seventeen?

—Yep.

—Little old for fourteen don't you think?

—What can I do?

—Seventeen is a wild age.

—Seventeen is anarchy.

—I was atrocious when I was seventeen. Absolutely atrocious.

—Likewise.

—Drunk driving was the least of it.

—When you think about it now you turn pale.

—And *I* wasn't crazy, some of those guys they were flat crazy.

—I knew a few.

—I mean they thought blood on the saddle was the *plan*, man.

—Don't remind me.

—Talk about behavior.

—Yes.
—Boy this was behavior.
—Yes.
—You can tell them to wait but what do you tell them after you tell them to wait?
—Tell them to keep their ass the hell out of Grandmother's house.
—Not very likely.
—Not very likely.
—Well at least we gave them plain names.
—Plain, but beautiful.
—Steal a kid. Begin all over again.
—Tear it up, tear it up, tear it up.
—Or get us to the glade.
—The heat of the glade.
—The damned nymphs have to be somewhere.
—Beautiful necks for biting.
—Soft anthropological bites.
—Bosomed nymphs, nymphs with a stripe of hair . . .
—Polka nymphs, red-eyed nymphs, drudge nymphs, bombous nymphs . . .
—Nymphs in warmup suits, Mohawks, clown nymphs . . .
—The splendid language of their hair . . .

OVERNIGHT TO MANY
DISTANT CITIES

To Marion

*They called for more structure, then, so we brought in some big
hairy four-by-fours from the back shed and nailed them into
place with railroad spikes. This new city, they said, was going to
be just jim-dandy, would make architects stutter, would make
Chambers of Commerce burst into flame. We would have our
own witch doctors, and strange gods aplenty, and site-specific
sins, and humuhumunukunukuapuaa in the public fish bowls.
We workers listened with our mouths agape. We had never
heard anything like it. But we trusted our instincts and our
paychecks, so we pressed on, bringing in color-coated steel from
the back shed and anodized aluminum from the shed behind
that. Oh radiant city! we said to ourselves, how we want you to
be built! Workplace democracy was practiced on the job, and
the clerk-of-the-works (who had known Wiwi Lönn in Finland)
wore a little cap with a little feather, very jaunty. There was
never any question of hanging back (although we noticed that
our ID cards were of a color different from their ID cards); the
exercise of our skills, and the promise of the city, were enough.
By the light of the moon we counted our chisels and told stories
of other building feats we had been involved in: Babel, Chandigarh, Brasilia, Taliesin.*

   *At dawn each day, an eight-mile run, to condition ourselves
for the implausible exploits ahead.*

   *The enormous pumping station, clad in red Lego, at the
point where the new river will be activated . . .*

   *Areas of the city, they told us, had been designed to rot, fall
into desuetude, return, in time, to open space. Perhaps, they
said, fawns would one day romp there, on the crumbling brick.
We were slightly skeptical about this part of the plan, but it
was, after all, a plan, the ferocious integrity of the detailing
impressed us all, and standing by the pens containing the fawns
who would father the fawns who might some day romp on the
crumbling brick, one could not help but notice one's chest bursting with anticipatory pride.*

High in the air, working on a setback faced with alternating bands of gray and rose stone capped with grids of gray glass, we moistened our brows with the tails of our shirts, which had been dipped into a pleasing brine, lit new cigars, and saw the new city spread out beneath us, in the shape of the word FASTIGIUM. Not the name of the city, they told us, simply a set of letters selected for the elegance of the script. The little girl dead behind the rosebushes came back to life, and the passionate construction continued.

Visitors

IT'S THREE o'clock in the morning.

Bishop's daughter is ill, stomach pains. She's sleeping on the couch.

Bishop too is ill, chills and sweating, a flu. He can't sleep. In bed, he listens to the occasional groans from two rooms away. Katie is fifteen and spends the summer with him every year.

Outside on the street, someone kicks on a motorcycle and revs it unforgivingly. His bedroom is badly placed.

He's given her Pepto-Bismol, if she wakes again he'll try Tylenol. He wraps himself in the sheet, pulls his t-shirt away from his damp chest.

There's a radio playing somewhere in the building, big-band music, he feels rather than hears it. The steady, friendly air-conditioner hustling in the next room.

Earlier he'd taken her to a doctor, who found nothing. "You've got a bellyache," the doctor said, "stick with fluids and call me if it doesn't go away." Katie is beautiful, tall with dark hair.

In the afternoon they'd gone, groaning, to a horror movie about wolves taking over the city. At vivid moments she jumped against him, pressing her breasts into his back. He moved away.

When they walk together on the street she takes his arm, holding on tightly (because, he figures, she spends so much of her time away, away). Very often people give them peculiar looks.

He's been picking up old ladies who've been falling down in front of him, these last few days. One sitting in the middle of an intersection waving her arms while dangerous Checkers curved around her. The old ladies invariably display a superb fighting spirit. "Thank you, young man!"

He's forty-nine. Writing a history of 19th Century American painting, about which he knows a thing or two.

Not enough.

A groan, heartfelt but muted, from the other room. She's awake.

He gets up and goes in to look at her. The red-and-white cotton robe she's wearing is tucked up under her knees. "I just threw up again," she says.

"Did it help?"

"A little."

He once asked her what something (a box? a chair?) was made of and she told him it was made out of tree.

"Do you want to try a glass of milk?"

"I don't want any milk," she says, turning to lie on her front. "Sit with me."

He sits on the edge of the couch and rubs her back. "Think of something terrific," he says. "Let's get your mind off your stomach. Think about fishing. Think about the time you threw the hotel keys out of the window." Once, in Paris, she had done just that, from a sixth-floor window, and Bishop had had visions of some Frenchman walking down the Quai des Grands-Augustins with a set of heavy iron hotel keys buried in his brain. He'd found the keys in a potted plant outside the hotel door.

"Daddy," she says, not looking at him.

"Yes?"

"Why do you live like this? By yourself?"

"Who am I going to live with?"

"You could find somebody. You're handsome for your age."

"Oh very good. That's very neat. I thank you."

"You don't try."

This is and is not true.

"How much do you weigh?"

"One eighty-five."

"You could lose some weight."

"Look, kid, gimme a break." He blots his forehead with his arm. "You want some cambric tea?"

"You've given up."

"Not so," he says. "Katie, go to sleep now. Think of a great big pile of Gucci handbags."

She sighs and turns her head away.

Bishop goes into the kitchen and turns on the light. He wonders what a drink would do to him, or for him—put him to sleep? He decides against it. He turns on the tiny kitchen TV and spends a few minutes watching some kind of Japanese monster movie. The poorly designed monster is picking up handfuls of people and, rather thoughtfully, eating them. Bishop thinks about Tokyo. He was once in bed with a Japanese girl during a mild earthquake, and he's never forgotten the feeling of the floor falling out from underneath him, or the woman's terror. He suddenly remembers her name, Michiko. "You no butterfly on me?" she had asked, when they met. He was astonished to learn that "butterfly" meant, in the patois of the time, "abandon." She cooked their meals over a charcoal brazier and they slept in a niche in the wall closed off from the rest of her room by sliding paper doors. Bishop worked on the copy desk at *Stars & Stripes*. One day a wire photo came in showing the heads of the four (then) women's services posing for a group portrait. Bishop slugged the caption LEADING LADIES. The elderly master sergeant who was serving as city editor brought the photo back to Bishop's desk. "We can't do this," he said. "Ain't it a shame?"

He switches channels and gets Dolly Parton singing, by coincidence, "House of the Rising Sun."

At some point during each summer she'll say: "Why did you and my mother split up?"

"It was your fault," he answers. "Yours. You made too much noise, as a kid, I couldn't work." His ex-wife had once told Katie this as an explanation for the divorce, and he'll repeat it until its untruth is marble, a monument.

His ex-wife is otherwise very sensible, and thrifty, too.

Why do I live this way? Best I can do.

Walking down West Broadway on a Saturday afternoon. Barking art caged in the high white galleries, don't go inside or it'll get you, leap into your lap and cover your face with kisses. Some goes to the other extreme, snarls and shows its brilliant teeth. O art I won't hurt you if you don't hurt me. Citizens parading, plump-faced and bone-faced, lightly clad. A young black boy toting a Board of Education trombone case. A fellow with oddly-cut hair the color of marigolds and a roll of roofing felt over his shoulder.

Bishop in the crowd, thirty dollars in his pocket in case he has to buy a pal a drink.

Into a gallery because it must be done. The artist's hung

twenty EVERLAST heavy bags in rows of four, you're invited to have a bash. People are giving the bags every kind of trouble. Bishop, unable to resist, bangs one with his fabled left, and hurts his hand.

Bloody artists.

Out on the street again, he is bumped into by a man, then another man, then a woman. And here's Harry in lemon pants with his Britisher friend, Malcolm.

"Harry, Malcolm."

"Professor," Harry says ironically (he is a professor, Bishop is not).

Harry's got not much hair and has lost weight since he split with Tom. Malcolm is the single most cheerful individual Bishop has ever met.

Harry's university has just hired a new president who's thirty-two. Harry can't get over it.

"*Thirty-two!* I mean I don't think the board's got both oars in the water."

Standing behind Malcolm is a beautiful young woman.

"This is Christie," Malcolm says. "We've just given her lunch. We've just eaten all the dim sum in the world."

Bishop is immediately seized by a desire to cook for Christie—either his Eight-Bean Soup or his Crash Cassoulet.

She's telling him something about her windows.

"I don't care but why under my windows?"

She's wearing a purple shirt and is deeply tanned with black hair—looks like an Indian, in fact, the one who sells Mazola on TV.

Harry is still talking about the new president. "I mean he did his dissertation on *bathing trends*."

"Well maybe he knows where the big bucks are." There's some leftover duck in the refrigerator he can use for the cassoulet.

"Well," he says to Christie, "are you hungry?"

"Yes," she says, "I am."

"We just ate," Harry says. "You can't be hungry. You can't possibly be hungry."

"Hungry, hungry, hungry," she says, taking Bishop's arm, which is, can you believe it, sticking out.

Putting slices of duck in bean water while Christie watches "The Adventures of Robin Hood," with Errol Flynn and Basil Rathbone, on the kitchen TV. At the same time Hank Williams Jr. is singing on the FM.

"I like a place where I can take my shoes off," she says, as Errol Flynn throws a whole dead deer on the banquet table.

Bishop, chopping parsley, is taking quick glances at her to see what she looks like with a glass of wine in her hand. Some people look good with white wine, some don't.

He makes a mental note to buy some Mazola—a case, maybe.

"Here's sixty seconds on fenders," says the radio.

"Do you live with anybody?" Christie asks.

"My daughter is here sometimes. Summers and Christmas." A little tarragon into the bean water. "How about you?"

"There's this guy."

But there had to be. Bishop chops steadfastly with his Three Sheep brand Chinese chopper, made in gray Fusan.

"He's an artist."

As who is not? "What kind of an artist?"

"A painter. He's in Seattle. He needs rain."

He throws handfuls of sliced onions into the water, then a can of tomato paste.

"How long does this take?" Christie asks. "I'm not rushing you, I'm just curious."

"Another hour."

"Then I'll have a little vodka. Straight. Ice. If you don't mind."

Bishop loves women who drink.

Maybe she smokes!

"Actually I can't stand artists," she says.

"Like who in particular?"

"Like that woman who puts chewing gum on her stomach—"

"She doesn't do that any more. And the chewing gum was not poorly placed."

"And that other one who cuts off parts of himself, *whittles* on himself, that fries my ass."

"It's supposed to."

"Yeah," she says, shaking the ice in her glass. "I'm reacting like a bozo."

She gets up and walks over to the counter and takes a Lark from his pack.

Very happily, Bishop begins to talk. He tells her that the night before he had smelled smoke, had gotten up and checked the apartment, knowing that a pier was on fire over by the river and suspecting it was that. He had turned on the TV to get the all-news channel and while dialing had encountered the opening credits of a Richard Widmark cop film called "Brock's Last Case" which he had then sat down and watched, his faithful Scotch at his side, until five o'clock in the morning. Richard Widmark was one of his favorite actors in the whole world, he told her, because of the way in which Richard Widmark was able to convey, what was the word, resilience. You could knock Richard Widmark down, he said, you could even knock Richard Widmark down repeatedly, but you had better bear in mind while knocking Richard Widmark down that Richard Widmark was pretty damn sure going to bounce back up and batter your conk—

"Redford is the one I like," she says.

Bishop can understand this. He nods seriously.

"The thing I like about Redford is," she says, and for ten minutes she tells him about Robert Redford.

He tastes the cassoulet with a long spoon. More salt.

It appears that she is also mighty fond of Clint Eastwood.

Bishop has the sense that the conversation has strayed, like a bad cow, from the proper path.

"Old Clint Eastwood," he says, shaking his head admiringly. "We're ready."

He dishes up the cassoulet and fetches hot bread from the oven.

"Tastes like real cassoulet," she says.

"That's the ox-tail soup mix." Why is he serving her cassoulet in summer? It's hot.

He's opened a bottle of Robert Mondavi table red.

"*Very* good," she says. "I mean I'm surprised. Really."

"Maybe could have had more tomato."

"No, really." She tears off a fistful of French bread. "Men are quite odd. I saw this guy at the farmer's market on Union Square on Saturday? He was standing in front of a table full of greens and radishes and corn and this and that, behind a bunch of other people, and he was staring at this farmer-girl who was wearing cut-offs and a tank top and every time she leaned over to grab a cabbage or whatnot he was getting a shot of her breasts, which were, to be fair, quite pretty—I mean how much fun can that be?"

"Moderate amount of fun. Some fun. Not much fun. What can I say?"

"And that plug I live with."

"What about him?"

"He gave me a book once."

"What was it?"

"Book about how to fix home appliances. The dishwasher was broken. Then he bought me a screwdriver. This really nice screwdriver."

"Well."

"I *fixed* the damned dishwasher. Took me two days."

"Would you like to go to bed now?"

"No," Christie says, "not yet."

Not yet! Very happily, Bishop pours more wine.

Now he's sweating, little chills at intervals. He gets a sheet from the bedroom and sits in the kitchen with the sheet draped around him, guru-style. He can hear Katie turning restlessly on the couch.

He admires the way she organizes her life—that is, the way she gets done what she wants done. A little wangling, a little nagging, a little let's-go-take-a-look and Bishop has sprung for a new pair of boots, handsome ankle-height black diablo numbers that she'll wear with black ski pants . . .

Well, he doesn't give her many presents.

Could he bear a Scotch? He thinks not.

He remembers a dream in which he dreamed that his nose was as dark and red as a Bing cherry. As would be appropriate.

"Daddy?"

Still wearing the yellow sheet, he gets up and goes into the other room.

"I can't sleep."

"I'm sorry."

"Talk to me."

Bishop sits again on the edge of the couch. How large she is!

He gives her his Art History lecture.

"Then you get *Mo*-net and *Ma*-net, that's a little tricky, *Mo*-net was the one did all the water lilies and shit, his colors were blues and greens, *Ma*-net was the one did Bareass On the Grass and shit, his colors were browns and greens. Then you get Bonnard, he did all the interiors and shit, amazing light, and then you get Van Guk, he's the one with the ear and shit, and Say-zanne, he's the one with the apples and shit, you get Kandinsky, a bad mother, all them pick-up-sticks pictures, you get my man Mondrian, he's the one with the rectangles and shit, his colors were red yellow and blue, you get Moholy-Nagy, he did all the plastic thingummies and shit, you get Mar-cel Duchamp, he's the devil in human form. . . ."

She's asleep.

Bishop goes back into the kitchen and makes himself a drink. It's five-thirty. Faint light in the big windows.

Christie's in Seattle, and plans to stay.

Looking out of the windows in the early morning he can sometimes see the two old ladies who live in the apartment whose garden backs up to his building having breakfast by candlelight. He can never figure out whether they are terminally romantic or whether, rather, they're trying to save electricity.

Financially, the paper is quite healthy. The paper's timberlands, mining interests, pulp and paper operations, book, magazine, corrugated-box, and greeting-card divisions, film, radio, television, and cable companies, and data-processing and satellite-communications groups are all flourishing, with over-all return on invested capital increasing at about eleven per cent a year. Compensation of the three highest-paid officers and directors last year was $399,500, $362,700, and $335,400 respectively, exclusive of profit-sharing and pension-plan accruals.

But top management is discouraged and saddened, and middle management is drinking too much. Morale in the newsroom is fair, because of the recent raises, but the shining brows of the copy boys, traditional emblems of energy and hope, have begun to display odd, unattractive lines. At every level, even down into the depths of the pressroom, where the pressmen defiantly wear their square dirty folded-paper caps, people want management to stop what it is doing before it is too late.

The new VDT machines have hurt the paper, no doubt about it. The people in the newsroom don't like the machines. (A few say they like the machines but these are the same people who like the washrooms.) When the machines go down, as they do, not infrequently, the people in the newsroom laugh and cheer. The executive editor has installed one-way glass in his office door, and stands behind it looking out over the newsroom, fretting and groaning. Recently the paper ran the same stock tables every day for a week. No one noticed, no one complained.

Middle management has implored top management to alter its course. Top management has responded with postdated guarantees, on a sliding scale. The Guild is off in a corner, whimpering. The pressmen are holding an unending series of birthday parties commemorating heroes of labor. Reporters file their stories as usual, but if they are certain kinds of stories they do not run. A small example: the paper did not run a Holiday Weekend Death Toll story after Labor Day this year, the first time since 1926 no Holiday Weekend Death Toll story appeared in the paper after Labor Day (and the total was, although not a record, a substantial one).

Some elements of the staff are not depressed. The paper's very creative real-estate editor has been a fountain of ideas, and his sections, full of color pictures of desirable living arrangements, are choked with advertising and make the Sunday paper fat, fat, fat, fat. More food writers have been hired, and more clothes writers, and more furniture writers, and more plant writers. The bridge, whist, skat, cribbage, domino, and vingt-et-un columnists are very popular.

The Editors' Caucus has once again applied to middle management for relief, and has once again been promised it (but middle management has Glenfiddich on its breath, even at breakfast). Top management's polls say that sixty-five per cent of the readers "want movies," and feasibility studies are being conducted. Top management acknowledges, over long lunches at good restaurants, that the readers are wrong to "want movies" but insists that morality cannot be legislated. The newsroom has been insulated (with products from the company's Echotex division) so that the people in the newsroom can no longer hear the sounds in the streets.

The paper's editorials have been subcontracted to Texas Instruments, and the obituaries to Nabisco, so that the staff will have "more time to think." The foreign desk is turning out language lessons ("Yo temo que Isabel no venga," "I am afraid that Isabel will not come"). There was an especially lively front page on Tuesday. The No. 1 story was pepperoni—a useful and exhaustive guide. It ran right next to the slimming-your-troublesome-thighs story, with pictures.

Top management has vowed to stop what it is doing—not now but soon, soon. A chamber orchestra has been formed among the people in the newsroom, and we play Haydn until the sun comes up.

Affection

How do you want to cook this fish? How do you want to cook this fish? Harris asked.
What?
Claire heard: How do you want to cook this fish?
Breaded, she said.
Fine, Harris said.
What?
Fine!
We have not slept together for three hundred nights, she thought. We have not slept together for three hundred nights.
His rough, tender hands not wrapped around me.
Lawnmower. His rough, tender hands wrapped around the handles of the lawnmower. Not around me.
What?
Where did you hide the bread crumbs?
What?
The bread crumbs!
Behind the Cheerios!
Claire telephoned her mother. Her mother's counsel was broccoli, mostly, but who else was she going to talk to?
What?
You have to be optimistic. Be be be. Optimistic.
What?
Optimistic, her mother said, they go through phases. As they get older. They have less tolerance for monotony.
I'm monotony?
They go through phases. As they grow older. They like to think that their futures are ahead of them. This is ludicrous, of course—
Oh oh oh oh.
Ludicrous, of course, but I have never yet met one who didn't think that way until he got played out then they sink into a comfortable lassitude take to wearing those horrible old-geezer hats . . .
What?

Hats with the green plastic bills, golf hats or whatever they are—

Harris, Claire said to her husband, you've stopped watering the plants.

What?

You've stopped watering the plants my mother always said that when they stopped watering the plants that was a sure sign of an impending marital breakup.

Your mother reads too much.

What?

Sarah decided that she and Harris should not sleep together any longer.

Harris said, What about hugging?

What?

Hugging.

Sarah said that she would have a ruling on hugging in a few days and that he should stand by for further information. She pulled the black lace mantilla down to veil her face as they left the empty church.

I have done the right thing the right thing. I am right.

Claire came in wearing her brown coat and carrying a large brown paper bag. Look what I got! she said excitedly.

What? Harris said.

She reached into the bag and pulled out a smeary plastic tray with six frozen shell steaks on it. The steaks looked like they had died in the nineteenth century.

Six dollars! Claire said. This guy came into the laundromat and said he was making deliveries to restaurants and some of the restaurants already had all the steaks they needed and now he had these left over and they were only six dollars. Six dollars.

You spent six dollars on *these*?

Other people bought some too.

Diseased, stolen steaks?

He was wearing a white coat, Claire said. He had a truck.

I'll bet he had a truck.

Harris went to see Madam Olympia, a reader and advisor. Her office was one room in a bad part of the city. Chicken wings burned in a frying pan on the stove. She got up and turned them off, then got up and turned them on again. She was wearing a t-shirt that had "Buffalo, City of No Illusions" printed on it.

Tell me about yourself, she said.

My life is hell, Harris said. He sketched the circumstances.

I am bored to tears with this sort of thing, Madam Olympia said. To tears to tears.

Well, Harris said, me too.

Woman wakes up in the middle of the night, Madam Olympia said, she goes, what you thinkin' about? You go, the float. She goes, is the float makin' us money or not makin' us money? You go, it depends on what happens Wednesday. She goes, that's nice. You go, what do you mean, you don't understand *dick* about the float, woman. She goes, well you don't have to be nasty. You go, I'm *not* being nasty, you just don't *understand*. She goes, so why don't you tell me? Behind this, other agendas on both sides.

The float is a *secret*, Harris said. Many *men* don't even know about the float.

To tears to tears to tears.

Right, Harris said. How much do I owe you?

Fifty dollars.

The community whispered: Are they still living? How many times a week? What is that symbol on your breast? Did they consent to sign it? Did they refuse to sign it? In the rain? Before the fire? Has there been weight loss? How many pounds? What is their favorite color? Have they been audited? Was there a his side of the bed and a her side of the bed? Did she make it herself? Can we have a taste? Have they stolen money? Have they stolen stamps? Can he ride a horse? Can he ride a steer? What is his best time in the calf scramble? Is there money? Was there money? What happened to the money? What will happen to the money? Did success come early or late? Did success come? A red wig? At the Junior League? A red dress with a red wig? Was she ever a Fauve? Is that a theoretical position or a real position? Would they do it again? Again and again? How many times? A thousand times?

Claire met Sweet Papa Cream Puff, a new person. He was the house pianist at Bells, a club frequented by disconsolate women in the early afternoons.

He was a huge man and said that he was a living legend.
What?
Living legend, he said.
I didn't name the "Sweet Papa Cream Puff Blues" by that name, he said. It was named by the people of Chicago.
Oh my oh my oh my, Claire said.
This musta been 'bout nineteen twenty-one, twenty-two, he said.
Those was wonderful days.
There was one other man, at that time, who had part of my fame.
Fellow named Red Top, he's dead now.
He was very good, scared me a little bit.
I studied him.
I had two or three situations on the problem.
I worked very hard and bested him in nineteen twenty-three. June of that year.
Wow, Claire said.
Zum, Sweet Papa Cream Puff sang, zum zum zum zum *zum*.
Six perfect treble notes in the side pocket.

Sarah calls Harris from the clinic in Detroit and floors him with the news of her "miscarriage." Saddened by the loss of the baby, he's nevertheless elated to be free of his "obligation." But when Harris rushes to declare his love for Claire, he's crushed to learn that she is married to Sarah. Hoping against hope that Harris will stay with her, Sarah returns. Harris is hung over from drinking too much the night before when Sarah demands to know if he wants her. Unable to decide at first, he yields to Sarah's feigned helplessness and tells her to stay. Later, they share a pleasant dinner at the Riverboat, where Claire is a waiter. Harris is impressed to learn that Sarah refused to join in his mother's plan to dissuade him from becoming a policeman. Claire is embracing Harris before his departure when Sarah enters the office. When Harris is caught shoplifting, Claire's kid sister, terrified at having to face a court appearance, signs for his release. Missing Sarah terribly, Harris calls her from New Orleans; when she tells him about becoming chairwoman of Claire's new bank, he hangs up angrily. Although they've separated, his feelings for Claire haven't died entirely, and her growing involvement with his new partner, Sarah, is a bitter pill for him to swallow, as he sits alone drinking too much brandy in Sarah's study. Sarah blazes with anger when she finds Claire in the hotel's banquet office making arrangements for Harris's testimonial dinner, as Sarah, her right leg in a cast, walks up the steps of the brownstone and punches Claire's bell, rage clearly burning in her eyes.

Sarah visited Dr. Whorf, a good psychiatrist.
Cold as *death*, she said.
What?
Cold as *death*.
Good behavior is frequently painful, Dr. Whorf said. Shit you know that.
Sarah was surprised to find that what she had told Dr. Whorf was absolutely true. She was fully miserable.
Harris drunk again and yelling at Claire said that he was not drunk.
I feel worse than you feel, she said.
What?
Worse, she said, wooooooooorrrssse.
You know what I saw this morning? he asked. Eight o'clock in the morning. I was out walking.
Guy comes out of this house, wearing a suit, carrying an attaché case.
He's going to work, right?
He gets about ten steps down the sidewalk and this woman comes out. Out of the same house.
She says, "James?"
He turns around and walks back toward her.
She's wearing a robe. Pink and orange.
She says, "James, *I . . . hate . . . you.*"
Maybe it's everywhere, Claire said. A pandemic.
I don't think that, Harris said.

This is the filthiest phone booth I've ever been in, Harris said to Sarah.
What?
The *filthiest phone booth* I have ever been in.
Hang up darling hang up and find another phone booth

thank you for the jewels the pearls and the emeralds and the onyx but I haven't changed my mind they're quite quite beautiful just amazing but I haven't changed my mind you're so kind but I have done the right thing painful as it was and I haven't changed my mind—

He remembered her standing over the toothpaste with her face two inches from the toothpaste because she couldn't see it without her contacts in.

Freud said, Claire said, that in the adult, novelty always constitutes the condition for orgasm.

Sweet Papa looked away.

Oh me oh my.

Well you know the gents they don't know what they after they own selves, very often.

When do they find out?

At the eleventh hour let me play you a little thing I wrote in the early part of the century I call it "Verklärte Nacht" that means "stormy weather" in German, I played there in Berlin oh about—

Claire placed her arms around Sweet Papa Cream Puff and hugged the stuffing out of him.

What?
What?
What?
What?

By a lucky stroke Harris made an amount of money in the market. He bought Claire a beautiful black opal. She was pleased.

He looked to the future.

Claire will continue to be wonderful.

As will I, to the best of my ability.

The New York Times will be published every day and I will have to wash it off my hands when I have finished reading it, every day.

What? Claire said.

Smile.

What?

Smile.

I put a name in an envelope, and sealed the envelope; and put that envelope in another envelope with a spittlebug and some quantity of boric acid; and put that envelope in a still larger envelope which contained also a woman tearing her gloves to tatters; and put that envelope in the mail to Fichtelgebirge. At the Fichtelgebirge Post Office I asked if there was mail for me, with a mysterious smile the clerk said, "Yes," I hurried with the envelope to London, arriving with snow, and put the envelope in the Victoria and Albert Museum, bowing to the curators in the Envelope Room, where the wallpaper hung down in thick strips. I put the Victoria and Albert Museum in a still larger envelope which I placed in the program of the Royal Danish Ballet, in the form of an advertisement for museums, boric acid, wallpaper. I put the program of the Royal Danish Ballet into the North Sea for two weeks. Then, I retrieved it, it was hanging down in thick strips, I sent it to a machine-vask on H. C. Andersen Boulevard, everything came out square and neat, I was overjoyed. I put the square, neat package in a safe place, and put the safe place in a vault designed by Caspar David Friedrich, German romantic landscape painter of the last century. I slipped the vault into a history of art (Insel Verlag, Frankfurt, 1980). But, in a convent library on the side of a hill near a principal city of Montana, it fell out of the history of art into a wastebasket, a thing I could not have predicted. I bound the wastebasket in stone, with a matchwood shroud covering the stone, and placed it in the care of Charles the Good, Charles the Bold, and Charles the Fair. They stand juggling cork balls before the many-times-encased envelope, whispering names which are not the right one. I put the three kings into a new blue suit, it walked away from me most confidently.

Lightning

EDWARD CONNORS, on assignment for *Folks*, set out to interview nine people who had been struck by lightning. "Nine?" he said to his editor, Penfield. "Nine, ten," said Penfield, "doesn't matter, but it has to be more than eight." "Why?" asked Connors, and Penfield said that the layout was scheduled for five pages and they wanted at least two people who had been struck by lightning per page plus somebody pretty sensational for the opening page. "Slightly wonderful," said Penfield, "nice body, I don't have to tell you, somebody with a special face. Also, struck by lightning."

Connors advertised in the *Village Voice* for people who had been struck by lightning and would be willing to talk for publication about the experience and in no time at all was getting phone calls. A number of the callers, it appeared, had great-grandfathers or grandmothers who had also been struck by lightning, usually knocked from the front seat of a buckboard on a country road in 1910. Connors took down names and addresses and made appointments for interviews, trying to discern from the voices if any of the women callers might be, in the magazine's terms, wonderful.

Connors had been a reporter for ten years and a freelancer for five, with six years in between as a PR man for Topsy Oil in Midland-Odessa. As a reporter he had been excited, solid, underpaid, in love with his work, a specialist in business news, a scholar of the regulatory agencies and their eternal gavotte with the Seven Sisters, a man who knew what should be done with natural gas, with nuclear power, who knew crown blocks and monkey boards and Austin chalk, who kept his own personal hard hat ("Welltech") on top of a filing cabinet in his office. When his wife pointed out, eventually, that he wasn't making enough money (absolutely true!) he had gone with Topsy, whose PR chief had been dropping handkerchiefs in his vicinity for several years. Signing on with Topsy, he had tripled his salary, bought four moderately expensive suits, enjoyed (briefly) the esteem of his wife, and spent his time writing either incredibly dreary releases about corporate doings or speeches in praise of free enterprise for the company's C.E.O., E. H. ("Bug") Ludwig, a round, amiable, commanding man of whom he was very fond. When Connors' wife left him for a racquetball pro attached to the Big Spring Country Club he decided he could afford to be poor again and departed Topsy, renting a dismal rear apartment on Lafayette Street in New York and patching an income together by writing for a wide variety of publications, classical record reviews for *High Fidelity*, *Times* Travel pieces ("Portugal's Fabulous Beaches"), exposés for *Penthouse* ("Inside the Trilateral Commission"). To each assignment he brought a good brain, a good eye, a tenacious thoroughness, gusto. He was forty-five, making a thin living, curious about people who had been struck by lightning.

The first man he interviewed was a thirty-eight-year-old tile setter named Burch who had been struck by lightning in February 1978 and had immediately become a Jehovah's Witness. "It was the best thing that ever happened to me," said Burch, "in a way." He was a calm, rather handsome man with pale blond hair cut short, military style, and an elegantly spare (deep grays and browns) apartment in the West Twenties which looked, to Connors, as if a decorator had been involved. "I was coming back from a job in New Rochelle," said Burch, "and I had a flat. It was clouding up pretty good and I wanted to get the tire changed before the rain started. I had the tire off and was just about to put the spare on when there was this just terrific crash and I was flat on my back in the middle of the road. Knocked the tire tool 'bout a hundred feet, I found it later in a field. Guy in a VW van pulled up right in front of me, jumped out and told me I'd been struck. I couldn't hear what he was saying, I was deafened, but he made signs. Took me to a hospital and they checked me over, they were amazed—no burns, nothing, just the deafness, which lasted about forty-eight hours. I figured I owed the Lord something, and I became a Witness. And let me tell you my life since that day has been—" He paused, searching for the right word. "*Serene*. Truly serene." Burch had had a great-grandfather who had also been struck by lightning, knocked from the front seat of a buckboard on a country road in Pennsylvania in 1910, but no conversion had resulted in that case, as far as he knew.

Connors arranged to have a *Folks* photographer shoot Burch on the following Wednesday and, much impressed—rarely had he encountered serenity on this scale—left the apartment with his pockets full of Witness literature.

Connors next talked to a woman named MacGregor who had been struck by lightning while sitting on a bench on the Cold Spring, New York, railroad platform and had suffered third-degree burns on her arms and legs—she had been wearing a rubberized raincoat which had, she felt, protected her somewhat, but maybe not, she couldn't be sure. Her experience, while lacking a religious dimension per se, had made her think very hard about her life, she said, and there had been some important changes (*Lightning changes things*, Connors wrote in his notebook). She had married the man she had been seeing for two years but had been slightly dubious about, and on the whole, this had been the right thing to do. She and Marty had a house in Garrison, New York, where Marty was in real estate, and she'd quit her job with Estée Lauder because the commute, which she'd been making since 1975, was just too tiring. Connors made a date for the photographer. Mrs. MacGregor was pleasant and attractive (fawn-colored suit, black clocked stockings) but, Connors thought, too old to start the layout with.

The next day he got a call from someone who sounded young. Her name was Edwina Rawson, she said, and she had been struck by lightning on New Year's Day 1980 while walking in the woods with her husband, Marty. (*Two Martys in the same piece?* thought Connors, scowling.) Curiously enough, she said, her great-grandmother had also been struck by lightning, knocked from the front seat of a buggy on a country road outside Iowa City in 1911. "But I don't want to be in the magazine," she said. "I mean, with all those rock stars and movie stars. Olivia Newton-John I'm not. If you were writing a book or something—"

Connors was fascinated. He had never come across anyone who did not want to appear in *Folks* before. He was also slightly irritated. He had seen perfectly decent colleagues turn amazingly ugly when refused a request for an interview. "Well," he said, "could we at least talk? I promise I won't take up much of your time, and, you know, this is a pretty important experience, being struck by lightning—not many people have had it. Also you might be interested in how the others felt . . ." "Okay," she said, "but off the record unless I decide otherwise." "Done," said Connors. *My God, she thinks she's the State Department.*

Edwina was not only slightly wonderful but also mildly superb, worth a double-page spread in anybody's book, *Vogue*, *Life*, *Elle*, *Ms.*, *Town & Country*, you name it. Oh Lord, thought Connors, there are ways and ways to be struck by lightning. She was wearing jeans and a parka and she was beautifully, beautifully black—a considerable plus, Connors noted automatically, the magazine conscientiously tried to avoid lily-white stories. She was carrying a copy of *Variety* (not an actress, he thought, *please* not an actress) and was not an actress but doing a paper on *Variety* for a class in media studies at NYU. "God, I love *Variety*," she said. "The stately march of the grosses through the middle pages." Connors decided that "Shall we get married?" was an inappropriate second remark to make to one newly met, but it was a very tough decision.

They were in a bar called Bradley's on University Place in the Village, a bar Connors sometimes used for interviews because of its warmth, geniality. Edwina was drinking a Beck's and Connors, struck by lightning, had a feeble paw wrapped around a vodka-tonic. Relax, he told himself, go slow, we have half the afternoon. There was a kid, she said, two-year-old boy, Marty's, Marty had split for California and a job as a systems analyst with Warner Communications, good riddance to bad rubbish. Connors had no idea what a systems analyst did: go with the flow? The trouble with Marty, she said, was that he was immature, a systems analyst, and white. She conceded that when the lightning hit he had given her mouth-to-mouth resuscitation, perhaps saved her life; he had taken a course in CPR at the New School, which was entirely consistent with his cautious, be-prepared, white-folks' attitude toward life. She had nothing against white folks, Edwina said with a warm smile, or rabbits, as black folks sometimes termed them, but you had to admit that, qua folks, they sucked. Look at the Trilateral Commission, she said, a perfect example. Connors weighed in with some knowledgeable words about the Commission, detritus from his *Penthouse* piece, managing to hold her interest through a second Beck's.

"Did it change your life, being struck?" asked Connors. She frowned, considered. "Yes and no," she said. "Got rid of Marty, that was an up. Why I married him I'll never know. Why he married *me* I'll never know. A minute of bravery, never to be repeated." Connors saw that she was much aware of her own beauty, her hauteur about appearing in the magazine was appropriate—who needed it? People would dig slant wells for this woman, go out into a producing field with a tank truck in the dead of night and take off two thousand gallons of somebody else's crude, write fanciful checks, establish Pyramid Clubs with tony marble-and-gold headquarters on Zurich's Bahnhofstrasse. What did he have to offer?

"Can you tell me a little bit more about how you felt when it actually hit you?" he asked, trying to keep his mind on business. "Yes," Edwina said. "We were taking a walk—we were at his mother's place in Connecticut, near Madison—and Marty was talking about whether or not he should take a SmokeEnders course at the Y, he smoked Kents, miles and miles of Kents. I was saying, yes, yes, do it! and whammo! the lightning. When I came to, I felt like I was burning inside, inside my chest, drank seventeen glasses of water, chug-a-lugged them, thought I was going to bust. Also, my eyebrows were gone. I looked at myself in the mirror and I had zip eyebrows. Looked really funny, maybe improved me." Regarding her closely Connors saw that her eyebrows were in fact dark dramatic slashes of eyebrow pencil. "Ever been a model?" he asked, suddenly inspired. "That's how I make it," Edwina said, "that's how I keep little Zachary in britches, look in the *Sunday Times Magazine*, I do Altman's, Macy's, you'll see me and three white chicks, usually, lingerie ads...."

The soul burns, Connors thought, having been struck by lightning. Without music, Nietzsche said, the world would be a mistake. Do I have that right? Connors, no musician (although a scholar of fiddle music from Pinchas Zuckerman to Eddie South, "dark angel of the violin," 1904–1962), agreed wholeheartedly. Lightning an attempt at music on the part of God? Does get your attention, Connors thought, *attempt* wrong by definition because God is perfect by definition.... Lightning at once a *coup de théâtre* and career counseling? Connors wondered if he had a song to sing, one that would signify to the burned beautiful creature before him.

"The armadillo is the only animal other than man known to contract leprosy," Connors said. "The slow, friendly armadillo. I picture a leper armadillo, white as snow, with a little bell around its neck, making its draggy scamper across Texas from El Paso to Big Spring. My heart breaks."

Edwina peered into his chest where the cracked heart bumped around in its cage of bone. "Man, you are one sentimental taxpayer."

Connors signaled the waiter for more drinks. "It was about 1880 that the saintly armadillo crossed the Rio Grande and entered Texas," he said, "seeking to carry its message to that great state. Its message was, squash me on your highways. Make my nine-banded shell into beautiful lacquered baskets for your patios, decks and mobile homes. Watch me hayfoot-strawfoot across your vast savannas enriching same with my best-quality excreta. In some parts of South America armadillos grow to almost five feet in length and are allowed to teach at the junior-college level. In Argentina—"

"You're crazy, baby," Edwina said, patting him on the arm.

"Yes," Connors said, "would you like to go to a movie?"

The movie was "Moscow Does Not Believe in Tears," a nifty item. Connors, Edwina inhabiting both the right and left sides of his brain, next interviewed a man named Stupple who had been struck by lightning in April 1970 and had in consequence joined the American Nazi Party, specifically the Horst Wessel Post #66 in Newark, which had (counting Stupple) three members. *Can't use him*, thought Connors, *wasting time*, nevertheless faithfully inscribing in his notebook pages of viciousness having to do with the Protocols of Zion and the alleged genetic inferiority of blacks. *Marvelous, don't these guys ever come up with anything new?* Connors remembered having heard the same routine, almost word for word, from an Assistant Grand Dragon of the Shreveport (La.) Klan, a man somewhat dumber than a bathtub, in 1957 at the Dew Drop Inn in Shreveport, where the ribs in red sauce were not bad. Stupple, who had put on a Nazi armband over his checked flannel shirt for the interview, which was conducted in a two-room apartment over a failing four-lane bowling alley in Newark, served Connors Danish aquavit frozen into a block of ice with a very good Japanese beer, Kirin, as a chaser. "Won't you need a picture?" Stupple asked at length, and Connors said, evasively, "Well, you know, lots of people have been struck by lightning . . ."

Telephoning Edwina from a phone booth outside the Port Authority Terminal, he learned that she was not available for dinner. "How do you feel?" he asked her, aware that the question was imprecise—he really wanted to know whether having been struck by lightning was an ongoing state or, rather, a one-time illumination—and vexed by his inability to get a handle on the story. "Tired," she said, "Zach's been yelling a lot, call me tomorrow, maybe we can do something . . ."

Penfield, the *Folks* editor, had a call on Connors' service when he got back to Lafayette Street. "How's it coming?" Penfield asked. "I don't understand it yet," Connors said, "how it works. It changes people." "What's to understand?" said Penfield, "wham-bam-thank you ma'am, you got anybody I can use for the opening? We've got these terrific shots of individual bolts, I see a four-way bleed with the text reversed out of this saturated purple sky and this tiny but absolutely wonderful face looking up at the bolt—" "She's black," said Connors, "you're going to have trouble with the purple, not enough contrast." "So it'll be subtle," said Penfield excitedly, "rich and subtle. The bolt will give it enough snap. It'll be nice."

Nice, thought Connors, what a word for being struck by lightning.

Connors, trying to get at the core of the experience—did being struck exalt or exacerbate pre-existing tendencies, states of mind, and what was the relevance of electro-shock therapy, if it was a therapy?—talked to a Trappist monk who had been struck by lightning in 1975 while working in the fields at the order's Piffard, New York, abbey. Having been given permission by his superior to speak to Connors, the small, bald monk was positively loquacious. He told Connors that the one deprivation he had felt keenly, as a member of a monastic order, was the absence of rock music. "Why?" he asked rhetorically. "I'm too old for this music, it's for kids, I know it, you know it, makes no sense at all. But I love it, I simply love it. And after I was struck the community bought me this Sony Walkman."

Proudly he showed Connors the small device with its delicate earphones. "A special dispensation. I guess they figured I was near-to-dead, therefore it was all right to bend the Rule a bit. I simply love it. Have you heard the Cars?" Standing in a beet field with the brown-habited monk Connors felt the depth of the man's happiness and wondered if he himself ought to re-think his attitude toward Christianity. It would not be so bad to spend one's days pulling beets in the warm sun while listening to the Cars and then retire to one's cell at night to read St. Augustine and catch up on Rod Stewart and the B-52's.

"The thing is," Connors said to Edwina that night at dinner, "I don't understand precisely what effects the change. Is it pure fright? Gratitude at having survived?" They were sitting in an Italian restaurant called Da Silvano on Sixth near Houston, eating tortellini in a white sauce. Little Zachary, a good-looking two-year-old, sat in a high chair and accepted bits of cut-up pasta. Edwina had had a shoot that afternoon and was not in a good mood. "The same damn thing," she said, "me and three white chicks, you'd think somebody'd turn it around just once." She needed a *Vogue* cover and a fragrance campaign, she said, and then she would be sitting pretty. She had been considered for *Hashish* some time back but didn't get it and there was a question in her mind as to whether her agency (Jerry Francisco) had been solidly behind her. "Come along," said Edwina, "I want to give you a back rub, you look a tiny bit peaked."

Connors subsequently interviewed five more people who had been struck by lightning, uncovering some unusual cases, including a fellow dumb from birth who, upon being struck, began speaking quite admirable French; his great-grandfather, as it happened, had also been struck by lightning, blasted from the seat of a farm wagon in Brittany in 1909. In his piece Connors described the experience as "ineffable," using a word he had loathed and despised his whole life long, spoke of lightning-as-grace and went so far as to mention the descent of the Dove. Penfield, without a moment's hesitation, cut the whole paragraph, saying (correctly) that the *Folks* reader didn't like "funny stuff" and pointing out that the story was running long anyway because of the extra page given to Edwina's opening layout, in which she wore a Mary McFadden pleated tube and looked, in Penfield's phrase, approximately fantastic.

That guy in the back room, she said. He's eating our potatoes. You were wonderful last night. The night before that, you were wonderful. The night before that, you were terrible. He's eating our potatoes. I went in there and looked at him and he had potato smeared all over his face. Mashed. You were wonderful on the night that we met. I was terrible. You were terrible on the night we had the suckling pig. The pig, cooking the pig, put you in a terrible mood. I was wonderful in order to balance, to attempt to balance, your foul behavior. That guy with the eye patch in the back room is eating our potatoes. What are you going to do about it?

What? he said.

What are you going to do about it?

He's got a potato masher in there?

And a little pot. He holds the little pot between his knees. Mashes away with his masher. Mash mash mash.

Well, he said, he's got to live, don't he?

I don't know. Maybe so, maybe not. You brought him home. What are you going to do about it?

We have plenty of potatoes, he said. I think you're getting excited. Getting excited about nothing. Maybe you'd better simmer down. If I want frenzy I'll go out on the street. In here, I want calm. Clear, quiet calm. You're getting excited. I want you to calm down. So I can read. Quietly, read.

You were superb on the night we had the osso buco, she said. I cooked it. That seemed to strike your fancy. You appreciated the effort, my effort, or seemed to. You didn't laugh. You did smile. Smiled furiously all through dinner. I was atrocious that night. Biting the pillow. You kept the lights turned up, you were reading. We struggled for the rheostat. The music from the other room flattered you, your music, music you had bought and paid for, to flatter yourself. Your good taste. Nobody ever listens to that stuff unless he or she wants to establish that he or she has supremely good taste. Supernal *good taste.*

Did you know, he said, looking up, *that the mayor has only one foot? One real foot?*

Cooking the pig put you in a terrible mood. The pig's head in particular. You asked me to remove the pig's head. With a saw. I said that the pig's head had to remain in place. Placing the apple in a bloody hole where the pig's neck had been would be awful, I said. People would be revolted. You threw the saw on the floor and declared that you could not go on. I said that people had been putting the apple in the pig's mouth for centuries, centuries. There were twenty people coming for dinner, a mistake, of course, but not mine. The pig was stretched out on the counter. You placed the pig on two kitchen chairs which had been covered with newspaper, the floor had been covered with newspaper too, my knee was on or in the pig's back, I grasped an ear and began to saw. You were terrible that night, threw a glass of wine in a man's face. I remember these things.

Kinda funny to have a mayor with only one foot.

The man said he was going to thump you. I said, Go ahead and thump him. You said, No one is going to thump anybody. The man left, then, red wine stains staining his pink cashmere sweater quite wonderfully. You were wonderful that night.

They say, he said, *that there are flowers all over the city because the mayor does not know where his mother is buried. Did you know that?*

Captain Blood

WHEN CAPTAIN BLOOD goes to sea, he locks the doors and windows of his house on Cow Island personally. One never knows what sort of person might chance by, while one is away.

When Captain Blood, at sea, paces the deck, he usually paces the foredeck rather than the afterdeck—a matter of personal preference. He keeps marmalade and a spider monkey in his cabin, and four perukes on stands.

When Captain Blood, at sea, discovers that he is pursued by the Dutch Admiral Van Tromp, he considers throwing the women overboard. So that they will drift, like so many giant lotuses in their green, lavender, purple and blue gowns, across Van Tromp's path, and he will have to stop and pick them up. Blood will have the women fitted with life jackets under their dresses. They will hardly be in much danger at all. But what about the jaws of sea turtles? No, the women cannot be thrown overboard. Vile, vile! What an idiotic idea! What could he have been thinking of? Of the patterns they would have made floating on the surface of the water, in the moonlight, a cerise gown, a silver gown . . .

Captain Blood presents a façade of steely imperturbability.

He is poring over his charts, promising everyone that things will get better. There has not been one bit of booty in the last eight months. Should he try another course? Another ocean? The men have been quite decent about the situation. Nothing has been said. Still, it's nerve-racking.

When Captain Blood retires for the night (leaving orders that he be called instantly if something comes up) he reads, usually. Or smokes, thinking calmly of last things.

His hideous reputation should not, strictly speaking, be painted in the horrible colors customarily employed. Many a man walks the streets of Panama City, or Port Royal, or San Lorenzo, alive and well, who would have been stuck through the gizzard with a rapier, or smashed in the brain with a boarding pike, had it not been for Blood's swift, cheerful intervention. Of course, there are times when severe measures are unavoidable. At these times he does not flinch, but takes appropriate action with admirable steadiness. There are no two ways about it: when one looses a seventy-four-gun broadside against the fragile hull of another vessel, one gets carnage.

Blood at dawn, a solitary figure pacing the foredeck.

No other sail in sight. He reaches into the pocket of his blue velvet jacket trimmed with silver lace. His hand closes over three round, white objects: mothballs. In disgust, he throws them over the side. One *makes* one's luck, he thinks. Reaching into another pocket, he withdraws a folded parchment tied with ribbon. Unwrapping the little packet, he finds that it is a memo that he wrote to himself ten months earlier. "*Dolphin*, Captain Darbraunce, 120 tons, cargo silver, paprika, bananas, sailing Mar. 10 Havana. *Be there!*" Chuckling, Blood goes off to seek his mate, Oglethorpe—that laughing blond giant of a man.

Who will be aboard this vessel which is now within cannon-shot? wonders Captain Blood. Rich people, I hope, with pretty gold and silver things aplenty.

"Short John, where is Mr. Oglethorpe?"

"I am not Short John, sir. I am John-of-Orkney."

"Sorry, John. Has Mr. Oglethorpe carried out my instructions?"

"Yes, sir. He is forward, crouching over the bombard, lit cheroot in hand, ready to fire."

"Well, fire then."

"Fire!"

BAM!

"The other captain doesn't understand what is happening to him!"

"He's not heaving to!"

"He's ignoring us!"

"The dolt!"

"Fire again!"

BAM!

"That did it!"

"He's turning into the wind!"

"He's dropped anchor!"

"He's lowering sail!"

"Very well, Mr. Oglethorpe. You may prepare to board."

"Very well, Peter."

"And Jeremy—"

"Yes, Peter?"

"I know we've had rather a thin time of it these last few months."

"Well it hasn't been so bad, Peter. A little slow, perhaps—"

"Well, before we board, I'd like you to convey to the men my appreciation for their patience. Patience and, I may say, tact."

"We knew you'd turn up something, Peter."

"Just tell them for me, will you?"

Always a wonderful moment, thinks Captain Blood. Preparing to board. Pistol in one hand, naked cutlass in the other. Dropping lightly to the deck of the engrappled vessel, backed by one's grinning, leering, disorderly, rapacious crew who are nevertheless under the strictest buccaneer discipline. There to confront the little band of fear-crazed victims shrinking from the entirely possible carnage. Among them, several beautiful women, but one really spectacular beautiful woman who stands a bit apart from her sisters, clutching a machete with which she intends, against all reason, to—

When Captain Blood celebrates the acquisition of a rich prize, he goes down to the galley himself and cooks *tallarínes a la Catalana* (noodles, spare ribs, almonds, pine nuts) for all hands. The name of the captured vessel is entered in a little book along with the names of all the others he has captured in a long career. Here are some of them: the *Oxford*, the *Luis*, the *Fortune*, the *Lambe*, the *Jamaica Merchant*, the *Betty*, the *Prosperous*, the *Endeavor*, the *Falcon*, the *Bonadventure*, the *Constant Thomas*, the *Marquesa*, the *Señora del Carmen*, the *Recovery*, the *Maria Gloriosa*, the *Virgin Queen*, the *Esmerelda*, the *Havana*, the *San Felipe*, the *Steadfast* . . .

The true buccaneer is not persuaded that God is not on his side, too—especially if, as is often the case, he turned pirate after some monstrously unjust thing was done to him, such as being press-ganged into one or another of the Royal Navies when he was merely innocently having a drink at a waterfront tavern, or having been confined to the stinking dungeons of the Inquisition just for making some idle, thoughtless, light remark. Therefore, Blood feels himself to be devout *in his own way*, and has endowed candles burning in churches in most of the great cities of the New World. Although not under his own name.

Captain Blood roams ceaselessly, making daring raids. The average raid yields something like 20,000 pieces-of-eight, which is apportioned fairly among the crew, with wounded men getting more according to the gravity of their wounds. A cut ear is worth two pieces, a cut-*off* ear worth ten to twelve. The scale of payments for injuries is posted in the forecastle.

When he is on land, Blood is confused and troubled by the life of cities, where every passing stranger may, for no reason, assault him, if the stranger so chooses. And indeed, the stranger's mere presence, multiplied many times over, is a kind of assault. Merely having to *take into account* all these hurrying others is a blistering occupation. This does not happen on a ship, or on a sea.

An amusing incident: Captain Blood has overhauled a naval vessel, has caused her to drop anchor (on this particular voyage he is sailing with three other ships under his command and a total enlistment of nearly one thousand men) and is now interviewing the arrested captain in his cabin full of marmalade jars and new perukes.

"And what may your name be, sir? If I may ask?"

"Jones, sir."

"What kind of a name is that? English, I take it?"

"No, it's American, sir."

"American? What is an American?"

"America is a new nation among the nations of the world."

"I've not heard of it. Where is it?"

"North of here, north and west. It's a very small nation, at present, and has only been a nation for about two years."

"But the name of your ship is French."

"Yes it is. It is named in honor of Benjamin Franklin, one of our American heroes."

"*Bon Homme Richard?* What has that to do with Benjamin or Franklin?"

"Well it's an allusion to an almanac Dr. Franklin published called—"

"You weary me, sir. You are captured, American or no, so tell me—do you surrender, with all your men, fittings, cargo and whatever?"

"Sir, I have not yet begun to fight."

"Captain, this is madness. We have you completely surrounded. Furthermore there is a great hole in your hull below the waterline where our warning shot, which was slightly miscalculated, bashed in your timbers. You are taking water at a fearsome rate. And still you wish to fight?"

"It is the pluck of us Americans, sir. We are just that way. Our tiny nation has to be pluckier than most if it is to survive among the bigger, older nations of the world."

"Well, bless my soul. Jones, you are the damnedest goatsucker I ever did see. Stab me if I am not tempted to let you go scot-free, just because of your amazing pluck."

"No sir, I insist on fighting. As founder of the American naval tradition, I must set a good example."

"Jones, return to your vessel and be off."

"No, sir, I will fight to the last shred of canvas, for the honor of America."

"Jones, even in America, wherever it is, you must have encountered the word 'ninny.'"

"Oh. I see. Well then. I think we'll be weighing anchor, Captain, with your permission."

"Choose your occasions, Captain. And God be with you."

Blood, at dawn, a solitary figure pacing the foredeck. The world of piracy is wide, and at the same time, narrow. One can be gallant all day long, and still end up with a spider monkey for a wife. And what does his mother think of him?

The favorite dance of Captain Blood is the grave and haunting Catalonian *sardana*, in which the participants join hands facing each other to form a ring which gradually becomes larger, then smaller, then larger again. It is danced without smiling, for the most part. He frequently dances this with his men, in the middle of the ocean, after lunch, to the music of a single silver trumpet.

A woman seated on a plain wooden chair under a canopy. She is wearing white overalls and has a pleased expression on her face. Watching her, two dogs, German shepherds, at rest. Behind the dogs, with their backs to us, a row of naked women kneeling, sitting on their heels, their buttocks as perfect as eggs or o's—oo oo oo oo oo oo oo. In profile to the scene, Benvenuto Cellini, in a fur hat.

Two young women wrapped as gifts. The gift-wrapping is almost indistinguishable from ordinary clothing, perhaps a shade newer, brighter, more studied than ordinary clothing. Each young woman holds a white envelope. Each envelope is addressed to "Tad."

Two young women, naked, tied together by a long red thread. One is dark, one is fair.

Large (eight by ten feet) sheets of white paper on the floor, eight of them. The total area covered is about four hundred square feet; some of the sheets overlap. A string quartet is playing at one edge of this area, and irregular rows of formally dressed spectators sit in gilt chairs across the paper from the players. A large bucket of blue paint has been placed on the paper. Two young women, naked. Each has her hair rolled up in a bun; each has been splashed, breasts, belly, thighs, with blue paint. One, on her belly, is being dragged across the paper by the other, who is standing, gripping the first woman's wrists. Their backs are not painted. Or not painted with. The artist is Yves Klein.

Nowhere—the middle of it, its exact center. Standing there, a telephone booth, green with tarnished aluminum, the word PHONE and the system's symbol (bell in ring) in medium blue. Inside the telephone booth, two young women, one dark, one fair, facing each other. Their naked breasts and thighs brush lightly (one holding the receiver to the other's ear) as they place calls to their mothers in California. In profile to the scene, at far right, Benvenuto Cellini, wearing white overalls.

Two young men, wrapped as gifts. They have wrapped themselves carefully, tight pants, open-throated shirts, shoes with stacked heels, gold jewelry on right and left wrists, codpieces stuffed with credit cards. They stand, under a Christmas tree big as an office building, and women rush toward them. Or they stand, under a Christmas tree big as an office building, and no women rush toward them. A voice singing Easter songs, hallelujahs.

Georges de La Tour, wearing white overalls (Iron Boy brand) is attending a film. On the screen two young women, naked, are playing Ping-Pong. One makes a swipe with her paddle at a ball the other has placed just over the net and misses, bruising her right leg on the edge of the table. The other puts down her paddle and walks gracefully around the table to examine the hurt; she places her hands on either side of the raw, ugly mark . . . Georges de La Tour picks up his hat and walks from the theatre. In the lobby he purchases a bag of M & Ms which he opens with his teeth.

The world of work: Two young women, one dark, one fair, wearing web belts to which canteens are attached, nothing more. They are sitting side-by-side on high stools (oo oo) before a pair of draughting tables, inking-in pencil drawings. Or, in a lumberyard in Southern Illinois, they are unloading a railroad car containing several hundred thousand board feet of Southern yellow pine. Or, in the composing room of a medium-sized Akron daily, they are passing long pieces of paper through a machine which deposits a thin coating of wax on the back side, and then positioning the type on a page. Or, they are driving identical Yellow cabs which are racing side-by-side up Park Avenue with frightened passengers, each driver trying to beat the other to a hole in the traffic. Or, they are seated at adjacent desks in the beige-carpeted area set aside for officers in a bank, refusing loans. Or, they are standing bent over, hands on knees, peering into the site of an archeological dig in the Cameroons. Or, they are teaching, in adjacent classrooms, Naked Physics—in the classroom on the left, Naked Physics I, and in the classroom on the right, Naked Physics II. Or, they are kneeling, sitting on their heels, before a pair of shoeshine stands.

Two young women, wearing web belts to which canteens are attached, nothing more, marching down Broadway again. They are followed by an excited crowd, bands, etc.

Two women, one dark and one fair, wearing parkas, blue wool watch caps on their heads, inspecting a row of naked satyrs, hairy-legged, split-footed, tailed and tufted, who hang from hooks in a meat locker where the temperature is a constant 18 degrees. The women are tickling the satyrs under the tail, where they are most vulnerable, with their long white (nimble) fingers tipped with long curved scarlet nails. The satyrs squirm and dance under this treatment, hanging from hooks, while other women, seated in red plush armchairs, in the meat locker, applaud, or scold, or knit. Hovering near the thermostat, Vladimir Tatlin, in an asbestos tuxedo.

Two women, one dark and one fair, wearing parkas, blue wool watch caps on their heads, inspecting a row of naked young men, hairy-legged, many-toed, pale and shivering, who hang on hooks in a meat locker where the temperature is a constant 18 degrees. The women are tickling the men under the tail, where they are most vulnerable, with their long white (nimble) fingers tipped with long curved scarlet nails. The young men squirm and dance under this treatment, hanging from hooks, while giant eggs, seated in red plush chairs, boil.

Conversations with Goethe

November 13, 1823

I WAS walking home from the theatre with Goethe this evening when we saw a small boy in a plum-colored waistcoat. Youth, Goethe said, is the silky apple butter on the good brown bread of possibility.

December 9, 1823

Goethe had sent me an invitation to dinner. As I entered his sitting room I found him warming his hands before a cheerful fire. We discussed the meal to come at some length, for the planning of it had been an occasion of earnest thought to him and he was in quite good spirits about the anticipated results, which included sweetbreads prepared in the French manner with celery root and paprika. Food, said Goethe, is the topmost taper on the golden candelabrum of existence.

January 11, 1824

Dinner alone with Goethe. Goethe said, "I will now confide to you some of my ideas about music, something I have been considering for many years. You will have noted that although certain members of the animal kingdom make a kind of music— one speaks of the 'song' of birds, does one not?—no animal known to us takes part in what may be termed an organized musical performance. Man alone does that. I have wondered about crickets—whether their evening cacophony might be considered in this light, as a species of performance, albeit one of little significance to our ears. I have asked Humboldt about it, and Humboldt replied that he thought not, that it is merely a sort of tic on the part of crickets. The great point here, the point that I may choose to enlarge upon in some future work, is not that the members of the animal kingdom do not unite wholeheartedly in this musical way but that man does, to the eternal comfort and glory of his soul."

Music, Goethe said, is the frozen tapioca in the ice chest of History.

March 22, 1824

Goethe had been desirous of making the acquaintance of a young Englishman, a Lieutenant Whitby, then in Weimar on business. I conducted this gentleman to Goethe's house, where Goethe greeted us most cordially and offered us wine and biscuits. English, he said, was a wholly splendid language, which had given him the deepest pleasure over many years. He had mastered it early, he told us, in order to be able to savor the felicities and tragic depths of Shakespeare, with whom no author in the world, before or since, could rightfully be compared. We were in a most pleasant mood and continued to talk about the accomplishments of the young Englishman's countrymen until quite late. The English, Goethe said in parting, are the shining brown varnish on the sad chiffonier of civilization. Lieutenant Whitby blushed most noticeably.

April 7, 1824

When I entered Goethe's house at noon, a wrapped parcel was standing in the foyer. "And what do you imagine this may be?" asked Goethe with a smile. I could not for the life of me fathom what the parcel might contain, for it was most oddly shaped. Goethe explained that it was a sculpture, a gift from his friend van den Broot, the Dutch artist. He unwrapped the package with the utmost care, and I was seized with admiration when the noble figure within was revealed: a representation, in bronze, of a young woman dressed as Diana, her bow bent and an arrow on the string. We marveled together at the perfection of form and fineness of detail, most of all at the indefinable aura of spirituality which radiated from the work. "Truly astonishing!" Goethe exclaimed, and I hastened to agree. Art, Goethe said, is the four per cent interest on the municipal bond of life. He was very pleased with this remark and repeated it several times.

June 18, 1824

Goethe had been having great difficulties with a particular actress at the theatre, a person who conceived that her own notion of how her role was to be played was superior to Goethe's. "It is not enough," he said, sighing, "that I have mimed every gesture for the poor creature, that nothing has been left unexplored in this character I myself have created, willed into being. She persists in what she terms her 'interpretation,' which is ruining the play." He went on to discuss the sorrows of managing a theatre, even the finest, and the exhausting detail that must be attended to, every jot and tittle, if the performances are to be fit for a discriminating public. Actors, he said, are the Scotch weevils in the salt pork of honest effort. I loved him more than ever, and we parted with an affectionate handshake.

September 1, 1824

Today Goethe inveighed against certain critics who had, he said, completely misunderstood Lessing. He spoke movingly about how such obtuseness had partially embittered Lessing's last years, and speculated that it was because Lessing was both critic and dramatist that the attacks had been of more than usual ferocity. Critics, Goethe said, are the cracked mirror in the grand ballroom of the creative spirit. No, I said, they were, rather, the extra baggage on the great cabriolet of conceptual progress. "Eckermann," said Goethe, "*shut up.*"

Well we all had our Willie & Wade records 'cept this one guy who was called Spare Some Change? 'cause that's all he ever said and you don't have no Willie & Wade records if the best you can do is Spare Some Change?

So we all took our Willie & Wade records down to the Willie & Wade Park and played all the great and sad Willie & Wade songs on portable players for the beasts of the city, the jumpy black squirrels and burnt-looking dogs and filthy, sick pigeons.

And I thought probably one day Willie or Wade would show up in person at the Willie & Wade Park to check things out, see who was there and what record this person was playing and what record that person was playing.

And probably Willie (or Wade) would just ease around checking things out, saying "Howdy" to this one and that one, and he'd see the crazy black guy in Army clothes who stands in the Willie & Wade Park and every ten minutes, screams like a chicken, and Willie (or Wade) would just say to that guy, "How ya doin' good buddy?" and smile, 'cause strange things don't bother Willie, or Wade, one bit.

And I thought I'd probably go up to Willie then, if it was Willie, and tell him 'bout my friend that died, and how I felt about it at the time, and how I feel about it now. And Willie would say, "I know."

And I would maybe ask him did he remember Galveston, and did he ever when he was a kid play in the old concrete forts along the sea wall with the giant cannon in them that the government didn't want any more, and he'd say, "Sure I did." And I'd say, "You ever work the Blue Jay in San Antone?" and he'd say, "Sure I have."

And I'd say, "Willie, don't them microphones scare you, the ones with the little fuzzy sweaters on them?" And he'd say to me, "They scare me bad, potner, but I don't let on."

And then he (one or the other, Willie or Wade) would say, "Take care, good buddy," and leave the Willie & Wade Park in his black limousine that the driver of had been waiting patiently in all this time, and I would never see him again, but continue to treasure, all my life, his great contributions.

Henrietta and Alexandra

ALEXANDRA WAS reading Henrietta's manuscript.

"This," she said, pointing with her finger, "is inane."

Henrietta got up and looked over Alexandra's shoulder at the sentence.

"Yes," she said. "I prefer the inane, sometimes. The ane is often inutile to the artist."

There was a moment of contemplation.

"I have been offered a thousand florins for it," Henrietta said. "The Dutch rights."

"How much is that in our money?"

"Two hundred sixty-six dollars."

"Bless Babel," Alexandra said, and took her friend in her arms.

Henrietta said: "Once I was a young girl, very much like any other young girl, interested in the same things, I was exemplary. I was told what I was, that is to say a young girl, and I knew what I was because I had been told and because there were other young girls all around me who had been told the same things and knew the same things, and looking at them and hearing again in my head the things I had been told I knew what a young girl was. We had all been told the same things. I had not been told, for example, that some wine was piss and some not and I had not been told . . . other things. Still I had been told a great many things all very useful but I had not been told that I was going to die in any way that would allow me to realize that I really was going to die and that it would be all over, then, and that this was all there was and that I had damned well better make the most of it. That I discovered for myself and covered with shame and shit as I was I made the most of it. I had not been told how to make the most of it but I figured it out. Then I moved through a period of depression, the depression engendered by the realization that I had placed myself beyond the pale, there I was, beyond the pale. Then I discovered that there were other people beyond the pale with me, that there were quite as many people on the wrong side of the pale as there were on the right side of the pale and that the people on the wrong side of the pale were as complex as the people on the right side of the pale, as unhappy, as subject to time, as subject to death. So what the fuck? I said to myself in the colorful language I had learned on the wrong side of the pale. By this time I was no longer a young girl. I was mature."

Alexandra had a special devotion to the Sacred Heart.

THEORIES OF THE SACRED HEART
LOSS AND RECOVERY OF THE SACRED HEART
CONFLICTING CLAIMS OF THE GREAT CATHEDRALS
THE SACRED HEART IN CONTEMPORARY ICONOGRAPHY
APPEARANCE OF SPURIOUS SACRED HEARTS AND HOW
   THEY MAY BE DISTINGUISHED FROM THE TRUE ONE
LOCATION OF THE TRUE SACRED HEART REVEALED
HOW THE ABBÉ ST. GERMAIN PRESERVED THE TRUE
   SACRED HEART FROM THE HANDS OF THE BARBARIANS
WHY THE SACRED HEART IS FREQUENTLY REPRESENTED
   SURMOUNTED BY A CROWN OF THORNS
MEANING OF THE TINY TONGUE OF FLAME
ORDERS AND CEREMONIES IN THE VENERATION OF THE
   SACRED HEART
ROLE OF THE SACRED HEART SOCIETY IN THE VENERATION
   OF THE SACRED HEART

Alexandra was also a member of the Knights of St. Dympna, patroness of the insane.

Alexandra and Henrietta were walking down the street in their long gowns. A man looked at them and laughed. Alexandra and Henrietta rushed at him and scratched his eyes out.

As a designer of artificial ruins, Alexandra was well-known. She designed ruins in the manners of Langley, Effner, Robert Adam and Carlo Marchionni, as well as her own manner. She was working on a ruin for a park in Tempe, Arizona, consisting of a ruined wall nicely disintegrated at the top and one end, two classical columns upright and one fallen, vines, and a number of broken urns. The urns were difficult because it was necessary to produce them from intact urns and the workmen at the site were often reluctant to do violence to the urns. Sometimes she pretended to lose her temper. "*Hurl the bloody urn, Umberto!*"

Alexandra looked at herself in the mirror. She admired her breasts, her belly, and her legs, which were, she felt, her best feature.

"Now I will go into the other room and astonish Henrietta, who is also beautiful."

Henrietta stood up and, with a heaving motion, threw the manuscript of her novel into the fire. The manuscript of the novel she had been working on ceaselessly, night and day, for the last ten years.

"Alexandra! Aren't you going to rush to the fire and pull the manuscript of my novel out of it?"

"No."

Henrietta rushed to the fire and pulled the manuscript out of it. Only the first and last pages were fully burned, and luckily, she remembered what was written there.

Henrietta decided that Alexandra did not love her enough. And how could nuances of despair be expressed if you couldn't throw your novel into the fire safely?

Alexandra was sending a petition to Rome. She wanted her old marriage, a dim marriage ten years old to a man named Black Dog, annulled. Alexandra read the rules about sending petitions to Rome to Henrietta.

"All applications to be sent to Rome should be written on good paper, and a double sheet, 8⅛ inches × 10¾ inches, should be employed. The writing of petitions should be done with ink of a good quality, that will remain legible for a long time. Petitions are generally composed in the Latin language, but the use of the French and Italian languages is also permissible.

"The fundamental rule to be observed is that all petitions must be addressed to the Pope, who, directly or indirectly, grants the requested favors. Hence the regulation form of address in all petitions reads *Beatissime Pater*. Following this the petition opens with the customary deferential phrase *ad pedes Sanctitatis Vestrae humillime provolutus*. The concluding formula is indicated by its opening words: *Et Deus* . . . expressing the prayer of blessing which the grateful petitioner addresses in advance to God for the expected favor.

"After introduction, body and conclusion of the petition have been duly drawn, the sheet is evenly folded length-wise, and on its back, to the right of the fold line, are indited the date of the presentation and the petitioner's name.

"The presentation of petitions is generally made through an agent, whose name is inscribed in the right-hand corner on the back of the petition. This signature is necessary because the agent will call for the grant, and the Congregations deliver rescripts to no one but the agent whose name is thus recorded. The agents, furthermore, pay the fee and taxes for the requested rescripts of favor, give any necessary explanations and comments that may be required, and are at all times in touch with the authorities in order to correct any mistakes or defects in the petitions. Between the hours of nine and one o'clock the agents gather in the offices of the Curial administration to hand in new petitions and to inquire about the fate of those not yet decided. Many of them also go to the anterooms of secretaries in order to discuss important matters personally with the leading officials.

"For lay persons it is as a rule useless to forward petitions through the mails to the Roman Congregations, because as a matter of principle they will not be considered. Equally useless, of course, would be the enclosing of postage stamps with such petitions. Applications by telegraph are not permitted because of their publicity. Nor are decisions ever given by telegraph."

Alexandra stopped reading.

"Jesus Christ!" Henrietta said.

"This wine is piss," Alexandra said.

"You needn't drink it then."

"I'll have another glass."

"You wanted me to buy California wine," Henrietta said.

"But there's no reason to buy absolute vinegar is there? I mean couldn't you have asked the man at the store?"

"They don't always tell the truth."

"I remember that time in Chicago," Alexandra said. "That was a good bottle. And afterwards . . ."

"How much did we pay for that bottle?" Henrietta asked, incuriously.

"Twelve dollars. Or ten dollars. Ten or twelve."

"The hotel," Henrietta said. "Snapdragons on the night table."

"You were . . . exquisite."

"I was mature," Henrietta said.

"If you were mature then, what are you now?"

"More mature," Henrietta said. "Maturation is a process that is ongoing."

"When are you old?" Alexandra asked.

"Not while love is here," Henrietta said.

Henrietta said: "Now I am mature. In maturity I found a rich world beyond the pale and found it possible to live in that world with a degree of enthusiasm. My mother says I am deluded but I have stopped talking to my mother. My father is dead and thus has no opinion. Alexandra continues to heap up indulgences by exclaiming 'Jesus, Mary and Joseph!' which is worth an indulgence of fifty days each time it is exclaimed. Some of the choicer ejaculations are worth seven years and seven quarantines and these she pursues with the innocent cupidity of the small investor. She keeps her totals in a little book. I love her. She has to date worked off eighteen thousand years in the flames of Purgatory. I tell her that the whole thing is a shuck but she refuses to consider my views on this point. Alexandra is immature in that she thinks she will live forever, live after she is dead at the right hand of God in His glory with His power and His angels and His whatnot and I cannot persuade her otherwise. Joseph Conrad will live forever but Alexandra will not. I love her. Now we are going out."

Henrietta and Alexandra went walking. They were holding each other's arms. Alexandra moved a hand sensuously with a circular motion around one of Henrietta's breasts. Henrietta did the same thing to Alexandra. People were looking at them with strange expressions on their faces. They continued walking, under the shaped trees of the boulevard. They were swooning with pleasure, more or less. Someone called the police.

Speaking of the human body, Klee said: One bone alone achieves nothing.

Pondering this, people placed lamps on all of the street corners, and sofas next to the lamps. People sat on the sofas and read Spinoza there, an interesting glare cast on the pages by the dithering inconstant traffic lights. At other points, on the street, four-poster beds were planted, and loving couples slept or watched television together, the sets connected to the empty houses behind them by long black cables. Elsewhere, on the street, conversation pits were chipped out of the concrete, floored with Adam rugs, and lengthy discussions were held. Do we really need a War College? *was a popular subject. Favorite paintings were lashed to the iron railings bordering the sidewalks, a Gainsborough, a van Dongen, a perfervid evocation of Umbrian mental states, an important dark-brown bruising of Arches paper by a printer of modern life.*

One man hung all of his shirts on the railing bordering a sidewalk, he had thirty-nine, and another was brushing his teeth in his bathrobe, another was waxing his fine moustache, a woman was marking cards with a little prickly roller so that her husband, the gambler, would win forever. A man said, "Say, mon, fix me some of dem chitlins you fry so well," and another man said, "Howard, my son, I am now going to show you how to blow glass"—he dipped his glass-blowing tube into a furnace of bubbling glass, there on the street, and blew a rathskeller of beer glasses, each goldenly full.

Inside the abandoned houses subway trains rushed in both directions and genuine nameless animals ate each other with ghastly fervor—

Monday. Many individuals are grasping hold of the sewer grates with both hands, a manifestation, in the words of S. Moholy-Nagy, of the tragic termination of the will to fly.

The Sea of Hesitation

"IF JACKSON had pressed McClellan in White Oak Swamp," Francesca said. "If Longstreet had proceeded vigorously on the first day at Second Manassas. If we had had the 40,000 pairs of shoes we needed when we entered Maryland. If Bloss had not found the envelope containing the two cigars and the copy of Lee's Secret Order No. 191 at Frederick. If the pneumonia had not taken Jackson. If Ewell had secured possession of Cemetery Heights on the first day of Gettysburg. If Pickett's charge . . . If Early's march into the Valley . . . If we had had sufficient food for our troops at Petersburg. If our attack on Fort Stedman had succeeded. If Pickett and Fitzhugh Lee had not indulged in a shad bake at Five Forks. If there had been stores and provisions as promised at Amelia Court House. If Ewell had not been captured at Saylor's Creek together with sixteen artillery pieces and four hundred wagons. If Lee had understood Lincoln—his mind, his larger intentions. If there had been a degree of competence in our civilian administration equal to that exhibited by the military. Then, perhaps, matters would have been brought to a happier conclusion."

"Yes," I said.

Francesca is slightly obsessed. But one must let people talk about what they want to talk about. One must let people do what they want to do.

This morning in the mail I received an abusive letter from a woman in Prague.

Dear Greasy Thomas:
You cannot understand what a pig you are. You are a pig, you idiot. You think you understand things but there is nothing you understand, nothing, idiot pig-swine. You have not wisdom and you have no discretion and nothing can be done without wisdom and discretion. How did a pig-cretin like yourself ever wriggle into life? Why do you exist still, vulgar swine? If you don't think I am going to inform the government of your inappropriate continued existence, a stain on the country's face . . . You can

expect Federal Marshals in clouds very soon, cretin-hideous-swine, and I will laugh as they haul you away in their green vans, ugly toad. You know nothing about anything, garbage-face, and the idea that you would dare "think" for others (I know you are not capable of "feeling") is so wildly outrageous that I would laugh out loud if I were not sick of your importunate posturing, egregious fraud-pig. You are not even an honest pig which is at least of some use in the world, you are rather an ocean of pig-dip poisoning everything you touch. I do not like you at all.

Love,
Jinka

I read the letter twice. She is certainly angry. But one must let people do what they want to do.

I work for the City. In the Human Effort Administration. My work consists of processing applications. People apply for all sorts of things. I approve all applications and buck them upwards, where they are usually disapproved. Upstairs they do not agree with me, that people should be permitted to do what they want to do. Upstairs they have different ideas. But "different ideas" are welcomed, in my particular cosmos.

Before I worked for the City I was interested in changing behavior. I thought behavior could be changed. I had a B.A. in psychology, was working on an M.A. I was into sensory deprivation. I did sensory deprivation studies for a while at McGill and later at Princeton.

At McGill we inhabited the basement of Taub Hall, believed to be the first building in the world devoted exclusively to the study of hatred. But we were not studying hatred, we were doing black-box work and the hatred people kindly lent us their basement. I was in charge of the less intelligent subjects (the subjects were divided into less intelligent and more intelligent). I spent two years in the basement of Taub Hall and learned many interesting things.

The temperature of the head does not decrease in sleep. The temperature of the rest of the body does.

There I sat for weeks on end monitoring subjects who had half Ping-Pong balls taped over their eyes and a white-noise generator at 40db singing in their ears. I volunteered as a subject and, gratified at being assigned to the "more intelligent" group, spent many many hours in the black box with half Ping-Pong balls taped over my eyes and the white-noise generator emitting its obliterating whine/whisper. Although I had some intricate Type 4 hallucinations, nothing much else happened to me. Except . . . I began to wonder if behavior *should be* changed. That there was "behavior" at all seemed to me a small miracle.

I pondered going on to stress theory, wherein one investigates the ways in which the stressed individual reacts to stress, but decided suddenly to do something else instead. I decided to take a job with the Human Effort Administration and to try, insofar as possible, to let people do what they want to do.

I am aware that my work is, in many ways, meaningless.

A call from Honor, my ex-wife. I've promised her a bed for her new apartment.

"Did you get it?"

"Not yet."

"Why not?"

"I've been busy. Doing things."

"But what about the bed?"

"I told you I'd take care of it."

"Yes but when?"

"Some people can get their own beds for their new apartments."

"But that's not the point. You promised."

"That was in the first flush of good feeling and warmth. When you said you were coming back to town."

"Now you don't have any good feeling and warmth?"

"Full of it. Brimming. How's Sam?"

"He's getting tired of sleeping on the couch. It's not big enough for both of us."

"My heart cries out for him."

She's seeing Sam now, that's a little strange. She didn't seem to take to him, early on.

Sam. What's he like? Like a villain. Hair like an oil spill, mustache like a twist of carbon paper, high white lineless forehead, black tights and doublet, dagger clasped in treacherous right hand, sneaks when he's not slithering. . . .

No. That's incompletely true. Sam's just like the rest of us: jeans, turtleneck, beard, smile with one chipped tooth, good with children, backward in his taxes, a degree in education, a B.Ed. And he came with the very best references too, Charlotte doted, Francine couldn't get enough, Mary Jo chased him through Grand Central with the great whirling loop of her lariat, causing talk— But Honor couldn't see him, in the beginning. She's reconsidered. I wish she hadn't thrown the turntable on the floor, a $600 B & O, but all that's behind us now.

I saw this morning that the building at the end of the street's been sold. It stood empty for years, an architectural anomaly, three-storied, brick, but most of all, triangular. Two streets come together in a point there, and prospective buyers must have boggled at the angles. I judged that the owners decided to let morality go hang and sold to a *ménage à trois*. They'll need a triple bed, customized to fit those odd corners. I can see them with protractor and Skilsaw, getting the thing just right. Then sweeping up the bedcrumbs.

She telephones again.

"It doesn't have to be the best bed in the world. Any old bed will do. Sam's bitching all night long."

"For you, dear friend, I'll take every pain. We're checking now in Indonesia, a rare albino bed's been sighted there . . ."

"Tom, this isn't funny. I slept in the bathtub last night."

"You're too long for the bathtub."

"Do you want Sam to do it?"

Do I want Sam to do it?

"No. I'll do it."

"Then *do* it."

We were content for quite a while, she taught me what she'd majored in, a lovely Romance tongue, we visited the country and when I'd ask in a pharmacie for a razor they'd give me rosewater. I'm teasing her, and she me. She wants Sam. That's good.

Francesca was reading to me.

"This is the note Lee wrote," she said. "Listen. 'No one is more aware than myself of my inability for the duties of my position. I cannot even accomplish what I myself desire. How can I fulfill the expectations of others? In addition I sensibly feel the growing failure of my bodily strength. I have not yet recovered from the attack I experienced the past spring. I am becoming more and more incapable of exertion, and am thus prevented from making the personal examinations and giving the personal supervision to the operations in the field which I feel to be necessary. I am so dull making use of the eyes of others I am frequently misled. Everything, therefore, points to the advantages to be derived from a new commander. A younger and abler man than myself can readily be obtained. I know that he will have as gallant and brave an army as ever existed to second his efforts, and it would be the happiest day of my life to see at its head a worthy . . .'"

Francesca stopped reading.

"That was *Robert E. Lee*," she said.

"Yes," I said.

"The leader of all the armies of the Confederacy," she said.

"I know."

"I wanted him to win. So much."

"I understand."

"But he did not."

"I have read about it."

Francesca has Confederate-gray eyes which reflect, mostly, a lifelong contemplation of the nobility of Lee's great horse, Traveller. I left Francesca and walked in the park, where I am afraid to walk, after dark. One must let people do what they want to do, but what if they want to slap you upside the head with a Stillson wrench and take the credit cards out of your pockets? A problem.

The poor are getting poorer. I saw a poor man and asked him if he had any money.

"Money?" he said. "Money thinks I died a long time ago."

We have moved from the Age of Anxiety to the Age of Fear. This is of course progress, psychologically speaking. I intend no irony.

Another letter from Jinka.

Undear Thomas:
The notion that only man is vile must have been invented to describe you, vile friend. I cannot contain the revulsion that

whelms in me at the sight of your name, in the Prague telephone book, from your time in Prague. I have scratched it out of my copy, and scratched it out of all the copies I could get my hands on, in telephone booths everywhere. This symbolic removal of you from the telephone booths of our ancient city should not escape your notice, stinking meat. You have been erased and the anointment of the sick, formerly known as Extreme Unction, also as the Last Rites, is what I have in mind for you, soon. Whatever you are doing, stop it, drear pig. The insult to consciousness afforded by your project, whatever it is, cannot be suffered gladly, and I for one do not intend to so suffer. I have measures not yet in the books, and will take them. What I have in mind is not shallots and fresh rosemary, gutless wonder, and your continued association with that ridiculously thin Robert E. Lee girl has not raised you in my esteem, not a bit. One if by land and two if by sea, and it will be sudden, I promise you. Be afraid.

                Cordially,
                Jinka

I put this letter with the others, clipped together with a paper clip. How good writing such letters must make her feel!

Wittgenstein was I think wrong when he said that about that which we do not know, we should not speak. He closed by fiat a great amusement park, there. Nothing gives me more pleasure than speaking about that which I do not know. I am not sure whether my ideas about various matters are correct or incorrect, but speak about them I must.

I decided to call my brother in San Francisco. He is a copy editor on the *San Francisco Chronicle* (although he was trained as a biologist—he is doing what he wants to do, more or less). Because we are both from the South our conversations tend to be conducted in jiveass dialect.

"Hey," I said.

"Hey," he said.

"What's happening? You got any girl copy boys on that newspaper yet?"

"Man," Paul said, "we got not only girl copy boys we got *topless* girl copy boys. We gonna hire us a reporter next week. They promised us."

"That's wonderful," I said. "How are you feeling?"

"I'm depressed."

"Is it specific or nonspecific?"

"Well," Paul said, "I have to read the paper a lot. I'm ready to drop the bomb. On us."

One must let people do what they want to do. Fortunately my brother has little to say about when and where the bomb will be dropped.

My other friend is Catherine. Catherine, like Francesca, is hung up on the past. She is persuaded that in an earlier existence she was Balzac's mistress (one of Balzac's mistresses).

"I endured Honoré's grandness," she said, "because it was spurious. Spurious grandness I understand very well. What I could not understand was his hankering for greatness."

"But he *was* great," I said.

"I was impatient with all those artists, sitting around, hankering for greatness. Of course Honoré was great. But he didn't know it, at the time, for sure. Or he did and he didn't. There were moments of doubt, depression."

"As is natural."

"The seeking after greatness," said Catherine, "is a sickness, in my opinion. It is like greed, only greed has better results. Greed can at least bring you a fine house on a grand avenue, and strawberries for breakfast, in a rich cream, and servants to beat, when they do not behave. I *prefer* greed. Honoré was greedy, in a reasonable way, but what he was mostly interested in was greatness. I was stuck with greatness."

"Yes," I said.

"You," Catherine said, "are neither great nor greedy."

"One must let people be—" I began.

"Yes," Catherine said, "that sounds good, on the surface, but thinking it through—" She finished her espresso, placed the little cup precisely on the little saucer. "Take me out," she said. "Take me to a library."

We went to a library and spent a pleasant afternoon there.

Francesca was stroking the brown back of a large spayed cat—the one that doesn't like me.

"Lee was not without his faults," she said. "Not for a moment would I have you believe that he was faultless."

"What was his principal fault?"

"Losing," she said.

I went to the Art Cinema and saw a Swedish film about a man living alone on an island. Somebody was killing a great many sheep on the island and the hero, a hermit, was suspected. There were a great many shots of sheep with their throats cut, red blood on the white snow, glimpses. The hermit fixed a car for a woman whose car had broken down. They went to bed together. There were flashbacks having to do with the woman's former husband, a man in a wheelchair. It was determined that somebody else, not the hermit, had been killing the sheep. The film ended with a car crash in which the woman was killed. Whiteout.

Should great film artists be allowed to do what they want to do?

Catherine is working on her translation of the complete works of Balzac. Honoré, she insists, has never been properly translated. She will devote her life to the task, she says. Actually I have looked at some pages of her *Louis Lambert* and they seem to me significantly worse than the version I read in college. I think of Balzac in the great statue by Rodin, holding his erect (possibly overstated) cock in both hands under his cloak of bronze. An inspiration.

When I was in the black box, during my SD days, there was nothing I wanted to do. I didn't even want to get out. Or perhaps there was one thing I wanted to do: Sit in the box with the half Ping-Pong balls taped over my eyes and the white-noise generator standing in for the sirens of Ulysses (himself an early SD subject) and permit the Senior Investigator (Dr. Colcross, the one with the bad leg) to do what *he* wanted to do.

Is this will-lessness, finally? Abulia, as we call it in the trade? I don't think so.

I pursue Possibility. That's something.

There is no moment that exceeds in beauty that moment when one looks at a woman and finds that she is looking at you in the same way that you are looking at her. The moment in which she bestows that look that says, "Proceed with your evil plan, sumbitch." The initial smash of glance on glance. Then, the drawing near. This takes a long time, it seems like months, although only minutes pass, in fact. Languor is the word that describes this part of the process. Your persona floats toward her persona, over the Sea of Hesitation. Many weeks pass before they meet, but the weeks are days, or seconds. Still, everything is decided. You have slept together in the glance.

She takes your arm and you leave the newsstand, walking very close together, so that your side brushes her side lightly. Desire is here a very strong factor, because you are weak with it, and the woman is too, if she has any sense at all (but of course she is a sensible woman, and brilliant and witty and hungry as well). So, on the sidewalk outside the newsstand, you stand for a moment thinking about where to go, at eleven o'clock in the morning, and here it is, in the sunlight, that you take the first good look at her, and she at you, to see if either one has any hideous blemish that has been overlooked, in the first rush of good feeling. There are none. None. No blemishes (except those spiritual blemishes that will be discovered later, after extended acquaintance, and which none of us are without, but which are now latent? dormant? in any case, not visible on the surface, at this time). Everything is fine. And so, with renewed confidence, you begin to walk, and to seek a place where you might sit down, and have a drink, and talk a bit, and fall into each other's eyes, temporarily, and find some pretzels, and have what is called a conversation, and tell each other what you think is true about the world, and speak of the strange places where each of you has been (Surinam, in her case, where she bought the belt she is wearing, Lima in your case, where you contracted telegraph fever), and make arrangements for your next meeting (both of you drinking Scotch and water, at eleven in the morning, and you warm to her because of her willingness to leave her natural mid-morning track, for you), and make, as I say, arrangements for your next meeting, which must be this very night! or you both will die—

There is no particular point to any of this behavior. Or: This behavior is the only behavior which has point. Or: There is some point to this behavior but this behavior is not the only behavior which has point. Which is true? Truth is greatly overrated, volition where it exists must be protected, wanting itself can be obliterated, some people have forgotten how to want.

When he came to look at the building, with a real-estate man hissing and oozing beside him, we lowered the blinds, muted or extinguished lights, threw newspapers and dirty clothes on the floor in piles, burned rubber bands in ashtrays, and played Buxtehude on the hi-fi—shaking organ chords whose vibrations made the plaster falling from the ceiling fall faster. The new owner stood in profile, refusing to shake hands or even speak to us, a tall thin young man suited in hopsacking with a large manila envelope under one arm. We pointed to the plaster, to crevasses in the walls, sagging ceilings, leaks. Nevertheless, he closed.

Soon he was slipping little rent bills into the mailboxes, slip slip slip slip slip. In sixteen years we'd never had rent bills but now we have rent bills. He's raised the rent, and lowered the heat. The new owner creeps into the house by night and takes the heat away with him. He wants us out, out. If we were gone, the building would be decontrolled. The rents would climb into the air like steam.

Bicycles out of the halls, says the new owner. Shopping carts out of the halls. My halls.

The new owner stands in profile in the street in front of our building. He looks up the street, then down the street—this wondrous street where our friends and neighbors live in Christian, Jewish, and, in some instances, Islamic peace. The new owner is writing the Apartments Unfurn. ads of the future, in his head.

The new owner fires the old super, simply because the old super is a slaphappy, widowed, shot-up, black, Korean War-sixty-five-per-cent-disability-vet drunk. There is a shouting confrontation in the basement. The new owner threatens the old super with the police. The old super is locked out. A new super is hired who does not put out the garbage, does not mop the halls, does not, apparently, exist. Roaches prettyfoot into the building because the new owner has stopped the exerminating service. The new owner wants us out.

We whisper to the new owner, through the walls. Go away! Own something else! Don't own this building! Try the Sun Belt! Try Alaska, Hawaii! Sail away, new owner, sail away!

The new owner arrives, takes out his keys, opens the locked basement. The new owner is standing in the basement, owning the basement, with its single dangling bare bulb and the slightly busted souvenirs of all our children's significant progress. He is taking away the heat, carrying it out with him under his coat, a few pounds at a time, and bringing in with him, a few hundred at a time, his hired roaches.

The new owner stands in the hall, his manila envelope under his arm, owning the hall.

The new owner wants our apartment, and the one below, and the two above, and the one above them. He's a bachelor, tall thin young man in cheviot, no wife, no children, only buildings. He's covered the thermostat with a locked clear-plastic case. His manila envelope contains estimates and floor plans and draft Apartments Unfurn. ads and documents from the Office of Rent and Housing Preservation which speak of Maximum Base Rents and Maximum Collectible Rents and under what circumstances a Senior Citizen Rent Increase Exemption Order may be voided.

Black handprints all over the green of the halls where the new owner has been feeling the building.

The new owner has informed the young cohabiting couple on the floor above us (rear) that they are illegally living in sin and that for this reason he will give them only a month-to-month lease, so that at the end of each and every month they must tremble.

The new owner has informed the old people in the apartment above us (front) that he is prepared to prove that they do not actually live in their apartment in that they are old and so do not, in any real sense, live, and are thus subject to a Maximum Real Life Estimate Revision, which, if allowed by the City, will award him their space. Levon and Priscilla tremble.

The new owner stands on the roof, where the tomato plants are, owning the roof. May a good wind blow him to Hell.

Terminus

SHE AGREES to live with him for "a few months"; where? probably at the Hotel Terminus, which is close to the Central Station, the blue coaches leaving for Lyons, Munich, the outerlands . . . Of course she has a Gold Card, no, it was not left at the florist's, absolutely not . . .

The bellmen at the Hotel Terminus find the new arrival odd, even furtive; her hair is cut in a funny way, wouldn't you call it funny? and her habits are nothing but odd, the incessant pumping of the huge accordion, "Malagueña" over and over again, at the hour usually reserved for dinner . . .

The yellow roses are delivered, no, white baby orchids, the cream-colored walls of the room are severe and handsome, tall windows looking down the avenue toward the Angel-Garden. Kneeling, with a sterilized needle, she removes a splinter from his foot; he's thinking, *clothed, and in my right mind*, and she says, now I lay me down to sleep, I mean it, Red Head—

They've agreed to meet on a certain street corner; when he arrives, early, she rushes at him from a doorway; it's cold, she's wearing her long black coat, it's too thin for this weather; he gives her his scarf, which she wraps around her head like a babushka; tell me, she says, how did this happen?

When she walks, she slouches, or skitters, or skids, catches herself and stands with one hip tilted and a hand on the hip, like a cowboy; she's twenty-six, served three years in the Army, didn't like it and got out, took a degree in statistics and worked for an insurance company, didn't like it and quit and fell in love with him and purchased the accordion . . .

Difficult, he says, difficult, difficult, but she is trying to learn "When Irish Eyes Are Smiling," the sheet music propped on the cream marble mantelpiece, in two hours' time the delightful psychiatrist will be back from his Mexican vacation, which he spent in perfect dread, speaking to spiders—

Naked, she twists in his arms to listen to a sound outside the door, a scratching, she freezes, listening; he's startled by the beauty of her tense back, the raised shoulders, tilted head, there's nothing, she turns to look at him, what does she see? The telephone rings, it's the delightful psychiatrist (hers), singing the praises of Cozumel, Cancun . . .

He punches a hole in a corner of her Gold Card and hangs it about her neck on a gold chain.

What are they doing in this foreign city? She's practicing "Cherokee," and he's plotting his next move, up, out, across, down . . . He's hired in Flagstaff, at a succulent figure, more consulting, but he doesn't want to do that any more, they notice a sullen priest reading his breviary in the Angel-Garden, she sits on a bench and opens the *Financial Times* (in which his letter to the editor has been published, she consumes it with intense comprehension), only later, after a game of billiards, does he begin telling her how beautiful she is, no, she says, no, no—

I'll practice for eighteen hours a day, she says, stopping only for a little bread soaked in wine; he gathers up the newspapers, including the *Financial Times*, and stacks them neatly on the cream-colored radiator; and in the spring, he says, I'll be going away.

She's setting the table and humming "Vienna"; yes, she says, it will be good to have you gone.

They're so clearly in love that cops wave at them from passing cruisers; what has happened to his irony, which was supposed to protect him, keep him clothed, and in his right mind? I love you so much, so much, she says, and he believes her, sole in a champagne sauce, his wife is skiing in Chile—

And while you sit by the fire, tatting, he says . . .

She says, no tatting for me, Big Boy . . .

In the night, he says, alone, to see of me no more, your good fortune.

Police cars zip past the Hotel Terminus in threes, sirens hee-hawing . . .

No one has told him that he is *a husband*; he has learned nothing from the gray in his hair; the additional lenses in the lenses of his spectacles have not educated him; the merriment of dental assistants has not brought him the news; he behaves as if *something* were possible, still; there's whispering at the Hotel Terminus.

He decides to go to a bar and she screams at him, music from the small radio, military marches, military waltzes; she's confused, she says, she really didn't mean that, but meant, rather, that the bell captain at the Hotel Terminus had said something she thought offensive, something about "Malagueña," it was not the words but the tone—

Better make the bed, he says, the bed in which you'll sleep, chaste and curly, when I'm gone . . .

Yes, she says, yes that's what they say . . .

True, he's lean; true, he's not entirely stupid; yes, he's given up cigarettes; yes, he's given up saying "forgive me," no longer uses the phrase "as I was saying"; he's mastered backgammon and sleeping with the radio on; he's apologized for his unkind remark about the yellow-haired young man at whom she was not staring— And when a lover drifts off while being made love to, it's a lesson in humility, right?

He looks at the sleeping woman; how beautiful she is! He touches her back, lightly.

The psychiatrist, learned elf, calls and invites them to his party, to be held in the Palm Room of the Hotel Terminus, patients will dance with doctors, doctors will dance with receptionists, receptionists will dance with detail men, a man who once knew Ferenczi will be there in a sharkskin suit, a motorized wheelchair— Yes, says the psychiatrist, *of course* you can play "Cherokee," and for an encore, anything of Victor Herbert's—

She, grimly: I don't like to try to make nobody bored, Hot Stuff.

Warlike music in all hearts, she says, why are we together?

But on the other hand, she says, *that which exists is more perfect than that which does not* . . .

This is absolutely true. He is astonished by the quotation. In the Hotel Terminus coffee shop, he holds her hand tightly.

Thinking of getting a new nightie, she says, maybe a dozen.

Oh? he says.

He's a whistling dog this morning, brushes his teeth with tequila thinking about *Geneva*, she, dying of love, shoves him up against a cream-colored wall, biting at his shoulders . . . Little teed off this morning, aren't you, babe? he says, and she says, fixin' to prepare to get mad, way I'm bein' treated, and he says, oh darlin', and she says, way I'm bein' jerked around—

Walking briskly in a warm overcoat toward the Hotel Terminus, he stops to buy flowers, yellow freesias, and wonders what "a few months" can mean: three, eight? He has fallen out of love this morning, feels a refreshing distance, an absolution— But then she calls him *amigo*, as she accepts the flowers, and says, *not bad*, *Red Head*, and he falls back into love again, forever. She comes toward him fresh from the bath, opens her robe. Goodbye, she says, goodbye.

The first thing the baby did wrong was to tear pages out of her books. So we made a rule that each time she tore a page out of a book she had to stay alone in her room for four hours, behind the closed door. She was tearing out about a page a day, in the beginning, and the rule worked fairly well, although the crying and screaming from behind the closed door were unnerving. We reasoned that that was the price you had to pay, or part of the price you had to pay. But then as her grip improved she got to tearing out two pages at a time, which meant eight hours alone in her room, behind the closed door, which just doubled the annoyance for everybody. But she wouldn't quit doing it. And then as time went on we began getting days when she tore out three or four pages, which put her alone in her room for as much as sixteen hours at a stretch, interfering with normal feeding and worrying my wife. But I felt that if you made a rule you had to stick to it, had to be consistent, otherwise they get the wrong idea. She was about fourteen months old or fifteen months old at that point. Often, of course, she'd go to sleep, after an hour or so of yelling, that was a mercy. Her room was very nice, with a nice wooden rocking horse and practically a hundred dolls and stuffed animals. Lots of things to do in that room if you used your time wisely, puzzles and things. Unfortunately sometimes when we opened the door we'd find that she'd torn more pages out of more books while she was inside, and these pages had to be added to the total, in fairness.

The baby's name was Born Dancin'. We gave the baby some of our wine, red, white, and blue, and spoke seriously to her. But it didn't do any good.

I must say she got real clever. You'd come up to her where she was playing on the floor, in those rare times when she was out of her room, and there'd be a book there, open beside her, and you'd inspect it and it would look perfectly all right. And then you'd look closely and you'd find a page that had one little corner torn, could easily pass for ordinary wear-and-tear but I knew what she'd done, she'd torn off this little corner and swallowed it. So that had to count and it did. They will go to any lengths to thwart you. My wife said that maybe we were being too rigid and that the baby was losing weight. But I pointed out to her that the baby had a long life to live and had to live in the world with others, had to live in a world where there were many, many rules, and if you couldn't learn to play by the rules you were going to be left out in the cold with no character, shunned and ostracized by everyone. The longest we ever kept her in her room consecutively was eighty-eight hours, and that ended when my wife took the door off its hinges with a crowbar even though the baby still owed us twelve hours because she was working off twenty-five pages. I put the door back on its hinges and added a big lock, one that opened only if you put a magnetic card in a slot, and I kept the card.

But things didn't improve. The baby would come out of her room like a bat out of hell and rush to the nearest book, Goodnight Moon *or whatever, and begin tearing pages out of it hand over fist. I mean there'd be thirty-four pages of* Goodnight Moon *on the floor in ten seconds. Plus the covers. I began to get a little worried. When I added up her indebtedness, in terms of hours, I could see that she wasn't going to get out of her room until 1992, if then. Also, she was looking pretty wan. She hadn't been to the park in weeks. We had more or less of an ethical crisis on our hands.*

I solved it by declaring that it was all right *to tear pages out of books, and moreover, that it was all right to* have torn *pages out of books in the past. That is one of the satisfying things about being a parent—you've got a lot of moves, each one good as gold. The baby and I sit happily on the floor, side by side, tearing pages out of books, and sometimes, just for fun, we go out on the street and smash a windshield together.*

The Mothball Fleet

It was early morning, just after dawn, in fact. The mothball fleet was sailing down the Hudson. Grayish-brown shrouds making odd shapes at various points on the superstructures. I counted forty destroyers, four light cruisers, two heavy cruisers, and a carrier. A fog lay upon the river.

I went aboard as the fleet reached the Narrows. I noticed a pair of jeans floating on the surface of the water, stiff with paint. I abandoned my small outboard and jumped for the ladder of the lead destroyer.

There was no one on deck. All of the gun mounts and some pieces of special equipment were coated with a sort of plastic webbing, which had a slightly repellent feeling when touched. I watched my empty Pacemaker bobbing in the heavy wake of the fleet. I called out. "Hello! Hello!"

Behind us, the vessels were disposed in fleet formation—the carrier in the center, the two heavy cruisers before and behind her, the destroyer screen correctly placed in relation to the cruisers, or as much so as the width of the channel would allow. We were making, I judged, ten to twelve knots.

There was no other traffic on the water; this I thought strange.

It was now about six-thirty; the fog was breaking up, a little. I decided to climb to the bridge. I entered the wheelhouse; there was no one at the wheel. I took the wheel in my hands, tried to turn it a point or two, experimentally; it was locked in place.

A man entered from the chartroom behind me. He immediately walked over to me and removed my hands from the wheel.

He wore a uniform, but it seemed more a steward's or barman's dress than a naval officer's. His face was not unimpressive: dark hair carefully brushed, a strong nose, good mouth and chin. I judged him to be in his late fifties. He re-entered the chartroom. I followed him.

"May I ask where this . . ."

"Mothball fleet," he supplied.

"—is bound?"

He did not answer my question. He was looking at a chart.

"If it's a matter of sealed orders or something . . ."

"No no," he said, without looking up. "Nothing like that." Then he said, "A bit careless with your little boat, aren't you?"

This made me angry. "Not normally. On the contrary. But something—"

"Of course," he said. "You were anticipated. Why d'you think that ladder wasn't secured?"

I thought about this for a moment. I decided to shift the ground of the conversation slightly.

"Are there crews aboard the other ships?"

"No," he said. I felt however that he had appreciated my shrewdness in guessing that there were no crews aboard the other ships.

"Radio?" I asked. "Remote control or something?"

"Something like that," he said.

The forty destroyers, four light cruisers, two heavy cruisers, and the carrier were moving in perfect formation toward the open sea. The sight was a magnificent one. I had been in the Navy—two years as a supply officer in New London, principally.

"Is this a test of some kind?" I asked. "New equipment or—"

"You're afraid that we'll be used for target practice? Hardly." He seemed momentarily amused.

"No. But ship movements on this scale—"

"It was difficult," he said. He then walked out of the chartroom and seated himself in one of the swivel chairs on posts in front of the bridge windows. I followed him.

"May I ask your rank?"

"Why not ask my name?"

"All right."

"I am the Admiral."

I looked again at his uniform which suggested no such thing.

"Objectively," he said, smiling slightly.

"My name is—" I began.

"I am not interested in your name," he said. "I am only interested in your behavior. As you can see, I have at my disposal forty-seven brigs, of which the carrier's is the most comfortable. Not that I believe you will behave other than correctly. At the moment, I want you to do this: Go down to the galley and make a pot of coffee. Make sandwiches. You may make one for yourself. Then bring them here." He settled back in his seat and regarded the calm, even sea.

"All right," I said. "Yes."

"You will say: 'Yes, sir,'" he corrected me.

"Yes, sir."

I wandered about the destroyer until I found the galley. I made the coffee and sandwiches and returned with them to the bridge.

The "Admiral" drank his coffee silently. Seabirds made passes at the mast where the radar equipment, I saw, was covered with the same plastic material that enclosed the gun installations.

"What is that stuff used for the mothballing?" I asked.

"It's a polyvinylchloride solution which also contains vinyl acetate," he said. "It's sprayed on and then hardens. If you were to cut it open you'd find inside, around the equipment, four or five small cloth bags containing silicate of soda in crystals, to absorb moisture. A very neat system. It does just what it's supposed to do, keeps the equipment good as new."

He had finished his sandwich. A bit of mustard had soiled the sleeve of his white coat, which had gold epaulets. I thought again that he most resembled not an admiral but a man from whom one would order drinks.

"What is your mission?" I asked, determined not to be outfaced by a man with mustard on his coat.

"To be at sea," he said.

"Only that?"

"Think a bit," he said. "Think first of shipyards. Think of hundreds of thousands of men in shipyards, on both coasts, building these ships. Think of the welders, the pipefitters, the electricians, naval architects, people in the Bureau of the Budget. Think of the launchings, each with its bottle of champagne on a cord of plaited ribbons hurled at the bow by the wife of some high official. Think of the first sailors coming aboard, the sea trials, the captains for whom a particular ship was a first command. Each ship has a history, no ship is without its history. Think of the six-inch guns shaking a particular ship as they were fired, the jets leaving the deck of the carrier at tightly spaced intervals, the maneuvering of the cruisers during this or that engagement, the damage taken. Think of each ship's log faithfully kept over the years, think of the Official Naval History which now runs, I am told, to three hundred some–odd very large volumes.

"And then," he said, "think of each ship moving up the Hudson, or worse, being towed, to a depot in New Jersey where it is covered with this disgusting plastic substance. Think of the years each ship has spent moored next to other ships of its class, painted, yes, at scheduled times, by a crew of painters whose task it is to paint these ships eternally, finished with one and on to the next and back to the first again five years later. Watchmen watching the ships, year in and year out, no doubt knocking off a little copper pipe here and there—"

"The ships were being stockpiled against a possible new national emergency," I said. "What on earth is wrong with that?"

"I was a messman on the *Saratoga*," he said, "when I was sixteen. I lied about my age."

"But what are your intentions?"

"I am taking these ships away from them," he said.

"You are stealing forty-seven ships from the government of the United States?"

"There are also the submarines," he said. "Six submarines of the Marlin class."

"But why?"

"Remember that I was, once, in accord with them. Passionately, if I may say so, in accord with them. I did whatever they wished, without thinking, hated their enemies, participated in their crusades, risked my life. Even though I only carried trays and wiped up tables. I heard the singing of the wounded and witnessed the burial of the dead. I believed. Then, over time, I discovered that they were lying. Consistently. With exemplary skill, in a hundred languages. I decided to take the ships. Perhaps they'll notice." He paused. "Now. Do you wish to accompany me, assist me?"

"More than anything."

"Good." He moved the lever of the bridge telegraph to Full Ahead.

Now that I am older I am pleased to remember. Those violent nights. When having laid theorbo aside I came to your bed. You, having laid phonograph aside, lay there. Awaiting. I, having laid aside all cares and other business, approached. Softly so as not to afright the sour censorious authorities. You, undulating restlessly under the dun coverlet. Under the framed, signed and numbered silverprint. I, having laid aside all frets and perturbations, approached.

Prior to this, the meal. Sometimes the meal was taken in, sometimes out. If in, I sliced the onions and tossed them into the pot, or you sliced the chanterelles and tossed them into the pot. The gray glazed pot with the black leopard-spot meander. What an infinity of leeks, lentils, turnips, green beans we tossed into the pot, over the years. Celery.

Sometimes the meal was taken out. There we sat properly with others in crowded rooms, green-flocked paper on the walls, the tables too close together. Decent quiet servitors in black-and-white approached and with many marks of respect and good will, fed us. Tingle of choice, sometimes we elected the same dish, lamb in pewter sauce on one occasion. Three yellow daffs and a single red tulip in the tall slender vase to your right. My thumb in my martini nudging the olives from the white plastic sword.

Prior to the meal, the Happy Hour. You removed your shoes and sat, daintily, on your feet. I loosened my tie, if the day's business had required one, and held out my hand. You smashed a glass into it, just in time. Fatigued from your labors at the scriptorium where you illuminated manuscripts having to do with the waxing/waning fortunes of International Snow. We snuggled, there on the couch, there is no other word for it, as God is my witness. The bed awaiting.

I remember the photograph over your bed. How many mornings has it greeted me banded with the first timorous light through the blind-slats. A genuine Weegee, car crash with prostrate forms, long female hair in a pool of blood shot through booted cop legs. In a rope-molding frame. Beside me, your form, not yet awake but bare of dull unnecessary clothing and excellently positioned to be prowled over. After full light, tickling permitted.

Fleet through the woods came I upon that time toward your bed. A little pouch of mealie-mealie by my side, for our repast. You, going into the closet, plucked forth a cobwebbed bottle. On the table in front of the couch, an artichoke with its salty dip. Hurling myself through the shabby tattering door toward the couch, like an (arrow from the bow) (spear from the hand of Achilles), I thanked my stars for the wisdom of my teachers, Smoky and Billy, which had enabled me to find a place in the labor market, to depart in the morning and return at night, bearing in the one hand a pannier of periwinkles and in the other, a disc new-minted by the Hot Club of France.

Your head in my arms.

Wrack

—Cold here in the garden.
—You were complaining about the sun.
—But when it goes behind a cloud—
—Well, you can't have everything.
—The flowers are beautiful.
—Indeed.
—Consoling to have the flowers.
—Half-way consoled already.
—And these Japanese rocks—
—Artfully placed, most artfully.
—You must admit, a great consolation.
—And Social Security.
—A great consolation.
—And philosophy. Furthermore.
—I read a book. Just the other day.
—Sexuality, too.
—They have books about it. I read one.
—We'll to the woods no more. I assume.
—Where there's a will there's a way. That's what my mother always said.
—I wonder if it's true.
—I think not.
—Well, you're driving me crazy.
—Well you're driving me crazy too. Know what I mean?
—Going to snap one of these days.
—If you were a Japanese master you wouldn't snap. Those guys never snapped. Some of them were ninety.
—Well, you can't have everything.
—Cold, here in the garden.
—Caw caw caw caw.
—You want to sing that song.
—Can't remember how it goes.
—Getting farther and farther away from life.
—How do you feel about that?
—Guilty but less guilty than I should.

—Can you fine-tune that for me?
—Not yet I want to think about it.
—Well, I have to muck out the stable and buff up the silver.
—They trust you with the silver?
—Of course. I have their trust.
—You enjoy their trust.
—Absolutely.
—Well we still haven't decided what color to paint the trucks.
—I said blue.
—Surely not your last word on the subject.
—I have some swatches. If you'd care to take a gander.
—Not now. This sun is blistering.
—New skin. You're going to complain?
—Thank the Lord for all small favors.
—The kid ever come to see you?
—Did for a while. Then stopped.
—How does that make you feel?
—Oh, I don't blame him.
—Well, you can't have everything.
—That's true. What's the time?
—Looks to be about one.
—Where's your watch?
—Hocked it.
—What'd you get?
—Twelve-fifty.
—God, aren't these flowers beautiful!
—Only three of them. But each remarkable, of its kind.
—What are they?
—Some kind of Japanese dealies I don't know.
—Lazing in the garden. This is really most luxurious.
—Listening to the radio. "Elmer's Tune."
—I don't like it when they let girls talk on the radio.
—Never used to have them. Now they're everywhere.
—You can't really say too much. These days.
—Doesn't that make you nervous? Girls talking on the radio?
—I liked H. V. Kaltenborn. He's long gone.
—What'd you do yesterday?
—Took a walk. In the wild trees.
—They spend a lot of time worrying about where to park their cars. Glad I don't have one.

—Haven't eaten anything except some rice, this morning. Cooked it with chicken broth.

—This place is cold, no getting around it.

—Forgot to buy soap, forgot to buy coffee—

—All right. The hollowed-out book containing the single Swedish municipal bond in the amount of fifty thousand Swedish crowns is not yours. We've established that. Let's go on.

—It was never mine. Or it might have been mine, once. Perhaps it belonged to my former wife. I said I wasn't sure. She was fond of hiding things in hollowed-out books.

—We want not the shadow of a doubt. We want to be absolutely certain.

—I appreciate it. She had gray eyes. Gray with a touch of violet.

—Yes. Now, are these your doors?

—Yes. I think so. Are they on spring hinges? Do they swing?

—They swing in either direction. Spring hinges. Wood slats.

—She did things with her eyebrows. Painted them gold. You had the gray eyes with a touch of violet, and the gold eyebrows. Yes, the doors must be mine. I seem to remember her bursting through them. In one of the several rages of a summer's day.

—When?

—It must have been some time ago. Some years. I don't know what they're doing here. It strikes me they were in another house. Not this house. I mean it's kind of cloudy.

—But they're here.

—She sometimes threw something through the doorway before bursting through the doorway herself. Acid, on one occasion.

—But the doors are here. They're yours.

—Yes. They seem to be. I mean, I'm not arguing with you. On the other hand, they're not something I want to remember, particularly. They have sort of an unpleasant aura around them, for some reason. I would have avoided them, left to myself.

—I don't want to distress you. Unnecessarily.

—I know, I know, I know. I'm not blaming you, but it just seems to me that you could have let it go. The doors. I'm sure you didn't mean anything by it, but still—

—I didn't mean anything by it. Well, let's leave the doors, then, and go on to the dish.

—Plate.

—Let's go on to the plate, then.

—Plate, dish, I don't care, it's something of an imposition, you must admit, to have to think about it. Normally I wouldn't think about it.

—It has your name on the back. Engraved on the back.

—Where? Show me.

—Your name. Right there. And the date, 1962.

—I don't want to look. I'll take your word for it. That was twenty years ago. My God. She read R. D. Laing. Aloud, at dinner. Every night. Interrupted only by the telephone. When she answered the telephone, her voice became animated. Charming and animated. Gaiety. Vivacity. Laughter. In contrast to her reading of R. D. Laing. Which could only be described as punitive. O.K., so it's mine. My plate.

—It's a dish. A bonbon dish.

—You mean to say that you think that *I* would own a bonbon dish? A sterling-silver or whatever it is bonbon dish? You're mad.

—The doors were yours. Why not the dish?

—A *bonbon* dish?

—Perhaps she craved bonbons?

—No no no no no. Not so. Sourballs, perhaps.

—Let's move on to the shoe, now. I don't have that much time.

—The shoe is definitely not mine.

—Not yours.

—It's a woman's shoe. It's too small for me. My foot, this foot here, would never in the world fit into that shoe.

—I am not suggesting that the shoe is yours in the sense that you wear or would wear such a shoe. It's obviously a woman's shoe.

—The shoe is in no sense a thing of mine. Although found I admit among my things.

—It's here. An old-fashioned shoe. Eleven buttons.

—There was a vogue for that kind of shoe, some time back, among the young people. It might have belonged to a young person. I sometimes saw young persons.

—With what in mind?

—I fondled them, if they were fondleable.

—Within the limits of the law, of course.
—Certainly. "Young person" is an elastic term. You think I'm going to mess with jailbait?
—Of course not. Never occurred to me. The shoe has something of the pathetic about it. A wronged quality. Do you think it possible that the shoe may be in some way a *cri de coeur*?
—Not a chance.
—You were wrong about the dish.
—I've never heard a *cri de coeur*.
—You've never heard a *cri de coeur*?
—Perhaps once. When Shirley was with us?
—Who was Shirley?
—The maid. She was studying eschatology. Maiding part-time. She left us for a better post. Perfectly ordinary departure.
—Did she perhaps wear shoes of this type?
—No. Nor was she given to the *cri de coeur*. Except, perhaps, once. Death of her flying fish. A cry wrenched from her bosom. Rather like a winged phallus it was, she kept it in a washtub in the basement. One day it was discovered belly-up. She screamed. Then, insisted it be given the Last Rites, buried in a fish cemetery, holy water sprinkled this way and that—
—You fatigue me. Now, about the hundred-pound sack of saccharin.
—Mine. Indubitably mine. I'm forbidden to use sugar. I have a condition.
—I'm delighted to hear it. Not that you have a condition but that the sack is, without doubt, yours.
—Mine. Yes.
—I can't tell you how pleased I am. The inquiry moves. Progress is made. Results are obtained.
—What are you writing there, in your notes?
—That the sack is, beyond a doubt, yours.
—I think it's mine.
—What do you mean, *think*? You stated . . . Is it yours or isn't it?
—I think it's mine. It seems to be.
—Seems!
—I just remembered, I put sugar in my coffee. At breakfast.
—Are you sure it wasn't saccharin?

—White powder of some kind . . .

—There is a difference in texture . . .

—No, I remember, it was definitely sugar. Granulated. So the sack of saccharin is definitely not mine.

—Nothing is yours.

—Some things are mine, but the sack is not mine, the shoe is not mine, the bonbon dish is not mine, and the doors are not mine.

—You admitted the doors.

—Not wholeheartedly.

—You said, I have it right here, written down, "Yes, they must be mine."

—Sometimes we hugged. Lengthily. Heart to heart, the one trying to pull the other into the upright other . . .

—I have it right here. Written down. "Yes, they must be mine."

—I withdraw that.

—You can't withdraw it. I've written it down.

—Nevertheless I withdraw it. It's inadmissible. It was coerced.

—You feel coerced?

—All that business about "dish" rather than "plate"—

—That was a point of fact, it was, in fact, a dish.

—You have a hectoring tone. I don't like to be hectored. You came here with something in mind. You had made an a priori decision.

—That's a little ridiculous when you consider that I have, personally, nothing to gain. Either way. Whichever way it goes.

—Promotion, advancement . . .

—We don't operate that way. That has nothing to do with it. I don't want to discuss this any further. Let's go on to the dressing gown. Is the dressing gown yours?

—Maybe.

—Yes or no?

—My business. Leave it at "maybe."

—I am entitled to a good, solid, answer. Is the dressing gown yours?

—Maybe.

—Please.

—Maybe maybe maybe maybe.
—You exhaust me. In this context, the word "maybe" is unacceptable.
—A perfectly possible answer. People use it every day.
—Unacceptable. What happened to her?
—She made a lot of money. Opened a Palais de Glace, or skating rink. Read R. D. Laing to the skaters over the PA system meanwhile supplementing her income by lecturing over the country as a spokesperson for the unborn.
—The gold eyebrows, still?
—The gold eyebrows and the gray-with-violet eyes. On television, very often.
—In the beginning, you don't know.
—That's true.
—Just one more thing: The two mattresses surrounding the single slice of salami. Are they yours?
—I get hungry. In the night.
—The struggle is admirable. Useless, but admirable. Your struggle.
—Cold, here in the garden.
—You're too old, that's all it is, think nothing of it. Don't give it a thought.
—I haven't agreed to that. Did I agree to that?
—No, I must say you resisted. Admirably, resisted.
—I did resist. Would you allow "valiantly"?
—No no no no. Come come come.
—"Wholeheartedly"?
—Yes, okay, what do I care?
—*Wholeheartedly*, then.
—Yes.
—*Wholeheartedly.*
—We still haven't decided what color to paint the trucks.
—Yes. How about blue?

On our street, fourteen garbage cans are now missing. The garbage cans from One Seventeen and One Nineteen disappeared last night. This is not a serious matter, but on the other hand we can't sit up all night watching over our garbage cans. It is probably best described as an annoyance. One Twelve, One Twenty-two and One Thirty-one have bought new plastic garbage cans at Barney's Hardware to replace those missing. We are thus down eleven garbage cans, net. Many people are using large dark plastic garbage bags. The new construction at the hospital at the end of the block has displaced a number of rats. Rats are not much bothered by plastic garbage bags. In fact, if I were ordered to imagine what might most profitably be invented by a committee of rats, it would be the plastic garbage bag. The rats run up and down our street all night long.

If I were ordered to imagine who is stealing our garbage cans, I could not. I very much doubt that my wife is doing it. Some of the garbage cans on our street are battered metal, others are heavy green plastic. Heavy green plastic or heavy black plastic predominates. Some of the garbage cans have the numbers of the houses they belong to painted on their sides or lids, with white paint. Usually by someone with only the crudest sense of the art of lettering. One Nineteen, which has among its tenants a gifted commercial artist, is an exception. No one excessively famous lives on our street, to my knowledge, therefore the morbid attention that the garbage of the famous sometimes attracts would not be a factor. The Precinct says that no other street within the precinct has reported similar problems.

If my wife is stealing the garbage cans, in the night, while I am drunk and asleep, what is she doing with them? They are not in the cellar, I've looked (although I don't like going down to the cellar, even to replace a blown fuse, because of the rats). My wife has a yellow Pontiac convertible. No one has these anymore but I can imagine her lifting garbage cans into the back seat of the yellow Pontiac convertible, at two o'clock in the

831

morning, when I am dreaming of being on stage, dreaming of having to perform a drum concerto with only one drumstick . . .

On our street, twenty-one garbage cans are now missing. New infamies have been announced by One Thirty-one through One Forty-three—seven in a row, and on the same side of the street. Also, depredations at One Sixteen and One Sixty-four. We have put out dozens of cans of D-Con but the rats ignore them. Why should they go for the D-Con when they can have the remnants of Ellen Busse's Boeuf Rossini, for which she is known for six blocks in every direction? We eat well, on this street, there's no denying it. Except for the nursing students at One Fifty-eight, and why should they eat well, they're students, are they not? My wife cooks soft-shell crabs, in season, breaded, dusted with tasty cayenne, deep-fried. Barney's Hardware has run out of garbage cans and will not get another shipment until July. Any new garbage cans will have to be purchased at Budget Hardware, far, far away on Second Street.

Petulia, at Custom Care Cleaners, asks why my wife has been acting so peculiar lately. "Peculiar?" I say. "In what way do you mean?" Dr. Maugham, who lives at One Forty-four where he also has his office, has formed a committee. Mr. Wilkens, from One Nineteen, Pally Wimber, from One Twenty-nine, and my wife are on the committee. The committee meets at night, while I sleep, dreaming, my turn in the batting order has come up and I stand at the plate, batless . . .

There are sixty-two houses on our street, four-story brownstones for the most part. Fifty-two garbage cans are now missing. Rats riding upon the backs of other rats gallop up and down our street, at night. The committee is unable to decide whether to call itself the Can Committee or the Rat Committee. The City has sent an inspector who stood marveling, at midnight, at the activity on our street. He is filing a report. He urges that the remaining garbage cans be filled with large stones. My wife has appointed me a subcommittee of the larger committee with the task of finding large stones. Is there a peculiar look on her face as she makes the appointment? Dr. Maugham has bought a shotgun, a twelve-gauge over-and-under. Mr. Wilkens has bought a Chase bow and two dozen hunting arrows. I have bought a flute and an instruction book.

If I were ordered to imagine who is stealing our garbage cans, the Louis Escher family might spring to mind, not as culprits but as proximate cause. The Louis Escher family has a large income and a small apartment, in One Twenty-one. The Louis Escher family is given to acquiring things, and given the size of the Louis Escher apartment, must dispose of old things in order to accommodate new things. Sometimes the old things disposed of by the Louis Escher family are scarcely two weeks old. Therefore, the garbage at One Twenty-one is closely followed in the neighborhood, in the sense that the sales and bargains listed in the newspapers are closely followed. The committee, which feels that the garbage of the Louis Escher family may be misrepresenting the neighborhood to the criminal community, made a partial list of the items disposed of by the Louis Escher family during the week of August eighth: one mortar & pestle, majolica ware; one English cream maker (cream is made by mixing unsalted sweet butter and milk); one set green earthenware geranium leaf plates; one fruit ripener designed by scientists at the University of California, plexiglass; one nylon umbrella tent with aluminum poles; one combination fountain pen and clock with LED readout; one mini hole-puncher-and-confetti-maker; one pistol-grip spring-loaded flyswatter; one cast-iron tortilla press; one ivory bangle with elephant-hair accent; and much, much more. But while I do not doubt that the excesses of the Louis Escher family are misrepresenting the neighborhood to the criminal community, I cannot bring myself to support even a resolution of censure, since the excesses of the Louis Escher family have given us much to talk about and not a few sets of green earthenware geranium leaf plates over the years.

I reported to my wife that large stones were hard to come by in the city. "Stones," she said. "Large stones." I purchased two hundred pounds of Sakrete at Barney's Hardware, to make stones with. One need only add water and stir, and you have made a stone as heavy and brutish as a stone made by God himself. I am temporarily busy, in the basement, shaping Sakrete to resemble this, that and the other, but mostly stones—a good-looking stone is not the easiest of achievements. Ritchie Beck, the little boy from One Ten who is always alone on the sidewalk during the day, smiling at strangers, helps me. I once bought him a copy of Mechanix Illustrated, *which I myself read avidly as a boy. Harold, who owns Custom Care Cleaners and also owns a Cessna, has offered to fly over our street at night and drop bombs made of lethal dry-cleaning fluid on the rats. There is a channel down the Hudson he can take (so long as he stays under eleven hundred feet), a quick left turn, the bombing run, then a dash back up the Hudson. They will pull his ticket if he's caught, he says, but at that hour of the night . . . I show my wife the new stones. "I don't like them," she says. "They don't look like real stones." She is not wrong, they look, in fact, like badly-thrown pots, as if they had been done by a potter with no thumbs. The committee, which has named itself the Special Provisional Unnecessary Rat Team (SPURT), has acquired armbands and white steel helmets and is discussing a secret grip by which its members will identify themselves to each other.*

There are now no garbage cans on our street—no garbage cans left to steal. A committee of rats has joined with the Special Provisional committee in order to deal with the situation, which, the rats have made known, is attracting unwelcome rat elements from other areas of the city. Members of the two committees exchange secret grips. My wife drives groups of rats here and there in her yellow Pontiac convertible, attending important meetings. The crisis, she says, will be a long one. She has never been happier.

The Palace at Four A.M.

My father's kingdom was and is, all authorities agree, large. To walk border to border east-west, the traveler must budget no less than seventeen days. Its name is Ho, the Confucian term for harmony. Confucianism was an interest of the first ruler (a strange taste in our part of the world), and when he'd cleared his expanse of field and forest of his enemies, two centuries ago, he indulged himself in an *hommage* to the great Chinese thinker, much to the merriment of some of our staider neighbors, whose domains were proper Luftlunds and Dolphinlunds. We have an economy based upon truffles, in which our forests are spectacularly rich, and electricity, which we were exporting when other countries still read by kerosene lamp. Our army is the best in the region, every man a colonel—the subtle secret of my father's rule, if the truth be known. In this land every priest is a bishop, every ambulance-chaser a robed justice, every peasant a corporation and every street-corner shouter Kant himself. My father's genius was to promote his subjects, male and female, across the board, ceaselessly; the people of Ho warm themselves forever in the sun of Achievement. I was the only man in the kingdom who thought himself a donkey.

—FROM THE *Autobiography*

I AM writing to you, Hannahbella, from a distant country. I daresay you remember it well. The King encloses the opening pages of his autobiography. He is most curious as to what your response to them will be. He has labored mightily over their composition, working without food, without sleep, for many days and nights.

The King has not been, in these months, in the best of spirits. He has read your article and declares himself to be very much impressed by it. He begs you, prior to publication in this country, to do him the great favor of changing the phrase "two disinterested and impartial arbiters" on page thirty-one to "malign elements under the ideological sway of still more malign elements." Otherwise, he is delighted. He asks me to tell you that your touch is as adroit as ever.

Early in the autobiography (as you see) we encounter the words: "My mother the Queen made a mirror pie, a splendid thing the size of a poker table . . ." The King wishes to know if poker tables are in use in faraway lands, and whether the reader in such places would comprehend the dimensions of the pie. He continues: ". . . in which reflections from the kitchen chandelier exploded when the crew rolled it from the oven. We were kneeling side-by-side, peering into the depths of a new-made mirror pie, when my mother said to me, or rather her celestial image said to my dark, heavy-haired one, 'Get out. I cannot bear to look upon your donkey face again.'"

The King wishes to know, Hannahbella, whether this passage seems to you tainted by self-pity, or is, rather, suitably dispassionate.

He walks up and down the small room next to his bedchamber, singing your praises. The decree having to do with your banishment will be rescinded, he says, the moment you agree to change the phrase "two disinterested and impartial arbiters" to "malign elements," etc. This I urge you to do with all speed.

The King has not been at his best. Peace, he says, is an unnatural condition. The country is prosperous, yes, and he understands that the people value peace, that they prefer to spin out their destinies in placid, undisturbed fashion. But *his* destiny, he says, is to alter the map of the world. He is considering several new wars, small ones, he says, small but interesting, complex, dicey, even. He would very much like to consult with you about them. He asks you to change, on page forty-four of your article, the phrase "egregious usurpations" to "symbols of benign transformation." Please initial the change on the proofs, so that historians will not accuse us of bowdlerization.

Your attention is called to the passage in the pages I send which runs as follows: "I walked out of the castle at dusk, not even the joy of a new sunrise to console me, my shaving kit with its dozen razors (although I shaved a dozen times a day, the head was still a donkey's) banging against the Walther .22 in my rucksack. After a time I was suddenly quite tired. I lay down under a hedge by the side of the road. One of the bushes above me had a shred of black cloth tied to it, a sign, in our country, that the place was haunted (but my head's enough to frighten any ghost)." Do you remember that shred of black cloth, Hannahbella? "I ate a slice of my mother's spinach pie and considered my situation. My princeliness would win me an evening, perhaps a fortnight, at this or that noble's castle in the vicinity, but my experience of visiting had taught me that neither royal blood nor novelty of aspect prevailed for long against a host's natural preference for folk with heads much like his own. Should I en-zoo myself? Volunteer for a traveling circus? Attempt the stage? The question was most vexing.

"I had not wiped the last crumbs of the spinach pie from my whiskers when something lay down beside me, under the hedge.

"'What's this?' I said.

"'Soft,' said the new arrival, 'don't be afraid, I am a bogle, let me abide here for the night, your back is warm and that's a mercy.'

"'What's a bogle?' I asked, immediately fetched, for the creature was small, not at all frightening to look upon and clad in female flesh, something I do not hold in low esteem.

"'A bogle,' said the tiny one, with precision, 'is not a black dog.'

"Well, I thought, now I know.

"'A bogle,' she continued, 'is not a boggart.'

"'Delighted to hear it,' I said.

"'Don't you ever *shave*?' she asked. 'And why have you that huge hideous head on you, that could be mistaken for the head of an ass, could I see better so as to think better?'

"'You may lie elsewhere,' I said, 'if my face discountenances you.'

"'I am fatigued,' she said, 'go to sleep, we'll discuss it in the morning, move a bit so that your back fits better with my front, it will be cold, later, and this place is cursed, so they say, and I hear that the Prince has been driven from the palace, God knows what that's all about but it promises no good for us plain folk, police, probably, running all over the fens with their identity checks and making you blow up their great balloons with your breath—'

"She was confusing, I thought, several issues, but my God! she was warm and shapely. Yet I deemed her a strange piece of goods, and made the mistake of saying so.

"'Sir,' she answered, 'I would not venture upon what's strange and what's not strange, if I were you,' and went on to say that if I did not abstain from further impertinence she would commit sewerpipe. She dropped off to sleep then, and I lay back upon the ground. Not a child, I could tell, rather a tiny woman. A bogle."

The King wishes you to know, Hannahbella, that he finds this passage singularly moving and that he cannot read it without being forced to take snuff, violently. Similarly the next:

"What, precisely, is a donkey? As you may imagine, I have researched the question. My *Larousse* was most delicate, as if the editors thought the matter blushful, but yielded two observations of interest: that donkeys came originally from Africa, and that they, or we, are 'the result of much crossing.' This urges that the parties to the birth must be ill-matched, and in the case of my royal parents, 'twas thunderously true. The din of their calamitous conversations reached every quarter of the palace, at every season of the year. My mother named me Duncan (var. of Dunkey, clearly) and went into spasms of shrinking whenever, youthfully, I'd offer a cheek for a kiss. My father, in contrast, could sometimes bring himself to scratch my head between the long, weedlike ears, but only, I suspect, by means of a mental shift, as if he were addressing one of his hunting dogs, the which, incidentally, remained firmly ambivalent about me even after long acquaintance.

"I explained a part of this to Hannahbella, for that was the bogle's name, suppressing chiefly the fact that I was a prince. She in turn gave the following account of herself. She was indeed a bogle, a semispirit generally thought to be of bad character. This was a libel, she said, as her own sterling qualities would quickly persuade me. She was, she said, of the utmost perfection in the female line, and there was not a woman within the borders of the kingdom so beautiful as herself, she'd been told it a thousand times. It was true, she went on, that she was not of a standard size, could in fact be called small, if not minuscule, but those who objected to this were louts and fools and might usefully be stewed in lead, for the entertainment of the countryside. In the matter of rank and precedence, the meanest bogle outweighed the greatest king, although the kings of this earth, she conceded, would never acknowledge this but in their dotty solipsism conducted themselves as if bogles did not even exist. And would I like to see her all unclothed so that I might glean some rude idea as to the true nature of the sublime?

"Well, I wouldn't have minded a bit. She was wonderfully crafted, that was evident, and held in addition the fascination surrounding any perfect miniature. But I said, 'No, thank you. Perhaps another day, it's a bit chill this morning.'

"'Just the breasts then,' she said, 'they're wondrous pretty,' and before I could protest further she'd whipped off her mannikin's tiny shirt. I buttoned her up again meanwhile bestowing buckets of extravagant praise. 'Yes,' she said in agreement, 'that's how I am all over, wonderful.'"

The King cannot reread this section, Hannahbella, without being reduced to tears. The world is a wilderness, he says, civilization a folly we entertain in concert with others. He himself, at his age, is beyond surprise, yet yearns for it. He longs for the conversations he formerly had with you, in the deepest hours of the night, he in his plain ermine robe, you simply dressed as always in a small scarlet cassock, most becoming, a modest supper of chicken, fruit and wine on the sideboard, only the pair of you awake in the whole palace, at four o'clock in the morning. The tax evasion case against you has been dropped. It was, he says, a hasty and ill-considered undertaking, even spiteful. He is sorry.

The King wonders whether the following paragraphs from his autobiography accord with your own recollections: "She then began, as we walked down the road together (an owl pretending to be absent standing on a tree limb to our left, a little stream snapping and growling to our right), explaining to me that my father's administration of the realm left much to be desired, from the bogle point of view, particularly his mad insistence on filling the forests with heavy-footed truffle hounds. Standing, she came to just a hand above my waist; her hair was brown, with bits of gold in it; her quite womanly hips were encased in rust-colored trousers. 'Duncan,' she said, stabbing me in the calf with her sharp nails, 'do you know what that man has done? Nothing else but ruin, absolutely ruin, the whole of the Gatter Fen with a great roaring electric plant that makes a thing that who in the world could have a use for I don't know. I think they're called volts. Two square miles of first-class fen paved over. We bogles are being squeezed to our knees.' I had a sudden urge to kiss her, she looked so angry, but did nothing, my history in this regard being, as I have said, infelicitous.

"'Duncan, *you're not listening*!' Hannahbella was naming the chief interesting things about bogles, which included the fact that in the main they had nothing to do with humans, or nonsemispirits; that although she might seem small to me she was tall, for a bogle, queenly, in fact; that there was a type of blood seas superior to royal blood, and that it was bogle blood; that bogles had no magical powers whatsoever, despite what was said of them; that bogles were the very best lovers in the whole world, no matter what class of thing, animal, vegetable, or insect, might be under discussion; that it was not true that bogles knocked bowls of mush from the tables of the deserving poor and caused farmers' cows to become pregnant with big fishes, out of pure mischief; that female bogles were the most satisfactory sexual partners of any kind of thing that could ever be imagined and were especially keen for large overgrown things with ass's ears, for example; and that there was a something in the road ahead of us to which it might, perhaps, be prudent to pay heed.

"She was right. One hundred yards ahead of us, planted squarely athwart the road, was an army."

The King, Hannahbellia, regrets having said of you, in the journal *Vu*, that you have two brains and no heart. He had thought he was talking not-for-attribution, but as you know, all reporters are scoundrels and not to be trusted. He asks you to note that *Vu* has suspended publication and to recall that it was never read by anyone but serving maids and the most insignificant members of the minor clergy. He is prepared to give you a medal, if you return, any medal you like—you will remember that our medals are the most gorgeous going. On page seventy-five of your article, he requires you, most humbly, to change "monstrous over-reaching fueled by an insatiable if still childish ego" to any kinder construction of your choosing.

The King's autobiography, in chapters already written but which I do not enclose, goes on to recount how you and he together, by means of a clever stratagem of your devising, vanquished the army barring your path on that day long, long ago; how the two of you journeyed together for many weeks and found that your souls were, in essence, the same soul; the shrewd means you employed to place him in power, against the armed opposition of the Party of the Lily, on the death of his father; and the many subsequent campaigns which you endured together, mounted on a single horse, your armor banging against his armor. The King's autobiography, Hannahbella, will run to many volumes, but he cannot bring himself to write the end of the story without you.

The King feels that your falling-out, over the matter of the refugees from Brise, was the result of a miscalculation on his part. He could not have known, he says, that they had bogle blood (although he admits that the fact of their small stature should have told him something). Exchanging the refugees from Brise for the twenty-three Bishops of Ho captured during the affair was, he says in hindsight, a serious error; more bishops can always be created. He makes the point that you did not tell him that the refugees from Brise had bogle blood but instead expected him to know it. Your outrage was, he thinks, a pretext. He at once forgives you and begs your forgiveness. The Chair of Military Philosophy at the university is yours, if you want it. You loved him, he says, he is convinced of it, he still cannot believe it, he exists in a condition of doubt. You are both old; you are both forty. The palace at four A.M. is silent. Come back, Hannahbella, and speak to him.

I am, at the moment, seated. On a stump in the forest, listening. Ireland and Scotland are remote, Wales is not near. I will rise, soon, to hold the ladder for you.

Tombs are scattered through the tall, white beanwoods. They are made of perfectly ordinary gray stone. Chandeliers, at night, scatter light over the tombs, little houses in which I sleep with the already-beautiful, and they with me. The already-beautiful saunter through the forest carrying plump red hams, already cooked. The already-beautiful do not, as a rule, run.

Holding the ladder I watch you glue additional chandeliers to appropriate limbs. You are tiring, you have worked very hard. Iced beanwater will refresh you, and these wallets made of ham. I have set bronze statues of alert, crouching Indian boys around the periphery of the forest, for ornamentation. For ornamentation. Each alert, crouching Indian boy is accompanied by a large, bronze, wolf-like dog, finely polished.

I have been meaning to speak to you. I have many pages of notes, instructions, quarrels. On weighty matters I will speak without notes, freely and passionately, as if inspired, at night, in a rage, slapping myself, great tremendous slaps to the brow which will fell me to the earth. The already-beautiful will stand and watch, in a circle, cradling, each, an animal in mothering arms—green monkey, meadow mouse, tucotuco.

That one has her hips exposed, for study. I make careful notes. You snatch the notebook from my hands. The pockets of your smock swing heavily with the lights of chandeliers. Your light-by-light, bean-by-bean career.

I am, at this moment, prepared to dance.

The already-beautiful have, historically, danced. The music made by my exercise machine is, we agree, danceable. The women partner themselves with large bronze hares, which have been cast in the attitudes of dancers. The beans you have glued together are as nothing to the difficulty of casting hares in the attitudes of dancers, at night, in the foundry, working the bellows, the sweat, the glare. The heat. The glare.

I AM, AT THE MOMENT . . .

Thieves have been invited to dinner, along with the deans of the chief cathedrals. The thieves will rest upon the bosoms of the deans, at night, after dinner, after coffee, among the beanwoods. The thieves will confess to the deans, and the deans to the thieves. Soft benedictions will ensue.

England is far away, and France is but a rumor. Pillows are placed in the tombs, potholders, dustcloths. I am privileged, privileged, to be able to hold your ladder. Tirelessly you glue. The forest will soon exist on some maps, tribute to the quickness of the world's cartographers. This life is better than any I have lived, previously. Beautiful hips bloom and part. Your sudden movement toward red kidney beans has proved, in the event, masterly. Everywhere we see the already-beautiful wearing stomachers, tiaras of red kidney beans, polished to the fierceness of carnelians. No ham hash does not contain two red kidney beans, polished to the fierceness of carnelians.

Spain is distant, Portugal wrapped in an impenetrable haze. These noble beans, glued by you, are mine. Thousand-pound sacks are off-loaded at the quai, against our future needs. The deans are willing workers, the thieves, straw bosses of extraordinary tact. Your weather reports have been splendid: the fall of figs you predicted did in fact occur. I am, at the moment, feeling very jolly. Hey hey, I say. It is remarkable how well human affairs can be managed, with care.

Overnight to Many Distant Cities

*A*GROUP *of Chinese in brown jackets preceded us through the halls of Versailles.* They were middle-aged men, weighty, obviously important, perhaps thirty of them. At the entrance to each room a guard stopped us, held us back until the Chinese had finished inspecting it. A fleet of black government Citroëns had brought them, they were much at ease with Versailles and with each other, it was clear that they were being rewarded for many years of good behavior.

Asked her opinion of Versailles, my daughter said she thought it was overdecorated.

Well, yes.

Again in Paris, years earlier, without Anna, we had a hotel room opening on a courtyard, and late at night through an open window heard a woman expressing intense and rising pleasure. We blushed and fell upon each other.

Right now sunny skies in mid-Manhattan, the temperature is forty-two degrees.

In Stockholm we ate reindeer steak and I told the Prime Minister . . . That the price of booze was too high. Twenty dollars for a bottle of J & B! He (Olof Palme) agreed, most politely, and said that they financed the army that way. The conference we were attending was held at a workers' vacation center somewhat outside the city. Shamelessly, I asked for a double bed, there were none, we pushed two single beds together. An Israeli journalist sat on the two single beds drinking our costly whiskey and explaining the devilish policies of the Likud. Then it was time to go play with the Africans. A poet who had been for a time a Minister of Culture explained why he had burned a grand piano on the lawn in front of the Ministry. "The piano," he said, "is not the national instrument of Uganda."

A boat ride through the scattered islands. A Warsaw Pact novelist asked me to carry a package of paper to New York for him.

Woman is silent for two days in San Francisco. And walked

through the streets with her arms raised high touching the leaves of the trees.

"But you're *married*!"

"But that's *not my fault*!"

Tearing into cold crab at Scoma's we saw Chill Wills at another table, doing the same thing. We waved to him.

In Taegu the air was full of the noise of helicopters. The helicopter landed on a pad, General A jumped out and walked with a firm, manly stride to the spot where General B waited—generals visiting each other. They shook hands, the honor guard with its blue scarves and chromed rifles popped to, the band played, pictures were taken. General A followed by General B walked smartly around the rigid honor guard and then the two generals marched off to the General's Mess, to have a drink.

There are eight hundred and sixty-one generals now on active service. There are four hundred and twenty-six brigadier generals, three hundred and twenty-four major generals, eighty-seven lieutenant generals, and twenty-four full generals. The funniest thing in the world is a general trying on a nickname. Sometimes they don't stick. "Howlin' Mad," "Old Hickory," "Old Blood and Guts," and "Buck" have already been taken. "Old Lacy" is not a good choice.

If you are a general in the field you will live in a general's van, which is a kind of motor home for generals. I once saw a drunk two-star general, in a general's van, seize hold of a visiting actress—it was Marilyn Monroe—and seat her on his lap, shrieking all the while "R.H.I.P.!" or, Rank Has Its Privileges.

Enough of generals.

Thirty per cent chance of rain this afternoon, high in the mid-fifties.

In London I met a man who was not in love. Beautiful shoes, black as black marble, and a fine suit. We went to the theatre together, matter of a few pounds, he knew which plays were the best plays, on several occasions he brought his mother. "An American," he said to his mother, "an American I met." "Met an American during the war," she said to me, "didn't like him." This was reasonably standard, next she would tell me that we had no culture. Her son was hungry, starving, mad in fact, sucking the cuff buttons of his fine suit, choking on the cuff buttons of his fine suit, left and right sleeves jammed into his mouth—he was not in love, he said, "again not in love, not in love again." I put him out of his misery with a good book, Rilke, as I remember, and resolved never to find myself in a situation as dire as his.

In San Antonio we walked by the little river. And ended up in Helen's Bar, where John found a pool player who was, like John, an ex-Marine. How these ex-Marines love each other! It is a flat scandal. The Congress should do something about it. The IRS should do something about it. You and I talked to each other while John talked to his Parris Island friend, and that wasn't too bad, wasn't too bad. We discussed twenty-four novels of normative adultery. "Can't *have* no adultery without adults," I said, and you agreed that this was true. We thought about it, our hands on each other's knees, under the table.

In the car on the way back from San Antonio the ladies talked about the rump of a noted poet. "Too big," they said, "too big too big too big." "Can you imagine going to bed with him?" they said, and then all said "No no no no no," and laughed and laughed and laughed and laughed and laughed.

I offered to get out and run alongside the car, if that would allow them to converse more freely.

In Copenhagen I went shopping with two Hungarians. I had thought they merely wanted to buy presents for their wives. They bought leather gloves, chess sets, frozen fish, baby food, lawnmowers, air conditioners, kayaks. . . . We were six hours in the department store.

"This will teach you," they said, "never to go shopping with Hungarians."

Again in Paris, the hotel was the Montalembert . . . Anna jumped on the bed and sliced her hand open on an open watercolor tin, blood everywhere, the concierge assuring us that "In the war, I saw much worse things."

Well, yes.

But we couldn't stop the bleeding, in the cab to the American Hospital the driver kept looking over his shoulder to make sure that we weren't bleeding on his seat covers, handfuls of bloody paper towels in my right and left hands . . .

On another evening, as we were on our way to dinner, I kicked the kid with carefully calibrated force as we were crossing the Pont Mirabeau, she had been pissy all day, driving us crazy, her character improved instantly, wonderfully, this is a tactic that can be used exactly once.

In Mexico City we lay with the gorgeous daughter of the American ambassador by a clear, cold mountain stream. Well, that was the plan, it didn't work out that way. We were around sixteen and had run away from home, in the great tradition, hitched various long rides with various sinister folk, and there we were in the great city with about two t-shirts to our names. My friend Herman found us jobs in a jukebox factory. Our assignment was to file the slots in American jukeboxes so that they would accept the big, thick Mexican coins. All day long. No gloves.

After about a week of this we were walking one day on the street on which the Hotel Reforma is to be found and there were my father and grandfather, smiling. "The boys have run away," my father had told my grandfather, and my grandfather had said, "Hot damn, let's go get 'em." I have rarely seen two grown men enjoying themselves so much.

Ninety-two this afternoon, the stock market up in heavy trading.

In Berlin everyone stared, and I could not blame them. You were spectacular, your long skirts, your long dark hair. I was upset by the staring, people gazing at happiness and wondering whether to credit it or not, wondering whether it was to be trusted and for how long, and what it meant to them, whether they were in some way hurt by it, in some way diminished by it, in some way criticized by it, good God get it out of my sight—

I correctly identified a Matisse as a Matisse even though it was an uncharacteristic Matisse, you thought I was knowledgeable whereas I was only lucky, we stared at the Schwitters show for one hour and twenty minutes, and then lunched. Vitello tonnato, as I recall.

When Herman was divorced in Boston . . . Carol got the good barbeque pit. I put it in the Blazer for her. In the back of the Blazer were cartons of books, tableware, sheets and towels, plants, and oddly, two dozen white carnations fresh in their box. I pointed to the flowers. "Herman," she said, "he never gives up."

In Barcelona the lights went out. At dinner. Candles were produced and the shiny langoustines placed before us. Why do

I love Barcelona above most other cities? Because Barcelona and I share a passion for walking? I was happy there? You were with me? We were celebrating my hundredth marriage? I'll stand on that. Show me a man who has not married a hundred times and I'll show you a wretch who does not deserve the world.

Lunching with the Holy Ghost I praised the world, and the Holy Ghost was pleased. "We have that little problem in Barcelona," He said, "the lights go out in the middle of dinner." "I've noticed," I said. "We're working on it," He said, "what a wonderful city, one of our best." "A great town," I agreed. In an ecstasy of admiration for what is we ate our simple soup.

Tomorrow, fair and warmer, warmer and fair, most fair. . . .

FROM
FORTY STORIES

Chablis

MY WIFE wants a dog. She already has a baby. The baby's almost two. My wife says that the baby wants the dog.

My wife has been wanting a dog for a long time. I have had to be the one to tell her that she couldn't have it. But now the baby wants a dog, my wife says. This may be true. The baby is very close to my wife. They go around together all the time, clutching each other tightly. I ask the baby, who is a girl, "Whose girl are you? Are you Daddy's girl?" The baby says, "Momma," and she doesn't just say it once, she says it repeatedly, "Momma momma momma." I don't see why I should buy a hundred-dollar dog for that damn baby.

The kind of dog the baby wants, my wife says, is a Cairn terrier. This kind of dog, my wife says, is a Presbyterian like herself and the baby. Last year the baby was a Baptist—that is, she went to the Mother's Day Out program at the First Baptist twice a week. This year she is a Presbyterian because the Presbyterians have more swings and slides and things. I think that's pretty shameless and I have said so. My wife is a legitimate lifelong Presbyterian and says that makes it O.K.; way back when she was a child she used to go to the First Presbyterian in Evansville, Illinois. I didn't go to church because I was a black sheep. There were five children in my family and the males rotated the position of black sheep among us, the oldest one being the black sheep for a while while he was in his DWI period or whatever and then getting grayer as he maybe got a job or was in the service and then finally becoming a white sheep when he got married and had a grandchild. My sister was never a black sheep because she was a girl.

Our baby is a pretty fine baby. I told my wife for many years that she couldn't have a baby because it was too expensive. But they wear you down. They are just wonderful at wearing you down, even if it takes years, as it did in this case. Now I hang around the baby and hug her every chance I get. Her name is Joanna. She wears Oshkosh overalls and says "no," "bottle," "out," and "Momma." She looks most lovable when she's wet, when she's just had a bath and her blond hair is all wet and she's wrapped in a beige towel. Sometimes when she's watching television she forgets that you're there. You can just look at her. When she's watching television, she looks dumb. I like her better when she's wet.

This dog thing is getting to be a big issue. I said to my wife, "Well you've got the baby, do we have to have the damned dog too?" The dog will probably bite somebody, or get lost. I can see myself walking all over our subdivision asking people, "Have you seen this brown dog?" "What's its name?" they'll say to me, and I'll stare at them coldly and say, "Michael." That's what she wants to call it, Michael. That's a silly name for a dog and I'll have to go looking for this possibly rabid animal and say to people, "Have you seen this brown dog? Michael?" It's enough to make you think about divorce.

What's that baby going to do with that dog that it can't do with me? Romp? I can romp. I took her to the playground at the school. It was Sunday and there was nobody there, and we romped. I ran, and she tottered after me at a good pace. I held her as she slid down the slide. She groped her way through a length of big pipe they have there set in concrete. She picked up a feather and looked at it for a long time. I was worried that it might be a diseased feather but she didn't put it in her mouth. Then we ran some more over the parched bare softball field and through the arcade that connects the temporary wooden classrooms, which are losing their yellow paint, to the main building. Joanna will go to this school some day, if I stay in the same job.

I looked at some dogs at Pets-A-Plenty, which has birds, rodents, reptiles, and dogs, all in top condition. They showed me the Cairn terriers. "Do they have their prayer books?" I asked. This woman clerk didn't know what I was talking about. The Cairn terriers ran about two ninety-five per, with their papers. I started to ask if they had any illegitimate children at lower prices but I could see that it would be useless and the woman already didn't like me, I could tell.

What is wrong with me? Why am I not a more natural person, like my wife wants me to be? I sit up, in the early morning, at my desk on the second floor of our house. The desk faces the street. At five-thirty in the morning, the runners are already out, individually or in pairs, running toward rude red health. I'm sipping a glass of Gallo Chablis with an ice cube in it, smoking, worrying. I worry that the baby may jam a kitchen knife into an electrical outlet while she's wet. I've put those little plastic plugs into all the electrical outlets but she's learned how to pop them out. I've checked the Crayolas. They've made the Crayolas safe to eat—I called the head office in Pennsylvania. She can eat a whole box of Crayolas and nothing will happen to her. If I don't get the new tires for the car I can buy the dog.

I remember the time, thirty years ago, when I put Herman's mother's Buick into a cornfield, on the Beaumont highway. There was another car in my lane, and I didn't hit it, and it didn't hit me. I remember veering to the right and down into the ditch and up through the fence and coming to rest in the cornfield and then getting out to wake Herman and the two of us going to see what the happy drunks in the other car had come to, in the ditch on the other side of the road. That was when I was a black sheep, years and years ago. That was skillfully done, I think. I get up, congratulate myself in memory, and go in to look at the baby.

On the Deck

THERE IS a lion on the deck of the boat. The lion looks tired, fatigued. Waves the color of graphite. A grid placed before the lion, quartering him, each quarter subdivided into sixteen squares, total of sixty-four squares through which lion parts may be seen. The lion a dirty yellow-brown against the gray waves.

Next to but not touching the lion, members of a Christian motorcycle gang (the gang is called Banditos for Jesus and has nineteen members but only three are on the deck of the boat) wearing their colors which differ from the colors of other gangs in that the badges, insignia, and so on have Christian messages, "Jesus is LORD" and the like. The bikers are thick-shouldered, gold earrings, chains, beards, red bandannas, a sweetness expressed in the tilt of their bodies toward the little girl wearing shiny steel leg braces who stands among them and smiles—they have chosen her as their "old lady" and are collecting money for her education.

To the right of the Christian bikers and a bit closer to the coils of razor wire forward of the lion is a parked Camry (in profile) covered with a tarp and tied down with bright new rope, blocks under the wheels, the lower half of its price sticker visible on the window not completely covered by canvas. The motor is running, exhaust from the twin tailpipes touching the thirty-five burlap-wrapped bales stacked at the back of the car. There is someone inside the car, behind the wheel. This person is named Mitch. The exhaust from the car irritates the lion, whose head rolls from side to side, yellow teeth bared.

In front of the tied-down red Camry, a man with a nosebleed holding a steel basin under his chin. The basin is full of brown blood, brown-stained blooms of gauze. He holds the basin with one hand and clutches his nose with the other. His blue-and-red-striped shirt is bloody. "Hello," he says, "hello, hello!" Gray institutional pants and brown shoes. There's a tree, an eight-foot western fir, in a heavy terra-cotta pot between his legs. He appears to be trying to avoid bleeding on the tree.

"They don't have anything I want," he says. A basketball wedged between the upper branches on the left side. Immediately to the left and forward of the fir tree, a yellow fifty-five-gallon drum labeled in black letters PRISMATEX, a hose coiled on top of it; bending over the PRISMATEX, her back turned, a young woman with black hair in a thin thin yellow dress. Concentrate on the hams.

The tilting of the deck increases; spray. The captain, a red-faced man in a blue blazer, sits in an armchair before the young woman, a can of beer in his right hand. He says: "I would have done better work if I'd had some kind of encouragement. I've met a lot of people in my life. I let my feelings carry me along." At the captain's knee is the captain's dog, a black-and-white Scottie. The dog is afraid of the lion, keeps looking back over his shoulder at the lion. The captain kisses the hem of the young woman's yellow dress. There's a rolled Oriental rug bound with twine in front of the Scottie, and in front of that a child's high chair with a peacock sitting in it, next to that a Harley leaning on its kickstand (HONK IF YOU LOVE JESUS in script on the gas tank). The owner of the boat, sister of the woman in the yellow dress, is squatting by the Harley cooking hot dogs on a hibachi, a plastic bag of buns by her right foot. A boyfriend lies next to her, playing with the bottom edge of her yellow shorts. "Sometimes she's prim," he says. "Don't know when you wake up in the morning what you're going to get. I'm really not interested just now. At some point you get into it pretty far, then it becomes frightening."

"A smooth flight isn't totally dependent on the pilot," says the next man. There's a bucket of raw liver between his knees, liver for the lion, he's up to his elbows in liver. Next, a shuffleboard court and two men shoving the brightly colored disks this way and that with old battered M-1 rifles. "I put two forty-pound sacks of cat food in the bed and covered them neatly with a blanket but she still didn't get the message." Further along, a marble bust of Hadrian on a bamboo plant stand, Hadrian's marble curls curling to meet Hadrian's marble beard, next to that someone delivering the mail, a little canvas pushcart containing mail pushed in front of her, blue uniform, two shades of blue, red hair. "Everyone likes mail, except those who are afraid of it." Everyone gets mail. The captain gets mail, the Christian bikers get mail, Liverman gets mail, the woman in the scandal-dress gets mail. Many copies of *Smithsonian*. A man sitting in a red wicker chair.

Winter on deck. All of the above covered with snow. Christmas music.

Then, spring. A weak sun, then a stronger sun.

You came and fell upon me, I was sitting in the wicker chair. The wicker exclaimed as your weight fell upon me. You were light, I thought, and I thought how good it was of you to do this. We'd never touched before.

Opening

THE ACTORS feel that the music played before the curtain rises will put the audience in the wrong mood. The playwright suggests that the (purposefully lugubrious) music be played at twice-speed. This peps it up somewhat while retaining its essentially dark and gloomy character. The actors listen carefully, and are pleased.

The director, in white overalls and a blue work shirt, whispers to the actors. The director is tender with the actors, like a good father, calms them, solicits their opinions, gives them aspirin. The playwright regards the actors with the greatest respect. How sweetly they speak! They have discovered meanings in his lines far beyond anything he had imagined possible.

> ARDIS: But it's always that way, always.
> PAUL: Not necessarily, dear friend. Not necessarily.

The rug on the set was done by a famous weaver, indeed is a modern classic, and costs four thousand dollars. It has been lent to the production (for program credit) as has the chrome-and-leather sofa. No one steps on the rug (or sits on the sofa) oftener than necessary.

The playwright studies the empty set for many hours. Should the (huge, magnificent) plant be moved a few inches to the left? The actors are already joking about being upstaged by the plant. The actors are gentle, amusing people, but also very tough, and physically strong. Many of their jokes involve scraps of dialogue from the script, which become catchphrases of general utility: "Not necessarily, dear friend. Not necessarily."

In the rehearsal room the costume designer spreads out his sketches over a long table. The actors crowd around to see how they will look in the first act, in the second act. The designs sparkle, there is no other word for it. Also, the costume designer is within the budget, whereas the set designer was eighteen thousand over and the set had to be redesigned, painfully.

An actor whispers to the playwright. "A playwright," he says, "is a man who has decided that the purpose of human life is to describe human life. Don't you find that odd?" The playwright, who has never thought about his vocation in quite this way, does find it odd. He worries about it all day.

The playwright loves the theatre when it is empty. When it has people in it he does not love it so much; the audience is a danger to his play (although it's only sometimes he feels this). In the empty theatre, as in a greenhouse, his play grows, thrives. Rehearsals, although tedious in the extreme and often disheartening—an actor can lose today something he had yesterday—are an intelligent process charged with hope.

The actors tell stories about other shows they've been in, mostly concerning moments of disaster onstage. "When I did *Charity* in London—" In the men's dressing room, one of the actors tells a long story about a female colleague whose hair caught fire during a production of *Saint Joan*. "I poured Tab on it," he says. Photographs are taken for the newspapers. The playwright goes alone for lunch to a Chinese restaurant which has a bar. He is the only one in the group who drinks at lunchtime. The temperate, good-natured actors vote in all elections and vehemently support a nuclear freeze.

PAUL: You've got to . . . transcend . . . the circumstances. Know what I mean?
REGINA: Easier said than done, boyo.

The playwright makes a shocking discovery. One of his best exchanges—

ARDIS: The moon is beautiful now.
PAUL: You should have seen it before the war.

—freighted with the sadness of unrecapturable time, is also to be found, almost word for word, in Oscar Wilde's *Impressions of America*. How did this happen? Has he written these lines, or has he remembered them? He honestly cannot say. In a fit of rectitude, he cuts the lines.

The producer slips into a seat in the back of the house and watches a scene. Then he says, "I love this material. I *love* it."

The playwright asks that the costume worn by one of the actresses in the second act be changed. It makes her look too little-girlish, he feels. The costume designer disagrees but does not press the point. *Now my actress looks more beautiful*, the playwright thinks.

The opening is at hand. The actors bring the playwright small, thoughtful gifts: a crock of imported mustard, a finely printed edition of Ovid's *Art of Love*. The playwright gives the actors, men and women, little cloth sacks containing gold-wrapped chocolates.

The notices are good, very good.

> LIGHTS UP THE SKY OVER
> OFF-BROADWAY AND STIMULATES
> MEN'S MINDS
> —*Cue*

The actors are praised, warmly and with discrimination. People attend the play in encouraging numbers. At intermission the lobby is filled with well-dressed, enthusiastic people, discussing the play. The producer, that large, anxious man, steams with enthusiasm. The critics, he tells the playwright, are unreliable. But sometimes one has good fortune. The play, he tells the playwright, will remain forever in the history of the theatre.

After the show closes, the director purchases the big, spiky plant that appeared, burning with presence, throughout the second act. The actors, picking up their gear, pause to watch the plant being loaded onto a truck. "Think he can teach it to go to the corner for coffee and a Danish?" "Easier said than done, boyo."

In his study, the playwright begins his next play, which will explore the relationship between St. Augustine and a Carthaginian girl named Luna and the broken bones of the heart.

Sindbad

THE BEACH: Sindbad, drowned animal, clutches at the sand of still another island shore.

His right hand, marvelous upon the pianoforte, opens and closes. His hide is roasted red, his beard white with crusted salt. The broken beam to which he clung to escape his shattered vessel lies nearby.

He hears waltzes from the trees.

He should, of course, rouse himself, get to his feet, gather tree fruits, locate a spring, build a signal fire, or find a stream that will carry him toward the interior of this strange new place, where he will encounter a terrifying ogre of some sort, outwit him, and then take possession of the rubies and diamonds, big as baseballs, which litter the ogre's domains, wonderfully.

Stir your stumps, sir.

Classroom: It's true that the students asked me to leave. I had never taught in the daytime before, how was I to know how things were done in the daytime?

I guess they didn't like my looks. I was wearing shades (my eyes unused to so much light) and a jacket that was, admittedly, too big for me. I was rather prominently placed toward the front of the room, *in* the front of the room to be precise, sitting on the desk that faced their desks, fidgeting.

"Would you just, please, leave?" the students said.

The chair had asked me, "How'd you like to teach in the daytime? Just this once?" I said that I could not imagine such a thing but that I would do my very best. "Don't get carried away, Robert," she said, "it's only one course, we've got too many people on leave and now this damnable flu . . ." I said I would prepare myself carefully and buy a new shirt. "That's a good idea," she said, looking closely at my shirt, which had been given to me by my younger brother, the lawyer. He was throwing out shirts.

Sindbad's wives look back: "I knew him, didn't you know that I knew him?"

"I didn't think that a person such as you could have known him."

"Intimately. That's how well I knew him. I was his ninth wife."

"Well of course you were more in the prime of life then. It was more reasonable to expect something."

"He treated me well, on the whole. In the years of our intimacy. Many gowns of great costliness."

"You'd never know it to look at you. I mean now."

"Well I have other things besides these things. I don't wear my better things all the time. Besides gowns, he gave me frocks. Shoes of beaten lizard."

"Maybe jewels?"

"Rubies and diamonds big as baseballs. I seem to remember a jeweled horsewhip. To whip my horses with. I rode, in the early mornings, on the cliffs, the cliffs overlooking the sea."

"You had a sea."

"Yes, there was a sea, adjacent to the property. He was fond of the sea."

"He must have been very well-off then. When I knew him he was just a merchant. A small merchant."

"Yes, he'd begun as a poor person, tried that for a while, didn't like it, and then ventured forth. Upon the sea."

The Beaux-Arts Ball: At the Beaux-Arts Ball given by the Art and Architecture Departments I saw a young woman wearing what appeared to be men's cotton underwear. The undershirt was sleeveless and the briefs, cut very high on the sides, had the designer's name ("EGIZIO") in half-inch red letters stitched around the waistband.

"Who are you?" I asked.

She raised her hands, which were encased in red rubber gloves. "Lady Macbeth," she said. Then she asked me to leave.

So I went out into the parking lot carrying my costume, a brightly polished English horn. If anyone had asked me who I was I had intended saying I was one of Robin Hood's merry men. One of the students followed me, wanted to know if I had a wife. I answered honestly that I did not, and told her that if you taught at night you weren't allowed to have a wife. It was a sort of unwritten law, understood by all. "You're not allowed to have a wife and you're not allowed to have a car," I told her honestly.

"Then what are you doing in this parking lot?" she asked. I showed her my old blue bicycle, parked between a Camaro and a Trans Am. "Do you have a house?" she asked, and I said that I had a room somewhere, with a radio in it and one of those little refrigerators that sit upon a table.

Sindbad's first emporium in Baghdad: When we opened Sindbad's we did not anticipate the good results we obtained almost immediately.

The people leaped over the counters and wrested the goods from our hands and from the shelves behind the counters.

Stock boys ran back and forth between the stockrooms and the counters. We had developed patterns of running back and forth so that Stock Boy A did not collide with Stock Boy B. Some warped, some woofed.

We had always wanted a store and had as children played "store" with tiny cedar boxes replicating real goods. Now we had an actual store, pearl-colored with accents of saturated jade.

Every day, people leaped over the counters and wrested goods from the hands of our brave, durable clerks. Our store was glorious, glorious. The simple finest of everything, that was what we purveyed. Often people had been wandering around for years trying to find the finest, lost, uncertain. Then they walked through our great bronze doors resonant with humming filigree. There it was, the finest.

Even humble items were the finest of their kind. Our straight pin was straighter than any other straight pin ever offered, and pinned better, too.

Once, a little girl came into the store, alone. She had only a few gold coins, and we took them from her, and made her happy. We had never, in our entire careers as merchants, seen a happier little girl as she left the store, carrying in her arms the particular goods she had purchased with her few, but real, gold coins.

Once, a tall man came into the store, tall but bent, arthritis, he was bent half-double, but you could tell that he was tall, or had been tall before he became bent, three or four lines of physical suffering on his forehead. He asked for food. We furnished him with foodstuffs from Taillevent in Paris, the finest, and not a centime did we charge him. Because he was bent.

In our pearl-colored store we had a pearl beyond price, a tulip bulb beyond price, and a beautiful slave girl beyond price. These were displayed behind heavy glass set in the walls. No offer for these items was ever accepted. They were beyond price. Idealism ruled us in these matters.

The students: "Would you please leave now?" they asked. "Would you please just leave?"

Then they all started talking to each other, they turned in their seats and began talking to each other, the air grew loud, it was rather like a cocktail party except that everybody was sitting down, the door opened and a waiter came in with drinks on a tray followed by another waiter with water chestnuts wrapped in bacon on a tray and another waiter with more drinks. It was exactly like a cocktail party except that everybody was sitting down. So I took a drink from a tray and joined one of the groups and tried to understand what they were saying.

Tennis: Yes, he could do this sort of thing all day. Something he can go home and talk about (assuming that he gets back to Baghdad alive), how he played tennis with two ogres tall as houses and brought them to their knees. Each ogre has a single red eye in the middle of his forehead and a single wire-rimmed lens framing the eye. He can sucker the one on the left out of position merely by glancing at the one on the right before he serves, and anything placed to the left of the one on the right is invariably missed, the one on the right has no backhand whatsoever. So how-he-played-tennis-with-two-ogres will be added to the repertoire, two female ogres following the game intently, their two staring eyes with the single tinted lenses turning right, left, right, left, the sun bursting off the lenses like the beams of two lighthouses. . . .

At night: At night, the Department's offices are empty. The cleaning women make their telephone calls, in Spanish, from Professor This's office, from Professor That's office, taking care of business. The parking lots are infernos of yellow light.

Sitting one night on the steps of the power plant I saw a man carrying a typewriter, an IBM Selectric III. I judged him to be one of those people who stole typewriters from the university at night. "Can you type?" I asked him. He said, "Shit, man, don't be a fool." I asked him why he stole typewriters and he said, "Them mothers ain't got nothin' else worth stealin'." I was going to suggest that he return the typewriter, when another man came out of the darkness carrying another typewriter. "This mother's *heavy*," he said to the first, and they went off together, cursing. An IBM Selectric III weighs approximately forty pounds.

The students, no doubt, whispered about me:

"I heard this is the first time he's taught in the daytime."

"They wouldn't *let* that sucker teach in sunlight 'cept that all the real teachers are dead."

"Did you get a shot of that coat? Tack-eeee."

I stood in the corridor gazing at them from behind my shades. What a good-looking group! I thought. In the presto of the morning, as Stevens puts it.

Experience: Sindbad learns nothing from experience.

A prudent man, after the first, second, third, fourth, fifth, sixth, and seventh voyages, would never again set foot on a ship's deck. Every vessel upon which he has ever embarked has either headed for the bottom not two days out of port or marooned him, has been stove in by a gigantic whale (first voyage), seduced into distraction by jubilant creatures of the air (second voyage), stolen by apelike savages no more than three feet high (third voyage), crushed by a furious squall (fourth voyage), bombed from the air by huge birds carrying huge rocks (fifth voyage), or dashed against a craggy shore (sixth voyage) by the never-sleeping winds.

But there is always a sturdy (wooden trough, floating beam, stray piece of wreckage from the doomed vessel) to cling to, and an island (garnished with rubies and diamonds, large quantities of priceless pearls, bales of the choicest ambergris) to pillage. Sindbad never fails to return to Baghdad richer than before, with many sumptuous presents for the friends and relatives who gather at his house to hear the news of his latest heroic impertinence.

Sindbad is not a prudent but a daring man. In *Who's Who at Sea* he is listed, disapprovingly, as an "adventurer."

Water cannon: The graduates don't wish to leave the campus. We'll have to blast them out. I say "we" because I identify with the administration although no member of the administration has asked my opinion on the matter. I think water cannon are the means of choice. I have never seen a water cannon except in TV news reports from East Germany but it seems to be an effective and relatively humane means of blasting people out of there. I wouldn't mind having a water cannon of my own. There are certain people I wouldn't mind blasting.

The grounds crew was standing at the edge of the field, waiting to fold the folding chairs. The band was putting away its instruments. The graduates must have had some boards stashed away among the trees. They began building lean-tos, many of them leaned against the Science Building, some against the Student Center. Cooking fires were lit, the graduates squatted around the cooking fires, roasting corn on spits. Totem poles were erected before the lean-tos. The provost went to the microphone. "Time to go, time to go," he said. The graduates refused to leave.

Waltzes: Sindbad gets to his feet, shakes himself, and heads toward the tree line. Waltzes? The music is exotic to him, he has never heard such music before. He congratulates himself that on his eighth voyage the world can still reward him with new enchantments.

Teaching: I reentered the classroom and fixed them with my fiercest glare. I began to teach. They had to put down their drinks and shrimp on toothpicks and listen.

It was true, I said, that I had never taught in the daytime before, and that my refrigerator was small and my jacket far, far too baggy.

Nonetheless, I said, I have something to teach. Be like Sindbad! Venture forth! Embosom the waves, let your shoes be sucked from your feet and your very trousers enticed by the frothing deep. The ambiguous sea awaits, I told them, marry it!

There's nothing out there, they said.

Wrong, I said, absolutely wrong. There are waltzes, sword canes, and sea wrack dazzling to the eyes.

What's a sword cane? they asked, and with relief I plunged into the Romantics.

Rif

LET ME tell you something. New people have moved into the apartment below me and their furniture is, shockingly, identical to mine, the camelback sofa in camel-colored tweed is there as are the two wrong-side-of-the-blanket sons of the Wassily chair and the black enamel near-Mackintosh chairs, they have the pink-and-purple dhurries and the brass quasi-Eames torchères as well as the fake Ettore Sottsass faux-marble coffee table with cannonball legs. I'm shocked, in a state of shock—
 —I taught you that. Overstatement. You're shocked. You reel, you fall, you collapse in Rodrigo's arms, complaining of stress. He slowly begins loosening your stays, stay by stay, singing the great *Ah, je vois le jour, ah, Dieu*, and the second act is over.
 —You taught me that, Rhoda. You, my mentor in all things.
 —You were apt Hettie very apt.
 —I was apt.
 —The most apt.
 —Cold here in the garden.
 —You were complaining about the sun.
 —But when it goes behind a cloud—
 —Well, you can't have everything.
 —The flowers are beautiful.
 —Indeed.
 —Consoling to have the flowers.
 —Half-consoled already.
 —And these Japanese rocks.
 —Artfully placed, most artfully.
 —You must admit, a great consolation.
 —And our work.
 —A great consolation.
 —God, aren't these flowers beautiful.
 —Only three of them. But each remarkable, of its kind.
 —What are they?
 —Some kind of Japanese dealies, I don't know.

—Lazing here in the garden. This is really most luxurious.

—I think that they provide, the company provides, a space like this, in the middle of this vast building, it's—

—Most enlightened.

—It drains away. The tensions.

—We still haven't decided what color to paint the trucks.

—I said blue.

—Surely not your last word on the subject.

—I have some swatches. If you'd care to take a gander.

—Not now. This sun is blistering.

—New skin. You're going to complain?

—Those new people. Upstairs. They make me feel bad. Wouldn't you feel bad?

—It's not my furniture that's being replicated in every detail. Every last trite detail. So I don't feel bad. The implications don't—

—I have something to tell you, Rhoda.

—What, Hettie?

—We're having a thirteen-percent reduction-in-force. A rif. You're in line to be riffed, Rhoda.

—I am?

—If you take early retirement voluntarily you get a better package. If I have to release you, you get less.

—How much less?

—Rounds out at about forty-two percent. Less.

—Well.

—Yes.

—I'll need something to do with myself. I am young yet Hettie. Relatively speaking.

—Very relatively very.

—What about the windows?

—What about them?

—They need washing. Badly in want of washing.

—You? Washing windows?

—Maybe work my way up through the ranks. Again.

—Your delicate hands in the ammonia-bright bucket—I can't see it.

—Is cheese alive when it's killed? My daughter asked me that she's beginning to get the hang of things.

—Perhaps too early?

—On schedule I would say. The windows radiate filth, building-wide. I can do it.

—I will plunge the dagger into my breast before I send you to Support Services.

—All part of the program, Hettie.

—Will I be okay without you, Rhoda?

—Fine, Hettie, fine. My parting advice is, cut the dagger.

—The only person I ever stuck with it was Bruce.

—He smiled slightly as he slid to the floor, a vivid pinkness obscuring the Polo emblem on his chest.

—He was most gracious about it, called it a learning experience.

—Most gracious. Above and beyond.

—I remember the year we got the two-percent increase.

—Then the four-percent increase.

—Then the eight-percent across-the-board cut.

—The year the Easter bonus came through.

—Our ups and downs.

—Wonderful memories, wonderful.

—Bruce. Mentor-at-large. First he was your Bruce. Then he was my Bruce.

—Taught me much, Bruce.

—That's what they're for. To teach. That's how I regarded him. That's why I took him.

—A good poke too, not a bad poke, fair poke not too bad a poke.

—Mentoring away. Through dark and dank.

—Yes.

—He always said you cast him off like an old spreadsheet.

—I remember a night in California. I've always hated California. But on this night, in California, he by God taught me lost-horse theory. Where you have a lost horse and have to find it. Has to do with the random movement of markets and the taming of probability. I was by God *entranced*.

—Well we've moved beyond that now haven't we?

—If you say so Hettie.

—I mean we don't want to get hung up on the Bruce question at this late date.

—What good would it do? He's gone.

—He thought he could cook.
—He prided himself upon his cooking.
—He couldn't cook.
—He could do gizzards. Something about gizzards that engaged his attention.
—Nothing he could do I couldn't do better. In addition, I could luxuriously stretch out my naked, golden leg. He couldn't do that.
—His, a rather oaklike leg covered with lichen.
—Oh he was a sturdy boy. Head like a chopping block. Many's the time I tried to bash the new into it.
—Your subtle concept shattered upon the raw butchered surface.
—And when it was necessary to put him out to pasture—
—Did we flinch? We did not flinch.
—Grazing now with all the other former vice-presidents in Kentucky.
—Muzzle-deep in the sweetest clover.
—I have the greatest of expectations, still.
—Of course you do. Part of the program.
—My expectations are part of the program?
—The soul of the program.
—No no no no. My expectations come from within.
—I think not. Blown into being, as it were, by the program.
—My expectations are a function of my thinking. My own highly individuated thinking which includes elements of the thought of Immanuel Kant and Harry S. Truman.
—Absolutely. Unique to you.
—Furthermore I'm going to bust out of this constraining smothering retrograde environment at the first opportunity. I give you fair warning.
—Why tell me? I'm the mere window person.
—To me, Rhoda, you will always be the rock upon which my church is founded.
—Why you ragged kid, you ain't got no church.
—I ain't?
—At most, a collection plate.
—I circulate among the worshipers, taking tithes.
—It's a living. Put a bunch of tithes one on top of another, you have a not inconsiderable sum.

—The priestly function, mine. The one who understands the arcanum, me.

—Also you get to herd the flock. Tell the flock to flock here, to flock there.

—Divine inspiration. That's all it is. Nothing to it.

—You yourself awash in humility all the while.

—I can do humility.

—Don't wave the dagger. The argument of the third act, as it spreads itself before us, is perfectly plain: If we recognize ourselves to be part of a larger whole with which we are in relations, those relations and that whole cannot be created by the finite self but must be produced by an absolute all-inclusive mind of which our minds are parts and of which the world-process in its totality is the experience. Don't wave the dagger.

—I'll bare my breast, place the point of the knife upon its plump surface. Then explain the issues.

—I tell you people lust for consummation. They see a shining dagger poised above a naked breast, they want it shoved in.

—I wonder what it would have been like. If I'd had another mentor. One less sour, perhaps.

—You'd be a different person, Hettie.

—I would, wouldn't I. Strange to think.

—Are you satisfied? You needn't answer.

—No, I'm not. You taught me that. Not to be satisfied.

—The given can always be improved upon. Screwed around with.

—You were a master. Are a master. Wangling and diddling, fire and maneuver.

—I can sit and watch my daughter. Scrape the city off her knees and tell her to look both ways when she crosses the street.

—They have to learn. Like everybody else.

—Maybe I'll teach her to look only to the left. Not both ways.

—That's wrong. That's not right. It's unsafe.

—The essence of my method.

—You were a wild old girl, Rhoda. I'll remember.

—I was, wasn't I.

—We still haven't decided what color to paint the trucks.

—Blue?

Jaws

How is William to prove to Natasha that he still loves her? That's the problem I'm working on, mentally, as I check the invoices and get the big double-parked trucks from the warehouses unloaded and deal with all the people bringing in aluminum cans for redemption. Benny, this black Transit cop who had ordered a hot pastrami on rye with mustard from our deli and then had to rush out on a call, is now eating his hot pastrami and telling me about this woman who was hanging out of a sixth-floor window over on Second Avenue where he and his partner couldn't get at her. "She wouldn't come in," Benny says. "I said, go ahead and fly, Loony-tunes. I shouldn't have said that. I made an error."

I understand how that could be. This woman wanted to blend her head with Second Avenue and mess up the honor of the Transit Police, probably because somebody didn't love her anymore. Mutilation, actual or verbal, is usually taken as an earnest of sincere interest in another person. Verbal presentations, with William and Natasha, are no good. So many terrible sentences drift in the poisoned air between them, sentences about who is right and sentences about who works hardest and sentences about money and even sentences about physical appearance—the most ghastly of known sentences. That's why Natasha bites, I'm convinced of it. She's trying to say something. She opens her mouth, then closes it (futility) on William's arm (sudden eloquence).

I like them both, so they both tell me about these incidents and I rationalize and say, well, that's not so terrible, maybe she's under stress, or maybe he's under stress. I neglect to mention that most people in New York are under some degree of stress and few of them, to my knowledge, bite each other. People always like to hear that they're under stress, makes them feel better. You can imagine what they'd feel if they were told they weren't under stress.

Natasha is a small woman with dark hair and a serious, concerned face. Good teeth. She wears trusty Canal Street–West

Broadway pants and shirts and is maybe twenty-six. I met her three years ago when she came over to my little cubicle at the A&P at Twelfth Street and Seventh to cash a check, one that William had signed. Of course she didn't have the proper ID, since she wasn't William. But she was so embarrassed that I decided she was okay. "He's a little peculiar about money," she told me, and *I* was embarrassed. I thought, what's with this guy? I thought he was probably some kind of monster, in a minor way. Then one day he came in to cash a check himself. "Why don't you put your wife on your account?" I asked him. "I cash her checks because I know her, but sometimes I'm not here. Also, she must have trouble other places. I mean, I'm not telling you how to run your life."

William blushed. You don't see that much blushing at A&P Twelfth Street. He was wearing a suit, a gray Barney's pin-striped number, and had obviously just come from work. "She has a tendency to overspend," he said. "It's not her fault. She was born to wealth and her habits never left her, even when she married me. When we had a joint account she never entered the checks in her checkbook. So we were always overdrawn and I finally closed the account and now we do it this way."

When Natasha found out about William's affair with the girl at the office, I should say woman at the office, she came straight to me and told me everything. "It was at the office picnic in Central Park," she said. "Everybody was playing badminton, okay? In bare feet. William was playing and I noticed that he had a piece of silver duct tape around his big toe. He had a cut, he said. William uses duct tape for everything. Our place is practically held together with duct tape. And then later on I noticed that this rather pretty girl was playing with a piece of duct tape on her ankle. She'd scraped her ankle. And that told me the story, right there. I confronted him with it and he admitted it. It was as simple as that."

Well, romance is not unknown at the A&P. We are an old and wise organization and have seen much. We are not called The Great Atlantic and Pacific for nothing, we contain multitudes and sometimes people lock gazes across the frozen rabbit parts and the balloon goes up, figuratively speaking. I counseled forbearance. "Don't come down too hard on him," I said. "William is clearly in the wrong in this matter, that gives you a certain edge. Don't harangue or threaten or cry and weep. Calm, rational understanding is your mode. Politically, you're way out in front. Act accordingly."

I think this was psychologically acute advice. It was the best I had to offer. What she did was, she bit him again. On the shoulder, in the shower. He was in the shower, he told me, and suddenly there was this horrible pain in his left shoulder and this time she did break the skin. He had to slug her in the hipbone to make her let go. "It's the only time I've ever hit her," he said. He poured Johnnie Walker Black over the wound and slapped a piece of duct tape on it and took a room at the Mohawk Motor Inn, on Tenth Avenue.

William has not only not proved to Natasha that he still loves her but alienated her still further, because of the thing with Patricia, who he's not seeing anymore, in that way. Furthermore he's been in the Mohawk Motor Inn for a week, and that can get to you. Nothing breaks down a man accustomed to at least some degree of domestic felicity more than a week at a Motor Inn, however welcoming. He walks over in the mornings from the Mohawk for a bagel with dilled cream cheese and to find out if Natasha's been around. I have to be, and have been, strictly impartial. "She was in," I say. "She's butterflying a leg of lamb tonight. Marinating it for six hours in soy sauce and champagne. I don't myself think the champagne is a good idea but she got some recipe from somewhere—"

"From her sister," William says. "Danni spreads champagne on hot dog buns. Rex, what do you think?"

"Go home," I say. "Praise the lamb."

"How do I know it won't be the spinal cord next?"

"Hard to get to. Probably couldn't even dent it."

"I feel like I'm married to some kind of animal."

"Our animal nature is part of us and we are part of it."

So he goes back to their apartment on Charles Street and they have a festive evening with the lamb and candles. They go to bed together and in the middle of the night she bites him on the back of the leg, severing a tendon just above the knee. A real gorilla bite. I can't understand it. She's a really nice woman, and pretty, too.

"You can't bite your way through life," I say to her. She's just seen William in his semi-private room at St. Vincent's.

"The physical therapist says there'll be a slight limp," she says, "forever. How could I have done that?"

"Passion, I guess. Feeling run rampant."

"Will he ever speak to me again?"

"What'd he say at the hospital?"

"Said the food was lousy."

"That's a beginning."

"He doesn't feel for me anymore. I know it."

"He keeps coming back. However chewed upon. That's got to prove something."

"I guess."

I don't believe that we are what we do although many thinkers argue otherwise. I believe that what we do is, very often, a poor approximation of what we are—an imperfect manifestation of a much better totality. Even the best of us sometimes bite off, as it were, less than we can chew. When Natasha bites William she's saying only part of what she wants to say to him. She's saying, *William! Wake up! Remember!* But that gets lost in a haze of pain, his. I'm trying to help. I give her a paper bag of bagels and a plastic container of cream cheese with shallots to take to him, and for herself, an A&P check-cashing application with my approval already initialed in the upper right-hand corner. I pray that they will be successful together, eventually. Our organization stands behind them.

Bluebeard

"NEVER OPEN that door," Bluebeard told me, and I, who knew his history, nodded. In truth I had a very good idea of what lay on the other side of the door and no interest at all in opening it. Bluebeard was then in his forty-fifth year, quite vigorous, the malaise that later claimed him—indeed enfeebled him—not yet in evidence. When he had first attempted to put forward his suit, my father, who knew him slightly (they were both clients of Dreyer, the American art dealer), refused him admittance, saying only, "Not, I think, a good idea." Bluebeard sent my father a small Poussin watercolor, a study for *The Death of Phocion*; me he sent, with astonishing boldness, a black satin remarque nightgown.

Events progressed. My father could not bring himself to part with the Poussin, and in very short order Bluebeard was a fixture in our sitting room, never without some lavish gift—a pair of gold cruets attributed to Cellini, a cut-pile Aubusson fire-extinguisher cover. I admit I found him very attractive despite his age and his nose, the latter a black rocklike object threaded with veins of silver, a feature I had never before seen adorning a human countenance. The sheer energy of the man carried all before it, and he was as well most thoughtful. "The history of architecture is the history of the struggle for light," he said one day. I have latterly seen this remark attributed to the Swiss Le Corbusier, but it was first uttered, to my certain knowledge, in our sitting room, Bluebeard paging through a volume of Palladio. In fine, I was taken; I became his seventh wife.

"Have you tried to open the door?" he asked me, in the twelfth month of our (to that point) happy marriage. I told him I had not, that I was not at all curious by nature and was furthermore obedient to the valid proscriptions my husband might choose to impose vis-à-vis the governance of the household. This seemed to irritate him. "I'll know, you know," he said. "If you try." The silver threads in his black nose pulsated, light from the chandelier bouncing from them. He had at that time a project in view, a project with which I was fully in sympathy: the restoration of the south wing of the castle, bastardized in the eighteenth century by busybodies who had overlaid its Georgian pristinity with Baroque rickrack in the manner of Vanbrugh and Hawksmoor. Striding here and there in his big India-rubber boots, cursing the trembling masons on the scaffolding and the sweating carpenters on the ground, he was all in all a fine figure of a man—a thing I have never forgotten.

I spent my days poring over motorcar catalogues (the year was 1910). Karl Benz and Gottlieb Daimler had produced machines capable of great speed and dash and I longed to have one, just a little one, but could not bring myself to ask my husband (my ever-generous husband) for so considerable a gift. Where did I want to go, my husband would ask, and I would be forced to admit that *going somewhere* was a conception alien to our rich, full life at the castle, only forty kilometers from Paris, to which I was allowed regular visits. My husband's views on marriage—old-fashioned if you will—were not such as to encourage promiscuous wanting. If I could have presented the Daimler phaeton as a toy, something to tootle about the grounds in, something that enabled him to laugh at my inadequacies as a pilot of the machine (decimation of the rosebushes), then he might have, with a toss of his full, rich head of hair, acceded to my wish. But I was not that intelligent.

"Will you never attempt the door?" he asked one morning over coffee in the sunroom. He had just returned from a journey—he always returned suddenly, unexpectedly, a day or two before he had planned to do so—and had brought me a Buen Retiro white biscuit clock two meters high. I repeated what I had told him previously: that I had no interest in the door or what lay behind it, and that I would gladly return the silver key he had given me if his mind would be eased thereby. "No, no," he said, "keep the key, you must have the key." He thought for a moment. "You are a peculiar woman," he said. I did not know what he meant by this remark and I fear I did not take it kindly, but I had no time to protest or plead my ordinariness, for he abruptly left the room, slamming the door behind him. I knew I had angered him in some way but I could not for the life of me understand precisely how I had erred. Did he *want* me to open the door? To discover, in the room behind the door, hanging on hooks, the beautifully dressed carcasses of my six predecessors? But what if, contrary to informed opinion, the beautifully dressed carcasses of my six predecessors were not behind the door? What was? At that moment I became curious, and at the same time, one part of my brain contesting another, I contrived to lose the key, in the vicinity of the gazebo.

I had trusted my husband to harbor behind the door nothing more than rotting flesh, but now that the worm of doubt had inched its way into my consciousness I became a different person. On my hands and knees on the brilliant green lawn behind the gazebo I searched for the key; looking up I saw, in a tower window, that great black nose, with its veins of silver, watching me. My hands moved nervously over the thick grass and only the thought of the three duplicate keys I had had made by the locksmith in the village, a M. Necker, consoled me. What was behind the door? Whenever I placed my hands on it the thick carved oak gave off a slight chill (although this may have been the result of an inflamed imagination). Exhausted, I gave up the search; Bluebeard now knew that I had lost something and could readily surmise what it was—advantage to me, in a sense. At dusk, from a tower window, I saw him trolling in the grass with a horseshoe magnet dangling from a string.

I had taken care that the duplicate keys manufactured for me by M. Necker had also been coated with silver, were in every way exact replicas of the original, and could with confidence present one on demand if my husband required it. But if he had been successful in finding the one I had lost but concealed that fact (and concealment was the very essence of his nature), and I presented one of the duplicates as the original when the original lay in his pocket, this would constitute proof that I had reproduced the key, a clear breach of trust. I could, of course, simply maintain that I had in fact lost it—this had the virtue of being true—meanwhile concealing from him the existence of the counterfeits. This seemed the better course.

He sat that night at the dining table slicing a goose with a prune-and-foie-gras stuffing (taking the best parts for himself, I observed) and said without preamble, "Where do you meet your lover, Doroteo Arango?"

Doroteo Arango, the Mexican revolutionary leader known to the world as Pancho Villa, was indeed in Paris at that moment, raising funds for his sacred and just cause, but I had had little contact with him and was certainly not yet his lover although he had pressed my breasts and tried to insinuate his hand underneath my skirt at the meeting of 23 July at my aunt Thérèse Perrault's house in the Sixteenth at which he had spoken so eloquently. The strange Mexican spirit tequila had been served, golden in brandy snifters. I had not taken exception to his behavior, assuming that all Mexican revolutionary leaders behaved in this way, but he had persisted in sending me, hand-delivered by hard-riding vaqueros in Panhards, bottles of the pernicious liquor, one of which my husband was now waving in my face.

I told him I had purchased a few bottles to assist the cause, much as one might buy paper flowers from schoolchildren, and that Arango was a well-known celibate with a special devotion to St. Erasmus of Delft, the castrate. "You gave him my machine gun," Bluebeard said. This was true; the Maxim gun that usually rested in a dusty corner of the castle's vast attic had been transferred, under cover of night, to one of the Panhards not long before. I had a truly frightful time wrestling the thing down the winding stairs. "A loan only," I said. "You weren't using it and he is pledged to rid Mexico of Díaz's vile and corrupt administration by spring at the latest."

My husband had no love for the Díaz regime—held, in fact, a portfolio of Mexican railroad bonds of the utmost worthlessness. "Well," he growled, "next time, ask me first." This was the end of the matter, but I could see that his trust in me, not absolute in the best of seasons, was fraying.

My involvement with Père Redon, the castle's chaplain, was then, I blush to confess, at its fiery height. The handsome young priest, with his auburn locks and long, straight, white nose . . . It was to him that I had entrusted the three duplicate keys to the locked door and the eleven additional duplicate keys that I had caused to be made by the village's second locksmith, a M. Becque. Redon had hidden one key behind each of the Bronzino plaques marking the chapel's fourteen Stations of the Cross, and since the chapel was visited by my husband only at Christmas and Easter and on his own name day, I felt them safe there. Still, the cache of my letters that Redon kept in a small crypt carved out of the reverse side of the altar table worried me, even though he replastered the opening most skillfully each time he added a letter. The nun's habit that I wore during the midnight Sabbats organized by the notorious Bishop of Troyes, in which we, Redon and I, participated (my shame and my delight, my husband drunk and dreaming all the while), hung chastely in the same closet that held Constantin's Mass vestments—cassock and chasuble, alb and stole. The ring Constantin had given me, unholy yet cherished symbol of our love, remained in its tiny velvet casket on the altar itself, within the tabernacle, stuffed behind pyx, chalice, and ciborium. The chapel was in the truest sense a sanctuary, all thanks to a living and merciful God.

"You must open the door," Bluebeard said to me one afternoon at croquet—I had just hit his ball off into the shrubbery—"even though I forbid it." What was I to make of this conundrum?

"Dear husband," I said, "I cannot imagine opening the door against your wishes. Why then do you say I *must* open it?"

"I change the exhibit from time to time," he said, grimacing. "You may not find, behind the door, what you expect. Furthermore, if you are to continue as my wife, you must occasionally be strong enough to go against my wishes, for my own good. Even the bluest beard amongst us, even the blackest nose, needs on occasion the correction of connubial give-and-take." And he hung his head like a lycée boy.

"Very well then," I said. "Give me the key, for as you know I have lost mine."

He withdrew from his waistcoat pocket a silver key, and, leaving the game, I entered the castle and walked up the grand staircase to the third étage. Before I could reach the cursed portal, a house servant flourishing a telegram intercepted me. "For you, Madame," she said, all rosy and out of breath from running. The message read "930177 1886445 88156031 04344979" and was signed "EVERLAST." Coded of course, and the codebook far from me at this moment, recorded on fragile cigarette papers tightly rolled and concealed within the handlebars of my favorite yellow bicycle, "A" to "M" in the left handlebar, "N" to "Z" in the right handlebar, in the bicycle shed. "Everlast" was M. Grévy, the Finance Minister. What calamity was he announcing, and was he telling me to buy or sell? My entire fortune, as distinct from my husband's, rested upon the Bourse; Everlast's timely information, which had increased the value of my holdings in most satisfactory fashion, was vital to its continued existence. I'm finished, I thought; I'll wear rags and become secretary to a cat-seller. I longed to rush to the bicycle shed, yet my intense curiosity about the contents of the prohibited chamber exerted the stronger sway. I turned the key in the lock and plunged through the door.

In the room, hanging on hooks, gleaming in decay and wearing Coco Chanel gowns, seven zebras. My husband appeared at my side. "Jolly, don't you think?" he said, and I said, "Yes, jolly," fainting with rage and disappointment. . . .

Construction

I WENT to Los Angeles and, in due course, returned, having finished the relatively important matter of business which had taken me to Los Angeles, something to do with a contract, a noxious contract, which I signed, after the new paragraphs were inserted and initialed by all parties, tiresome business of initialing numberless copies of documents reproduced on onionskin, which does not feel happy in the hand. One of the lawyers wore a woven straw Western hat with a snake hatband. He had an excessive suntan. The hatband displayed as its centerpiece the head of a rattlesnake with its mouth stretched and the fangs touchable. Helen made a joke about it, she does something in the West Coast office, I'm not sure what it is but she is treated with considerable deference, they all seem to defer to her, an attractive woman, of course, but also one who manifests a certain authority, a quiet authority, had I had the time I would have asked someone what she was "all about," as we say, but I had to get back, one cannot spend all one's time in lawyers' offices in Los Angeles. Although it was January and there was snow, blizzarding even, elsewhere, the temperature was in the fifties and the foliage, the collection of strange-looking trees, not trees but something between a tree and a giant shrub, that distinguishes the city, that hides what is less prepossessing than the trees—I refer to the local construction—which serves as a screen or scrim between the eye and the local construction, much of it admirable no doubt, the foliage was successfully carrying out its function, making Los Angeles a pleasant, reticent, green place, which fact I noticed before my return from Los Angeles.

The flight back from Los Angeles was without event, very calm and smooth in the night. I had a cup of hot chicken noodle soup which the flight attendant was kind enough to prepare for me; I handed her the can of chicken noodle soup and she (I suppose, I don't know the details) heated it in her microwave oven and then brought me the cup of hot chicken noodle soup which I had handed her in canned form, also a number of drinks which helped make the calm, smooth flight more so. The plane was half empty, there had been a half-hour delay in getting off the ground which I spent marveling at a sentence in a magazine, the sentence reading as follows: "[Name of film] explores the issues of love and sex without ever being chaste." I marveled over this for the full half-hour we sat on the ground waiting for clearance on my return from Los Angeles, thinking of adequate responses, such as "Well we avoided *that* at least," but no response I could conjure up was equal to or could be equal to the original text which I tore out of the magazine and folded and placed, folded, in my jacket pocket for further consideration at some time in the future when I might need a giggle. Then deplaning and carrying my bag through the mostly deserted tunnels of the airport to the cab rank, I obtained a cab driven by a black man who was, he said, leaving the cab business to begin a messenger service and had that very morning taken delivery on a truck, a 1987 Toyota, for the purpose and was, as soon as his shift ended, going to not only show the 1987 Toyota to his mother but also pick up his car insurance. He asked me what I thought about the economy and I said that I thought it would continue to do well, nationally, for a time but that the local economy, by which I meant that of the whole region, would I thought not do as well, because of structural problems. He then told me a story about being in the jungle in Vietnam with a fellow who had been there for seventeen months and got a letter from his wife in which she announced that she was pregnant but (and I quote) "hadn't been doing anything," and that his colleague, in the jungle, had then gone crazy, and I said, "Seventeen months, what was he doing there for seventeen months?" the normal tour being one year, and he said, "He extended," and I said, "He extended?" and he said, "Yeah, extended," and I said, "*Then he was crazy before he got the letter*," and he said, "Bingo!" and we both said, "Hoo hoo," in healthy fashion. He dropped me off in front of my building and I went upstairs and made a thickish cup of Hot Spiced Cider from an envelope of Hot Spiced Cider Mix that I had acquired free when I bought the bottle of Tree Top Apple Cider that was in my refrigerator, and took off my tie, and sat there, in my house, on my return from Los Angeles.

I thought about the food that I had had in Los Angeles and about what I had to do next, the next day, the next several days, and of course about the long-range plan. I sat there in the darkened room without a shirt (I had taken off my shirt) thinking about the food I had had in Los Angeles, the rather ordinary Tournedos Rossini, the rather too down-to-earth Huevos Rancheros in a very expensive place that nevertheless presented its Huevos Rancheros on a *tin plate*, and its coffee in *cracked blue enamel mugs*, the Chuck Wagon was its name. Breakfast there with Helen, who had an air of authority, one could not immediately fathom its source and I was too tired, after a long night in Los Angeles, too tired or insufficiently interested, to ask the questions, either of her associates or my associates or of Helen directly, that would have allowed me to fathom the sources of her authority in Los Angeles, Los Angeles being to me a place where one went, of necessity, at rare intervals, to sign and/or initial or renegotiate whatever needed such attention. I noticed very little about the place, the shrubs or trees, saw a bit of the ocean from my hotel-room window, saw an old woman in a green bathrobe on the balcony of the building opposite, at the same level, the eleventh floor, and wondered if she was a guest or if she was one of those persons who clean the place; if she was one of those persons who clean the place it seemed unlikely that she would come to work in a green bathrobe and I am sure that she wore a green bathrobe, but she did not resemble a guest or tenant, she had a bent broken stooped losing-the-game look of the kind that defines the person who is not winning the game. Seldom am I in error about such things, the eidetic memory as we say, saw a figure of some kind possibly female atop the Mormon temple, the figure seemed to be leading the people somewhere, onward, presumably, saw several unpainted pictures on the street, from the windows of the limousine in which I was moved from place to place, Pietàs mostly, one creature holding another creature in its arms, at bus stops, mostly. Los Angeles.

I thought about sand although I saw no sand in Los Angeles, they told me that there were beaches in the vicinity; the bit of ocean I had seen from the window of my hotel room on Wilshire implied sand but I saw no sand during my not extensive stay in Los Angeles, where I signed various documents having to do with the long-range plan, which I sat thinking about in the dank without my shirt upon my return from Los Angeles. I mentally compared our city to Los Angeles, a competition in which our city was not found inferior, you may be sure, a weighing of values in which our city was not given short weight, you may be sure. In the matter of madhouses alone we surpass Los Angeles. To say nothing of our grand boulevards and taverns (where never, never would one be served Huevos Rancheros on a tin plate) and our excellent mayor who habitually meets the City Council with a Holy Bible clenched between his teeth. But I had no desire to get into a slanging match with the city of Los Angeles, in my mind, and so turned my mind to the problem at hand, the long-range plan.

I was considering the long-range plan, pressing upon me in all its immensity, the eight-hundred-and-seventy-six-million-dollar long-range plan for which I have been repeatedly criticized by my associates and by their associates and, who knows, by associates of the associates of my associates, with particular reference to the vast underground parking facility, when my mother telephoned to ask what the left-hand page of a book is called. My mother often calls me at two o'clock in the morning because she has trouble sleeping. "Recto," I said, "it's either recto or verso, I don't remember which is which, look it up, how are you?" My mother said that she was fine except for horrible nightmares when she did manage to get to sleep, horrible nightmares involving the long-range plan. I had taken the eight-hundred-and-seventy-six-million-dollar long-range plan home to show my mother some months previously, she studied the many-hundred-page printout and then announced that, very probably, it would give her nightmares. My mother is a disciple of Schumacher, the "small" man, a disciple of Mumford, a disciple (moving backward in time) of Fourier, and a disciple most recently of François Mitterrand, she wonders why we can't have a President like that, a real Socialist who also speaks excellent French. My mother is somewhat out of touch with present realities and feels that property is theft and feels that my father taught me the wrong things (although I feel that much of what my father taught me, in his quite bold and dramatic way, his quite bold and dramatic and let it be acknowledged self-dramatizing way, was of great use to me later—the épée, the leveraged buyout, Chapter 11—although had he really loved me he would have placed more stress, perhaps, on air conditioning, the manufacture, sale, installation, and maintenance of air conditioning). My problem with the long-range plan was not ethical, like my mother's, but practical: Why am I doing this?

It is not easy, it is not the easiest thing, to go through life asking this sort of question, this sort of poignant and noxious question that poisons and makes poignant (I detest poignancy!) one's every can of chicken noodle soup or cup of Hot Spiced Cider, afflicting equally morning, noon, and night (I sleep no better than my mother does), infecting calm seriousness and the will-to-win. *For America*, I say to myself, *for America*, and that works sometimes but sometimes it does not; *for America* is better than *because I can* and not as good, not as sweetly persuasive, as *movement of historical forces*, which is itself less convincing than either *what else?* or *why not?* Where in this, I ask myself, where in all this "construction" (and the vast underground parking facility alone will extend from here to St. Louis, or very near), where in all this is the (and we do not fail to notice, do not fail to notice, the constructive associations clustering about the word "construction," the hugely affirmative and congratulatory overtones clinging like busy rust to the word "construction") answer to the question, Why am I doing this?

What else? Why not?

There remained the mystery of Helen, whose moods, her aggressive moods, her fearful moods, her celebratory, resentful, and temporizing moods, remained to be plumbed, thoroughly plumbed. Thoroughness is the key to avoidance of noxious and life-ruining questions, perplexing, noxious, and life-ruining questions which threaten the delicate principle, construction. Construction is like a little boy growing up or an old man winding down or a middle-aged man floundering in the soup, where not infrequently I find that boiling lobster, myself. The spread (margarine, disease) of the physical surround can be like a spill of mixed motives or like an irruption of the divine (New Jerusalem, vast underground parking facility) or like decay in the sense of spoliation of an existing unshrubbed unbuilt swamp or Eden, these are the three categories under which construction may be subsumed, the word "subsumed" itself sounds like a soil test. But if one spends (and on the word "spend" I wish to dwell not at all) one's time thinking about these issues one loosens one's grasp on other issues, bond issues, for example, on leverage and the honest use of materials and density and building codes which vary fearfully from locality to locality and tax wrinkles and the golden section and 1% for art and 100% locations and cul-de-sacs and the Wiener Werkstätte and seals-and-cladding and fast skinning and cure of paints and the beveling of glass and how to clinch a nail and how to sleep well, at night, in the vast *marché aux puces* of my calling. . . .

The next day, pausing only to instruct my secretary, Rip, to throw our messenger business to Hubie the former cabdriver, who had given me his card, I flew back to Los Angeles to begin understanding the mystery of Helen.

Letters to the Editore

*T*HE EDITOR *of* Shock Art *has hardly to say that the amazing fecundity of the LeDuff–Galerie Z controversy during the past five numbers has enflamed both shores of the Atlantic, at intense length. We did not think anyone would care, but apparently, a harsh spot has been touched. It is a terrible trouble to publish an international art-journal in two languages simultaneously, and the opportunities for dissonance have not been missed. We will accept solely one more correspondence on this matter, addressed to our editorial offices, 6, Viale Berenson, 20144 Milano (Italy), and that is the end. Following is a poor selection of the recent reverberations.*

Nicolai PONT
Editore

SIRS:

This is to approximate a reply to the reply of Doug LeDuff to our publicity of 29 December which appeared in your journal and raised such possibilities of anger. The fumings of Mr. LeDuff were not unanticipated by those who know. However nothing new has been proved by these vapourings, which leave our points untouched, for the most part, and limp off into casuistry and vague threats. We are not very intimidated! The matters of substantial interest in our original publicity are scatheless. Mr. LeDuff clearly has the opinion that the readers of *Shock Art* are dulls, which we do not. Our contention that the works of Mr. LeDuff the American are sheer copyings of the work of our artist Gianbello Bruno can be sustained by ruthless scholarship, of the type that Mr. LeDuff cannot, for obvious reasons, bear to produce. But the recipient of today's art-scene is qualified enough to judge for himself. We need only point to the 1978 exposition at the Galerie Berger, Paris, in which the "asterisk" series of Bruno was first inserted, to see what is afoot. The Amercian makes the claim that he has been painting asterisks since 1975—we say, if so, where are these asterisks? In what collections? In what expositions? With what documentation? Whereas the accomplishment of the valuable Bruno is fully documented, by the facts and other printed materials, as was brought out in our original publicity. That LeDuff has infiltrated the collectors of four continents with his importunity proves nothing, so much so as to be dismissive and final.

Of course the fully American attitude of the partisans of LeDuff, that there is nothing except America, is evident here in the apparently fair evaluation of the protagonists which is in fact deeply biased in the direction of their native land. The manifestation of Mr. Ringwood Paul in your most recent number, wherein he points out (correctly) that the asterisks of LeDuff are six-pointed versus the asterisks of Bruno which have uniformly five points, is not a "knockout blow." In claiming severe plastic originality for LeDuff on this score, Mr. Paul only displays the thickness of entrenched opinion. It is easy, once one has "borrowed" a concept from another artist, to add a little small improvement, but it is not so easy to put it back again without anyone noticing! Finally, the assertion of the estimable critic (American again, we understand!) Paula Marx that the moiré effect achieved by both Bruno and LeDuff by the superimposition of many asterisks on many other asterisks is an advancement created by LeDuff alone and then adduced by Bruno, is flatly false. Must we use carbon-dating on these recent peintures to establish truth, as if we were archeologists faced with an exhausted culture? No, there are living persons among us who remember. To support this affair with references to the "idealism" of the œuvre of LeDuff is the equivalent of saying, "Yes, mostly his shirts are clean." But the clean shirt of LeDuff conceals that which can only throw skepticism on this œuvre.

Bernardo BROWN
H. L. AKEFELDT
Galerie Z
Milan

Sirs:

The whole thing is to make me smile. What do these Americans want? They come over here and everyone installs them in the best hotels with lavish napery, but still, complaints of every kind. Profiting unduly from the attentions of rich bourgeois, they then emplane once again for America, richer and thoughtful of coming again to again despoil our bourgeois. Doug LeDuff is a pig and a child, but so are his enemies.

Pino Vitt
Rome

Caro Nikki—

May I point out the facility of the LeDuff–Galerie Z debate that you have allowed to discolor your pages for many months now? Whether or not you were admirable in your decision to accept for publication the Galerie Z advertisings defaming LeDuff (whom I personally feel to be a monger of dampish wallpaper) is not for me to state, although you were clearly incredible, good faith notwithstanding. I can only indicate, from the womb of history, that both LeDuff and Bruno have impersonated the accomplishments of the Magdeburg Handwerker (May 14, 1938).

Hugo Timme
Düsseldorf

Sirs:

The members of the surface Group (Basel) are unfalteringly supportive of the immense American master, Doug LeDuff.

Gianni Arnan
Michel Pik
Zin Regale
Erik Zorn
Basel

EDITORE (if any)
Shock Art
MILANO

The most powerful international interests of the gallery-critic-collector cartel have only to gain by the obfuscations of the LeDuff–Galerie Z bickerings. How come you have ignored Elaine Grasso, whose work of now many years in the field of parentheses is entirely propos?

Magda BAUM
Rotterdam

SIRS:

Shock Art is being used unforeseeably in this affair. The asterisk has a long provenance and is neither the formulation of LeDuff nor of Bruno either, in any case. The asterisk (from the Greek *asteriskos* or small star) presents itself in classical mythology as the sign which Hera, enraged by yet another of Zeus's manifold infidelities, placed on the god's brow while he slept, to remind him when he gazed in the mirror in the morning that he should be somewhere else. I plead with you, Sig. Pont, to publish my letter, so that people will know.

G. PHILIOS
Athens

CARO PONT,

It was kind of you to ask me to comment on the good fight you are making in your magazine. A poor critic is not often required to consult on these things, even though he may have much better opinions than those who are standing in the middle, because of his long and careful training in ignoring the fatigues of passionate involvement—if he has it!

Therefore, calmly and without prejudice toward either party, let us examine the issues with an unruffled eye. LeDuff's argument (in *Shock Art* #37) that an image, once floated on the international art-sea, is a fish that anyone may grab with impunity, and make it his own, would not persuade an oyster. Questions of primacy are not to be scumbled in this way, which, had he been writing from a European perspective, he would understand, and be ashamed. The brutality of the American rape of the world's exhibition spaces and organs of art-information has distanciated his senses. The historical aspects have been adequately trodden by others, but there is one category yet to be entertained—that of the psychological. The fact that LeDuff is replicated in every museum, in every journal, that one cannot turn one's gaze without bumping into this raw plethora, LeDuff, LeDuff, LeDuff (whereas poor Bruno, the true progenitor, is eating the tops of bunches of carrots)—what has this done to LeDuff himself? It has turned him into a dead artist, but the corpse yet bounces in its grave, calling attentions toward itself in the most unseemly manner. But truth cannot be swallowed forever. When the real story of low optical stimulus is indited, Bruno will be rectified.

Titus Toselli DOLLA
Palermo

January

THE INTERVIEW took place, appropriately enough, on St. Thomas in the U.S. Virgin Islands. Thomas Brecker was renting a small villa, before which a bougainvillaea bloomed, on the outskirts of Charlotte Amalie. Brecker was wearing an orange-red tie with a light blue cotton shirt and seemed very much at ease. He has a leg brace because of an early bout with polio but it does not seem to inhibit his movement, which is vigorous, athletic. At sixty-five, he has published seven books, from Christianity and Culture *(1964) to, most recently,* The Possibility of Belief, *for which he won the Van Baaren Prize awarded annually by Holland's Groningen Foundation. While we talked, on a sultry day in June 1986, a houseboy attended us, bringing cool drinks on a brown plastic tray of the sort found in cafeterias. From time to time we were interrupted by Brecker's son Patrick, six, who seemed uncomfortable when out of sight of his father.*

INTERVIEWER

You were a journalist when you began, I believe. Can you tell us something about those years?

BRECKER

I wasn't much of a journalist, or I wasn't a journalist for very long, two or three years. This was on a small paper in California, a middle-sized daily, a Knight-Ridder paper in San Jose. I started out doing all the routine things, courts, police, city hall, then they made me the religion writer. I did that for two years. It was not a choice assignment, it was very much looked down upon, one step above being an obituary writer, what we called the mort man. Also, in those days it was very difficult to print anything that might be construed as critical of any given religion, even when you were dealing with the problems a particular church might be having. So many things couldn't be talked about: abortion, mental illness among the clergy, fratricidal behavior among churches of the same denomination. Now that's all changed.

INTERVIEWER

And that got you interested in religion.

BRECKER

Yes. It was very good experience and I'm grateful for it. I began to think of religion in a much more practical sense than I'd ever thought about it before, what the church offered or could offer to people, what people got from the church in a day-to-day sense, and especially what it did to the clergy. I saw people wrestling with terrible dilemmas, gay priests, ministers who had to counsel people against abortion when abortion was obviously the only sane solution to, say, the problem of a pregnant thirteen-year-old, women who could only be nurses or teachers when they felt they had a very powerful vocation for the priesthood itself—I came to theoretical concerns by way of very practical ones.

INTERVIEWER

You did your undergraduate work at UCLA, I remember.

BRECKER

Yes. In chemistry, of all things. My undergraduate degree was in chemical engineering, but when I got out there were no jobs so I took the first thing that was offered, which was this fifty-dollar-a-week newspaper thing in San Jose. So after working on the paper, I went back to the university and studied first philosophical anthropology and then religion. I ended up at the Harvard Divinity School. That would be the late forties.

INTERVIEWER

You did your dissertation with Tillich.

BRECKER

No. I knew him and of course he was of enormous importance to all of us. He was at Harvard until '62, I believe. He had an apartment on Chauncy Street in Cambridge, on the second floor, he used to have informal seminars at home, some of which I attended. But he wasn't my dissertation director, a man named Howard Cadmus was.

INTERVIEWER
Your dissertation dealt with acedia.

BRECKER
In the forties that sort of topic was more or less in the air. And of course it's interesting, that sort of sickness, torpor, one wonders how it arises and how it's dealt with, and it's real and it has a relation, albeit a negative one, to religion. The topic was maybe too fashionable but I still think the dissertation was respectable, a respectable piece of work if not brilliant.

INTERVIEWER
What was the burden of the argument?

BRECKER
The thesis was that acedia is a turning toward something rather than, as it's commonly conceived of, a turning away from something. I argued that acedia is a positive reaction to extraordinary demand, for example, the demand that one embrace the *good news* and become one with the mystical body of Christ. The demand is extraordinary because it's so staggering in terms of changing your life—out of the ordinary, out of the common run. Acedia is often conceived of as a kind of sullenness in the face of existence; I tried to locate its positive features. For example, it precludes certain kinds of madness, crowd mania, it precludes a certain kind of error. You're not an enthusiast and therefore you don't go out and join a lynch mob—rather you languish on a couch with your head in your hands. I was trying to stake out a position for the uncommitted which still, at the same time, had something to do with religion. I may have been right or wrong, it doesn't much matter now, but that's what I was trying to do.

Acedia refuses certain kinds of relations with others. Of course there's a concomitant loss—of being with others, intersubjectivity. In literature, someone like Huysmans exemplifies the type. You could argue that he was just a 19th Century dandy of a certain kind but that misses the point, which is that something brought him to this position. As ever, fear comes into it. I argued that acedia was a manifestation of fear and I think that's true. Here it would be a fear of the need to submit, of joining the culture, of losing that much of the self to the culture.

INTERVIEWER

The phrase "the need to submit"—you're consistently critical of that.

BRECKER

It has parts, just like anything else. There's a relief in submission to authority and that's a psychological good. At the same time, we consider submission a diminishment of the individual, a ceding of individual being, which we criticize. It's a paradox which has to do with competing goods. For example, how much of your own autonomy do you cede to duly constituted authority, whether civil or churchly? And this is saying you're not coerced. We pay taxes because there's a fairly efficient system of coercion involved, but how much fealty do you give a government which is very often pursuing schemes which you, as an individual, using your best judgment, consider quite mad? And how much submission to a church, quite possibly the very wrongheaded temporary management of a church, whether it's a local vestry with ten deacons of suspect intelligence or Rome itself? Christ tells us not to throw the first stone, and that's beautiful, but at some point somebody has to stand up and say that such-and-such is nonsense—which is equivalent to throwing stones.

On the other hand, how much value should be attached to individual being? I take a clue from the fact that we *are* individual beings, that we're constructed that way, we're unique beings. That's also the root of many of our problems, of course.

INTERVIEWER

You're well-known for critiques of contemporary religion, but also for what might be called an esthetic distaste for some aspects of modern religion.

BRECKER

If you're talking about television evangelism and that sort of thing, it's a waste of time to be critical. I begin speaking from the position that I'm a fool and an ignoramus, which is true enough and not just a rhetorical device, and having said that, I can also say that these performances give me very little to think about. There's so little content that there's almost nothing to talk about. A sociologist might profitably study the phenomenon but that's about it. You note the sadness in the fact that so many people draw some kind of nourishment from what is really a very thin version of religion. On the other hand, people like Harvey Cox, who speaks about "people's religion," by which I take him to mean religion in nontraditional forms or mixed traditions or even what might be called bastard forms, have a point too—it can't be disregarded, it has to be thought about. Not that Cox was talking about television specifically. He's thinking, after Tillich, about the theology of culture as a whole. His generosity is what's admirable, and I don't mean that as a way of saying that his thought is not.

INTERVIEWER

Still, the whole thing, the millions of people watching and mailing in their money, is an example of what you characterize as the need to submit.

BRECKER

It's that, certainly. But I'd rather talk about submission at the other end of the scale—say the Catholic bishops in regard to Rome, or St. Augustine, any of the classic saints, very strong figures, bending to what they think or feel to be the will of God. Here you have the most sophisticated people imaginable, people for whom religion has been a central concern all their lives, people who have in every sense earned the right to speak on this sort of question, and you find a joyous submission. The other end of the scale from what we were speaking of as the madness of crowds. That's got to be respected but at the same time it can be examined, because the final effect is precisely submission. What is to be said of this kind of very informed, very sophisticated submission? That it reflects a proper, even admirable humility? It does. Or is it an abdication of responsibility? It's that too, or can be.

INTERVIEWER

The question is one of degree, then. How much you give up.

BRECKER

The question is, rather, what is proper to man? The right way to proceed in regard to these matters can be argued in so many ways, and has been, that the individual can be forgiven for chucking the whole business, giving up religion entirely, and many people do. Still, the question remains. Is a particular position a reasoned position or is it rather a matter of personality, or even pride, the *non serviam*? If it is a reasoned position, how do you deal with the finitude of human reason? What should be trusted, reason or authority? Authority or the individual cast of mind?

INTERVIEWER

To get back to fear, why is it so central in your schema?

BRECKER

It has to do with the problem of finitude, of which fear is an aspect. A mind without limit would have no fear, not even the fear of death. There'd be nothing to fear. Death, for example, would be understood so perfectly that it could contain nothing that could perturb the mind. It's the kind of thing the Eastern religions aim at. Obviously, we'll never get there, to this kind of serenity, because of the limits of human understanding.

But we are most ingenious, most ingenious. One of the finest religious inventions is the concept of absolution. I fall into error, confess it, and you give me absolution, or somebody gives me absolution. That cleansing—itself a very human idea, the washing-away—is of interest. It prevents us from being worse and worse, from in some sense stewing in our own juices. It makes new directions possible. It's just a bloody marvelous conception, and there are others just as good, of which the idea of life after death is merely the first example. Life-after-death may be seen as coercive, or as providing hope, or as pure metaphor, or as absolute fact. What's the truth of the matter? I don't know.

INTERVIEWER

But people can get that from psychiatry, absolution. Admittedly, with greater difficulty.

BRECKER

And perhaps greater efficacy. But as an immediate thing, the fact of absolution is inspired. Although there's a downside to that too, in that it restores one to the ranks of the blessed and the idea of there being a class of persons whom we agree to call blessed is a bit worrisome. There's something psychologically worrisome about there being *the blessed*. I like better the notion that we are all sinners, from a psychological point of view. A sinner who knows himself to be a sinner is always tense, cautious, morally speaking.

INTERVIEWER

What influence would you say your books have had? What do you consider your audience?

BRECKER

Books are dealt with in different ways by professionals in a particular discipline and by ordinary readers. I try to write for both. Let's say I write a book, a book dealing with the kinds of things we've been talking about. And you sit down to read my book. But let's also say that you're a specialist and you turn at once to the index—more or less to see where my book originated, if that's the right word. And going through the index you note, say, references to Alfred Adler, Hannah Arendt, Martin Buber, Dostoevsky, Huizinga, Konrad Lorenz, Otto Rank, Max Weber, and Gregory Zilboorg. So you feel you've read my book or at least have a pretty good sense of where it's coming from, as people say nowadays. You might, with great courtesy, then skim the text in search of unfamiliar ideas, etc. etc. Or to see what I got wrong.

As for influence, I think it's very slight, tiny. I've yet to meet anyone who's been influenced in any important way by my books. I've met lots of people who want to argue particular points, which leaves me at a bit of a disadvantage. I'm not so much interested in resolving varying Christologies or in debating specific religious ideas, techniques of atonement, for example.

INTERVIEWER
Can you accept a disinterested objectivity as finally normative, in regard to historical Christianity?

BRECKER
I've never found a disinterested objectivity. You have to view each tradition in the context of its own historical particularity, and these invariably militate against what might be called a disinterested stance. Very often people establish validity through the construction of a criterion, or a series of criteria, which they then satisfy. The criteria can be very elaborate. It's a neat way of proceeding.

The "good news" is always an announcement of a reconciliation of the particular into the universal. I have a lifelong tendency not to want to be absorbed into the universal, which amounts to saying a lifelong resistance to the forms of religion. But not to religious thought, which I consider of the greatest importance. It's a paradox, maybe a fruitful one, I don't know. Looking at myself, I say, hubris, maybe, the sin of pride, again, but this feeling exists and at least I can look at it, try to understand it, try to figure out how widespread it is. That is, are there others who feel this way? Again a paradox, a movement toward the universal: I don't want to be the only one who wants to be out on a limb. Or I'm seeking validation from outside, etc. etc.

INTERVIEWER
On the question of—

BRECKER
Remember that I was the opposite of a charismatic figure, not a leader, not even a preacher. Perhaps because I had polio and was on crutches and all that. Polio might be said, by a shrink, to be the basis of my psyche in that it set me apart, involuntarily, and it may be that that apartness persisted, as a habit of mind. It would be curious if that accounted for my career, so-called. There are just too many variables to enable you to judge the quality of your own thought. Truth rests with God alone, and a little bit with me, as the proverb says.

Also, there's no progress in my field, there's adding-on but nothing that can truthfully be described as progress. Religion is not susceptible to *aggiornamento*, to being brought up to date, although in terms of intellectual effort the impulse is not shoddy either. It's one of the pleasures of the profession that you are always in doubt.

BRECKER

I think about my own death quite a bit, mostly in the way of noticing possible symptoms—a biting in the chest—and wondering, Is this it? It's a function of being over sixty, and I'm maybe more concerned by how than when. That's a . . . I hate to abandon my children. I'd like to live until they're on their feet. I had them too late, I suppose.

BRECKER

Heraclitus said that religion is a disease, but a noble disease. I like that.

BRECKER

Teaching of any kind is always open to error. Suppose I taught my children a little mnemonic for the days of the month and it went like this: "Thirty days hath September, April, June, and November, all the rest have thirty-one, except for January, which has none." And my children taught this to their children and other people, and it came to be the conventional way of thinking about the days of the month. Well, there'd be a little problem there, right?

BRECKER

I can do without certitude. I would have liked to have had faith.

BRECKER

The point of my career is perhaps how little I achieved. We speak of someone as having had "a long career" and that's usually taken to be admiring, but what if it's thirty-five years of persistence in error? I don't know what value to place on what I've done, perhaps none at all is right. If I'd done something with soybeans, been able to increase the yield of an acre of soybeans, then I'd know I'd done something. I can't say that.

UNCOLLECTED STORIES

Basil from Her Garden

A: In the dream, my father was playing the piano, a Beethoven something, in a large concert hall that was filled with people. I was in the audience and I was reading a book. I suddenly realized that this was the wrong thing to do when my father was performing, so I sat up and paid attention. He was playing very well, I thought. Suddenly the conductor stopped the performance and began to sing a passage for my father, a passage that my father had evidently botched. My father listened attentively, smiling at the conductor.

Q: Does your father play? In actuality?

A: Not a note.

Q: Did the conductor resemble anyone you know?

A: He looked a bit like Althea. The same cheekbones and the same chin.

Q: Who is Althea?

A: Someone I know.

Q: What do you do, after work, in the evenings or on weekends?

A: Just ordinary things.

Q: No special interests?

A: I'm very interested in bow-hunting. These new bows they have now, what they call a compound bow. Also, I'm a member of the Galapagos Society, we work for the environment, it's really a very effective—

Q: And what else?

A: Well, adultery. I would say that's how I spend most of my free time. In adultery.

Q: You mean regular adultery.

A: Yes. Sleeping with people to whom one is not legally bound.

Q: These are women.

A: Invariably.

Q: And so that's what you do, in the evenings or on weekends.

A: I had this kind of strange experience. Today is Saturday, right? I called up this haircutter that I go to, her name is Ruth, and asked for an appointment. I needed a haircut. So she says she has openings at ten, ten-thirty, eleven, eleven-thirty, twelve, twelve-thirty— On a Saturday. Do you think the world knows something I don't know?

Q: It's possible.

A: What if she stabs me in the ear with the scissors?

Q: Unlikely, I would think.

A: Well, she's a good soul. She's had several husbands. They've all been master sergeants, in the Army. She seems to gravitate toward N.C.O. Clubs. Have you noticed all these little black bugs flying around here? I don't know where they come from.

Q: They're very small, they're like gnats.

A: They come in clouds, then they go away.

A: I sometimes think of myself as a person who, you know what I mean, could have done something else, it doesn't matter what particularly. Just something else. I saw an ad in the Sunday paper for the C.I.A., a recruiting ad, maybe a quarter of a page, and I suddenly thought, It might be interesting to do that. Even though I've always been opposed to the C.I.A., when they were trying to bring Cuba down, the stuff with Lumumba in Africa, the stuff in Central America . . . Then here is this ad, perfectly straightforward, "where your career is America's strength" or something like that, "aptitude for learning a foreign language is a plus" or something like that. I've always been good at languages, and I'm sitting there thinking about how my résumé might look to them, starting completely over in something completely new, changing the very sort of person I am, and there was an attraction, a definite attraction. Of course the maximum age was thirty-five. I guess they want them more malleable.

Q: So, in the evenings or on weekends—

A: Not every night or every weekend. I mean, this depends on the circumstances. Sometimes my wife and I go to dinner with people, or watch television—

Q: But in the main—

A: It's not that often. It's once in a while.

Q: Adultery is a sin.

A: It is classified as a sin, yes. Absolutely.

Q: The Seventh Commandment says—
A: I know what it says. I was raised on the Seventh Commandment. But.
Q: But what?
A: The Seventh Commandment is wrong.
Q: It's wrong?
A: Some outfits call it the Sixth and others the Seventh. It's wrong.
Q: The whole Commandment?
A: I don't know how it happened, whether it's a mistranslation from the Aramaic or whatever, it may not even have been Aramaic, I don't know, I certainly do not pretend to scholarship in this area, but my sense of the matter is the Seventh Commandment is an error.
Q: Well if that was true it would change quite a lot of things, wouldn't it?
A: Take the pressure off, a bit.
Q: Have you told your wife?
A: Yes, Grete knows.
Q: How'd she take it?
A: Well, she *liked* the Seventh Commandment. You could reason that it was in her interest to support the Seventh Commandment for the preservation of the family unit and this sort of thing but to reason that way is, I would say, to take an extremely narrow view of Grete, of what she thinks. She's not predictable. She once told me that she didn't want me, she wanted a suite of husbands, ten or twenty—
Q: What did you say?
A: I said, Go to it.
Q: Well, how does it make you feel? Adultery?
A: There's a certain amount of guilt attached. I feel guilty. But I feel guilty even without adultery. I exist in a morass of guilt. There's maybe a little additional wallop of guilt but I already feel so guilty that I hardly notice it.
Q: Where does all this guilt come from? The extra-adulterous guilt?
A: I keep wondering if, say, there is intelligent life on other planets, the scientists argue that something like two percent of the other planets have the conditions, the physical conditions, to support life in the way it happened here, did Christ visit each

and every planet, go through the same routine, the Agony in the Garden, the Crucifixion, and so on . . . And these guys on these other planets, these lifeforms, maybe they look like boll weevils or something, on a much larger scale of course, were they told that they couldn't go to bed with other attractive six-foot boll weevils arrayed in silver and gold and with little squirts of Opium behind the ears? Doesn't make sense. But of course our human understanding is imperfect.

Q: You haven't answered me. This general guilt—

A: Yes, that's the interesting thing. I hazard that it is not guilt so much as it is inadequacy. I feel that everything is being nibbled away, because I can't *get it right*—

Q: Would you like to be able to fly?

A: It's crossed my mind.

Q: Myself, I think about being just sort of a regular person, one who worries about cancer a lot, every little thing a prediction of cancer, no I don't want to go for my every-two-years checkup because what if they find something? I wonder what will kill me and when it will happen, and I wonder about my parents, who are still alive, and what will happen to them. This seems to be to me a proper set of things to worry about. Last things.

A: I don't think God gives a snap about adultery. This is just an opinion, of course.

Q: So how do you, how shall I put it, pursue—

A: You think about this staggering concept, the mind of God, and then you think He's sitting around worrying about this guy and this woman at the Beechnut Travelodge? I think not.

Q: Well He doesn't have to think about every particular instance, He just sort of laid out the general principles—

A: He also created creatures who, with a single powerful glance—

Q: The eyes burn.

A: They do.

Q: The heart leaps.

A: Like a terrapin.

Q: Stupid youth returns.

A: Like hockey sticks falling out of a long-shut closet.

Q: Do you play?
A: I did. Many years ago.
Q: Who is Althea?
A: Someone I know.
Q: We're basically talking about Althea.
A: Yes. I thought you understood that.
Q: We're not talking about wholesale—
A: Oh Lord no. Who has the strength?
Q: What's she like?
A: She's I guess you'd say a little on the boring side. To the innocent eye.
Q: She appears to be a contained, controlled person, free of raging internal fires.
A: But my eye is not innocent. To the already corrupted eye, she's—
Q: I don't want to question you too closely on this. I don't want to strain your powers of—
A: Well, no, I don't mind talking about it. It fell on me like a ton of bricks. I was walking in the park one day.
Q: Which park?
A: That big park over by—
Q: Yeah, I know the one.
A: This woman was sitting there.
Q: They sit in parks a lot, I've noticed that. Especially when they're angry. The solitary bench. Shoulders raised, legs kicking—

A: I've crossed both major oceans by ship—the Pacific twice, on troopships, the Atlantic once, on a passenger liner. You stand out there, at the rail, at dusk, and the sea is limitless, water in every direction, never-ending, you think *water forever*, the movement of the ship seems slow but also seems inexorable, you feel you will be moving this way forever, the Pacific is about seventy million square miles, about one-third of the earth's surface, the ship might be making twenty knots, I'm eating oranges because that's all I can keep down, twelve days of it with thousands of young soldiers all around, half of them seasick— On the Queen Mary, in tourist class, we got rather good food, there was a guy assigned to our table who had known Paderewski, the great pianist who was also Prime Minister of

Poland, he talked about Paderewski for four days, an ocean of anecdotes—

Q: When I was first married, when I was twenty, I didn't know where the clitoris was. I didn't know there was such a thing. Shouldn't somebody have told me?
A: Perhaps your wife?
Q: Of course, she was too shy. In those days people didn't go around saying, This is the clitoris and this is what its proper function is and this is what you can do to help out. I finally found it. In a book.
A: German?
Q: Dutch.

A: A dead bear in a blue dress, face down on the kitchen floor. I trip over it, in the dark, when I get up at 2 A.M. to see if there's anything to eat in the refrigerator. It's an architectural problem, marriage. If we could live in separate houses, and visit each other when we felt particularly gay— It would be expensive, yes. But as it is she has to endure me in all my worst manifestations, early in the morning and late at night and in the nutsy obsessed noontimes. When I wake up from my nap you don't *get* the laughing cavalier, you get a rank pigfooted belching blunderer. I knew this one guy who built a wall down the middle of his apartment. An impenetrable wall. He had a very big apartment. It worked out very well. Concrete block, basically, with fibre-glass insulation on top of that and sheet-rock on top of that—
Q: What about coveting your neighbor's wife?
A: Well on one side there are no wives, strictly speaking, there are two floors and two male couples, all very nice people. On the other side, Bill and Rachel have a whole house. I like Rachel but I don't covet her. I could covet her, she's covetable, quite lovely and spirited, but in point of fact our relationship is that of neighborliness. I jump-start her car when her battery is dead, she gives me basil from her garden, she's got acres of basil, not literally acres but— Anyhow, I don't think that's much of a problem, coveting your neighbor's wife. Just speaking administratively, I don't see why there's an entire

Commandment devoted to it. It's a mental exercise, coveting. To covet is not necessarily to take action.

Q: I covet my neighbor's leaf blower. It has this neat Vari-Flo deal that lets you—
A: I can see that.

Q: I am feverishly interested in these questions.
Q: Ethics has always been where my heart is.
Q: Moral precepting stings the dull mind into attentiveness.
Q: I'm only a bit depressed, only a bit.
Q: A new arrangement of ideas, based upon the best thinking, would produce a more humane moral order, which we need.
Q: Apple honey, disposed upon the sexual parts, is not an index of decadence. Decadence itself is not as bad as it's been painted.
Q: That he watched his father play the piano when his father could not play the piano and that he was reading a book while his father played the piano in a very large hall before a very large audience only means that he finds his roots, as it were, untrustworthy. The father imagined as a root. That's not unusual.
Q: As for myself, I am content with too little, I know this about myself and I do not commend myself for it and perhaps one day I shall be able to change myself into a hungrier being. Probably not.
Q: The leaf blower, for example.

A: I see Althea now and then, not often enough. We sigh together in a particular bar, it's almost always empty. She tells me about her kids and I tell her about my kids. I obey the Commandments, the sensible ones. Where they don't know what they're talking about I ignore them. I keep thinking about the story of the two old women in church listening to the priest discoursing on the dynamics of the married state. At the end of the sermon one turns to the other and says, "I wish I knew as little about it as he does."

Q: He critiques us, we critique Him. Does Grete also engage in dalliance?

A: How quaint you are. I think she has friends whom she sees now and then.

Q: How does that make you feel?

A: I wish her well.

Q: What's in your wallet?

A: The usual. Credit cards, pictures of the children, driver's license, forty dollars in cash, Amex receipts—

Q: I sometimes imagine that I am in Pest Control. I have a small white truck with a red diamond-shaped emblem on the door and a white jumpsuit with the same emblem on the breast pocket. I park the truck in front of a subscriber's neat three-hundred-thousand-dollar home, extract the silver canister of deadly pest killer from the back of the truck, and walk up the brick sidewalk to the house's front door. Chimes ring, the door swings open, a young wife in jeans and a pink flannel shirt worn outside the jeans is standing there. "Pest Control," I say. She smiles at me, I smile back and move past her into the house, into the handsomely appointed kitchen. The canister is suspended by a sling from my right shoulder, and, pumping the mechanism occasionally with my right hand, I point the nozzle of the hose at the baseboards and begin to spray. I spray alongside the refrigerator, alongside the gas range, under the sink, and behind the kitchen table. Next, I move to the bathrooms, pumping and spraying. The young wife is in another room, waiting for me to finish. I walk into the main sitting room and spray discreetly behind the largest pieces of furniture, an oak sideboard, a red plush Victorian couch, and along the inside of the fireplace. I do the study, spraying the Columbia Encyclopedia, he's been looking up the Seven Years' War, 1756–63, yellow highlighting there, and behind the forty-five-inch RCA television. The master bedroom requires just touches, short bursts in her closet which must avoid the two dozen pairs of shoes there and in his closet which contains six to eight long guns in canvas cases. Finally I spray the laundry room with its big white washer and dryer, and behind the folding table stacked with sheets and towels already folded. Who folds? I surmise that she folds. Unless one of the older children, pressed into service, folds. In my experience they are unlikely to fold. Maybe the au pair. Finished, I tear a properly made out receipt from my receipt book and present it to the young wife. She scribbles her name in the appropriate space and hands it back to me. The house now stinks quite palpably but I know and she knows that the stench will dissipate in two to four hours. The young wife escorts me to the door, and, in parting, pins a silver medal on my chest and kisses me on both cheeks. Pest Control!

A: Yes, one could fit in in that way. It's finally a matter, perhaps, of fit. Appropriateness. Fit in a stately or sometimes hectic dance with nonfit. What we have to worry about.

Q: It seems to me that we have quite a great deal to worry about. Does the radish worry about itself in this way? Yet the radish is a living thing. Until it's cooked.

A: Grete is mad for radishes, can't get enough. I like frozen Mexican dinners, Patio, I have them for breakfast, the freezer is stacked with them—

Q: Transcendence is possible.

A: Yes.

Q: Is it possible?

A: Not out of the question.

Q: Is it really possible?

A: Yes. Believe me.

Edwards, Amelia

AMELIA EDWARDS was washing the dishes when she noticed that a dish that she had already washed had a tiny piece of spinach stuck to the back of it.

I am not washing these dishes well, she thought. I am not washing these dishes as well as I used to wash them.

Mrs. Edwards stopped washing the dishes, even though half of them remain unwashed in the sink. She dried her arms on a paper towel and went into the bedroom. She sat down on the bed. Then she stood up again and looked at the bed.

The bedspread had been placed on the bed in a somewhat sloppy manner. She thought: I am not making the bed as well as I used to.

She sat down on the bed again and stared at the floor. Then her eyes moved to the corner of the room near the closet. In the corner, in the place where the two walls met, there was a gray dustball the size of an egg.

I have not vacuumed this room correctly, she thought. Is it because I am thirty-eight now?

No. Thirty-eight is young, relatively.

I am young and vigorous. George is handsome and well paid. We are going to Hawaii in June.

I wonder if I should have a drink?

Mrs. Edwards went out to the kitchen and looked at the vodka bottle.

Then she looked at the plate with the bit of spinach stuck to the back. She scratched the spinach from the plate with her fingernail. She poured some vodka into a glass. She went to the refrigerator to get some ice cubes, but when she opened the door to the freezing compartment it came off in her hands.

Mrs. Edwards regarded the door to the freezing compartment, a rectangular piece of white plastic.

The door to the freezing compartment has come off, she thought.

She placed it on the floor next to the refrigerator. Then she moved a tray of ice cubes from the freezing compartment and made herself a vodka-tonic. The telephone rang. Mrs. Edwards did not answer it. She was sitting on the bed looking at her vodka-tonic. The telephone rang eleven times.

Perhaps I should listen to some music?

Mrs. Edwards arose and walked into the living room. She found an Angel record. "Don Giovanni Highlights," with Eberhard Wächter, Joan Sutherland, and Elisabeth Schwarzkopf. She placed the record on the turntable and switched on the amplifier. Then she sat down and listened to the music.

She remembered something she had read in the newspaper:

GIRL, 8, FOUND SLAIN

Mrs. Edwards drank some of her vodka-tonic. Then she noticed that something was wrong with the music. The turntable was slow. The music was dragging.

She got up and lifted the arm of the turntable to see if there was anything the matter with the needle. She scratched the needle with her finger. A scratching noise came out of the speakers. Behind the cabinet on which the turntable sat— between the back of the cabinet and the wall—there was a pair of black socks.

Black socks, she thought.

Mrs. Edwards turned off the amplifier and carried the black socks to the closet. She placed them in the dirty clothes hamper.

Take clothes to laundromat, she thought.

Then she went into the kitchen and made herself another vodka-tonic.

Which she did not drink. She placed the second vodka-tonic on the small table beside the big chair in the living room and looked at it.

I used to put lime juice in my vodka-tonics, she thought. Now I just put in the vodka and the tonic, and the ice. When did I stop putting in the lime juice? I remember buying limes, slicing limes, squeezing limes . . .

If we had had children, I could have interested myself in the problems of children.

I once won a prize for whistling with crackers in my mouth, she remembered. I whistled best. At a birthday party. When I was eight.

The telephone rang again. Mrs. Edwards did not answer it. Because she was afraid it was the Telephone Company calling about the telephone bill. The Telephone Company had already called once about the telephone bill. She had told the woman from the Telephone Company that she would send a check right away but had not done so.

The telephone bill is one hundred and twelve dollars, she thought.

I can pay it on the fifteenth. Or I can send them a check and forget to sign it. I have not done that for a long time. Probably that would work, at this time.

Mrs. Edwards drank some of the second vodka-tonic.

Do I not put the lime juice in because of the war? she wondered. The incredible war? Is that why I don't put the lime juice in?

Behind her—that is, behind the chair in which she was sitting—a large picture fell off the wall. There was a sound of glass breaking.

Mrs. Edwards did not turn around to look.

I never liked that picture. George liked that picture. Our taste in pictures differs. I like Josef Albers. George does not understand what Josef Albers is all about. Only I understand what Josef Albers is all about. Our tastes differ. I have not been courted properly in three years. It is ridiculous to have a reproduction of Marie Laurencin hanging in one's home. In the living room.

Once, I would have refused to have a reproduction of Marie Laurencin hanging in my home.

Not that she is bad. She is not bad at all. She is rather good, if one likes that sort of thing. Once, I would have fought about it. Tooth and nail.

She thought: A long time ago.

She thought: Did I remember to have photostats made, front and back, of the two checks for $16.22 each that the Internal Revenue Service says we didn't send in for the maid's Social Security for the first two quarters of 1970? That we did send? Because I have the cancelled checks?

No, I did not. I must take the check to the photostat place and have the photostats made front and back and then send them with a letter to the Internal Revenue Service.

I will not have another vodka-tonic. Because I have will power.

When I lived in the city I had a dog. I would go out and walk my dog at ten o'clock in the morning. I would see all the other people walking their dogs. We would smile at one another over our dogs.

If I have will power, why don't I take my anti-alcohol pills? Because I would rather drink.

Marie Laurencin had a good time. In life. Relatively. 1885–1956.

Am I a standard-issue American alcoholic housewife? Assembled by many hands, like a Rambler, like a Princess telephone?

But there is my love for the work of Josef Albers.

But perhaps every one of us has a wrinkle—kink would not be too strong a word—which enables us to think of ourselves as . . . Marginal differentiation, as they call it in George's business.

Three years.

Mrs. Edwards looked at her fingernails. There was a time, she thought, when I cared about my cuticles.

Mrs. Edwards thought about Duke Ellington. She knew everything about Ellington there was to know. She thought about Johnny Hodges, Harry Carney, Ivie Anderson, Tricky Sam Nanton, Ray Nance the fiddler, Jimmy Blanton. She thought especially hard about Barney Bigard. She thought about "Transblucency," "What Am I Here For?," and "East St. Louis Too-dle-oo." This music had made her happy, when she was young.

But the turntable—

I have done something wrong, she thought.

At this point, the water, which had been accumulating for many days, walked up the stairs from the basement and presented itself in the living room.

Living room, Amelia thought. What does that mean?

There is water on the floor of the *living room*.

Chagall is soft, she thought. All those floating lovers. Kissing above the rooftops. He has radically misperceived the problem.

The telephone rang but Mrs. Edwards did not answer it, because she knew the caller was a professional woman-terrorizer who was not very good at it: too tentative. She had talked to him before. His name was Fred.

I do not want to talk to Fred today.

Mrs. Edwards looked at herself and noticed that she had forgotten to put any clothes on. When she had gotten up, after George had left for the office. She was not wearing any clothes.

Then she went into the kitchen and washed the rest of the dishes. Very well, very well indeed. Very carefully. Nobody could object to the way she washed them, nobody in the whole world.

A Man

A FIREMAN woke up one morning to find that his left hand was gone.

My left hand! he thought.

Then he thought: This is going to be damned inconvenient.

The fireman cursed for a while. "God damn it! Jesus, Mary, and Joseph! God damn it to Hell! Bloody Hell! Dumb ass! Christ Almighty! Son of a bitch!"

But the stump is not bad-looking, he reflected. A neat separation. Not offensive to the eye.

He got out of bed and took a shower. Washing his right side, which he customarily did with his left hand, was difficult. It was also difficult to dry himself with one hand. Usually he took a large brown towel in both hands and zipped it back and forth across his back. But he discovered that one cannot zip a towel with one hand. One can only flop a towel with one hand.

Putting on socks with one hand is not easy. Shaving, however, presented no particular problems.

At the firehouse nobody said anything about the hand. Firemen are famously tactful and kind to each other. Harvey read *The New York Times* until there was an alarm. Then he put on his rubber coat and boots and climbed up on the engine in his regular place, second from left, in the back.

"No," the captain said.

"What do you mean, 'No'?"

"You can't go to the fire," the captain said. "You don't have any left hand."

"I can cradle the hose in my arms as one would a baby and pull it in the right direction!"

"Get down off there, Harvey. We're in a hurry."

Harvey stood in the empty firehouse.

My livelihood is threatened! he thought.

My livelihood!

And it wasn't even an on-the-job injury. It was, rather, a "mysterious occurrence." No compensation!

He sat down in a chair. He placed his fireman's hat on top of *The New York Times.*

I must face this problem intelligently. But what is intelligently? Prosthesis? Prosthetic device concealed under black glove? A green glove? A blue glove? The cops wear white gloves on traffic duty. But a man would be a fool to wear a white glove to a fire. A brown suede driving glove from Abercrombie—the Stirling Moss model? Probably there is such a thing in the world.

He got up and went to the place in the firehouse where the whiskey was hidden and had a shot, neat.

He thought: Why don't we buy better whiskey for the firehouse? This stuff tastes like creosote.

A twelve-year-old girl who hung around the firehouse a lot entered at this moment.

"Harvey," she said. "How come you aren't out on the run with the rest of the men?"

Harvey waved his stump in the air.

"What's with the hand?" the girl asked. "I mean, where is it?"

"It fell off, or something, last night, while I was sleeping."

"What do you mean, *fell off*? Was it in bed with you when you woke up? Or on the floor? Or under the bed?"

"It was just . . . missing."

"Man, that's *strange*," the girl said. "God, I mean that's *weird*. It gives me a funny feeling. Let's talk about something else." Then she paused. "Is there anything I can do? I could go out on your runs with you. Function as your extra hand, as it were." There was a look of childish eagerness in her eyes.

The fireman thought: This child is childish. But a good kid.

"Thank you, Elaine," he said. "But it wouldn't work. There'd be union problems and stuff." Delicately he avoided mentioning that she was a twelve-year-old girl.

"I've been studying the Civil Service exam for fire lieutenant," Elaine said, producing a study guide to the Civil Service examination for fire lieutenant published by Arco Publishing Co. "I know it backwards and forwards. Ask me anything. Just dip in anywhere and ask me anything. At random. I know the answers."

"Elaine," Harvey said, "would you mind letting me alone for a little while? I have to think about something."

Silently the little girl withdrew.

A hook? Harvey wondered.

The next day at the firehouse Harvey was playing chess with his friend Nick Ceci. He consciously made all his moves with his new artificial hand in its black glove. Every time Harvey moved, a lot of the pieces fell off the board. Nick said nothing. He just picked up the pieces off the floor and put them back in their proper places. The alarm bell rang.

Harvey climbed up on the back of the engine, second from left.

"Get down off there, Harvey. For God's sake," the captain said. "This is a serious business we're in, firefighting. Quit screwing around."

"But I have this new hand!"

"Yes, but it's no good," the captain replied. "I don't want to hurt your feelings, Harvey, but that hand is just a piece of junk."

"I paid two hundred and twelve bucks for it!"

"You got taken," the captain said. "I cannot risk the safety of my men on a possibly fallible plastic-and-metal hand which looks to me unsound and junky. I must use my best judgment. That is why I am captain, because I have good judgment. Now will you get your ass down from there and let us get out of here?"

Harvey hung up his rubber coat and went home to Staten Island. He spent some time looking at a picture of his mother, who was dead. In the picture his mother was reading a book.

I am a finished fireman, he thought. But yet, a human being, I have courage, resiliency—even hope. I will remold myself into something new, by reading a lot of books. I will miss firehouse life, but I know that other lives are possible—useful work in a number of lines, socially desirable activities contributing to the health of the society . . .

The fireman told himself a lot more garbage of this nature.

Then he told himself some true things:

(1) Women do not like men with one hand as much as they like men with two hands.

(2) His fake hand was a piece of expensive junk, like a gold jeweled bird that could open its mouth and sing, and also tell the time.

(3) He had only $213.09 in the bank, after having paid for the hand.

(4) God had taken his hand away for a reason, because God never does anything mindlessly, appearance notwithstanding.

(5) God's action *in re* the hand could only be regarded as punitive. It could hardly be regarded as a reward or congratulations.

(6) Therefore he, Harvey Samaras, either had done something wrong or, more specifically, *been* something wrong.

(7) His mother was dead. His father was dead. All his grandmothers and grandfathers were dead, as were his uncles, aunts, and cousins.

(8) He had never had the guts to marry anybody, although Sheila had wanted to get married.

(9) No children were his.

(10) Reading a lot of books would solve nothing.

(11) As he had grown older he had become less brave. That time at the P.S. 411 fire . . .

(12) In essence, he had failed to improve. He had failed to become a better man.

(13) There were mitigating circumstances—his very poor education, for example.

(14) Having a gold jeweled bird that could open its mouth and sing and also tell the time was in no sense as good as having an ordinary left hand.

(15) He did not know what he had done wrong. But he knew that a better man would have, somehow, done better.

(16) But how?

(17) How does that arise, that condition of being a better man?

(18) Reading a lot of books?

(19) But to be honest, he did not want to be a better man. All he wanted to do was drink and listen to music.

(20) He did not love anybody, really.

(21) No one loved him, particularly. Nick Ceci was friendly but probably that was just his nature, to be friendly.

(22) We are all replaceable parts, like a bashed-in fender on a

Maverick. His left hand was a replaceable part of an organism that was itself replaceable.

(23) His death, his own death, would not be noticed by the world, would not make the slightest difference to the world.

(24) He would live anyhow.

(25) Poorly.

Tickets

I HAVE decided to form a new group and am now contemplating the membership, the prospective membership, of my new group. My decision was prompted by a situation that arose not long ago vis-à-vis the symphony. We say "the symphony" because there is only one symphony orchestra here, as opposed to other cities where there are several and one must distinguish among them. The situation had to do with an invitation my wife received from Barbet, the artist, to attend the symphony with him on the evening of the ninth of March.

My wife, as it happened, was already planning to attend the performance of the ninth of March with her friend Morton. Barbet had extra tickets and wanted my wife to join his group and was gracious enough to enlarge his invitation to include my wife's friend, Morton. My wife could join his group, Barbet said, and took special pains to make clear that this invitation extended to Morton also. My wife responded, with characteristic warmth, with a counter-invitation, saying that she already had tickets for the ninth of March including extra tickets, that Barbet was most welcome to join her group, the group of my wife and Morton, and that the members of Barbet's group were also most welcome to join my wife's group, the group consisting, at that moment, of herself and Morton. My wife had previously asked me, with the utmost cordiality, if I wished to go to the symphony with her on the ninth of March, despite being fully apprised of my views on the matter of going to the symphony.

I had replied that I did not care to join her at the symphony on the occasion in question, but had inquired, out of politeness, what the program was to be, although my wife is fully aware that my views on the symphony will never change. My views on the symphony are that only the socially malformed would choose to put on a dark suit, a white shirt, a red tie, and so on, black shoes, and so on, and go to the symphony, there to sit pinned between two other people, albeit one of them one's own warm and sweet-smelling wife, for two hours or more, listening to music that may very well exist, in equally knowing and adroit performances, in one's own home, on records. That is to say that such people, the socially malformed (my wife, of course, excepted), go to the symphony out of extramusical need, clear extramusical need. But because of the raging politeness that always obtains between us I asked her what the program was to be on the ninth of March, and she told me that it was to be an all-Laurenti evening.

Laurenti is a composer held in quite high esteem hereabouts, perhaps less so elsewhere but of that I cannot judge, he is attached to the symphony as our composer-in-residence. It was to be, she told me, an all-Laurenti performance with just a bit of Orff by way of curtain-raiser, the conductor of the symphony, Gilley, which he pronounces "Gil-lay," having decided that Orff would make an appropriate, even delicious, curtain-raiser for Laurenti. While I am respectful of Laurenti's tragedy, what is called in some circles Laurenti's tragedy— that he has not a shred of talent of any description—still the prospect of sitting tightly wedged between two other human beings for the length of an all-Laurenti evening would have filled me with dismay had I not been aware that the invitation from my wife was perfectly pro forma. It appears that Gilley is sleeping with Mellow the new first-desk cellist, who sits at the head of the cellos with her golden cornrows, or so it is said at the Opera-Cellar, where I have a drink from time to time, especially often during the rather hectic period when my wife was both chairperson of the Friends of French Art Fandango and head whipper-in for the Detached Retina Ball.

It could be relied upon that Barbet, being an artist, would respond with enthusiasm to the notion of yet another disastrous all-Laurenti evening, possibly with the idea of mocking Laurenti behind his hand, although Barbet, as an artist, would not literally mock Laurenti behind his hand but rather in speech, or ironic speech rotten with wit. Barbet, being an artist of a particular kind, no doubt feels that a mocking attitude is appropriate to an artist of his kind, known not only hereabouts but in much larger cities, cities with two and even three distinct symphony orchestras, not even counting a Youth Symphony or one maintained by the Department of Sanitation. Barbet's reputation rests, not unimpressively, upon his "Cancellation" paintings—or simply "cancellations," in the language of his métier—a form he is believed to have invented and in which he displays his rotten wit along with the usual exhausting manual dexterity. The "cancellations" are paintings in which a rendering of a well-known picture, an Edvard Munch, say, has superimposed on it a smaller, but yet not small, rendering of another but perhaps not so well known picture, an El Lissitzky, say, for example the "Untitled" of 1919–20, a rather geometrical affair of squares and circles, reds and blacks, whose impetuses not only contest, contradict, the impetuses of the Munch, the Scandinavian miserablism of the Munch, but effectively *cancel* it, an action one can see taking place before one's eyes. I must say in his defense (because what Barbet is doing, has been doing all his life as a painter, is fundamentally indefensible), I must say in Barbet's defense that the contestation between the two paintings he has chosen to superimpose, one on the other, is of a very high order, is of substantial visual interest just *as paint*, and that the way the historically unrelated paintings relate to each other *as forms or collections of forms* is a value in addition to the value one awards the destructive act that is the soul of Barbet's painting, as much as the decayed wit displayed in titling these things "Improved Painting #1," "Improved Painting #2," "Improved Painting #19"—all these values must be taken into account in deciding whether or not Barbet should be shot, on the basis of ill will. But because Barbet is one of our few, our very few, genuine artists, we embrace him. This is not to say that the work of many other painters not our own is not similarly indefensible and that they, too, from a strictly construed moral-aesthetic standpoint, should not be shot. There are forty-four examples of Barbet's work in the museum, I refer to our quite grand local museum, in which my wife's family's money has had quite an important role over the years; it can be imagined how much I detest the phrase "provincial museum" but there is no other way of describing the place, which is, of course, quite grand, with its old part done in the classical mode and its new part done in a mode that respects the classical mode to the point of being indistinguishable from the classical mode but is also fresh, new, contemporary, and ironic.

This Morton who has been my wife's friend for ten years at least, who is forever calling her on the telephone so that I have come to recognize his voice although I have never met him—I recognize not only his voice but the characteristic pause before he asks if my wife is there, the freighted pause, I recognize that and say yet, Morton, just a moment, I'll see if she's in—this Morton, on the other hand, is a singer, and thus has no irony. He has, however, a legitimate interest in the symphony, as well as a truly frightening voice, easily recognized, a bass voice of remarkable color and strength, and patina; it is not wrong to add "patina" since this Morton is a man of a certain age, not old in any sense, but not young either, and of course not new to my wife, whose constant companion he has been for the past ten years. Morton does not go to the symphony or to musical occasions of any sort merely to make jokes or scoff behind his hand. And considered in the light of the possible attendance of someone like Morton, a sage and well-tempered listener, even some of Laurenti is perhaps worth hearing, the "Songs" perhaps, which draw from reviewers notices that begin "Among the best, perhaps, of this fluent but uneven composer's efforts are the 'Songs.'" I must tell you that last night I slept with my wife, I use the term "slept with" in the sense of congress, it was four-fifteen in the morning and I awoke with an itch to sleep with my wife, who was sleeping beside me as she has every night for the past fifteen years or thereabouts. My wife appeared to me to be a young person, that was interesting, I of course have no idea how I appeared to her but she appeared to me to be a young person and together after arduous endeavor we achieved quite sublime heights of sexual communion, such as one does not often achieve, we achieved that, at about four-fifteen in the morning, last night, the children sleeping soundly, the dog awake, she said in the morning, "Good morning, sexy boy."

It is the case that Barbet actively dislikes Morton, whereas Morton is absolutely indifferent to Barbet. Morton acts upon Barbet like a rug that makes you ill, a rug that is your own rug, clean, in good condition, not frayed or stained, but suddenly looking at the rug you are made ill, a wind around the heart, looking at the gray, green, and yellow rug, with its melon-shaped figure, purchased, yes, at Klecksel's, where the very best recent rugs, V'Soke and the like, are to be found (as well as both Klecksel and Jeri, his girlfriend, yes, even Klecksel has a girlfriend, so bounteous/fortunate are the times, even Klecksel has a girlfriend and the two are always at the symphony, or at the opera, or at the ballet, giving one very odd feelings, in that the person who sells you rugs, whom you regard as a rug person, someone who swims into your ken when rugs are an issue, and then swims out again when the issue has been resolved, must also be regarded as part of a social pair on quite another plane, and not just part of a social pair but part of a set of *new lovers*, God help us all), illness ensues. Morton is a very fine singer, a bass with the opera, where he sings Hunding in "Die Walküre," Méphistophélès in "La Damnation de Faust," etc. I find a slightly nasal quality to his singing, but perhaps I am imagining it. He is a handsome fellow, of course, my wife's self-regard would not allow her to be seen out with anyone who is not a handsome fellow. The nose is quite large but there is, I suppose, no necessary connection between the quite large nose and the slightly nasal quality he brings to Hunding or Méphistophélès or Abul in "Der Barbier von Baghdad," the last a role in which his comic flair, what is called in the newspaper his comic flair, is employed to great advantage. I have seen him many times at the opera (which offers something for the eye as opposed to the symphony where one can watch the kettledrums going out of tune) and have found his performances juicy and his comic flair endurable and have chosen him as a member of my new group, an honor he may, of course, decline.

My group will be unlike any existing group, will exist in contradistinction to all existing groups, over against all existing groups, will be in fine an anti-group, given the ethos of our city, the hysterical culture of our city. My new group will contain my wife, that sugarplum, and her friend Morton and a Gypsy girl and a blind man and will take its ethos from the car wash. My new group will march along the boulevards shouting "Let's go! Let's go!" with the enthusiasm of the young men at the car wash who are forever shouting "Let's go! Let's go!" to inspirit their fellows, if there is a moment of quiet at the car wash someone will take up the cry "Let's go! Let's go!" and then others will take up the cry "Let's go! Let's go!" shouting "Let's go! Let's go!" over and over, as long as the car wash washes.

CHRONOLOGY

NOTE ON THE TEXTS

NOTES

Chronology

1931 Born Donald Barthelme, Jr., on April 7 in Philadelphia, Pennsylvania, the first child of Helen Bechtold and Donald Barthelme, Sr. (Helen Bechtold [1907–1995], a Philadelphia native, was a teacher, writer, and aspiring actress. Donald, Sr. [1907–1996], the son of a prominent lumberyard owner in Galveston, Texas, was an architecture student at the University of Pennsylvania, where he met Helen, and went on to become a demanding and outspoken champion of modernist architecture, an acolyte of Mies van der Rohe, Eero Saarinen, and Le Corbusier. His aesthetic greatly influenced Donald, Jr., with whom he nevertheless quarreled frequently. Helen and Donald, Sr., married in June 1930, and after graduation he went to work for a Philadelphia architecture firm that also employed Louis Kahn. Helen put aside a career of her own and devoted herself to raising a family, which eventually included five children, all of whom became writers of one sort or another.)

1932 Family moves to Galveston, where father, unable to find an architecture job in Philadelphia, works for grandfather's lumberyard. Sister Joan is born.

1937 Family moves to Houston, where father joins the architecture firm of John F. Staub. Starts classes at St. Anne's School, run by the Basilian order of the Catholic Church. Along with the conventional subjects, Donald's brothers later recall, it also teaches guilt.

1939 Brother Peter born. Father, about to go into business for himself, builds house of his own design in the new West Oaks neighborhood on the suburban edge of Houston. A low, flat-roofed, copper-clad rectangle with irregular projections, it's so unusual that it becomes a kind of tourist attraction. On Sundays, Donald later recalls, people would park their cars out front and stare, and sometimes the family would come out and do high kicks in a chorus line. Inside, the place is a constant remodeling project. The furniture is Aalto, Eames, and pieces designed by Donald, Sr., and then built by the children.

1943 Brother Frederick born. Starts classes at St. Thomas Catholic High School, also run by the Basilians, where he is an indifferent student but excels at writing. Begins reading *The New Yorker* and decides he wants to write for it someday. Becomes interested in jazz and takes up the drums. Plays so often and so loudly that both the family and the neighbors begin to complain.

1947 Brother Steven born. Accused of plagiarism by a teacher who says his papers are too good for a high-school student. Probably for this reason, also denied the editorship of the school paper, *The Eagle*.

1948 Wins awards for poetry and short stories but, still angry at losing the editorship, leaves school one afternoon in February and hitchhikes to Mexico City with a friend. Tracked down by angry father and grandfather and brought back to Houston, where he refuses to continue attending St. Thomas. Transfers to Mirabeau B. Lamar High, a public school in the wealthy River Oaks neighborhood, where he again distinguishes himself with his writing. Begins smoking and drinking and going on joyrides in his father's white Corvette.

1949 Graduates from Lamar and, against father's objections, joins a small jazz band that tours East Texas. In September enrolls at the University of Houston, where his father is now a professor in the architecture department. Studies journalism and begins writing for the college newspaper, the *Daily Cougar*.

1951 Though only a sophomore, becomes editor of the *Cougar*, youngest student ever to hold that post; also begins Sunday drama column for the Houston *Post*. Argues with father again, leaves home, and with three friends moves into a dilapidated house in a scrappy neighborhood, across from a burger joint.

1952 Marries Marilyn Marrs, a graduate student working on a degree in French literature at Rice, and they move into an apartment in downtown Houston. While still attending classes at the university, works on the night desk at the *Post* and has regular beat reviewing movies, plays, and concerts.

1953 Drafted into the army and assigned to the 37th Infantry Division, based at Camp Polk in Ohio. After basic training, reassigned to Fort Lewis, in Tacoma, Washington, and then ordered to Korea, where he arrives on July 27, the day the armistice agreement ending the war is signed. Army wants to send him to baking school, but he wangles a spot in the Public Information Office at Division Headquarters, near the Korean town of Chorwon. Begins writing what he calls "The Great American Novel," which has since disappeared.

1954 Promoted to corporal. Visits Tokyo, where he hangs out at jazz clubs and visits brothels. Transferred to Seoul, and then, having been put on reserve status (as he remains for the next six years), returns to Houston.

1955 Re-enrolls at the University of Houston and takes up his old arts beat at the *Post*. Marriage grows distant, partly because of the long separation and his frequent drinking. In a Restoration drama course, meets Herman Gollob, a fellow Texan and Korean War vet, who becomes a lifelong friend and later, an editor at Little, Brown, publishes Barthelme's first book. Leaves Marrs and with Gollob and two friends rents a run–down Charles Addams-ish house downtown. Becomes protégé of Maurice Natanson, a professor at the university, who instills in him a lasting love of philosophy, Kierkegaard especially.

1956 Hired by the public relations department at the University of Houston and put in charge of *Acta Diurna*, the faculty newsletter, which he renames *Forum* and transforms into a full-fledged weekly arts magazine. Seeks out and publishes work of up-and-coming writers such as Norman Mailer, Walker Percy, and William Gass. In October, divorces Marilyn Marrs and a week later marries Helen Moore, a former journalism student at the university, whom he has known for years and who now works at a Houston ad agency. At a newsstand discovers the work of Samuel Beckett, who becomes a transformative influence on his own writing.

1957 Helen suffers series of miscarriages, which leave her and Barthelme bereft. Begins quarreling with the board of *Forum*, which resists many of his editorial innovations, arguing that he is assuming "too much interest, background, and mental acuteness on the part of *Forum*'s readers."

1960 Fed up, he resigns from *Forum*. Works on fiction and helps Helen design ads for her agency. Joins board of the Contemporary Arts Association, for which he organizes

	exhibitions, writes catalogue copy, and arranges poetry readings and stagings of innovative theater.
1961	Becomes part-time director of the CAA's art museum, and in May visits New York City for the first time, to attend a writers' conference at Wagner College on Staten Island. Meets Lynn Nesbit, a young agent at the Sterling Lord Agency, who agrees to represent him.
1962	Recruited by the art critic Harold Rosenberg to become the managing editor of *Location*, an avant-garde arts magazine starting up in New York, resigns from the CAA and moves to Manhattan, while Helen remains at her job in Houston. Visits jazz clubs almost nightly, attends art-world parties, becomes passionate moviegoer. Helen takes temporary leave from her job but can't adjust to New York, and they agree to separate. By now, drinking so much that people have begun to notice.
1963	Becomes romantically involved with Nesbit, who sells one of his stories to *Harper's Bazaar*. Moves into rent-controlled apartment on West 11th Street near Sixth Avenue, which will become his permanent New York address. Sells first story to *The New Yorker*, "L'Lapse," a parody of Antonioni movies, and begins long friendship with Roger Angell, one of the fiction editors there, who champions his work against the objections of several colleagues. Wins a crucial admirer in William Shawn, the editor-in-chief, and in midsummer signs agreement giving the magazine first look at everything he writes.
1964	*Location* folds after just two issues. Turns to writing full-time, and in April publishes first book, the story collection *Come Back, Dr. Caligari*, which is warmly reviewed for the most part and sells out its modest advance. At Christmastime travels to Denmark, where he visits Kierkegaard's grave and meets and falls in love with Birgit Egelund-Peterson, daughter of a science professor. Writes Helen and suggests divorce.
1965	Meets new downstairs neighbors at West 11th Street, Kirkpatrick Sale, a writer, and wife Faith, a book editor, and begins long friendship. Travels with Birgit in Europe and then splits time between rented flat in Copenhagen and a small farm owned by her family. In October, returns to

	New York with Birgit, now pregnant. Daughter Anne born November 4.
1966	Wins Guggenheim Fellowship.
1967	*The New Yorker* devotes most of its February 18 issue to "Snow White," a novel by Barthelme that is a retelling of the Grimm brothers' fairy tale with some Disney thrown in. Published in book form a month later, it becomes an unlikely best seller and one of the most talked-about novels of the year. Has brief affair with Grace Paley, a Greenwich Village neighbor. Drinking more than ever.
1968	Splits time between New York and Denmark as marriage begins to unravel, in part because Birgit is in the early stages of Huntington's disease, suffering memory lapses and unpredictable bouts of sadness or anger. Nor does his drinking help. Publishes collection *Unspeakable Practices, Unnatural Acts*.
1970	Beset by money problems, taking on most of the child care, nevertheless publishes *City Life*, one of his strongest collections, in which many of the pieces are collages of a sort, illustrated by engravings cut from old books. It's chosen as an alternate Book of the Month Club selection, an honor that Barthelme at first tries to decline.
1971	Birgit hospitalized for a drug overdose, and after recovering she and Barthelme separate. Publishes a children's book, *The Slightly Irregular Fire Engine, or the Hithering, Thithering Djinn*, which wins the National Book Award for children's literature.
1972	Birgit moves back to Denmark, leaving Anne with Barthelme. Begins affair with Marianne Frisch, wife of the Swiss novelist Max Frisch. Also has affair with Karen Kennerly, a writer and, later, executive director of PEN, who at the time is dating Miles Davis. Publishes *Sadness*, a more personal collection, with fewer collage elements. Receives Zabel Award for achievement in writing from the American Academy of Arts and Letters. Becomes romantically involved with Marion Knox, a reporter-researcher at *Time* magazine, whom he meets while shopping at the Jefferson Market. Teaches writing at SUNY Buffalo. With Mark Mirsky, starts *Fiction* magazine, a tabloid devoted to experimental writing.

1973	Divorces Birgit Egelund-Peterson. Teaches writing at Boston University.
1974	Publishes collection *Guilty Pleasures*. Becomes visiting distinguished professor at City College of New York.
1975	Publishes *The Dead Father*, a novel in extended dialogue form, about a son trying to dispose of a giant, monumental parent. It's chosen by *The New York Times Book Review* as one of the best books of the year.
1976	Publishes *Amateurs*, fourth book in four years. Considered by some a lesser effort than *Sadness* and *City Life*, nevertheless receives generally warm reviews.
1978	Marries Marion Knox and the couple honeymoons in Barcelona.
1979	Inducted into the American Academy of Arts and Letters. Publishes collection *Great Days*, in which many of the stories are dialogues, stripped of the usual Barthelmesque flourishes. Does six-week stint filling in for Pauline Kael as *The New Yorker*'s film critic.
1980	Publishes *Sixty Stories*, an anthology of what he considers his best published work, which is enthusiastically received.
1981	In need of money, accepts one-year appointment to teach creative writing at the University of Houston. Begins living half of the year there and half in New York.
1982	Daughter Katherine born January 13. Awarded tenure at the University of Houston and made head of the creative writing department, where he quickly establishes himself as a beloved and influential teacher and an energetic and inspiring administrator.
1983	In New York, where he still returns every summer, convenes what comes to be known as the Postmodern Dinner. The guest list includes Thomas Pynchon (who fails to show up), John Barth, William Gaddis, Robert Coover, John Hawkes, Kurt Vonnegut, Walter Abish, and Susan Sontag. Publishes *Overnight to Many Distant Cities*, story collection interlarded with short interchapters.
1984	Birgit Egelund-Peterson commits suicide in Copenhagen.
1986	Helps organize 48th International PEN Conference in New York, which ends in acrimony all around. Publishes

Paradise, a novel about a divorced architect who finds himself sleeping with three lingerie models. Gets mixed response, and even Barthelme himself is ambivalent about it.

1987 Publishes *Forty Stories*, another anthology of previously published work, and, in collaboration with the artist Seymour Chwast, *Sam's Bar*, an illustrated book of made-up bar conversations.

1988 Hospitalized for throat cancer, undergoes surgery and radiation. Gives up drinking and smoking. Receives Rea Award for the Short Story.

1989 Awarded fellowship by the American Academy in Rome, finishes draft of *The King*, a novel that will be published posthumously. In early June is hospitalized again with a recurrence of throat cancer; drifts in and out of lucidity. Slips into a coma and dies on June 23.

Note on the Texts

This volume prints the texts of seven complete short story collections by Donald Barthelme published from 1964 to 1983, along with twenty-three stories first published in book form in Barthelme's retrospective collections *Sixty Stories* (1981) and *Forty Stories* and four additional stories that were uncollected during Barthelme's lifetime.

Barthelme took great care in preparing his story collections, which extended even to the selection of cover art. The ordering and presentation of the stories in these volumes were not haphazard or casual and express his authorial intentions for each collection. For this reason, although Barthelme later revised some of the stories after their first book publication, the texts printed here are uniformly those of the first American book publications, printed as they appeared in these volumes. The list below provides publication information for each of the story collections organized by first book publication, listing for each story its prior periodical publication and subsequent inclusion, where applicable, in *Sixty Stories* (abbreviated "SS") or *Forty Stories* (abbreviated "FS").

Come Back, Dr. Caligari (Boston: Little, Brown and Company, 1964).

    Florence Green Is 81. *Harper's Bazaar*, April 1963, pp. 130–31, 200, 209, 217.

    The Piano Player. *The New Yorker*, August 31, 1963, p. 24.

    Hiding Man. As "The Hiding Man," *First Person* 1 (Spring–Summer 1961): 65–75.

    Will You Tell Me? *Arts and Literature* 1 (1964): 68–76.

    For I'm the Boy Whose Only Joy Is Loving You. As "For I'm the Boy," *Location* 1 (Summer 1964): 91–93.

    The Big Broadcast of 1938. *New World Writing* 20 (1962): 108–20.

    The Viennese Opera Ball. *Contact* 10 (June 1962): 42–44.

    Me and Miss Mandible. As "The Darling Little Duckling at School": *Contact* 7 (February 1961): 17–28.

    Marie, Marie, Hold On Tight. *The New Yorker*, October 12, 1963, pp. 49–51.

    Up, Aloft in the Air.

    Margins. *The New Yorker*, February 22, 1964, pp. 33–34.

    The Joker's Greatest Triumph.

    To London and Rome. *Genesis West* 2 (Fall 1963): 35–38.

    A Shower of Gold. *The New Yorker*, December 28, 1963, pp. 33–37.

Unspeakable Practices, Unnatural Acts (New York: Farrar, Straus and Giroux, 1968)

    The Indian Uprising. *The New Yorker*, March 6, 1965, pp. 34–37. SS.

    The Balloon. *The New Yorker*, April 16, 1966, pp. 46–48.

    This Newspaper Here. *The New Yorker*, February 12, 1966, pp. 28–29.

    Robert Kennedy Saved from Drowning. *New American Writing* 3 (April 1968): 107–116. SS.

    Report. *The New Yorker*, June 10, 1967, pp. 34–35. SS.

    The Dolt. *The New Yorker*, November 11, 1967, pp. 56–58.

    The Police Band. *The New Yorker*, August 22, 1964, p. 28.

    Edward and Pia. *The New Yorker*, September 25, 1965, pp. 46–49.

    A Few Moments of Sleeping and Waking. *The New Yorker*, August 5, 1967, pp. 24–26. FS.

    Can We Talk. *Art and Literature* 5 (Summer 1965): 148–50.

    Game. *The New Yorker*, July 31, 1965, pp. 29–30.

    Alice. *The Paris Review* (Summer 1968): 25–31. SS.

    A Picture History of the War. *The New Yorker*, June 20, 1964, pp. 28–31.

    The President. *The New Yorker*, September 5, 1964, pp. 26–27.

    See the Moon? *The New Yorker*, March 12, 1966, pp. 46–50.

City Life (New York: Farrar, Straus and Giroux, 1970)

    Views of My Father Weeping. *The New Yorker*, December 6, 1969, pp. 56–60. SS.

    Paraguay. *The New Yorker*, September 6, 1969, pp. 32–34. SS.

    The Falling Dog. *The New Yorker*, August 3, 1968, pp. 28–29. SS.

    At the Tolstoy Museum. *The New Yorker*, May 24, 1968, pp. 28–29. SS.

    The Policemen's Ball. *The New Yorker*, June 8, 1968, p. 31. SS.

    The Glass Mountain. SS.

    The Explanation. *The New Yorker*, May 4, 1968, pp. 44–46. SS.

    Kierkegaard Unfair to Schlegel. *The New Yorker*, October 12, 1968, pp. 53–55. SS.

    The Phantom of the Opera's Friend. *The New Yorker*, February 7, 1970, pp. 26–27.

    Sentence. *The New Yorker*, March 7, 1970, pp. 34–36.

    Bone Bubbles. As "Mouth," *The Paris Review* 48 (Fall 1969): 189–202.

    On Angels. *The New Yorker*, August 9, 1969, p. 29. SS.

    Brain Damage. *The New Yorker*, February 21, 1970, pp. 42–43.

City Life. First published in two parts in *The New Yorker*, January 18, 1969, pp. 31–32, and *The New Yorker*, June 2, 1969, pp. 32–37. SS.

Sadness (New York: Farrar, Straus and Giroux, 1972)
Critique de la Vie Quotidienne. *The New Yorker*, July 17, 1971, pp. 26–29. SS.
Träumerei. SS.
The Genius. *The New Yorker*, February 20, 1971, pp. 38–40. FS.
Perpetua. *The New Yorker*, February 26, 1972, pp. 30–31. FS.
A City of Churches. *The New Yorker*, April 22, 1972, pp. 38–39.
The Party. *The New Yorker*, June 3, 1972, pp. 30–31. SS.
Engineer-Private Paul Klee Misplaces an Aircraft Between Milbertshofen and Cambrai, March 1916. *The New Yorker*, April 3, 1971, pp. 33–34 FS.
A Film. *The New Yorker*. Published precursors to this story include a "Notes and Comments" piece in *The New Yorker*, June 13, 1970; "A Film," *The New Yorker*, September 26, 1970; and "Flying to America," *The New Yorker*, December 4, 1971. FS, as "The Film."
The Sandman. *The Atlantic*, September 1972, pp. 62–65. SS.
Departures. *The New Yorker*, October 9, 1971, pp. 42–44. FS.
Subpoena. *The New Yorker*, May 29, 1971, p. 33.
The Catechist. *The New Yorker*. November 13, 1971, pp. 49–51. FS.
The Flight of Pigeons from the Palace. As "The Show," *The New Yorker*, August 8, 1970, pp. 26–29. FS.
The Rise of Capitalism. *The New Yorker*, December 12, 1970, pp. 45–47. SS.
The Temptation of St. Anthony. *The New Yorker*, June 3, 1972, pp. 34–36. FS.
Daumier. *The New Yorker*, April 1, 1972, pp. 31–36. SS.

Amateurs (New York: Farrar, Straus and Giroux, 1976)
Our Work and Why We Do It. *The New Yorker*, May 5, 1973, pp. 39–41. SS.
The Wound. *The New Yorker*, October 15, 1973, pp. 36–37. FS.
110 West Sixty-first Street. *The New Yorker*, September 24, 1973, pp. 33–34. FS.
Some of Us Had Been Threatening Our Friend Colby. *The New Yorker*, May 26, 1973, pp. 39–40. FS.
The School. *The New Yorker*, June 17, 1974, p. 28. SS.
The Great Hug. *The Atlantic*, June 1975, pp. 44–45. SS.

I Bought a Little City. *The New Yorker*, November 11, 1974, pp. 42–44. SS.

The Agreement. *The New Yorker*, October 14, 1974, pp. 44–45.

The Sergeant. *Fiction* 3 (2–3): 24–25. SS.

What to Do Next. *The New Yorker*, March 24, 1973, pp. 35–37.

The Captured Woman. *The New Yorker*, June 28, 1976, pp. 22–25. SS.

And Then. *Harper's*, December 1973, pp. 87–89.

Porcupines at the University. *The New Yorker*, April 25, 1970, pp. 32–33. FS.

The Educational Experience. *Harper's*, June 1973, pp. 62–65. FS.

The Discovery. *The New Yorker*, August 20, 1973, pp. 26–27.

Rebecca. *The New Yorker*, February 24, 1975, pp. 44–45. SS.

The Reference. *Playboy*, April 1974, pp. 163, 186–87.

The New Member. *The New Yorker*, July 15, 1974, pp. 28–30.

You Are as Brave as Vincent Van Gogh. *The New Yorker*, March 18, 1974, p. 34.

At the End of the Mechanical Age. *The Atlantic*, June 1973, pp. 52–55. SS.

Great Days (New York: Farrar, Straus and Giroux, 1979)

The Crisis. *The New Yorker*, October 24, 1977, pp. 42–43. SS.

The Apology. *The New Yorker*, February 20, 1978, pp. 35–37.

The New Music. *The New Yorker*, June 19, 1978, pp. 29–30, and as "Momma," *The New Yorker*, October 2, 1978, pp. 32–33.

Cortés and Montezuma. *The New Yorker*, August 22, 1977, pp. 25–26. SS.

The King of Jazz. *The New Yorker*, February 7, 1975, pp. 31–32. SS.

The Question Party. *The New Yorker*, January 17, 1977, pp. 32–34.

Belief. University of Houston *Forum* 13 (Winter 1976): 47–49.

Tales of the Swedish Army. *The New Yorker*, December 26, 1977, pp. 23–24.

The Abduction from the Seraglio. *The New Yorker*, January 30, 1978, pp. 30–31. SS.

The Death of Edward Lear. *The New Yorker*, January 2, 1971, p. 21. SS.

Concerning the Bodyguard. *The New Yorker*, October 16, 1978, pp. 36–37. FS.

The Zombies. *The New Yorker*, April 25, 1977, p. 35. SS.

Morning. *The New Yorker*, May 1, 1978, pp. 36–37. SS.

On the Steps of the Conservatory. *The New Yorker*, February 21, 1977, pp. 33–36. SS.

The Leap. *The New Yorker*, July 31, 1978, pp. 27–29. SS.

Great Days. *Partisan Review* 4.3 (1977): 501–11. FS.

From *Sixty Stories* (New York: G. P. Putnam's Sons, 1981)
    Eugénie Grandet. *The New Yorker*, August 17, 1968, pp. 24–25.
    Nothing: A Preliminary Account. *The New Yorker*, December 31, 1973, pp. 26–27.
    A Manual for Sons. As "Manual for Sons," *The New Yorker*, May 12, 1975, pp. 40–50.
    Aria. *The New Yorker*, March 12, 1979, p. 37.
    The Emerald. *Esquire*, November 1979, pp. 92–105.
    How I Write My Songs. As "How I Write My Songs, by Bill B. White," *The New Yorker*, November 27, 1978, pp. 36–37.
    The Farewell. As "The Farewell Party," *Fiction* 6.2 (1980): 12–16.
    The Emperor. *The New Yorker*, January 26, 1981, p. 31.
    Thailand. *The New Yorker*, December 29, 1980, pp. 33–35.
    Heroes. *The New Yorker*, May 5, 1980, pp. 36–37.
    Bishop. *The New Yorker*, August 4, 1980, pp. 27–28.
    Grandmother's House. As "Grandmother," *The New Yorker*, September 3, 1979, pp. 26–28.

Overnight to Many Distant Cities (New York: G. P. Putnam's Sons, 1983)
    They called for more structure . . .
    Visitors. *The New Yorker*, December 14, 1981, pp. 38–41.
    Financially, the paper . . . As "Pepperoni," *The New Yorker*, December 1, 1980, p. 43.
    Affection. *The New Yorker*, November 7, 1983, pp. 45–47.
    I put a name in an envelope . . . *Joseph Cornell Exhibition Catalogue* (New York: Leo Castelli Gallery, 1976); *Ontario Review* 5 (Fall–Winter 1976): 50.
    Lightning. *The New Yorker*, May 3, 1982, pp. 42–45.
    That guy in the back room . . .
    Captain Blood. *The New Yorker*, January 1, 1979, pp. 26–27.
    A woman seated on a plain wooden chair . . . Parts earlier published in "Presents," *Penthouse*, December 1977, 106–10.
    Conversations with Goethe. *The New Yorker*, October 20, 1980, p. 49.
    Well we all had our Willie & Wade records . . . *Harper's*, June 1979.
    Henrietta and Alexandra. As "Alexandria and Henrietta," *North American Review* 12 (1971): 82–87.
    Speaking of the human body . . .
    The Sea of Hesitation. As "Over the Sea of Hesitation," *The New Yorker*, November 11, 1972, pp. 40–43.
    When he came . . .
    Terminus.
    The first thing the baby did wrong . . .

The Mothball Fleet. *The New Yorker*, September 11, 1971, pp. 34–35.

Now that I am older . . .

Wrack. *The New Yorker*, October 21, 1972, pp. 36–37.

On our street . . . As "Sakrete," *The New Yorker*, September 26, 1983, pp. 34–35.

The Palace at Four A.M. *The New Yorker*, October 17, 1983, pp. 46–49.

I am, at the moment . . . Includes material from unpublished story "Among the Beanwoods," published posthumously in Kim Herzinger (ed.), *Flying to America: 45 More Stories* (Emeryville, CA: Shoemaker & Hoard, 2007).

Overnight to Many Distant Cities. *The New Yorker*, January 1, 1979, pp. 26–27.

From *Forty Stories* (1987)

Chablis. *The New Yorker*, December 12, 1983, p. 49.

On the Deck. *The New Yorker*, January 12, 1987, p. 37.

Opening. *The New Yorker*, October 22, 1984, p. 41.

Sindbad. *The New Yorker*, August 27, 1984, pp. 30–32.

Rif.

Jaws. *The New Yorker*, August 17, 1987, pp. 20–21.

Bluebeard. *The New Yorker*, June 16, 1986, p. 33.

Construction. The New Yorker, April 29, 1985, pp. 34–36.

Letters to the Editore. *The New Yorker*, February 25, 1972, pp. 34–35.

January. *The New Yorker*, April 6, 1987, pp. 40–41.

Uncollected Stories. The texts are taken from Kim Herzinger (ed.), *Flying to America: 45 More Stories* (Emeryville, CA: Shoemaker & Hoard, 2007).

Edwards, Amelia. *The New Yorker*, September 9, 1972, pp. 34–36.

A Man. *The New Yorker*, December 30, 1972, pp. 26–27.

Basil from Her Garden. *The New Yorker*, October 21, 1985, pp. 36–37.

Tickets. *The New Yorker*, March 6, 1989.

This volume presents the texts of the original printings chosen for inclusion here, but it does not attempt to reproduce nontextual features of their typographic design. The texts are presented without change, except for the correction of typographical errors. Spelling, punctuation, and capitalization are often expressive features and are not altered, even when inconsistent or irregular. The following is a list of typographical errors corrected, cited by page and line number: 40.3, acohol,; 85.33, it it; 86.15, yeoman; 109.12, this; 148.1, rysstafel; 184.10, owning; 217.18, doing."; 420.10, "Rupert."; 427.26, he if uses; 591.36, her.; 666.15, augensheinlich; 707.27, wedge; 832.38, Wilkins; 899.12–13, reconcilation; 914.35, it for; 923.29, Bal.

Notes

In the notes below, the reference numbers denote page and line of this volume (the line count includes headings but not blank lines). No note is made for material that is sufficiently explained in context, nor are there notes for material included in standard desk-reference works such as Webster's Eleventh Collegiate, Biographical, and Geographical dictionaries or comparable internet resources such as Merriam-Webster's online dictionary. Foreign words and phrases are translated only if not translated in the text or if words are not evident English cognates. Quotations from Shakespeare are keyed to *The Riverside Shakespeare*, edited by G. Blakemore Evans (Boston: Houghton Mifflin, 1974). Quotations from the Bible are keyed to the King James Version. For further biographical information than is contained in the Chronology and Introduction, see Tracy Daugherty, *Hiding Man: A Biography of Donald Barthelme* (New York: St. Martin's, 2009).

COME BACK, DR. CALIGARI

1.1 DR. CALIGARI] The hypnotist villain of *The Cabinet of Dr. Caligari* (1920), German film directed by Robert Wiene (1873–1938) with Werner Krauss (1884–1959) in the starring role.

3.13 Quemoy and Matsu] In September 1954 the People's Republic of China Communists began shelling Quemoy and Matsu, islands in the Formosa (Taiwan) Strait occupied by the Chinese Nationalists, and in January 1955 attacked other Nationalist-held islands along the coast. After Congress passed a resolution authorizing the President to defend Quemoy and Matsu, the Eisenhower administration warned in March that an attack on the islands could result in the use of tactical nuclear weapons by the United States. The Communists halted their shelling of the islands on May 1, 1955, but resumed it on August 23, 1958. Eisenhower responded by sending naval forces to the region and declaring in a televised address on September 11 that the United States would resist aggression in the Formosa Strait. The Chinese halted their bombardment on October 6, 1958, ending the crisis.

3.16 Famous Writers School] Correspondence course cofounded in 1961 by the Random House publisher Bennett Cerf (1898–1971), the prolific magazine writer John D. Ratcliff (1903–1973), and the illustrator Alfred Dorne (1906–1965), modeled on the Famous Artists School cofounded by Dorne. Later the Writers School was the subject of an investigative report into its dubious practices by the English writer Jessica Mitford (1917–1996) in *The Atlantic*, July 1970.

3.21 Herman Kahn] American mathematician and military strategist (1922–1983), founder of the conservative Hudson Institute, author of *On Thermonuclear War* (1960) and *Thinking About the Unthinkable* (1962).

5.25 Joe Weider] Canadian-born bodybuilder, magazine publisher, and fitness and nutrition entrepreneur (1919–2013).

5.36 Pamela Hansford Johnson] English novelist (1912–1981), author of twenty-seven novels, including *This Bed Thy Centre* (1935) and *The Unspeakable Skipton* (1959).

6.2 *Graf Zeppelin*] German airship that provided commercial passenger service from 1928 to 1937.

6.3–4 Mandrake the Magician] Syndicated comic strip, created by Lee Falk (1911–1999), that began its long run in 1934.

6.8 *Lakehurst*] The German passenger airship Hindenburg caught fire and crashed at the Lakehurst Naval Air Station in New Jersey on May 6, 1937.

7.28–29 "It is closing time in the gardens of the West Cyril Connolly."] A remark made by Cyril Connolly (1903–1974) in 1949 in *Horizon*, the magazine he cofounded and edited: "It is closing time in the gardens of the West and from now on an artist will be judged only by the resonance of his solitude or the quality of his despair."

7.32–33 "Before the flowers of friendship faded friendship faded Gertrude Stein."] *Before the Flowers of Friendship Faded Friendship Faded* (1931), work by the American writer Gertrude Stein (1874–1946).

8.9 Chiang's] Chinese nationalist leader Chiang Kai-shek (1887–1975).

8.14 Egmont] Font developed by the Dutch designer and artist S. H. de Roos (1877–1962).

9.2–3 "Remarks are not literature,"] An aphorism of Gertrude Stein, first recorded in her book *The Autobiography of Alice B. Toklas* (1933).

9.14–15 Henry James writes fiction . . . painful duty Oscar Wilde] Cf. "The Decay of Lying" (1889), essay by the Anglo-Irish writer Oscar Wilde (1854–1900).

9.20 the Andrew Sisters] Popular swing-era vocal trio.

9.36 Norman Brokenshire] Canadian-born American radio and television announcer (1898–1965) known as "Sir Silken Speech."

10.11 Captain Mid-night] Titular hero of a serialized radio program (1938–49) that was the basis for films and television programs as well as a comic strip.

10.30 Onward Christian] Cf. "Onward, Christian Soldiers," hymn with words (1864) by Sabine Baring-Gould (1834–1924) and music (1871) by Sir Arthur Sullivan (1842–1900).

11.1–2 "An army . . . truth"] From "For Christ the King" (1932), Catholic youth anthem written by Fr. Daniel A. Lord (1888–1955).

11.13   Tempelhof] West Berlin's airport during the Cold War.

14.34   *Parsifal*] Opera (1882) by the German composer Richard Wagner (1813–1883).

14.38–15.7   Wellfleet . . . Edmund Wilson . . . Bunny] For much of his life the American literary critic Edmund Wilson (1895–1972), nicknamed "Bunny," lived in Wellfleet, Massachusetts, on Cape Cod.

15.37   Coriolanus.] Eponymous protagonist of a tragedy by Shakespeare, based on the fifth-century B.C.E. Roman general Gaius Marcius Coriolanus.

16.4   *The Rise and Fall*] The best-selling popular history *The Rise and Fall of the Third Reich* by William L. Shirer (1904–1993).

16.12   Pinetop Smith] Blues pianist (1904–1929) whose most famous composition is "Pine Top's Boogie Woogie" (1928).

16.16   Altman's.] Upscale New York department store, 1865–1989.

18.31   Sons and Daughters of I Will Arise] Fictional Birmingham, Alabama, social organization of African Americans invented by the writer and playwright Octavus Roy Cohen (1891–1959).

22.17   *Bride of Frankenstein*] Film (1935) directed by James Whale (1889–1957). The other film titles mentioned in this story are those of real B-movies.

28.25   Hyacinth Girl.] See lines 35–36 of *The Waste Land* (1922) by the American poet T. S. Eliot (1888–1965): "You gave me hyacinths first a year ago; / They called me the hyacinth girl."

28.26–27   It is a portrait . . . development.] From the introduction to *A Hero of Our Time* (1840–41), novel by the Russian writer Mikhail Lermontov (1814–1841).

31.32   Bergson] The French philosopher Henri Bergson (1859–1941) whose works include *Creative Evolution* (1907).

32.7   Matson Line] Passenger shipping line for a company that also transported freight.

33.25   the fall of Ethiopia] Italy declared Ethiopia an Italian province in May 1936 upon occupying Addis Ababa, having forced the country's emperor Haile Selassie (1892–1975) into exile.

34.2–3   Joel S. Goldsmith's books on the oneness of life] The American lecturer and author Joel S. Goldsmith (1892–1964) was the founder of the nonsectarian spiritual movement The Infinite Way, also the title of the first of his more than fifty books.

34.13   Cow on the Roof or something like that] Le Bœuf sur le Toit (The Ox on the Roof), Parisian cabaret renowned as a haunt of modernist artists and other cultural figures during the interwar years.

34.33 Rambler] Affordable automobile manufactured in the postwar period by the American Motors Corporation.

36.2–3 *For I'm the Boy . . . You*] A line from "Remember Me?", song with words by Al Dubin (1891–1945), music by Harry Warren (1893–1981), from the musical comedy *Mr. Dodd Takes the Air* (1937).

37.25 Mallarmé] French poet and critic Stéphane Mallarmé (1842–1898), whose works include the experimental poem *Un coup de dés jamais n'abolira le hazard* (A Throw of the Dice Will Never Abolish Chance, pub. 1914).

42.26 Tuesday Weld] Film and television actor (b. 1943), a child and teen star in the 1950s and 1960s with a tempestuous personal life.

47.24 Conrad Veidt] German actor (1893–1943) whose many film roles included *The Cabinet of Dr. Caligari* (see note 1.1) and *Casablanca* (1942).

48.1–2 *DE REZKE*] De Reszke cigarettes, manufactured by the London-based firm J. Millhoff & Co. Branded as "the aristocrat of cigarettes," they were named after the Polish opera singer Jean de Reszke (1850–1925).

52.10–11 *Ideal Marriage* by Th. H Van De Velde, M.D.] *Ideal Marriage: Its Physiology and Technique* (1928), title of English translation of the sex manual *Het volkomen huwelijk* (1926) by the Dutch gynecologist Theodoor Hendrik van de Velde (1873–1937).

52.30 Carmen Lambrosa] A fictional actor.

55.35–36 Meyer Davis] American bandleader and musical entrepreneur (1893–1976) who presided over a group of orchestras catering to high-society events.

59.9–10 Lester Lannin] Lester Lanin (1907–2004), American bandleader whose orchestras, like Meyer Davis's, specialized in high-society events.

59.30 Leon Jaroff] Editor and science writer (1927–2012) for *Time* magazine.

61.38 Emile Myerson] "Man does metaphysics just as he breathes, involuntarily and, above all, usually without realizing it." From *De l'explication dans les sciences* (On Explanation in the Sciences, 1921), by the Polish-born French philosopher of science Émile Meyerson (1859–1933).

62.2–3 Abbey Lincoln . . . La Plante] The jazz singer and songwriter Abbey Lincoln (1930–2010) and the actor Laura La Plante (1904–1996), whose roles were mostly in the silent film era.

64.8 *Sounds of Sebring*] Series of LP records, 1956–62, 1964, featuring recordings taken during the annual twelve-hour auto race held in Sebring, Florida, accompanied by commentary about the race.

69.10 "Debbie's Date Insults Liz!"] Debbie Reynolds (1932–2016) and Elizabeth Taylor (1932–2011) were involved in a highly publicized and sensationalized feud after it became known that Taylor was having an affair with Reynolds's first husband Eddie Fisher (1928–2010), who married Taylor after a divorce from Reynolds in 1959.

75.1 *Marie, Marie, Hold on Tight*] From T. S. Eliot's *The Waste Land*, lines 15–16.

75.12 COGITO ERGO] Latin: I think, therefore, from Descartes's dictum "I think, therefore I am."

77.29–30 "What Is To Be Done?" . . . famous revolutionary catchword] Title of Vladimir Lenin's 1902 political pamphlet.

81.2 BUCK] Buck Rogers, space adventurer who first appeared in *Amazing Stories* in 1928 and the comic strip adapted from it in 1929, *Buck Rogers in the 25th Century*, and later in radio, movies, and television.

87.13 old poet of the city Constantine Cavity."] A play on the name of the Greek poet Constantine Cavafy (1863–1933).

89.7 science has its reasons that reasons knows not of,"] Cf. "Le cœur a ses raisons que la raison ne connaît point" (The heart has its reasons of which reason knows nothing), from the *Pensées*, collection of philosophical and theological observations by the French philosopher Blaise Pascal (1623–1662) first published posthumously in 1669–70.

89.16–17 "In the Blue . . . Williams."] "In the Blue of Evening" (1943), hit song by Al D'Artega (1907–1998) and Tom Adair (1913–1988) for Tommy Dorsey & His Orchestra, with Frank Sinatra singing vocals; "Long Ago (and Far Away)," song with music by Jerome Kern (1885–1945) and lyrics by Ira Gershwin (1896–1983), introduced by Rita Hayworth and Gene Kelly in the film *Cover Girl* (1944); "Who?", song from the Broadway musical *Sunny* (1925) with music by Jerome Kern and lyrics by Oscar Hammerstein II (1895–1960) and Otto Harbach (1873–1963); fictional poem dedicated to the American poet and physician William Carlos Williams.

90.33 *liaisons dangéreuses*] French: dangerous liaisons, from the title of the novel (1782) by French writer Pierre Choderlos de Laclos (1741–1803).

91.16 *Wozzeck*.] Opera (1925) by the Austrian composer Alban Berg (1885–1935).

91.29–31 "Red Boy Blues," . . . "Edward"] "Red Boy Blues" (1957) and "Gigantic Blues" (1956), compositions by jazz saxophonist Lester Young (1909–1959); "That's All" (1952), song written by Bob Haymes (1923–1989) and Alan Brandt (1923–2003); "Muggles" (1928), composition by jazz trumpeter, composer, and singer Louis Armstrong (1901–1971); "Edward," traditional ballad about a murder.

91.38–39 "I Didn't Know . . . "Misty."] "I Didn't Know What Time It Was," song from stage musical *Too Many Girls* (1939) with music by Richard Rodgers

(1902–1979), lyrics by Lorenz Hart (1895–1943); "Misty" (1954), composition by jazz pianist and composition Erroll Garner (1921–1977).

94.4   objective correlative] Aesthetic concept formulated by T. S. Eliot in his essay "Hamlet and His Problems" (1919): "The only way of expressing emotion in the form of art is by finding an 'objective correlative'; in other words, a set of objects, a situation, a chain of events which shall be the formula of that particular emotion."

94.20   "Carl Maria von Weber,"] German composer (1786–1826).

95.17   John Hawkes] American fiction writer and playwright (1925–1998) whose works include *The Lime Twig* (1961), *Second Skin* (1961), and *Adventures in the Alaskan Skin Trade* (1985); a friend of Barthelme's and like him often labeled as a postmodernist.

96.30–32   Villon . . . 'If I Were King'] The life of the French poet François Villon (ca. 1431–1463), who was imprisoned on charges of theft in 1462, was dramatized in *If I Were King* (1901), play by the Irish writer and politician Justin Huntly McCarthy (1859–1936), adapted into a film in 1938.

99.23   the "Warsaw Concerto."] Composition (1941) for piano and orchestra by the English composer Richard Addinsell (1904–1977) written for the film *Dangerous Moonlight*.

100.18   "Cornish Rhapsody"] Piano composition (1944) by the English composer Hubert Bath (1883–1945) featured in the film *Love Story* (1944). Like "Warsaw Concerto," it was written in the style of Rachmaninoff.

100.22   "Flying Dutchman!"] A legendary ghost ship associated with the tale of a sea captain selling his soul to the devil, after which he was doomed to sail for eternity.

101.15   *Où est mon livre?*] French: Where is my book? The following French phrases on this page are Where is your book?, Where is his book?, All that happened in 1924, and Phone me one of these days.

101.32   *Grit*] Publication founded in 1882 aimed at a rural audience, often sold by youngsters and teenagers.

105.3   Mark Schorer] American critic, academic, and fiction writer (1908–1977), the author of *Sinclair Lewis: An American Life* (1961).

106.30   Aqueduct] Horse-racing facility in Queens, New York.

114.1   *A Shower of Gold*] In Greek mythology Zeus, disguised as a shower of gold, impregnated the Greek princess Danaë.

115.8–10   "*You* may not be interested in absurdity . . . *you*."] Cf. the remark often attributed to the Russian revolutionary Leon Trotsky (1879–1940), "You may not be interested in war, but war is interested in you."

116.39 Giacometti stickman] The Swiss-born sculptor Alberto Giacometti (1901–1966) is best known for his elongated sculptures of human figures.

117.12 I-Thou relationship] Relationship between the individual and God articulated by the German Jewish philosopher and theologian Martin Buber (1878–1965) in *I and Thou* (1923).

117.14–15 In the end one experiences only oneself, Nietzsche said] In *Also Sprach Zarathustra* (*Thus Spoke Zarathustra*), Third Part (1884), by the German philosopher Friedrich Nietzsche (1844–1900).

117.30–32 "Like Pascal said, "The natural misfortune . . . console us."] From *Pensées*, section 2, no. 139.

118.6–7 biography of Nolde] Emile Nolde (1867–1956), German expressionist artist.

118.24–25 early seventeenth-century engraving by Franz van der Wyngaert . . . in which a cat piano appears] *La Lecture du grimoire* (*Reading the Book of Spells*) by Frans van den Wyngaerde (1614–1679), Flemish printmaker and publisher.

118.29–30 'The Martyrdom of St. Sebastian'] Incidental music by the French composer Claude Debussy (1862–1918) for a theater piece (1911) by the Italian writer Gabriele D'Annunzio (1863–1938).

118.30 'Romeo and Juliet' overture] Orchestral composition (third and final version, 1880) by the Russian composer Pyotr Ilyich Tchaikovsky (1840–1893), known particularly for its Love Theme.

118.30–31 'Holiday for Strings'?] Instrumental hit single (1944) by David Rose and His Orchestra composed by its leader, David Rose (1910–1990).

119.3 *pour-soi*] French: for itself, a term in existentialist philosophy, in particular that of the French philosopher Jean-Paul Sartre (1905–1980), who opposed the being-in-itself (*en soi*) of other philosophers, which precedes all action, to the more creative existentialist conception of being-for-itself.

119.29 A.I.R.] Artist in residence.

119.39 *engagé*] French: committed, often said of intellectuals who involve themselves in public debates or activism.

121.18 BAD FAITH] Bad faith (*la mauvaise foi*) is a key concept in Jean-Paul Sartre's existentialism as discussed in his *L'Être et le néant* (*Being and Nothingness*, 1943).

122.3–4 a man singing "Golden Earrings"] Title song from the movie *Golden Earrings* (1947) by Victor Young (1899–1956), Jay Livingston (1915–2001), and Ray Evans (1915–2007), a hit record in its first release as a single for singer Peggy Lee.

UNSPEAKABLE PRACTICES, UNNATURAL ACTS

124.1 *Herman Gollub*] Book editor, publishing executive, and author, a friend of Barthelme's who was his apartment-mate for a while.

125.5 Mark Clark] U.S. Army general (1896–1984) who commanded forces in World War II and the Korean War.

125.21 Fauré's 'Dolly'] Suite of six piano compositions for four hands (1898) by the French composer Gabriel Fauré (1845–1924).

126.11–12 bottles of Black & White] A blended Scotch whiskey.

126.33 Korzybski] Polish-born philosopher Alfred H. Korzybski (1879–1950), founder of the field of general semantics, outlined in *Science and Society* (1933).

127.11 Chester Nimitz] U.S. Navy admiral (1885–1966), commander of the U.S. Pacific fleet during World War II.

127.16 I.R.A.] Irish Republican Army.

127.24 George C. Marshall] Military officer and government official (1880–1959), U.S. Army chief of staff during World War II and U.S. secretary of state, 1947–49, who helped to create the European Recovery Program, known as the Marshall Plan.

128.18 Skinny Wainwright] Lieutenant General Jonathan Wainwright (1883–1953), commander of U.S. and Filipino forces during World War II, the highest-ranking American POW during the war after his capture by the Japanese in 1942.

128.21–22 former king of Spain, a Bonaparte . . . New Jersey] Joseph Bonaparte (1768–1844), who had been king of Spain, 1808–13, acquired the land for his Point Breeze estate in Bordentown, New Jersey, in 1816 and lived in the United States until 1839.

128.25 Valéry] The French poet and critic Paul Valéry (1871–1945).

128.33 Gabrieli, Albinoni, Marcello] The Italian composers Giovanni Gabrieli (ca. 1554/1557–1612), Tommaso Albinoni (1671–1751), and Benedetto Marcello (1686–1739).

129.1 *serviette*] French: napkin.

129.22 Abraham Lincoln Brigade] Unit of American volunteers who fought on the Republican side in the Spanish Civil War.

129.24–25 Frank Wedekind] German playwright (1864–1918), author of *Frühlings Erwachen* (*Spring's Awakening*, 1891).

129.35 Gustave Aschenbach.] Gustave von Aschenbach, dying protagonist of Thomas Mann's novella *Death in Venice* (1912), who becomes obsessed with a beautiful Polish youth named Tadzio.

130.29   Emery Roth & Sons.] Architecture firm founded by the Hungarian-born architect Emery Roth (1871–1948), a prolific builder of apartment buildings, hotels, and other buildings in New York City from the 1920s through the 1980s.

130.33   Jean-Luc Godard] Jean-Luc Godard (b. 1930), French-Swiss filmmaker at the forefront of the French New Wave whose films include *Breathless* (1959) and *Alphaville* (1965).

135.27   Alamo Chili House] Restaurant on West 44th Street with a statue of a giant iguana on the roof, which closed in the 1970s.

135.29–30   Gallery of Modern Art] Art museum on Columbus Circle in Manhattan exhibiting the collection of Huntington Hartford II (1911–2008), heir to the A&P retail grocery fortune.

138.15   EEC."] European Economic Commission, the forerunner of the European Union.

138.35   "bonne chance!"] French: good luck.

140.12   Heinrich von Kleist] German writer (1777–1811) whose works include the novella *Michael Kohlhaas* (1810).

141.4–5   rock around the clock interviewing Fabian] A conflation of the single "Rock Around the Clock" (1952), best known in the recording by Bill Haley & His Comets, with the long-running syndicated television variety show *American Bandstand*, hosted by Dick Clark (1929–2012); the teen singer and actor Fabian (Fabian Forte, b. 1943) rose to fame with his hit "Turn Me Loose" (1959).

142.1   *Robert Kennedy Saved from Drowning*] Cf. the title of the satirical French film *Boudu sauvé des eaux* (*Boudu Saved from Drowning*, 1932), directed by Jean Renoir (1894–1979).

143.35   *Unknown Towns (Rimbaud)*] See *Une Saison en enfer* (*A Season in Hell*, 1873), prose poem by the French poet Arthur Rimbaud (1854–1891): "nous voyagerons, nous chasserons dans les déserts, nous dormirons sur les pavés des villes inconnues, sans soins, sans peines" (we will travel, we will hunt in the deserts, we will sleep on the pavement of unknown towns, without cares, without worries).

144.1   MÖBEL . . . MEUBLES] German and French words for furniture, respectively.

144.30–33   *Karsh of Ottawa* . . . Churchill thing . . . Hemingway thing] The Armenian-Canadian portrait photographer Yousef Karsh (1908–2002) photographed Winston Churchill during a 1941 visit to Canada in an image that soon graced the cover of *Life* magazine and was widely circulated around the world; among Karsh's many other celebrity subjects was Ernest Hemingway.

147.9   Sidi-Madani] Village in Algeria.

149.24–25 Poulet . . . Marivaux] The Belgian literary critic Georges Poulet (1902–1991) addressed the work of the eighteenth-century French playwright Pierre Marivaux (1688–1763) in *La distance intérieure* (*The Interior Distance*, 1952).

151.12 os calcis] The heel bone.

151.22 Isambard Kingdom Brunel] Pioneering English civil engineer (1806–1859).

153.20 "Nothing mechanical is alien to me,"] Cf. the Latin dictum "Nihil humanum mihi alienum puto" (Nothing human is alien to me) from *Heauton Timorumenos* (*The Self-Tormenter*) by the Roman playwright Publius Terentius Afer, known as Terence (c. 186–c. 159 B.C.E.).

161.3–4 Seville, to see if hell was a city much like] See *Man and Superman* (1905), play by the Anglo-Irish playwright George Bernard Shaw (1856–1950), act III: "As saith the poet, Hell is a city much like Seville," adapting as well a remark by Percy Bysshe Shelley in "Peter Bell the Third" (1819) about London.

162.24–25 Steve Canyon recruiting posters] *Steve Canyon*, comic strip, 1947–88, created by Milton Caniff (1907–1988), adapted into a television show, 1958–59, its titular hero a pilot in the U.S. Air Force.

163.9 "Perdido."] Jazz composition (1942) by the trombonist and composer Juan Tizol (1900–1984), with lyrics (1944) by Ervin Drake (1919–2015) and Hans Lengsfelder (1903–1979).

165.8 the Marat/Sade] Common abbreviated title of the play *The Persecution of Jean-Paul Marat by the Inmates of the Asylum of Charenton Under the Direction of the Marquis de Sade* (1963) by the German playwright Peter Weiss (1916–1982).

165.30–31 *Life* magazine with a gold-painted girl on the cover] The actor Shirley Eaton (b. 1937), who was shown as a corpse covered in gold paint in the James Bond film *Goldfinger*, was featured on the cover of *Life* on November 6, 1964.

166.6 Round Tower.] Seventeenth-century architectural landmark in central Copenhagen constructed as an observatory.

166.27–28 Eddie Constantine] American comic actor (1917–1993) who starred in B-movies in Europe, including a recurring role as the agent Lemmy Caution.

166.33 Ross Macdonald] Canadian-born American crime novelist (pseud. Kenneth Millar, 1915–1983), creator of the detective Lew Archer and author of many books, including *The Moving Target* (1949), *The Galton Case* (1959), and *Black Money* (1966).

167.17–18 "*Ich verstehe nicht*,"] German: I don't understand.

169.38–39 princesses. . . . archaeologist] Danish queen Margrethe II (b. 1940), who as crown princess made her first visit to an archaeological excavation in Egypt in 1962.

170.2 "We Shall Overcome."] Protest folk song often sung at civil rights demonstrations.

170.8 Finn Viderø] Danish organist and composer (1906–1987).

172.14 *wienerbrød*] Danish pastry (lit. "Vienna bread") known simply as a "Danish" outside Denmark.

173.3 *The Interpretation of Dreams*] English translation of Sigmund Freud's *Die Traumdeutung* (1899).

173.27 *blufaerdighedskraenkelse*] Danish: indecent exposure.

173.29 *Joan Baez*] Folksinger and political activist (b. 1941).

173.35–36 We be of one blood, thee and I.] Version of the recurring line spoken by the boy Mowgli to animals in *The Jungle Book* (1894) by Rudyard Kipling (1865–1936).

175.5 Anthony Powell] English novelist (1905–2000), author of the twelve-volume novel cycle *A Dance to the Music of Time* (1951–75).

175.12 *Madam Cherokee's*] Spiritualist in Manhattan's Greenwich Village. See Barthelme's *Here in the Village* (1978): "I went last week to see Madam Cherokee, my Reader and Spiritual Advisor, who maintains premises on Orchard Street devoted, as it were, to pulling the teeth of the future."

176.1 *La vache!*] French expression to express surprise (literally "The cow!").

178.4–6 "Mrs. Miniver" . . . Flynn] The novel *Mrs. Miniver* (1940) was written by the English writer Jan Struther (1901–1953), not the English novelist, playwright, journalist, and critic J. B. Priestley (1894–1984). Its 1942 screen adaptation starred Greer Garson (1904–1996) and Walter Pidgeon (1897–1984) but not Errol Flynn (1909–1959), known for his swashbuckling movie roles.

180.15 "The Mark of Zorro."] Adventure film (1940) starring Tyrone Power (1914–1958) and Linda Darnell (1923–1965).

183.36 USAFI course] Correspondence course offered by the United States Armed Forces Institute.

186.16 Brahms' "Guten abend, gut Nacht,"] The "Wiegenlied" (1868; often referred to as "Brahms's Lullaby"), op. 49, no. 4, by Johannes Brahms (1833–1897).

189.14 Poujadist] Poujadism was an anti-establishment economic populist movement in France during the 1950s.

190.4–5 Babar books . . . elephants] Babar the Elephant is the anthropomorphic hero of a series of French children's books beginning with *Histoire de Babar* (1931), written and illustrated by Jean de Brunhoff (1899–1937).

190.19 Tinguely] The Swiss artist Jean Tinguely (1925–1991).

192.12 Klinger's] The German symbolist artist Max Klinger (1857–1920).

194.24 Brye . . . Marshall Blücher] On the morning of June 16, 1815, two days before the Battle of Waterloo, Wellington met with the Prussian field marshal Gebhard Leberecht von Blücher (1742–1819) at the latter's headquarters at the windmill of Bussy on the heights of the Belgian village of Brye to discuss their cooperation against Napoleon's forces.

195.9–12 essay by Paul Goodman . . . antidote")] From "A New Deal for the Arts," essay by the social critic, novelist, and poet Paul Goodman (1911–1972) first published in *Commentary* in January 1964.

195.14–15 Mr. and Mrs. Beck of the Living Theatre] Judith Malina (1926–2015) and Julian Beck (1925–1985), husband-and-wife founders of the experimental Living Theatre company.

196.22 Benning.] Fort Benning, U.S. Army post near Columbia, Georgia.

196.25 Leonard Wood] U.S. Army training facility in Missouri.

196.26–27 a little more grape, Capt. Gregg] Cf. "a little more grape, Capt. Bragg," remark attributed to Zachary Taylor (1784–1850) during the Battle of Buena Vista, February 23, 1847, and used as a slogan for Taylor's victorious 1848 presidential campaign.

197.2–4 battle of Borodino . . . Valmy] Battle of Borodino, September 7, 1812, French victory over Russian forces about seventy miles west of Moscow during the Napoleonic Wars. Battle of Arbela, Alexander the Great's decisive defeat in 331 B.C.E. of the Persian army led by Darius III at Gaugamela, about thirty miles from the city of Arbela (present-day Arbil, Iraq). Battle of the Metaurus, Roman victory in 207 B.C.E. over the Carthaginians in a battle fought near the Metaurus River in Italy during the Second Punic War. Battle of Châlons or Battle of the Catalaunian Plains, fought in Gaul in 451 C.E. by Roman forces and Germanic allies against the Huns under the command of Attila, with neither side conclusively victorious. Battle of Pultowa or Poltava, July 8, 1709, a Russian victory over the Swedish Empire in the Great Northern War. Battle of Valmy, French victory against Prussian and Austrian forces on September 20, 1792, the first victory of French revolutionary forces against regular armies.

198.35 'Johnny Got a Zero.'] Hit song (1943) popular during World War II ("Zero" was a Japanese fighter aircraft), words by Mack David (1912–1993), music by Vee Lawnhurst (1905–1992).

199.9   On the third] October 3, 1864; the sentences following, describing events in northern Georgia, are taken directly from W. Birkbeck Wood and J. E. Edmunds, *A History of the Civil War in the United States, 1861–65* (1905).

199.32   Yusef Lateef] Jazz musician and composer (1920–2013).

200.22   Gregg] Union cavalry general David McMurtrie Gregg (1833–1916).

200.23   Fitzhugh Lee] Confederate cavalry general (1835–1905).

204.11   'Struttin' with Some Barbecue,'] Recording (1927) by Louis Armstrong and His Hot Five.

204.15–16   "The Gypsy Baron."] Operetta (1885) by the Austrian composer Johann Strauss, Jr. (1825–1899).

205.32   Henri Bendel] High-end retailer of women's fashions and accessories on Fifth Avenue, founded in 1896.

208.23   Rutherford] The British physicist Ernest Rutherford (1871–1937).

209.30   Komsomol] Soviet Communist Party youth organization.

211.13   Skinner box] Common name for a chamber used by behavioral scientists to observe animals' responses to stimuli as forms of conditioning; it was created by the American scientist and psychologist B. F. Skinner (1904–1990) while he was a graduate student.

211.30   Palestrina] The Italian composer Giovanni Pierluigi da Palestrina (1525?–1594).

211.36   Gog] In Jewish eschatological tradition, Israel's battle against barbarian enemies led by the tribes Gog and Magog was prophesied to be one of the major events preceding the reign of the Messiah; they are also referred to in Revelation 20:7–8.

212.3   the Elgar] *Pomp and Circumstance*, or "The Land of Hope and Glory," op. 39, no. 1 (1901), march by the English composer Edward Elgar (1857–1934) customary at graduations.

212.7–8   admiral . . . the Coral Sea] A reference to the Battle of the Coral Sea, May 7–8, 1942, in the Pacific.

216.10   "Is there any value that has value?"] From the *Tractatus Logico-Philosophicus* of the Austrian philosopher Ludwig Wittgenstein (1889–1951), Proposition 6.41.

216.29   Minnesota Multiphastic Muzzle Map] Cf. the Minnesota Multiphasic Personality Inventory, a widely used psychological test, the first iteration of which was published in 1943.

216.31   "Stella by Starlight,"] Popular song (1944), music by Victor Young (1899–1956), lyrics by Ned Washington (1901–1976).

217.31–32 "Mr. W. B. Yeats Presenting . . . Queen of the Fairies."] Drawing (1904) by the English novelist, essayist, and caricaturist Max Beerbohm (1872–1956).

CITY LIFE

220.1 Roger Angell] Writer and editor (b. 1920), Barthelme's longtime friend and editor at *The New Yorker*.

234.7–8 *Teníamos grandes deseos de conocerlo*,"] Spanish: We really wanted to meet you.

240.1 *The Falling Dog*] The title and the story are an allusion to a series of sculptures and paintings featuring a "Falling Man" figure as depicted by the self-taught American artist Ernest Trova (1927–2009).

241.11 Sax Rohmer] English novelist (pseud. Arthur Henry Ward, 1883–1959) best known for inventing Dr. Fu Manchu, a Chinese master criminal.

241.16–17 Olympia Press] Publishing house founded in Paris in 1953 that published erotica as well as experimental literary works by Samuel Beckett, William S. Burroughs, and Georges Bataille, among others.

241.33 Baskin, Bacon, Landseer] American artist Leonard Baskin (1922–2000); English artist Francis Bacon (1909–1992); English painter Edwin Landseer (1802–1873) who specialized in animals.

253.1 story of Tolstoy's] "The Three Hermits" (1886).

255.5–6 Nekrasov, and Fet] The Russian poets Nikolay Nekrasov (1821–1878) and Afanasy Fet (1820–1892).

258.34 Vercingetorix] Gallic chieftain (c. 82–46 B.C.E.), leader of a revolt against Roman rule that was crushed by Julius Caesar.

260.1 *The Glass Mountain*] Polish fairy tale about a princess whose golden mountaintop castle can only be entered by a man who, bearing a golden apple plucked from a tree on the mountainside, completes a perilous climb up the slope where many have previously failed. In the version given by Hermann Kletke, the tale was included in *The Yellow Fairy Book* (1894), edited by Andrew Lang, which is quoted here on p. 263.

262.7–8 "A weakening . . . a close."] From *The Hidden Order of Art* by the Austrian-born British aesthetic theorist Anton Ehrenzweig (1908–1966), published posthumously in 1967.

262.34 M. Pompidou] Georges Pompidou (1911–1974), France's prime minister, 1962–68.

264.2–3 "In some centuries . . . energies."] From *Shakespeare and Spiritual Life* (1924) by the English poet John Masefield (1878–1967).

270.17 Schumann Festival.] Recurring festivals featuring the works of the composer Robert Schumann (1810–1856) in his hometown of Zwickau and in other German cities.

275.1 *Kierkegaard . . . Schlegel*] The Danish philosopher and religious thinker Søren Kierkegaard (1813–1855); the German philosopher and man of letters Friedrich Schlegel (1772–1829).

276.38 Sierra Maestra types] Supporters of the Cuban Revolution.

278.14–16 quoted Nietzsche . . . many a bad night] In *Jenseits von Gut und Böse* (*Beyond Good and Evil*, 1886).

281.37 Hitchcock-Truffaut book] *Hitchcock/Truffaut* (1966) by the French filmmaker François Truffaut (1932–1984), based on conversations with the English director Alfred Hitchcock (1899–1980).

282.33–34 Mme. Boucicault, widow of the department-store owner.] Marguerite Boucicault (1816–1887), the widow of the cofounder of Paris's Bon Marché department store, made significant contributions to its operations and was a philanthropist.

285.2–3 his great work *Don Juan Triumphant*] The name of the fictional opera composed by Erik (or the Phantom), the protagonist of *The Phantom of the Opera* (1910), novel by the French writer Gaston Leroux (1868–1927).

285.34 Christine] Christine Daaé, singer with whom the Phantom is in love.

286.10 The acid] The Phantom's face has been disfigured by acid in the novel's 1943 film adaptation but not in the novel itself.

286.36–37 *The Secret of the Yellow Room*.] Novel by Leroux published in 1907.

287.7–8 "*All men that are ruined . . . natural propensities,*"] From "Letters on a Regicide Peace," letter 1 (1796), by the Anglo-Irish philosopher and social theorist Edmund Burke (1729–1797).

293.1 Bulwer-Lytton] The English novelist, playwright, and politician Edward Bulwer-Lytton (1803–1873).

293.17 Robert-Houdin] The French illusionist, watchmaker, and popular Parisian performer Jean-Eugène Robert-Houdin (1805–1871).

293.33 Mr. Christopher medal] The devotional St. Christopher medal depicts the patron saint of travelers.

294.3 Moholy-Nagy] László Moholy-Nagy (1895–1946), Hungarian-born artist who worked across media, and especially in photography, painting, and design; he taught at the Bauhaus, an experimental school of art and design in Weimar, Germany, 1923–28.

294.35 Tugendhat House] Villa Tugendhat, modernist residence (1928–30) in Brno, Czechoslovakia, designed by Ludwig Mies van der Rohe (1886–1969) and Lilly Reich (1885–1947).

297.34 *bozzetti*] Italian: sketches.

298.24 King Lud] Legendary pre-Roman British king, reputed to have founded London.

302.11 Swedenborg] Emanuel Swedenborg (1688–1772), Swedish theologian, philosopher, and mystic.

302.25–30 "Some of the most intelligent . . . not clothed."] From Swedenborg's *Heaven and Its Wonders and Hell, from Things Heard and Seen* (1758).

306.4 *Toynbee's*] The English historian Arnold Toynbee (1889–1975).

317.3 "*Masters of War*"] Song (1963) by Bob Dylan (b. 1941).

317.14 "*Me and My Winstons*,"] Commercial jingle from a television advertisement for Winston cigarettes.

320.5–11 original gravure . . . picture of a tree] *Le 16 Septembre*, etching by the Belgian artist René Magritte (1898–1967) after his 1955 painting.

325.29 "Victimas de Pecado,"] *Victimas del Pecado* (*Victims of Sin*, 1950), Mexican film directed by Emilio Fernández (1904–1986).

326.2 great singer Moonbelly] The name suggests a fusion of the folk and blues singer, songwriter, and guitar virtuoso Leadbelly (Huddie Ledbetter, 1889–1949) and the blind Manhattan street performer and avant-garde musician Moondog (Louis Hardin, 1916–1999), known as "the Viking of Sixth Avenue."

326.5 Vercingetorix] See note 258.34.

328.30 Sacred Rota] The Vatican's foremost tribunal.

330.18 Hector Guimard] Not a trombone player but a French architect and designer (1867–1942) at the forefront of the art nouveau movement.

331.22–23 As Goethe said . . . is green.] From the lines spoken by Mephistopheles in the first part (1808) of Goethe's drama *Faust*, scene 7, lines 2038–39.

SADNESS

334.1 *To Kirk . . . Starr*] Kirkpatrick Sale (b. 1937), writer, political theorist, and environmentalist, and his wife the editor Faith Sale (1936–1999) lived in the same building as Barthelme in New York City; she would be the editor of Barthelme's collection *Sixty Stories* at G. P. Putnam's Sons. Barthelme's friend Harrison Starr was a film producer and director.

335.1 *Critique de la Vie Quotidienne*] *Critique of Everyday Life*, title of three-volume study published from 1947 to 1981 by the Marxist French sociologist, philosopher, and theorist Henri Lefebvre (1901–1991), as well as a description more broadly of one of the chief emphases of his work.

335.7 "*Femmes enceintes . . . de bifteck cru!*"] French: Pregnant women, don't eat raw steak!

335.13 Arne Jacobsen] Danish architect and designer (1902–1971).

335.14–15 "*Une Maison Qui Capte la Nature.*"] French: A House That Captures Nature.

335.16 *actualité* pieces] Current events pieces, articles about the present.

337.2–3 St. Catherine of Siena . . . Pope Gregory] Over three months in Avignon in 1376 and through later correspondence, Catherine of Siena (1347–1380) mounted a successful campaign to persuade Pope Gregory XI (c. 1329–1378) to restore the papacy to Rome.

339.9 "Intimations of mortality,"] Cf. the title of William Wordsworth's poem "Ode: Intimations of Immortality from Recollections of Early Childhood" (1807).

342.24 best Piagetian principles.] Ideas about child development put forth by the Swiss psychologist Jean Piaget (1896–1980).

343.1 *Träumerei*] Title ("Dreaming") of a piece in Robert Schumann's piano suite *Kinderszenen* (*Scenes of Childhood*, 1838).

343.11 *Nelson Mass* of Haydn] The D-minor *Missa in Angustiis* (*Mass for Troubled Times*, 1798) by Joseph Haydn (1732–1809).

343.17 Spontini] The Italian composer Gaspare Spontini (1774–1851), whose works include the opera *Agnes von Hohenstaufen* (1827).

343.24 a Putzi] The nickname of the Hungarian composer Franz Liszt (1811–1886).

343.28 bringing in the sheaves.] Title of hymn with words (1874) by Knowles Shaw (1834–1878), sung most often to music (1880) by George Minor (1845–1904).

344.11 Mascagni] Pietro Mascagni (1863–1945), Italian composer of operas, most notably *Cavalleria Rusticana* (1890).

344.28 the persistence of memory] Title of well-known painting (1931) by the Spanish surrealist painter Salvador Dalí (1904–1989) depicting melting clocks.

345.23 Glazunov] The Russian composer Alexander Glazunov (1865–1936).

353.3 Parke-Bernet] New York City auction house that became part of Sotheby's.

356.14 Marshal Foch] The French military leader Ferdinand Foch (1851–1929), supreme commander of the allied forces in the final months of World

War I and the official who accepted Germany's surrender on November 11, 1918.

358.11 *Sturmgeschütz*] A German armored vehicle of the Second World War.

359.9 Poets' Corner] Section of Westminster Abbey in London dedicated to tombs and commemorative monuments of poets and writers, including Chaucer, Spenser, Dickens, and Tennyson.

366.4 Bonnard.] Pierre Bonnard (1867–1947), French painter, member of the avant-garde artists' group known as the Nabis.

367.14 *Osservatore Romano* . . . Diet of Worms] *L'Osservatore Romano*, daily newspaper of the Vatican; Diet of Worms, assembly of the Holy Roman Empire in the German city of Worms in 1521 that unsuccessfully demanded that Martin Luther repudiate his views.

369.15 d'Alembert] Jean le Rond d'Alembert (1717–1783), French mathematician who co-edited the *Encyclopedia* with Diderot.

373.8 Walden] The German artist and gallerist Herwarth Walden (pseud. Georg Lewin, 1879–1941), whose Sturm Gallery in Berlin exhibited Klee's works.

376.3 Dreyer] The Danish filmmaker Carl Dreyer (1889–1968), director of *The Passion of Joan of Arc* (1928) and *Gertrud* (1964), among other films.

376.9 Dziga-Vertov] Soviet filmmaker (1896–1954) of films such as *The Man with the Movie Camera* (1929) and *Three Songs of Lenin* (1934), a leader of a movement in Soviet cinema.

376.35–37 Correlation . . . according to Hagman.] In Elmer R. Hagman, "A Study of Fears of Children of Pre-School Age," *Journal of Experimental Education* (December 1932).

377.17 quoting Nietzsche] See *Morgenröte* (*Daybreak*, 1881), section 153.

378.25 *Finlandia*] Orchestral and choral work (1899) by the Finnish composer Jean Sibelius (1865–1957).

378.26 I. F. Stone] Left-wing investigative journalist (1907–1989).

378.39–379.1 the change of Philomel, by the barbarous king] Quoted from T. S. Eliot's *The Waste Land*, part II, line 99, referring to the ancient Greek story of the rape of Philomela by King Tereus of Thrace, who also cut out her tongue; she was later transformed into a nightingale.

379.1 ¡*huelga!*] Spanish: strike.

379.2 Mongo Santamaria] Cuban-born conga drummer and bandleader (1917–2003).

379.2–3 St. John of the Cross] Spanish priest, mystical writer, and poet (1542–1591).

379.3 Melmoth the Wanderer] Eponymous protagonist of novel (1820) by the Irish writer Charles Robert Maturin (1782–1824) about a man who has sold his soul to the devil.

381.15 *Victory through Air Power!*] Wartime Disney animated documentary (1943) based on the book (1942) by the Russian-born pilot and aircraft designer Alexander de Seversky (1894–1974).

381.18 China Clipper] A Martin M-130, flying boat built for Pan American Airways that made transpacific flights for mail and passenger service, 1933–45.

381.19 Flying Wings] Aircraft without a fuselage or tail.

381.24 Spads and Fokkers] Planes made, respectively, by the French aircraft manufacturer SPAD (an acronym of Société pour l'aviation et ses dérivés), in operation 1911–21, and by the Dutch-based manufacturer Fokker.

395.33–34 "Let's Burn Down the Cornfield."] Song (1970) by the singer, songwriter, and composer Randy Newman (b. 1943).

396.10–11 "Bye Bye Baby . . . Baby."] "Bye Bye Baby," song from the musical *Gentleman Prefer Blondes* (1949), lyrics by Leo Robin (1900–1984), music by Jule Styne (1905–1994).

399.17 Charles Evans Hughes] American jurist (1862–1948) who served as a Supreme Court justice in 1910–16, secretary of state in 1921–25, and chief justice in 1930–41.

405.6 Scheler] Max Scheler (1874–1928), German phenomenologist philosopher and author of *On the Eternal in Man* (1960) and *The Nature of Sympathy* (1970).

410.7 Grand Cham] Cf. "The Grand Cham" (1922), story published in *Adventure* magazine by the American fiction writer Harold Lamb (1892–1962), and the "great Cham," as Samuel Johnson was sometimes called.

419.10–11 *"studiare da un punto . . . di un—"*] Italian: study from a formalistic and semiological point of view the relationship between a text's language and the codification of a—.

420.6–7 St. Paul says] In 1 Corinthians 7.

420.29 Simone Simon] French film actor (1910–2005) whose Hollywood films include *The Devil and Daniel Webster* (1941) and *Cat People* (1942).

420.30 Raymond Radiguet] French writer (1903–1923), author of the novel *Le Diable au Corps* (*The Devil in the Flesh*, 1923); not an actor.

421.14 Casals] The Spanish cellist Pablo Casals (1876–1973).

430.9 VISTA] Volunteers in Service to America, national poverty relief program.

431.1 *Daumier*] The French artist Honoré Daumier (1808–1870), known for his political caricatures and satirical tableaux of French social life.

431.6 self-slaughter] See Shakespeare, *Hamlet*, I.ii.129–32: "O that this too too sullied flesh would melt, / Thaw, and resolve itself into a dew! / Or that the Everlasting had not fix'd / His canon 'gainst self-slaughter!"

431.20 Messalina] Empress Messalina Valeria (d. 48 C.E.), wife of the Roman emperor Claudius (r. 41–54 C.E.), notorious for her promiscuity.

442.21 "I must have the new . . . world."] From *Clymène* (1671) by the French poet Jean de la Fontaine (1621–1695).

445.24 Brann the Iconoclast] William Cowper Brann (1855–1898), owner and editor of *The Iconoclast*, published in Waco, Texas. He was shot to death by a reader angry over a published attack on Baylor University; Brann mortally wounded his attacker.

AMATEURS

448.1 *Grace Paley*] American short story writer (1922–2007), with whom Barthelme was briefly romantically involved.

449.24 Alice Cooper] Stage name of Vincent Furnier (b. 1948), provocative rock performer known for his neogothic persona onstage.

450.2 I saw the figure 5 writ in gold] Cf. *I Saw the Figure 5 in Gold* (1928), painting by American artist Charles Demuth (1883–1935), whose title and conception were inspired by lines from "The Great Figure" (1920), poem by the American poet William Carlos Williams.

468.6 Gristede's] New York City grocery-store chain.

472.19 Busoni] The Italian composer and pianist Ferruccio Busoni (1866–1924).

473.9–10 Grace Under Pressure] Definition of "guts" made by Ernest Hemingway (1899–1961) in a profile by Dorothy Parker in *The New Yorker*, November 30, 1929.

477.10 Orson Welles picture] *Citizen Kane* (1941).

478.14–15 the late Huey P. Long] American lawyer and populist Democratic politician (1893–1935) known as "The Kingfish," who was governor of Louisiana, 1928–32, and U.S. senator from 1932 to 1935, when he was assassinated.

482.5–6 HACHARD & CIE?] French art-poster company.

483.25 stone soup] Reference to a folktale in which a traveler arrives in a village and boils a cauldron of water with a stone in it, then convinces the residents to help him make soup by contributing ingredients they had been hoarding.

485.29 TDY] Temporary duty.

485.34 I.G.] Inspector general. "Bird colonel" is full colonel, not a lieutenant colonel.

489.13 R.A.] Regular army.

490.12 Andromache!] In *The Iliad*, the wife of Hector, who was taken captive when Troy fell.

494.1 Bengal Lancers] Regiments in the British Indian Army during British colonial rule of India.

494.4 "Love of Life,] Soap opera on CBS television, 1951–80.

494.9 Landseer] See note 241.33.

498.38 A. E. Housman] English poet (1859–1936), author of *A Shropshire Lad* (1896).

506.11 *désabusé*] French: disillusioned.

507.27–28 Hyde Park . . . President,"] Springwood, the estate of Franklin Delano Roosevelt (1882–1945), is in Hyde Park, New York.

512.2–3 "AND NOW . . . heart,"] From "Stardust," song (1927) by Hoagy Carmichael (1899–1981), first recorded as an instrumental; Mitchell Parish (1900–1993) added lyrics in 1929.

512.20 "De bustibus . . . disputandum,"] Cf. "De gustibus non est disputandum," Latin maxim meaning "There's no disputing matters of taste."

514.9 Merle Travis] Country singer, guitarist, and songwriter (1917–1983).

514.21 Sonny and Cher show] *The Sonny & Cher Comedy Hour*, CBS television variety show, 1971–74, 1976–77 (when it was called *The Sonny and Cher Show*), hosted by the singers and actors Sonny Bono (1935–1998) and Cher (Cherilyn Sarkisian, b. 1946).

517.4 Fisher King] Figure in Arthurian legend, discussed in *From Ritual to Romance* (1920), study by the British medievalist Jessie L. Weston (1850–1928), and appearing in T. S. Eliot's *The Waste Land*, as does the Arthurian locale the Chapel Perilous mentioned later in this story.

518.6–7 steady-state cosmologists, Bondi, Gold, and Hoyle] The three mathematicians and cosmologists who in 1948, working at Cambridge University, proposed the steady-state model to explain the universe: the Vienna-born mathematician Hermann Bondi (1919–2005), the Vienna-born astrophysicist Thomas Gold (1920–2004), and English mathematician and astronomer Fred Hoyle (1915–2001).

518.9 Merzbau] Sculptural installation (c. 1923–37) by the German artist Kurt Schwitters (1887–1948), constructed in the artist's studio in Hanover. The installation was a kind of three-dimensional collage, with stalactite-like columns and cavelike recesses in which Schwitters placed small objects he had come upon or that put him in mind of friends.

518.9–10 Van de Graaff machine] Van de Graaf generator, an electrostatic generator invented in 1929 by Robert J. Van de Graaf (1901–1967).

518.23 Sergeant Preston of the Yukon] Eponymous hero of a television series broadcast on CBS, 1955–58, a Western starring Richard Simmons (1913–2003).

518.23–24 Sam Browne belt] A belt invented by the British general Samuel Browne (1824–1901) and worn by U.S. Army officers; it has a supporting strap over the right shoulder.

530.29 the true gen.] Phrase used by Ernest Hemingway in a 1945 letter to Malcolm Cowley: "The gen is RAF slang for intelligence, the hand out at the briefing. The *true gen* is what they know but don't tell you. The true gen very hard to obtain."

530.31 galgenspiel] German: hangman (the game).

540.14–15 Saint-Exupéry . . . Night flight?] Antoine de Saint Exupéry (1900–1944), French author and pilot, wrote several books on aviation, including *Vol de nuit* (Night Flight, 1931) and *Terre des hommes* (translated as *Wind, Sand and Stars*, 1939).

540.32–33 *From Ritual to Romance*, by Jessie L. Weston] See note 517.4.

541.22 BOAC] British Overseas Airways Corporation, a precursor to British Airways.

542.19 Hopper] The American painter Edward Hopper (1882–1967).

550.31–32 A. F. of L.] American Federation of Labor.

GREAT DAYS

552.1 *Thomas B. Hess*] American art curator (1920–1978) and longtime editor of the magazine *ARTnews*.

554.14 Broadcasting House] London headquarters of the BBC.

555.15–16 the sexy part of *Tristan und Isolde*.] "Liebesnacht," the love duet in act 2 of Richard Wagner's opera *Tristan und Isolde* (1865).

557.3–4 Leskov's] The Russian journalist, novelist, and short story writer Nikolai Leskov (1831–1895).

563.16 Athene's statue] The Palladium, a wooden statue in ancient Troy that was supposed to ensure that the city could not be conquered. According to legend it was stolen by Diomedes and Odysseus during the Trojan War.

565.30 Great Lyceum.] School just beyond the city boundary of Athens established by Aristotle.

567.36   Eckermann's *Conversations with Goethe.*] Collection of Goethe's remarks (1832–33) gathered by his literary assistant Johann Peter Eckermann (1792–1854) and an account of their relationship. The quote, made by Goethe on April 2, 1825, is taken from Eckermann's book.

568.10   the G.I. Bill.] Officially called the Servicemen's Readjustment Act (1944), federal legislation that guaranteed veterans access to higher education and provided tuition funding.

568.22   Momma didn't 'low] Reference to the American folk song "Momma Don't Allow."

569.15   Eleusinian mysteries] Ancient Greek religious rites performed in honor of Demeter, the Greek goddess of corn, who allowed nature to be reborn in the spring, when her daughter Persephone returned from the underworld.

571.37–38   whom the Lord loveth He chasteneth] From Hebrews 12:6: "For whom the Lord loveth he chasteneth, and scourgeth every son whom he receiveth."

572.1–2   *Un Coup de Dés*] See note 37.25.

573.37–38   Hite Report.] *The Hite Report on Female Sexuality* (1976) by the American-born German sex researcher Shere Hite (1942–2020).

576.26   Doña Marina] La Malinche, an enslaved Nahua woman who was given to Hernando Cortés in 1519 and who served as Cortés's interpreter and adviser during the conquest of Mexico; she was the mother of a son by Cortés.

576.30   Father Sanchez?] Miguel Sánchez (1594–1674), a Mexican priest who was the author of the first published account (1648) of the Virgin of Guadalupe, a representation of a dark-skinned Virgin Mary who appeared to one of the first Christian converts in North America, Juan Diego, on December 9, 1531.

578.10–11   Cuitlahuac] Cuitláhuac (c. 1476–1520), Aztec leader who resisted the Spanish conquest, most notably during the expulsion of Cortés's forces from Tenochtitlán in 1520; he died shortly afterward during a smallpox outbreak.

578.27–28   Juan de Escalante] Spanish military officer (d. 1519) accompanying Cortés.

581.22   *schnell*] German: fast.

582.17–18   Chalchihuitlicue] Water goddess of the Aztecs.

582.28   "I am the State!"] Remark by the French king Louis XIV (1643–1715, r. 1643–1715): "L'état, c'est moi!"

582.37–39 Pitalpitoque . . . Tendile."] Pitalpitoque and Tendile were Aztec governors who met with Cortés; Quintalbor was a chief said to resemble Cortés in appearance.

596.15 I.T.U.] International Typographical Union, a now defunct labor union.

598.5 APC] Armored personnel carrier.

598.26 Swedish poet Bodil Malmsten] Also a novelist and memoirist (1944–2016), whose books include *The Price of Water in Finistère* (2001).

600.14–15 Kulicke frames] Modern frames designed by the American frame designer, artist, and businessman Robert M. Kulicke (1924–2007).

601.1 *The Abduction from the Seraglio*] Title of Mozart's 1782 opera.

601.2 Butler building] Prefabricated metal building designed and produced by Butler Manufacturing.

601.18 Waylon Jennings] Country music singer, guitarist, and songwriter (1937–2002).

601.27 Darvon] Opioid painkiller containing propoxyphene, formerly a prescription medication but now banned in the United States.

602.33 Sea & Ski] Brand of suntan lotion.

605.1 *Edward Lear*] English poet and artist (1812–1888), the author of nonsense poems collected in *A Book of Nonsense* (1846).

605.18–19 the words of Lear's great friend, Tennyson] From the verse play *Becket* (1884) and "The Brook" (1855), respectively, by the English poet Alfred, Lord Tennyson (1809–1892).

609.16 *Emmanuelle Around the World*] *Emanuelle: Perché violenza alle donne?* (1977), softcore pornographic Italian film starring Laura Gemser (b. 1950).

609.20–21 *Remember 17 June?*] Marshal Philippe Pétain (1856–1951), addressing the nation as France's newly appointed premier on June 17, 1940, called for a stop to fighting against the German invasion; he would lead the government, headquartered in Vichy, that collaborated with the Germans throughout the war. In 1945 he was tried and convicted of treason.

614.37 patassas] A type of freshwater fish found in Louisiana.

617.13 Mowgli] See note 173.35–36.

617.15 Scriabin] Russian composer Alexander Scriabin (1872–1915).

617.21 Cuisine Minceur] French: Lean Cuisine.

619.4 Eternal Return?] Throughout his writings Friedrich Nietzsche explored the idea of eternal recurrence, in which everything perpetually repeats itself.

619.7 "One O'Clock Jump,"] Jazz composition (1937) by Count Basie (1904–1984), a standard; it inspired "Two O'Clock Jump" (1939), composition by the trumpeter and bandleader Harry James (1916–1983).

619.23 Bomba the Jungle Boy] Protagonist of a series of boys' adventure books written by different authors under the pseudonym Roy Rockwood, 1926–38, and of several films, 1949–55.

622.19–20 loaf or a fish? . . . Christian imagery] Referring to one of the miracles of Jesus, in which five loaves and two fish were multiplied to feed thousands.

625.9 Coushatta Indian] Indigenous nation also called Koasati (the name of their language) whose members live mostly in Louisiana, Texas, and Oklahoma.

630.22 "I think that I shall never see"] From "Trees" (1913), poem by the American poet Joyce Kilmer (1886–1918).

630.37–631.1 Bessie Smith . . . Franklin.] The blues singer Bessie Smith (1894–1937); Alice Babs, stage name of Alice Nilson (1924–2014), Swedish singer and actor who performed songs in jazz and other genres; the British singer-songwriter Joan Armatrading (b. 1950); R&B superstar Aretha Franklin (1942–2018).

631.5 Sweet Emma Barrett] Jazz pianist and singer (1897–1963) from New Orleans.

631.7 *Das Lied von der Erde*] Symphonic piece with vocal parts (*The Song of the Earth*, 1909) by Gustav Mahler (1860–1911).

631.18 Z.P.G.] Zero population growth.

632.12 Cardinal Spellman] Francis Spellman (1889–1967), Roman Catholic archbishop of New York, 1939–67.

632.20 William of Ockham.] English philosopher and theologian (1285–1349).

632.20–21 Vienna Circle] A group of philosophers whose ideas were associated with logical positivism. It flourished in the interwar years and included among its members its cofounder Moritz Schlick (1882–1936), Otto Neurath (1882–1945), and Rudolf Carnap (1891–1970).

632.21 The Frankfurt School] Marxist-oriented circle of social and cultural theorists including the German-Jewish thinkers Theodor Adorno (1903–1969), Max Horkheimer (1895–1973), and Herbert Marcuse (1898–1979).

632.21 Manichaeus.] Persian philosopher (also Mani or Manes, 215–276), who taught that the universe is divided between the forces of good and evil.

632.21 Peirce.] The American pragmatist philosopher Charles Sanders Peirce (1839–1914).

632.21–22 Occasionalism.] The philosophical belief that restricts causation to the actions of God, a view associated with but not limited to the French philosopher Nicholas Malebranche (1638–1715).

632.26 Self-slaughter.] See note 431.6.

633.29 Purity of heart is to will one thing.] From the title of Kierkegaard's "On the Occasion of a Confession: Purity of Heart Is to Will One Thing" (1847).

634.11 Walkin' my baby back home] Title of song (1930), lyrics by Roy Turk (1892–1934), music by Fred Ahlert (1892–1953).

636.5 "How High the Moon."] Jazz song (1940), music by Morgan Lewis (1906–1968), lyrics by Nancy Hamilton (1908–1985).

639.18 Oni of Ife.] Ooni of Ife, title for the traditional ruler of the Yoruba kingdom of Ife-Ife.

639.21 "Vulcan and Maia."] Painting (c. 1585) by the Flemish artist Bartholomäus Spranger (1546–1611).

641.23 "Tancred Succored by Ermina."] Painting (1660) by the Lucchese artist Pietro Ricchi (1606–1675).

642.39 "Portia Wounding Her Thigh."] Painting (1664) by the Bolognese artist Elisabetta Sirani (1638–1665).

643.1–2 "Wolfram . . . Corpse of Her Lover."] Painting (1812–20) by Swiss-born English painter Henry Fuseli (1741–1820).

644.6 Delacroix] French artist Eugène Delacroix (1798–1863)

FROM SIXTY STORIES

651.31 John Graham!] American modernist artist (1881–1961).

658.13–14 *esse est percipi*] Latin: to be is to be perceived, the idea at the core of the Anglo-Irish philosopher George Berkeley's (1685–1753) subjective idealism.

659.2 *pain*] French: bread.

659.15 Gorgias] Rhetorician (c. 485–c. 380 B.C.E.) who came to Athens from the Sicilian town of Leontini, the author of the lost work *On That Which Is Not, or Nature*.

659.19 Athos, Porthos, or Aramis] The individual Three Musketeers in the novel (1844) of that name by the French writer Alexandre Dumas *père* (1802–1870).

660.4–5 Heidegger suggests that "Nothing nothings"] Cf. "Das Nichts selbst nichtet" (Nothing nihilates of its own) in "What Is Metaphysics?" (1929), lecture by the German philosopher Martin Heidegger (1889–1976).

660.28–29   *Charlie Is My Darling*] A traditional Scottish song.

660.35   "Do not go gentle into that good night"] Title and recurring line of the villanelle "Do Not Go Gentle into That Good Night" (1947) by the Welsh poet Dylan Thomas (1914–1953).

660.37   says Beckett's Krapp] In *Krapp's Last Tape* (1958), play by the Irish playwright and novelist Samuel Beckett (1906–1989).

660.38–661.1   rape of Lucrece . . . Tarquin? . . . Shakespeare] As recounted by the Roman historian Livy, the Roman noblewoman Lucretia was raped by the son of the Lucius Tarquinius Superbus (Tarquin the Proud), the legendary seventh and final king of Rome. After her rape Lucretia committed suicide; reaction to her death precipitated the overthrow of the Roman monarchy. The episode is the basis for Shakespeare's narrative poem *The Rape of Lucrece*.

660.39–661.2   raglan sleeves . . . Lord Raglan] The raglan sleeve, which extends to the collar in one piece, was designed for FitzRoy James Henry Somerset, 1st Baron Raglan (1788–1855), British military officer who had lost an arm due to injuries sustained at the Battle of Waterloo.

663.32–33   cloud of unknowing] Title of an anonymous treatise of Christian mysticism written in the later fourteenth century.

666.16   *augenscheinlich*] German: apparent.

670.2   Flee from the wrath to come] Cf. Luke 3:7.

675.5   Knights of the Invisible Empire.] The Ku Klux Klan.

675.33   "Publish and be damned!"] See the remark of the British scientist and author Jacob Bronowski (1908–1974), "If a man is a scientist, like me, he'll always say 'Publish and be damned.'"

676.17   *hors concours*] French: out of the competition.

677.25–26   Remember ye not . . . things?] 2 Thessalonians 2:5.

678.6   *gardes-bébés*] French: babysitters.

678.33   Rupert's Land] Prince Rupert's Land, historical designation of the area comprising the Hudson Bay drainage basin in Canada.

680.17   "Genevieve, Oh Genevieve."] "Sweet Genevieve" (1869), song with lyrics by George Cooper (1840–1927), music by Henry L. Tucker (1826–1882).

681.12–13   the great Peripatetic] Aristotle.

684.8   Man Mountain Dean] Pseudonym of Georgia-born wrestler and entertainer Frank S. Leavitt (1890–1953).

684.16–17   the salt losing its savor . . . air.] See Matthew 5:13 ("Ye are the salt of the earth: but if the salt have lost his savor, wherewith shall it be salted?")

and Matthew 6:26–28 ("Behold the fowls of the air: for they sow not, neither do they reap, nor gather into barns, yet your heavenly father feedeth them").

685.37 long tall Sally] Hit record (1955) for Little Richard (pseud. Richard Penniman, 1932–2020).

686.5 Malraux] The French novelist and cultural critic André Malraux (1901–1976).

689.20 *Oui, je sais.*] French: Yes, I know.

692.10 the famous one] Sybil Leek (1917–1982), English occultist, astrologer, columnist, and author who settled in the United States in the 1960s and became widely known for her *Diary of a Witch* (1968) and other writings on supernatural phenomena.

707.15 it was a dark and stormy night] From the opening line of English novelist Edward Bulwer-Lytton's *Paul Clifford* (1830), often parodied.

710.15 Ghost Dance] Reference to a late nineteenth-century pan-Indian religious movement originating among the Northern Paiutes of Nevada, which promised the renewal of the world and a reunification of the living and the dead. Its most important ritual was a ceremonial round dance repeated on successive nights.

722.28 *mot juste.*] French: the precise word.

725.1 *The Emperor*] In a 1981 interview Barthelme noted that this story was inspired by "the so-called First Emperor, Ch'in Shih Huang Ti" (Pinyin: Qín Shǐ Huáng; 260–210 B.C.E.), the founder of the Qin dynasty and the first ruler of a unified China.

725.27 assassin Ching K'o] Jing Ke (d. 225 B.C.E.) died in a failed assassination attempt on the future Emperor Qín.

728.16–17 Gilda. . . . sizzling blouse.] Rita Hayworth (1918–1987) played the title character of the 1946 film *Gilda*.

731.3 OD] Olive drab.

734.12–14 glass . . . darkly.] Cf. 1 Corinthians 13:12.

737.13–14 "You shall not . . . Bryan.] From the "cross of gold" speech delivered by William Jennings Bryan (1860–1925) at the Democratic Convention in Chicago, July 9, 1896.

738.15–16 according to Alfred Frankenstein.] In his entry on the American artist John Frederick Peto (1854–1907) in the exhibition catalog *The Reality of Appearance: The Trompe l'œil Tradition in American Painting* (1970) by the American art historian, music critic, and musician Alfred Frankenstein (1906–1981). Frankenstein also wrote a monograph on the American painter William Michael Harnett (1848–1892), mentioned just below, in *After the*

Hunt: William Harnett and Other American Still Life Painters, 1870–1900 (1953).

741.2 as Colonel Thursday] In *Fort Apache* (1948), Western directed by John Ford (1894–1973).

741.10 Robert Young says: "Sanka] The film and television actor Robert Young (1907–1998) was a television spokesman for Sanka instant decaffeinated coffee.

742.13 Poulenc to Bob Wills] The French avant-garde composer Francis Poulenc (1899–1963); the Western swing bandleader, fiddle player, singer, and songwriter Bob Wills (1905–1975).

742.15–16 Jim Dine . . . Richard Hamilton.] The American pop artist Jim Dine (b. 1935); the Italian metaphysical painter Giorgio de Chirico (1888–1978); the German surrealist artist Hans Bellmer (1902–1975), active in France; the English Pop artist Richard Hamilton (1922–2011).

743.34 "I'm an Old Cowhand."] "I'm an Old Cowhand (on the Rio Grande)" (1936), song by Johnny Mercer (1909–1976), written for the film *Rhythm on the Range*, in which it was sung by Bing Crosby.

748.37 blood on the saddle] Title of an anonymous cowboy ballad.

OVERNIGHT TO MANY DISTANT CITIES

752.1 *Marion*] Barthelme's wife Marion Knox Barthelme (1944–2011).

753.14 *Wiwi Lönn*] Wivi Lönn (1872–1966), Finnish architect.

753.20–21 *Chandigarh, Brasilia, Taliesin.*] Planned city in India designed by the Swiss architect Le Corbusier (1887–1965); planned city designed as Brazil's new capital and inaugurated in 1960, designed by the Brazilian architects Lúcio Costa (1902–1998) and Oscar Niemeyer (1907–2012); the estate of the American architect Frank Lloyd Wright (1867–1959) near Spring Green, Wisconsin, parts of which were rebuilt twice after two separate fires.

754.6 *FASTIGIUM.*] An architectural term for a pediment or end gable as well as a word used to describe the height of a fever.

762.4–5 Bareass On the Grass] Sardonic reference to Édouard Manet's painting *Le Déjeuner sur l'herbe* (1863).

763.18 *VDT*] Video display terminals.

763.29 *Guild*] The Newspaper Guild of New York.

767.33 Junior League?] Charitable aid organization of upper-class young women founded in 1901 by a railroad magnate's daughter, Mary Harriman (1881–1934).

767.34 a Fauve?] Member of Les Fauves (French for "Wild Beasts," as they were dismissively described by a critic in 1905), an early twentieth-century European art movement whose central figures included the French artists Henri Matisse (1869–1954), André Derain (1880–1954), and Maurice de Vlaminck (1876–1958).

770.17 "Verklärte Nacht"] Title of composition ("Transfigured Night," 1899) for string sextet, op. 4, by the Austrian-born composer Arnold Schoenberg (1874–1951).

771.26–27 *Charles the Good, Charles the Bold, and Charles the Fair.*] Charles I, Count of Flanders (1083–1127); Charles, the final duke of Burgundy (1433–1477); Charles IV of France (1294–1328).

772.27 Seven Sisters] Term coined by Italian government official Enrico Mattei (1906–1962) to describe the seven oil companies Standard Oil of New Jersey, Royal Dutch Shell, Anglo Persian Oil Company, Standard Oil of New York, Standard Oil of California, Gulf Oil, and Texaco.

776.32–33 Without music, Nietzsche said, the world would be a mistake.] In *Götzen-Dämmerung* (*Twilight of the Idols*, 1888), "Maxims and Arrows," 33.

777.31 Protocols of Zion] *Protocols of the Elders of Zion*, fraudulent document forged by Russian police officials exposing a purported plot of Jews and Freemasons to subvert Christian civilization and create a world state; published in Russia in 1902, it was translated into German, English, French, Polish, and other languages in the 1920s.

779.4 the Cars] Pop-rock band with numerous hit singles, starting with "Just What I Needed" in 1978.

779.10 Rod Stewart and the B-52s.] Rod Stewart (b. 1945), English rock star who was lead singer of The Faces and has enjoyed a successful solo career; the B-52s, New Wave band whose earliest popular success was "Rock Lobster" (1979).

782.1 *Captain Blood*] Hero of the adventure novel *Captain Blood* (1922) by the Italian-born English novelist Rafael Sabatini (1875–1950) and its many sequels.

787.6 *Benvenuto Cellini*] Italian painter, goldsmith, sculptor, and writer (1500–1571).

787.25–26 *Yves Klein.*] French artist (1928–1962) whose use of nude female models as a means of applying paint to the canvases of his "Anthropometry" paintings is described here.

788.11 *Georges de La Tour*] French artist (1593–1652) whose paintings often feature striking images illuminated by candlelight and set against dark backgrounds.

789.14 *Vladimir Tatlin*] Russian constructivist artist (1885–1953), best known for his unrealized architectural design *Monument to the Third International* (1919–20).

790.1 *Conversations with Goethe*] See note 567.36.

790.26 Humboldt] The German naturalist and explorer Alexander von Humboldt (1769–1859).

792.12 Lessing.] The German philosopher, playwright, and scholar Gotthold Ephraim Lessing (1729–1781).

796.32–33 Langley . . . Marchionni] The English architect and landscape gardener Batty Langley (1696–1751), also the author of numerous books on building and architectural design; the German architect Joseph Effner (1687–1745), who served as court architect of Bavaria; the influential Scottish neoclassical architect and designer Robert Adam (1728–1792); the Italian architect Carl Marchionni (1702–1786), who among his other projects contributed designs to the Villa Alboni in Rome.

797.36 *Beatissime Pater*] Latin: Holy Father.

797.37–38 *ad pedes Sanctitatis Vestrae humillime provolutus*] Latin: humbly kneeling at the feet of Your Holiness.

800.1–2 *Klee said: One bone alone achieves nothing.*] In the Swiss artist Paul Klee's *Pedagogical Sketchbook* (1925). The remark by the German-born art historian and architectural critic Sybil Moholy-Nagy (1903–1971) at lines 800.30–31 is taken from her introduction to her English translation of Klee's book, published in 1953.

810.5 *Buxtehude*] Dieterich Buxtehude (c. 1637–1707), German-Danish organist and composer.

812.10 "Malagueña"] Popular song by the Cuban composer and pianist Ernesto Lecuona (1896–1963), originally part of his *Suite Andalucía* (1933).

812.30 "When Irish Eyes Are Smiling,"] Popular song (1912), lyrics by Chauncey Olcott (1858–1932) and George Graff, Jr. (1886–1973), music by Ernest R. Ball (1878–1927).

813.7 "Cherokee,"] Jazz song (1937) by the English bandleader and composer Ray Noble (1903–1978).

813.21 "Vienna"] "Wien, du Stadt meiner Traüme" (Vienna, City of My Dreams, 1914) by the Austrian composer Rudolf Sieczynski (1879–1952).

814.22 Ferenczi] Sándor Ferenczi (1873–1933), Hungarian psychoanalyst who collaborated with Freud.

814.24–25 of Victor Herbert's] Victor Herbert (1859–1924) was an American composer of operettas, including *The Fortune Teller* (1898), *Babes in Toyland* (1903), *Mlle. Modiste* (1905), and *The Red Mill* (1906).

814.29–30 *that which exists . . . does not*] From the ontological argument for the existence of God first put forth in the *Proslogion* (c. 1077–1078) of Anselm of Canterbury (1022–1109) and later developed by René Descartes, among other philosophers.

817.17 Goodnight Moon] Young children's book (1947), written by Margaret Wise Brown (1910–1952) and illustrated by Clement Hurd (1908–1988).

822.33 *Weegee*] Pseudonym of Arthur Fellig (1899–1968), American photographer known for his photographs of crime and accident scenes in New York City, among other urban subjects.

823.14 *Hot Club of France.*] Hot Club de France, organization devoted to jazz.

825.31 "Elmer's Tune."] Big-band song (1941) written by Sammy Gallop (1915–1971), Dick Jurgens (1910–1995), and Elmer Albrecht (1901–1959).

825.36 H. V. Kaltenborn.] Radio commentator and journalist (1878–1965) whose broadcasts were heard in millions of American households in the 1930s and 1940s.

827.10 R. D. Laing.] Scottish psychiatrist and author (1927–1989) whose books include *The Divided Self* (1960) and *Knots* (1970).

835.1 *The Palace at 4 A.M.*] Sculpture (1932) made of wood, glass, wire, and string by Alberto Giacometti (see note 116.39).

838.14 *Larousse*] French dictionary.

846.11 Parris Island] Marine Corps training base in South Carolina.

847.30 Schwitters] See note 518.9.

FROM FORTY STORIES

858.15 *Charity*] Drama (1874) by English playwright W. S. Gilbert (1836–1911).

858.17 *Saint Joan*] Play (1950) by the Irish playwright George Bernard Shaw (1856–1950).

866.5–8 Wassily . . . Ettore Sottsass] Modern furniture: the Wassily Chair, designed by the Hungarian-born architect and furniture designer Marcel Breuer (1902–1981); designers of the other pieces of furniture alluded to are the Scottish architect and designer Charles Rennie Mackintosh (1868–1928), the American furniture and industrial designers Charles Eames (1907–1978) and Ray Eames (1912–1988), and the Italian architect and designer Ettore Sottsass (1917–2007).

866.13 *Ah, je vois le jour, ah, Dieu*] French: Ah, I see the day, ah, God.

873.40 St. Vincent's] Hospital in Greenwich Village, 1849–2010.

875.1–2 *Bluebeard* . . . that door,"] In the folktale of Bluebeard, best known in the version by French fabulist Charles Perrault (1628–1703), Bluebeard tries to murder his wife Fatima after she opens a closet in his château against his express orders and discovers the corpses of his previous wives. He is himself killed by her brothers.

875.9 Dreyer, the American art dealer] Martin Dreyer (1909–2001) and Margaret Webb Dreyer (1911–1976) founded and operated the Dreyer Galleries in Houston, 1959–75.

876.4 Vanbrugh and Hawksmoor.] The English architect and playwright John Vanbrugh (1664–1726) and the English architect Nicholas Hawksmoor (c. 1661–1736), who assisted Vanbrugh on his Castle Howard and Blenheim Palace.

876.28–29 Buen Retiro] Real Fábrica del Buen Retiro, porcelain manufacturer in Madrid.

878.10 Panhards] Automobile produced by the French motor vehicle company Panhard, founded in 1887.

878.36 Bronzino] Florentine mannerist artist Agnolo di Cosimo di Mariano (1502–1572).

883.29–30 a figure . . . atop the Mormon temple] The angel Moroni, who according to the testimony of Joseph Smith (1805–1844), in 1823 revealed to him the location of golden tablets containing the scripture Smith later translated as the Book of Mormon.

884.31–32 disciple of Schumacher . . . of Fourier] The German-born British economist E. F. Schumacher (1911–1977), author of *Small Is Beautiful* (1973) and a well-known advocate for global sustainability; the American social and architecture critic Lewis Mumford (1895–1990); the French economic reformer and utopian social theorist Charles Fourier (1772–1837).

886.8–9 Wiener Werkstätte] Austrian design company that produced modern furniture, ceramics, clothing, and jewelry, founded in 1903 by Koloman Moser (1868–1918) and Josef Hoffmann (1870–1956).

886.11 *marché aux puces*] French: flea market.

893.27 Tillich] The German-born theologian Paul Tillich (1886–1965), author of *The Courage to Be* (1952) and *Dynamics of Faith* (1957).

894.32 Huysmans] Joris-Karl Huysmans (1848–1907), pen name of the French novelist and art critic Charles-Marie-Georges Huysmans (1848–1907), best known for *À Rebours* (*Against the Grain*, 1884) and *La-Bas* (*Down There*, 1891).

896.8 Harvey Cox, who speaks about "people's religion,"] In *The Seduction of the Spirit: The Use and Misuse of People's Religion* (1973) by the American theologian Harvey Cox (b. 1929).

897.8 *non serviam?*] Latin: I will not serve.

898.22 Alfred Adler] Austrian psychoanalyst (1870–1937), founder of a psychoanalytic school that he called Individual Psychology.

898.23–24 Huizinga . . . Otto Rank.] The Dutch historian and social theorist Johan Huizinga (1872–1945), whose books include *Herfsttij der Middeleeuwen* (*The Autumn of the Middle Ages*, 1919) and *Homo Ludens* (1938); the Austrian zoologist and animal behaviorist Konrad Lorenz (1903–1989), author of *King Solomon's Ring* (1949) and *On Aggression* (1963); the Austrian Freudian psychoanalyst Otto Rank (1884–1939), author of *Das Trauma der Geburt* (*The Trauma of Birth*, 1924).

898.23–24 Gregory Zilboorg.] Russian-born psychoanalyst (1890–1959) whose books include *Mind, Medicine, & Man* (1943) and *Psychoanalysis and Religion* (1962).

900.1–2 *aggiornamento*, to being brought up to date] This Italian word for modernization was used by Pope John XXIII and others to characterize the aims of the reformist Second Ecumenical Council of the Vatican, 1962–65, popularly known as Vatican II.

UNCOLLECTED STORIES

904.20 the stuff with Lumumba] Patrice Lumumba (1925–1961), a leader of the Congolese independence movement, was the first prime minister of the Congo, June 23–September 5, 1960. He was arrested on December 1 by troops loyal to Colonel Joseph Mobutu and shot on January 17, 1961, by Katanga secessionists led by Moise Tshombe, with possible CIA involvement in the assassination.

914.21 Josef Albers] German-born American artist and teacher (1888–1976), an experimental formalist who was one of the key figures of the Bauhaus movement.

914.25 Marie Laurencin] French modernist painter (1885–1956).

915.12 Rambler . . . Princess telephone?] See note 34.33; lightweight telephone introduced in 1959 by Bell, widely marketed to teenaged girls and their families.

915.22 Johnny Hodges] Longtime alto saxophonist (1906–1970) for the Duke Ellington Orchestra who also led his own big band from 1950 to 1955. The other members of Ellington's band named here are the saxophonist and clarinetist Harry Carney (1910–1974); the singer Ivie Anderson (1904–1949); the trombonist "Tricky Sam" Nanton (1904–1946); the violinist, trumpet player, and singer Ray Nance (1913–1976); the double bassist Jimmie Blanton (1918–1942); and the clarinetist Barney Bigard (1906–1980). The Ellington compositions named are from 1946, 1942, and 1926, respectively.

918.8 Stirling Moss model?] Driving gloves produced by Dents, named for the champion British Formula One race car driver Stirling Moss (1929–2020).

923.14 Orff] The German composer Carl Orff (1895–1982), whose works include the orchestral cantata *Carmina Burana* (1937).

924.9 El Lissitzky] Russian artist, architect, and designer (1890–1941).

926.12 "Die Walküre" . . . "Le Damnation de Faust,"] Operas (1870; 1846) by Richard Wagner and Hector Berlioz, respectively.

926.19 "Der Barbier von Baghdad,"] Comic opera (*The Barber of Baghdad*, 1858) by the German composer Peter Cornelius (1824–1874).

*This book is set in 10 point ITC Galliard, a face designed
for digital composition by Matthew Carter and based
on the sixteenth-century face Granjon. The paper is acid-free
lightweight opaque that will not turn yellow or brittle with age.
The binding is sewn, which allows the book to open easily and lie flat.
The binding board is covered in Brillianta, a woven rayon cloth
made by Van Heek–Scholco Textielfabrieken, Holland.
Composition by Publishers' Design and Production Services, Inc.
Printing by Sheridan Grand Rapids, Grand Rapids, MI.
Binding by Dekker Bookbinding, Wyoming, MI.
Designed by Bruce Campbell.*